JENKINS' EAR

"You need not fear but posterity will be ever glad to know the absurdity of their ancestors. The foolish will be glad to know they were as foolish as they, and the wise will be glad to find themselves wiser. You will please all the world then; and if you recount miracles you will be believed so much the sooner."

Thomas Gray to Horace Walpole

JENKINS' EAR

*A Narrative Attributed to
Horace Walpole, Esq.*

by

ODELL SHEPARD
&
WILLARD SHEPARD

THE MACMILLAN COMPANY: NEW YORK

1951

TO WHOM IT MAY CONCERN:

I, William Cole, an obscure English clergyman, am writing these words in mid-November of the year of Our Lord 1782 and the sixty-eighth year of my age. They are meant to go with and to vouch for a strange narrative, herein called "Jenkins' Ear," a true copy of which I am now handing on to those readers as yet unborn for whom it was mainly intended. I believe it to be the work of the Honourable Horace Walpole, youngest son of England's first Prime Minister and now even more illustrious in his own right than on account of his father. My reasons for this belief, and also for my somewhat qualified faith in the veracity of the document itself, demand a clear statement. This I am the more willing to make because it is probably the last service I shall be able to render one who for more than half a century has honoured me with his friendship.

"Jenkins' Ear" was brought to my door exactly twenty-seven years ago, on the fifteenth day of November, 1755, by Mr. Walpole's man-servant Louis. For that sole purpose he had journeyed down from Arlington Street in London to the village of Bletchley, Bucks, of which at the time I was Rector. He was ushered into my library, I remember, where I was imprisoned by the gout, and there, with the sigh of one completing an important if not a hazardous mission, laid a large stoutly wrapped bundle on the desk before me. By his master's direction he asked for, and got, my written assurance that the bundle had reached me in good condition, with its several seals of wax unbroken. Then he had a comfortable chat in the kitchen with my housekeeper over a mug of ale, meanwhile avoiding any mention of recent events at Strawberry Hill. This Louis was a discreet young man, acquainted with the frailties of women, remarkably well spoken, and a devoted servant.

The bundle, when at last I had it open, proved to contain a manuscript extending to nine hundred and seventeen demy quarto leaves of excellent paper written on only one side. From beginning to end it was written in the clear and handsome chirography, as familiar to me as the shape of the letters now flowing from my quill, of Horace Walpole. This I assert and affirm on my honour as a gentleman, a clergyman, and a scholar.

No such solemn asseveration would be called for, I am well aware, if I could now transmit the original manuscript as it came to me; for surely some scrap or two of my friend's handwriting will survive, for purposes of comparison, the two hundred years he and I wish to bridge. Indeed there will be found among the papers I am bequeathing to the British Museum—with the strict injunction, by the way, that they are not to be opened for many years after my death—no less than one hundred and seventy letters written from him to me; and doubtless a few of his two hundred other correspondents will take a similar care. The fact is, however, that during almost three decades of hard and frequent use the holograph of "Jenkins' Ear" has been so marred by deletions, additions, corrections, and occasional sharp rejoinders as to render it, for any eyes but mine, well nigh illegible. My sole and insufficient excuse for such intrusion is that in more than one place, as the reader will see, Mr. Walpole seems to expect and even invite it. Often he speaks as though we were telling this tale together, and refers to my discretion matters about which he pretends, at least, to be in doubt. Thus encouraged, and at times all but prodded, I have gone by little and little much too far. Beginning with a modest attempt to castigate his occasionally licentious language, I soon found myself shortening interminable sentences, inserting marks of quotation where I knew he was using the words of other men, adding necessary punctuation, and changing neologisms such as "smuckle" and "serendipity" and "womanagement" into words that can be found in Dr. Johnson's Dictionary.

In all this I did not, perhaps, greatly exceed the privilege of an editor who is also a friend. There were many evidences that Mr. Walpole had written, as usual, at top speed, and nothing showed that he had ever looked through the completed text. He had filled nine hundred and odd pages in less than three weeks, some of them while sitting in the House of Lords ostensibly listening to the Speech from the Throne. As mere penmanship the feat was impressive, but it left little time for thinking.

Because Mr. Walpole, in spite of what looks like a promise, has never mentioned "Jenkins' Ear" to me, I have not felt free to broach the subject to him by word of mouth or by pen, and thus it has seemed to me that I remained the sole protector of his repute in those ages to come whose good opinion he values far beyond that of his contemporaries. My sense of the responsibility involved has added not a little to the burden of my declining years. Again and again I have debated with myself whether I had the right to let a man of such rank and distinction go before Posterity as a fribble, a zany, a scoffer at religion, and a fleerer at his King.

This I say not to excuse my conduct but only to show that the problem I faced was difficult and painful. Eventually it irritated and angered me to the point where I began to wreak my wrath upon the manuscript itself. When the gout was more than usually raging in my members I sometimes scored out whole paragraphs and pages, or wrote in the margins such exclamations as "Absurd," "Frivolous," "Incredible," and "Intolerable." One of the critical terms I most favored at such times was "No!" and another was "Out!" Occasionally I answered back, dashing down my rejoinders diagonally across the text. Also I wrote scores and hundreds of notes, and in these I laboured chiefly not to clarify the document but to show its inaccuracies, improbabilities, and other shortcomings.

The years have brought me to a more temperate view of "Jenkins' Ear." Not yet by any means does it seem to me the kind of thing that a gentleman ought to put forth for Posterity to remember him by, but that is for him to decide—or, rather, he did decide it long ago, and perhaps has never since given the matter a second thought. Also I have come to realize that much of what I once took for gratuitous insult is only the play of Mr. Walpole's sometimes bewildering humour, and that his frequent appeals for my help are due to his warmth of heart. What he has mainly wanted of me is that I should serve as a faithful custodian and transmitter of his narrative. Therefore I have spent several weeks in making a fair copy of the manuscript as it came to me, neither adding nor subtracting nor changing one word or mark of punctuation. All my notes have gone, along with the holograph, into the fire.

There is a personal satisfaction in having finished this task, but a good custodian does not think of himself alone. My thought goes forward to those who will read "Jenkins' Ear" when I am dust, and I cannot but ask how much of it they will understand. Mr. Walpole has everywhere assumed that they will be closely acquainted not only with the history of our time, its politics and society and manners and leading personages, but also with him, with his villa, his friends and servants, even his little dog. Yes, the reason why he does not say that the dog he owned in 1755 was a King Charles spaniel is that he expects everyone in "the good time coming" to know that much. Now it is easily possible, and greatly to be hoped, that twentieth-century readers will be much better informed than we are, but it does not follow that their knowledge will be about us. Conceivably, they may have other preoccupations, and in the degree that they grow wiser may think of us less and less.

This is perhaps a gloomy view, but a lifetime devoted to antiquarian studies has convinced me that the Past is seldom so well remembered as it hoped to be and that the dead are more mortal than they expected. Therefore I shall jot down here a few facts about our time which the readers of "Jenkins' Ear" will need to have in mind.

The Ear itself, I emphatically assert to begin with, is not imaginary but a tangible object which I myself have seen and, somewhat reluctantly, handled. Its astonishing influence in human affairs—precipitating our war with Spain in 1739, contributing to the downfall of Sir Robert Walpole's Peace Ministry, facilitating the rise of Prussia as a military power, enabling the followers of the exiled James Stuart to perpetrate the Jacobite Rebellion of 1745, and thus rendering inevitable the embroilment of Europe and the Western World—is a thing which the twentieth century may forget without escaping its consequences. Indeed it may be that those consequences, increasingly vast and dire, will not be exhausted until the sea is dry and the heavens crack and human history is rolled up as a scroll. At the very least, as I now see more clearly than anyone could in 1755, the Ear is a theme for historic and prophetic meditation as deep as the ancient myth of the Apple of Discord or even the lie that was told in the Garden of Eden.

Yet I affirm again that the Ear itself is no myth. Sceptical readers who doubt that it ever existed will find their answer in the newspapers of our day and in early numbers of The Gentleman's Magazine. There too will be found numerous references to the Jacobite Rebellion and also to the fact that in October, 1755, England was expecting an invasion from France with the Young Pretender at its head. Hundreds of flat-boats and thousands of soldiers had been assembled at Dunkirk across the Channel, and we on our side were making ready to meet them with armed encampments, fire-ships, floating castles at the river-mouths, and concentrations of the Fleet. All this was common knowledge at the time, but so far as I am aware no one except Mr. Walpole, and he only in this narrative, has ever suggested a reason why that invasion was not finally attempted. The strange reason he gives or implies can be refuted only by those who know a better one.

I speak of "Jacobites" and "the Young Pretender" as though the names would always be familiar, but in fact they have rapidly faded since the accession, twenty-two years ago, of His Gracious Majesty George the Third. Jacobitism—that is, the belief that the House of Stuart is entitled by Divine Right to the Throne of England—is now a faint memory, and when we occasionally speak of the Young Pretender we think of a man past sixty who is drinking himself to death. —Such at least is the report of our spies, but toward the end of "Jenkins' Ear" there will be found a prophecy that just such reports will be made and that they will not be true.

With Jacobitism, a political heresy to which men of my cloth are often prone, I have never been tainted. My tendency is to accept constituted authority, and this in my lifetime has been represented for me by my ecclesiastical superiors and by three King Georges, all of the House of Hanover. I could wish that these monarchs had been less German and more intelligent, but in my judgement the main thing is that they have unquestionably been our Kings, and fully entitled as such to our respectful obedience.

That is the attitude of a Hanoverian Tory. Now Mr. Walpole, by inheritance if not by reasoned conviction, is a Whig. He feels that real power should rest not with the King but with Parliament, yet for Parliament itself, although he has long served as a member, he has no high regard. Authority of any kind he is wont to decry and deride. It is to me a wonder, as I look back, that such a difference has never endangered our friendship.

But now to proceed. In addition to the things in "Jenkins' Ear" which future readers may not understand there may be some which they cannot believe. At any rate that was my own experience during my first perusal. I remember reading on and on until far after midnight, so "ensorcelled"—it is Mr. Walpole's word—that I could scarce keep my tobacco-pipe alight and the fire on my hearth shrank to a handful of embers, yet most of the time convinced that the tale had been cleverly concocted, out of almost nothing, to amuse a house-bound friend. If I could think that, with my knowledge of the many minute particulars in which the narrative agrees with, explains, and illumines historical fact, the readers of two centuries hence will be even more likely to regard it as a trivial fiction.

My notes might have prevented that misconception, but now that they are gone the readiest way of vouching for "Jenkins' Ear" will be to record the stages by which my own disbelief has been, for the most part, overcome. Such a record should be the more persuasive because I am by nature and training a highly sceptical person, and have long been accustomed to the close scrutiny of manuscripts in which the possibility of fraud is always present.

The general truth of this document is proved to my satisfaction by its congruity with facts of which I have independent knowledge. My previous awareness that an invasion was intended by France is one example out of many. Moreover, I am well acquainted with Mr. Walpole's villa and the region about it. I have the advantage of intimate acquaintance with three of the main persons in the narrative, for Mr. Henry Conway and Mr. George Selwyn were my school-mates and Mr. John Chute of the Vyne has long been my friend. Mrs. Catherine Clive I have never met, nor do I aspire to do so, but the fact of her existence is notorious and everyone knows that in her long career as an actress she has excited, in various ways, much amusement.—In this place I should like to make it clear, speaking as a bachelor, that she lives at Strawberry Hill with her brother, an Irishman by the name of Raftor, whose residence there has done something to preserve appearances.

These, then, are real people—I use the present tense because all of them are still living—and their familiar names and characters could not fail of a persuasive effect. Even in my first reading I said to myself that if Mr. Walpole were fabricating this tale he would scarcely include so many scenes, persons, and events with which he knew me to be familiar. And that argument, I may add, was sustained some ten years later when he produced "The Castle of Otranto," a work of pure fiction entirely negligent of historic fact, of probability, and of common sense.

Thus I gradually came to accept the larger part of what my friend told me about a series of events at Strawberry Hill in October, 1755.

"The larger part," I say, and I may as well name a few items to which my faith does not extend. Lord and Lady Madlands I take to be creatures of fancy, meant to protect some neighbor of Mr. Walpole's —Lord Radnor, perhaps, considering that he lived at the time just across the road and had a number of Chinese pagodas on his grounds —from the imputation of Jacobitism. Needless to say, I do not believe that Mr. Walpole saw a unicorn by moonlight in his garden, or that the ghost of the late Alexander Pope appeared there and was driven thence by a gesture which no gentleman could conceivably make. These things and others of like sort are the figments, I take it, of a wildly irresponsible imagination, just as the vision of King Henry the Eighth on the river is obviously due to unaccustomed potations of Abingdon ale.

And yet the very presence of these incredible assertions in "Jenkins' Ear" has, surprisingly, the effect of validating the narrative in its main tenor. They show, I mean, that it was written in a mood of intense excitement which no ordinary event could have caused. The same effect is given by the frequently breathless and headlong mode of expression wherein every fault and felicity of Mr. Walpole's usual writing is inflated, exaggerated, exalted, to meet some momentous occasion. Hitherto his friends have known him as an amusing embroiderer of the truth, and here to be sure he embroiders still, but upon what a magnificent fabric! In these pages he calls himself, justly, a carver of cherry-stones, but for once it is the terrene globe that he chisels.

Asking myself what could have wrought this change, I could think of nothing adequate except what my friend himself alleges: the sudden appearance at Strawberry Hill of the Young Pretender, or at least of his plenipotentiary agent. That indeed, and perhaps that alone, could have shaken his disposition so far beyond the former reaches of his soul. Therefore I have finally come to accept even Blandison, though without being quite sure what that involves, the promised occasion on which Mr. Walpole and I were to discuss the man's identity having never arrived. I only know that this stranger came out of mystery and returned whence he came, as indeed we all do.

My growing confidence in the record of events at Strawberry Hill did not at first include all the stories told there. The account of the Jacobite Rebellion agreed well enough with what I already knew, but the Honourable John Byron's tale of shipwreck, many things related

TO WHOM IT MAY CONCERN

by Lieutenant Morris about his Patagonian adventures, and Mr. James Adair's scenes of life and death in the American wilderness, were as strange to me as "Gulliver's Travels." To believe, for example, that eleven naked Indians could capture and terrorize a man-of-war packed with soldiers was beyond my power until I discovered three printed accounts of that incident, none of which Mr. Walpole had used in his version. He depended upon an eye-witness.

In further corroboration of "Jenkins' Ear" I shall now set down a list of the books, gradually assembled over a period of twenty years, upon which my own belief in the subordinate stories it contains is largely based. They are as follows:

A Voyage to the South Seas in His Majesty's Ship *Wager* in the Years 1740-41, by John Bulkeley and John Cummins. London, 1743.

A True Journal of a Voyage to the South Seas and Round the World, by Pascoe Thomas. London, 1745.

The Sequel to Bulkeley and Cummins' Voyage to the South Seas, by Alexander Campbell, late Midshipman of the *Wager*. London, 1747. (Suppressed soon after publication, probably by the Admiralty Office.)

A Voyage Round the World by George Anson, Esq., Compiled by Richard Walter, M.A. London, 1748.

Second edition and fourth printing of Bulkeley and Cummins, containing an account of the court-martial and also the narrative, here printed for the first time, of Isaac Morris. Published in Philadelphia, 1756.

The Narrative of the Honourable John Byron, Written by Himself. London, 1768.

History of the American Indians, by James Adair, Esq. London, 1775.

The reader will see that three items on this list—that is, if the narrative of Isaac Morris is counted separately—are the work of persons who at an earlier time told their stories by word of mouth in Mr. Walpole's library. Divergencies between their spoken and their written accounts are probably due to the fact that they would speak more frankly to a small group of acquaintances, all of whom had a strong motive for secresy, than they would do when writing for publication. This applies especially to the Honourable John Byron, who produced his fascinating but rather confused "Narrative" many years after the events it describes and at a time when his position in His Majesty's Navy forbade any hint that he had once sympathized with alleged mutineers.

I think I have now covered most of the matters about which readers of "Jenkins' Ear" in the distant future are likely to be incredulous, doubtful, or uninformed. Perhaps I ought to say that the Maze at Hampton Court is an actual place, already several centuries old and bidding fair to last as much longer. Horn Fair, I regret to say, is actual also, and it descends every year to a greater depth of depraved imbecility. Of John Wesley, sometimes erroneously styled "Reverend," the same sad admission must be made. He really exists, and continues at almost eighty to foment strife and dissension both within and without the Established Church. Dr. Samuel Johnson, also an actual figure, has achieved at the age of seventy-three a fame which renders all the more shocking the scurrilous treatment accorded him in these pages. Of Hal Pudsey I can only say that I hope he has gone to his reward.

Thus I might go on to a tedious length, but all the while I should be asking myself what good such assurances could do if it should turn out that quite the least believable thing about "Jenkins' Ear" is the author of it. For I cannot be sure that the now famous name of Horace Walpole will be widely familiar in times to come. No doubt it deserves to be so, but, as Sir Thomas Browne reminds us, "the iniquity of Oblivion blindly scattereth her poppy, and deals with the memory of men without respect to merit of perpetuity."

Mr. Walpole is not what I should call a probable man, and the list of his incongruities if drawn up in full would make him look almost incredible. I shall not attempt such an enumeration, partly because this document itself reveals him as both harsh and tender, brilliant and foolish, timorous and brave, vain of his outward advantages but unaware of his inward virtue, and a man who even while jesting at reputation still hopes and believes that his name will live forever.

Mr. Walpole has laid many a trap for posthumous fame. His country house is one of these, and his collection of curiosities—now including a desiccated human ear—is another. To these we may add his poems and essays and memoirs, his account of Royal and Noble Authors, his Anecdotes of Painting, his regrettable attempts at prose

fiction and blank-verse drama, his printing press, his amateur antiquarianism, and his oddities of expression and manner and opinion.
Surely all these, one fancies him saying, should suffice in number if
not in quality to hold attention for many generations.

Yet I think it is mainly upon his correspondence that Mr. Walpole
depends for the survival of his name—and this with good reason, because it is in his letters that the best of the man shines forth: his longing, I mean, to be liked by many and beloved by at least a few. This
is the deepest thing in him, and comes nearest to what Pope called a
"master passion." It has driven his quill across and down many
thousands of pages all meant for his friends whether living or yet unborn. Between the two kinds he makes little distinction except for his
faith that the people of the future will be greatly superior to us. Those
who read my present words will be better judges of that than I, but
they can scarcely be unmoved by the fact that every letter he writes is
intended ultimately for them. The underlying motive of each one,
moreover, is not entirely selfish. He speaks not solely for himself but
also for us, to you.

"Jenkins' Ear" is one more of the numberless shallops of paper this
man has set afloat on the river of time, all bearing one message, one
plea: "Don't forget us, we beg you! Don't let us die utterly! In the
great age we shall never see and can but dimly imagine may these
words of ours, at least, live on!"

WILLIAM COLE
Milton, near Cambridge
November 15, 1782

To The Reverend William Cole
Bletchley Parsonage by Fenny Stratford
Buckinghamshire

Strawberry Hill
Twickenham, Middlesex
October, 1755

Dear William:

Here is a letter to be kept under lock and key at all times when it is not in your hands. It must be kept with the fact in mind that in these degenerate days both women and servants are able to read, and that what they read in private letters they are likely to tell. Furthermore, I request that when you have read it through—and have made, of course, your customary corrections—you will bury it deep among those writings of your own which you are determined that no one now living shall see. Thereafter you will please mention its existence to no human being by tongue or by pen, and will say never a word of the events it records.

My reasons for this request are cogent. One is that ever since the execution of the Scotch Lords, some ten years ago, I have felt a strong disgust for that ungracefully public demise which the law prescribes for persons convicted of treason. Death coming in almost any gentlemanly form I hope I shall be able to greet with a courteous smile, but decapitation by the hangman's axe is a mode of dismissal from this world's room which, even with the example of an English king to recommend it, no man of *bon ton* would choose.

And then, too, I have a modest reputation to maintain, or to lay in your charge, which beheading would not improve. Even at the best, supposing that treason could not be proved against me, the suspicion that I had done a brave, a patriotic, perhaps even a thoughtful thing would be ruinous. (I don't say, mind you, that I have; but you know

1

how people talk.) And even more calamitous would be the whisper that Horace Walpole had written a serious letter showing signs of not only a head but a heart. —I should then have to start life all over again.

That would be rather a pity, for thus far I have played the fribble and feather-pate with some success. No doubt I began with natural gifts, but to them I have added a laborious art somewhat like that which a fine lady uses in preparing herself for a ball. Possibly you have heard, if it is permitted to mention such things to The Cloth, how she pads out her hips and pulls in her waist and bulges her bosom, then takes her health from one pot of paint, her youth from another, her innocence from a third, and her tall coiffure from the horse. She draws upon all the three kingdoms of Nature to produce a master-piece of artificiality. Now my own efforts of this sort are compara-tively slight, but at least I may say that I have made the most of a moderate endowment of folly. Take this gay toy of a house from which I write, this architectural counterpart of its owner. To begin with—I can say this to a friend who knows the fact already—it was a coachman's cottage, tiny, simple, and little more impressive than a mushroom pushed up in one night from the sod. But look at it today and you see an elaborate fraud, a card-castle flimsily pasted together, glittering with tinsel and bestuck with painted glass to make a brave show.

Have I told you the sincerest encomium that Strawberry Castle has ever received? It was the spontaneously profane outcry of a lady com-ing up from her barge and catching her first glimpse. "Oh, Lord!" she screamed, at a distance, and then, coming nearer, "Oh, God!" and finally, quite overwhelmed, "Jesus! What a *house*!" I blushed, I stam-mered my thanks, I bowed as Kitty Clive does when acknowledging the plaudits of Drury Lane. For those frank words could only mean that as a comic actor I had succeeded. Even my house was comic.

You, to be sure, have not seen the place in its present stage of retro-gression toward the Gothic Ages. You know that I have an embattled wall here and there, with crenellations of lath and plaster; but unless you come soon—Well, what would you say to a moat, portcullis, and drawbridge? You are aware that I have Cardinal Wolsey's red hat and the tobacco pipe of Admiral Tromp, but you are ignorant that I have recently acquired the Ear. —Whose Ear? Come and see. Mean-while, I only say, the Ear!

Now, sir, it is a main secret of retaining public esteem never to disappoint public expectation. Once a man has played successfully in a given role, he must go on playing it to the end. His mask is taken for the face God gave him, and by tearing it off he gains only the name of a hypocrite.

But you, as a clergyman and a Tory, must already understand this. It provides the best excuse I can think of for your stubborn support, even in talk with me, of certain irrational opinions, political and ecclesiastic. Even Kitty Clive understands it now, though she had to pay dear for the knowledge. Not content with clear supremacy on the comic stage, she must needs aspire to play Shakespeare's Portia. We argued and pled, all but wept, but she would play Portia. And play it she did for half a scene—until the laughter drove her off in tears. It has been estimated that a good five pounds of Kitty were lost that night in tears alone. And it was not that she lacked the brains, the voice, the aplomb, the presence. Of all that and more she has enough for a dozen queens of tragedy. But the main thing was, and is, that Mrs. Catherine Clive belongs to the public domain, and has no right to run off with herself or make any alterations without public consent —which will never be granted.

You see my drift. I too must live down to what is expected of me. My duty is to confirm the syllogism that whereas the sons of great men are always fribbles and Horace Walpole is the son of an extremely great man, therefore Horace Walpole must be a fribble, as his friend Gray puts it, "of purest ray serene." Hitherto I have given satisfaction. If it now became known that I have written such a letter as you are about to read, I should lose either my head or my sinecures.

Another main reason why this letter should lie perdue for at least two hundred years is that the people of our time are not worth writing for. I have come, indeed, to such a contempt for the human race as one sees it today in England that I would rather have its blame than its praise, and prefer its neglect to either. You need not be told that the world about us is stupid and cruel and vulgar, for you have shown your estimate of it by thinking mostly about times gone by and writing for times to come. In these pages I shall be following your good example. Of the past I know far less than you do, but I yield to no man in my hopes for a future worthy of the best that I, at any rate, can think, feel, and say. I even hope that in the good time coming there will be no more gout.

This disease has long been your familiar companion—a fact which proves that virtue, in which you abound, is no preventive. And neither, I may add, is leanness, which decidedly you have not. Truly, there is no justice in nature. My father, it is well known, was a lover of flesh-pots and a looker upon the wine when it was red; yet gout never touched him. On the other hand I, whom you know to be a long meager monk of a fellow, a nibbler at biscuits and sipper of iced water—I have the gout, or it has me, oh . . .! For the last few days it has made a monopod of me, a mere seated statue of my late un-lamented self. Now why should I pay for the vices of another man without enjoying his pleasures? You clergymen will please consider this question, seriously, in conclave. I await a prompt answer.

Meanwhile I admit that there has been revelry and feasting at Strawberry Castle. During all last week we entertained here, as some would say, royally. Scarce a bite did I eat, and barely a sip for polite-ness did I drink in that time; but such a week, such company, such high intrigue and deep play, were enough to bring on not merely the gout but an apoplexy. Would that you had been here! I am yet be-wildered, amazed, astonished. Were it not that Mr. Chute took down the greater part in shorthand, I should now be thinking it all a wild impossible dream. But his transcribed notes lie before me, and I find that he heard and saw what I did, shared with me the most dreadful temptation that can be offered in our time to any Englishman. Mr. Chute, I remind you, has no dreams, tells no lies.

And so to my story of the most wonderful week I have ever lived— a story involving many lives, but chiefly my own. I shall not write it well, of course, for what is commonly called good writing is my abomination. The chief pains I shall take—except for those thrust upon me by my great toe—will be to take no pains. For, say what you will of me in other regards, I belong to the rapidly disappearing species called "gentlemen," of whom the simplest definition is that what they cannot do easily they will not do at all. In any case I could not, even if I would, imitate the voluminous lexicographical tumefac-tions of Samuel Johnson's verbal elephantiasis.

For once, moreover, I have something to say. I have continents, seas to traverse, and many a hitherto unknown region of my own self to explore. As I look forward into these unwritten pages the vision of the rounded world stands majestic before me, with some cloudy hint of how every life is entwined with every other, how things near are one with those afar, and each passing moment is glorified, like a drop of dew at sunrise, by all that has been or will be. A strange mood comes upon me, which I am sure the late Alexander Pope would have despised, and whether to call it frenzy or inspiration I know and care not. Enough that I must write as it shall decide. I must snatch me a quill from the spread eagle's wing and make it whistle with speed.

But compose yourself, William. Perhaps all I mean by that tirade is to prepare you for a letter surprising not only in what it relates but in the manner and mood of the relation—most of all, it may be, in the length. Hitherto, I call you to witness, my letters have mostly been brief as a parson's grace when he dines with a fox-hunting squire; but now I am feelingly persuaded that epistolary longitude is sometimes a virtue. Just now we both have the gout, and I propose that we enjoy it all we can.

Behold me, then, by the triple-pointed window in my new library with my bandaged left leg resting on a chair and my right hand rejoicing as a strong man to run a race. Let us see which will end first: the gout or the present epistle. My little dog, dozing beside me in the weak October sunshaft, hopes, if I understand him, that both of them will be endless, so that never again will his master be lured away by such trumpery nonsense as the debates in the House of Commons. Ponto thinks well of the gout, and approves of long letters. I trust that your Busy does also.

Busy will be in your lap as you sit by the fire at Christmas, one bandaged leg on a chair, this letter in your right hand and a tobacco-pipe in your left. Most clearly I see you there now as you turn these pages, steadily holding the gout at leg's length away, unheeding the wind at the door and the early dark and that chill at the heart which no bachelor's fire can ever quite dispel. You think you are housebound, do you? For months you have not crossed your threshold? Well then, let us see what arrangements can be made.

Read, William, and wonder, and be silent. Lay what plans you think fit for letting Posterity know that Horace Walpole wore his cap and bells with something of a brain beneath them, and used his fool's bauble to defend his name and his country. —Meanwhile you will not forget that I have The Ear, and that it awaits your astonished inspection.

SUNDAY

Promptly at nine on that first morning—can it have been less than two weeks ago?—I was waked by my man drawing the curtains of my bed.

"Good morning, Louis," said I. "What's the weather?"

"I wish you an amusing day, your Honour. The weather is propitious. I have observed an unseasonable number of pleasure-craft upon the Thames. Three private coaches, not to mention several less elegant vehicles, have passed the gate since I arose. The contents of one coach have descended to wonder at the house and make exclamations of astonishment. Five gentlemen on horseback have done likewise. In short, we may expect a day of amusing events, to be enjoyed *al fresco*."

"That is, Louis, you think it won't rain. I disagree with you."

"It is very well, sir. —May I serve your tea?"

"Do. But what's that letter you're fiddling with?"

"A communication from Madlands, sir. It has arrived but at this moment. The man-servant has urged me that I should bring it to your instantaneous attention."

"Well, why not? While I'm drinking my tea—it's too hot, as usual —you may tell me what the letter says."

"I have not presumed to peruse it, sir; but the man-servant has communicated to me its quiddity."

"Ah, Louis, if you have a worse fault than reading your master's letters it is this degrading habit of taking your English from the new dictionary by Samuel Johnson, that Grub Street hack! How many times . . . But come! The 'quiddity'!"

"My Lord of Madlands and his Lady invite you, sir, together with the other gentlemen in your house and Mrs. Catherine Clive of Cliveden, to partake of breakfast with them in the Chinese pagoda at twelve o'clock, noon, today."

"H'm. Twelve o'clock, eh? What will George Selwyn say if we try to drag him out of bed at eleven?"

"I would respectfully suggest that the remarks of Mr. Selwyn will be worth all the effort. In addition, my Lord of Madlands—as I understand from his serving-man—offers suitable apologies for the brevity of the notice, but declares that he is now in the entertainment of a gentleman, recently from abroad, the whom he believes you will find amusing."

" 'Amusing,' you say, for the third time in one minute. Louis, where did you get that word—from the serving-man, the new dictionary, or the letter itself?"

I took the letter, glanced through it, and there the word was—chosen not by Lord Madlands, to be sure, but by his secretary.

"You rascal!" said I, striving to sound really shocked and stern. "Is there nothing that your gluttonous curiosity stops short of?"

Louis' blush, though rare, is worth waiting for. After a moment's hesitation he replied: "But, sir, pray consider how few opportunities a poor young Swiss has enjoyed for studying the language of the English upper classes in their correspondence! The works of Samuel Johnson, who is no gentleman, do not assist. Those of Samuel Richardson, though composed in the epistolary form, are what one would expect of a shopkeeper. As for Judge Fielding's *Tom Jones,* I understand that it has not your approval."

My frown melted. "Well done, Louis!" I exclaimed. "Decidedly well done! In covering guilt with flattery you have little to learn from the upper classes of England. —But now go and call my cousin and Mr. Chute. George Selwyn may sleep until eleven. Send a message to Mrs. Clive. Have some one step over to Madlands and say that we'll be there at twelve. While you're gone I may think up a fresh reason for the belief that I should have the first reading of my letters."

* * *

Louis was not disappointed in the "remarks" of George Selwyn, nor was he wrong about the weather. Except in Italy, perhaps, I have never known an October noon more benign than that into which we stepped forth. The sky was brimmed and dripping with the twitter of a thousand invisible larks. After the heavy rains of these last weeks— and you will remember that in early June we had a Noachian deluge

—the grass of my lawn and meadow was vivid as newly split emerald. A few white roses were blooming by the gate, with butterflies among them. How I envied those gorgeous creatures under no obligation to "partake of breakfast" in a damp pagoda! Down in the meadow my two cows and dozen sheep and little shepherd boy—his value is solely pictórial—were sensibly drowsing in the sunshine. The gilded weather-cock stood perfectly still, all ablaze. The boats on the polished Thames lay quiet as though in a picture, with no motion of any poised oar, any slack-hung sail.

But Mother Nature, after all the handsome things Jemmy Thomson has said about her in his *Seasons*—each of them a full year long!— needs no encouragement from me. Deception, no doubt, was her motive in looking so handsome just then, as it commonly is when females adorn themselves. That calm and guileless demeanor was meant to hide the danger that lay for us five just ahead.

Lord and Lady Madlands were awaiting us at the end of the gravelled avenue. They evidently had in mind a portrait by young Gainsborough as they stood there posed, arm in arm, with the bastard Greek portico for a background and a droop of golden leaves over-head. Yet I, if asked, should have suggested Hogarth's pencil, and Conjugal Fidelity as the theme. One saw at a glance that this woman would never be tempted to deceive her lawful spouse, and that he—to judge from the grip on his arm of those bejewelled talons—would be ever faithful to her. My Lord's marriage, you are to understand, was a sacrifice not to Aphrodite but to Plutus, that much more respect-able and persevering god.

But you must paint your own picture, William, of this fond pair. Make sure that my Lord shall stand enormous as a monument to his vintner and his cook, even as the decorated bones of his lady do to the skill of her lady's-maid. Pastoral simplicity is her present affecta-tion, in accord with the fact that our breakfast, in Louis' phrase, is "to be enjoyed *al fresco.*" Depict her, then, as an aged *ingénue,* stu-diously and expensively girlish, who has just come up from milking the cows but has stopped on the way to plaster her face with paint and load her fingers with rings. To show her simplicity she must wear a flat-crowned hat of the shepherdess style—if you can find a shep-herdess for a model—adorned with the Jacobite emblem, a white cockade. Give her slippers of silk for comfort and convenience in trip-ping through the morning's dew, and a dairy-maid's long white apron for Heaven knows what reason. So much for attire; but into her needling black eyes you must manage to concentrate all the calculating worldliness that a clergyman can imagine. My Lord's eyes are to be small, pale blue, dim, and therefore trustful, like those of a familiar barnyard quadruped with a large appetite. Try to give him just enough brains for the accumulation of great wealth while leaving him stupid enough to think wealth extremely important, even sufficient. Put a bob-wig on him, for he is bald and subject to colds. Clap a gold-headed cane and a three-cornered hat under his free arm. On the hat there must be a white cockade, because his guests are all Whigs, and won't like it.

(What a relief to get that matter out of the way without saying anything unpleasant about my neighbors! Descriptions of people bore me almost as much as raptures about landscape. In this instance, fortunately, I have contrived to let you do all the work.)

The gentleman from abroad, my Lady told us as we came up, was already at the pagoda, where breakfast would be served *"tout de suite."* She accepted Henry Conway's arm, coyly. I walked with her husband.

"Who are those horsemen?" I asked him as we rounded the left wing of the house.

"Eh? Horsemen? Don't see any horsemen. No."

"Use your glass, my Lord. I see ten or a dozen of 'em—fifteen, indeed—down there at the foot of the meadow. They aren't dressed for a hunt, and there are no hounds."

He adjusted his eyeglass—as usual, with difficulty. "Why, curse me," said he at last, puffing, "if they a'n't! Horsemen, begad! In fact, riders! Yes."

"Are they guests of yours, my Lord?"

"Eh? Guests, you say? How should I know? Ask my Lady. She'll tell you."

"Are they living here at Madlands?"

"Living here! Certainly not. Too dangerous. Yes. —That is, no."

"Why dangerous?"

"What say? Why dangerous? Well, by gad! Came with Blandison, didn't they? He's dangerous, a'n't he? I ask you that. Yes or no?"

"I can't say, my Lord, not having the privilege of the gentleman's acquaintance."

"Heh! Heh! Don't know Blandison, eh? Thought everybody knew

Blandison. But he knows you, Mr. Walpole. Yes. Here he comes now. Yes."

Some one had come out at the door of the pagoda and was walking to meet us—a tall man, well shaped, with no hat, dressed in black. He held himself well, and walked like a gentleman. There was nothing in the least ostentatious in his attire, unless it might be his flowing peruke of a sort I remembered seeing occasionally, years ago, in Paris and Rome. As he came closer, I saw that he was at least as handsome as my cousin Henry Conway. On his left hand he wore a ring, large and massy, of silver. One would take him to be a good swordsman, an excellent horseman, used to the chase and perhaps the tented field. He seemed to be of about my age, or perhaps a year or two younger. There was something bold if not scornful in the way he scanned us, as though he knew that one of our number had spent most of his life in drawing-rooms and seldom ventured far from home unless in a chariot or a sedan chair. You, William, will be able to picture that one as he stepped rather mincingly forward on his tiptoes, his knees slightly bent, clutching his hat between his two hands, to meet this lordly stranger.

My Lady elbowed her husband aside to do the honours, and I heard myself introduced as "the Honourable Horatio Walpole" to "the Reverend Mr. Blandison." Then those in my party were introduced. Kitty Clive, I could see, was deeply impressed. Never had I known her to look so intently at any man, even at me. Besides, there was the shock—no less—of hearing this man styled "Reverend." Of course I had long known that the clergy of our isle, ranging downward from William Cole to the pestilent insects that buzz about every episcopal palace, are of many sorts; but never had I seen a clergyman before like this one.

If I were a concocter of fiction, now, I might here describe how my Lady arranged that I should walk on, and then sit at breakfast, with "the Parson." Trifles of that sort keep us yawning for hours in *Clarissa Harlowe* and *Tom Jones* whilst the story, if there is one, waits. Judge Fielding, as though leading a donkey with a handful of hay, draws his reader through a thousand pages of mire to find out who gave birth to a scapegrace who should never have been born at all. As for Richardson, he writes about nothing but seduction, everlastingly procrastinated. 'Tis true that, the more we learn about the females concerned, the better we understand the procrastination. But why not a little sympathetic understanding, now and then, of the reader?

I myself, though a man of erring walk, have tried, at least, to keep the eleventh commandment: Thou shalt not bore. This rule is of special force in writing to one's friends, and therefore I hope that you will find in these pages, amidst much that is frivolous, nothing wearisome, stupid, or dull. What I should find tedious to read, I forbear to write.

On this principle, and also out of Christian charity, I omit all description of the Madlands wilderness, its assembly of moss-grown gods and goddesses listening to an oration by a noseless Cicero, and even of the pagoda. As this was an English breakfast I need not say that it was Gargantuan, miserably cooked, wretchedly served, and cold. 'Tis nothing to the purpose how often my Lady cried across the table's length, "Stop gobbling, my Lord!" or else "My Lord! Don't drool!" Cousin Conway was pouring silence in at her right ear, the better one of the two, and George Selwyn slept at her left. Mr. Chute was thoughtful. Kitty Clive, across the table from me, was obviously excited about something. At the moment I thought this was due to the excellent opportunity she was having for the study of my Lady, who has long served as the model of her most ludicrous affectations in comedy parts. But that, you will soon see, was a bad guess.

Meanwhile, I was mainly concerned with the talk of the man at my right hand. Mr. Chute's conversation is more judicious, but then it is seldom anything else. George Selwyn's is often as witty, but you know how George opens one eye for one sentence and then drops off again, exhausted. Blandison—for I find that I cannot use his absurd title— never drowses, or lets his listeners do so. During that breakfast and the week that followed I heard him talk on a hundred topics—always easily, often eloquently, yet never with the least hint of parade. He spoke Italian and French better than I do. He showed himself at home in Paris, Rome, and Florence as though he had lived in each of them always. He apparently had the Odes of Horace and the Bible by heart, for although he often misquoted them it was always by intention.

You will think, William, that I have been dazzled. So I have. You may fear that I have been blinded. Wait and see.

Halfway through the breakfast my Lord happened to mention, between two mouthfuls, that he was a charter member of the Sublime Society of Beefsteaks, which, as you should know, is one of the most select and exalted of London's numberless clubs. Blandison, realizing that this was like to be the only remark vouchsafed by our host during the meal, made the most of it. He told us how the Society had been formed, in 1735, and called the roll of its more distinguished members, past and present. From there he went on at a hand-gallop through a bewildering list of clubs with odd names: the Pandemonium, the Man Hunters, the Surly, the Atheistical, the Quacks, the Thieves, the Scatter-Wits, the Hustle-Farthings, the Broken Shop-Keepers, the Small Coalman's Music Club, the Lady's Lap-Dog Club, the Kit-Cat Club, the Humbugs Club, the Anonymous Club, and some twenty others. It was a bewildering display of knowledge, memory, and nimble wit.

"One thing I don't like about your list," sang out Kitty Clive when he paused for breath, "is that most of those clubs are Jacobite. One can tell from their very names."

"What names do you especially refer to, Mrs. Clive?"

"Oh, the Quacks, the Scatter-Wits, the Thieves, and the Broken Shop-Keepers."

"Do you prefer the Mug Houses, madam?"

"Decidedly I do; and also the Calf's Head Club, founded to put down Jacobites and keep them down."

"Oh, I didn't know that, Kitty," George Selwyn drawled. "I thought they were just for putting down ale. —Of course, it doesn't always *stay* down."

That helped a little, and so did Blandison's pleasant laughter. "When it comes to putting down ale," said he, "there's the Club of Jenkins' Ear. They've learned to keep it down by putting other drinks on top."

"Whiskey, I suppose."

"How did you guess, Mrs. Clive?"

"It wasn't a guess. Everyone knows that whiskey is the Jacobite drink. Things are getting so that you can smell a Jacobite as far off as you can see his white cockade."

"Kitty's talking as though she'd had some herself," said Selwyn. "On an empty stomach, too."

"Harold," said my Lord to the servant at his elbow, "bring us out a decanter of whiskey."

"Yes, my Lord. Scotch or Irish, my Lord?"

"Scotch. Highland malts. —But don't drink any."

"Certainly not, my Lord."

My cousin Conway then asked about the Club of Jenkins' Ear—quite the oddest name, he said, that he had ever heard. Was it confined to Jacobites, or might it include an occasional Tory who worshipped the King but not the Pope?

Blandison seemed eager to reply. Any one might join, he said, who had taken part in the War of Jenkins' Ear. "This means, Colonel Conway," he went on, "that you yourself are eligible as a hero of Fontenoy and Culloden. The club was founded, to be sure, by persons out of sympathy with the policy of Robert Walpole, but no discrimination has ever been made against that great Minister's party—or, for that matter, against highwaymen, pickpockets, spies, burglars, or, for a climax, politicians. I myself am a member, so that you see not even the clergy are excluded."

"Ah, but they might have let you in under several of those other headings," said Kitty Clive, gazing steadily at him from under her brows with a look at once roguish and severe. I caught that look, and instantly knew that Kitty liked Blandison, as one good swordsman does another. Nor could she have liked him the less for the way he tossed back his handsome head and smiled gaily at her.

Harold came in with the whiskey, and Blandison helped himself in a manner which I should call generous.

"Are we to learn anything about the Club of Jenkins' Ear?" asked my cousin.

Blandison emptied his glass. "I can tell you," said he, "when and how it was formed, as well as why. The gentlemen present would, I think, find the story interesting; but about the ladies I am not sure."

"If you're thinking of me," Kitty said, "I shall stay and hear it."

"Mrs. Clive," spoke a shrill harsh voice, "it is the privilege of the hostess to decide when the ladies shall leave the table."

"Oh, certainly! Of course I shall remain not as a lady but as an actress. You know an actress can hear anything, and sooner or later she does hear most things."

"Eh? What say? Any girls in this story, Blandison? Eh?"

"No girls, my Lord."

"Oh. No girls." And my Lord composed himself for slumber.

"The Club of Jenkins' Ear," Blandison began, "was formed on the nineteenth day of October, 1739, a few hours after the declaration of the war of that name. I was present and helped to found it. Ever since, although much of my life has been spent out of England, I have been an active member, always cheerfully paying the few shillings a year that suffice for its dues.

"You see that I begin by speaking of myself, and I ask your permission to go on in that way because my experience may stand for that of many. Let me say, then, that in 1739 I was young, hopeful, active, and in search of adventure. Of that there had been little enough in the years of what I may call my education. My fortune was yet to make, and there was nothing in my ancestry, my habits and training, or indeed in my natural abilities, to suggest that it should be won by toil. For good or ill, I come of a stock accustomed to actions that stir the blood. Few of my forebears were docile, ducking, obedient men. Some of them have lived in exile and others have died on the scaffold; but whilst they were alive they did live, and when they died they left their country poorer in manhood. Boredom was the one thing they feared, and they worshipped chiefly the Goddess of Fortune.

"This is what all English gentlemen, whether aware of their inheritance or not, may say. They are the products of those seven hundred years in which the descendants of the Norman conquerors ruled England in peace and war. Seven centuries can establish a habit, a tradition. Consequently, there were many English gentlemen in and about the year 1739 who felt defrauded. Look where they might, they found few shreds of the stuff of daring that had once made England great. Twenty years of sluggish prosperity had dulled the edge of the country's resolution. Fat faces, of the sort long ago battered down by William the Conqueror, were now all that one saw in places of power. In the Church, in Parliament, in the Court, on the Throne itself, stupidity reigned."

My cousin, red in the face, called out: "You will kindly omit the insults, sir, and get on to Jenkins' Ear."

"Don't be impatient, Henry," George Selwyn drawled. "The vulture is in full flight."

This interruption, though it came from my friends and was meant in defence of my father, I almost resented, just as I often do the derisive outcries from my side of the House when William Pitt's eloquence is filling that dull place with splendour. I recalled the famous occasion when my father stood smiling, his arms folded, and heard himself magnificently berated in the House of Commons by the leader of the Opposition. At one point, unable to control his admiration, he cried "Bravo! Bravo, Colonel Yorke!"

"Let's hear this man out," I said. "Our turn may come later."

"Mr. Walpole's generosity," Blandison continued, "makes it all the more awkward for me to say, in his presence, anything adverse to his father. In what I do say you will understand that I speak not of the man, whom I never knew, but of the Prime Minister—and indeed not so much of him as of his influence. Sir Robert Walpole himself was by no means stupid; he only established and maintained stupidity until it became the national habit. Nothing shows that he was a coward, but he gave his country the reputation of cowardice so that even the Spaniards felt that they might flout and insult us at will. I have heard that Robert Walpole himself was a good horseman and rode hard to hounds, yet he pulled England down from horseback and destroyed what was left of her chivalry. When he came to office there was still a remnant amongst us of that knighthood which had gathered round the banners of the Royal Martyr. When he left it, England was a land of merchants, and whatever honour, virtue, beauty, and manhood she had left were for sale. Her legitimate king, James the Third, was living in exile, and on the throne of the Stuarts there sat a stranger, a dullard, a barbarian from a barbarous land, the Elector of Hanover!"

"Why," Kitty exclaimed, "this parson would make a wonderful actor! I must tell Mr. Garrick about him at once. —To be sure, he has the notion that he's fitted for tragic parts, but a few catcalls would cure him of that."

" 'Catcalls,' madam?"—and we could see that he was really at a loss.

"Oh, you don't know about catcalls. Well, sir, we must try to instruct you."

"Sir," said Mr. Chute, "you will find an entertaining essay on the topic in one of Mr. Addison's Spectator papers. He says there that the catcall has been known to damp the ardour of the boldest generals and to frighten heroes off the stage."

"But what it is mainly good for," George Selwyn added, "is to stop a man who starts to tell a story at a breakfast table and then tries to make a political speech instead."

"George," said I, "for once I don't agree with you. The catcall is a test of good temper, and a man meets that test when he takes it with a smile and goes on."

Blandison did smile, and continued: "Now for that story of Jenkins' Ear, which some of you have been so eager for that you could scarcely wait through the introduction. Let's go back to that nineteenth of October, 1739, and to the crowd waiting in St. Stephen's Yard for the outcome of a momentous debate in Parliament. This crowd had assembled the day before to observe the ancient rites of Horn Fair down the river; but the customary orgies of that holiday had been postponed so that they might be employed to celebrate the defeat of the great peace Minister. Mr. Horace Walpole, I believe, was then in Europe with his friend Thomas Gray, but you other gentlemen may remember the turbulent multitude that surged about Westminster Hall and the two Houses. All London seemed to be there, shouting 'Horns! Horns!—War with Spain!—Remember Jenkins' Ear!—Down with Walpole!—Send Old Bob back to Norfolk! —We *will* have war!—Horns! Horns!' "

"If beasts could talk," George interjected, "I suppose that's what they would say—or bellow."

"It was England one heard there," said Blandison, "calling for war. Two youngsters, both of them now famous, stood beside me. One was John Byron, son of Lord Byron of Newstead Abbey, a Tory. The other was Augustus Keppel, son of the Earl of Albemarle, a Tory. Neither one was old enough to have any political opinions of his own, but both felt and resented the shame of Robert Walpole's recent bargain with Spain—that shopkeeper's bill called the 'Spanish Convention' in which he had merely charged her so much per insult, apparently willing to put up with any number of other insults so long as she paid the market price. When they shouted 'Down with Old Bob!' they meant 'Up with Old England!'

"Such a cry, with the force behind it of all the manhood left in our country, was not to be withstood. At last the vote was taken, and out marched the heralds from Westminster Hall, proclaiming war with Spain. Through St. Stephen's Yard and on into the Strand they went, amidst the hurrahs and the tossed-up caps of the crowd. The news rushed ahead so that before we reached St. Clement Danes all the steeples of London seemed to be reeling with grandsire triples and treble bob majors. Such a dance of bells the old city had never known. The very walls shook. We could scarcely hear one another shout."

Blandison reached for the decanter. I said: "You evidently enjoyed that occasion, sir."

"I did, greatly."

"But while you and the other noisy boys were having your frolic there was a man thrice your age, sir, and with a thousand times your responsibility, who stood at his window in Downing Street and listened sadly—not on his own account—to the drunken uproar. I was in Europe then, as you have somehow learned, but I have been told by those who were with him what my father said."

"Oh?"

"He said: 'Aye, let them ring the bells now, for soon enough, God knows, they will be wringing their hands.' "

"Oh, indeed!—It was a tolerable pun."

"What! Is that all you see in it?—But the years, sir, have proved those words true. 'Twas the bells and the shouts that were false."

"Now, Horatio," came Kitty Clive's voice, with the soft bubblement of laughter we all love beneath the tone of reproof, "you must *not* interrupt. Pray continue, Parson Blandison."

"You were marching up the Strand toward Jenkins' Ear," my cousin reminded him.

"The Ear! The Ear!" Selwyn chanted, pounding the table. "Down with Old Bob! We want the Ear!"

"Very well, you shall have it.—As we approached Fleet Street we saw that the crowd was gathering, just inside Temple Bar, about a heavy-jowled youth in a coach. Someone was handing him up a tankard of ale, and there was a hurrah for 'The Prince! The Prince of Wales!' He stood up in the coach and made a few remarks which I could not hear and in any case should not have understood, having never mastered the Hanoverian *patois*. I suppose, however, that they were about what he planned to do to the Spaniards, for then there were more hurrahs and he dipped his broad red face into the tankard, reminding me of sunset over the ocean.

"Flinching away from that spectacle, my attention was caught by a placard, hastily scrawled, stuck up in a window of the Rose Tavern close at hand. There I managed to read something like these words: 'The original Robert Jenkins who is a master mariner of the brig *Rebecca* and grower of the identical ear so cruelly cut and torn off his head by a Spanish sea-captain which has been sat upon by a committee of the House of Commons and found ample warrant for the present glorious war with Spain and the expulsion of Mr. Robert Walpole from his Majesty's Ministry may be seen within by any gentlemen who wish to converse with same and witness said ear for themselves in an excellent state of preservation in addition to one full quart of Abingdon ale drawn from the wood just received from Berkshire upon payment at the door of three shillings per gentleman to avoid a crowd and exclude those who have no pretensions to that honourable title.'

"Here, thought I, was a nobler sight than that of a corpulent foreigner drinking in the street. Here was a man who had actually lost flesh for his country instead of putting it on at England's expense. Besides, the opportunity to avoid the smell and din of that crowd was moderately priced, I felt, at three shillings. I think I paid three times that sum at the door, and took Keppel and Byron in with me."

"You seem to have been of two minds," Mr. Chute dryly observed, "with regard to that crowd. —Did you like it, or did you not?"

Blandison paused for several seconds, considering. Then he said: "It was a necessary tool, but filthy."

"Ah, yes. We are to infer, then, that you do not like filth, but that you think the end may sometimes justify the means. Pray continue."

"The Rose Tavern at Temple Bar—quite different from that of the same name in Covent Garden—is not one of the more commodious inns of London; and until that October day when its fame began it had not been among the more prosperous. Damp, dark, fusty, with only a few candles and no fire burning, with a hundred-year-old smell about it of rats and wet boots and sailors' tobacco, it seemed a fit place . for the concocting of low villainies and paltry crimes, for guttural whisperings in the corners of men who drew their hats low over their eyes and sucked at short, black pipes. And yet the place was packed, when we entered, with 'gentlemen'—at least if the possession of three shillings is a sufficient warrant for that 'honourable title.' They were all facing one way, some standing on tiptoe, some on chairs, and a few on the rickety tables, striving to catch a glimpse of the hero and partial martyr whose weary, half-drunken voice could just be heard above the jostling in the room and the shouts from outside.

"The most remarkable thing about that room was a huge mural painting, some twenty feet long, that covered the wall farthest from the door. Keppel, Byron, and I walked across the room while the voice droned on, to examine this picture. It represented a field of chivalric battle near the sea, with a number of mounted knights in

armour and richly emblazoned shields and a fallen knight on the
ground with his hands upraised as though pleading for mercy. The
painting was dark with filth, and the light in the room was dim, yet
we could make out that here was a relic, at least two centuries old, of
what Mr. Horace Walpole calls the Gothic Ages and I the Age of
Glory.

"Meanwhile the voice we had heard when we entered was reciting
some formula, evidently learned by rote. We caught at first only
random phrases, but on the third or fourth repetition we could piece
them together thus: '. . . sailed from J'maica . . . sugar an' rum . . .
off Havana Spanish guard-coaster. . . calls me sea-thief like all British
seamen . . . breaks open me hatches an' chests . . . hists me to yard-arm
an' drops me down . . . hists me up an'—'

" 'Git on with it, Master Jenkins,' some one sharply commanded.
'Tell 'em what ye said to Pulteney an' Pitt an' Vernon.'

" 'What say? Can't talk without rum. I been talkin' for hours.
I'm dry.'

"A tapster pushed through the crowd, nipperkin held forth. 'Now,
Master Jenkins,' said he, 'that's eight drams ye've had, and we wants
ye to tell 'em 'bout the *year*, an' *show* it to 'em. They ha'n't paid their
good money jest to hear how many times ye was histed an' bumped.
They wants the *year*, Master Jenkins—the *year*!'

" 'Ar—but I a'ready *tol*' 'em 'bout that.'

" 'Not to these here gen'lemen ye ha'n't. These here is *new* gen'lemen.'

" 'What say? Ar. . . . But fust-off I drinks me my nipperkin—
see? That's the un'erstandin', ain't it? One showin' o' the year, one
nipperkin? Ain't that right? I arsks yeh as one honest man to 'nother.'

" 'Git it down, Master Jenkins! Git it *down*!'

"While it was going down I bethought me of an expedient for catching a glimpse of this famous and beneficent organ. To the gentleman
standing next me I said: 'Did you know that his Royal Highness is at
this moment drinking success to the war just outside the tavern?'
—'What, the Prince of Wales, himself?' he asked. —'Frederick, the
Heir Apparent, no less,' I replied.

"The rumour spread rapidly, so that soon there was a general
exodus of three-shilling gentlemen from the tavern, and Byron,
Keppel, and I enjoyed an unobstructed view of Master Jenkins in the

act of draining the final drop. Hardly more than a dozen others in whom curiosity had triumphed over patriotism now lingered beside the table.

"Cynical persons, devoid of faith and the prophetic spirit, might have sneered at what we saw. To the eye of the flesh, Master Jenkins was an uninspiring, even a dismal sight. For one thing, the many nipperkins of Jamaica rum which he had earned and consumed that day had made him drunk. For another, one could see that this was his chronic condition, and that he would never voluntarily change it. His eyes were bleared and his hands so shook that, although he used both of them in lifting and holding his nipperkin, a good portion of the liquor had been spilled on the table-top, or down his coat. He was not old in years, but his sodden, putty-coloured face was scored by the mean iniquities and petty lies that mire a man's spirit and teach him nothing. What wit he had left, one would say, was mainly used in cadging for one more dram. Many such derelicts adrift on the seas of life we all have seen, and turned away in disgust. The one thing that marked this man off as unusual was the enormous wig rakishly cocked on the left side of his head—a wig dark brown in original hue but now faded, filthy, and loathsomely tenanted.

"Now it happens that I am curious in the lore and history of wigs. Even in 1739 I had begun to collect specimens of the various styles, ancient and modern, male and female: the periwig, the grizzle-bag, the fox-ear, the full bottom, the natty scratch, the natural fly, the Spanish fly, the spencer, the twisted and forelocked campaign, the dignified Blenheim, the curled cauliflower, the elegant Ramilie, and the magnificent allonge. With this knowledge at my disposal, I saw at once that Master Jenkins was wearing a late surviving example of the 'water-dog,' a wig affected by coachmen at about the time when the Dutch Hofstadter called William of Orange usurped the throne of the Stuarts. In other words, his wig might well be fifty years old—and this, I need scarcely add, is a venerable age in plocacosmology. Mr. Horace Walpole, with his passion for old medals and mediaeval armour, will understand how I longed to add it to my collection—how proudly I would have set it beside the auburn wig, recently discovered in the Roman catacombs, which was worn in disobedience of her bishop by a Christian lady of fourteen centuries ago. And yet I restrained myself. I considered that Jenkins' water-dog in my hands could serve only the ignoble pride of possession, but that on him it was the mark of a surprising modesty. Instead of flaunting his celebrated disauriculation, he hid it from the eyes of men beneath this enormous wig, contenting himself with occasional exhibitions of the ear alone.

"I am not myself a collector of ears. Mr. Walpole, whose virtuosity extends far beyond mine, would perhaps have known how to value the specimen that lay before us on the table, but for me it had no intrinsic attractions. Its resemblance to the human ear, that delicately whorled and rose-tinted portal of the temple of sound, was no longer apparent. 'Twas a mere shred of leather—flat, shapeless, wrinkled, and bleached by long pickling. I confessed to myself a certain disappointment.

"This, of course, was absurd. I made the common error of supposing that causes must be commensurate with their effects. A wise man standing at the source of the Thames would say: 'Though thy beginning is but small, yet thy latter end shall be greatly enlarged—Solomon, 8, 3.' Just so, as I gazed at Jenkins' Ear, I should have foreseen its huge and numberless consequences. I charge myself with a lack of faith, a failure in prophecy.

"Yet all of us knew, as we stood there and gazed, that here was an ear already rampant, militant, triumphant. On that very day it had helped to break a poltroon peace and to loosen the grip of a mercantile ministry upon an England made by and for gentlemen.

" 'Master Jenkins,' said I, looking him in the eyes and pointing to what lay on the table, 'is this the object you showed to the Committee of the House of Commons?'

" 'Objick?' said he. 'Objick! When a man's gone an' growed a year, sir, an' got 'tached to it, like the way I useter be to this 'un, 'e don't egzackly enjy 'earin' it called a "objick"! Not by no means 'e don't. It 'arrows 'is best feelin's an' makes 'im tur'ble dry, like 's if 'e don't 'ave a nipperkin this minute 'e 'll die o' thirst.'

"We laughed at the rascal—evidently not so drunk but that he could contrive to get more so—and I gave the necessary order.

" 'Well, then,' I continued, 'is this the ear you showed them?'

" 'Cer'ly is. I don't 'ave but jest the one loose ear to show, even to King Garge 'isself."

"The tapster came up with a full nipperkin, but for the moment he held it out of Jenkins' reach. 'Tell the gen'lemen how you lost the year,' said he.

" 'Lost it I never did. I 'ung on to it. That 'ar ear sleeps under me pillow, like it useter on top.'

" 'Well then, how they took it off.'

" 'Oh, ar. Wal, thisheer Spanish cap'n 'e comes me up the side with a cutlass atween 'is teeth an' "Confess or die !" sezee. I tells 'im they ain't no more money but what he'd took out o' me pockets a'ready, the which was four guineas, four doubloons, an' one pistole.'

" 'Now ! Now !' cried the tapster. 'Now we're comin' to it. What next, Master Jenkins ?'

" 'Why, next he grabbed aholt o' me year an' laid 'is cutlass 'long-side o' me 'ead, an'—'

" 'Which side, Master Jenkins ?' I inquired.

" 'The right side, o' course. Can't ye see it's me right ear ?'

" 'Oh, to be sure. I was confused by observing that your wig is pulled down on the left side. But continue, Master Jenkins. What happened next ?'

" 'Why, then 'e cuts an' 'e cuts an' 'e—'

" 'No, no,' exclaimed the tapster. 'Ye mean, 'e *tore* !'

" 'Oh, yeah : 'e tore off me year an'—an' throwed it in me face, an' then—an' then 'e says as 'ow 'e'd like to do the same for King Garge.' "

" 'H'm !' said I. 'Not a bad idea. That Spanish captain must have been a good Jacobite. —But did you make any reply ?'

" 'Why, why, I c'mended me soul to God an' me cause to me country."

" 'Excellent, Master Jenkins. Excellent ! Did you use those words at the time, or did some one else—perhaps a member of the Com-mittee, years afterwards—make them up for you ?'

" 'Oh, well, o' course, them words, it was Mr. William Pitt made 'em up; an' then Mr. Pulteney 'e says them words 'll pull down Old Bob an' start a war an' bring in a million volunteers.'

" 'With the help of the ear, of course.'

" 'Yeah. I showed 'em the year. Mr. Pulteney an' Mr. Pitt an' Cap'n Vernon, they liked the year. They didn't call it no "objick." Proba'ly Mr. Bob Walpole, *'e* would' a' called it a "objick".'

" 'Master Jenkins, I apologize for that expression. It was spoken in ignorance and unwarranted disrespect. I can now see that your ear is destined for lasting fame. If not in beauty, then in its influence it may rival "the face that launched a thousand ships and burnt the topless towers of Ilium." —But do drink your dram, Master Jenkins. You have fairly earned it.'

" 'Ar,' he replied, in a tone oddly compounded of truculence and pathos, 'but by rights I've earned me not 'ere a nipperkin an' there a can. I've earned me kegs o' rum—aye, an' bar'ls, puncheons, 'ogs'eads. I'm a 'ero, sirs; that's w'at I be, an' 'eroes by rights oughter be kep' in their drink by a grateful country.'

"From that speech—in which I scarcely think any play upon 'ear' and "ero' was intended—the now powerful and populous Club of Jenkins' Ear spontaneously sprang. 'Gentlemen,' said I, turning to those who stood beside me, 'I propose that we band ourselves together in a brotherhood, the main concern of which shall be that the proprietor of the Ear, like Jason's fleece, shall never be dry. Second only to that should be our resolve that the glorious war this day begun shall always be known as the War of Jenkins' Ear. Our club, I think, should bear the same honorable cognomen; and its membership should be open to all persons who take part in that war—or, rather, to all the gentlemen among them who show themselves worthy of that title by the annual payment of three shillings into our treasury. I suggest that our funds be administered by mine host of the Rose for the maintenance in liquor during the term of his natural life of our patron saint, Master Jenkins. —Do we agree?'

"The vote was passed by vociferous acclamation. Then our host was called in, and was easily persuaded to allow us the use of his tavern as our permanent headquarters. We are now, I believe, the largest club in London, and, though our dues have never been raised, one of the more affluent. For some time we have been able to supply Master Jenkins not only with his alcoholic necessities but with certain comforts and decencies of life. Moreover, we have extended and solidified his fame. Every evening, and far into the night, he is to be seen in the Painted Room, as we call it, with a crowd of admirers about him. One thinks of Ben Jonson at the Mermaid in the old days, or of Dryden smoking his pipe at Button's; but the attraction wielded by Master Jenkins is of a different sort. Men go there to see, not to hear him. They gather about his table and stare at the man, at the water-dog wig which I think has never once been removed since I first saw him, but, most of all, at the Ear."

"But once more about that strange picture," Mr. Chute interrupted. "You have examined it closely, have you? And you are quite certain that it represents a scene of chivalric contest and glory?"

"Oh, yes; quite. The horses, the armour, the banners and emblazoned shields leave no doubt on that head. The figures are dim, to be sure, as England's glory is also, but one sees at a glance what they represent."

"Thank you. And this Rose Tavern, you say, is inside of Temple Bar?"

"A few steps inside of it, yes; and that, I suppose, is farther than any of you gentlemen have ever ventured. However, a theme more fit for this occasion is the wonderful diversity of the men who come to that table in the corner. There one may see highwaymen and parsons, nabobs from Calcutta and Connecticut yeomen, Highlanders deprived of their tartans, Indians from the Mississippi, pickpockets and squires, Hanoverian Tories and Jacobites and Whigs, peers and bishops and pimps and members of Parliament, all eager to gaze for the first or the twentieth time at the magnetic Ear which once turned the course of their lives and still draws and holds them together.

"The Ear is smooth and papery now, worn thin by thousands of fingers, and, as it were, refined by some vague awareness of its own fame. Lying there in the candlelight, it seems to shine with a faint lustre or inward glow. While gazing at it one forgets its origin as one does the source of the Thames, and thinks only of the many strange and violent ways in which its influence has gone out to the ends of the earth.

"I have said that this talisman, charm, symbol, or holy relic—this 'objick' if you prefer—unites all the veterans of the War of Jenkins' Ear. Equally true it would be to say that the sight of it sends each one of them back along paths of memory which he alone can travel. I know about this because I am one of those veterans, and also because I have talked with many men beside that table. To one of them the Ear recalls the capture of a Spanish galleon laden with gold; to another it brings the sight of naked Indian women diving for sea-eggs off the coast of Patagonia; to a third comes the burning of Canton; and still another returns to an upper room in the town of Derby where for hour after hour the debate went on whether he should withdraw his triumphant forces back to the Highlands and certain defeat or should march forward to London and the throne. On almost any night of the year, while Master Jenkins snores and the Ear shines in the candlelight with the phosphorescence of decay, one may hear talk at that table involving four continents, three oceans, and many desolate isles. There one hears tales of mutiny, shipwreck, murder, starvation, sudden riches, utter defeat, and unhoped-for, impossible victory. One is taken back

to the siege of Louisburg, to Fontenoy, and to Dettingen, where even
the Hanoverian usurper fought almost like an English king. One
returns to Prestonpans, to Falkirk, to Culloden, and hears again the
skirl of the Highland pipes in the driving snow with the brave old
Jacobite songs ringing through them—

> Hey, Johnnie Cope, are ye waukin' yet?
> Or are your drums a-beatin' yet?
> If ye were waukin' I wad wait
> To gang to the coals i' the mornin'."

You would have been astonished, William, by the sudden explosive
force with which those wild, all but meaningless words were uttered.
Blandison's voice shook with some strong excitement. But this was
over in a moment. With the self-possession of an experienced actor
who, having dropped his mask, recovers and readjusts it as though
nothing had happened, he went on speaking:

"I ask your pardon. That old song always excites me, and whilst
I was quoting it there came to mind a Highlander whom I met one
night at Jenkins' table. His right arm was gone. He told me where he
had lost it and . . .

"But now, ladies and gentlemen, I have told you enough to indicate
that Jenkins' Ear ought never to be omitted from any list of the
clubs of London that bear strange names."

After a brief pause my cousin said: "And yet, for my part, I never
heard of this club before."

"Nor I," said George Selwyn.

"Ah, but that is natural, surely," Blandison replied. "The headquarters of the Jenkins' Ear, as I have told you, are in the City of
London. You gentlemen seldom visit that city. You know Westminster, Whitehall, St. James, and the rest of that marshy region
once given over to lepers and frogs but now to the Hanoverians. What
can you tell me, though, about Little Britain, Gunpowder Alley, or
Shoe Lane? Mr. Selwyn, I believe, has for many years drawn a
considerable salary as Surveyor of the Melting at the Mint. Quite
possibly he knows where the Mint is. But has he ever actually witnessed a melting?"

"Certainly not!" George answered without opening his eyes. "I
hear they do it at nine in the morning, and I'm seldom up so late."

"Just so. —And take another example. Mr. Horace Walpole is

curious in old buildings. London Tower is the oldest building in London. What can he tell me about the strength of its gates and how long it would stand a siege?"

"What Horace knows about that," my cousin cut in, "he may not feel free to tell you. I myself would say that any Jacobite planning to take the Tower had better think first about how he is going to get there without being killed. If he does get there, say by the Traitor's Gate, he will be killed soon after."

"Step by step, as you say, sir. At present, I am only trying to suggest how it happens that these gentlemen are ignorant of the Club of Jenkins' Ear. Another point I would make is that they are all members of White's in St. James' Street. To be sure, the members of White's know one another, which is of course a high privilege; but it excludes a good many other things which may be important."

To that remark we members of White's could think of no immediate rejoinder. Even Kitty was silenced by the man's effrontery. But then, more important for the moment than any possible retort were the questions that shouted in our minds: What is the basis of this self-confidence? What lies behind it—and what, perhaps, ahead?

The full urgency, as we felt it, of these questions cannot be conveyed to you, William, by mere black marks on white paper. I have done my utmost to suggest the effects of Blandison's talk:—its flash, its play, its range, its shifts of mood, and, above all, its prevading mockery. Of course I have left out a good many words of his and unconsciously foisted some of my own; but that is a slight defect in comparison with the total inability of written words, though set down by the Recording Angel, to render back again out of silence the sound of a living voice.

Do you agree that the swift quiescence of voices, the death of every tone in its moment of birth, is one of the most sorrowful aspects of our mortality? It makes every moment of life a farewell, a forgetting. I can recall a thousand things that my mother said to me—things merry and sad, wise and foolish. Her words come back every hour of the day; but the tones of her voice—I listen and listen for year after year, and they do not return. Ah, let us hope that the posterity for which we write will find out some way of holding back all noble and beloved tones from the tomb!

Never, I think, have I heard a voice more worthy than Blandison's of such perpetuation. It is not my opinion alone but also that of Kitty Clive, that what the man said at the Madlands' breakfast table was made memorable chiefly by his magnificent skill in the use of a grand instrument. Kitty calls it a skill, and admires it as such. From her first glimpse of him she saw Blandison as an actor. She also felt, and more than once said, that it seemed unfair to ordinary mortals for an actor to have a voice equally fit for all parts at once. It was mainly his voice, she told us from the start, that made Blandison fascinating, and therefore dangerous.

That, I think, was going too far, because there was also the mystery of his origin. Here was a man obviously of the upper classes, striking in appearance, at once bold and suave in manners, with powers of speech that would distinguish him in any salon or drawing-room; yet this man we had never seen before, or so much as heard of. He seemed to know London, England, and Europe remarkably well, but Europe and England and London were unacquainted with him. Somehow he had learned about the idlest jesting of White's Coffee House; but never had we heard mention at White's of such a man. What bushel had hidden this light? Behind what disguises had he concealed himself alike from fame and from scandal?

*   *   *

Questions of that sort were, I may say, raging in me as our breakfast party broke up and we stepped out into the October sunshine. Indeed, they absorbed my thoughts so completely that I have now no recollection of how Blandison singled me out and led me, with his hand on my arm, not toward Strawberry Hill but in the direction of the hermitage that looks out over the river. On ahead of us there were eight or ten of the horsemen I had seen while on my way to the pagoda. Now as then they seemed to be doing nothing in particular, nor was there any discernible reason for their being there; yet they appeared to be aware of our approach.

"A day like this in October is not English weather," Blandison was saying as we entered the hermitage and sat down on the wooden bench facing the Thames. "It makes me think of Juan Fernandez in June."

"Juan Fernandez!" I exclaimed. "Do you mean Robinson Crusoe's island?"

"In a way it belongs to him and always will, even though he never existed and Daniel Defoe was never there. In another way it might be called Dampier's island, Selkirk's, Shelvocke's, Captain Stradling's, or, best of all, Commodore Anson's. He lived there for three months in 1741."

"Ah, that would be during the War of Jenkins' Ear."

"Precisely."

"You took part in that war?"

"As I have already said, I did so, in more than one way. That was long ago; yet somehow, as I was saying, a scene like this takes me back. I suppose it must be the serenity of the light on the Thames and the woods of Richmond Hill, for certainly there is no likeness in the landscape. This English scene is small, smooth, worn by long human use, but the view from El Yunque on Juan Fernandez is savage, enormous. It takes in, first, a chaos of jagged black rocks confusedly piled as though by a drunken giant; next, the palms and tangled green wilderness; then the endless, leisurely roll of the breaker that creams and combs and crashes on the sands below; and, farther, the five thousand miles of purple Pacific between you and China. Mingled in with the crash of the breaker you hear the bark of a thousand seals and the roar of sea elephants. From overhead comes the call of a raven, wonderfully delicate and ethereal, sifted by distance, with the cope of the sky for a sounding-board."

For a minute or two there was silence between us as we gazed out over the vivid meadow and stream. Then I said: "Why do you tell me these things?"

"Because, sir," he answered, "I value your good opinion, and would not have you think that my remarks back there at the pagoda represented all that I have in me."

"They represented a good deal," said I, "—that is, a good many kinds of men. Some of those kinds I have not been accustomed to admire."

"That I should not expect; for, in fact, neither do I. What I do expect of you is the realization that a man may be forced, say by the circumstances of his birth, to assume a role which he would not have chosen. —Am I right or wrong in believing that Mr. Horace Walpole has done just that?"

"You ask a question, sir, after two hours of acquaintance with me, which a friend might ask after many years."

"I accept the reproof, of course; but let me point out that such a friend would have no need of that haste which, as Dante tells us, 'takes the dignity from every action.' He would not be, as I am, in danger."

"What sort of danger?"

"The word itself will, for the moment, suffice. Meanwhile you have agreed, I take it, that you are playing a part—or, rather, many parts —not wholly of your choosing but more or less imposed by your being the inevitably famous son of a famous man. Not for one waking moment do you forget this, any more than a skilful actor forgets his audience while upon the stage. You live behind many masks, Mr. Walpole. One you wear in the House of Commons, another at White's, a third in your house in Arlington Street, a fourth at Strawberry Hill, to say nothing of those you don as a collector, as a virtuoso, as a scholar, as a poet, and as a dilettante. Nay, I put it to you whether you have not a different mask for each of your friends and correspondents, and still another—perhaps the deepest disguise of all—which you assume while writing your endless letter to posterity."

"Sir," said I, "that last statement, at any rate, is false. Besides that, we are strangers, and I know not by what right—"

But Blandison's smile was so disarming—I may say so warm and friendly—that my indignation did not last through the sentence. Nothing had yet so clearly shown the beguiling charm of this man as the fact that in a moment or two I was smiling also.

"'Strangers'?" said he. "'Tis a cold word, and one which I hope you will not wish to use again. For, surely, we have much in common. There is, for one thing, that need of incessant disguises. The fool confuses acting with deceit, but we know it as a fine art demanding the utmost powers of united body and mind. We understand, also, that it lies in no man's choice what parts he shall play, but only whether he shall play them, as we do, well. —Why, then, need we be strangers? Is it that you think I should be unable to keep pace with you in any of your numerous interests—in your knowledge, say, of painting, or of royal authors, or of the war that brought your father's great career to a close? Or is it that Mr. Horace Walpole, so highly favoured by the Goddess Fortuna, is most fortunate in this, that he already has all the friends his heart can hold, and so is never at a loss, never sad, never lonely?"

But this will suffice to illustrate Blandison's skill in anointing the wounds left by insult with the oils of flattery. I admit that I was soothed and pleased, yet somehow I kept half a wit about me that went on asking what he was leading up to, what he wanted of me.

Well, at last it came—his audacious and astonishing request that I invite him to spend a week with me at Strawberry Hill! It came so swathed and perfumed, half concealed in a dozen cunning enticements, that I almost felt an invitation was being extended to me. Blandison managed to do like a consummate gentleman a thing which, one minute before, I should have said that no gentlemen would think of attempting.

He began by saying that he was obliged, for reasons with which he would not bore me, to spend a week in the Twickenham region, and then appealed to my sympathies by a courteous reference to his present hosts. There would be no difficulty, he thought, in explaining the transfer to my Lord and my Lady without giving offence. From there he went on to say that he had long wished to make my acquaintance, to visit Strawberry Hill, and to see my collections; that this desire had been increased by our talk in the pagoda, and had been so heightened by his interest in my guests—and here he named them, with a word of discerning appreciation for each—that now he felt it would be a grievous neglect of Fortuna's promptings not to make his present bold suggestion. "The opportunity does not often come my way," said he, "for such talk and laughter, such *noctes cenaeque deum,* as we might have; and experience has taught me to take such chances when they come. If you agree— Who knows? For one thing, I might provide some materials for the memoir which I understand you are planning of the period that began with the War of Jenkins' Ear. As you know, there is little yet written about that epoch; but if you would care to talk with a few of those who played some part in its chief events, that might be arranged."

What does one say in such circumstances? What does one do? Or, rather, did I have any choice? As I recall it, my feeling was that of embarrassment—for Blandison; and what I chiefly wanted was to save him from the confusion which I should have felt in his place. This put refusal out of the question. There remained for me to decide only the manner of accepting his proposal, and what conditions I should name.

Yet I did not abandon all caution. After thanking him for his kind suggestion and expressing my confidence that the week he offered would be delightful to me and my guests, I intimated that he knew a good deal more about us than we did about him. You should have seen him throw back his head and laugh. "Ah, well," said he, "you must not expect every one to be as famous as you and your friends. If there is any mystery about me I have made almost indecent haste to reduce it, and have even asked for a week of your company in which to dispel it altogether."

"Perhaps, then," said I, "you will tell me about those horsemen— who they are and why they are here. My Lord of Madlands seemed to be somewhat confused when I asked him."

"My Lord is always confused; but there's no secret about those men. They call themselves followers of mine, and I call them my companions. Their present business is to see that I am not interrupted. Most of them—not counting my man-servant, who rides a horse when not otherwise engaged—are gentlemen temporarily living in reduced circumstances. —Would you care to meet their leader?"

"It would be a pleasure," I replied, dishonestly.

The fact was that the look of them as they stood there facing us, uncovered, holding their mounts by the bridles, brought to mind the gentleman in reduced circumstances who stopped my coach in Hyde Park some years ago and nearly blew my brains out. Yet they were not ill dressed; their weapons and other accoutrements were excellent; their horses were splendid, and they had with them a magnificent stallion, evidently held in reserve for some rider not now of their number.

Twenty feet from the group Blandison stopped walking, and I, of course, also. One of the horsemen came forward with his mount beside him. At ten feet off he paused and made a deep bow. Then, looking respectfully at Blandison, he spoke one surprising word: "Sire?"

"Mr. Horace Walpole," said Blandison, "allow me to present my friend Sir Edward Livermore."

We bowed, and murmured the conventional nothings.

"Mr. Walpole," Blandison continued, speaking rapidly, "has invited me to spend the coming week with him at his villa across the road. Wishing to make some return, I have offered to bring down a few members of the Club who have interesting stories to tell about their personal experiences in the War of Jenkins' Ear. You will please to have writing materials brought at once to the pagoda. In fifteen minutes, have Richard Beston ready to ride to London with a letter to the Honourable John Byron, who is living just now with his sister, Lady Carlisle, in Soho Square. Byron will choose the narrators and see that they reach Strawberry Hill, by coach and in his company, not later than two o'clock tomorrow afternoon. They will come prepared to spend a week and will be lodged either at Madlands or at one of the inns of the neighbourhood. I shall make my own excuses to Lord and Lady Madlands. Your duties during the week will be as before. Please report to me every morning at eight o'clock, at the outer gate of Strawberry Hill. That is all."

No sooner had Sir Edward turned away than Blandison began talking to me, walking me back to the gate, leaving me no chance to edge in a word. Indeed, if there had been time for a word I should not have had the breath, so astonished I was by the man's assumption that his proposal had already been accepted.

* * *

My friends were awaiting me in the Prior's Garden, which, as you remember, extends along the northern front of the house behind the embattled wall. Kitty's face was almost pale. My cousin paced up and down the path, looking stern and soldierly, with his hands clenched. Mr. Chute was sitting on the little stone bench, leaning forward, his face between his hands. George Selwyn's eyes, both of them, were wide open. Something, clearly, had struck them "all of a heap," yet I was so full of my own news that I could not wait to hear theirs. —"What do you think?" I burst out. "You could never guess! That man, that, that— Well, he has asked me—that is, he has invited himself to come here and spend a week!"

Kitty Clive threw up her hands in a gesture that would have done credit to a tragedy queen, but for several seconds no one spoke. Then she said: "You agreed, I'm sure!"

"Well, I did not refuse. How could I? He made it so—so plausible, and, in a way, so attractive."

"Of course. So did the Snake in the Garden!"

"What do you mean, Kitty? After all, he's a gentleman, and I think you like him."

With a slight nod of the head and glance of the eye she reminded us that the windows of the servants' hall, looking out over the garden, were open. "Let's go up to the Library," she said.

She led the way. You can see the five of us leaving the garden, passing the saint and altar and holy-water basin of the Oratory, winding through the tiny Cloister, climbing the stairs in the Gothic gloomth of the lanthorne (a spelling I much prefer), stepping gingerly past the hollow iron men of the Armoury—in short, making a half-minute tour of the Middle Ages, and emerging at last into the eighteenth-century light, warmth, and delicately proportioned amplitudes of my new Library which, or the like of which, you have never yet beheld. Shall I pause to describe that tempered splendour, bold, ever bold, but never too bold, of leather-bound learning, richly carved wood and stone, painted glass, and then, over all, the ceiling glorious with "the boast of heraldry, the pomp of power?" Shall I try to make you see the room, twenty-eight feet long by twenty wide, in which the gorgeous butterfly that Strawberry Hill is destined to become is at last beginning to uncrumple its wings? Half a dozen instincts vociferate "Yes!" They insist that I ought at least to say something about the triple window looking eastward across the loveliest river in the world and richly emblazoned above with old azure and crimson sanctities. "Yes!" cries the pride of possession, and all the amateur antiquarian in me echoes, "Yes!" But I reply, like Lord Madlands: "That is, I mean, "No!" We have more serious business on hand."

I lighted two candles before we sat down, not because we needed them, but—I scarcely know why. Then I said: "Now, Kitty, what was that you were saying about a snake?"

"And you said I liked him, didn't you? Well, I do. So did Eve, poor woman! You said he's a gentleman. Of course. Satan has beautiful manners, when they suit his purpose."

"Oh, come! This isn't Drury Lane."

"Tell him, Kitty," said my cousin. "What's the good of drawing it out?"

"Horry," said she—and I can see her now as she turned to face me, excited, anxious, perplexed—"people don't think up things like this to put into a play. This is true, and dreadfully dangerous to us all—most of all, to you."

"What is, Kitty?"

"Let your cousin tell you."

"Nonsense!" said he. "Out with it, Kitty. It's your notion."

" 'Notion'! —I tell you, Henry Conway, I know what I'm talking about. This man, Horry, who calls himself Parson Blandison is really the Young Pretender. To English Jacobites he's Prince Charles Edward, and to the Scotch he's Bonnie Prince Charlie. During the uprising of the Forty-five you called him 'The Boy'; but you can see for yourself that he's a man now. Here in England, and especially at Strawberry Hill, he's about the most dangerous man alive."

I gasped, and stared—first at her and then at each of the others. For several seconds the only sound in the room was the slow, soft ticking of the clock. My little dog came over from the fireplace and rested his muzzle on my knee, looking up with an expression of confidence, even admiration, such as I seldom see in the eyes of my human friends.

"That's Kitty's notion," my cousin repeated. "She can't prove it, and has no evidence. We've always heard that the Young Pretender is an idiot and a cripple who—"

"You mean," Kitty broke in, "that we always *had* heard such things until the Young Pretender came over in the Rebellion of Forty-five and terrified this country to within an inch of her life. That was not the work of a cripple or an idiot but of the man we saw today."

"You go too fast," said I. "Horace Mann—he's our Minister in Florence, and knows more about the Prince than any of us—has always said that the handsome young soldier who landed in Scotland was a Jacobite cheat."

"What does that mean?"

"Probably that he was a double, an agent of some sort, but not the real man."

"Nonsense! Spies always report what their employers want to hear, and we English believe whatever they say because it saves us the trouble of thinking."

"Horace Mann is not a spy," I answered. "What's more, I myself have seen the true Prince more than once, at the Jacobite Court in Rome. The man we met today did not in the least remind me of Prince Charles Edward."

"It's fifteen years since you were in Rome, but I saw this man less than five years ago at Lady Primrose's house in Essex Street. —We all know Lady Primrose, and how she has gone on posing as a Jacobite after most people forgot what the word means. Well, that night she was showing us a life-size portrait of a man she called 'the Prince of Wales.' We knew she couldn't mean Prince Frederick because the man in the portrait was really princely, and finally she gave us the full name, Prince Charles Edward Louis Philip Casimir Stuart. It was just then that the man who had sat for the portrait walked through the crowd and stood beside his own picture. He was the man we met today at Madlands."

"Very well," said Mr. Chute, and he rose from his chair and began pacing the length of the room with his hands under his coattails. "Kitty Clive has quick eyes, she remembers faces, and she knows a few interesting facts. The question is: What do those facts mean? For my part, I'm not convinced that her solution is the only one they will support. What's to hinder, for instance, that this Parson Blandison is a mere adventurer, a gambler for high stakes, who, taking advantage of some resemblance to Charles Edward, has charmed a few foolish women like Lady Primrose and Lady Madlands into accepting him as—as the Prince?"

"But—"

"Just a moment, Kitty. I know there are difficulties in my supposition, but so there are in yours. For one thing, you may have been a bit hasty in your confidence that Lady Primrose knew and spoke the truth when she said that the portrait was that of Charles Edward. What chance has she ever had of seeing the man who properly bears that name? I am told that she has never been outside of England; and there is no proof that he has ever been farther inside it than the town of Derby, the southernmost point he reached in his foray of Forty-five. You will scarcely suggest that she was one of his camp-followers in that uprising, for, whatever you may think of her, Charles Edward is not, I believe—or at least was not then—that kind of man."

"And neither, if you would care to know," said Kitty, "is Parson Blandison."

"Ah. There you speak with authority. It is a thing to know. But now, once more, the weak point in your argument is the testimony of Lady Primrose. If she got in touch with the Young Pretender after the Forty-five, then she did a thing which all our English agents and spies in Europe were trying to do, but failed. Even Horace Mann, in Florence, lost sight of him. Charles Edward sank into a rumour, a wandering name. All that we heard of him was that he was drinking himself to death."

"Yes," George Selwyn interrupted, "on Scotch whiskey. The only mistake those English spies made was in underestimating his capacity."

"Let's be serious," Mr. Chute went on "The chances are a thousand to one that Lady Primrose was either deceived or else, for some reason, wanted to deceive other people. The story Mrs. Clive tells about that party, with the melodramatic appearance from nowhere of the portrait's original, does not correspond with my notion of the way things spontaneously happen. I would say that the whole affair in Essex Street was concocted, crudely. It does not by any means prove Mrs. Clive's contention that Blandison is the Young Pretender."

"And neither," said I, "have you proved that he is not."

"No. I agree."

"You think," I went on, "that there is one chance in a thousand that the man we met today may be Charles Edward. What I ask is, can we afford to neglect that chance? If only a Jacobite agent, the man is dangerous; but if he is what Kitty Clive thinks, why, then—"

Mr. Chute suddenly turned about and faced me with the cold blue glitter in his eyes which shows that his mind is rushing through half a dozen intermediate ideas to an inevitable conclusion. "Horatio," he exclaimed—for that is what he calls me when strongly moved—"you have made the most sensible remark I have heard today."

"I'm sorry, sir," I stammered. "I didn't mean to. I won't do it again."

"Now don't try to spoil it. Your meaning is, of course, that since we don't know, and can't find out, whether Blandison is or is not the Young Pretender, we must treat him as if we knew him to be that very person."

Between you and me, William, I was not aware of meaning just that; but I'm so often credited with more folly than I possess that I sometimes let an imputation of wisdom pass unchallenged.

"Yes," Mr. Chute continued in his half-humorous pontifical manner, "the decision reached by the son of England's greatest Prime Minister is approved, without qualification, by the grandson of Oliver Cromwell's great speaker in the Long Parliament, Sir Chaloner Chute. I take it that we all agree. From this decision we draw an immediate and practical consequence: this man, this Charles Edward Blandison, is to be entertained, according to his own request, for a week at Strawberry Hill."

"I don't see that," my cousin objected. "Why should we take the risk? If he should turn out to be really Charles Edward, entertaining him here would be treason. —Think what the Tories would make of it!"

"Then, General, what do you suggest?"

"Why, naturally, turning him over to the authorities."

"And they are?"

"Well, say—say King George."

"General Conway, this matter is serious. We have no time for idle jesting."

My cousin looked abashed.

"Why not turn him over to the Army then?" George Selwyn suggested.

"That's so," said my cousin, rising, squaring his broad shoulders, and gazing severely at George just as the rest of us were about to laugh. "You do well to remind me that I wear the King's coat, and that it is my duty to defend the realm against invaders."

"But Blandison has fifteen horsemen," I reminded him. "They would prevent you from getting any help."

"I shall need no help. I shall call the fellow out. His fifteen brigands will be of no use to him when he stands at the end of my sword."

"That's heroic of you," said George, "but according to the code of the duello any Prince of the Blood may ignore a challenge."

"Then, sir, I shall publish him as a coward!"

"Where? How? By what name? The Town would laugh if you said that about the man who gave us all such a fright ten years ago. As for this Parson Blandison, no one has ever heard his name. People would say you were making him up, to enhance your own reputation."

"Oh, no, no!" Kitty cried impatiently. "Don't you see, General, that if he's only an agent it would do no good to kill him? On the other hand, if you should kill the true Prince on Horry's land that would be the end of all of us."

After a moment my cousin sat down again.

"The thing to do," said George, "is to have the Twickenham beadle order this ambiguous parson to cease and disperse and abscond from these parts, taking his highwaymen with him. Or again—yes, now I have it—let's tell my Lord of Madlands that Blandison is carrying on an amorous intrigue with his Lady."

"George Selwyn," Kitty scolded, "you will either behave yourself or leave the room. Don't you know that our lives are at stake, and perhaps the freedom of England?"

"I know that the part of England where we now sit is ruled by a tyrannical queen."

"Very well; and she says we must have this man here on his own terms, and treat him as well as we can. If we don't he'll go elsewhere, and make more trouble. Horry must send off his invitation at once."

"But there's a thing you don't know yet," said I. "Blandison is bringing down four or five members of his Jenkins' Ear Club to tell us stories."

"Humph! Stories!"—from my cousin. "More likely they'll be more highwaymen. —And does he expect you to put them up in your house?"

"No; they'll be lodged at the King's Head in Twickenham, or else at Madlands. His motive in bringing them, I think, is to contribute something toward the entertainment, or perhaps to fill out the time and make it seem more reasonable for him to stay a week."

"But why a week?"

"That I don't know, Henry, and can't guess."

"At least," said Kitty, "we must have the club members to dinner."

"I suppose so," said I. "And how about Madlands? Must he come to dinner too?"

"Certainly. Tonight, at any rate. And so must she."

"Oh, merciful God!"

We reflected in silence. Then Mr. Chute sighed and said, about no one in particular: "One can make a shrewd guess at what God thinks of money by looking at the people he gives it to."

"All the best moralists," George drawled, gazing up at the Walpole shield in the ceiling so that we saw only the whites of his eyes, "keep telling how terrible it is to have too much money. Why can't some wiseacre mention not having enough? It's a commoner complaint. Almost epidemic."

"Now don't let's get philosophic," said Kitty. "We have business on hand. Horry, you must go and write your letters. The sun, you see, is setting."

*   *   *

When I got back to the library my friends were drinking tea. They had lighted three more candles, so that there was one for each of us. A good fire was burning on the hearth. The scene was peaceful, almost domestic, needing only a cat. The room was filled with a golden and rosy light such as a poet might dream of and a painter would never forget. You can scarcely imagine how warmly it lay on the great old books, how it gilded the little clock given long ago by Henry the Eighth to Anne Boleyn, and transfigured the faces of my friends.

Have you known such instants, William, and wondered whence they come, what they mean? They may last for only a heartbeat, yet each is somehow immortal. Ah, sir, if Horace Walpole ever becomes religious it will not be by persuasion of the Thirty-nine Articles but— may we say like St. Paul?—with the help of one of these blindingly beautiful moments that "into glory peep."

Perhaps it was not the fading light of the afterglow alone, but also the thought of our friendship, that brought heaven into the room. For my part, I welcomed the danger we were in because we were going to share it. —But then there was something more: a faint sorrow, a hint of grief, an undertone of farewell. That pitiless clock on the chimneypiece ticked so audibly on and on. Shadows were blotting the glow. Kitty's last words seemed to reverberate, deepen, and darken. It was as though each of us said to the others: "Let us now, more than ever, be faithful and kind,—for the sun, you see, is setting."

*   *   *

"You tell him, Kitty," my cousin said as I sipped my tea.

"Well, Horry," she began, "we've agreed about a few things while you were away. If you don't like them you can say so, and then we'll show you where you're wrong. —But, first, is he coming to dinner?"

"I have asked him to."

"Then he will. Where's Margaret putting him?"

"In the north bedchamber."

"I see—so that he can signal to his highwaymen and get signals from them. And where will his servant sleep?"

"With Louis."

"Good! —Did you think of that, or Margaret?"

"I did."

"Wonderful! You must be growing up."

"Oh, nothing like that! There really wasn't any other place to put him; and, besides, I thought Louis would appreciate the chance to study the language used by gentlemen of the road."

"Say what you may, sir, I suspect you of using your wits, as Louis will certainly use his. —But now for our decisions. The first is that all four of us are staying here all this week. Drury Lane can wait, and Parliament isn't in session, so that we are all at your service."

I got up from my chair, suddenly, to poke at the fire. "Bless your kind, brave hearts," I managed to say with my back turned. "Most people would leave the house tonight, before dinner."

"Well, there are only four of us, but—"

"But the right four, and enough to turn this card-castle into a fortress."

"Thank you, Horry. But don't get the notion we're being so very brave. For what danger is there? Only one of us knows who this man is, and she sees no chance of convincing the others. You gentlemen really think he's only some kind of Jacobite. Well, there's no law against entertaining that sort of people."

"No, indeed. It's quite the fashion. Every one keeps a pet Jacobite these days."

"Very well; on this question we hold five different opinions. No one can charge us with conspiracy. Suppose it should come out that Parson Blandison is what I say, and that he stayed here. I should go to the scaffold—or perhaps it's the stake that they send women to for treason—insisting, truly, that you four would not listen to me, that arguments had no effect upon you, and that you were all too ignorant and sleepy and stupid to know what you were doing. —Every one would believe me."

"But the stake, Kitty?" said George. "You tried a tragic part once, and it simply wouldn't do."

"Well, then, we're all safe, and Parson Blandison will be the only one who's doing a really reckless thing. As the Young Pretender, don't forget, he comes here with a price of thirty thousand pounds on his head, and he knows we know it."

"That's true," murmured Mr. Chute into his teacup. "I hadn't thought of that. The offer, I think, has never been withdrawn."

"It has not," said my cousin.

"If Kitty is right," said I, "she can make herself a rich woman, and hold up her head with Lady Madlands."

"Thirty thousands pounds!" George drawled. "What a wager at White's! Almost thou persuadest me to turn informer."

"But don't forget," laughed Kitty, "that when the Young Pretender heard about that reward he immediately offered *thirty* pounds—leaving out the thousands—for the head of King George. You wouldn't hurt a man who could say a thing like that!"

"Ah, well, no. Let him come. I mean— You get me all confused, Kitty! I mean, let this Parson Blandison come, this new flame of yours, pretending that he's the Pretender."

"Let him come! He *is* coming, call him what you like. We couldn't stop him now if we wanted to. He'll be here for a week, almost a member of the family, watching us, listening, guessing, and finding things out. This man can say just as good things as you can, George Selwyn; and he also can keep awake. He thinks faster and farther than any of us except Mr. Chute. He knows more than all of us put together. In fact it amazes me—considering his ignorance—how much he knows. And then, on top of all, he's a grand actor—and that means, of course, a grand person."

"But, Kitty," I objected, "you were saying a moment ago that Blandison isn't dangerous, and now you make him out a serious threat."

"You're right, Horry. I suppose George put me off by his notion that such a man can be defeated by a few *bons mots*. But then, too, I have to consider—even more than you gentlemen do—his charm. He doesn't care much for women; but they, let me tell you, care for him. He knows it, and he's a tempter."

"Do you expect to be tempted, Kitty?" asked George.

She smiled, at the fire. After a moment she said, almost shyly: "Naturally, I hope so."

Then we all laughed, and she went on: "It would do me good. It's years since anyone—well, what you mean; and my virtue needs exercise."

"Who's being overconfident now?" I asked. "You've called this man a snake in the garden, and that reminds us of what happened to Eve."

"Yes; that she fell. But since then we women—or some of us— have made a closer study of snakes."

"In other words," said George, "you don't expect to fall? You don't —ah—plan to?"

Again that smile—withdrawn, enigmatic, womanly. "We shall see," she said, softly. "Or rather, I shall."

Mr. Chute's level, serious voice broke into our musing. "Now there's the question," said he, "why the man should want to come here at all. As I understand it, he has given no reason except a wish to escape from Madlands. That, to be sure, is plausible; but I would suggest that he went there in the first place only as a step toward Strawberry Hill. He may feel that the home of Horace Walpole is a safer place of hiding, if that's what he wants, than that of a notorious Jacobite. What he certainly feels is that the son of Sir Robert Walpole would be a great support for the Jacobite cause. One sees how that news would sweep through the country, raising questions again of the Hanoverian right, rousing Tory hopes now all but dead. —Why, yes; whether we think of him as Mrs. Clive does, or regard him as the Young Pretender's 'double' or agent or spy, his main purpose here is to make a convert. Of course, he will not succeed. What remains to be seen is not whether any of us will 'fall,' but whether we can defeat him so soundly that the House of Stuart will never try this sort of thing again. If we can, if we do ... Mrs. Clive thinks we have a chance."

"Yes," said she, "there's a chance. Whether it's a good one, I don't yet know; but I see where it lies and something of how we can use it. Arguments, reason, and thinking things out will never defeat this man. His self-assurance, what some people might call his arrogance, is unconquerable. We have to get inside him. We must reach not his head but his heart."

"Has he one?" I asked.

"He has, but doesn't know it. That's part of the ignorance I spoke of. The man has been everywhere—except inside himself. He knows everything—except the man whom, at present, he calls Parson Blandison. Why, I don't suppose he even knows that he is lonesome, lost, and hopeless. That mask he wears fools him more than it does any intelligent woman. The polished shield he carries to cover his heart is only his mirror. He wants the world to think—and he really believes, himself—that he is all made of shining metal like one of those suits of armour you have upstairs. —Well, he *is* hard in a way, and he certainly *does* shine; but there's a man inside."

"How did you find that out?"

"Oh, don't you remember? It was when he spoke those lines from some old Scottish Jacobite song: 'Hey, Johnnie Cope, are ye waukin' yet?' and the rest. His voice shook as he said them; and then, just after, there was that about the Highlander who had lost his right arm in the Forty-five. —Well, I've told you that he's a grand actor; but just there, for a moment, he forgot his part and became himself. There were tears in his eyes—not from an onion nor yet the whiskey. What I learned just then is what we must keep in mind all week: this hard, brilliant man can be moved, even to tears, by the suffering of others—especially that of men whose misery he brought upon them."

"Ah, I see it!" said I. "You mean, Kitty, that we might defeat him by showing what another Jacobite uprising would cost."

"Yes, or what the last one did."

"There's the execution of the Scottish Lords," George Selwyn suggested.

"To be sure, George," Kitty answered. "We could give you a chance to tell that favorite story again."

"And there's Culloden," said my cousin.

"There again. General Conway can tell us about Culloden. —And then there are the members of the Club coming down from London. We don't know who they'll be or what they'll talk about, but they can hardly make another Stuart uprising look attractive."

"Even Blandison," said I, "doesn't know who the story-tellers will be. He's leaving the choice to his friend Byron; and Byron will have to take whomever he can find. Blandison, no doubt, is depending upon the Goddess Fortuna, but she may send some one like that one-armed Highlander."

"She may," Kitty agreed; "but we mustn't depend upon any such fickle female. We must play our own parts—or, rather, overplay them, a little."

"What on earth do you mean?" my cousin asked. "Tell us, Kitty."

"Well, now, for you, General Conway, I mean that you must do a good deal of marching up and down the room, looking stern, heroic, extremely handsome, and, in general, like a—general. Every two or three minutes you must jerk out a command, like 'Tell us, Kitty!' On no account must you ever pretend to any ability to think for yourself. Mr. Chute, on the other hand, must never show any power to do anything but think. George Selwyn must try to look even more exhausted than usual, and the question about what exhausts him must remain a mystery. But for Horry"—here she laid her warm hand on my cold one—"I have no suggestions. He always overacts all his parts, and he always will."

"But what's the purpose of this—this play-acting?" my cousin inquired. "Blandison will take us for a pack of fools!"

"Why, of course! But he already does, and we mustn't disappoint him. If he should come to suspect that we are normally intelligent he would take fright and ride off to some place where we couldn't work on him. Thus far, we have done well. Only fools, he is now saying to himself, would have allowed him to invite himself into this house for a week and then dictate what should be done here. All we have to do now is to continue on that same line—never crossing him, never seeming to question his motives, always grateful to him for every suggestion he makes about ways and means of turning the country upside-down."

"And what happens," Mr. Chute inquired, "if we fail?"

Kitty looked at him steadily for several seconds, and then replied, "We fail."

She once told me that an actress playing the part of Lady Macbeth has a choice among seven different ways, each with its own quite separate meaning, of speaking those two words. On this occasion she chose the best way.

"But I can tell you, Kitty," my cousin continued, ignoring these niceties, "that all this pretending in order to beat a pretender goes against the grain with me. I'm a soldier. I've fought at Culloden and Dettingen and Fontenoy and—"

"Yes, yes! You can say all that later—and then you can tell us how much good it did for you to fight, win, and lose in those places."

"But this woman's way of yours is—"

"—is the only way of beating a man so that he will stay beaten."

"Humph! By play-acting!"

"Yes, in short, madam, 'Humph!'" said George. "And by woman-agement."

"And when a woman has beaten two men down so far that they have nothing but 'Humph' left to say, then it's time for her to go and get dressed for dinner so that she can beat them some more."

Kitty rose, and we four men with her. "General Conway will see me over to Cliveden," she said. "I always feel so safe with a soldier."

At the door she turned again towards us. I see her standing there now, her hand on my cousin's arm, the candlelight agleam on her sprigged green muslin, and touching the soft auburn hue—or is it bronze?—of her hair. Oh, that Joshua Reynolds had been there, or even Van Loo! Her eyes sparkled with merriment and determination at once. "Now, gentlemen," said she, "I know you all hate to do anything useful; but this 'play-acting' isn't going to be extremely laborious. You don't have to learn any lines, attend any rehearsals, or even sit for a make-up. You've been practising your parts all your lives, and are now letter-perfect. Even if some slight exertion should be called for, you might consider that you have lived for many years, and lived well, on England's bounty. Now England needs you. Place-men, to the rescue! —But come, General. I must not be late for the opening scene."

* * *

Few things are less enlivening to me than an account of what other people have had for dinner, how they liked it, and what they managed to say between mouthfuls. The fact is, I do not recall what Mrs. Margaret set before us on that Sunday evening; but I have the word of Kitty Clive—an expert in such matters—that it was sufficient in quantity and good in kind. She also says that the talk was good at her end of the table, where she had Blandison at her right hand. At my own right I had Lady Madlands, to whom my tyrannical conscience obliged me to pay an almost exclusive attention. Therefore it was only by snatches of a word here and there that I heard what was going on ten feet away. Something there was about Patagonian giants—you know how giants of any kind, anywhere, have always enthralled my fancy—and a good deal about the Captain John Byron who was arriving from London on the morrow. He was the one, I gathered, who knew about the giants. One of the Byrons of Newstead Abbey in Sherwood Forest, this Captain seemed to be. Yet all these abbeys and giants and forests were borne away and drowned in the flood of my Lady's talk about her rheumatism and the execrable liver of my Lord. I listened to her with my right ear, wishing meanwhile that it were stone-deaf. I even contributed a few symptoms of my own. Not a word, however, did I say concerning the gout, for in that blissful epoch of ten days ago it was still to me only a word.

We gentlemen did not linger long at table after the two ladies had left it. No sooner had we rejoined them in the Library than Lady Madland set up a cry for whisk. I should have foreseen this. A brave man, realizing as I long have that whisk is becoming the opium of the English nation, would have declared that he had built Strawberry Hill for the sole purpose of providing a retreat from the tyranny of Edmond Hoyle. Instead, I called for cards and two tables. At one of them I sat down with Lady Madlands, who became my partner on the cut. Kitty Clive and Blandison at the other table engaged George Selwyn and my Lord. It was agreed—at Blandison's suggestion—that we should keep the same partners throughout the evening, and that Hoyle's rule of silence should not apply. Therefore, as we might have expected, Blandison talked almost continuously for hour after hour—regaling us with gossip of Parisian salons and the Papal court, the latest scandals from Venice and the death of Queen Caroline, with descriptions of Pacific volcanoes and of sea elephants, with accounts of gambling in China and a general history—beginning with the ancient Persians—of cock-fighting. Whether because of this somewhat distracting talk or because that Goddess Fortuna of his was smiling upon him, he and Kitty won so considerable a sum that I shall not divulge it to posterity. At our table, naturally, I lost, but lost to my friends, one of whom carries a purse chronically flat. Thus, although the evening was misspent, the outcome was mutually agreeable.

And what an odd thing that is, if one considers it a moment! For years I have tried to persuade that friend to accept half my income. But no, he will not. His "pride" is stronger than his love. Yet this friend is more than willing, he is overjoyed, to win from me on the turn of a card what he would never take as a gift! Surely, not even the code of the duello is more absurd than that.

Thus our Sunday came to a close. I fear that some of its diversions and anxieties will not accord with a clergyman's notion of keeping the Sabbath holy. Well, sir, no one knows better than you do the depravity of my spiritual state, and perhaps the worst of it is that I am unrepentant. Frankly speaking, I disapprove of this partiality to the youngest day of the week, whilst the other poor six are treated as though they had no souls to save. Read on, then, before you condemn me quite, and see what was done here before the week was out.

We rose from the card-tables at two in the morning. Kitty Clive told me, at her cottage door, that she thought we had made a good start. "I could see that you, at least, were enjoying yourself," said I. "And that, of course, is the main thing."

MONDAY

"Good morning, Louis," said I, some eight hours later. "What's the outlook for the day?"

"Good morning, your Honour. The weather is still salubrious. There has been a remarkable cessation of traffic along the road and upon the Thames. No letters or messages have been received. The Reverend Mr. Blandison conversed for half an hour, beginning at eight, with Sir Edward Livermore. They conversed in the Prior's Garden. Although the windows of the Servants' Hall chanced to be open, I overheard nothing of their conversation."

"You surprise me, Louis. As a usual thing you are so good at overhearing."

"I thank you, sir. —May I serve your tea?"

"Do. Are the other gentlemen up?"

"All but Mr. Selwyn. Mr. Chute will await your coming, at eleven, in the summerhouse at Cliveden. Mrs. Clive herself has been walking in her garden and singing."

"What! Singing in her garden?"

"Yes, sir. I took the liberty of thinking it unusual, sir, and especially at an hour so matutinal. She was singing 'Under the Greenwood Tree.' The words are by William Shakespeare, and the music has been composed by Mr. Thomas Arne. It is a beautiful song."

"Quite," said I. To so learned and observant a young man it seemed unnecessary to add that the song's refrain is "Come hither, come hither, come hither."

"This tea," I said, "is too hot. —Is there any more news?"

"Only that the Honourable John Byron will arrive by coach before two o'clock with four other members of the Club of Jenkins' Ear. These are to be a Mr. Morris, a Mr. James Adair—both of whom I understand to be gentlemen—a man from the Colony of Connecticut called John Chester, and a person by the Christian name of Jeremy."

47

"Ah," said I, setting down the teacup, "I'm glad we're to have a 'person' and a 'man.' They will add variety and extend your acquaintance with the language used by the lower classes. —But how did you learn all this, Louis? Did Blandison tell you?"

"No, sir. The Reverend Mr. Blandison tells me nothing, sir; and if he should condescend to do so I should still wish to draw my own conclusions."

"How, then?"

"Richard Beston, sir, who is the Reverend Mr. Blandison's manservant when not otherwise engaged, has been my source of information. He it was who conveyed the message to the Honourable John Byron. He returned at two o'clock. It has been arranged that he shall sleep in my room. I make bold to say that the arrangement has been well considered—except that he snores."

"Ah! Too bad! Does he talk in his sleep?"

"Upon that matter I shall be in a better position to report tomorrow morning."

"Does he talk in his cups?"

"Again, my brief acquaintance would not justify the present expression of an opinion. I fear, however, that he is abstemious, sir."

"What a deplorable virtue in a highwayman! But try him, Louis, with the best our cellar affords. We need to find out who and what his master really is."

"So I have gathered, sir. In addition, my own curiosity has been aroused. The Reverend Mr. Blandison is an amusing gentleman, with remarkable powers of speech. I shall endeavor to pluck out the heart of his mystery."

"Then our problem is as good as solved. —Don't let me detain you any longer."

*　　*　　*

The mood of friendly banter in which Louis and I indulge ourselves at what we call my levee is fit, no doubt, for my first waking moments, but I seldom carry it far into the day. It died that Monday morning as soon as he had closed the door, and the full gravity of my situation—so far, at least, as I then understood it—came upon me for the first time. On the day before, you will understand, and until I dropped asleep, exhausted, at two in the morning, I had been hurried on by I knew not what compelling impulse, and given scarce a moment for collecting my own thoughts. Other people—mostly Blandison, but also my friends—had done nearly all the thinking, talking, deciding, and I had been swept along by them as though I had no mind, no wish even, of my own. Looking back, I saw that I had behaved like a weakling, and I was ashamed. Also I felt a little as though I had been imposed upon, and I was mildly indignant.

I say "mildly," and to that I might add the word "confusedly," because of the difficulty I felt in singling out the object of my indignation. You will take this, perhaps, as another sign of my feeble-mindedness, because it will seem obvious to you that Blandison had been from the start the head and forefront of all offending. Ah, well, I can only ask you to read on—meanwhile keeping it in mind that from the start I had liked this man.

Was I really indignant after all, or did I merely feel that I ought to be so? An Englishman's house is said to be his castle, and my castle had been taken and entered—not by storm but by what George Selwyn would soon be calling "blandishments." My conqueror had spent the night under my roof. He confidently expected to spend there several more nights and days—using my home as a refuge, as a lurking-place from which to sally forth on some adventure which might involve me and mine in ruin. I remember saying to myself that surely it is the very essence of insult for one man to use another as a mere convenience, and that there can be no graver sin against the rites of hospitality than that of a guest who deliberately endangers the house that shelters him.

For danger there was here, certainly. Suppose this Blandison should turn out to be in fact the Young Pretender—or, for that matter, his double, or his agent—and that his presence in England was in some way connected with that gathering of French troops and transports at Dunkirk of which my cousin had heard in London only the week before. —On the other hand, he and I now stood in that relationship of host and guest which is older by far, and more sacred, than any law that parliaments can enact or kings pronounce. Besides that, although no promises had been made or asked on either side, we were both of us—or so I meant to assume until the contrary was proved—gentlemen.

Against this danger I had no defence except what now seemed to me the all but hopeless attempt to dissuade Blandison from his purpose by appealing, as one might say, to his better nature. That had been Kitty's notion. For my part I thought I had never seen a man less susceptible to the kind of education that works upon the will and the inward impulses. It was natural, I thought, for a woman to think of a man as more vulnerable than he really is, and I doubted whether we should be able to find any crack or crevice in the armour of self-assurance that clothed my guest from top to toe.

Well then, here was one of those occasions on which I hasten to find out what Mr. Chute has to say. In less than twenty minutes after Louis left my chamber I too was out of it and down the stairs and on my way to Kitty Clive's summerhouse. As I went along I saw that she was still walking—barefooted, as her way is on dewy mornings—in her garden. Her "Come hither" song had evidently achieved its purpose, for Blandison was walking beside her. She had taken his arm, and was looking up at him from under her chip bonnet with just that expression of merry comradeship which she had so often in times past turned upon me.

Yes, as you are thinking, William, that look gave me a perceptible twinge.

Blandison did not see me going up to the door of the summerhouse, but Kitty Clive, as she told me later, did. That may have added something—who can say?—to the warmth of her gaze at her companion.

Kitty has built this tiny summerhouse—one-roomed, thatch-roofed, with a double window toward the river and a small single one behind —since you were here, and unless you make haste to come again you will never see it, so crazed it is and only waiting for the first brisk wind from the west. Kitty calls it her "green room" and uses it for learning her lines when the weather will not let her sit in the great oaken shell which I have placed just outside the larger window. It does look theatrical, but then too it reminds one of that other side of Kitty's nature which she expressed when she wrote me not long ago: "Tho' I am now representing women of qualitty and coblers wives &c &c to crowded houeses"—I give you her exact words and spelling —"and flattering applause; the characture I am most desirous to act well is a good sort of countrey gentlewoman at twickenham." This explains, no doubt, the thatched roof, for which I can think of no other justification. It combines oddly with the painted glass in the window, pieced together out of bits gathered from ancient churches far and near for which I have no present use. —And then too, think of that old glass which for centuries had echoed back nothing but the Psalter and Litany having to listen now to the speeches of Lady Wishfort in Congreve's *Way of the World*!

Mr. Chute was sitting at the table near the window, engaged, he said, in writing shorthand notes of everything he could remember about the events, remarks, and plans of the preceding day. You know that note-taking habit of his, and we have agreed that it is in keeping with the clear, orderly, perspicuous habit of his thought. He writes notes as I do letters—except, of course, that they are addressed to himself. At his home in Hampshire I have seen thousands of them, all carefully filed away—for what reason, I cannot guess, because what he has once written down he remembers forever.

He made light of the fears—or, let us say, the anxieties—that had got me so abruptly out of bed, pointing out that each of them had been considered in our conference of the day before, that a plan of action had been agreed upon, and that now we had only to put that plan into execution. "First gather your facts," said he, ticking the points off on his fingers; "then think them into order and meaning; then decide what to do about them; and, finally, act." When I pointed out that the "facts" we had thus far gathered were almost frighteningly few he replied, first, that he thought we had a good many, and, second, that a sensible man never clutters his mind with more information than he needs for the task in hand. From there he went on to speak about the method of thought devised by Sir Francis Bacon and the wonderful results it had achieved in Sir Isaac Newton's discoveries. I failed to see the connection of all this with what he had rightly called "the task in hand," but it was wonderfully comforting to find him not in the least dismayed or perplexed. If he was not, then why should I be? More and more as he talked on, I approached the feeling of security, with something in it of a willing dependence, which I used to have while listening to my father. The differences between Mr. John Chute of the Vyne and Sir Robert Walpole of Houghton and Downing Street are many and great, but both of them have had the faculty of making me feel, without resentment, rather like a child.

I wish that you knew this man better, William, for I love to have my friends love one another. Why should mere politics—the fact that he is an inveterate, perhaps even a violent, Whig while you are what you are—stand like a high stone wall between two good men? And even in political opinion are you really far asunder? Mr. Chute regards royalty as an expensive bauble, corrupting and enfeebling every one concerned, and you think it a holy thing enjoined by the Monarch of Heaven. That disagreement admits of no compromise, but you and he do agree that royalty is a necessary thing—as he thinks, because of the childishness of the people. He goes on to say that since we must have a monarch it is well to have a weak and stupid one— and is that not rather close to the position of you Hanoverian Tories? You would have been satisfied entirely had you seen the vigour with which Mr. Chute set to work to keep the Elector of Hanover upon the throne.

For the rest, he is, as you know, a sound scholar, an enthusiastic antiquarian, and a Christian far more nearly orthodox than one, at least, of your present friends. You would not, or should not, like him the less because he is inclined to be a little old-fashioned in opinion as he is in his dress. He is at times somewhat brusque, and he does not suffer fools gladly—a fact which would in no way affect you, and is, besides, easily forgiven by all who know that for almost thirty years he has suffered villainously with the gout. With better health he might have been a great figure in Parliament, as his grandfather was in the time of Cromwell; but he would have been a splendid failure at Court. His manners are those of a highly cultivated country squire, and good enough for me. He is the Mentor of our group, talking little but thinking all the while. He represents reason among us, as wit is incarnated by George Selwyn, martial courage by my cousin Conway, and womanly wisdom by Kitty Clive.

And yet the word "reason" does not cover the ground. I never hear other people praising this man's mind without saying, either to them or to myself: "Ah, but if only you knew the warmth of his heart, and how faithful a friend he can be!" He is not quite old enough to be my father, but I have a notion that his feeling for me is somewhat paternal. Perhaps I have said enough to show that I would by no means resent such a feeling, and that I regard him with the mingling of love and veneration proper to a son.

Mr. Chute is a good deal grayer now than he was when you met him here some years ago. He is thinner, too, and somewhat less robust, yet no one would call him an old man. His clear blue eyes grow larger year by year, and his nose makes one think more and more of an eagle, but it seems to us that the masculine force and speed of his mind are steadily increasing. The pain he endures every hour of the night and day—I know a little more about this now than I did ten days ago—seems rather to attenuate and refine than to weaken him. Let me add that a good part of whatever is good in this house is of his design, and that much the same thing may be said of the house's owner.

Well, you see how I ramble and rattle on when I begin talking about my friends. Now let's get back to the summerhouse on that Monday morning. Mr. Chute was still praising Sir Isaac Newton, one of his heroes, when we heard voices outside the double window, which stood slightly ajar. Kitty and Blandison were approaching the oaken shell. We fell silent—so as not to interrupt them, you understand—and Mr. Chute's lead pencil began to move across the page.

"Why, no," Kitty was saying, "you're completely and absurdly mistaken. Of course it's flattering to a woman of my age and figure, and I suppose I ought to thank you, but, really, I thought you had better eyes, and more wit."

"As I said before, madam," came Blandison's voice from just below the window, the two of them having seated themselves by this time in the oaken shell, "I intended no discourtesy. I was only putting two and two together and making four."

"No, sir," Kitty gurgled, "you were trying to put one and one together in a way they don't go, and making a ridiculous blunder."

"I accept your word for that, of course, and I apologize; yet you will perhaps agree that the mistake was natural."

"Why, yes—to an ignoramus, to one who has seen just nothing of life; but scarcely to the accomplished, quick-witted man that Parson Blandison would like to appear."

"Come, come, madam! You are a famous actress, and one of your most triumphant parts is that of Lady Wishfort in Congreve's *Way of the World.*"

"Yes, I'm an actress, and a good one, and I do play that part well. Do you know why? It's because I *play*, but do not *live* it. —You, of course, are an actor too. In some ways you too are a good one. You have fine natural gifts; but, if you care for a professional opinion, they are at present obscured by what I must call your ignorance."

"Ignorance, madam?" Blandison exclaimed, in a tone that brought a smile to Mr. Chute's grave face and almost made me laugh aloud.

"Or, if you prefer, stupidity. I myself should not prefer it, because ignorance can be cured and stupidity is hopeless. —But the main thing is that either one of them will be fatal to your success in the part you are playing just now on the stage of Strawberry Hill."

Blandison rallied after a few seconds, for we heard him say: "Suppose we assume, then, that my fault lies in ignorance. —May I hope that you will attempt a cure?"

"That's the very thing to which I shall devote all my energies during this coming week. In fact, I'm beginning now."

"Oh?"

"Yes. There's no time to be lost. You have grown a hard shell about that ignorance of yours, so that it's going to be no easy thing to get at. What you don't know seems to you not worth knowing. You think the good of life is in being clever and subtle and hard. It isn't. Wise people are simple. You think you're deceiving others, as no doubt you often do; but the person you deceive most of all is yourself."

For what seemed a long time, then, we were left to wonder how Blandison was taking this attack. Would he resent it? Would he try to turn it aside by ridicule or a change of topic? Would he rise and walk away? But we could only wait, with little glances at each other to express our admiration of Kitty's boldness. She was matching Blandison's audacity with her own, and going beyond it. And of course we kept it in mind that every word she spoke was addressed, in her firm belief, to Prince Charles Edward Louis Philip Casimir Stuart, who might some day be King of England.

At length we heard Blandison speaking, in a tone which showed at any rate that he was not angry. "Won't you yourself be a little simpler," the voice said, "and tell me what you think I most need to know?"

After a brief pause the answer came: "Yes, I think I can tell you in one short word. That word is 'love.'"

There was no reply. The silence grew and grew. It was startling, shocking, incredible. Even now I can scarcely believe it, and I do not yet know all that it meant.

Kitty's voice was low and grave when she spoke again, and we thought that she and Blandison must have risen from the shell. "Parson Blandison," said she, "you have come here for reasons which we understand only in part, but I should like to have you know that we are glad to have you with us. As the acknowledged Queen of Strawberry Hill, I welcome you."

"Thank you, madam."

"I think we are all going to have a good time together, for you really are a most amusing clergyman."

"Again, I thank you!"

"Yes, a good time; and possibly a profitable one for us all—excepting, perhaps, Lord and Lady Madlands. —May I make one request?"

"You need only name it."

"That if we should play again at whisk the partners shall be the same as they were last night. Lord Madlands can well afford to lose, and some of us others need to win."

"Ah, Mrs. Clive, let us be partners in all things!"

"Agreed. There's my hand. —And now I am sure that you have much to do. Horry will want to show you his house, and your friends will soon be arriving from London. —Haven't we had a good talk!"

"At least, you have given me much to think about."

"Shall we meet here tomorrow?"

"If you will only sing 'Come hither' I shall take it as a command."

"Oh," Kitty laughed, her voice growing fainter in the distance, "I'm always singing that song. And I will show you, Parson Blandison, that I too can lay my little plots and plans. Yes, and even—who knows?—I might teach you something."

"I'm sure you can teach me many things. But what have you especially in mind?"

"Oh, something—about—love."

And at that they must have parted. A few seconds later we heard Kitty singing on the path to her cottage:

> "Who doth ambition shun
> And loves to live i' the sun . . .
> Come hither, come hither, come hither!
> Here shall he see
> No enemy
> But winter and rough weather."

* * *

You would never guess, William, what especially took Blandison's fancy as he and Mr. Chute and I went the rounds of what some one has called my "oyster-grotto-like profanation." It was not the tiny central hall in which I have caught and enclosed the very soul of the

Gothic past, not the lean windows fattened by painted-glass saints, not Mr. Chute's College of Arms in miniature, not my treasury of books by and about Madame de Sévigné, not even the noble new Refectory or the Library above it where I am now writing. The fact is, I fear, that Blandison has lived too long amidst what is called good taste to have any deep understanding of a venerable barbarism. He lacks that instinct for ruins, charnels, and screech-owls which has led you and me on so many romantic peregrinations. To be sure, he spoke politely of my collections, and paused for some time before Eckardt's portraits of my father and mother, as though surprised that parents of mine could have looked so intelligent. His eyes really lighted up, though, when we came to the delicately carved antelopes that adorn the balustrade of the staircase, each of them, you remember, supporting the Walpole shield.

"What's this! What's this!" said he. "I was not aware that the Walpoles use the antelope as their supporter."

I replied that it had been holding up our arms ever since the days of Sir Terry Robsart, the Crusader.

"H'm! Indeed! That goes back farther than I had thought our European knowledge of the animal extended. —Of course you know that its name comes from the late Greek word *antholops,* meaning Unicorn."

My Greek, I told him, had never been much, and was now in ruins. Blandison thought that a pity, and suggested that my interest in Gothic was in some way connected with it. From there he launched into a discourse about antelopes and unicorns which, though learned exceedingly, was neither dull nor pedantic. There was a good deal about the use of the unicorn's horn for the detection and cure of poison—two things, he said, which the horns of the antelope could not do at all. I was told that the unicorn has always been a symbol of courage and fidelity, whereas the antelope is notoriously a fickle, capricious, irresolute beast, afraid of its own shadow. The unicorn, he said, was the legitimate king of beasts, and the lion a mere usurper. Then he shot the question at me: "Do you know, Mr. Walpole, how and when the unicorn came to be used as a supporter of the Royal Arms of England?"

Unfortunately, because I could see that this was what he had been leading up to all along, I did not. I was even a little ashamed, not only because this was the sort of thing an Englishman might be expected to know but for the reason that I have spent some time—under your guidance, William, and that of Mr. Chute—in the study of heraldry.

"It came in with the House of Stuart," Blandison declared, in a tone unmistakably triumphant. "The unicorn had always been the Stuart supporter, and the first King James brought it with him. Wherever you see the arms of an English king, even though they be borne today by a foreign upstart, you see the Stuart unicorn in his glory— argent, armed, crined, unguled, gorged with a coronet of *crosses patées* and *fleurs de lis,* with a chain extending from the crown between the forelegs and reflexed over the back, all or."

I had just the breath to remind Blandison that the Royal Arms of England are supported also by a lion. "Degraded," he thought, would be a more suitable word; and from there he went on to discuss what he called the "natural antipathy" between the lion and the unicorn. This he attributed to abject cowardice in the one and, in the other, a total absence of fear. "Hang a lion's skin in the open air," said he, "and let a unicorn approach it, upwind, by as close as a mile, and what happens? All the hair falls off the skin as the result of sheer terror."

How did he expect me to take that assertion—as a statement of fact or as some kind of allegory? In what sense, if in any, did he believe it?

"But there's one clear advantage," I suggested, "which the lion has over the unicorn: he really exists. I've seen one."

"Oh, you mean in the Tower, I suppose, where the Hanoverians keep so much of their plunder. Yes, they naturally would have a few lions there, in captivity, afflicted by mange and vermin. It might occur to a thoughtful man that the reason why they have no unicorn is that they couldn't catch one."

And there again was that note of triumph in Blandison's voice. The thought flashed upon me that perhaps he was not talking about any mere animal, real or alleged, but about a man who had lived for ten years with a price of thirty thousand pounds on his head and had never been taken. Our agents and spies in Europe had reported many rumours of this man. He was here, he was there, he was planning this and that, they had written, but always he had eluded pursuit. Then for months and years at a time there had been no reports, no conjectures even, so that one came to ask whether this man was still living—or, indeed, had ever lived.

But now Blandison was speaking again. "I see, Mr. Walpole," said he, "and grieve to see it, that you are an infidel. It seems to me a shocking thing that one who has been to such pains and expense in gathering the mere debris of the Gothic ages should lack the faith of that great time, and should disbelieve in its sacred animal on no better grounds than that he has never seen it. —May I inquire whether you have ever seen, with your own eyes, an antelope?"

"I have not."

"And yet you believe in its existence."

"I do."

"Why?"

"On the authority, I suppose, of those who have seen it."

"Then let me tell you, sir, that there is at least ten times as much and as good authority for the existence of the unicorn as for that of the antelope. In the Bible, for example, the unicorn is mentioned again and again, but the antelope not once. I suppose you will scarcely ask for better authority than the Word of God. I trust you will not oppose Holy Writ with the pestilent heresy of Ole Wurm, who taught, well over a hundred years ago, that this glorious beast is really a sort of whale. If you do, I shall overwhelm you with citations from Thomas Bartholinus *De Unicornu Observationes Novae,* who draws his 'authority' from six hundred different writers, sir, in twelve different languages."

To avoid this avalanche I hastily declared that I had no intention of disputing Holy Writ.

"Well then, sir, you must believe in unicorns."

"Oh, I do! I do!"

"Very well. And you will recall that in the Bible this animal invariably represents a chieftain or sovereign."

That fact, I said, had escaped my attention.

"It is, however, a fact," said he. "And now, Mr. Walpole, in return for your kindness in showing me your antiquities, I show you the only one of my own that I happen to have with me. This silver ring"—and he drew it from his finger—"is of no great age, having been made, I think, by Benvenuto Cellini, at Rome, in his younger manhood. That would be, say, two hundred and thirty years ago, and far short of the Ages of Faith; yet you can see that Cellini believed in unicorns, even as he did in salamanders, or in Leda and the divine swan."

I took the ring to the window, where Mr. Chute and I examined it closely with a magnifying glass. It was all of silver, heavy and large, yet delicate—a signet-ring, much worn by use. On the bezel there was carved, in relief, a tiny landscape in which a unicorn stood facing a waterfall, the spirals of his horn clearly marked. There was a crescent moon in the sky, and some hint of clouds. The thing was so spirited, or perhaps I should say so virile, and yet at the same time so minutely precise, that I could easily believe it the work of Benvenuto—whose medals, of course, I know fairly well. It made me feel, as I gazed, that now I really had seen a unicorn. Just that is what I said to Blandison as I gave the ring back.

He seemed pleased at that, and smiled as he slipped the ring on his finger. "You have seen one," said he, "and in your own house."

"I begin to get an inkling of what you are hinting at," I replied. "That does not necessarily mean that I accept your suggestions, but—"

"No. As I said before, Mr. Walpole, you are a man of little faith."

Blandison then told us how the ancient position of the unicorn has been usurped in modern times by the rhinoceros, a clumsy beast of cavernous maw and foul breath, wearing a stumpy spike on his snout. This creature, said he, was ugly enough for infidels to feel at home with and never doubt his existence, but there was the disadvantage that whatever the rhinoceros touched was defiled.

It became evident as Blandison went on about these two animals, one of them ideal and the other actual, that he was working out a kind of allegory wherein faith and doubt were contrasted, truth and fact were sharply distinguished, past and present were praised and blamed. He made the unicorn stand for the Gothic ages and the House of Stuart while the rhinoceros represented the present time and the actual ruler of England. In all this there was much of that audacity, not to say arrogance, which had so astonished us during the Madlands breakfast. Mr. Chute and I found it hard to remember that this man had been completely silenced, hardly more than an hour ago, by Kitty Clive. He seemed to need another lesson in humility, and the chance for it came when he said that the one thing missing in that old chivalric picture at the Rose Tavern was a unicorn.

"By the way," said Mr. Chute, "I think you told us yesterday that the Rose stands inside Temple Bar."

"Yes, sir. Just inside."

"That is not so, as any sedan-chair man in London could tell you. The Rose could not have survived to the present day had it not stood to begin with outside the gate. It is undoubtedly one of our oldest buildings, and was at first a monastic hospice kept for wayfarers who arrived after the gates were closed. A club of antiquarians of which I am a member has studied the building closely and has found that the main part of it, including the Painted Room, is of the fourteenth century. The painting which you described was also studied in evidence. We washed the wall, made measurements and drawings, matched the pigments of one side with those of the other, and found older paint—much older—beneath the present surface. —May I ask how long it has been since you were last at the Rose?"

Blandison admitted that he had paid his last visit there "some years ago."

"Ah. That explains the error you made yesterday in saying that the picture on the wall represents a scene of chivalric contest. It does not. At present that picture is a crude and vulgar daub showing a scene on shipboard in which the captain is having his ear torn off by the leader of a boarding-party."

"Why! But that is a desecration!"

"Yes, sir. Whoever may have been responsible, it is. But it may relieve your indignation to learn that the picture has been desecrated five separate times to suit the needs of five separate ages. We have found that the earliest painting showed the conversion of St. Paul, who was stricken with a great darkness outside Damascus and so might be considered the patron saint of benighted travellers. The second one, superimposed, is perhaps a century younger. It represents Jonah cast up by a whale, and is therefore suited to the time when London was becoming a seaman's town. The third, really chivalric, depicts the capture of Francis the First at Pavia. The fourth shows the capture of Charles the First of England at the time when London was the main strength of Parliament against the Stuarts. The fifth is the one you saw years ago. It is not really chivalric, for it represents the rescue of the Palatine Elector by a member of the Tufton family which then—some eighty years back—owned the tavern. The present painting uses many of the old figures—for the sign-painter, of course, never works harder than he has to—and Master Jenkins lying on the deck is probably in much the same position as St. Paul just fallen from his horse. There is, however, a striking difference in the significance of those two figures. Are we to judge from your enthusiastic remarks of yesterday that you prefer the figure of Master Jenkins? Which comes closer to your ideal of chivalric glory: the saint or the sot? And let me leave with you this further question: While retaining all you can of the pure gold of your dreams, had you not better learn to mix it with a little more of ascertained fact?"

Blandison did not reply. He stood and gazed at his silver ring, shining vividly now as he held it out into the sunshaft that slanted through a painted pane. All three of us, I think, welcomed the interruption when Louis appeared at the door to announce the arrival of the Honourable John Byron.

"Ah," said I, glancing at the clock, "he comes early. Good!"

"I took the liberty of asking him to do so, and to come alone," Blandison explained. "He and I will wish to make certain arrangements before the other members of the Club arrive."

"He will be welcome," I said. "Where have you left him, Louis?"

"In the waiting-room, your Honour. He appears to be interested in the Venetian prints."

"Show him into the Great Parlour, and ask Margaret to set seven places. —Tell her not to forget the whiskey."

"You don't need to provide whiskey for me," Blandison said, with a swift return to his friendly manner, as we three walked to the parlour. "I haven't lost my taste for good wine."

I told him that my cellar was at his disposal, and that I even had a good supply of beer for any of his friends who might prefer it. This, he said, was fortunate, as he did not yet know what particular friends John Byron had found available on such short notice, and so could not foresee their tastes in the important matter of drink.

The Honourable John Byron—or, as we soon came to call him, the Captain—was gazing out of the window with his back toward us as we entered the parlour. He looked tall and thin as he stood there, his hands nervously clasping and unclasping behind him, for that first second or two; and there came to me an impression, of which I could not rid myself in the days that followed, that here was a man of one dimension, a linear man. The cue of his sandy hair, unpowdered and smoothly combed, was tied with a plain black ribbon. His snuff-coloured coat was well made and without ornament of any sort. His breeches, stockings, and shoes were black.

The effect of Quakerish sobriety which these habiliments alone might have given was corrected at once when the man turned about, almost with a jerk, and came toward us. He smiled with every feature—with his strangely twisted mouth, his large and luminous gray eyes, and even, it seemed to me, with his crooked nose. His right shoulder was lower than the left, and if I am not mistaken his ears were out of balance. I saw that the single line to which I had reduced him was a wavering one.

Well, here I am, William, in one of those descriptions which I've already told you that I detest; but I find that it's not, after all, an intolerable bore—this effort to make you see, and like, a man whom I liked at first sight. His smile seemed to come from inside him, as though from some natural spring of gaiety. Good humour and the spirit of comradeship looked out of his eyes and spoke in his voice as he greeted Blandison and then was introduced to me and to Mr. Chute. "Yes, I know that I'm an odd spectacle," he seemed all the while to be saying. "Let's enjoy it together."

The Captain told us that he and the four members of the Club whom he had brought with him had made the journey from London quite comfortably that morning in less than two hours, and that they were well ensconced at the King's Head Tavern and the Eel Pie House, delighted with their rooms, with the river and village and, as it appeared, with the universe in general. His friends, he said, were all for the time at leisure, and glad of the opportunity to spend a week "far from the madding crowd's ignoble strife."

"You read poetry, Mr. Byron," said I.

"It would have been stupid of me," he answered, "not to have glanced through my sister's copy of Mr. Gray's magnificent poem when I knew that I was about to meet Mr. Gray's illustrious friend."

Was not this rather well turned, William?—I mean not for wit, but for the grace, the good nature.

The Captain said that his companions would reach the house promptly at two, having eaten in the village. Our lunch, I told him, would be served at one o'clock, and that would leave half an hour for the talk which he and Blandison wished to have. With this arrangement, Mr. Chute and I left the two men together.

Oh, yes; just here I had better remind you of the odd hours we keep at Strawberry Hill. At nine in the morning I have tea, with bread and butter, in bed. At one comes what I call "lunch" and George Selwyn "breakfast," served either in the Blue Room looking out toward the Thames or in the Refectory. Tea comes at four or thereabouts, wherever we happen to be, and dinner at eight. By this arrangement I make a sharp distinction between country hours and those of the

Town. Furthermore, I save sunlight for my agricultural duties: quarrelling with my gardener, chatting with the shepherd-boy, and feeding the goldfish.

*   *   *

Taking out Lord and Lady Madlands and putting Captain Byron in their place made a huge difference between the meal of Monday noon and the one I had just managed to live through the night before. We had a "merry" time, in all the meanings of that old, deep, many-coloured English word. There was laughter in it a plenty, but laughter that had no malice or poison and left no wound. Frankly, I was surprised to see how little the effects of the ridiculous depend upon ridicule. And Blandison too may have learned something by the observation that in order to command an occasion of this sort a man does not have to talk all the time, or to be mysterious, or eloquent, or even handsome. Blandison behaved rather well. He showed, as he had said, that he could enjoy good wine. He showed that he could listen to the talk of another man and enjoy it—a test I should not have expected him to meet. But then, we all behaved well, in our several ways. I was proud of us.

The Captain and I had some talk about Newstead Abbey as an example of Gothic architecture, and I told him of course about the delightful half-day that you and I spent there some years ago. He is fond of his birthplace, though not so much of the house and ruins as of the great old "Pilgrim Oak" and other trees of Sherwood Forest round about; but his acquaintance with it is what you would expect from the fact that most of his life, since he was sixteen or so, has been spent at sea. He is now, I should say, about thirty-two. I learned that he is a younger son of the fourth Lord Byron, the first of that line being, as you probably remember, John, Baron Byron, who fought with such astonishing vigour and gallantry, along with his five brothers, under the banner of the first Charles. He went into exile with Charles's son, and died abroad, so that he might well be called a Jacobite of the original and most impassioned strain. All the more, therefore, was I pleased—and, indeed, relieved—to find that the Captain, like William Cole, is staunchly, even outspokenly, a Tory, but of the Hanoverian, or anti-Jacobite, sort. For that meant, you see, that Blandison was not trying to overwhelm us, as he so easily might have done, with people of his own persuasion. Was this due to his having no other choice, to a careless oversight, to magnanimity, or to his trust in the Goddess Fortuna? The answer to that question is one of the many with regard to Blandison which I shall probably never know.

One thing I observed about the Captain, as we all did, was that he ate, as the saying goes, "just enough to keep a bird alive." He was rallied about this by Kitty Clive, herself a good trencherwoman, who offered once or twice to eat what he had left on his plate—an offer which caused in Louis, who was serving at table, a sudden shocked raising of the eyebrows. "Yes," said Byron, "my friends are always laughing at my contemptible appetite. The fact is that I was starved in my boyhood and have never got over it."

"What!" said I. "At Newstead Abbey?"

"No, not there, but in other places less bountifully supplied. The coast of Patagonia was one of them." The tone of his voice and a momentary grimness in his face prevented any comment.

We were all diverted by the Captain's account of the perplexities into which Blandison's message of the day before had suddenly thrown him, how he had been roused from his afternoon nap at his sister's house in Soho Square by Richard Beston's thunder at the door, and then they two—a sailor ashore and a highwayman in temporary retirement—had sallied into the deserted Sunday streets to gather historians of the War of Jenkins' Ear. Of course they went directly to the Rose in Fleet Street, and found it, as usual, full. Then began the real problem: out of these forty or fifty veterans, many of them drunk and as many more wordlessly stupid, what four or five to choose who would be presentable and worth listening to at Strawberry Hill? The landlord of the Rose, although tremulously eager to do anything he could for "the Reverend Mr. Blandison," had not seemed to grasp this problem in all its niceties and ramifications. Astonishing to relate, he had never heard of Strawberry Hill, and the name Walpole suggested nothing to him but "Old Bob." Neither was Master Jenkins much help, for he was asleep beyond rousing, the Ear firmly clutched in his right hand. Jenkins and the host excepted, there was apparently not a man in the room that Byron knew by sight—so huge and scattered throughout the world is the present membership of this Club, and the group gathered there at headquarters at any given time so completely a matter of chance. "Or at any rate," Captain Byron mused, smiling at us all to take off the curse of the philosophy, "what we mortals in our ignorance call 'chance,' not knowing what we mean and often doubting whether any such thing exists. What was it that drew our attention, as we stood there, peering about through the tobacco smoke, to four men sitting quietly together over their mugs at a table near the bow-window, with the light of the setting sun turning the reek of their pipes to azure? Parson Blandison, I think, would call it chance. My own notion is that Destiny, Fate, or what some people call Providence, took hold of events and began to arrange them as we two walked across to those four—all sober, all decently dressed and clean, all of them obviously intelligent—and asked permission to join them.

" 'Join us, Captain Byron?' one of them exclaimed, rising from his stool so abruptly that it fell to the floor. 'Don't you remember Isaac Morris, after all we've been through together?'

"Then I did recall my old comrade—a tall, dark man, grown far beyond the stature of the midshipman I once had familiarly known. We shook hands, and I sat down beside him. Pipes and beer were brought for Beston and me, and we all began to talk.

"The oldest of them, well over fifty, was Jeremy Tinker—a wizened little man in brown with tired blue eyes and a low, patient, weary voice. His left hand was crippled—by an Indian arrow, he told me. Yes, he said, he knew a good deal about that War of the Ear. More than enough. When I asked whether he would care to tell his story to a group of friendly listeners he said, with a sigh, that he would rather not, that it was a thing he had for years been trying to forget. —'Not that I ever can,' said he, 'but to tell it, Mr. Byron! Oh, no! It was dreadful, sir!'.

" 'And yet,' I replied, 'you come here to the Rose, where everyone thinks and talks about that war.'

" 'Ah, yes; I know. I try not to, but—but a man has to have some place to go, Mr. Byron.'

" 'Aw, cheer up, now, Jer'my!' sang out the much younger man on my left. 'Drink yer beer and be thankful 'tain't bilge-water. Why, hell, man, hyar we set warm an' dry, mugs in hand an' pipes a-drawrin'! Wal, I mean to say, ain't this hyar a damn sight better 'n bein' et up by cannibals?'

"With that, Mr. John Chester of New London, Connecticut, stood up and rendered us a song in a voice that sounded, in that low-raftered room, really tremendous. It made the rum-glasses shake on the shelf at the bar, and temporarily aroused Master Jenkins himself. I think we're all going to like John Chester. He's really much more a farmer than a sailor, and he tells me that most of his neighbours in New London are both at once. His language is sometimes a little hard to follow, and it smells of the barnyard as much as of tar. He thinks, by the way, Mr. Walpole, that you are working a farm here at Strawberry Hill, and you are likely to have a good deal of advice about growing Indian corn and the breeding of cattle."

The Captain went on to tell us about the last man of the group, Mr. James Adair, aged about forty, who had spent many years in the American wilderness near the Mississippi River, living actually in the wigwams of the Creek, Choctaw, Chickasaw, and Cherokee Indians, and who had witnessed the effects of the war even amongst those savage tribes. This Adair, Byron said, was not merely well educated but a scholar. —He was just telling how fortunate a thing it seemed to him that these four men were all able, willing, and glad to spend a week at Twickenham when Louis whispered in my ear that four strangers—they had not given him their names, and two of them at least were rather odd-looking—were now at the door and asking to see Captain Byron.

*   *   *

We were fourteen in all, the Madlands people having joined us for the afternoon, as we sat, half an hour later, in the Library. Louis was with us to keep the fire, pour the wine, serve tea, and extend his education. 'Twas a scene to warm the heart of any bachelor, with enough elegance about it, lent by the long, lofty room, but more of that solid comfort for which we English, say what you will against us on other accounts, have an unparalleled genius. With the possible exception of little Jeremy Tinker—and even he was thawing out under the influence of my really excellent Madeira, administered by Kitty—every one already felt at home. John Chester, indeed, had thrown off his coat and lighted his pipe—a sort of thing which I had never supposed could happen at Strawberry Hill. For a second or two I gasped, and what I may call my inward eyebrows were raised at least half an inch. Outwardly, however, I think I gave no sign of astonishment, and in three puffs I was saying to myself: "Well, Horace Walpole, why not? Most of the smoke goes up the chimney, and, in any case, John Chester is your guest."

According to the arrangement which he and Blandison had worked out together, Captain Byron was sitting in what we called the "Speaker's Chair." The light from the tall triple window was falling full upon his lean, brown, mobile face. I see the Captain, in memory —and so should you, William, when you try to imagine him—in constant motion. He thinks and feels, apparently, with his body as a whole, so that the tale he told us was, you might say, narrated as much to the eye as to the ear. Mostly we watched the changing lights of his eyes, but also the swift, restless gestures of his hands. Recollection of a storm made him roll and rock in his chair—and I say "made him" because there was no hint in all this of anything studied. The story swept through him, making the whole man for the time its servant. —For example, when once he was speaking of a ship's gunner in great torment of mind, he suddenly sprang from his chair and paced the floor of the Library as though it were a deck, his head bowed, his brows darkly knit, his teeth clenched. He became that gunner.

"Parson Blandison has told you," Byron began, "about the declaration of war and the founding of our Club. You can imagine how all that excitement in St. Stephen's Yard, along the Strand, and then at the Rose, would work on the nerves of a lad not yet sixteen, a schoolboy in London on holiday. The sight of Master Jenkins and his ear made me rather sick, I admit; but then of course I had Parson Blandison with me—although I'm not sure that he had at that time taken holy orders—to explain how I ought to think and feel about such a spectacle. Also I had Augustus Keppel, even younger than I but with five years at sea already behind him. Like Keppel I was a second son, and so had been consigned to the Navy almost as though I had come into the world with the King's broad arrow on my brow. Therefore I did not need either young Blandison's eloquence or Keppel's promptings to see the beginnings of what Jenkins' Ear would mean in my life. It would take me out of school, which I hated. It would relieve my father and elder brother of a person whose possibly permanent departure from Newstead Abbey they would be able to bear without heartbreak. It would take me to sea in wartime, when promotion is rapid, so that I should not have to dawdle my life away as a midshipman until gray hairs made me a laughingstock for beardless boys. —Ah, yes, a beneficent ear it seemed to me, for all its disgustfulness, and a war neatly timed to suit the convenience of John Byron."

Here he paused, brushed his hair back with both hands, and glanced from face to face, smiling. Then he leaned forward, rested his elbows on his knees, made the shape of a heart with the fingers of his two hands, and stared at the floor. "Yet I don't know," he went on. "I'm not sure that what I've just told you isn't too calculating for the boy I then was to have felt or thought. What a hard thing it is—don't you ladies and gentlemen find it so?—to be fair in later life to one's own childhood and youth! We grow hard, and forget as much as we learn. Base metal is mixed with the gold, and night begins before noonday. No doubt I thought also about my mother, my home, and certain beloved old oaks of Sherwood Forest as I stood there gazing at the Ear in the candle-shine. Perhaps I vaguely foresaw that the Ear would filch from me what was left of my boyhood. At any rate, that is what it did.

"Almost any other thing would have done this if the Ear had not, for at fifteen I was already beginning to feel that lust for danger, change, and roving which has been the curse of all Byrons. There's a wild streak in us. The Byrons of Sherwood Forest go back to the times of Robin Hood—or he comes down to ours.

"However that may be, I shared to the full the excitement of that hour at the Rose, and although I had not touched a drop of liquor I went into the street with my head reeling. 'Hurrah! Hurrah!' the crowd yelled and roared, and 'Long life to old Jenkins!' and 'Health to the Ear!' There must have been some one in that crowd who knew that Parson Blandison is a wonderful orator, for they seized him as he came out of the tavern door and lifted him to the top of a sedan chair, demanding a speech. I believe he never refuses such a demand. A few phrases of what he said come back to me: 'Rise from your sloth, you manhood of England! Wake from your dreams, you sluggards of London! Shout, dance, and sing for the war! Throw down your cards and dice, you perfumed dandies of St. James; cast away your sham crutches, you sturdy beggars and clapperdudgeons of St. Giles; for England is going to war! We shall send Robert Walpole home; we shall break the power of Spain; we shall free the seas for England's ships; we shall come back laden with Spanish gold; and the Ear, the Ear shall be avenged!' "

Kitty clapped her hands at this burst of mock-thunder, and both the Captain and Blandison bowed a smiling acknowledgment from their chairs.

"After such a speech," Byron continued, "there followed, naturally, a mighty preparation and girding for war throughout the land. When I stopped, the next day, at old John Hall's gunsmithery in Cheapside to buy a fowling-piece I found him almost too busy to serve me. Already, he said, Jenkins' Ear had brought him a Tower contract for five hundred muskets, at a good price, and already he was distracted. No iron for those muskets was to be had at any price. Three of his apprentices had run away the night before, no doubt to join the fleet, and there would be no help from any one to bring them back. Two journeymen had told him that they wanted to leave the shop at once and set up for themselves. John Hall, in order words, was facing ruin as an immediate result of the prosperity brought by the war.

"And so it was throughout London as I walked the streets that morning. From out of the fog there spread a vast rumble and clatter and din, as though some iron giant were rousing from sleep. I heard the very beat of his heart in the thud of numberless hammers rapping home the heads of casks, drifting trunnels through planks and frames, knocking oakum into seams, setting spokes into hubs, shaping daggers and swords on the anvil. For a mind somewhat given to flights of fancy, as mine was then and perhaps is still, it was easy to imagine that these hammers of London—yes, and soon of all England—were knocking at the walls, already half crumbled, of Spain. For my country— what English lad bred as I had been could escape the thought?—was as young, I believed, as I myself, and as guileless, as certain of victory.

"Home again at Newstead Abbey, waiting for a midshipman's appointment, I heard all day in Sherwood the crashing fall of oaks that had sheltered Robin Hood and Maid Marian. The Ear had need of them now, and soon, shaped into futtocks and knees and gaudy figureheads, they would be tossing on vast rollers of the sea halfway round the world. Part of my childhood expired with their violent deaths, yet there was comfort in the hope that whither they went I too might go.

"It was a weary time for me, those weeks and months at home with little to do but read the tales of old wars in which my forefathers had fought, to wander about the ever dwindling forest with my fowling-piece, gaining skill with my weapon which was to serve me both well and ill in a distant land.

"One thing that made this period of waiting irksome to me was the knowledge that Admiral Vernon, even before the declaration of war, had sailed for the Spanish Main to fulfil his boast that he could take Porto Bello with only six ships. The news that he had done precisely that, in a quick and easy victory, reached Newstead Abbey in the late winter. Glorious news it seemed, for no one took any account at the time of the fact that Vernon had struck at an almost defenceless port without warning, and before the defenders could know that war had been declared—an act little short of piracy. Neither did I or any one then consider that he had left his task half done—that if only he had gone on to take Panama, like Sir Henry Morgan the buccaneer, he might have garrisoned and held that central link in Spain's American empire and so changed the course of history.

"Every one can now see that Admiral Vernon's raid at Porto Bello was not a remarkably glorious affair, that it added nothing to England's honour and little to her power. Indeed I think it may be the conclusion of the historians that it did us more harm than good, and this for the reason that the popular acclaim for Admiral Vernon caused a corresponding neglect, for the time, of a man enormously more able. Also it brought about a meagre and niggardly provision for a naval exploit compared with which the expedition against Porto Bello was mere boy's play. —What the Prime Minister may have thought about the matter, I have never learned, probably because his calm and judicious voice was by that time almost silenced. Am I right, Mr. Walpole, in thinking that Vernon's victory was interpreted as a defeat for your father?"

"In so far as his enemies could bring that about," I replied, "you are right. Of course he had opposed the war from the start, and his view was shared by many others after Vernon's dismal failure at Cartagena."

"All of us," said Byron, "are old enough to recall that failure, and how Vernon's star sank as that of a really great commander rose slowly and serenely into the zenith of fame. I mention this only to show how grievously I was disappointed when at last a letter came notifying my father that I had been approved for a berth in another squadron then fitting out. The letter was signed by Commodore George Anson—a name which at that time I had never heard.

"My parents went with me as far as London, and what I chiefly recall of the journey is that the roads were blocked again and again by herds of cattle on the way from the Scottish border, raising great clouds of dust. They too, like the oaks of Sherwood and the sixteen-year-old riding with the coachman, were bound for the high seas.

"I shall leave out all the bustle, tears, advice, and leave-taking that went on after our arrival in London. Behold me, then, on the top of the Portsmouth coach, with my friend Augustus Keppel beside me, bound for the same squadron. In no time we made friends with our jovial coachman. The guard let us sound his long brass horn as we entered the villages, and all along the country lanes we were greeted by the calls of children, squeals of outraged pigs, and the cackling and fluttering of fowls. Thus Kingston, Esher, and Wisley whirled past us. At Ripley we stopped at the Talbot Inn for fresh horses. Keppel and I went with the coachman and guard into the taproom and, following their example, ordered bread, cheese, and porter.

" 'So ye're off for some o' Jack Spaniard's gold,' said the coachman, with his mouth full.

"We nodded agreement.

" 'Here's luck to ye, then'—and his face was eclipsed by his tankard. 'If I war a game young cockerel the likes o' ye, I'd be goin' along. —What say, Ben?'

" 'Not me !' the guard replied. 'I druther be a-drownded in good dry dust, the which we must all come to, than in the salt sea.'

" 'Don't ye pay 'im no mind, young gentlemen,' the coachman laughed. 'Pore ol' Ben's a Methody, an' turble sad. 'Sides that, o' course, guards ain't got much brains. A-settin' back there on the tail o' the coach, all shook to a jelly, how could they? 'Tain't in nater.'

"Ben did look sad at that, and also bored, as though he had heard it before ; but the coachman drained his tankard and continued : 'These be smart lads, I tell ye, Ben. Next time they rides with us we'll hear the jolly doubloons a-jinglin' in their pockets all the way to Lunnon Town. They're goin' out to jine Ammiral Vernon, don't ye for-get—an' look what he's gone an' done even afore they get there. Took Porto Bello, he has, without hardly a shot, an' captered a hundred coachfuls o' Spanish gold ! —Wal now, with these brisk lads to help 'im . . . I mean to say, Ben, even only a guard an' a Methody oughter see what I mean. These lads will come home as rich as earls—jukes, mebbe. Why, Ben, they'll be rich enough to stand us the drinks.'

"Naturally, we stood them the drinks, and then confessed, sadly enough, that we were sailing not to reinforce the already triumphant squadron of Admiral Vernon but with Commodore George Anson. The coachman looked astonished, then pained. 'Anson? Anson?' said he, shaking his head. 'Never heard tell o' no sech animile. He must 'a' come up like a rat through the hawsehole, an' not come up very far. No Anson ever rode with me. No.'

"From then on it was a different story. Apparently we were not, after all, cut out for wealth and fame, but for lives of miserable obscurity. As we rode onward the coachman sank into a gloom as deep as the guard's, which the tankards of porter we supplied at Guildford and Godalming and Petersfield could not dispel. Morever, the very tavern signs along the road bore witness against our hopes. Newly painted, with the old red lions and white swans still showing beneath the fresh colors, the Vernon Heads and Vernon Arms, the Admiral Vernons and the Vernon's Victories blazoned the fame of the man with whom Keppel and I were not to sail. Not once did we see the name of Anson.

"Darkness was falling as we rattled through the crooked lanes of Portsmouth, smelling the tar and the salt air, catching the first gleam of candles in the windows, hearing calls and curses in many strange tongues, and watching at the corners for the hedge of masts and yards that seemed to block the shoreward ends of all the lanes and streets. Keppel and I were set down with our baggage, including my conspicuous fowling-piece, at the Blue Posts Inn on the Hard. 'Good huntin' to ye, yer Honour,' the coachman shouted as he drove off. 'Bring us back a few Spanish fowl!'

"The taproom of the Blue Posts looked a cheerful place. We went directly to the fire, hoping to dry our clothes and stop the chattering of our teeth, for we had been soaked through by the rain that poured upon us during the last two hours of our journey. The room was crowded with seamen, stamping and roaring to the tunes set by a tipsy fiddler who stood on one of the tables: 'The *Ruby* and Benbow fought the French, fought the French . . .' The din and the stench were all but overpowering to us two lads, just come from the open air. Never before had I known or imagined such smells as that room contained, although since then, of course, I have encountered others that have made them, in comparison, like the perfumes of Araby.

"We must have looked rather forlorn as we stood there gazing about, for before long one of the roisterers, moderately sober, came over and asked us our business. 'The *Centurion,* eh? Anson's ship,' said he, when he heard our reply, spitting contemptuously into the fire. 'Too bad! Too bad! Oh, what a rotten shame for two smart up-standin' lads like you, *with* a fowling-piece!'

"The pity of our situation seemed to affect him much as it had the coachman. He brooded over it, staring at the fire. Then he turned about and, with a mighty voice and upheld hand, quieted the room. 'I say,' he called out, 'here's a piece o' hard luck as breaks a man's 'eartstrings, it do. Look at 'em standin' 'ere, these two stout an' brave young English gentlemen *with* a fowling-piece as ye'd ever wish to see. An' where d'ye think they're bound for? Ye'd never guess it, boys, an' I 'ates to tell ye, but out it will. 'Tis the *Centurion* they're arskin' for—that wormy, waterlogged, crank old tub—when they mought 've vyaged along of us to riches an' glory!'

"'Are you and these others going out to join Admiral Vernon?' I asked.

"'That we be, me lad—us an' twenty thousand more. We'll make the strongest fleet that ever sailed the seas. With Vernon to lead us, we'll take Panama, Peru, South Americy, an' lug home all their gold.'

"I glanced at Keppel and found that he was looking at me with a gleam of hope in his eyes. Well, thought I, he ought to know more than I do about such matters, after his five years as a midshipman. But then came another thought—that I, now sixteen, was his senior by several months, and must not lead him astray. 'We're listed for the *Centurion,*' said I, with what firmness I could muster.

"Our acquaintance did not think that an insuperable difficulty. Young gentlemen, he said, often changed their minds. No one had seen us come in here, and certainly no one would blab to Anson. We might change our names if we liked—and, by the way, what were our names?

"He looked considerably impressed when he heard them. 'Anyhow,' said he, 'I'll call you two gentlemen, if you don't mind, by your first names. —Look here, my dear,' he called to a barmaid. 'I want you to meet my friends Jack an' Gus. Treat 'em like you do me, an' bring us three mugs o' flip.'

"That flip, stiff with gin and steaming from the poker, soon made us forget our wet clothes, the stench of the room, the tangle of voices, and the fact that this man who asked us to call him Bill was a total stranger. After the second mug he was our confidential friend, at the bottom of the third our profound philosopher, and before we had finished the fourth we realized that we loved him as a brother.

"Then things began to happen which at the time I did not understand, and, later on, could not clearly remember. We were out in the dark and the rain, all of us, with our hats pulled low and cudgels in our hands, stealing quietly along like thieves. Bill was there as our leader, keeping a close watch on us two boys. His presence quelled such wild suspicions as that these fellows were Spaniards in disguise, perhaps Jacobites even, planning to capture Portsmouth, burn the royal dockyard, and sail away with the shipping in the harbour.

"We soon learned, of course, that our expedition was entirely lawful, patriotic, and beneficent in purpose; quite necessary to the defense of those glorious liberties of which all Englishmen are so justly proud. Yes, if silence had not been demanded by the nature of our task, we might well have marched along singing, 'Britons never, never, never will be slaves!' At least it must have been with that noble sentiment in mind that we ran down, cudgelled, and bound every man or boy that we encountered in the streets and lanes and alleys, that we entered taverns and took both landlords and guests, that we broke down doors barred against us and dragged away fathers and sons, that we stormed into bawdyhouses and tore men from the arms of screaming, half-clad women. We lighted fires on hearthstones to smoke out any who might have taken refuge in chimneys. We beat up featherbeds and smashed the locks of cupboards and chests. In one house we found mourners sitting about a coffin upon which a corpse was lying. Our gang tipped the body to the floor, ripped off the coffin-lid, and hauled out an exceedingly belligerent young man.

"Once in the street, our prisoners—if that is the right word for men who would soon be defending England's freedom—were tied wrist to wrist, so that they could walk but not run, unless the whole forty or fifty ran together, in single file.

"All this made a bad enough introduction of a dreamy youth to the calling in which he meant to spend his life; but of a sudden it was worse. At the meeting of two dark lanes we came to a smithy not yet closed for the night. One of the women who had followed us, clawing and scratching and biting, dashed into the shop, scooped up a bucket of live coals, and sprayed us with them through the open door. Then the smith, a gnarled runt of a fellow bare to the waist, ran out and cleared a way for himself through our gang with a white-hot iron. Our friend Bill brought him down with a blow on the back of the skull. Just as we were pinioning the smith and Bill was telling us that he ought to be worth six shillings, we were struck by a second gang, larger than ours and at least as savage. It came at us out of the dark with the force of a hurricane that knocks a ship on her beam ends and tears off her clothes before a boatswain can find his whistle. I was lifted off my feet and crushed against the wall by their onset, but thus gained a moment to look about me in the faint red light from the forge. A huge bull-necked, carrot-haired fellow was leading them, beating his way with a club through our gang toward our Bill. 'It's them damned water-drinkers from Old Grog's fleet,' he was yelling. 'It's Vernon's men, boys! Knock 'em down! Grab 'em up! We'll turn 'em over to Anson for a shillin' a head!' With that he reached Bill, and our Bill disappeared. A few seconds later he must have reached me, for there my recollections of that night in Portsmouth end."

Here Captain Byron paused and took a sip from the glass of claret that Louis had set at his elbow. He was not smiling as he glanced from face to face—looking longest and most thoughtfully, perhaps, at Blandison. Mr. Chute was waving his right hand to limber his wrist, tired out by the swift pace of Byron's talk. John Chester, rising from his chair, emptied his pipe into the fire and filled it again from a leathern pouch. The bowl was light-red in hue, made of some soft and velvety stone. "Injun," he said it was, and a gift from his friend King Uncas. James Adair added that "pipestone" of that sort is found in only one place, far out beyond the Great Lakes, and that for ages it has been an important article of Indian commerce. I gladly accepted Chester's offer to send me a pipe like his when he got home. It will look handsome enough in my collection beside Admiral Tromp's, and, as for the frightful smell, I suppose I can boil that out.

"Being knocked on the head," the Captain resumed, "is the customary way of entering His Majesty's Navy. In my boyhood it had already become so much a matter of routine that, although I really wanted to enter the Navy, and had an appointment, it could not be omitted. Still, for those of you who have never experienced the blow of a belaying-pin on the base of the brain, I may say that there is something brusque and abrupt about it which tends to cool a young man's patriotic fervour. And then to be forced into giving what one has already offered . . . Well, you see my point.

"I came back to consciousness—wet through, bloody, cramped, with every nerve jerking, my head feeling as large as a barrel—to find myself tightly wedged amongst ten or twelve other 'prizes' in the bottom of a ship's longboat. A dreary dawn was breaking through the drizzle. I shook with cold; my head ached; I felt sure that I was dying, and rather hoped so. Gradually, however, my sight cleared and my thoughts swam into some connection. Apparently we were being rowed across a harbour, for the spars of tall ships passed over our heads and were lost behind, to be replaced by more and more. It seemed we were pulling through a large fleet, and the glimpse I caught of a row of lighted gun-ports suggested that these might be naval vessels. The Navy? England's Navy? Could this be the vast squadron that was gathering at Portsmouth for the reinforcement of Admiral Vernon? Why, surely, it was! I was going out, as I had so mightily hoped, to fight under Vernon! —I glanced back over my shoulder and saw there, sitting at the tiller three feet away, that same bull-necked, redheaded brute who had crashed into our gang by the smithy the night before—the leader of Commodore Anson's press-gang.

"Then I really did want to die. Instead, I had to listen while we rowed the whole length of Vernon's fleet to the derisive catcalls from the decks: 'Ahoy, there! Y'ain't a-goin' out with Anson, be ye? Ye cain't eggspeck the *Centurion* will hold all the men in that 'ar longboat. They'll sink her, sartin. Fack is, she's a'ready gone down, with her Capting an' one starved rat aboard.' But the man at the tiller was not one to take ridicule in silence. He pointed out—in language which I forbear to quote, for he was a boatswain's mate and spoke as such—that he was bringing off this morning five boatfuls of prizes, fully half of whom he had captured from the Vernon press-gang. He suggested, furthermore, that if they should care to look for the leader of that same besotted and vilely diseased horde of ruffians they might find him scrubbing the necessary houses in the head of His Majesty's Ship *Centurion*.

"And here is an odd thing in human nature, or at least in mine: I had not listened for two minutes to this exchange of amenities before I felt myself taking sides with the man at the tiller of our longboat. His name, I learned from his shouting it, was Bill—Bill Cheney—and in complete forgetfulness of the violence he had done me, as also of my recent devotion to another person with that name, I began to think of him as our spokesman and champion, the defender of Commodore

Anson and of the *Centurion* against all sneers and aspersions. This, remember, was before I had seen the Commodore or had heard one word in his favour. What I owed to him and Bill Cheney at that moment was only a brutal blow on the head, yet then and there it was, ladies and gentlemen, that I began to be Commodore Anson's faithful servant, as I hope I have shown myself ever since.

" 'A brutal blow,' I have called it"—here the Captain stroked the back of his head with his hand. "But, in spite of the misery it cost me then and thereafter, I have often thought that Bill Cheney and his belaying-pin were a godsend in deep disguise. Parson Blandison, as you may all know, is fond of showing that Master Jenkins' Ear changed the lives of multitudes. I agree. My own life has been profoundly affected by the Ear; and so has that of every person in this room. Yet our destinies are not decided by one thing only but by an infinite number, from which we select a few. Among those few I count that blow. The Ear alone might have sent me to share the defeats and the long decline of Admiral Vernon. The blow saved me from that for —other things."

"And yet, Captain," said Mr. Chute, "do you really feel that your life has been controlled by such accidents—supposing for the moment that the whole affair of Jenkins' Ear really was accidental, and not a deliberate, more or less clever fraud?"

"Perhaps I simplify too much, Mr. Chute, for the sake of the story. What do you think?"

"Nothing very clear or helpful, and I ask pardon for breaking in with my doubts. Still, it seems to me that each of us deals with such chances freely, and according to his own nature."

"But does one freely choose that nature?"

"Not all at once; but, little by little, I think, yes. The cards we hold are dealt by chance. We decide how to play them."

"And even that chance in the deal," said George Selwyn, opening his eyes for a swift glance at Blandison and then closing them again, "—I have heard that some people know how to reduce it."

Quick as a sensitive woman to catch the faintest tone of dissension, Byron gathered us in again with his thoughtful smile. "You gentlemen," he said, "have taken me off my soundings. It's my fault, of course, for pretending to be a philosopher. In fact, I'm only a sailor who has spent a good deal of time out under the stars at sea, with nothing to do but think."

"Wal then, Cap'n, why the hell not *talk* like a sailor?" inquired John Chester of Connecticut, now lighting his pipe with a live coal he had taken from the fire with his fingers—an astonishing performance! "Sailor-talk is good 'nough talk for these hyar folks, iffen only ye leave out some o' the words. —Mought larn 'em summat."

I give you this man's language, William, as accurately as I can, but with the caveat that my rendering falls far short of the fascinating actuality. Mr. Chute's record is of no help to me here, for shorthand, as he says, was made to fit the English, not the American, language. In the notes he has made for my perusal, John Chester's talk is translated into English, with a definite loss, I should say, in force and pungency. His impression seems to be that our friend from New London speaks bad English. I disagree. I think he speaks excellent, even admirable, American.

"If it's sailor-talk you want," Captain Byron continued, "I have it in plenty. I shall leave out, however, not only the words that Master Chester has in mind but a good many others which landsmen do not understand. There's a special language about ships, sails, masts and spars, cables and lanyards, which is no more admirable when used out of place than pedantry of any other kind. Were I to talk to you in Latin—as I could not—the ladies would feel slighted; and, similarly, if I should say, 'Starboard your helm—fore sheet, fore top-bowline, jib and staysail sheets let go!' it is possible that some of you gentlemen might be perplexed.

"Think of me as still lying in the bottom of the longboat, but now able to raise my aching head a few inches and look about. The anchorage of the *Centurion* was at the far end of the harbour, so that we had to row through the whole flotilla going out to help Vernon before we reached her. At last, however, we came to Anson's squadron of six vessels, and I could read their names and count their gun-ports. There was the *Gloucester* of fifty guns, the *Severn,* which also carried fifty, the *Pearl* with forty, the *Wager* with twenty-four, and the *Tryal* with eight. Also I had seamanship enough to recognize that the first four of these, like the sixty-gun *Centurion,* were ship-rigged—that is, each had three masts, fore, main, and mizzen, and also a bowsprit, the short spar projecting forward over the bow like the horn of the fabulous unicorn. The little *Tryal,* however, had only two masts and a bowsprit, and, as I later learned, she was rigged as a snow—but that is one of those pedantries that need not detain us."

"Don't forget the two merchant pinks, Captain," said Isaac Morris, "—the victuallers, *Anna* and *Industry.*"

"Forget them, Lieutenant, I never shall; for the *Anna,* at least, though not a man-o'-war, was as gallant a vessel as any that went along. Those two, however, were not lying with the squadron that morning— nor were they to do so for weeks to come. When they did join us I learned that a pink is masted like a ship, but is built with what the seamen call a 'lute' or 'tombstone'—a high, narrow, and raking stern which marks it off sharply from any other kind of vessel.

"And now, as we approached the flagship, that strange sense of allegiance which I had already felt for Bill Cheney, even for the longboat, began to include the whole squadron. That it was small, and composed of small vessels, none of them looking that day either smart or well found, only increased my feeling of loyal pride. I made the utmost of everything bright and strong that I could discern about them —as, for instance, their port-lids opened and triced up to show a blood-red checker against the dull brown of their sloping sides. The sight of the Commodore's broad red pennant flying from the main-topgallant mast head made my heart leap. A few strokes of the oars farther on we passed under the *Centurion's* bowsprit and figurehead—a rampant red lion with staring white eyeballs, bulging yellow cheeks, blue nostrils, and a wide roaring mouth that showed gold teeth and a red tongue. His claws were gold over black pads. He had a blue mane and two lashing tails, one for each side of the stem out of which he sprang. The carving was crude, but one saw that the *Centurion's* people loved their lion and took good care of his appearance. One of our oarsmen spoke affectionately to him as we passed by below.

"At this point there comes another blank in my recollections, for at my first effort to sit up in the boat and to grasp the ship's entry-ladder, I swooned away. Bill Cheney it was, I learned later on, that lugged me up that ladder, doused me with cold sea water, and then dragged me to the half-deck and the door of the Commodore's cabin. Many 'prizes' of the night before were waiting there—the blacksmith, my old friend Bill of the Blue Posts who had led Vernon's press-gang, the man we had found in the coffin, and a dozen others whom I had seen before—but Bill Cheney went at once to the head of the line. Two minutes later, still unable to walk or to stand, I was seated in the great cabin, 'coach,' or 'roundhouse,' the Commodore's headquarters.

"In spite of my still dazed condition, I saw that something remarkable was going on there. A large man in a snuff-coloured coat was sitting at a great oaken table, leaning far back and gazing wide-eyed, almost gaping, at a copper-coloured giant whose fierce dark eyes were fixed upon him from less than a yard away. The cabin's ceiling, though well over a fathom above the floor, was too low for this young Hercules, and he bent forward perforce, with his fists on the table-top, looking—in his fringed leather coat and with long black hair swinging free—a good deal like a wild beast ready to spring. Yet also he made me think of a hawk, an eagle, sighting its prey. Bird or beast, he was wild, untamably. How had this grand feral creature been taken, I wondered, in last night's raid? How had Cheney, or any ten such men armed with cudgels, subdued and got him aboard?

" 'Mr. Cheney,' gasped the man seated at the table, 'what—who— For God's sake, Mr. Cheney, what *have* we here?'

" 'Ar, it's only one o' them Yankee Injuns, Commodore. 'E won't bite. They's a lad jest outside what talks for 'im.'

" 'Bring him in, if you please. I feel a sudden need of more white men.'

"Bill Cheney reached out of the door and instantly produced a youth of normal size, with sandy hair and eyes of Saxon blue. 'I told 'em out thar,' said he as he entered, 'they warn't no use o' talkin' to Uncas 'thout me along. He never says nothin' but "Ugh!" when I ain't thar, an' not much more when I be.'

" 'Please give me your name,' said the Commodore .

" 'John Chester o' Quaker Hill, New London, Connecticut Colony, farmer, hunter, fisherman, shipbuilder, able seaman, carpenter, *an'* whaler. When times is slack I do me a little gravestone cuttin' on the side. Me an' Prince Uncas, hyar, we come across to see a patch o' the world. Heered tell ye're baound for strange parts, an' so we're glad to obleege, as the sayin' is, an' sign on.'

"The Commodore pulled out a handkerchief and trumpeted his nose to hide his astonishment. 'Do you mean to say that you two came aboard of your own free will?'

" 'Huh! How the hell else? —Ye didn't think that puny press-gang ye had in town last night could 'a' brung us! Why, let me tell you—'

" 'No. I see what you mean. How about this—ah—this Uncas? Is that his full name?'

" 'His Injun name 'd fill a hull book, but back in New London an'

round about we call him Prince Jonathan Uncas Gaines for short.
Ez for me, I'm his chum, an' so I jest calls 'im Uncas.'

" 'That's good,' said the Commodore. 'He needs all the shortening
we can give him.' And with that he entered the name in the muster-
book, writing slowly and biting his tongue the while. That done, he
looked up and asked: 'Is this man really a prince?'

" 'Don't he look it?'

" 'I have seen only one prince in my life, and between your friend
Uncas and Prince Frederick, heir apparent to the British throne, there
are several—ahem—differences. —What country is Uncas the Prince
of?'

" 'Mohegan kentry.'

" 'And of what nation, what people?'

" 'The Mohegans, o' course.'

" 'Don't say "o' course" to the Commodore, Chester!' Bill Cheney
ordered. 'An', likewise, say "Sir"!'

" 'And where's his palace, his throne, his— In short, where does he
live?'

" 'Why, hell, he lives all over the place. One night he'll be sleepin'
under Cochegan Rock or mebbe Larrabee Oak, an' then next night
you'll find 'im deep down like a woodchuck in Machimoodus Cave,
a good twenty mile off.'

" 'I see. But I must set down some place of residence for him.'

" 'Wal then, jest say Mohegan Village.'

" 'H'm. Mohegan Village. Yes. —Can he speak English?'

" 'He can; but he won't.'

" 'Will he obey orders?'

" 'No. Leastways, not iffen I don't ask 'im to. He's a prince, like
I told you; an' he don't *take* orders, he *gives* 'em.'

" 'So that here on shipboard we should always have to ask you first?'

" 'Eeah.'

" 'Can this prince do anything else—I mean, besides disregarding
orders and keeping his mouth shut?'

" 'He can run a hunderd mile 'thout stoppin', see in the dark, fight
a bobcat with his bare hands, go without food an' drink, build a
canoe out o' birch bark, make a fire in the rain, ketch a shark with a
spear, an' sech. But what Uncas is really good at is leap-dancin'.'

"The Commodore seemed to have some difficulty in choosing among
these varied accomplishments, of which only the ability to catch sharks

and see in the dark had any obvious bearing upon his present needs—although the going without food and drink was to prove useful before the voyage was over. But finally he inquired: 'Can the Prince sail a boat?'

" 'Why, sartin shore!'

" 'Don't say "sartin shore" to the Commodore,' snapped Cheney again. 'An' say "Sir," like I told yeh.'

" 'As one cap'n to another,' Chester went on, I said "sartin shore"; an' that 'ar is prezackly what I mean. Ain't me an' Uncas sailed from New to Old London in our own thirty-foot sloop, standin' watch an' watch alike?'

" 'Do you mean to assert,' the Commodore asked, throwing down his quill, 'that you two, alone, brought a sloop across the Atlantic Ocean?'

" 'Eeah. Took us six weeks, but hyar we be.'

" 'What will you do with your vessel?'

" 'Sold her in London Pool, at a good profit. Gungywamp oak. Built her ourselves, up to Mamacoke.'

" 'Well, well! Captain Chester, this is most remarkable! Speaking as one captain to another, I congratulate you, sir.'

" 'Thank you—sir.'

"There, or shortly thereafter, the conference with the two volunteers from Connecticut closed. I saw nothing of them during the voyage or in the years that followed, but since our meeting of yesterday Master Chester and I have struck up an acquaintance which I hope will increase and endure. He tells me that Prince Uncas has grown considerably since the one time I saw him, and has been for several years the King of his nation.

"Turning his gaze to me as these two left the room, the Commodore told me not to rise from the chair, and asked Cheney how badly I was hurt.

" 'Oh, sir,' said Bill, "e ain't really w'at a man 'd call *'urt!* I only guv 'im jest the reg'lar sleep-medicine wi' the twig to quiet 'im down; but, o' course, 'e's only young yet, an' 'is skull mebbe not proper growed.'

" 'H'm. —I believe there's a law against pressing men under eighteen, Mr. Cheney, as there certainly is against assault and battery. You must remember that you are a very powerful man.'

" 'Aye, aye, sir; I allus takes that 'ar into reck'nin'. Bill Cheney don't 'it too 'ard, not ever. Show 'im a 'ead for one second, an' 'e knows jest 'ow 'ard to 'it that 'ead, an' whar.'

" 'How old is this lad?'

" 'Sixteen, sir,' said I.

" 'Ah, sixteen. And your name?'

" 'John Byron.'

" 'I think I have heard that name before.'

"I said that he had heard it from my father, Lord Byron of Newstead Abbey, and that we had received his favourable reply; but that his letter of appointment, unfortunately, was in my valise—or so I hoped—at the Blue Posts Inn.

" 'Yes; now I remember; and I promised you appointment as a first-class volunteer. Is that right?'

"I agreed, perhaps with a private reflection that my actual coming aboard had had little of the voluntary about it.

" 'But you were then,' said he, 'only fifteen. At your present age you cannot be rated as a volunteer but only as a full midshipman. —Let me see, now.'

"The Commodore turned to his muster-book and began leafing through the pages while I sat and watched. He was a large man, as I have said, heavy and powerful in body and limb. His head, his face, his features were large, and his hands looked to me positively huge. Obviously, they had done much hard labour of the sort that falls to sailors before the mast. His expression was as kindly as it was firm, but the main thing that I saw in it then was the look of quiet and patient authority. He was a man, I felt, who would never need to raise his voice. Somehow it came to me that he too, like the lion of his figurehead, must be carved out of oak.

" 'Well, Mr. Byron,' he said, closing the book but keeping the place with one finger, 'it is as I feared: the *Centurion*'s complement of midshipmen is already filled. That will mean, I am sorry to say, that we must find a place for you in some other vessel of the squadron.'

"My heart sank. It had never occurred to me that I should serve anywhere but on the flagship.

"Anson opened the muster-book again and ran his finger down its columns. The finger paused several times, and then moved slowly on again. I could not then guess, but now I know, that at every pause and motion of that finger matters of high importance to me, questions involving even life and death, were decided. Finally, at almost the bottom of the page, it stopped, and the Commodore looked up.

" 'Now there's the *Wager*,' said he, musingly, 'where they have room for another midshipman. She's a sixth-rate, of about half the *Centurion*'s burden, and carries only one hundred and forty men. The *Wager* was purchased from the East India Company, and not built for a man-o'-war—though I don't say she is any the worse for that. She is to serve on this voyage mainly as a store-ship. All that won't sound attractive; but, on the other hand, promotion should be more rapid on a ship of that size than it can be here. She's a staunch vessel, not unlucky, and will see her fair share of whatever fighting we have. I'm sorry that I can't recall her other midshipmen, but I see here that their names are Mr. Henry Cozens, Mr. Alexander Campbell, and Mr. Isaac Morris. Captain Dandy Kidd of the *Wager,* though not in sound health, is, I believe, an excellent commander. The *Wager*'s midshipmen are in charge of their gunner, John Bulkeley, whom I know to be a man of strong religious faith and manly conduct. —All things considered, therefore, I assign you to the *Wager*, hoping that this will work out to your satisfaction and that we shall become better acquainted during the voyage. Mr. Cheney will see that your bruise is cared for at once by our surgeon, and will then arrange for your transport. I shall send you a letter of introduction to Captain Kidd.'

"With these words George Anson rose from his chair and helped me to rise from mine. I can see him now as he stood there and took my slender, trembling hand in his huge firm one, looking down at me with a fatherly kindness. He had on an old, worn, badly fitting, and wrinkled brown coat. His scratch wig was a little awry. On his right temple there was a splotch of ink, left I suppose by a wet quill hastily thrust over his ear. Nothing less resembling my boyish dreams of what a naval commander would look like could well be imagined. George Anson, I saw, was not even a gentleman in the tight, narrow meaning we have brought that word down to. What he was, essentially, I was too young, and too miserable at the moment, to guess. In fact it was to take me months of close association with another person of the same kind to realize that here—in the broad, deep sense which requires a certain emphasis—was a man."

Captain Byron took another sip of claret, and looked again round the room.

"I remember the *Centurion*'s surgeon plastering and binding my wounded head in a dark little room that stinks of stale blood. I see Bill Cheney, bare to the waist, barefooted, rowing me across to the *Wager*, his hair like a blown flame against the blue dance of the waves—and he telling me that I must win my first fight in the midshipman's berth, cost what it may and come when it will, and it probably will come today. I don't feel like fighting today. I feel faint, lost, forlorn. The strong drink of last night, the chill, the wet, the brutality, the blow on the head, the grief of leaving the flagship, the loss of a man I should soon have loved as a father, the separation also from Keppel—these things have come too thick and fast. Bill has to help me up the side of the chunky, blunt, deep-bellied *Wager*. Her hull needs paint, her ironwork is rusted; her deck is cluttered from bowsprit to taffrail with canvas, ropes coiled or loose, long-barrelled siege guns and artillery stores, huge bales of trading cloth, sea-chests, debris, filth, dirty unshaven sailors, and women lolling between the guns in shocking attitudes of lecherous debauch. One startled glance at all this, and I am led, stumbling, to Captain Dandy Kidd. He sits in his cabin like a man besieged, trying to pretend that he, not the bawdyhouses of Portsmouth, has control of the ship. Dandy Kidd is frightened, wizened, death-struck. Without a word or a smile he writes my name in his muster-roll and then tells me to see Gunner Bulkeley.

"The Gunner, when Bill and I found him at last in the midshipmen's berth, was another-guess kind of man. At first, coming down from the sunshine, I made out only that he was short, square, squat, as though built to fit and exactly fill the room where he stood. A stub of a man, he looked to be, on whom other men could securely rest down. The hand that reached for mine and shook it was short, square, warm, hard, and powerful. It was a kindly voice that spoke my name and bade me welcome. Then, as my eyes gathered light from the bull's-eye of thick glass let into the deck above and the farthing dip on the table, I saw more and more clearly a man with intelligent and straightforward blue eyes, close-cropped graying hair, bushy eyebrows in constant expressive motion, and a jaw apparently made of iron. —Yes, just as the Commodore had made me think of oak, Gunner John Bulkeley brought to mind a metal shaped under the hammer.

"The room was five feet and a half in height and ten feet square. In the middle stood a stout and ponderous oaken table, to serve for the midshipmen's mess and the surgeon's operations. The only other furniture was the sea-chests ranged along the wall—three of them; and I suddenly realized that I had no such thing, and must get one. Nets of onions and cheeses hung from the low beams; potatoes were heaped under the table; from nails driven into the bulkheads hung foul-weather clothes, hats, dirks, quadrants, sea-boots, and hammocks —all dripping, like the walls of the room, with moisture. Wedged in far aft on the orlop deck, below water-line, the room had no ventilation of any kind save what came down the hatchways. Not since the *Wager* was decked had one ray of sunshine struck in there. It stank with fumes beyond name or number, most of which rose from the bilge.

"Such was the greeting of my future home to my senses. For the mind and nerves it had another kind of torment. I had lived all my short life in large, lofty rooms and in the open air. On that account, probably, the feeling of suffocation and intolerable enclosure that came over me as I stood there was all the worse. I wanted to scream, but could not catch a breath. I wanted to dash out of that noisome den, but could not move. Instead, for the third time in twenty-four hours, I fainted.

"Poor boy!" Kitty said, in a soft voice utterly different from that she uses on the stage.

"Some time later," the Captain continued, "I awoke to find that Bill Cheney, John Bulkeley, and I were in a jolly-boat together, on the way to Portsmouth Hard. My friends explained that while I lay unconscious they had realized my need of a sea-chest and sea-clothes, perhaps also of a good dinner—for which dinner they had reason to think I was able to pay. After feeling in my pockets I replied that I should gladly buy a good dinner for the three of us at the Blue Posts. I did so, and whilst we were stowing a brisket of beef under hatches I was given far more than my money's worth of information and advice.

" 'Now I ben tellin' the young ge'man,' said Bill, with no pause in his eating and drinking, 'as 'ow he'll hev to fight one fight in the mids' mess, an' he better make it a good un.'

" 'Yes,' the Gunner agreed, 'that's true. I can't be there all the time, and when I'm away those boys are bound to fight till they find who's marster. An' ye're right, Mr. Cheney: there'll be but the one—with Mr. Alexander Campbell.'

" 'Why so?' said Bill.

" 'Because he's already fit the other two and licked 'em, being some twenty years old and they only youngsters. Mr. Morris he grabbed in his hammock an' choked, which is all they was to that fight. Mr. Cozens he waited an' cotched 'im sober, knowin' full well that nobody can lick Mr. Cozens when drunk. But that's how 'tis: he don't fight fair. Dirks, carvin' knives, belayin' pins, teeth, nails, below-the-belts, leg-jerks—Mr. Campbell, he'll use anything to get a man down, an' when he's down he kicks 'im, gentlemen, in the head.'

" 'In the 'ead, Mr. Bulkeley!' Bill exclaimed. 'Why, thisheer Midshipman Campbell he 'pears to me a reg'lar ol' bloody brute!'

" 'Mebbe. But more'n that he's a thief an' a liar an' a bully. That I do know.'

" 'A bully?' I inquired, having filled my hold with good beef. 'I've met that kind at school. Mostly, they're cowards.'

" 'That's right, Mr. Byron. So's this one. —Did you larn anything else at school?'

" 'Not much Latin and Greek, but a little about using my fists.'

" 'Good! In a midshipman's berth fists are more useful; and if you can use 'em to draw blood on Mr. Campbell, I do b'lieve he'll run. —Now, mind you, I don't say pick a fight with Mr. Campbell. That would be sinful. What I do say is, when he starts any hectorin'—as he will—then open fire! Mr. Campbell does not know how to use his fists, nor yet to keep his temper when fightin'. He fights wild, if you take my meanin', so as he wastes the most of his shots on air an' water, so to speak.'

" 'Let 'im waste 'em on the top o' your 'ead, Mr. Byron,' said Bill, 'whar they'll 'urt 'im wuss 'n they do you. Meanwhile, do you 'it 'im on the nose 'ard an' frequent; an' every time you do 'it 'is nose do you count that 'ar time out loud—one, two, three, an' et cetery—an' I lay you a quart by time you git to twenty Mr. Campbell 'e won't be thar.'

" 'That's a good plan, that countin',' the Gunner agreed. 'I use it when sarvin' the guns in battle. An' then too, in battle I'm all the time sayin' over some rhymes I found once in a book. I'll write 'em out for you, Mr. Byron, so's you can have 'em by heart for your fight; but here they be:

" 'Presence of Mind, and Courage in Distress
Are more than Armies to procure Success.
True Courage dwells not in a troubled Flood
Of mounting Spirits and fermenting Blood.

Lodg'd in the Soul, with Virtue over-rul'd
Inflam'd by Reason, and by Reason cool'd.
In times of Peace content to be unknown,
And only in the Field of Battle shown.'

"Bill Cheney, in spite of his obvious awe at the Gunner's learning, was not sure that poetry would be so efficacious in the actual combat as, say, brass knuckles; but the three of us finally agreed that if I could manage to recite Addison's lines from *The Campaign* and at the same time enumerate my contacts with the nose, the effect upon the enemy would be confusing. 'You do it,' said Bulkeley, 'this way:

" 'Presence of Mind *(One!)*, and Courage in Distress
Are more *(Two!)* than Armies to procure Success.
True Courage *(Three!)*
and et cetery.'

"Much more sage counsel of this sort I absorbed from my two friends along with the brisket of beef and the porter, so that by the time the sunlight slanted through the western window upon our table I felt that I had made many strides toward manhood. These friends believed that I could fight a man, and beat him. Therefore I believed that too. I resolved that there would be no more fainting away, no sickness at the dark and damp and stench of the midshipmen's berth, and no sign from me of the disgust I could not but feel at the conditions on the *Wager*'s deck. Thus I put my childhood behind me and walked out upon Portsmouth Hard arm-in-arm with a gunner and a boatswain's mate.

"My valise had somehow disappeared from the Blue Posts Inn. Even the serving-wench, whom my former friend had adjured to treat me as she did him, had never once—or so she said with a straight face—laid eyes on it. This loss of my papers and all my clothing except what I then had on would have been a more grievous blow if I had not found my fowling-piece leaning in the very corner where I had put it the night before. Still, I had many things to buy: a sea-chest, sea-boots, a midshipman's dirk, a rope of onions, a large Cheddar cheese, a keg of cider, and several slops—the sailor's term for his outer clothes and his bedding. The knowledge of my friends, and their determination that I should not be cheated, saved me several times as much in these purchases as our dinner had cost. Consequently, I went back to the *Wager* not only well equipped but with three gold pieces and some silver still in my pocket.

"Bill Cheney left us at the foot of the *Wager*'s ladder. I asked him to find my friend Keppel on the *Centurion* and tell him where I was. His last words, shouted from half a cable's length away, were something about 'top o' yer 'ead' and 'one-two-three.'

"The three other midshipmen were in the berth when the Gunner and I arrived. Curly-haired little Cozens was cleaning Campbell's boots. Mr. Isaac Morris, who is with us today, was engaged, if I remember, in mending Campbell's breeches. The great Campbell himself lay at full length—and he was long—on the table. He made no effort to rise as we entered, but surveyed me through half-shut eyes with a growing expression of contempt.

" 'Get up, please, Mr. Campbell,' the Gunner politely said.

"Campbell did not stir.

" 'Mr. Campbell, I ask you to rise and greet our new berth-mate.'

"No motion followed, except that the expression of contempt now approached a sneer. " 'Get up!'

" 'You get out, Gunner. Go mumble your damned Methodist prayers outside. This berth is for gentlemen!'

"With a sudden jerk of his left hand Bulkeley tipped the massive oaken table over as one might turn the page of a book. 'Now,' said he, even more quietly than before, 'you will please to rise, Mr. Campbell, set this table back on its legs, and greet the Honourable John Byron, son of Lord Byron of Newstead Abbey.'

"The introduction was not fortunate, either in the occasion or the wording, and Mr. Campbell took it with even less grace than might be expected. He did not meet the eyes of the Gunner, but stared at me, grinding out something to the effect that his greeting of me would come later on.

"Mr. Campbell, I could now see, was well over six feet tall. He had to crouch far forward to avoid the ceiling and the beams of the room. This was, of course, an interesting strategic fact. It would bring his otherwise inaccessible nose, a prominent feature, well within my range. As for the rest of him . . . But such things take longer in telling than they are worth, and so let me sum up Mr. Campbell's general appearance by saying only that I did not find it attractive. It is fair to add that his estimate of me seemed to be much the same.

"We had stood thus for perhaps ten seconds—Campbell and I staring and glaring, the Gunner grim, young Cozens and Morris hugely excited, breathless, confident at least of a fight—when some officer bawled from the deck above that the Gunner was wanted at once in the Captain's cabin. 'Aye, aye, sir!' Bulkeley replied, and instantly began gathering up every weapon or tool—dirks, swords, pistols, my fowling-piece, even the table knives and forks—that could do mortal injury. 'I can't keep you from fightin',' he said meanwhile, speaking rapidly. 'Fact is, for once, I don't want to. I'd like to stay an' enjy what's about to 'appen like Mr. Cozens will an' Mr. Morris, an' likewise the Honourable Mr. John Byron. But I'll be back to enjy the results, Mr. Campbell.'

"These last words were spoken as Bulkeley opened the door to his gun-room, just aft of our berth. There he deposited all our weapons in a heap and locked the door on them before he left us to go on deck. Then came Campbell's voice, choked by anger: '*Honourable,* eh? So *that's* what you expect us to call you! Well, I won't, see. You'll call *me* "the Honourable," that's what, an' I'll call *you* what you are!'

"I told him that the Gunner, not I, had used the title that distressed him, that I didn't want it, and that the name of 'Jack' was good enough for me.

" ' "Jackass," you mean now, don't you?' he snarled, ducking under a beam and coming closer. 'All right, then; that's your name. Cozens an' Morris, take notice: if you call this Johnny Newcome by any other name than "Jackass," I'll cut your hearts out. —Cozens, drop those boots! Jackass, you black 'em!'

"Now I don't want to pretend that there was anything heroic about my conduct in this affair. There was not. I had all the advantages, except in the reach of my arms. I had been in at least twenty fights at school, some of which I had lost and learned why. Campbell really was a coward, and I knew it. Furthermore, he was already in a rage, while I was recalling Gunner Bulkeley's charm: 'Presence of Mind and Courage in Distress, and et cetery.' Therefore I was able to smile and to say: 'If you ask me politely, Mr. Campbell, I'll black your boots as best I can; but at a command I will not.'

" 'Then I'll make you,' he growled, ducking to avoid a second beam, his fists swinging.

"This conduct clearly came under the head of what Gunner Bulkeley had called hectoring. Therefore, at the moment when Campbell's nose came on a level with mine, I smote it, hard, so that his head struck the beam behind with a clearly audible thud.

" 'That's *one*,' I shouted, and while he was still dazed by the blow on his head I was able to deliver two more attacks upon the same organ, counting aloud, 'That's *two* !' and 'That's *three* !' Blood spurted from his nose and ran down into his panting mouth. With a sweep of his arm across his face, he got some of it into his eyes. He looked murderous as he came at me with a rush and a storm of blows. One of them closed my left eye. Another, below the belt, knocked the breath out of me and sent me reeling. For an instant I thought I was through, but I managed to get round the table and catch a breath. He grinned, thinking me beaten, and reached into his pocket. 'Don't let him get his knife !' Cozens yelled. 'He'll kill you !'

"This, I saw, was true. 'Presence of Mind and Courage in Distress' were clearly called for. He had smeared more blood in his eyes and was blinking, half blinded, while fumbling in his pocket. With all my strength I lunged at the table, lifted its edge, and toppled it over. It fell with a crash on his toes, and his scream of agony rang through the half-dark that followed the fall of the tallow dip. There was just enough light breaking through the glass scuttle above to let me see him with my good eye as he stood pinned against the stout gun-room door, striving to free his feet, still trying to get at his clasp-knife. For a few seconds he was helpless, and during those seconds I counted, for the world to hear, 'Four,' 'Five,' 'Six,' and—well, and et cetery, paying exclusive attention to the one feature upon which I had begun. Remembering Bill Cheney's advice, I ' 'it 'im 'ard an' frequent,' and at each blow on the nose his head banged back against the lintel of the door. There was nothing heroic, I say again, or even brave, about this performance ; but it seemed necessary. Mr. Cozens and Mr. Morris enjoyed it extremely, to judge from their applause."

"That we did, Captain," said Morris, rubbing his hands and smiling broadly. "It set us free from a tyrant. A grand fight it was—and you have told it well."

"But go on, Cap'n, go on !" John Chester urged. " 'Tain't fair to leave 'im jest standin' thar, bein' punched on the nose ! Didn't he do nothin' back ?"

"He managed to get in one desperate blow. I saw it coming, and took it—again according to Bill Cheney's instructions—on the top of my head. It hurt my head severely, I remember, but also it sprained his thumb. He yelled for help and, after a while, begged for mercy. He got none of that until my count had reached well into the twenties. I stopped when he began to cry. He was not a pleasing sight."

"Why," said Kitty, throwing herself back so that her chair creaked, "I never heard of such a thing! But you *take* us there. He isn't in a play or a story. He's real! He's suffering! I'm sorry for him!"

"Yes, Mrs. Clive; so am I. I was at the time. I distinctly remember the revulsion of feeling that came in the very moment when it was clear that my victory was complete. Yet I saw, too, that he had to be vanquished once for all, if there was to be any peace or safety for the rest of us in that berth. I asked the other midshipmen to be quiet, and we let him sob and curse for a while. Gradually he quieted down. Then I politely requested him to hand over his knife, unopened. When this was done we lifted the table off his toes and got him to set it upright for the second time. The next thing was for him to black the boots of Mr. Cozens and Mr. Morris. When Gunner Bulkeley returned he was mending the rent in his own breeches by the light of the tallow dip, making a bad job of it because he had never learned to sew and the blood still bleared his eyes.

"The Gunner was so delighted by this domestic scene that he felt it should be witnessed and enjoyed by at least one other person. After a moment's consultation with us three lads he went away to get the Lieutenant, who, he told me, was the officer with final authority over all midshipmen.

"Lieutenant Robert Beans I can best describe by saying that at my first glimpse of him I began to calculate how many tallow dips could be made of his gross, fat body. What he lacked in height he made up in rotundity, bulges, and creases. Yet Mr. Beans had the quick intelligence so often seen in corpulent people. His little blue pig's eyes gleamed with delight as they glanced from Campbell to me and back again. 'Why, this is charming!' said he. 'It's delightful to see Mr. Campbell going in for housekeeping this way. I congratulate you, Mr. Byron, upon the new arrangements you have made on the very day of your arrival. The only question is how we can make them last, and about that I have an idea. —Mr. Campbell, stand up!'

"Campbell staggered to his feet, holding hard to the table-top.

" 'Look at me, Mr. Campbell. —I say, look at *me*! —Now, you're already plotting in your banged and bloody head how you can get back at these boys. You hope to do so in some sneaking way. Let me tell you that if any of them comes to the least harm, whether I can trace it to you or not, you will suffer the like at once. If one of them is killed, you will hang. If one is stabbed, so will you be. If one falls to the deck, you will fall. Is that clear?'

" 'Yes, sir.'

" 'One more thing: there is to be no more bullying in this berth, no cursing of your mates, no sneering or sulking or sour looks. You're to conduct yourself like a gentleman if you expect a gentleman's treatment. If you don't, for the first offence you'll be spread-eagled in the weather-rigging, and for the next, flogged. The Gunner will report to me every night. Now you may finish mending your breeches and then scrub this floor. —I wish you a pleasant evening.' "

"That, I should think," said my cousin, "left a dangerous situation."

"You are right, General Conway. The Lieutenant's bluster—for of course he threatened far more than he could have done—succeeded in frightening Campbell but also deepened his hatred. It drove him to seek out treacherous ways of revenge. For the time, however, he gave no more trouble in the berth. After a while he withdrew his presence.

"Campbell's animosity tended to draw the rest of us more closely together. Mr. Morris was my elder by several years, and on that account I saw less of him than I wished. He may be amused to learn that in those days I greatly admired his manly way of looking the dismallest facts in the face and, when they could not be changed, laughing at them. Situations and events that distressed me almost beyond endurance were to him only a part of the day's work. In other words, Mr. Morris was a grown man with the gift of humour, and I was still a boy—easily excited, highly emotional, and determined to get the utmost suffering out of every woe.

"A boy of that kind needs a father, and almost as much he needs another lad of his own age, or near it, for whom his feeling is warmly fraternal. Now it is true that I already had a brother and father in the way of the flesh; but they were far away, and moreover, for reasons that are no part of this story, my relations with them had never been close. On that account I took all the more delight in my friendship, deepening from day to day, with Gunner Bulkeley and Henry Cozens. I may as well say at once that I soon came to love these two—the Gunner because I needed him and Cozens because I thought he needed me.

"Henry Cozens was younger than I by several months, and even less ready for the shocks and dangers lying before us. His curly blond hair, blue eyes, and delicate complexion made him look, at times, hardly more than a child. He had, I think, the gayest, most generous and open-hearted disposition I have ever known. He was naturally good, kind, and well mannered. When I add that he was also remarkably intelligent you will see how fortunate I was in this companion. And yet there was this strange, sad thing: though still so young, Cozens had already acquired—I never knew how or where—a passion for strong drink, and when drink was in him he seemed of a sudden to put off his humanity and become a raging animal. All his friends knew this weakness of his, and were sorry for it. One of the things that brought the Gunner and me together was our wish to protect Henry Cozens as much as we could.

"He never quarrelled with me. There was never a hard word between us. In the cockpit, on deck, and up the masts, we were inseparable companions. He and I shared all our belongings, our thoughts, our hopes and fears. Nothing that happened to me was fully my own experience until I had told it to him; and every jest I heard among the men had to wait for its full effect until I saw the flash of his smile, heard the shout of his boyish laughter. Even now, after all these years, I often catch myself saying: 'I must remember to tell Henry Cozens about this.' At this moment I can see us two youngsters, down in the midshipmen's berth, reading by the light of a farthing dip a book he bought one day in Portsmouth. It was a battered, pigskinned copy of Shelvocke's *Voyage Round the World*, with the marks of many sailors' thumbs in the margins. We must have read it through several times, learning it almost by heart, meanwhile discussing with great eagerness the question whether George Shelvocke was a pirate. That question seemed to us one of high importance. As things turned out, we were right."

Again Captain Byron sipped his wine. My little dog Ponto rose from his mat by the fire, stretched, and yawned from the red curling tip of his tongue to the end of his quivering tail. Then he lay down again, curled up, and slowly closed his eyes. Anne Boleyn's clock rang its tiny chime and struck three delicate strokes.

"During the weeks that followed," Byron continued, "I learned more than in any other year of my life. For one thing, Cozens and I had to row over to the *Centurion* every morning and there take lessons in the mathematics of navigation from an impatient little Cornishman by the name of Pascoe Thomas. He was a good teacher, and we liked him. I've heard that he has since written a book and a good one, about the *Centurion*'s voyage. It might easily be better than the account by Richard Walter, Anson's Chaplain, which is written as though its author had never left the quarterdeck. Well, those lessons brought young Keppel and me together for three hours a day, and gave me a glimpse now and then of the Commodore. They let me see, too, that even in harbour and when seriously undermanned, a ship need not be, like the *Wager*, filthy and cluttered. But then, also, I had to learn every part of a ship—its name, place, and use—down to the smallest fid and treenail. I learned to climb the ratlines in a race with my comrades, to lay out on a yard, to reef and furl, to heave in the cable with the men at the capstan, to help cat the anchor, and a thousand more such things. They come fast to an eager lad, but it was a harder thing for me to command other men, thrice my age and with many times my experience. That is the worst aspect of the midshipman's life—to have men of sixty touching their caps to him, obeying his orders, meekly accepting his insolence, when he is still an ignorant boy.

"Hardest of all, though, in what I went through was the mere waiting, the coming up on deck day after day and seeing always the same shore-line, the same masts and hulls, with no sails set and no ripple along the bow. I had looked forward to action, storms, perhaps even battle. Instead, there we stuck, almost within hail of the land. This was bad for the crew. The officers lost control of their men, and the Captain was never once seen. Poisonous hatreds spread like a plague through the ship, along with unspeakable vices. Every night the *Wager* became a brothel. Every morning, at eight, we midshipmen had to oversee still half-drunken sailors told off to cleanse the deck of their midnight spewings.

"I do not mean to say, or suggest, that this debauchery was universal among us, that the other ships in harbour were not in like case, or, indeed, that it was more common on shipboard than in the alleys of Portsmouth and those of London itself. We had on the *Wager*, as I shall show, our due share of temperate, clean-living, upright men. Perhaps it was only that vices ordinarily hidden away were there almost publicly indulged, and were at any rate known to all. But then, too, you may try to imagine what horror, what loathing, would be felt by a decent lad of sixteen in the constant, unavoidable presence of men and women who had grown old in depravity.

"There were some eighty men and boys on the *Wager* when I joined her, and almost every one of these I saw, heard, talked and worked with, every day. The look, the gestures, the habits, as it seemed to me the very thoughts of each one, were burned, after the first few weeks, into my mind.

"You fortunate people, who can choose your associates and escape with a few of them into quiet places like Strawberry Hill, can know little about this, and I cannot tell you much. I would say, though, that there can be no closer association—not in a village, a convent, or family—than that forced upon the officers and crew of a ship, where each must depend upon all and all upon each. Think of a ship in a storm, though, and you will understand how everything may depend upon the men at the wheel, on the yards, and at the braces. In a calm, when every mind works upon every other, this interdependence is, if anything, greater. Strongest and most tyrannical it is in such weary waiting as we of the *Wager* endured in Portsmouth harbour.

" 'Now then, Mr. Byron,' said the Gunner one day, 'there's a few things I'd like to tell you about this expedition afore we sail—if we ever do. 'Tain't too late for your people to get you off, an' I wouldn't have you steerin' blind into misforten.'

"It was a torrid afternoon, I remember. Portsmouth Harbour was like a sheet of glass. Bulkeley, Morris, Cozens, and I had climbed to the maintop to catch whatever air might be stirring and to get as far as possible away from the stench of the ship.

" 'I know some of them already,' said I. 'Commodore Anson isn't popular like Admiral Vernon, and he's had trouble getting men.'

" 'Trouble! Why, sir, he's been in torment, not only about men but ships and stores and victuals, even orders. Look you, now: George Anson took this command from Sir Charles Wager, First Lord o' the Admiralty, in July, 1739. Now here it is eleven months later ,and we haven't a ship ready for sea. Partly it's a matter o' stores. Take this: the *Centurion* needed a new foremast. When it came, there was a rotten knot in it, eleven inches deep, reachin' halfway through. The Commodore objected, but the Dockyard people told him all the mast needed was a plug to stop the hole. He got no help from the Navy Office. Only a plug. And so he'll be tryin' to round Cape Horn with a mast that may snap in any gale.'

" 'Somebody,' Cozens said, 'must have pocketed the money for a good mast.'

" 'Right you are, young man. And somebody took the money for seventy-two puncheons o' prime beef ordered for the *Gloucester*. When they were delivered, forty-two of those puncheons were already stinkin'. —But there's no help for it. The good masts and good beef have all gone to Vernon.'

" 'And most of the good men, too,' said Morris.

" 'Ah, there's the worst of it—the men we haven't got; and likewise them we can't get rid of. We could do with plugged masts and putrid beef, young gentlemen; we could do with old sails sold for new, an' cordage mostly rotten; we could forget that the *Wager* was built long ago for the East India v'y'ge and not for battle nor yet Cape Horn. But look on the deck there below, and what have we? We have disease, filth, villainy, drunkenness, vice, and crime; but of men . . . Make no mistake, Mr. Byron, this v'y'ge will be unlucky. You can still leave it if you want. I don't ask you to leave. Your gain would be my loss. Yet I've thought it my duty to tell you how bad things be."

" 'We're short-handed, aren't we, Gunner?' said Morris. 'How much, now?'

" 'Three hundred men short in the squadron, yes. —I mean three hundred able seamen, and not the dregs caught by the press-gangs, or sent up from the jails and hospitals. Weeks ago, the First Lord o' the Admiralty ordered Sir John Norris—that's Vernon's man in the grand reinforcement fleet over there—to supply us. Sir John said he wanted those men for Vernon, and sent us not so much as one cook's boy.'

" 'But,' I gasped, 'that was disobedience!'

" 'Aye; it was all of that. O' course, if Sir John Norris had been a common seaman, then "mutiny" would have been the word and a yard-arm party the result.'

"Not anger or indignation, but a grim endurance of wrong was what we saw in the Gunner's eyes as he sat there on the maintop, erect in repose, and not so much leaning against the mast, one might say, as supporting it. He made me think of some stout iron clamp or holdfast shaped by the blacksmith's hammer to strengthen things less firm than itself.

"Do you see what I mean? I'm not sure that I bring the man before you—the bare-headed man, bare-chested, bare-footed, sitting there with his hard, hairy arms folded and staring off at Portsmouth through the heat-haze. Gunner Bulkeley is not the kind of man that ladies and gentlemen are likely to know—or, if they do, to admire. He

was not brilliant, you understand, nor amusing. He was ignorant of
most things that we know. I was to learn later on that he was a
Methodist—'converted,' as he put it, by the preaching of John Wesley.
In a company such as this, can one say worse? Still, as the days
passed, I was finding in John Bulkeley a man staunch, faithful, true,
and by far the best teacher I had ever known.

"The Gunner was gazing at Portsmouth so intently that Morris and
I turned about to look in the same direction. Something of interest—
we could not make sure quite what—was going on over there. A
number of large open boats lay at one of the docks, and a crowd of
men were slowly, awkwardly, embarking. They did not know how to
get into a boat. They had to be helped. Even from a distance they
looked feeble. Some, we saw, were crippled.

" 'Ye don't s'pose, now, do you, gentlemen, as these might be the
sojers we ben promised to take the place o' seamen?'

" 'Soldiers?' asked Morris and Cozens together.

" 'Yeah. Ha'n't you heard? It's a new way o' fightin' at sea which
the Lords of Admiralty just thought up. We're to have Colonel
Bland's regiment o' foot, I'm told, an' three comp'nies o' marchin'
men.'

" 'How will they help?' I asked.

" 'Help? —I b'lieve the understanding is they'll do everything. We
sailors 'll only be took along for the sea-air an' the sights. Anyhow,
there'll be no need o' gunners, nor yet midshipmen. When we sight a
Spanish ship the sojers 'll march aboard an' take her, an' that'll be
the end o' the war.'

"We sat silent then for several minutes, watching the slow approach
of the boats. Three were bound for the *Wager*. On the deck below us
all the men were by this time leaning over the rail. Little by little, as
they saw what the three boats held, their catcalls and jibes subsided.
When the newcomers came alongside, our people were perfectly still.
Peering down from the top, Bulkeley, Morris, Cozens, and I were
silent. The sight below was too pitiful, too shameful for words.

"Those boats were crowded with decrepit old men, white-haired,
white-bearded. Two of them had wooden legs, two carried crutches,
and one had an iron hook in place of a hand. One and all, they were
wizened, worn out, ready not for seafaring but for the grave. 'Chelsea
Hospital pensioners,' I heard Bulkeley say under his breath.

"That was precisely what we found them to be when we reached the deck and helped hoist them in by means of a boatswain's chair. They were old soldiers who had fought England's battles in many lands. Now England was sending them out to die at sea, thus saving the cost of their keep and their burial charges. From the *Wager*'s people, as they helped these forlorn old hulks to their quarters, I heard many expressions of wrath and compassion, strangely mingled.

"There had been five hundred of these pensioners in Portsmouth the day before, the boatmen told our Gunner, but during the night all those who were able to walk had disappeared. Thus the squadron got two hundred and fifty-nine aged cripples, not one of whom had any knowledge of the sea, in place of the three hundred sailors Anson had called for. In addition, the squadron had acquired the seeds of sundry diseases, destined to yield a huge crop.

"You will wonder what can have been the object of this cruelty. I have never made quite sure. Perhaps, as I have hinted, it was done to save money. Perhaps someone in high place was doing all he could to cripple our expedition—since, as we now know, the agents of Spain had great influence in causing the war, and were doubtless still powerful in Whitehall at that time. A darker possibility is that it was planned by the rich provision contractors on shore, so that their agents, the ships' pursers, could charge the government for the victuals and drink and wages of men who died on the voyage. But the opinion I incline to is that the decision was made in sheer stupidity and ignorance.

"That night I lay awake for hours in my hammock, thinking about these things and the Gunner's suggestion that it was not too late for me to leave the ship. I longed to leave. Visions of my home, of Sherwood Forest, even of my school and schoolmates, came before me— all of them hallowed by distance and shining with the lustre of childhood. But then, as I turned and tossed, I knew that I could not return—for one reason because I did not, at the bottom of my heart, want to. The ship was loathsome to me. This voyage, I now knew for myself without needing the Gunner's word, would be disastrous. Yet I was determined to take it and do my utmost for the ship. I had been mastered, you see, by that strange spirit of loyalty which I have mentioned before and shall speak of again.

"Among the misfortunes suffered by Anson's squadron before we set sail, the most serious of all was the delay. Our orders required us to round Cape Horn, a thing that is never easy in summer, but in winter should never be attempted. It was of utmost import that we should reach the Horn before the winter of that region began—that is, in April; and we had much to do on the way. You can therefore understand the anxiety of our Commodore, of the Gunner, and indeed of us all, as day followed day and the squadron did not sail.

"Our hold and lower decks were already filled with artillery and stores when we were ordered to take on board a large quantity of trucking cloth and other goods which the gentlemen of Whitehall imagined we might barter with the Spanish colonists of South America. Against this ridiculous scheme of trading with our enemies the Commodore had argued and pled with all his force; but the interests of private gain had overcome those of national honour. The gentlemen agents in charge of these goods had, it appeared, powerful friends at Court. George Anson probably injured what small reputation he had at Court by saying that he had no training or experience in facing an enemy with a sword in one hand and a roll of trucking-cloth in the other. But all would not do: the cloth was hoisted aboard and stowed somehow in a ship already overladen. How useful we found it later, you shall hear.

"We had some hopes of sailing when, on the eighth of August, the last small company of soldiers was brought aboard the squadron. Two hundred and ten young Marines they were, meant to take the place of the two hundred and forty invalids who had escaped at Portsmouth. We began to fear that Whitehall could not even count. As for military experience, these youngsters could neither load nor fire their muskets.

"Thus at last our squadron stood ready to sail—or as ready as it could ever be with rotting spars and sails aloft, stinking beef below, and mobs of miserable, debauched men on the gun-decks. The parting drams were drunk. Shore-women and pedlars were driven out, still clamouring for their money. On the tenth of August sails were hoisted, anchors lifted, and with a huge chorus of cheers we worked out of Portsmouth Harbour. But the cheers did not last long. Almost at once we were struck by headwinds that drove us to anchorage before nightfall off St. Helen's on the Isle of Wight.

"There we lay for the next forty days and nights while the west wind blew continually against us, as though striving to complete what human stupidity and greed had begun. I will not detain you with the story of how we tried to take advantage of every lull. Enough that we were exhausted by setting sail in vain almost daily, and also by the

alternation of hope and disappointment. The thing became a nightmare. We felt doomed to spend our lives in this meaningless, monotonous toil, still held in sight of England.

"On the eighteenth day of September, 1740, our imprisonment came
to its end. It was a drizzling, miserable day; but the wind, though still
against us, was light. Flood tide came at three in the afternoon, and at
two the flagship signalled that we should drift down the Channel with
the outgoing tide.

"My station was in the foretop, where I had little to do because no
sails were set. From that broad platform, forty feet above the deck,
I looked down at Bulkeley on the forecastle, taking the place of the
Boatswain, who was too drunk for duty, and directing the men as they
hove in the anchor cable. It was a quiet enough beginning. No one
cheered or sang. A fiddler scraped out a tune for the cold, wet men as
they tramped round the capstan. Then the anchor pulled free and we
began to crawl, to drift, with barely a perceptible motion at first but
little by little gathering way. The *Gloucester, Severn, Pearl, Tryal,*
and *Centurion* were also feeling the steady pull of the sea. The whole
squadron, which now included the two pinks, *Anna* and *Industry,* was
moving at last—moving against the breeze, and also, one might say,
against all that human agencies could do to detain it—to meet its
destiny. There was something mysterious, thrilling, sad in that motion,
and something that spoke to my heart in the whisper of little waves at
the bow. Death must be like this, I said to myself, when the will lets
go its hold and the spirit is drawn forth into strangeness. I stood there
for hours, listening and watching, while the rain fell, the first night
watch was set, the forecastle bell rattled out eight tinny strokes, and
night came down over England, the roadstead, and our eight ships
going out on the tide.

"Thus we went at a crawl, a creep, for some forty-eight hours,
until, off the Ram's Head, near Plymouth, we found, or were found
by, a fair wind at last. It scoured the sky and turned the sea in half
an hour from lead to dancing blue. Ah, how it comes back, that first
quiver and thrill of the ship I rode when the morning's breath changed
her to a living thing! What words can say, or what music sing, the
heart-shaking beauty of a ship's sway and plunge when she and the
wind are wedded? —I was sixteen, and that was my first morning
at sea.

"A broad, red, swallow-tailed pennant goes fluttering up the mizzen rigging of the flagship. When it reaches the peak the *Gloucester* begins her salute of thirteen guns to the flag of the Commodore. Then the *Severn* speaks, and the *Pearl*; even the little *Tryal*. On the deck below me I can see my friend John Bulkeley at his duties, pacing slowly between the guns, apparently measuring out the *Wager's* salute with his own strides. The heavy metal of the *Centurion* herself is added now. An instant before the bellow of each gun reaches our ears a puff of cotton—or so it looks—is suddenly pushed through the porthole from the inside of the vessel. Throughout the squadron the boatswains' pipes are twittering, topmen lay out on the yards aloft, waisters stand to the halliards on deck, officers are raising their speaking-trumpets, and then comes the call of the Commodore from the high poop of the flagship: 'Fore, main, and mizzen topsails—off gaskets, and sheet home!'

"Our officers repeat that order, for the words have not come clearly, but every man of us has heard the strong happy voice of George Anson setting his ships free from the land. Each of us shares, in his fashion, the Commodore's joy that now we shall have to face only the clean, honest dangers of the sea which, though they kill men's bodies, do not corrupt the mind and heart. The hatreds, poisons, and diseases we have brought from shore are forgotten. For the moment we are a band of brothers. The topmen are working furiously, gaily, at the gasket-knots, standing shoulder to shoulder along the yards.

" 'Waisters! Hoist topsails!'

"Have you heard the rhythmic calls, cries, and work-songs of sailors up the mast, at the capstan, or tailing to the halliards, how they make one man of many and mingle the beat of every heart with the throb of the waves and the tide? Hear them now, if you can, mixed in with the creaking of tackle-blocks, as the yards with their burden of canvas rise slowly, heavily, into the blue. The canvas flaps as it goes up, and bulges, catching the wind. All at once it turns into sails. Like the boughs of a thorn tree in April, the topmasts burst into bloom. Now the reef-points begin their tapping dance to the music the wind hums. The ship comes alive, and is singing. She begins to dance. Down, down goes the bow with a plunge that sends me reeling, and then up, up again with a strong slow swing comes the dripping spear of the bowsprit. She steadies now, and answers her helm, and seems to hear some command of the will or—who knows?—some call of her destiny. She is off, at last, on her way.

"All of us, I suppose, must hoard up memories of that kind, and go back to them year after year, still wondering what magic it is that surrounds and changes and glorifies them as an oyster turns a sand-grain into a pearl. Even now as I sit here I feel that first dip and toss of the ship, see the quiver and tilt of a gull's wing over the maintop, and suddenly catch my breath at the discovery—how have I missed it before?—that one of the three men pulling a rope beside me has only two fingers on his right hand. Another is wearing gold earrings. The bare back of the third is livid and ridged with wales left by the lash. All three of these men—Bosman, Callicutt, and MacCawl—show the marks of prolonged debauch, but the breath of the sea is already blowing them clean.

"These pictures shine like the memory of a sunrise that has ushered in a dismal day. For the fair wind did not last long. During most of the month we spent on the twelve-hundred-mile voyage to Madeira— a voyage often done in less than half the time—we fought for every league. Some of us never reached Madeira. After anchoring there in the harbour of Fonchiale, the Commodore found that there were a hundred and twenty-two men in the squadron too sick for duty. Fourteen had been buried at sea.

"There was nothing surprising in this. Prison fever had been brought aboard by men offered the choice between serving His Majesty at sea and hanging by the neck until they were dead. I fear that their choice was unwise, but they did not know when they made it that they would have to sleep in a dark, airless den with only twelve inches of lateral space allowed to each man. No prison is quite so bad as that, and death by the rope is less horrible than typhus or scurvy.

"The *Wager* was probably more crowded than the other vessels, because we had been obliged to stow most of the trucking-cloth as well as the artillery stores. I heard that on the *Centurion* each common seaman was allotted sixteen inches for his hammock-room."

"Yes, that's about right, I guess," John Chester declared, breaking into the thoughtful silence that followed. "I went down thar on the gun-deck, first night, along of Uncas. We took one smell o' the place, and then went an' slep' on the maintop the heft o' the v'y'ge."

"Was that the Commodore's orders?" asked Byron.

"Wal, say an invitation. When he saw they warn't a hammock half big enough for Uncas, an' him useter sleep mos'ly out o' door, why the

Old Man said what he wanted was a man up the mast who could see in the dark. I went along."

"Did you stay aloft all the time?"

"Aw, times we'd go down for another try at that 'ar swill they called 'burgoo', or mebbe a handful o' weevils. But mos'ly we et sea-gulls."

"Ah. Raw, I suppose?"

"Eeah. Raw sea-gulls keeps off scurvy. That's what Uncas said, an' likewise he ketched the sea-gulls."

"H'm. Why didn't the rest of us know about that?"

"'Twa'n't for lack o' tellin'; but ye can't drag an English sailor offen his weevils an' burgoo, no more 'n Mr. Walpole here away from his tea. Consekence was, most of 'em died. Me an' Uncas stayed alive."

Something was going on here, William, which I did not fully comprehend. Were these statements to be taken as literal fact, or as contributions to marine mythology? One has heard about sailors' "yarns," and you are perhaps familiar with the vulgar expression "pulling the leg." Well, what I more and more wanted to know, as I listened last week to John Chester, was whether, how, why, and to what extent our legs were being pulled—oh, never, you understand, with violence or malicious intent, but playfully, merrily, with delighted and often delightful small jerks and tweaks. Captain Byron seemed to know, and I judged that he thought they were. Also he seemed to feel that such treatment would do the legs of Strawberry Hill no harm. Certainly he felt, as we all did that this man from Connecticut was a godsend of whom we should make the utmost.

"After six months of fumbling through fog," said Byron, "and struggling with headwinds and lying idle in calms, Anson's squadron came, in March, 1741, to the desolate coast of Tierra del Fuego at the southern tip of South America. By that time the vessels were weakened and leaking. Their hulls were crusted with barnacles and long grass, their ironwork eaten by rust, their cordage rotting. Prison fever had been followed by scurvy, which was now killing a dozen men a day while a hundred others lay helpless in their crowded hammocks waiting for death. Captain Kidd of the *Wager* had died, and, after a brief interval under another commander, his place had been taken by one David Chepe, who had never held such authority before. The discipline of the *Wager*'s people had suffered in this swift succession of captains. The monotony of the voyage, the stench, the damp, the crowding below decks, the bad food, the excessive labour of those able to work at all, had sapped whatever enthusiasm they may have felt at the outset. All the men now knew, moreover, that a Spanish flotilla of greatly superior strength was in pursuit of them, so that even if they escaped the perils of the Horn they might still be destroyed by their human foes. Add to this the fear of foes supernatural that tightened upon them as winter came on and they approached the place of ordeal. No man on the *Wager* had ever sailed those seas before. There was no adequate map, on board, of the coast they were skirting, no sufficient chart of soundings and currents, but only a fifty-year-old book by Sir John Narborough who had been sent there by the second King Charles to make observations. Knowledge, therefore, gave way to surmise, and this in turn to the wild superstitions that had been gathering about Cape Horn since the time of Magellan.

"On the seventh of March we came into the long narrow channel that runs between Tierra del Fuego and Staten Land. This corridor of the sea is walled by vast crags that spire up into pinnacles of perennial snow. Not one green thing could we see, but only black rocks weirdly piled, rocks gigantic and jagged, vast precipices of rock gashed by chasms. On a day less innocently serene we should not have dared to enter there, and even on that blithe morning, with a sparkling sea about us and a following wind and tide to help us onward, we ought to have said that those rocks were clearly the gates of hell and that we would not be lured between them by any ruse of fair weather; but what we did say to one another as we ran merrily southward through the Straits—making the distance of eight leagues in less than two hours—was that now our toils and dangers were over, that we were coming into the calm and healthful Pacific, there to heal our sick, careen and cleanse our vessels, and gather the silver of Chile and gold of Peru. Ah, the gay calls, the laughter, the songs, the chirruping pipes and squeaking fiddles, that rang out from the deck and the mastheads that morning! We brought our sick up into sunlit air. During those two hours not one man in the squadron died. Midshipman Campbell spoke to me without a frown or a growl as we met for a moment in Captain Chepe's cabin. The Captain himself smiled at me, and that was not his custom. In fact the only man I can recall who did not look as though he had cast away all care was Gunner Bulkeley. 'Enj'y it while you can, Mr. Byron,' was all I could get him to say.

"Two hours of this we had, whether as a solace for six months of misery past or to deepen the disasters to come. Then, just as we reached open water, the sky darkened, the sea changed its hue, the tide turned against us, and we heard from the south a confused on-rushing clamour of wind and wave. A vast bellow of rage it was, as though some enormous herd of monsters riding the sea far off had snuffed our invasion. The sun went out. The north wind died. The sails hung slack, breathless. The ships stumbled in their stride and began to plouter and drift, idly swinging between the gone wind and the wind racing up from the unknown. On ahead, far ahead of the storm, came fear and sprang upon us and clutched every heart. It left our bodies for a later stroke but would shatter our wills at once. The *Tryal* and *Pearl* rode two miles away to the westward, their tall trucks ghostly against torn black skirts of cloud. Then came the *Centurion,* the *Gloucester,* the *Severn,* and *Anna,* with sea-room enough. The *Wager,* hindermost, was barely clear of the Straits. Close astern gloomed Staten Land, one black bristling rock with breakers leaping against it and numberless thousands of Cape pigeons, half flying and half blown, seeking shelter among its ice-hung cliffs. Toward that graveyard of ships some uncharted, unguessed-at current was sweeping us momently nearer and nearer.

"Before the orders could be called we topmen knew what must be done and were racing for the masts and up them and out on the yards to hand and reef canvas before the wind could strike, and hearing below in the lull a babel of shouts with the Boatswain's yell mixed in and the Captain's scream all lost in the howl of the storm increasing and rushing at us across the black water and the calls of my comrades beside me on the yard going fainter and farther off and leaving me alone with the gasp of my breath and the pound of my heart and the tightening grip of my fear. We had started the sheets and were hauling the buntlines when the first blast struck and stunned her. The sail leapt from our hands with a shriek and was ripped into frantic tatters that beat at our faces and hands, bound our legs and arms, tied us fast to the yard while the naked masts went swinging down and down and still down until the sea I thought lay within arm's reach of where I clung and I saw my shipmates huddled along the weather-rail of the canted deck far off to one side.

"Seconds went by like hours while we lay there, lashed by the flying canvas, clinging with broken finger-nails, flattened out by the thrust of a wind leaping straight from the southern pole. It came with a cry of hatred. It blotted out all other voices. Only by the look of their pale twisted mouths did I know that my topmates were yelling. In all the world there was left only one voice, one purpose, one will, and that was the wind's. Yet meanwhile the wind was rousing the sea. All black half a minute before, the huge heaving waste to southward was ridged now with pale crests of foam that jostled and climbed and towered and toppled and ran to be in at the kill while the ship lay helpless, struggling to right herself, trembling in every member, all her canvas gone, half her deck awash, and the cliffs as it seemed striding toward her as fast as the waves. 'It will take a great wave,' I thought, 'to throw her quite down, and at once she was struck in the flank by a billow that bore the full force of the wind and the tide. She gave a great lurch. Like a beast that feels its death-stroke she shuddered and reeled. The mast and the yard once more swept downward. —I said to myself that this was the end. I was wrong. It was the beginning.

"A ship under bare poles driven by such a wind upon such a coast has no least chance of living. If any man aboard the *Wager* is to live for half an hour a sail must instantly be bent on her mizzen to make her obey her helm and head into the wind. Every man on the deck over there knows that. Why, then, do they only stand and stare? Why does no one—the Captain, the Lieutenant, even the Boatswain—shout a command? Can it be that they are cowering away from the storm? Have they been washed overboard? But Gunner Bulkeley is there with that cluster of men by the rail, his gray head uncovered, his body bare to the waist, and pointing, not trying to outshout the tempest but only pointing, and then leading the way while six men move cautiously, painfully after him, lifting their wind-heavy hands and feet with huge effort, slowly, all but glued to the rail, the capstan, the mast, while the cliffs rush closer but yet moving inch by inch and foot by foot onward. Once, twice, and a third time in their long thirty-foot journey they are swamped by the seas running wild on the deck and then stagger up, streaming, partly stunned, partly drowned, and go on again, lashed together by one man's purpose and will, to find the driver and staysail somewhere in the smother of foam and bring them back to the mizzen and bend them there in the wind's shriek whilst every man of us holds his breath in an anguish of watching that fierce resolution whereby if the sails hold and the helm brings her round we may live a few hours longer."

Captain Byron had been speaking at a steadily increasing speed, his words tumbling forth and his sentences running each into the next so that Mr. Chute's pencil could catch only here and there a phrase and I have been forced to fall back upon language partly my own. Now he paused, leaning against the chimneypiece, and looked earnestly about the room. His gaze went again from face to face, and again lingered longest, I thought, upon Blandison's.

"Well, as you see, we lived," he continued. "Far better for many it would have been if they had not; but it was written that we should endure fiercer toils and more dreadful dangers. Those two sails held. The ship felt her helm, found her keel, faced into the tempest. Little by little we clawed off, the cliffs receded, breath returned, and Bosman, Callicutt, MacCawl and I crawled back to the foretop, trembling, and from there to the deck, like half-frozen flies.

"I have now told you a small part of what happened on the *Wager* during the first ten minutes of a storm that lasted, with a few brief and deceitful intervals, for ten weeks. I mean for ten weeks as you comfortable people here in England counted that time. To us they were an eternity of torment, struggle, and stress in which we seemed to be wrestling not with the wrath of the storm alone but against almighty powers. Yes, I tell you, there grew upon us the crippling conviction that our effort to get round Cape Horn was a sacrilegious attempt to invade a place where man had never been and had no right to be. Only so could we explain the dreadful and persistent force of the wind that beat every hour against us, or the determined might of the currents sweeping eastward round the coast. Something vastly more powerful than currents and winds, we felt, was baffling our skill and breaking our bodies and making ready to stifle our breath.

"But what can I make you see and feel and believe of all that? Does it help to say that for ten weeks our clothing and hammocks and blankets were never once dry, that we had no hot food or drink because no fire could be made in the galley, that our muscles were always cramped and many bones were broken by falls, that great seas often rushed the length of the deck bearing with them the corpses we had no time to thrust overside? Does it mean something that men burly and hale when the storm began were white-haired, palsied, wizened, and crazed before it ended? —But no. You cannot imagine the ceaseless howl of the wind in the rigging, the groans and screams of every timber, or the day-and-night-long bellow of the hungering sea as it prowled and shambled gigantic about us with derisive hootings and exultations. I cannot take you down into the damp, dark chill of the midshipmen's berth at midnight and make you hear the thunder of the tempest along the planks and the yells of Henry Cozens in the hammock beside me. Let me say, though, that one hour of such horror would leave a lifelong wound in the memory. We lived through it—or most of us did—for seventy days and nights. That was our preparation for what lay ahead.

"The wind did not, and could not, steadily increase. What did grow was the cold. Going aloft to shift sails when the wind lulled, we carried belaying-pins for knocking ice off the ropes, and even then they would not work through the frozen blocks. The sails themselves were often stiff with ice. Sails and cordage rotted fast in the frequent thawing and freezing. Never did we topmen venture out on the yards without expecting the footropes to break and let us fall to the deck or into the sea. This did in fact happen to one of our best sailors, as it did also on the *Centurion*.

Few of us had ever been south of the equator, and therefore it seemed to many a cruel and incomprehensible thing that as March passed into April and April into May the winter came down upon us. In the dreary night-watches one saw the men huddled pitifully together like sheep in a windy field. 'Hey, Bill,' one would say, 'here's a rum go! I can't feel me fingers, Bill!' 'That so? Well, nuther can I feel me toes. What be wrong wi' us, Tom?' Then a third voice would break in: 'Wrong? Aw, nothin' much. They be froze, mates; that's all.' 'But, froze? How c'n that be, Jack? They don't feel cold no more.' 'No, an' what's more they never will. They'll thaw out, come mornin', an' then they'll be green, an' surgeon he'll come with his axe an' chop 'em off short so's yer whole damn leg won't rot. I seen it done once on a Whitby whaler.'

"Of the loathsome disease called scurvy there is not much that I care to say. Like the cold, it increased among us from day to day while the storm went on, striking down young men as well as old, the strong with the weak, our best sailors along with men who should never have been brought aboard. It killed surely but slowly, and while its victims lay dying they had to be cared for. They lay packed, because we had no sick bay, among those who were still sound. Often they lay for many hours after death in their hammocks or on the deck. To our fears of a violent death you may add, therefore, the inescapable sight and stench of death by slow corruption.

"And how went it meanwhile with the *Wager* herself? She had never been a beautiful ship; but at starting, though much overladen, she had been staunch. Now she was battered, wrenched, rusted, and weary of the sea. Her mizzen had been put to great strain, we knew, in clawing off Staten Land. All her masts, we feared, must have been weakened by the perpetual pitch, toss, and roll. The hull, lifted high twenty times an hour on the wave-crests and then dropped with a staggering jolt into troughs of the sea—how long could that endure? I went down into the hold with Carpenter Cummins and watched the writhe and twist of the frames there, the agonized working of clamps, beams, and knees. Every timber was groaning, and from end to end of the hold rushed the water our pumps could not keep out. On deck I looked up a hundred times a day at the masts, yards, and rigging— that huge web of intricate, delicate strength woven by man's will and wit in ten thousand years. Could it hold firm a moment longer? Surely something must give—if not this shroud or backstay then some bolt, chain, channel, lanyard, deadeye, or tarred hempen strand. It mattered not which or what, for, like the muscles of a man's hand, they were all tied together, and should one shroud go then a mast would snap like a rotten carrot and pull down the others and leave us to flounder and sink and drown.

"There is one sort of proud affection felt by a sailor for his ship when she is fresh from the builder, taut and eager for the sea, and goes tripping or trampling from wave to wave with gay scorn of all opposition. A deeper love, though, and a nobler pride, comes when he sees her weary, worn, overwhelmed, and yet battling on with what strength she has left. It was so that we came to feel toward the *Wager*, the ship which perhaps we had scarcely loved at all, or been proud of, until this time of her peril. Even now I can see how my shipmates used to glance at one another with slow smiles of wonder when for the thousandth time, beyond all hope or possibility, she lifted herself up and over some monstrous billow that had meant to be her grave.

"You will think that I linger too long upon that image of a small death-laden ship stubbornly beating her way round the end of the world. You may not share my feeling that there is something gallant about it, as well as something mad. She might, of course, have turned back; and there were many times when, with slightly less care and devotion, she might have gone down. Instead, she went on, and miraculously held together while the furious questioning finger of the storm went probing for weakness, testing every fibre of rope and wood, each particle of iron. What is more wonderful, the crew held together, in spite of death, sickness, wounds, and all the demons of discord. I like to recall how for a while they stood united on the steep streaming deck, nearly frozen by flying spume and the icy breath of the Horn but with arms interlocked, sharing what warmth they had, fighting down the fears of each one with the courage of all, a dozen men holding to one man who had a hold on something, and steadily keeping death at bay it might seem by the mere dauntless stare of their eyes.

"That picture, if you care to know, is what comes back to me now most clearly. It has come many times in years past—always with a hint of beauty and a suggestion of meaning not easy to explain. —What would you say, Parson Blandison? On the *Centurion* you must have seen such things."

There was a pause then, William—a long one, and it grew awkward. We heard the clock strike four. At length Kitty said: "I think you had better go on, Captain. Perhaps he didn't hear your question."

"Or if he did," Byron continued, "he probably thinks I rush in where angels fear to tread. But you, Mrs. Clive, are partly responsible because you asked me to talk about myself. Now I've done enough of that. The time has come for John Byron, better known as 'Foul-Weather Jack,' to retire from this tale and let the facts speak.

"The seven ships of Anson's squadron kept together for three weeks, none of them suffering great damage. Then the *Gloucester*'s main-yard was lost, and Carpenter Cummins was sent from the *Wager* to make what repairs he could. While he was gone the *Wager*'s mizzenmast snapped, leaving her incapable of heading into the wind. She lagged behind her proper station in the squadron, and the Commodore ordered the *Gloucester* to send Mr. Cummins back to us. But it was two weeks before the longboat could bring him back, and when he had come there was nothing better than a studding-sail boom to be lashed to the stump as a jury rig, making a poor exchange for our old mast.

"The squadron was now breaking up. Early in April we lost sight of the *Severn* and *Pearl,* both of which abandoned the westward struggle and were blown back into the Atlantic. We felt they were cowards to give up, yet we ourselves could scarcely keep pace with the remaining other vessels.

"At six in the evening of the nineteenth of April the Master came on deck to take command of the second dog watch. Before going below the Gunner pointed over the forecastle and said: 'There's the Commodore's light, Master Clark. Do you set your course by that, and we shall hold our place.'

" 'Light? I see no light.'

" 'Why, Master, it's shining clear directly over the larboard bow. —Mr. Byron, can you see it?'

" 'Yes, certainly, Gunner. It's perfectly clear.'

"The Gunner went below, and in a few minutes I heard the voice of Captain Chepe: 'What's this—what's this, Master Clark? You can't see the *Centurion's* light?'

" 'No, Captain. It's my belief we've been following a will-o'-the-wisp.'

" 'Where are your eyes? It's right over the bow. You see it, don't you, Mr. Byron?'

" 'Yes, sir.'

" 'Very well, Master. You've heard what Mr. Byron says. You'll remember that he saw it clearly, and said so. —If you can't see it yourself, then bid one of the powder boys watch it for you.' "

With that Captain Chepe stamped away, leaving the old. half-blind Master in charge of the watch and the ship. That seemed to me unwise, but soon I too went below, being off duty and scarcely able to stand. In the morning the *Centurion* was out of sight. We never saw her again. On that same morning we had a glimpse of the *Gloucester* and the *Anna,* far ahead. They too disappeared—so far as we were concerned, for ever.

"Thus at last the storm had scattered our seven ships abroad and was making ready to destroy them one by one. We had not known how much we depended upon the occasional sight of a sail uplifted by some far-away billow and the red sternlight of the flag-ship rising and falling on ahead in the storm. Now we felt forgotten by all mankind.

Our struggle to survive lost its meaning. There came upon us a sense of loneliness harder to bear than the hunger and cold and cramp. It struck at the mind, froze the heart, and crippled the will. Our people fell apart into hostile groups. They began to refuse their duty.

"Gunner Bulkeley was in the Steward's room the next evening when a seaman entered to get his ration of bread. 'Steward,' the man growled, 'from now on I expecks to git me full tot o' water. —What's that you say? Cap'n's orders to hell! Now Commodore's gone, what's the Cap'n? From now on there'll be a change, an' I'll git me water!'

"The Gunner quieted this outbreak for the time and then went at once to Captain Chepe. He found him, not quite sober, in the cabin. 'I beg pardon, sir,' said he, 'but one o' the men has just now complained to the Steward about the ration o' water. He says he wants more, and is going to get it. He sounded ugly, sir. I thought you ought to know.'

" 'Ah, h'm,' the Captain replied, half yawning. 'It's a pity, Gunner, that you and the other officers can't attend to these trifles when I have so many cares upon me. —But who is this man?'

" 'Joseph King, sir. He's the brother of the Boatswain.'

" 'I see. That means he's probably a coward and a bully. Do you think a hundred lashes would serve the turn?'

" 'We're none of us strong just now, Captain, and we need every hand on board.'

" 'Well then, say fifty. Will that do?'

" 'If you ask my opinion, sir, I think it would be better for you to have a talk with Joseph King.'

" 'Talk! Good God, you must be losing your mind! When a Captain starts talking with his men he loses all their respect!'

" 'That might depend on what he says to them.'

" 'Don't answer me back. I'm captain of this ship, and a captain's orders are like the word of God. I can order this man five hundred lashes if I want, and see 'em laid on.'

" 'So you could, Captain Chepe. And then, too, you could order us to throw him overboard. That would be more merciful, an' the result would be the same: we should lose a good seaman out of the few we have left.'

" 'That's enough, Mr. Bulkeley. I have a good opinion of you in spite of all that Midshipman Campbell says, but there's a kind of talk I will not endure from any one. Is that clear?'

" 'I hear you, sir.'

" 'Very well. And now here are the keys to the arms chests. You will deliver a brace of pistols, double charged, to each officer. If there's any more grumbling, the officers will know what to do.'

" 'But, Captain—'

" 'Good day, Mr. Bulkeley. I have more important matters to consider'."

"More important!" my cousin Conway called out. "Why, Captain Byron, is that the way things are done in the Navy? That man should have been court-martialled."

"No doubt, General, but, however it may be in the Army, we sailors have to wait for a court-martial until all the harm has been done. In this instance, though, we were saved by the scurvy. Joseph King was soon laid by the heels along with the Boatswain and a dozen other malcontents, and the small remainder of the crew was kept fully occupied by the needs of the crippled ship. What most distressed the Gunner now was the course that the ship was sailing. The Captain's orders held her steadily north-northwest, and for night after night he had her laid to, so that she made little westing. According to the Gunner's calculation this meant that she was driving toward the land somewhat northwest of Cape Horn. Supposing, as we all did at the time, that we were making for the Island of Juan Fernandez, he was unable to comprehend the Captain's reason for following such a course. He lived in a great and growing perturbation of mind which was not decreased when I told him, about the tenth of May, that I had seen from the quarterdeck a large mass of rockweed floating by the ship.

" 'Well, what of it?' the Captain said when Bulkeley reported my observation. 'I'm not surprised. Are you?'

" 'Not so much surprised, sir, as alarmed. With this current from the west always pushin' against us and these steady strong winds from westward, with the ship under reefed courses and the mizzenmast gone, she must drive wholly to leeward—especially durin' those four nights hove-to—and now must be nigher the land than expected.'

" 'No nigher than I want. We must come in near the land. Don't you know that our rendezvous is at the Island of Nuestra Señora del Socorro, in latitude forty-four?'

" 'I hear that for the first time, sir.'

" 'At any rate, you hear it now. At St. Julian's we captains agreed with the Commodore that if we should be separated each of us would

wait for the others at Del Socorro, and proceed from there first
to Valdivia and then to Juan Fernandez.'

" 'Wait for how long, if you please?'

" 'That is none of your affair; but we were to wait there for two
weeks.'

" 'By this time, then, if the *Centurion* is still afloat, she has probably
reached Del Socorro and left it. No doubt she has as many sick men
as we, and the only place to cure them is Juan Fernandez.'

" 'That may be. It is none of your affair. I am the captain of this
ship.'

" 'By shaping our course for Juan Fernandez now we shall make
sure of finding the Commodore. If we proceed toward Del Socorro we
shall probably lose him, lose the *Wager,* and perhaps our lives.'

" 'Don't try to argue with me, Gunner. I tell you I'm bound and
determined to keep this rendezvous.'

" 'But sir, sir, the ship is at this moment all but a wreck. Our mizzen
is gone, our chain-plates and standing rigging afore and abaft all
broke. More than half our people are near dead with scurvy. Why, sir,
we have scarce a dozen to go aloft or stand at the wheel. What chance
should we have on a lee shore?'

"Captain Chepe's head jerked up and backward with a habitual
nervous twitch. 'All that,' he said, 'does not signify. The course will
be kept for Del Socorro. Good day.'

"She was held on that course for three days and nights of increasing
tempest. At two on the afternoon of the fourth day the Gunner, looking out from the foreyard where he was helping to set the sail, saw
land on the larboard beam, high land with many scattered hills and
one great hummock shaped like a human skull at the sea's edge. He
came off the yard at top speed, sliding down a backstay, and ran to
the Captain's cabin. A moment later I saw the Captain rush from
his door. His foot slipped on the icy planks of the quarterdeck, and he
fell backward down the after ladder. He was in great pain when we
lifted him, having wrenched his shoulder. Also, he was drunk. We
carried him to the Surgeon's cabin and left him there. The foreyard
had fallen while we were below, and the deck was cluttered with
tangled rigging and gear. At that time we had twelve men fit for duty
—twelve out of the one hundred and sixty with whom we sailed from
England. Among these were three midshipmen, the Lieutenant, the
Carpenter, the Gunner, the Master's Mate, and five ordinary seamen.

We twelve set to work for our lives to get sails on the masts, but no canvas could hold against the storm. The night came on, dreadful beyond description, and still we worked, stumbling and falling and shouting unheard in the darkness.

"At half an hour past four on the morning of May the fourteenth we felt a grinding shock. It made the ship shudder from stem to stern. For a moment as we stood there astonished, speechless, it seemed a not impossible hope that this was only another buffet of some gigantic billow such as we had felt before; but then, more violently, with a blow that laid her over, she struck again, unquestionably upon a rock, and was instantly smothered by a breaking wave. To me it is still a wonder how any survived that wave lunging suddenly out of the dark and tossing us about the deck like helpless billets of wood and then fumbling, fingering, licking at the hatches and the scuttles to find and drown the sick men below. But death had other plans. Jenkins' Ear had thought out more ingenious devices. The wave lifted us free of the rock. The ship staggered back to an even keel. The sounding-lead showed fourteen fathoms. We began to hope a little. The Mate took the wheel. It whirled like a spinning top. Our rudder was broken, we saw. We strove to steer by hauling and easing the sheets as the ship came to or fell off, darting and plunging here and there like a hunted creature until she struck a third time, bilged, grounded, and stood stock-still firmly wedged between two islets of rock a musket-shot from the shore. The dawn was beginning to break."

*　　*　　*

For a while Captain Byron was silent, sitting perfectly still. Not even with his eyes did he ask whether he was taking us there. Enough that he was there himself. He seemed to be listening—perhaps to the sound of breakers, that oldest and saddest sound in the world.

"There lay before us," he went on, " a coast desolate and bleak, strewn with rocks. The tall skull-shaped hill we had seen the day before loomed close at hand. It bore no tree, shrub, or blade of grass. Inland for as far as the dim light showed there was only rocks, snow, ice—a prospect, as the Gunner said, 'very dismal to behold.'

"Soon the quarterdeck was crowded with men, miraculously cured, who had long thought themselves unfit for any service. The Boatswain, who had not shown his face on deck for a month, was there with his

brother, and both were shouting that now the ship was a wreck every
man could do as he pleased. What they pleased to do was to break
into the spirit room, thus drawing off a considerable number of like
minds. Many others acted as though they had already been there.
Some were thumping about on their knees shouting prayers from
mouths more accustomed to cursing. Some raced up and down, yelling,
mere wild beasts in panic. A few lay helplessly rolling with every lurch
of the ship and slowly drowned before our eyes in the waves that
plunged over the rail. But most frightful of all to remember, like a
horror seen in nightmare, is that crazed giant wildly swinging a cutlass
who calls himself king of the country and is going, he says, to kill the
captain. He does kill one man nearly dead already and slashes at every
one within reach and has started for the cabin where Captain Chepe
still lies in bed when Gunner Bulkeley rushes at him and brings him
down with the blow of a belaying pin. He lies there stunned, bleeding,
and the Gunner reaches slowly for the cutlass, wipes the blood off the
blade on the prone man's hair, and walks close to the people shrinking
away from him on the quarterdeck as he eyes them earnestly, peering
hard into every face, taking his time, balancing to the jerk and lurch
of the tortured ship, holding the oaken pin in his left hand ready and
the cutlass in his right while the wind screams at us and the breakers
roar until at last he says, not shouting but so that every word rings
clear in the tumult: 'Are there any more kings of the country here?'

"There seem to be no more pretenders to the throne.

" 'Well then,' says he, 'we can go to work. With the rigging cleared
away she'll ride easier. Job Barnes and Sam Stook, ye've got your
knives: cut free these backstay halliards, and the shrouds too. Jack
Duck, pitch these dead men over the rail. Dick Noble, take five good
men and go find out what the Boatswain and his brother are up to. The
rest will come with me and help cut down the masts. —But cheerily,
men! We've been among breakers before. Staten Land couldn't kill
us, nor ten weeks of storm, nor yet twenty weeks of scurvy. Lay hold,
now! We'll get the masts down and the boats hoisted out and all go
ashore before night!'

"Gunner Bulkeley's resolute words and example postponed, at least,
the threatened chaos. The few of us able and willing to work at all
worked furiously during the rest of that day, expecting at every
moment that the hulk would give way beneath us. Before nightfall
we had cut away the masts and sheet anchor, had launched the barge

and cutter and yawl over the gunwale, and had sent away to land
most of the men, sick and well, along with the Captain, the Lieutenant,
and the officers of the Marines. At twilight, just before leaving the
ship, I went down to the midshipmen's berth to get what clothing and
other gear I could from my chest. Or rather, I went part way there.
At the after hatchway I heard the yells and curses of a dozen seamen,
crazed by drink, who were evidently carousing in the cockpit. The
Boatswain, also drunk, was staggering up the ladder with his arms full
of bottles, clothing, and other plunder in which my fowling-piece
was the most conspicuous object. He had my sea-boots also, and the
heavy coat I had particularly come for. All this however, he saw
fit to ignore, changing the subject as one might say before I had
time to speak. ' 'Tain't mut'ny, ye know, boy,' he snarled. 'Arter
shipwreck every man Jack looks out for hisself an' takes orders from
no man. That's admiralty law, the which you an' Dave Chepe an' your
Methody friends will obey or git cut up for fish-bait. —Now git out o'
here an' keep yer mouth shut. You hear me.'

"My 'Methody friends,' Gunner Bulkeley and Carpenter Cummins,
insisted for reasons which at the time I could not guess upon spending
the night on the wreck. They would give me no reasons. They ignored
the obvious danger that the ship might go down at any moment, and
also the danger they stood in from the Boatswain and his drunken
gang. Neither would they let me stay with them, but almost forced
me into the last boat that put off for the shore.

"Not until some time later did I understand their reasons, and how
they spent that dreadful night barricaded in the gun-room, guarding
the hatch to the powder magazine beneath their feet, the arms chest
lying open beside them in case of attack by the gang that was looting
the ship, and on the table before them the torn remnants of half a
dozen journal-books which they had found in their own and other
officers' cabins, and which had evidently been destroyed by some one
who intended that no true account of the loss of the vessel should be
preserved. There they sat the long night through, in chairs that were
lashed to ring-bolts in the deck, while the Carpenter held the stub of
candle in one hand and the ink-bottle in the other upon the tottering
table, while the water dripped from the opening deck above their
heads so that the Gunner was forced to hunch over those precious
sheets of paper on which he was painfully beginning to write a true
and fair account—in so far as he and the Carpenter could remember—

of all the events leading to the loss of the ship. They put no hatred into their journal—there was no room for that—but a plain statement of facts which might stand as evidence in a court-martial to save the necks of all the *Wager*'s people from the rope.

"But to return to myself: night was falling when, after a fierce struggle through the breakers, I felt firm ground underfoot. The rain fell in sheets. The wind and the sea yelled their wrath at our temporary escape. What we saw of the land was utterly desolate, barren, and dreary. Our sole comfort was the lee of the tall rock shaped like a skull which we at once named Mount Misery. Behind it, somewhat sheltered from the tempest, we found a ruinous hut made of boughs and rotting sealskins—perhaps not unlike the miserable shelter in which King Lear took refuge on the blasted heath. Captain Chepe and some of his more favoured officers—Lieutenant Beans, the Purser, the Surgeon, Alexander Campbell, and the officers of the Marines— had crept in there for the night, having no fire, no lamp, no food or drink, and little else to sustain them unless it were their lively fear that the Indians whose weapons they found scattered about on the ground might return in the darkness. The Lieutenant of the Chelsea Hospital invalids died there that night. Two men died under the great tree where the rest of us huddled until the dawn.

"It may seem that to men who had lived for ten weeks upon the point of perishing by shipwreck this coming ashore must have been a great joy. No such exultation was felt, however, as we looked about us in the morning light and saw that we had escaped immediate destruction only to face a death lingered out to the limits of misery. One hundred and forty men and boys—Marines included—most of them wasted by disease and the others worn to the bone by long battling with storm, had landed in the dead of winter upon what appeared to be an island of all but naked rock. Except for a few leafless trees we discerned no sign of life. Peering out through the driving rain between Mount Misery and the smaller hill close beside it, we saw what was left of the *Wager* still wedged between two rocks. There, in that broken hull so terribly pounded by breakers, dismasted, rudderless, its deck half awash, lay our food, drink, clothing, tools— all we had in the world whereby we might faintly hope to survive. So near she lay that we could see her tremble and writhe under each blow of the waves. Half a dozen of the drunkards and thieves we had left aboard were now wildly beckoning for help, their new freedom to do

as they pleased having begun to pall. Not until the waves calmed
somewhat in the afternoon could a boat reach them, and then I
steered the barge alongside the wreck and we took off the Gunner
and Carpenter with his tool-chest, and several of the gang. The Boatswain himself remained aboard with a few others for some days,
during which they showed their independence by firing one of the
quarterdeck four-pounders at the Captain's hut on shore.

"But the great event of that first day on the island was our first
meal. Few of us had eaten a morsel in forty-eight hours. I borrowed a
musket from Purser Harvey and, with three or four others, toiled
part way up Mount Misery. After much scrambling about in the rain
and the wind we found a number of frozen plants resembling wild
celery, extremely bitter and tough but, we hoped, not inedible. These
we took back to camp along with the cormorant or shag which, by
patient stalking, I had been able to kill with the musket. Our comrades
had started a fire of driftwood, and were trying to boil rainwater
scooped from the rocks in one of our two iron pots. The scene was
dreary beyond description. It made me think of how the invaders
of windy Troy had prepared their meals—except that they, as I
recalled my Homer, had commonly dined upon an ox well fattened,
five years old, and roasted whole. We plucked and singed our cormorant and dropped it, including the claws and beak, into the pot. Along
with it went two or three pounds of foul biscuit crumbs swept from
the galley floor which some one had brought from the ship in an old
cloth bag. Then we stood about the fire and watched Thomas Mac-
Lean, our white-haired cook—eighty-two years old, he was, by the
muster-roll—as he stirred the broth with an iron ladle. But sea-birds
boil so slowly that I can readily understand why Master Chester and
his Indian friend preferred to eat them raw. We must have stood
there for hours, shaking and blue with cold, while the thick black
smoke whirled about us and the rain beat heavily down. My cap, red
jacket, and breeches and shoes—they were all the clothes I had on,
or would have for months to come—gave me little protection. One of
our invalids, a man ripe for the grave when he first came aboard,
crawled a little to one side while we waited, not wishing to disturb
us, and died.

"At last a few bubbles rose to the surface of the pale, thin soup.
More and more bubbles rose, and burst. Peering hopefully into the

pot we saw our cormorant lying quite unchanged at the bottom. Someone prodded him with the point of a dirk and reported that his body
was still as tough as his beak and claws. But we could wait no longer.
Old MacLean ladled out the share of the Captain and his friends.
Then, looking round at us with a wry smile, 'Who's judge today?'
said he.

"John Jones, the Master's Mate, a thoroughly honest man whom
we all liked, was nominated and pushed forward. We blindfolded him
and made him stand with his back to the cook. 'Who's to have the
first one?' MacLean asked, stirring and dipping. 'Bill Oram,' said
Jones. Oram stepped briskly up, seized the ladle, and drank off the
gill of liquid it held at one gulp. The grimace he made was not encouraging to us others, but we were mainly concerned with the fact that
the two gallons of soup in the pot, allowing one gill to each man,
could be shared by not more than half our number. More eagerly,
therefore, than those who have never known hunger can well imagine,
we listened to Jones's impartial calling of name after name. We
watched the fortunate chosen go forward, gulp, make their faces of
shocked surprise, and then retire. They seemed to retire in some haste
and confusion, but this I put down at first to a courteous wish to
avoid the appearance of exulting over their comrades. Our butcher,
John Pitman, was the second choice—a man of huge appetite who
died later on of starvation. Then came a little man who broke his neck
the next day while hunting for limpets among the rocks. John Bosman
was called, one of my comrades in the foretop. He too was to starve,
and my face was the last thing he saw in life. Jacob Grindling had
his share—he whose body I found some days later among the rocks
of Mount Misery. And so I might go on; but well before the pot
was emptied those who had been first served began to show signs that
we had better not empty it at all. One saw in their faces not disgust
now but agony. They were seized by violent retchings. They clapped
their hands to their bellies, and 'Ah, that damned shag!' Bill Oram
cried out. 'It must 'a'ben dead for a month when Byron found it.
'Twas carrion, lads.' And then another: 'Nay, 't wa'n't the bird but
that hell-weed they called celery. We spend three months in dyin' o'
scurvy, an' the first plant we get does our business at last!'

"But I was unconvinced by these opinions. I picked up the cloth bag
that had held the biscuit crumbs, examined it closely, sniffed it, and

turned it inside out. 'Cook,' said I, 'you've been feeding us boiled tobacco.' Then I went and thanked John Jones for not calling my name.

"Some forty men were exceedingly sick all that day and the following night. Captain Chepe and his companions, having drunk larger portions of the broth, were the worst off. Midshipman Campbell suffered worst of all. I was told by Surgeon Elliot the next day that Campbell had come near to dying and held the whole thing against me."

"Wal, I'll be—I mean, what's the sense o' that?" John Chester exclaimed. "Arter all, ye'd only shot the bird."

"For Campbell that was enough. He declared to everyone who would listen that the flesh of the cormorant is deadly poison, that I had known this, and had meant to kill every officer and all the men whose names were called out—after consultation with me—by the Master's Mate. For listeners of a superstitious turn he added that the dead bird had been the guardian spirit of Mount Misery, and that nothing but dire misfortune was to be expected until its death had been avenged upon me. There were many, at first, who believed him."

"And all this went back," said Mr. Chute, "to your first meeting?"

"Yes. From that day he sought some revenge that would leave him safe. There were many times when he might have killed me outright by the thrust of a dirk or a sudden shove in the darkness; but two things held him back: fear of the Lieutenant and the wish to see me suffer. I think it gave him pleasure to let me live on aware of his hatred, not only for me but for my friends—the Gunner, the Carpenter, and Midshipman Cozens. When he went to live with the Captain—an extremely irregular and almost unheard-of thing—we foresaw trouble. It came, increasingly. Whatever went wrong with the ship was blamed upon us, and often what went right. Thus the loss of our mizzen was charged against Gunner Bulkeley, although every one knew that the Gunner had saved our lives by getting sail on that mast. Egged on by Campbell, the Captain grew more and more jealous of Bulkeley, and not the less because of his dependence upon the Gunner's seamanship and his influence with the crew. That had much to do with our shipwreck, by making Captain Chepe stubbornly refuse the Gunner's sound advice. After the wreck, when every one knew that the Gunner had been right and the Captain disastrously wrong, it went on working. To our bodily woes there was added the poison of jealousy, hatred, and fear.

"You will recall Boatswain King's remark to me that a captain's authority ended at the time of a wreck. That was true, and all the people knew it. Captain Chepe knew it, but was determined to ignore and defy the law as long as he could. He began by bluster and intimidation, went on to deceit and bribes and intrigue, and then finally tried to appeal to our sympathy by asserting that he was sick—as indeed he often was from overindulgence in brandy—and that his mind was burdened by cares past our comprehension.

"Though by no means a coward, Captain Chepe was a wrong-headed, violent weakling whose sole notion of authority was that his will or whim must prevail. As I have told you, he came to the command of the *Wager* merely because other commanders had died—much as any bigoted fool may come to the throne because he belongs to a certain family. On shipboard that dependence upon blind chance is more dangerous than it is in a realm. A king like George the Second, let us say, may be held in check by his wife, and one like the Second Charles has a Parliament to take into account. Captain Chepe had Midshipman Campbell. His attitude toward the rest of us was expressed by such remarks as 'It does not signify' or 'I have made up my mind, and you cannot change it,' or 'You rascal, I'm still your Captain, and I can blow your brains out!'

"Arrogancies of that sort, increasing in number and violence after the man's real authority was gone, and usually accompanied by his habitual backward jerk of the head, were hard for some of us to bear. There were several officers who took a strong dislike to Chepe's way of pulling at his sword while engaged in a discussion, and even, when debate grew warm, laying a loaded pistol on the table before him. They grew weary of his frequently iterated declaration that by far the greater number of us had been guilty of mutinous rebellion, and that he would see us hanged for it as soon as he got back to England. Captain Pemberton of the Marines, to name only one, was highly incensed at this conduct. Had it not been for the dissuasions of Gunner Bulkeley he would have taken authority into his own hands and put Chepe in irons."

In reply to a question from Blandison, Byron said that, although the Admiralty law on such matters has since been changed, Pemberton

had at the time a better right than Chepe to the command of the men
on the island, and that most of them would have been glad if he had
assumed it. "Then," said Blandison, "it was his duty to do so, and I
should like to hear what the Gunner could say to dissuade him."

Byron smiled at this, seeing the reference to the political situation
on quite a different island. "Why," said he, "Gunner Bulkeley argued
that deposing Chepe would breed dissension among us and destroy
what discipline we had left. He urged us to bear with the man to the
limit of our endurance, never questioning his right to command but
using every peaceable means of bringing him to reason."

"I see. He advocated the indolent policy he had seen at work here
in England: enduring a ruler with neither right nor fitness merely
because it might be some trouble to change him. —And did this work
out well on Wager Island?"

"The answer to that may appear," said Byron, "in what I have yet
to say."

"Ah; no doubt. Pray excuse my interruption."

"The Gunner felt sure, and so did we three who had remained with
him in the cockpit, that the man most to blame for the Captain's conduct
was Alexander Campbell. We believed, though we could not prove,
that Campbell had suggested to Chepe the plan of lagging deliberately
behind the squadron and then, after the Commodore had given us up,
going on the account, or, in other words, turning pirate. I still think
that he had that intention, for in no other way can I explain his neglect
of ordinary caution which led to our loss of the flagship, his lying
to for four nights when we should have been running westward, and,
again, his tarrying for months on Wager Island when he knew that
Anson would wait for him no more than two weeks.

"Our suspicion that Campbell had concocted this scheme was not
based upon mere hostility or upon the feeling that treachery of that
sort would more naturally occur to him than to Chepe. We all knew
that while he was still with us in the midshipmen's berth he had been
deeply interested in the copy of George Shelvocke's *Voyage Round the
World* which Henry Cozens had brought aboard at Portsmouth. Some
of you may have read that exciting book, and if so you will see that
in several ways Shelvocke's experience in the *Speedwell*, some twenty
years before we set out, was strangely parallel to ours in the *Wager*.
Thus he too was delayed for months in sailing from England, he had
a long and laborious voyage to the Horn, and he passed with extreme

difficulty and danger through the Straits Le Maire. The thing that would have caught the attention of Campbell, however, was that Shelvocke took the first opportunity to separate from Commodore Clipperton, under whom he was sailing, and that after that treacherous desertion he went on to secure for himself a considerable fortune.

"That book, then—after the day when Cozens was unable to find it in our berth—may have been the source of Campbell's suggestion to Chepe; but the hope of financial profit was not his main motive. He was also actuated by hatred of me and of all who had witnessed his humiliation. Above all he wanted a revenge that would leave him safe and unsuspected while he watched me suffer."

Captain Byron leaned forward, elbows on knees, and thrust his long, thin fingers into his hair. "My story is too long, I know," said he. "That's partly because I was asked to tell about the squadron and partly, as you see, because I can't help trying to understand what the story means. Fortunately, though, Lieutenant Morris has agreed to narrate most of what happened on the island in the time he and I spent there together. I'm glad of that for the reason that many of those events are a pain for me to remember. One of them in particular, the murder of Henry Cozens, I shall leave out entirely. I did not witness them all because Midshipman Campbell arranged that much of my time should be spent at the dangerous task of retrieving what stores could be got from the wreck. Some of the things I did see, moreover, are now like the visions of nightmare—vivid enough, to be sure, but subject to doubt whether they actually occurred. At times, looking back, I say to myself: 'Why, no, John Byron: you never went on that voyage, lived through that storm, or survived the horrors of the island. You were sent to a madhouse instead, and these scenes that haunt you now are only your recollected hallucinations.

"However that may be, I see myself lying prone on the *Wager*'s quarterdeck and angling with grapnels for the provisions lying deep in her submerged hold. Other live men are with me to help with the hoisting, but I feel alone with the dead. The water in the hold, though constantly churned by the wash of waves through the broken hull, is vile with the smell of death. Now and then my hooks, groping deep in the darkness, rake up a keg of liquor, a cask of flour or beef, perhaps a bale of trucking-cloth; but mostly they catch the wedged-in or floating bodies of men who died in their hammocks when the sea burst in upon them. As my eyes grow accustomed to the gloom I discern a dozen more of them down there who still bear the black stigma of scurvy. Also there are three or four of the Boatswain's gang whose night of doing as they pleased had ended with drowning. They revolve and sidle and drift and turn slowly over in the roil, like men still helplessly drunk, staring up at me with wide-open eyes. Most loathsome of all is the face of Timothy Triseat, late of Plymouth— not drowned, not killed by scurvy or drink, but throttled. In those bulging eyes what question, what entreaty? For a minute or more we stare at each other whilst I struggle to work the hook free. Then Timothy turns on his side in the water and looks away, disappointed, despairing.

"But I cannot forget that face, those eyes, that tongue. Timothy comes before me every hour of the day, though I may be miles from the wreck. He pursues me in my dreams. His entreaty changes to accusation. I go to the Captain and plead to have him and his companions lifted out of the hull and buried. Captain Chepe calls me white-livered. He says that the hull will soon break up and so save us the trouble. Campbell says they are saving those bodies, well pickled in brine, for me to eat when the time comes. If I make any more complaints, he says, it will come soon.

"In justice to Campbell and Chepe I ought to admit that the burial of those corpses would have involved much hard labour, for which we had little strength. Decent interment of the dead, moreover, is a task for men who themselves are somewhat confident of living. Besides, we had fallen during the storm into the habit of letting dead bodies lie about for some time unburied. That habit persisted after we went ashore.

"For weeks I was kept at this unusual kind of angling—perhaps on the ground that, as the son of a gentleman, I should devote all my time to sport. Then, having recovered my fowling-piece, but not my clothes, from the Boatswain, I went hunting every day. The first thing of importance that I found was the body of Jacob Grindling—he who, a twelvemonth before, had attempted to hide from the press-gang in Portsmouth by climbing into a coffin. He too had been strangled. His body, partially devoured by some wild beast or by the carrion birds of the region, lay among the rocks halfway up Mount Misery.

"Again I reported to the Captain, but he and Campbell agreed that Grindling had been a mutinous dog who did not deserve burial. Campbell recalled that there had been a long-standing quarrel between this

Grindling and James Mitchell, the Carpenter's Mate, who had recently deserted the camp, along with nine or ten others, and had gone away to the other side of the island. He thought that both of these deaths by strangling were the work of one man, and that if any one was to bury Grindling and Triseat, then it ought to be Mitchell.

"This I considered a shrewd guess and a sound suggestion, made by one who was likely to know about such things. But James Mitchell, we all knew, was unlikely to return for this or any other purpose. What I have called his desertion was in fact a flight, caused by the discovery that he and some others were plotting to blow up the Captain in the hut.

Mitchell was a man more dangerous than the Boatswain because more intelligent. Thus it was he that had been mainly responsible for the looting and riot on the *Wager* during the night of the wreck—that night on which he had opportunity not only for the throttling of Triseat but for much other deviltry. Like some tigers and sharks, he had come to delight in killing for its own sake. And yet I have sometimes thought that Mitchell was not, after all, a mere criminal. It is possible that he, like my friend Henry Cozens, was more sensitive than the rest of us and so suffered more from the horrors we all went through, even to the unhinging of his reason. Cozens, I knew, had been for some time out of his mind, and so was Carpenter Cummins on one occasion, though he as a rule was a mild man, excellent in his craft and deeply absorbed by his religion.

"Something of that sort seemed to be the opinion of the majority among us when it became known, not through anything I said, that Mitchell was suspected of murder. I will not assert that the people were unconcerned about the presence, or close neighbourhood, of this kind of madman, but it would be true to say that they blamed Mitchell less for the murders he was thought to have committed than they did Captain Chepe for his refusal to bury the victims.

"For murder, you see, is a serious offence in proportion to the value set upon human life, and with us that valuation was sinking from day to day. Death had become commonplace, and life an encumbrance. We believed that in some form or other death was coming soon to us all; and of the several ways in which it might come that of murder had at least the advantage of being swift. As for the laws of man and even the divine commandment, 'Thou shalt not kill,' you can scarcely imagine how remote they seemed to us in our condition.

"Soon after the Captain's refusal to have the body of Grindling buried the men began to hear, or to say they heard, a doleful voice crying out in the night, sometimes from the inward parts of the island, at others from beyond the breakers, but mostly from the rocky heights of Mount Misery. They imagined that it resembled the voice of Grindling, and that his ghost was demanding sepulture. At first my own opinion was that they had heard, as I also had done once or twice, the nocturnal cry of a wild beast ranging for prey; but this belief was considerably shaken by a strange experience the reality of which I could not doubt. In the middle of a moonlit night we were suddenly awakened by the lamentations, coming from the sea, of what certainly sounded like a human voice. A number of us ran at once to the shore and there saw, though indistinctly, what we took for the figure of a man swimming strongly among the breakers, but swimming—how can I help you to see it?—as though with his legs alone, with his body upright and half out of water, his arms reaching out toward us with a beseeching gesture. Some affirmed, later on, that this figure was translucent so that the moonlight shone through it. I did not see that, nor was I so sure as others that the woeful cries still sounding in the night came from that direction. Our own shouts were not answered, at least in any human language, nor did the figure approach us. It seemed, if you can at all understand me, to be at once swimming strongly and remaining still, as though caught there and unable with all its effort to pass some invisible barrier. We waited on the shore, gazing and listening, for a long time, too fearful to put off in a boat and yet too fascinated to return to our beds.

That mystery was never solved, but neither was it forgotten. It left us all uneasy, and some of us with the conviction that we should henceforth have to contend not merely with the hostile sea and the barren shore but with the powers of the spirit world. Some said that those of us who had seen this thing ought at once to bury Grindling, but a more vociferous party held that only the murderer could do that to any purpose. Thus they reached Campbell's conclusion by a different route; but, as I have explained, the murderer was not available. Therefore the corpse of Grindling lay there on the desolate mount for week after week, and many meanwhile believed that it was bringing the wrath of supernatural powers upon us as surely as iron draws lightning.

"Midshipman Campbell made another suggestion, more fit for his purposes. You recall that he had laid upon me all blame for the sickness caused by the cormorant soup—or, as I preferred to say, the broth of tobacco crumbs. He now extended that charge so as to hold me responsible for every ill that had befallen us, or would befall, from the day of our landing. The hint for this probably came from that book by Captain Shelvocke to which so much else of our trouble was due, for there he undoubtedly read the tale of a sailor called Hately who brought misfortune upon his ship by shooting an albatross. At any rate, Campbell easily convinced the greater number of our people that the bird I had killed on Mount Misery had been the guardian spirit of the island, and that every man of us must now suffer in expiation of my wicked deed. Those who believed him saw that it was their duty as well as their pleasure to make me suffer most of all. Thenceforward I saw nothing but hatred in their eyes, and heard from them only curses and revilings. To be known as my friend brought dark suspicion upon any man. My presence in any group was felt as a contamination. My life was saved by Campbell himself, who told those who wanted to kill me that my death would not be sufficient."

"But what arguments, what evidence did he use," Mr. Chute asked, "to support his absurd charge against you?"

"Alexander Campbell, sir, was a clever man, and he knew that the repeated and unsupported assertion of a lie is far more telling with the sort of minds he had to deal with than any amount of evidence. Furthermore, he worked through a few men, chosen for their exceptional stupidity. He convinced them, and they the others."

"Ah. —I suppose this notion about the cormorant must have laid Grindling's ghost."

"Not at all. The two superstitions lived on side by side. In the absence of Mitchell, however, nothing could be done for Grindling, but I was always there to suffer for the slaughtered bird."

Mr. Chute laid down his pencil and gazed at Byron in perplexity. "But, sir," said he, "to believe two contradictory things is not common sense."

Byron's smile, though courteous, was not approving. "Pray keep it in mind, Mr. Chute," he replied, "that whatever power of clear thinking some of us may once have had was by this time shattered.

I suggest that common sense is more readily maintained by comfortable people, sitting in quiet rooms with firelight and candles, than by desperate starving men on a wind-swept rock in the sea. The storm that had raged for so long about us had now entered our hearts and minds. It is a nightmare, a madness, that I am recording."

"I see."

"I have tried to show how that storm of madness began and increased. Its climax came, at least for me, when I accepted and bore the burden of guilt thrust upon me by Midshipman Campbell."

Mr. Chute stared. "You can't mean," he exclaimed, "that you agreed with him!"

"Yes. Even though I knew his devilish motive and method, I agreed that I had been guilty of sacrilege. I too came to believe that the bird I had killed had been the island's tutelar spirit, and that every woe we had since endured was part of the punishment of my sin."

"Sir," said Mr. Chute, "this is astonishing."

"It is so to me. I no longer understand it. Looking back through the years, I am amazed that I should have sunk so far below the level of ordinary intelligence. But that is because I no longer recall, or sufficiently allow for, the effect of long hunger and wet and cold, the drag of a fever-shaken body upon the mind, and the intolerable loneliness caused by those averted eyes and sidelong glances. There was, besides, my craving for some explanation of our miseries and disasters. At Newstead Abbey, in spite of its name, the Christian interpretation of life's mystery had not been much urged upon me. Even if it had been, I doubt whether the idea of a loving and almighty Father in Heaven—of a Father acquainted with all my woe and not wishing me to suffer beyond what was needful—would then have seemed to me a credible form of belief. Far more to the purpose then, if not now, was the older and once universal faith in the powers of malevolent evil. Benevolence I saw nowhere, but the works of the Kings of Darkness were visible all about me. If they needed a motive, what was easier than the surmise that they were avenging the murder of a bird beloved by them because it too had been evil?"

"Had it been a wicked bird, do you think?" George Selwyn asked. "Had it wasted its substance in riotous living?"

Byron did not smile. "Perhaps you remember," said he, "how in *Paradise Lost* the Arch Fiend perches 'like a cormorant' on the Tree of Life, 'devising death for them that live.' Something of that sort

I felt as I came upon the creature crouched there with outstretched wings on the summit of the rock, gazing down at our battered ship. To me it looked utterly abhorrent and loathsome. Hatred was in my heart as I aimed and fired and then twisted its neck many times, round and round."

"The Christian religion," said Kitty, "would have taught you that your sin was in that hatred, not in killing the bird."

"Possibly so, although I think that even Christianity teaches us to hate evil. You remind me, though, that all those who accepted Campbell's charge against me were members of England's Established Church. Of those who did not I recall only Gunner Bulkeley, Carpenter Cummins, and John Young, the Cooper. These three were the heretics among us, and they were despised for their heresy as much as was consistent with the respect they commanded in other regards. So far as I could see they were heretical—except for their lack of faith in the ghost of the cormorant—chiefly in the fact that they tried to make their religion work. They used to hold what they called 'prayer-meetings' on the *Wager* before the wreck. Later on, whenever the rain held off for an hour or two, they would climb the steep slope of Mount Misery—they called it Golgotha—and sing a hymn and pray. They had to make up their own prayers because the only book they had with them was a sort of tract called *The Christian Pattern*. All this was pitiful enough, no doubt, but it shows again to what lengths the human mind will go for an answer to its questions of whence and whither and why. Some solution it must have, for the thought that the things we endure have no meaning whatever—that way madness lies.

"These three Methodists were, next to Henry Cozens, my closest friends. In order to protect them from the hatred of Campbell, I did all that I could to make it appear that we had quarrelled and I had withdrawn from them. Among other things, I built myself a hut, large enough to lie down in, and there lived alone somewhat apart from the main camp.

"At that time I must have looked like a slightly animated skeleton, as perhaps you think I still do. My red jacket and black breeches, thin to begin with and now worn to tatters, hung on me like bags. My shoes I had made for myself, of sealskin. Having been excluded from the daily ration doled out at the Purser's tent, I subsisted upon limpets, mussels, crabs, and such barely edible plants as I could find.

Midshipman Campbell was living meanwhile in comparative comfort.
He and the Captain had free access to the rather large store of brandy
and other liquors which I had retrieved from the wreck. Besides
consuming far more than their due shares, they used this brandy as
a bribe in their constant intrigues against the Gunner and all others
who opposed them. Worse still, they used it to get their enemies drunk
and then punished them—in one terrible instance by death—for what
they had said or done in their frenzy.

"You may get some notion of our sufferings in these conditions
from the fact that forty-five men died on the island during the first
month of our stay there. That was nearly one in three of those who
had first come ashore. They died in many ways—not of scurvy, for
that was mysteriously cured soon after our landing, but of starvation,
poisoning, fatigue, falls from the rocks, drowning, and murder. Some
died merely because they had lost all desire to live. They were like
men swimming in the middle sea who at last throw up their hands
and sink.

"All things considered, then, one does not see what could have been
added to our miseries, or at least to mine, by a powerful malevolence
doing all it could to plague us. Let me tell you, though, that in the
midst of that evil time I found a companion, a fellow creature as
bewildered and forlorn as I was. Or rather, he found me. One day
when I was wandering in the rain, far from camp, on the dreariest
part of the island, there came running toward me among the rocks
a little black dog, short-haired, sharp-nosed, by no means handsome—
a dog accidentally left behind, I suppose, by the Indians who had been
there before our arrival. Like me, he was shivering with the cold and
wet. Like me, he was mere skin and bone. And then too, he was
lonely. From that moment we were friends. Wherever I went, he was
at my heels, always keenly suspicious of every human being that
approached me. At night he slept at my side, and indeed in my arms.
That was a way of sharing what warmth we had, and also a means of
mutual protection. He may have saved me from being strangled, and
I for a while preserved him from those who regarded him as merely
so much food.

"Ah, you may laugh, but I did not. I had seen them looking at him
sidelong, sizing him up, thinking how he would taste. I had heard
their talk about the relative merits of roast-dog and dog boiled in
a pot. In reply I had pointed out that my dog would provide only a

morsel for each of the company, and that he brought in every day far more food than there was on his emaciated body. That was true. His Indian master had made him an expert hunter of shellfish. He learned quickly from me to retrieve a bird that had fallen into the water. Again and again I saw him try, all alone, to drive fish toward the shore as the Indian dogs of Patagonia are trained to do in companies. —Ah, his eagerness to help, his fidelity, and, if I may be allowed the word, his love! They shone like the one star left in a sullen sky.

"But nothing could save him—no words of mine, no usefulness of his, and certainly not my dependence upon him for companionship. Midshipman Campbell came to my hut one morning—it was the first time he had been there—to say that the Captain wanted my dog and requested my presence at dinner on that same evening. Campbell was extremely polite. He pretended to admire the comfort and convenience of my miserable dwelling. Every word he spoke was charged with hatred. He took some pains to show what I knew already, that the whole cruel plan was of his hatching, and congratulated me upon this chance to exhibit and prove my recent change of feeling toward the Captain.

"What was I to do? Here was a demand, couched in the form of a request, for a thing which, if I refused it, would be taken. What would you have done, any of you, if you had been there—and especially if you knew that the safety of your friends, perhaps their lives, depended upon making the Captain think that you were now siding with him? Oh, I beg of you"—here Byron sprang from his chair, strode to the window, and stood with his back to us, his hands writhing behind him—"be fair if you can to that lonely, starved, broken-hearted youth of my name. Be more just in your judgment than I have ever managed to be. What choice was left? Do you say that I might have killed Campbell? But then what of Bulkeley and Cummins and Morris and . . .

"But no! Be as fair as you can, you still come back to the fact that I did give Campbell my dog and went that night to the dinner. Three weeks later I found where they had buried his paws. I dug them up, and—I ate them."

Byron turned suddenly round and faced us. He was pale. His eyes blazed. His voice shook as he shrilled out: "What is the horror of cannibalism compared to that? What savage, what beast would have done that thing? What—what devil?"

Mr. Chute looked up from his notes and quietly asked: "Do you want an answer?"

"Why, yes, sir, if you have one."

"Then it is that you, in the thing you did, were blameless, compared with the man who forced you to do it."

"Ah! 'Forced'!"—The words were ground out, fiercely, and Byron's eyes were still blazing.

George Selwyn sat up, opened both eyes, glanced at the clock, and drawled: "I do wish someone would try to force me to drink a dish of tea."

*　　*　　*

I nodded to Louis, and tea was served at once. It had been waiting for some time—dammed up, so to speak, just outside the library door until Byron should reach a period. Louis lighted the candles and laid fresh wood on the fire. We rose from our chairs—even Lord Madlands—and moved about the room. My little dog got up from his rug beside the fire, stretched, yawned, and then walked over to Byron for a few moments of wordless colloquy. I was glad that, although he is black and by no means handsome, he differs from Byron's Indian dog in having a blunt nose and long shaggy hair. I doubt, too, whether he knows how to drive fish.

John Chester would take no tea, and I sent a servant to bring him bread and cheese and another tankard of beer. He said that those three things are almost as good in England as in Connecticut, but that we are entirely ignorant of two other important articles of diet: baked beans and corn-bread.

Think of it, William! Try to imagine it! Baked beans! —As for corn-bread, of course I told him that all our English bread is made of corn; but this he stoutly denied. "Jest you take a look at the colour of it," said he, indignantly holding out a slice. "It's white, ain't it? Corn-bread's yaller. Thought everybody knew that much."

We should probably not have understood each other at all if Mr. James Adair had not come up at that moment and explained that in America the word "corn" is commonly taken to mean Indian maize—according to his account of it a most remarkable plant. So it may be, but no more remarkable than the men who grow in that country. Think of their taking one of our oldest English words and applying it to a vegetable which few Englishmen have ever so much as seen!

Ought this kind of thing to be allowed? What will it come to? Given time, will they not be running off with the English language entire?

This Mr. James Adair, as I should have told you long since if I were able to say everything at once, is, though not American by birth, a sufficiently remarkable man. I should say that he must be unique in appearance, turn of thought, and way of life. Either he does not know this or else he cares not at all who else may know it. I mean that he has no fear of singularity—or, for that matter, of anything else. He made a strange spectacle here last week in our timorous little Twickenham where the ghost of Alexander Pope still struts full four feet six inches tall and tyrannically forbids any aberration from the rules of decorum, reason, and common sense. Mr. Adair has heard of those rules, as he has of most things, but fails to see that they apply to him. He has read the works of Alexander Pope—I believe in a wigwam—and they have left him wondering whether there may not be even greater poets yet to come. I heard him remark to Mr. Chute one day that Pope might well bulk fairly large against the Twickenham background, or even in that minute district of London called "the Town," but that when read in the American forest or beside the Mississippi he left something to be desired. This, you see, is a way of looking at things to which you and I are not accustomed, but which may some day alter, perhaps even obliterate, many considerable reputations. Yes, there may come a time when the descendants of Englishmen dwelling out there beside that vast, scarcely pronounceable river—to say nothing of spelling it!—will regard the Thames as a negligible trickle, Twickenham as a fictitious name, and Strawberry Hill, Horace Walpole, possibly even the Reverend William Cole . . .

But this is gloomy, and I wander. What first catches the eye in Adair, and holds it, is his magnificent dress, made mostly of deerskins bleached to the hue of old ivory and adorned with beads and colored quills and strings of small shells, black and white, which he calls—and again there is the problem of spelling!—"wampumpeague." Even his shoes, or "moccasins," are of the same soft, beautiful material. They too are richly decorated. He wears his long black hair, as John Chester said, "Injun-fashion, like Uncas"—that is, not gathered in a cue but falling loosely to his shoulders. He stands six or eight inches taller than I do and has a powerful, manly shape and bearing. His eyes are large, black, quick-moving. He sits for hours at a time with no motion except of his eyes, seeing all that goes on, hearing everything, drawing his own conclusions, making no comment. This too, I suppose, is "Injun-fashion." I have known worse. When he does move you get a notion of the force held in check by his inward calm. He walks with a long, swift stride, silently, straight-toed, and as though he meant to keep on going for at least a hundred miles. One cannot picture him in a sedan chair. Strawberry Hill—not only the house but the grounds— was too small for him. You could see that he felt cramped, like an eagle in a parrot's cage. The grip of his hand at our first meeting made me think of how one lowers the voice in talking with an invalid—so easily, if he had not been careful, he might have crushed my bones.

For the rest, Mr. James Adair seems to have been born in North Ireland some forty-five years ago; but in blood and breeding he is Scotch. Call him Scotch-Irish, then, and say that there is the reason— for I can guess no other—why he has spent half his life, and will spend the rest of it, in the American wilderness. Where he picked up his Latin, Greek, and Hebrew he did not say; but it is certain that he has them, and also a fluent colloquial French, together with I know not how many Indian languages and dialects. He speaks of the Catawbas and Cherokees, Chickasaws and Choctaws, as you and I do of French-men and Italians—that is, as one who has lived familiarly among them as a guest and a friend. He has made a considerable fortune as an "Indian trader," and has recently lost a good part of it in troubles with James Glen, the Royal Governor of South Carolina—troubles which arose out of a conflict between the Governor's thoroughly English opinion that the Indians were created to enrich the English and Adair's odd notion that they are human beings.

Adair goes beyond that, in fact, and asserts that they are descend-ants of the "lost tribes of Israel"—an opinion which he urges and defends with vast erudition and complete neglect of common sense. To hear him and Blandison debating this question out in the Prior's Garden or over their wine was one of the more delightful entertain-ments we had during the week. Indeed, the recollection of those talks makes me wish that I had no story to tell in this letter and so might wander from theme to theme, in my habitual way, like a butterfly in a flowering meadow.

To be sure, that's what I am doing at present; but then, you see, it's tea-time, during which one naturally gabbles about whatever comes into one's head. We're all of us gabbling as we stand in groups or walk up and down or gaze out of the windows at the slowly darkening

Thames. Blandison is being polite to Lord and Lady Madlands, as he
has good reason to be. Mr. Chute and my cousin, at my request and
with the help of my best Madeira, are trying to make Jeremy Tinker
feel at home. Kitty Clive and George Selwyn, standing so near that
I overhear what they say, are talking with Captain Byron about his
story. He thinks it's too dismal for the time and place, and that they
must fear it will never come to an end.

"Dismal?" says George. "Dismal, with all those marvellous corpses?
Nonsense, sir! And that dog-banquet of yours made a perfect preparation for tea."

"As for coming to an end," Kitty adds, "we're not afraid that you
won't, but that you will."

"Oh yes," George goes on, "you will. At the rate you're killing your
people off, you'll be through by dinner-time—which is at eight, by the
way—and perhaps leave us a few minutes for dressing."

*　　*　　*

Whether or not the Captain found these remarks encouraging, he
started out at a brisker pace after we had returned to our chairs.
"Almost from the day of our landing," said he, "we survivors on
Wager Island were divided into two parties—or three if you count the
deserters. Some ten of us stood by the Captain, agreeing to go with
him up the western coast to the rendezvous at the Island of Del
Socorro. Eight times as many were convinced by Gunner Bulkeley
and Carpenter Cummins that there was no chance of overtaking the
Commodore, and that the best hope lay in going through the Straits
of Magellan and so back up the eastern coast of South America to
some port from which it would be possible to embark for home. With
this in view the larger company—or, that is, Carpenter Cummins with
such help as he could get—cut the longboat in two and enlarged it so
that it would hold, tightly packed, eighty men, in the meantime doing
all they could to bring the Captain over to their opinion. Chepe
promised and refused and promised again; but at no time did he really
intend to go in the longboat. As I have explained to you, he had plans
of a quite different sort. I did not agree with those plans. On the
contrary, I abhorred them. And yet . . .

"But all that belongs to Lieutenant Morris. He may suggest what
led me to a decision which, at the time, I left unexplained. I do not

care to explain it now, but will merely say that I am not ashamed of it and have never been sorry that it was made. At any rate, when the Gunner and his eighty men sailed away, about the middle of October, I remained on the island with Captain Chepe, Midshipman Campbell, and the rest of those who regarded me as an enemy and a spy.

"They treated me as such—not in any violent attempts upon my life, for they considered that for a time I might be more useful as a slave than as a corpse, but by abusive and contemptuous language, evil looks, concealment of their plans, and refusal to let me share in the provisions of flour and beef which the Gunner had left behind for our sustenance. This last mark of their hostility made no difference to me because, as I have said, I had long been going without my daily ration, but the Captain's decision that I was no longer to be trusted with my fowling-piece was a serious thing. Nearly all the shellfish along the shore had been consumed during the five months since the wreck. The *Wager* had now broken up, and no more valuable driftage was to be hoped for. What I mostly subsisted upon was the acrid plant I have called wild celery and another weed, not unlike cabbage in appearance, which went among us by the name of slaw. These I fried in the tallow of candle-ends secretly dealt out to me, one by one, by the Surgeon.

"Day by day, for some two months after the sailing of the long-boat, I grew weaker. I sank to the level of a famished animal, and, below that, to the level of a beast slowly losing even the instinct that bids it remain alive. My will let go its hold. For much of the time I must have been out of my mind, taking little notice of what went on about me. Among the few events I can now recall there was the occasion when three seamen were caught stealing flour from the store tent. One escaped, and was never seen again. The others were given four hundred lashes each and, as that did not quite kill them, were then banished to an islet of rock not far offshore. A week or so later their bodies were found there, cold and stiff."

"Two more corpses," George Selwyn murmured, ticking them off on his fingers.

"Yes, and more to the purpose, two fewer mouths to be fed—or three, counting him who ran away and starved in the woods. Thus, if we could no longer increase our food supply, we did at least reduce the number of consumers. Captain Chepe now had with him only eight persons, counting myself. These were Midshipman Campbell, Surgeon Elliot, Lieutenant Hamilton of the Marines, and four of Hamilton's men.

"Early in December—corresponding to England's July—we had one whole day on which it did not rain and even the wind subsided. I took advantage of it by getting the Marines to row me out to the scene of the wreck, and there I found three large casks lying some four fathoms down and held fast among the rocks. You can vaguely imagine the joy with which, an hour or two later, we brought those casks ashore, broke them open, and found that they contained salt beef not completely spoiled. Of this I was given my share—not on the ground that I had made the discovery but because I was soon to be needed as a steersman. For Captain Chepe now began to think of setting out on his piratical expedition, the plan being to make for the Island of Chiloé, some hundred leagues northward, and there to capture the first armed Spanish vessel that we might find.

"It is a familiar axiom of His Majesty's Navy that a single Englishman is the equal in combat of at least ten Spaniards; but even with this in mind Captain Chepe was doubtful whether his meagre troop of starvelings would be able to cut out, capture, and man a Spanish ship of war. Naturally, therefore, he began to think of the deserters still living on the other side of the island, and living as well as we were on provisions left with them by the Gunner. Thus, unless they had already consumed their portion, they would not reduce our store. The fact that most of them were cutthroats, and that their leader had reached and held his bad eminence by a murderous ferocity, rendered them none the less eligible as members of a pirate's crew. So, at any rate, the Captain and Midshipman Campbell believed. The rest of us had nothing to say in the matter.

"James Mitchell and his nine followers accepted the invitation not because they expected to enjoy our company but for the reason that the barge and the yawl, in our possession, were the only means they had of leaving the island. From their first coming among us they were a sullen lot, and not the less because the Captain at once obliged them to deliver up all their weapons to him and to put what food and drink they had left in the common stock. He would not, however, require Mitchell to bury the body of Grindling, and indeed I think that if he had given such an order it would not have been obeyed. Mitchell firmly denied that he had taken any part in the murder of Grindling, and he was heard to say that there was only one known murderer on the island—meaning, of course, David Chepe.

"Thus manned and thus led, we set forth, northward, on the fif-

teenth of December, 1741, having stowed all our provisions and gear
in the two boats. Captain Chepe and the Surgeon and I were in the
barge with nine men, and Midshipman Campbell, accompanied by
Lieutenant Hamilton of the Marines and six men, steered the yawl.
Both boats, overcrowded and heavily laden, swam low in the water,
and we saw at once that the repairs we had made upon them with our
poor tools and no help from the Carpenter had been badly bungled.
Although it was now the midsummer of that region, the weather was
good only in the respect that it gave due warning of worse to come.

"The wind, I remember, blew hard from the southwest that morning, with fleets of dark cloud driving before it and flaws of rain and
an incessant hurry of shade and shine. Yet the southwest was the wind
we had long awaited and now we could wait no longer but stumbled
into the boats at dawn and pushed off without a cheer—one of us
thinking the while of that so different departure long ago from the
Ram's Head off Plymouth where the fair wind found us and the
Commodore joyously shouting from the quarterdeck to almost nineteen hundred men and the trumpets speaking and the twitter of pipes
and the flags going up aflutter and the squadron beginning at last to
move as one body controlled by one purpose and will. Where now
might the flagship be, and the *Severn*, the *Pearl*, the *Tryal*, the *Anna*,
the *Gloucester?* Had Gunner Bulkeley's longboat, the *Speedwell*, gone
down by this time with her eighty men in one of the many tempests
that had swept the sea since her departure, or had she luckily fumbled
and groped through the intricate Straits of Magellan—held together
and helped onward, perhaps, by *The Christian Pattern*, so that now
she had rounded the Cape of the Virgin and was creeping and beating
and drifting up the Atlantic coast toward some friendly port and
home?—About all that we could only fear and hope, and our fears
and hopes were conflicting. It was certainly the wish of some amongst
us that neither the Gunner nor the Commodore might ever see England
again."

*   *   *

Captain Byron has risen from the Speaker's Chair and is moving
restlessly about the room. "Though our setting forth," he says, "was
in no way propitious, there came to me a few minutes of joy, whilst
we were struggling out through the tumble of breakers, at seeing the
hateful island which had been for seven months our home gradually

dwindle and fade. But Mount Misery, where I had shot the cormorant and Grindling's body lay still unburied, did not disappear. We were to see it again and again in the days that followed, until we began to feel that it was striding after us across the sea, and that we should never escape the spell of its power.

"I myself have not done so. It strides after me still in my dreams, and often my moments of happiest companionship are darkened by its shadow. Its image comes before me even now, as I have seen it a hundred times through the rain or lifting its huge bulk of blackness against the stars. Once more I look out from its blunted summit across the interminable tumult of waves, and share the anguish of those vast water-weeds, each one a forest in itself of enormously swaying branches and flapping fronds. I look down again from that height upon the bared ribs of the *Wager,* my first ship and most dearly beloved. Her too we must leave, like Grindling, to the teeth of the wind and the blind assault of the sea. We must leave here the body of Henry Cozens, pitifully slain. My own boyhood has died in agony on this gaunt mishallowed rock grown weary in gazing so long upon the Pacific's meaningless settle and heave. Surely no place on earth is more intolerant of man. It was once, I think, a peaked mountain, but its top was torn off long ago by some local Polyphemus and hurled after a retreating ship.

* * *

"For an hour or two of that first day we were able to use the full spread of our small, clumsy sails, and make good speed on our course. Then, little by little, the wind moved round to the west and freshened and we took one reef in the sails and the men bent to their oars and I at the tiller looked wondering out at the long green hills of water wind-carved, foam-streaked, white-crested, that steadily marched upon us in vast everlasting procession with such a majestic omnipotent tread and the width of the world's greatest ocean behind each wave and the depth below it and all about of that never-yet-fathomed sea. It was there, some eight leagues out from Wager Island, that I got a new notion of waves: not now as the sailor sees them in numberless multitudes from the deck of his ship or the masthead, but one by one as they come, each of them different from all the others and each a world by itself and the only world and perhaps the last in the instant it looms enormous above you with its mile-long wavering crest beginning to curl and . . ."

"Have a care now, Captain," said George Selwyn. "I knew a man once who got lost in a sentence like that and never came back."

"Better take a nip o' wine an' ketch your breath," Chester suggested.

Captain Byron did so, but his expression of a man gazing and listening far away did not change. "The wind grew to a gale," he said, "and we took a double reef and ran with the wind up the backs of the waves toward the land of which we knew nothing except that it must be near and rocky and would in all likelihood break and grind our frail boats to splinters. My work at the tiller was eased by this change in our course, and indeed the hardest thing I now had to do was to refrain from glancing over my shoulder at the waves racing toward us—yes, not to look back lest all of us, like Lot's wife, should be turned to salt. While facing the wind and the combers I had depended upon my own small skill, but now I had to learn faith in the barge, that she by some blind instinct would know how to save herself from the terror rushing behind. And that she did, wonderfully, time after time, yet with increasing labor, for every crest we outrode spilled into her gallons of spray, and her seams were opening in the strain. The men at the Captain's command dropped their oars and took to bailing with the three buckets we had and the kettle and the scoop and even their bare hands; but still she wallowed, and the men sat close together to take the seas on their backs and so prevent her from filling, and the Captain ordered first one cask of beef, then a second, and then our third and last to be thrown overboard—all our provisions and most of our gear, even the grapnel—while she rode lower and lower, more heavily, shipping more water from each succeeding wave. The yawl, we knew, could not be far off, for we had seen her once or twice on the top of a mountainous sea. Night was coming. We began to hear above the scream of the wind a crash of breakers on a lee shore. That was what we had expected, and somewhere on that shore we also expected to die. Dark cliffs loomed ahead, stormed by breakers, with black jagged rocks at their feet. A moment more and I should have let go the tiller and leapt into the surf when I caught a glimpse through the welter of what looked like an opening as it were of a little door among the rocks and made toward it with some help from two or three men at the oars and in a few seconds we found ourselves entering the mouth of a narrow creek which, after a few sharp bends, brought us into a shallow harbor sheltered from the wind and as smooth almost as a millpond. The yawl was there before us.

"So ended the first day of our piratical expedition, with what Gunner Bulkeley, if he had been with us, would have called an act of Divine Providence. However that may be, the day left us with tattered and leaking boats, drenched clothing, and nothing to eat. No one slept that night, during the first part of which it rained so hard that we could build no fire. Toward morning the wind shifted to the north, the sky cleared, and our wet garments froze on our backs.

"Let that day and night serve as example of the sixty that followed, some less miserable but others worse. We lived mostly on berries and limpets and sea-tangle. When even that sustenance failed us, we ate our shoes of sealskin. Night after night we were unable to land at all, and so lay upon our oars until morning. Once more, as on the island, many of us lost interest in living and all its concerns. The Captain and Midshipman Campbell seemed to forget even their hatred of me, and to feel that though I had meant to spy upon them it did not now matter because none of us would ever reach home.

"Of this indifference to life I recall a vivid instance. One morning, about a month after our departure from the island, the yawl was stove in and destroyed on the rocks. The barge could not hold our entire company, and it was therefore decided that four of the oldest Marines should be left on that desolate shore to fend for themselves. This, of course, was their death-warrant. After we had turned over to them the one musket we could spare, we shook hands, bade them farewell, and took to the oars. They gave us three cheers as we pulled away, and called out to us, each man raising his hand, 'God save the King!'

"That was all—except that when we got beyond the breakers some of us looked back and saw them, dwarfed by the distance and the crags now, helping one another across a hideous tract of rock, moving slowly, feebly, the strongest of them carrying the musket, going aimlessly as though well aware that any way they took would bring them straight and soon to their goal. We never saw them again, or heard any report of how and when and where they crossed into that undiscovered country. It is only in my dreams and waking visions, I suppose, that they return now and then, with a kind of grandeur about them. Their names were Smith, Hobbs, Hertford, and Corporal Crosslet."

* * *

I asked Louis, in a whisper, to fill the Captain's wineglass and lay more wood on the fire. No one else spoke. No one moved for a while.

And neither do you move, William. Like a man bewitched, you sit there at your window fifty miles northwest, as I am sitting by mine, forgetting the gout, your pastoral duties, and every private concern. You have forgotten almost your very name and the time of year. The Swiss cuckoo-clock on your bookshelf strikes unheeded. Your housekeeper sets your tea beside you, and it grows cold. The shouts of the village boys at play on Bletchley Common come faintly to your ears from amid the crash of Pacific breakers. When you look out of the window to rest your eyes you scarcely see the ivied wall near at hand of your little stone church, so spellbound you are by your vision of those four broken, starved old men standing far off on a desolate coast with their trembling hands held high.

What can be the meaning of this fascination? Why are both of us so loath to leave them there, to watch them dwindle with every stroke of the oars as our boat draws slowly away? Why should we care how feebly, like mid-winter flies on a windowpane, they wander off now among the rocks, still helping one another all they can? We understand that their work was done, and that henceforth they could only have been a burden. By this arrangement Providence was saving England the cost of their burial——supposing, that is, that they could ever have got home again. All this we agree to, and feel that it should be enough; yet from the crest of every wave we look back and peer and search that dreadful coast, unwilling to believe that they are gone.

One is glad that they had, at least, one another, so that again and again and again there could be that simple reticent gesture and phrase of farewell, meaning not much, to be sure, and yet much better than silence. But one of them, of course, the last one . . .

* * *

Byron went on to say that the discouragement of the sixteen men now carried in the barge alone was not wholly due to their physical woes. There had grown up among them a conviction that they were being pursued, thwarted, and tormented by the ghost of Jacob Grindling, and that they would meet nothing but disaster unless and until they returned to Wager Island and put that perturbed spirit at rest. Once more they heard, or said they did, the voice of Grindling from the midnight sea, calling not plaintively now but in wrath and derision. There were sullen complaints against Chepe, against Campbell and Mitchell, for their failure to bury Grindling's body before starting northward. These increased from grumblings to growls and direct accusations. The crisis came when the expedition had been a month on its way and after two futile attempts had been made to round a great cape called the Peninsula of Three Mountains. Then Chepe was told that unless he agreed to return to Wager Island, there to do whatever was still possible toward laying the ghost, he would be set ashore and left to shift for himself. From his point of view this was another mutiny; but the only condition he could make was that they try once more to get round the cape. They did try, they failed for the third time, and then turned about.

The return voyage also took a month, and one may guess at its difficulties from the fact that the distance from the peninsula to the island is scarcely more, in a straight line, than one hundred miles. Byron's recollection of this return was dim for the reason, he said, that during most of the time he had been more nearly dead than alive. What he chiefly recalled was the talk that went on among the men about the eating of sins and the funereal use of salt. On this strange topic he spoke with an unmistakable earnestness, brushing aside almost impatiently some idle jest of George Selwyn's to the effect that sin-eating, with or without salt, must be a new form of cannibalism. No, said he, it is a custom exceedingly ancient, and one still practiced in the region of Sherwood Forest, which no one brought up in a Christian country, believing to any extent in the doctrine of the Vicarious Atonement, ought to scorn. The Founder of the Christian religion, he said, was a sin-eater. George looked for a moment embarrassed, as of course all ladies and gentlemen do when religion is seriously mentioned—or, for that matter, sin.

Well, at any rate, it was agreed during the return voyage that mere burial of Grindling's body would not compensate for the many weeks in which that simple decency had been neglected. Something must be done for the man's soul, which, according to the account of those who had known him best, would need all the help it could get. For one thing, before they placed Grindling in the grave they would have to lay on his breast-bone at least a pinch of salt—an article of which, since the jettison of the salt beef, they had not among them a single grain. For another, it would be necessary to find some member of the company who would freely and willingly take the total load of Grindling's iniquities upon himself so that the murdered man might stand up on Judgment Day as innocent as a newborn child. That would be doing the thing "handsome," the men said, and after such a ceremony they might be allowed to go their ways with no more interference from the spirit world.

They soon discovered that a willing scapegoat would be harder to find than the necessary salt. James Mitchell, naturally enough, was first nominated for this office; but he, with blasphemous emphasis, refused to serve. Captain Chepe was then approached, on the ground that the ghost probably held him as culpable as Mitchell. The Captain firmly declined. So did Midshipman Campbell. Thus the three men who had most scornfully denied that the ghost could have any power whatever showed themselves not wholly devoid of faith.

But then came forward two volunteers. One was Surgeon Elliot, an intelligent and well educated man who said that, although he had no belief whatever in ghosts or in the possibility that one man could assume another's evil deeds, he was perfectly willing to go through any nonsensical ceremony that would conduce to the general peace and comfort. The other volunteer was the sailor John Bosman who had served under Byron on the topmast. He was the man, if you recall, who had only two fingers on his right hand—a foul-mouthed, quarrelsome fellow who lived primarily in the joyous recollection and eager expectation of debauchery. It was evident that Captain Byron had liked the man, for reasons he did not make clear. At any rate this Bosman offered his services quite cheerfully, though not at all for the Surgeon's reasons. He said that he was hopelessly damned already, and scarcely thought the additional load of Grindling's sins would sink him to any deeper hell. It seemed to him right and just, moreover, that the price of remission of sins should be paid not by the innocent but by one sinful man for another.

So there you are, William. As Madame de Sévigné wrote to her daughter after describing the torture and execution of the wicked Madame Voisin: "Que dites-vous de cette sorte de courage?" The Christian martyrs were sustained by hope. Apparently despair can serve, at need, quite as well.

But I see that I have anticipated a good part of what happened on the island when these would-be pirates got back there, considerably worse off than when they went away. You will be glad to learn that

what was left of Grindling's body was buried at last, with such ceremonial salt and ritualistic consumption—and assumption—of his iniquities that thereafter his ghost gave no more trouble. From that day,
in fact, the fortunes of Chepe's company took a turn for the better.
Just as their imaginations were beginning to dally with the charms of
cannibalism—one man whispering to another, let us say, that it had
the double advantage of increasing the supply of food while simul-
taneously reducing the demand—they discovered a few rotten pieces
of beef that had been cast up by the sea some miles from their huts.
Here, of course, was an act of Providence, not wholly unlike that
which provided a ram caught by its horns in the thicket at the moment
when Abraham was raising the knife to slay his son Isaac as a sacrificial victim. —Captain Byron, to be sure, would not agree that there
was anything providential about it. If a loving and almighty God
provided that beef and helped them to find it, then why, said he, did
it have to be rotten? Why too, on the same supposition, had it been
necessary to starve them for month after month until they were on
the point of eating human flesh? Several other such questions he
asked, all of them with what I fear you would think a sacrilegious
tendency.

Providence was in a more generous mood, or perhaps a less
ironic, when it sent to Wager Island, some days later, an Indian who,
besides being a resident of the Island of Chiloé, knew a way of getting
there without encountering the difficulties that had defeated the
earlier expedition. In addition, he knew enough Spanish so that Surgeon Elliot was able to arrange that he should guide the company to
Chiloé and take the barge in payment for the service.

On the sixth of March, 1742, the barge put forth again, northward.
Two sailors had died of starvation during the second stay on the
island, and a Marine had run away after being detected in a theft.
Chepe's company was thus reduced to thirteen, but as he had to take
along the Indian Cacique and his servant there were fifteen men in
the barge. There were also a good many dissensions and animosities.
The Captain and Lieutenant Hamilton of the Marines were not at
this time on speaking terms. Midshipman Campbell had lost the Captain's confidence—now extended to Surgeon Elliot alone. Byron himself was in extreme disfavour. All the men took it hard that Captain
Chepe would not share with any one except the Surgeon the large
piece of seal-meat given him by the Cacique. He held it in his lap all

day and used it for a pillow at night, so that his cheeks turned black
from the putrid grease. Everyone saw that the Captain's legs were
swelling with a kind of elephantiasis, and that the skin was peeling off
his body, but at least he was not starving. The stench of that rotten
meat became almost intolerable. To Byron in his delirium it had the
smell of envy, hatred, fear, greed, and essential evil. For him it took
the place of Grindling's ghost, and also of the sins that John Bosman
had eaten. James Mitchell began to plot against the Captain's life.

I have spoken of Byron's "delirium," but the word is too violent.
It suggests a kind of frenzy, and that, I should say, is just the opposite
of the state into which he sank on this second effort to reach the
Island of Chiloé. From his story and the way he told it—speaking
listlessly, almost sleepily, as though these things had happened to
some other man of whom he had vaguely heard—I judge that he must
have lived in a daze, a waking dream, accepting whatever pain and
terror and outrage was thrust upon him without surprise. Certainly
he looked and sounded like a man trying to recall a nightmare as he
sat, with his hands lying quiet on the arms of his chair, gazing out of
the darkened window and speaking in a monotonous voice.

"On the first night of our new voyage," he said, "we lay at a place
we called Sheep Island, perhaps because there were no sheep there, or
anything else to eat. On the second night, off Montrose Island, we
could not land, but lay on our oars. The third and fourth days we
spent at the hut of Martin the Cacique. He had no food to give us.
Under his direction we tried to row the barge up the rapid current of
a river. Thus we spent the fifth, sixth, and seventh days since our
departure from Wager Island. On the sixth one of our oarsmen
dropped dead. On the seventh, John Bosman died of starvation. On
the eighth we gave up our struggle with the current, were swept back
to the mouth of the river, and there buried the two dead men in
the sand.

"John Bosman had died at my feet while I sat rowing in his place.
Over and over, before he expired, he had begged for a mouthful of
seal-meat. Captain Chepe, sitting three feet away, had made no
answer, had not glanced at the dying man. That evening, after the
burial, he unwrapped his bundle of stinking seal and cut a large slice
for himself and another for the Surgeon. Then they two sat down by
their fire of driftwood—I can see at this moment how blue the flame

was with the salt of the sea—and fell to eating. They paid no attention to us. They pretended that we were not there.

"You scarcely believe this, and I only assert that it happened. You say it is not in human nature, and I wish you were right. Besides the brutal selfishness, you see the stupidity of this action, for Chepe's very life depended upon the strength of the oarsmen, and that fidelity which he did less than nothing to maintain. I see only one chance of your believing me, and that depends upon whether you yourselves have seen something of the same kind—say in England. As a sailor who has spent most of his life away from home I can only ask whether there are Englishmen who live upon the toil of others and yet refuse them the livelihood that would enable them to go on toiling. Or, still worse, have you ever known a man whose hopes and dreams wholly depended upon the fidelity of others and yet had no thought of faithfulness to those who served him? If you have known one such man, then Captain Chepe was not unique.

"The rest of us built a separate fire and supped on wild purslane. We had much wrathful talk meanwhile about the Captain's cruelty to Bosman. We recalled that he had seemed the strongest man of our number, so that the only reason we could give for his dying while we lived on was that the burden of Grindling's sins had overpowered him. This meant that in some sense he had died for us, and at once the question was raised—I think by James Mitchell—how we could save his soul from an eternal torment brought on by an act of pure generosity. The details of our discussion escape me now, but its outcome was a firm, concerted resolve. We rose from the fire as one man, took four oars from the barge, and dug up the body of Bosman. Then we went to the other fire and stood in a circle, nine men looking at two. James Mitchell the murderer was our spokesman. He spoke well, wasting no words, making no accusations, but giving Chepe and Elliot quite clearly to understand that one or the other of them would eat Bosman's sins—including, of course, those of Grindling—or else they would both be left in that place to starve.

"Captain Chepe began to bluster. Enfeebled and poisoned as he already was, he offered to fight Mitchell or any other man among us to decide who should serve as sin-eater. He went on to say that this now huge accumulation of sins should of course be assumed by the man who had brought them upon us by the murder of Grindling, and that we all knew who that man was. Surgeon Elliot at this point broke in—that tall, lean, powerful man who had somehow maintained his health and vigour through all our privations. What marked him still more, and made him mysterious, was his habit of keeping his thoughts and inward purposes—for one could not doubt that he had them—completely to himself. He was laughing now as he rose to his feet —not in derision but indulgently—as one does at the fears of children. He reminded us that he had already offered to eat Grindling's sins and said that now, if it would be any comfort to us, he was perfectly willing to assume those of Bosman as well. There was, of course, the question whether his atheism, along with his total lack of faith in the efficacy of sin-eating, might unfit him for this office; but that, said he, was for us to decide.

"Night was coming on as we stood there and briefly considered this problem, the shout of the sea increasing meanwhile and the exhumed body appearing to twitch with impatience in the flickering light of the fires. It was not a time or a place for fine discriminations. What we mainly wanted was to get that corpse back underground and that spirit appeased before the darkness fell. Therefore it was agreed— perhaps not for the first or last time in human history—that the value of a given ritual does not depend upon the faith or unfaith of those by whom it is performed. We accepted the Suregon's offer.

"James Mitchell then directed the Captain to open his bundle of seal-meat again and to cut a large slice for ceremonial use. He ignored Chepe's remark that the Surgeon could not be hungry, having just finished supper. After the first slice was cut he demanded another and larger one, pointing out that two souls were now involved, and that one of these had been exceedingly sinful. The Captain obeyed, with a bad grace. We then went and stood on one side of the corpse, telling the Surgeon to stand on the other. Mitchell laid the meat for a moment on Bosman's breast and then, taking it up again and holding it out toward the Surgeon: 'Walter Elliot,' said he, in a voice meant to sound like a clergyman's, 'do you freely and willingly pledge your immortal soul for the souls of John Bosman and Jacob Grindling, deceased, solemnly swearing that at the Last Assize you will confess to their sins all and sundry, take upon you their guilt, and suffer in their stead the punishment meted out by a righteously angered Judge, leaving them to go free of all blame and taint for ever, so help you God?'

" 'I do,' the Surgeon answered, smiling with amusement at what was to him mere rigmarole, and perhaps also at Mitchell's rather magnificent language. 'And furthermore,' he added, 'I sincerely hope it may do you some good.'

" 'Then here are the sins of John Bosman'—and Mitchell handed the smaller slice across the corpse. 'You will eat them as fast as you can, and then those of Jacob Grindling. We shall sit on this side of the fire and watch you eat them, partly to see that you don't throw a morsel away, and partly so that on Judgment Day there will be nine witnesses to hold you to your word. When you've got them all down we shall drive you out of camp and keep you out all night.'

" 'In other words, I'm to act as a scapegoat,' the Surgeon replied, still smiling. 'It's like something out of the Old Testament. But while we're about it, James Mitchell, haven't you a murder or two of your own which I might take over, and thus save you trouble later on?'

" 'Time enough for that,' said Mitchell, 'when it's proved that I've done any murders. Just now we all know that your crony David Chepe has committed at least two. If you want to eat those, you're welcome; but first we'll have to kill Chepe.'

" 'Let's get on with this business,' some one growled. 'It's getting dark.'

" 'Eat!' said Mitchell.

"Surgeon Elliot sat down on a rock and looked at the huge collop of putrid flesh in his hand. His smile faded. We could see him sicken. It was as though he smelled if not the stench of sin then certainly that of death. We watched him while he ate—slowly, laboriously, with effort and loathing. Mitchell handed the second slice across the body. For a while we sat and listened to the crash and roar of the breakers. The fires dwindled to a few relics of gold and crimson. Then the world was blotted out except for that foam-pale corpse and the vague crouching shape of the sin-eater. Place and time blurred out into everywhere and always as we waited there, silent, all but invisible each to each, we nine living men and one corpse on the coast dividing the half-known from things known not at all.

"At last a voice said, 'It is finished,' and we rose and sprinkled sea-water on the breast of the dead man and buried him and drove Walter Elliot away into the night with curses, flinging after him sticks, stones, and ashes."

"Did he die?" asked George Selwyn.

Byron ignored, or perhaps did not hear, that question. He sat for a time as though listening intently, still gazing out through the darkened window. Then he went on to relate his shocking discovery, at dawn of the following day, that the barge was gone, with all that it had contained. James Mitchell was gone, and with him six other men had disappeared. Only Chepe, Hamilton, and Campbell were in sight, and beginning now to rub their eyes and sit up in the places where they had slept on the sand.

While those three were away in search of the deserters, Surgeon Elliot crawled back into camp—hollow-eyed, death-struck. He had come back to lay upon Byron not his sins, he said, but a charge, an obligation; to see that Chepe was brought to trial in England for the murder of Cozens. Elliot declared that he himself had lived for months with this determination, and that it had enabled him to win the confidence of a man whom he despised and hated. "You must do it, Mr. Byron," he gasped out with feverish intensity. "You will do it because Henry Cozens was your closest friend and Chepe is your enemy. If you do not do it I shall drag you down to the hell I have lived in for all these weeks since I let Cozens die uncared for."

Byron was astonished by this revelation of tragic depth in a man whom he had always thought shallow and empty. He could scarcely believe that this was the man he had so often heard scoffing at spiritual things. Fog gathered about the two sitting there in the pearly light by the small gray pile of ashes. From the outer world came only the mournful crash and backwash of the billow; but nearer, enclosed within that old sorrow of the sea, was the voice that pled and appealed and threatened, striving to lay the sins of one soul upon another.

For it came to that, Byron felt. The very thing at which the Surgeon had so recently scoffed he was now urging, even demanding. His eyes glittered as he spoke, and the hand he laid on Byron's arm was burning. Fever was drinking his blood. Thus constrained, Byron solemnly swore that he would see Chepe brought to justice—adding, however, that this might not include trial for murder and the rope. With that promise the Surgeon was obliged to be content.

"Did he die?" George Selwyn asked again.

"Yes, Mr. Selwyn. He died a few days later. I dug his grave in the sand with my bare hands."

"And what would you say he died of—pangs of conscience, all those sins he had eaten, or rotten seal-meat?"

"I am not a physician, but I think I have heard the word 'complications.'

"Ah. —And did anyone eat his sins?"

"Not in the formal ceremony we had used for Grindling and Bosman. That neglect may have been the reason for the misfortunes we later on went through. I shall not narrate those miseries. Try to imagine how it felt to us four, in our dreadfully weakened condition, to struggle up the western coast of South America on foot. We were now to cross, inland, that same Peninsula of Three Mountains which we had failed to round, some months before, in our boats. There was no road, no path across it, but occasionally we had a choice between clambering over rocks and wading through swamps. All of us were bare-footed. What clothing we had left was in shreds. My shirt had long since rotted away. We had no utensils, no tools, and for weapons only the Captain's sword and my fowling-piece, for which there was now left but a single charge of powder and ball. Hamilton and Campbell and I subsisted on the food we could find as we went along—now and then a clam, here and there a gooseberry, and for *pièce de résistance* a bitter root recommended to us by the Indians. As for Chepe, he confined his diet to putrid seal-meat, of which he had acquired another supply soon after the death of the Surgeon. I think he did this largely to excite our envy and to show that he was still our Captain. The meat was wrapped in a large canvas bag which I carried, lashed to my head, in the daytime, and which he used at night for a pillow. Not once in that journey did he offer a morsel to any of his companions; and, indeed, if he had done so it would have been rejected. The stench of it was revolting, and so was the sight and smell of the man who made it his only food.

"If you were to ask why we did not simply walk away from Chepe, leaving him to enjoy his blubber while it lasted, I should answer that we were tied to him by strands we could not break: Campbell by self-interest, Lieutenant Hamilton by his quarrel with Captain Pemberton, and I by my promise to the Surgeon. And David Chepe knew this. Even though he must have realized that his very life depended upon us from day to day and hour to hour, he did not hesitate to play the tyrant—sending us on useless errands, making us cut his meat for him with his sword, and requiring us to carry him through the swamps and over rocks. His demands increased as his physical power of enforcing them diminished, so that before long we were acting as slaves to a man for whom we felt only contempt and loathing.

"On the last day of that journey we came to a quagmire through which we had to wade, often up to our knees and above them. I had eaten nothing that day except the stem of a succulent plant with an acid taste. Weakened as I was by months of starvation, the seal-meat strapped to my head was a grievous burden. Again and again I had to stand still and gasp for breath, while the blood from my torn feet and legs slowly stained the water about me. Thus, little by little, I fell behind my companions. They disappeared from sight. I heard no answer to my shouts. In my haste to overtake them, I fell into a stagnant pool and there came near drowning because of the burden on my head. When at last I pulled myself out of that weedy slime and lay exhausted on the bank, trying to think connectedly, I realized that another such fall would be fatal, and that if I went on wading at random through the swamp with the bundle of seal-meat on my head I should probably not survive the night. Accordingly I left the bundle in the fork of a tree, took careful note of that tree's position, and waded painfully onward."

Here Byron walked to the window and stood looking out into the dusk. For half a minute or more he was silent, so that we almost thought he would not continue at all. At last he said: "There followed one of the darkest hours of my life. I was starving, naked, exhausted, and utterly alone in the wilderness. If I should survive it could only be to go on in slavish subjection to a man I despised and who hated me. In addition, my guilty sense of responsibility for all our tribulations was an intolerable burden, but one which could not be laid aside like the bundle of seal-meat. As I now recall it, the one thing that kept me toiling onward was the thought that if I should live I might be of some service to Gunner Bulkeley.

"But somewhere in that lonely plodding and splashing I came upon a small island in the swamp, covered with flowering shrubs of the azalea kind. Wonderfully delicate and fresh those blossoms were, and of many colors. By themselves alone they would have been a delight, but among them I saw perhaps a score of birds no longer than my thumb, flashing in and out among the leaves or standing still in the air with wings moving so swiftly as to be all but invisible. Now and then one of them would plunge from a great height almost to the ground, and then instantly rise again in the same vertical line. Their level flight was swifter than the eye could follow, and only when one of them perched within reach of my hand did I realize that they were as wonderful in hue as in motion. The plumage of our English king-fisher is perhaps as beautiful, but is certainly less brilliant.

"For a long while I stood there watching those joyous creatures, giving thanks for their beauty, quite forgetting my woes, going out of myself and into their lives. When I moved on again I took their image with me, and I carry it still. The thought of the humming-bird is a lighter load to bear than that of the cormorant.

"It took me some hours to find the others. None of them spoke when I sat down beside them under a tree on the bank of a deep, dark river, and for my part I was willing to let my bleeding feet and legs tell their own story. At length, in a surly tone, Chepe asked what I had done with the bundle. I told him, and then took without a word of reply the profane abuse he poured upon me. While he spoke I was looking at him closely, thoughtfully, trying to decide a question which, at the moment, seemed to me important.

"You recall my promise to the Surgeon that I would see David Chepe 'brought to justice'—a form of words which left much leeway to my own opinion. That was fortunate because it looked to me less and less probable that I should ever lead him to the kind of punish-ment the Surgeon had wished him to get. There was little, after all, that I could do in the matter. I could stay with him and slavishly obey his every command, humour his every whim; but to get back to Eng-land with him, to bring against him the charge of murder, and to get an English court to take the word of a midshipman seventeen years old against a captain twice that age, was a different thing.

"I saw that even if my heart were in the task I should have scarcely one chance in a thousand of getting the man hanged.

"But now it occurred to me that this whole problem was being taken out of my hands. As I have said, I looked at Chepe closely and thoughtfully whilst he was pouring out his almost insane vituperation, and what I saw was at the same time loathsome and pitiful. His bloated skin hung on his bones like a loose flapping bag. His legs were swollen to the shape and size of millposts, for he was suffering from a kind of elephantiasis which the Indians of that region attribute to the eating of putrid seal. His puffed face was black with grime, his hair was matted, and the bush of beard from which his little swinish eyes peered out was foul with the grease of seal. Since the loss of

his sword somewhere on our way across the peninsula he had given
up all care of his person—taking no heed, for example, of the crawl-
ing verminous life that made one think, when as now he sat down to
rest, of a huge anthill. Chepe had sunk far below the level of the
clean, wholesome beasts, and his mind had sunk with his body. He
had forgotten where he was, how he had come there, and whither he
wished to go. He could not recall—nor, I think, did he wish to—the
names of his three companions. By this time he did not even know
his own name, which, easy as it should have been to live up to, he had
dishonoured. Two things only he kept in mind: his bundle of rotting
blubber and the conviction that he was still our captain. One human
trait, unknown to the beasts, he retained—greed.

"Well then, as I looked at Chepe and flinched away and looked
again with mingled horror and pity, I saw that to hang such a man
would only cut short his punishment and let him escape from full
justice. More dreadful by far than the hangman's rope would be the
doom of living with himself, bearing and eating his own sins. That
would be the justice not of man but of God, and I felt that it ought to
satisfy the ghost of Walter Elliot.

"I went back after the seal-meat and brought it to Chepe with a
lightness of heart, almost a gaiety, such as I had not felt since the
sailing of the squadron. 'Here you are, Mr. Chepe,' said I, handing
him the bundle and smiling as I spoke—really smiling, I mean, for all
my rancour was gone now. 'Here is your seal-meat. I have not eaten
any. From now on I shall not carry it again.'

"The pale little eyes peered out at me for a moment through the
thicket of beard and saw that I meant what I said. Chepe hesitated,
and then held out the bundle to Hamilton. He shook his head and
turned away. Campbell took it. Then the three of them hobbled down
the bank to an Indian canoe that had come for us during my absence.
I went with them, and helped Chepe into the canoe. When I offered to
get in myself he said to me, gruffly, 'You stay here.' I stood there
knee-deep in the swirl, watching them paddle away. A blood-red sunset was staining the water, the dark trees about me, the savage land.
It laid a tinge of gules on the snowy peaks of the Cordilleras a hundred
miles to the eastward. My heart leapt with a sudden wild exultation.
All at once, before I knew what I was doing or why, I heard myself
calling out, with my right hand raised: 'God save the King!' "

"Odd," George Selwyn murmured.

"Superb!" cried Kitty.

"What king?" I heard Blandison ask of himself.

"Oh, well," Byron continued, leaning forward now in his chair and making the shape of a heart again with his two hands, "no doubt it was boyish of me, and of course it was mere imitation, but something I had to do to express the joy that filled me. Then I washed myself in the fresh sweet water, trying to get rid of all stains of blood and the stench of dead seal. For some while, as the sky's colour faded and night crept down among the trees, I swam here and there in the river. It washed the ache of weariness from my bones. When I climbed up the bank and lay down under a tree the full darkness had come, but a darkness crowded with stars.

"You cannot think what a wonder they were, those stars which I had scarcely seen—or, at any rate, heeded, for months. A sailor is lost without stars. I had been lost, but now knew my way. The Pole Star, of course, was hidden by the bulge of the globe, but I had the Southern Cross."

"And also," Blandison put in, "you must have had the Unicorn."

"Oh, yes, over there by the Little Dog. But the Unicorn is a dim constellation, and nothing to steer by. It lies too far from the Pole."

"Didn't you have anything but stars?" Kitty wanted to know. "It all sounds so lonesome."

The clock was striking six, and Byron rose from his chair. "I have known worse companions than the stars," he said.

Some tone of finality in his voice made Kitty ask: "But aren't you going on?"

"Not now, if you please. As you see, I survived—largely by the help of friendly Indians. Later on I was to owe to the enemies of my country a happiness that easily counterbalanced all I had been through. —But that is the story of John Byron, and we are concerned with Jenkins' Ear. Besides, we must leave Mr. Selwyn time to dress for dinner."

TUESDAY

Louis did not call me next morning, at least in the usual way. He was moving about in my chamber when I awoke, and muttering there on the other side of the bed-curtains some outlandish jargon which made me fear for a moment that he had gone out of his head.

"Now there's his best lavender toggy," said he, *sotto voce,* hanging my coat on the back of a chair. "Over that we lay his embroidered little ben with the tick in the groper. Next come the kickseys, and I think ... Yes, I think we'll wear just the lavender kickseys today, and the gam-cases of partridge silk. As for a squeeze-clout, this rose one goes well enough with the lavender. —But now we must have a new-dabbled lally, and, while we're about it, a clean wipe too, a bird's-eye. Blandison wouldn't prig a bird's eye. He runs a different sneak. Get it clearly in mind, friend Louis, that Blandison is a royal scamp. He keeps his coppers clinking by doing flats on the broads. In other words, he's a sharp, and takes your Master for a flat.

"Well"—Louis fetched a sigh—"when you come to that you do have to admit that the Master is easily spoke to and soon had. Oh, it gives me the grue, the way he goes on with this queer Tom Pat, asking him here for a week with his unicorn ring and tame highwaymen. Not but what the scamp has a rum patter and lips a rum chaunt, but the way he's doing us over is enough to make a man nap the bib."

"Good morning, Louis," said I, drawing back the curtains, in a tone meant to suggest exceptional alertness of mind and strength of character. "What's the weather?"

The rascal pretended to be startled. "I wish you good morning, Your Honour," said he. The auspices appear to be favourable. The beauty of the day has been sullied, as yet, only by the Reverend Mr. Blandison in conference with his head highwayman. The gentlemen are still asleep. It is eight o'clock, sir."

158

"Eight o'clock! Why, that's the dead of night. What's the meaning of this?"

"I have taken the liberty, sir, of assuming that you will wish to make hay while the sun shines. The words, though vulgar, are apposite. They have been written by one Benjamin Franklin, an American. He also says, still more vulgarly, that the early bird catches the worm."

"Ah! You see what happens to worms that get out of bed at eight o'clock."

But Louis was in no mood for frivolity. He had observed, he said, both yesterday and this morning, a remarkable diminution of the vehicular traffic passing our gate, and almost a complete stoppage of navigation on the Thames. This had alarmed him, as an indication of the power which a certain person now in our midst could bring to bear, and he made so bold as to suggest that the time had come for me to make my own arrangements.

"Yes, yes," said I. "Quite so. —Am I to have any tea?"

"While it cools I would respectively remind you that Mrs. Catherine Clive will soon be singing 'Come hither.' Now, if you should manage to anticipate the Reverend Mr. Blandison in his rendezvous with her at the summerhouse it might conduce to the welfare of all parties."

"I see. This is what you mean by urging me to make my own arrangements. You turn me over to Mrs. Clive, and she gives me any further orders she may think needful. —Tea, please."

The young man neglected, in his perturbation, to lay a spoon on the saucer. "What I would propose," he said, "is a course of conduct with much more of the native hue of resolution. In the Honourable John Byron's narrative of yesterday we saw what dreadful things may happen when the captain of a ship neglects his duty. You, sir, are the captain of Strawberry Hill."

Take an hour for it, William, and see whether you can find the exactly right answer to that thrust. I took two seconds, and then said: "This tea is too hot."

"Oh—oh, I forgot the lap-feeder!" Louis exclaimed, handing me the teaspoon. "If you sip it out of the lap-feeder it won't burn your lispers."

Our eyes met, and we both smiled. In a moment we were laughing. I laughed so hard that I had to hand him the teacup, lest it spill over. Whatever wall dividing master from man there may have been between us was down, at least for that hour.

"And now," said I, when I was quiet again, "perhaps you will tell me what you mean by a 'queer Tom Pat.'"

"Why, sir, a 'Tom Pat' is a clergyman—either a true and a real one like the Reverend William Cole, in which case we call him 'rum,' or else a false clergyman like Parson Blandison. Any one ought to be able to see that he's a 'queer Tom Pat.' More than that, he's what we call a 'royal scamp,' a term by which we mean not at all that he has royal blood but only that he rides a horse and robs people without knocking them down. A 'foot scamp,' now, is quite another thing, far less genteel and well mannered."

"And all these wonderful new words I suppose you got last night from your roommate. —Does he talk in his cups?"

"No, your Honour. (By the way, we do not say 'roommate.' We say that he 'dorsed in my lumber.') I tried him with hot gin and brandy, but he would not split his bone-trap. Then I stayed awake to see whether he would snitch in his snooze, but he must have twigged that I was a queer rooster; and so we sat up together and made chin-music the rest of the darkey."

"But you learned nothing about Blandison?"

"Nicks. I learned about tollibon nans, queer plungers and running rumblers and smacking sams. I learned how to do a cock-o'-brass, a skylarker, and perhaps even a rum squeeze at the spell. Along toward dawn my new pal slanged me his mauley and said I should always be welcome on his beat in St. Giles; but about the royal scamp he kept his dubber mummed."

"Then, Louis," said I, handing him the empty teacup, "we shall have to go to work some other way. Please call Mr. Chute and ask him to be at the summerhouse, with pencil and paper, in half an hour. Ten minutes from now you may come back here for a note which I shall write to Mrs. Clive."

"Very good, Your Honour."

The young man looked decidedly pleased at this show of "native resolution" as he turned and left the room.

* * *

Everything went smoothly. A little before nine o'clock Kitty sang "Come hither" with all the seductive trills and roulades of a Drury Lane siren, and then disappeared into the summerhouse as though it were a cuckoo-clock. Blandison's disappointment when he came on the scene a few minutes later, and found only me awaiting him in the shell just outside the window, was well concealed. He sat down beside me and professed his pleasure at this opportunity for an uninterrupted talk with his host. We had a few things to say about the extraordinary effect of Byron's narrative—an effect which Blandison felt he could not hope to rival in his own contribution of the coming afternoon. Then, little by little, the talk veered to quite a different topic. Whichever one of us changed its course, the other was willing to go along.

"It is not every one," I heard myself saying, "who can play the fool in England with impunity. I am one of the few who can—or, at least, have hitherto done so. You know that; and there was one reason for your wish to come here."

His smile was friendly and indulgent as he replied: "Well, sir, you may choose your own words, but we both know that 'fool' is wide of the mark. Should Mr. Chute or Mrs. Clive call you that, and mean it, I think you would be deeply hurt. Morever, this 'impunity' you speak of might better, I think, be called freedom, for you really are one of the few men in England left free to think things out for themselves and then to enact their conclusions. That is why I have come here."

"Think them out for myself, you say; and yet you seem more than willing to offer assistance."

"I merely say that you are free, as of course you will remain so far as I am concerned. If your freedom is lost it will be for the reason that you do not use it. —Have you thought how swiftly it fusts and rots, unused, into that utterly other thing called safety? Have you considered this paradox, that whatsoever freedom a man has, great or small, turns at once into an obligation?"

"No doubt, Parson Blandison," said I, "this is an excerpt from one of your sermons. Please wake me up when you come to what you really mean."

His gaze, which had been wandering at large across the brimming Thames and the many-hued woods of Richmond, came slowly back and met, for three or four long seconds, my own. Rather a startling experience that was, for me. Not often do two persons look at each other so long and earnestly, with such intention to pierce below surfaces. Remember that we were sitting side by side in the oaken shell, so that our faces were less than two feet apart. Remember too what I have already said—or have I?—about the splendour of Blandison's large, strangely luminous eyes. If he were a woman there would have been odes about them, and probably duels. Yet their lustre, at that moment, was wholly of the surface. They did not shine, like Kitty Clive's, from within. I could not look into them, as he, I had little doubt, was penetrating mine.

"I mean," said he, quietly, at the end of those seconds, "to restore the Stuart family to the throne of England."

Again there was silence, broken only—or rather, adorned—by the dulcet jargoning of a blackbird perched on the ridgepole behind us. I let Blandison's sentence reverberate. Then I got up, walked a few paces across the lawn to Kitty's little garden, and plucked two late-blooming roses, a red one and a white. The white one I gave to Blandison.

He looked at it long, closely, and with that admiration for beautiful things which I had already seen in him more than once. "I thank you," said he at last. "You seem to know that the white rose is a Jacobite emblem."

"Every one knows that," I replied. "Is it not the original of the white cockade? Besides, over there in the house I have a silver plate in the shape of a five-petalled rose, with many Jacobite names engraved upon it. One of them, I recall, is that of Charles Edward Stuart, with the date of his birth."

"You say that you actually own this plate?"

"Why, yes. I've had it for years."

"Can you show it to me?"

"I think so. Of course it has no great value, being merely a relic of an enthusiasm now well forgotten; but probably I can dig it out of some pile of debris or other. I'll ask Louis to look for it."

"Pray do! —By the way, you say it bears the date of Charles Edward's birth. What was that date, if you recall?"

"Now let me see. Charles Edward Stuart—that would be the romantic youth whom people used to call the 'Young Pretender' and who called himself 'the Chevalier.' Boyish—wasn't it!—and also a little pathetic. But I think the date was— Yes, now I see it clearly: 'Charles Edward Stuart, Born December 20, 1720.' —Of course that date was according to the old calendar, and nowadays we should say December the thirty-first."

"Right!" he exclaimed. "Exactly right!" He brought his hand down so hard on the side of the shell that it must have hurt.

"Why, sir," said I with my society smile, "I'm delighted to be able to show you an object to which, rightly or wrongly, you attach such high importance."

"Well, but anything is important, surely, which has a bearing upon the heir apparent to the throne of England."

"Ah, but that heirship is not in this instance so apparent as you seem to think. For more than a hundred years the throne of England has been controlled by the English people. They decide who shall be king, and, occasionally, who shall not. Take the time when they drove the second James off the throne and out of the country. He stayed out, and he was a Stuart. Take that earlier time when they cut off the head of the first Charles—a Stuart."

"But, sir, that was a sacrilegious murder!"

"Call it what you like, it showed where the real power lay. —I have also in the house a copy of the order for Charles's execution. It hangs on the wall of my chamber. I call it England's Maior Carta. To me it is worth a shipload of silver plates with the names graven on them of sundry renegades and rebels."

It was one of the really admirable things about this man that he could keep his temper at times when most men in his place would have given way to wrath. He twirled the rose between his fingers, held it at arm's length, and then "I have told you in clear words," said he, "what I mean to do. Your answer has been to pluck two roses and give me one."

"Expecting you," I replied, "to remember the occasion, now just three hundred years ago, when two representatives of the Yorkist and Lancastrian houses met in a garden beside the Thames and there chose two roses, red and white, as their emblems. There followed a long, brutal war in which no one gained anything but England nearly died. —Do you begin to see what my answer meant?"

"Among other things, that you mean to oppose my purpose."

"Right!" I replied. "Exactly right!"

"My hope is, however, that when you have heard how certain my plan is to succeed, and have taken time to consider how its success will affect you and your friends, you may change your mind."

"Be so good as to tell me, first, how your success would affect my friends."

"That needs few words. You and many of your closest acquaintances, including at least two of the gentlemen now your guests, have lived mostly upon the income from various sinecures. I am not questioning the justice of those arrangements when I say that they are solely dependent upon the continued dominance of a certain political party. If that party should fall, what would become, say, of Strawberry Hill? On the other hand, suppose that the return of the Stuarts were made easier by the support of your name. —Mr. Walpole, among the faults of that family you cannot count ingratitude."

The blackbird, unable to compete with Blandison in seductive tones, had flown away. Ten drowsy strokes from the Twickenham church-tower climbed the hill. An elderly cricket, maudlin-drunk on dew and sunshine, was chinking somewhere near. Butterflies purple and golden and brown—I ought to know the names of them, they're so unmistakably my near relations—were sipping the dregs of October in Kitty's garden. Her pigeons, dazzling-white against the blue, went on with their morning drill high above the Thames. On the ruffled silver and blue of the water itself there was not one sail, wherry, or barge to be seen.

This must be the place I've been waiting for in which to mention the stillness that had settled upon Strawberry Hill, or round about it, since Blandison's arrival. Louis had been vaguely aware of it even on Monday morning when he reported "a remarkable cessation of traffic along the road and upon the Thames," and also that no letters or messages had been received. Now, twenty-five hours later, that report still held good, except that it required a certain emphasis. Not to hear any sound of wheel or of hooves for so long, or any voices from the river, not to receive one letter in two days or even catch the blast of the post-boy's horn, and then to look out across the water so many times an hour and find it still sailless, unoared—can you understand that I had begun to feel as though I were living behind thick walls of stone? Or rather, since that suggests imprisonment, let me say that this feeling was a little like what I suppose one would have in living on an island, more comfortable by far than the one Byron had told us about but not much less remote.

*   *   *

Blandison had seemed for a while to forget me, but at length he said: "A man so fortunate as you are, Mr. Walpole, soon comes to feel that almost any change would be a loss. You may have this quiet beauty about you, night and day, whenever you feel for a while somewhat weary of London. You have Mr. Chute's learning and wisdom for guide, and Mrs. Clive's gay charm for an endless delight. In the ordinary way you are not ambitious. What some men call power does not attract you. Of worldly goods you have always had, and may confidently expect to keep, at least enough. Your wish to serve England is satisfied in the House of Commons. —What, then, can I offer? How, as you might put it, can I tempt you?"

I declined to make any suggestions.

"Oh, happy man!" he laughed. "In heaven, then, they will have to provide you with an exact copy of Strawberry Hill as it is on this Tuesday morning, October the fourteenth, in the year of Our Lord seventeen hundred and fifty-five."

"Except for one thing," I replied. "I shall ask to have those horsemen of yours, now riding back from the village, removed."

"But even heaven, one hears, has its guardian angels."

"I felt safer before they arrived."

"Ah, well, safety! Who has it, except the dead? What wise man wants it?"

"Naturally, I can't say about wise men; but to me it has always meant much."

Blandison's voice, when he spoke again, was more vibrant, and I had a sense that he was moving into another phase of a planned attack. "Yes," he said, "I begin to understand how much it means to you. Pray forgive the intrusion, but it is as though life had at some time hurt you to the quick, so that you resolved never again to expose an inch of surface."

"Sir!" I cried out. "Do you—"

"Yes; that would help to explain your studied frivolity, your eagerness always to laugh first even at yourself, your fortress of lath and plaster, perhaps even your collection of hollow iron men."

"But this is intolerable!"

"And yet, do you not often feel that complete safety, supposing you could find and keep it, might some day pall? Think of growing old among idlers, still feeding on gossip, chronicling scandal, playing at life with doll-people who take the son of Sir Robert Walpole as merely another stuffed and painted doll! Is that the privilege which you and your friends are so anxiously protecting against an intruder?"

"We have not called you that."

"But that, I fear, is what you think me; and indeed there was something in the manner of my invitation to lend such a view some colour. However, now that I'm here, I differ from your other friends in wishing for you not an endless and stupefying security but risk, danger, loss and ruin perhaps—in a word, glory."

"Glory!" I exclaimed, trying to smile.

"I said 'glory' unashamed, though it is a word nowadays little understood. Let me remind you, therefore, that it does not mean wealth, fame, power, or success of any outward kind. The longing for glory is the noblest of passions, the manliest of virtues. It is a splendour in the mind and a grandeur of heart which the world cannot give or take away. Glory is the spirit of those same Gothic Ages which you have hitherto studied only in their frippery, trinkets, and gauds. You have tried to turn chivalry into a toy. I urge you to make it the rule of your life."

At a loss for anything of my own to say, I reached for a quotation. "A friend of mine has written," said I, "that 'the paths of glory lead but to the grave.'"

"They do; but does your platitudinous friend know any other paths that lead elsewhere? Shakespeare's Hotspur did not speak so, and neither did the Marquis of Montrose. You remember those manly lines:

> "He either fears his fate too much,
>   Or his desert is small,
> Who dares not put it to the touch,
>   To gain or lose it all."

"My recollection is," I replied, "that the man who wrote those lines died on the scaffold, at an early age."

"Ah, what does it signify where or when a man dies if he lives and dies well? Montrose was hanged, at your age or thereabout, after winning six brilliant battles for his King with a starveling snatched-up horde of Irish and wild Highlanders. He had thrown his total force, his name, his wealth, his love, his life, on the side of glory. Thus he achieved that tragic grandeur which is every true man's aspiration. Through no fault of his, but because the world was not worthy of him, he failed, magnificently."

"And you take me for another Montrose?"

"If I had not thought you capable of heroism I should not have come here. Now I begin to think that I may have been wrong in coming, for I find you sunk in safety and ease. A busy indolence is eating away the best of your years. More and more you convince yourself that England's degradation is none of your concern. Less and less do you protest against infamies which you cannot fail to see. Fear of ridicule keeps you silent when you ought to speak in wrath, and also it drives you into a cynical volubility when contempt should hold you silent. —Do you disagree?"

In spoken words, at any rate, I did not.

"And yet," he continued, "it has seemed to me that a sufficient motive for action might rouse you. I have wondered whether this might be found in your wish to cleanse an otherwise honourable name of certain charges which, without your help, will forever stand against it."

"What charges?" I demanded.

"I have in mind a sin, a sacrilege."

"Has it a clearer name?"

"Call it prostitution."

"Ah, that leaves the Walpoles out. I don't recall—"

"Who said that 'every man has his price,' and acted accordingly?"

"That was my father's blunt statement of a fact which, I think, had been observed before his time."

"But, sir, before his time it was not a fact. In the Civil Wars men fought on both sides for convictions passionately held. Now they will fight for nothing but gain. On both sides in those wars great families went willingly to ruin for causes really great. Now, look where you may, every man and woman is for sale."

"Not Kitty Clive," said I. "Not John Chute of the Vyne. And not Horace Walpole of Strawberry Hill."

With a smile, and in a tone which showed that he knew the precise extent of his audience, Blandison admitted that he had gone half an inch too far. Mrs. Clive, he said, could of course have whatever she wanted for the asking. Mr. Chute he described, not inaptly, as a survivor from the last great age. As for me, I had been raised above temptation when my father provided me with several lucrative sinecures. About other people, the facts were as well known to me as to him, and I loathed them as much. I too, said he, felt ashamed that the readiest way for an Englishman to secure high preferment in our time is, first, to acquire great wealth by any means fair or foul, and then to bribe this or that German mistress of a German usurper.

I declared with heat that my father had never done that; but the man seemed to know everything, and had all that he knew at instant command. "Why, certainly not!" said he. "As Chancellor of the Exchequer Sir Robert was able to operate on a much grander scale. He bribed the Queen herself, and so could afford to neglect her rivals in the King's affections."

"But," I cried, "he was her friend!"

"Ah, yes; and his 'friendship' for Queen Caroline cost England one hundred thousand pounds per year. —At the same time, of course, he was 'friendly' toward the King, in exactly the same amount."

"No doubt that was done," I suggested, attempting a smile, "to keep peace in the Royal Family."

"You try to dissemble your shame in various ways, Mr. Walpole; but, in the degree that you are an English gentleman, you feel it. All your life you have seen, and must have suffered in seeing, how the stain of corruption that bears your father's name spreads slowly outward and down from the Hanoverian Court into every phase of the nation's life."

I tried to deny any such knowledge, but was overborne. "You must know, for example," said he, "that Amelia Sophia de Walmoden wheedled a peerage out of the man you call George the Second for a 'friend' of hers who had shown his 'friendship' by a gift of twelve thousand pounds. You are aware that this same courtesan, for five thousand pounds, sold a bishopric to another 'friend,' a clergyman. —It was about her, by the way, that the usurper wrote from Hanover to his wife at Hampton Court: 'I know you will love the Walmoden, for she loves me.'"

I told him that, although amazingly well informed, he did the Walmoden wrong. "That affair of the bishopric," I said, "was not a commercial but a sporting transaction. The King's mistress laid a wager of five thousand pounds with her clerical friend that he would be appointed a bishop. He must have known that the odds were against him, for the appointment would have to come from the King, and he was known to act in such matters upon the advice of such women. Nevertheless, the clergyman took the bet, lost it, and—paid her."

"How amusing! How it must titillate a cynical taste to watch a

foreign whore debauching the clergy of England! But, sir, I have
known several true cynics in my time, and you are not one of them.
Behind your fashionable grimaces any one can discern a man who
loves his country and hates whatsoever degrades it."

The answer to this did not immediately come to mind.

"Am I right, Mr. Walpole, or wrong?"

But my thoughts were in a whirl. Never before had I been so rushed
at, bowled over, and trampled. —Or perhaps it was that I had seldom
before been taken, even by my closest friends, so seriously.

Blandison leaned back, crossed his legs, and snuffed once or twice
at the white rose. "We agree, then," he said, "that you feel these
defilements as a smear upon your personal honour. They are that, and
will so remain until you have done your utmost to cleanse England
of them."

"I agree to no such thing. It is utterly absurd to charge one man,
one family, with the sins of a nation."

That calmed him a little. He even allowed that England was already
far gone in corruption when Sir Robert came to power, and this because, having "hired herself a king, so called," she naturally assumed
that money could do anything. Once the shrine was profaned, as he
put it, what holiness was left in the temple?

I thanked him for a "handsome admission" which at least pointed
in the general direction of the truth. If only he would now go a step
farther and admit that even under the Stuart kings . . .

But he was not through with his charge against Sir Robert. Any
man, he said, who maintains and extends and profits by an evil
thing, even though he does not begin it, is guilty of that evil itself.
Equally culpable, in his opinion, is the man who, taking nothing for
himself, habitually sneers at the higher motives of human conduct and
panders to those that are base. This, he said, was precisely what my
father had done, and nothing I could urge about the necessity of
working with men and things as one finds them was of the least avail.

This may startle you, William, and I feel the shock of it even now.
Perhaps you cannot believe that an intelligent man of the world could
say such things and mean them. You may suspect that I have intentionally misled you in suggesting that there was something formidable
about a man who now turns out to have been a moralist, old-fashioned,
even naïve.

Let me say, then, that for my account of Blandison I claim no merit

other than simple fidelity in reporting what he said and did, together
with our conjectures about him in their order as they came. For, however such things are managed in fiction, it is clear that in actual life
we learn about people little by little—guessing right, guessing wrong,
looking now at one side and then at another, seeing at first only the
outside and then, perhaps, catching a flash from far within of something quite other than we expected. It is when those flashes come that
I, at least, begin to pay close attention. In other words, it is when a
character seems to contradict itself that it takes on the hues of life.

But do you develop that notion, or else leave it out. What I have to
say is, first, where I think this morality of Blandison's came from
and, second, what it meant to me.

It came out of the past, as he did. Wherever born, and of whatever
parentage, the man was a temporal foreigner—one of those waifs and
strays among the ages whom we call "modern" for no better reason
than that their bodies inhabit our time. Meanwhile their thoughts,
moods, hopes and fears, are elsewhere, not of our kind.

I may seem to talk nonsense, but at any rate it comes out of a long-
standing conviction. Often, when listening to an orator in the House,
I have felt that ancient Cato might have spoken thus, or Catiline, or
great-hearted Roland in the sombre pass of Roncevaux. And it is not
wholly a matter of eloquence. My cousin Conway, with no remarkable
powers of speech, keeps about him wherever he goes an air of forgotten grandeurs. Once in an old baronial hall hung with faded
banners I set a plumed helmet on his head, and instantly the world
was younger for me, and nobler, by three hundred years.

And now for the importance to me of Blandison's downright belief
in good and evil, fair and foul, right and wrong. Briefly, it made him
more dangerous, gave him the huge advantage of simplicity and directness as against—whatever I am. Had he been what is called a wicked
man, a brilliant man merely, a self-seeking adventurer, a gambler and
no more, or nothing but an actor superbly gifted and trained, why
then, with the help of my friends, I might have known how to treat
and perhaps to defeat him. But against a good man on fire, tempting
me to virtue, striving to seduce me into martyrdom, heroism, glory . . .
Oh, William!

Think, too, how I had been crippled for this encounter by those
Gothic ramblings on which you and Mr. Chute have guided my infant
steps. Blandison had heard about them. He seemed to know how often

and irresistibly I am lured away from our dull time by the glamour of the ages that can never change, dwindle, or fade. Therefore I could not merely look blank and stare when he spoke of "honour" and "glory." Moreover, he spoke of them not in your cool and erudite manner, as though he had discovered them in black-letter folios, in mouldering tombs, or amid the debris of castles long given over to foxes and owls. There was nothing in the least antiquarian about him. Instead of retreating into the past he came charging out of it, bringing it with him alive.

* * *

Blandison's purpose, you remember, was to show that the name of Walpole had been darkened by a cloud of obloquy which I alone could dispel. Let me spare you the further recital of his charges, most of them patently absurd, against my father. —Ah, but no; I must not omit the accusation that Sir Robert was the "only begetter" of that third, middle, or commercial class which is now bustling so briskly forward amongst us, elbowing right and left, and has already—so my informant averred—taken over the Parliament, the Court, and the Throne. You should have heard—yes, and seen, for it showed in his face—the disgust with which he described this *profanum vulgus*, as he called it, lifting a phrase from my namesake of long ago.

Blandison expressed a fear that all England might some day be overrun and subdued, flattened out, by these vulgarians to whom, he said, their ledgers are Holy Writ, bankers are priests, millionaires are heroes and saints, and the only god is Profit, the only devil Loss. In their language, I was told, such notions as glory, honour, and goodness are lumped together in the one word Wealth. They create nothing, but only collect. "Beauty," they spell with a double *o*. The Church, to them, is a means of keeping poor people quiet, and the armed forces exist solely for the protection of their money-bags.

"There is nothing behind these people," Blandison declared, warming to his theme, "—no experience of leadership, no love of the land, no skill in any craft. Neither is there anything within them except an omnivorous insatiable maw. Yet these are the people, Mr. Walpole, on whose behalf the Chevalier, ten years ago, was turned away. These, too, are the only people who will benefit by your refusal of my offer. Given forty years—you may live to see it—they will make England rich, mighty, coarse, crude, and intolerably dull. To prevent that desecration there is only one chance: that the gentlemen of England may rise in their wrath while there is yet time and take back their own."

*   *   *

Two of Blandison's arguments had some force. He pointed out that, however I might feel about the King, I need not hesitate to move against the present Ministry, Whig only in name, and composed of the very men who had forced Sir Robert's retirement.

"True," said I, "and the very men who devised that trick of Jenkins' Ear which, on Sunday, you described with evident delight."

"Sufficient unto the day," he replied, "is the argument thereof, and unto the year the trick. In 1739 Jenkins' Ear served us well; but we cannot depend upon it forever."

I suggested that if we could judge from the men who had taken my father's place, or even from Captain Byron's story, this Ear did not seem to be wholly beneficent. He agreed, even admitting that there had been a rapid deterioration in its influence since the start of the war with Spain. What that meant to him, however, was not that the trick had been evil but that we must now, and at once, devise a new one on a grander scale.

"At once," he said, and the phrase reminds me of the effect he made upon us all of a man in whose thoughts "Now or never" was continually sounding. That is not, to be sure, what one would deduce from his having a week to spend at Strawberry Hill, apparently doing little there except amuse himself and us. I would say, though, that Blandison had an unusual power of combining action with leisure. In spite of what he said to me in the hermitage on Sunday, we seldom saw him in haste; yet in one way and another he made every moment contribute to his purpose. He was like a man determined to reach a certain goal at a certain hour who has thought out precisely the time required for every stage of his journey.

Blandison's sense that the time of a deed is part of the deed itself was explicit in the second of the two arguments in which I saw some validity. "The Elector of Hanover," said he, "is nearing seventy, and if he dies in the next three years England will then have as regent the Duke of Cumberland, more appropriately called 'Billy the Butcher.' You know the man. In fact he was here only a few months ago, blundering about in your castle like Gulliver in Lilliput. Think of that hulking brute, if you can, as England's ruler, imitating his cousin Frederick of Prussia, making war to feed his vainglory, taxing out of existence all such places as this to support his armies! But even that is pleasanter to contemplate than what will be in store if ever the third of these Hanoverian Georges comes to the throne. Him you do not know; but I can tell you that in the span of his eighteen years he has accumulated an ignorance which, even when one remembers his ancestry, is phenomenal. He has been brought up on the one idea that what England most needs is a tyrant, and that idea is all that his head will ever hold.

"But now I have said enough. To sum up, I put the whole matter thus: the signal event of your lifetime will be the overthrow of a hired king and the return of England's true sovereign. In this action you will be conspicuous either by your participation or by your absence. —Which shall it be?"

* * *

We heard eleven strokes from the Twickenham tower. I could scarcely believe them, for to me the last sixty minutes had seemed thrice as many. I remember feeling a half-humorous compassion for Kitty Clive, so unused to sitting still and listening to other people. How tired Mr. Chute's hand must be, and how twingeous his poor gouty toe! And yet it was for Horace Walpole that I felt sorriest of all. What had he done to deserve this?

"I take it," said I at last, "that you are offering me a place in your band of highwaymen, but once more I fear that you flatter me. I cannot ride a horse like your gentlemen in reduced circumstances, and I have little skill with the weapons they carry. Besides, I could not possibly learn to take orders from you in the way of the person you call Sir Edward Livermore."

"You mistake the nature of my invitation," he replied, "but, what is more important, your tone suggests that you would reject any offer I might make."

"With the customary regrets, of the usual sincerity, I should."

"Well, sir, the sincerity of your regrets may increase."

And then indignation did speak out. "Sir," said I, turning sharply toward him, "it is just possible that you are trying to frighten me. If so, let me assure you that it will take more than your fifteen mounted ruffians to have any such effect. Your slight acquaintance with my affairs does not in the least daunt me. I am not impressed by your hints at mysterious shadows in your own life, or by what I know about the gathering just now of sixteen thousand soldiers and hundreds of transports on the French coast. All my fears of that sort I took out during the Rebellion of Forty-five, and I shall never have another such panic."

"Why, certainly not! But panic is nothing to the point. What I urge upon you is reason."

"Begin that word with a *t*, and I shall believe you."

"Let us leave the word 'treason' out of this discussion. It is an unpleasant name given to rebellions that have failed, and we are not interested in any such rebellions. Along with that word let us avoid all others that imply a moral turpitude. I am not tempting you to evil, but urging you to act upon the highest principles and noblest feelings of an English gentleman."

"Ah," said I, "how romantic and old-fashioned this sounds! You Jacobites are apparently unable to understand that England has grown up since the Stuart family decided to live abroad. You still hold to the hoary superstition about the 'divine right of kings' and yet want to talk about 'reason'! I tell you, sir, that here at home we have made other arrangements."

"Evidently. And do you know . . . But of course you can't imagine how amusing it is to hear the builder of Strawberry Castle, with a roomful of old armour rusting away upstairs, inveighing against things old-fashioned and romantic. Why, sir, this entire place is a deliberate anachronism. Take the painted glass in the window behind us. —It stands ajar, I see, as it did yesterday while I was talking with Mrs. Clive. —Well, that glass is older by far than the Family of Stuart, yet I see that you are attempting a restoration."

"Only corpses and madmen," said I, "are perfectly consistent. I put fifteenth-century glass into my eighteenth-century windows, but I do not assume while gazing through them that they give me the real hues of the outer world."

He smiled, and said: "You win that trick."

"Or again," I continued, "there's that Gothic armour. I collect it and show it to my friends, but for daily wear I prefer what my man has been learning from your man to call my 'toggy,' my 'kickseys,' and my 'squeeze-clout.' "

"You take another trick," said he, laughing almost out loud.

"But not the game?"

"Oh, by no means the game!"

"And yet, if you would only think a little more deeply about that armour . . ."

"How do you mean?"

"I mean that the notion of a living man encased in metal is really, if one dwells upon it, dreadful. One may smile at the awkwardness of getting into such a cage; one may laugh at the spectacle of the ironclad hero knocked off his horse and helplessly sprawling; he makes a ridiculous clatter of sollerets and cuishes and tassets as he lumbers along; but think of the loneliness inside that breastplate, the frantic dreams under the helmet, and the stupidity of his notion that so long as his skin is whole no one is injured! —Now, I am not trying to make a point, or even, as Byron puts it, to 'take you there.' For the pitiful thing is, sir, that you are there already. You are a man imprisoned in armour, and your friends at Strawberry Hill would like to help in getting you out."

That was a good speech, William, whoever says so, and perhaps it made some impression. There was a perceptible pause before Blandison said, laying a hand on my knee: "I thank you heartily, and all the rest of my new-found friends. —Just now we are considering whether you are to have any part in the restoration of the Stuarts."

"That happened ninety-five years ago."

"But history can repeat itself—and will."

"Your confidence is astonishing."

"At any rate, it is absolute."

"But, sir"—here I rose and stood leaning toward him with one foot on the edge of the shell—"you have not once chance in ten thousand."

"Oh?"

"No. You can do nothing without the French, and more than once you Jacobites have found them fickle allies. If they should try an invasion they would find us as much an island as ever, with a fleet now far stronger than theirs and an army, now ready and at home, larger by two-thirds than it was in the Forty-five."

"Naturally," Blandison cut in. "The hired German on the throne hires every year more German soldiers to keep him there."

"Consider too," I went on, "that the sound defeat of the last uprising is not forgotten. Neither is the blood-bath that followed. The few Jacobites we have left, though stupid exceedingly, have learned the

lesson of the axe and the hangman's rope. The youngsters who tossed
their caps for Charles Edward have had time to grow better brains.
Or, if not, then let them invite their French friends and their 'Young
Pretender' across the Channel. —By the way, he must be as old as
you are, and that's old enough to know better. —But, I say, let them
bring the boy over if they can. Should Charles Edward Stuart appear
in England at the head of a French army, that would be the surest way
of turning every Englishman against him forever."

Blandison gazed for some time at his white rose. I began to feel
foolish standing there, and sat down.

"You argue ably," he said at length, "and with conviction. Yet there
is much that you do not know, and more that you misunderstand."

He paused again, and then, turning to look into my eyes: "Mr.
Walpole," he said, "you would no more betray my confidence than you
would the Chevalier himself if he were here in my place. Supposing,
absurdly, that you should make the attempt, how could your message
escape my mounted gentlemen and those who are watching the river?
Therefore we may speak quite freely, and I assure you that what you
call the 'chance' of restoring the House of Stuart is in fact a certainty. French help will come if and when it is needed, together with
that of Prussia, Sweden, and Spain; yet the point you make that such
matters should be settled without foreign aid—a strange argument to
hear from a sound Hanoverian, by the way—is well understood and
agreed to in Jacobite headquarters. Furthermore, I should not advise
you to rest too heavily upon the notion that the Chevalier is still a
'boy,' and is therefore likely to repeat the obvious blunders of the
Forty-five. In fact it would be unwise for you to count upon his
making any blunders whatever."

"Ah, then," I groaned, "we are lost; for England never makes
anything else!"

"Laugh if you must," he went on, "but sensible men respect their
opponents. About this one you and your kind will do well to consider
that he knows precisely what he wants. You do not. He knows that
the thing he wants is not only his right but his obligation, and against
that assurance you can bring only the ignoble wish to keep those
privileges, unearned and for the most part unwarranted, which you
now have. On his side will be all the advantage of attack, and on yours
the blind confusion and divided counsels of a defence improvised at

the last moment. He can strike when and where he wishes, and you cannot be ready to meet him at all times and places."

"This grows more and more dreadful!" said I, leaning forward and covering my face with my hands. The tone of my voice was not, perhaps, so ironic as I intended.

"Count upon it," Blandison's words came on with a sound as of marching men, "that he will strike soon, close at hand, and hard. Not this time, as in the Forty-five, will he land far off, or depend upon chance-gathered forces, or try to fight his way down through England against forces steadily increasing as his decline. That, if you like, was the plan of a boy, depending too much upon the loyalty of Englishmen and the justice of his cause. The man has not wholly abandoned the dream; but he has learned to mingle it with fact. Therefore his blow will fall suddenly, without warning, upon the very heart of the Hanoverian power. It will be struck by men already gathered, trained, and true to their plighted word."

I managed one more groan, hoping that its sincerity would not be detected. Then, after an interval, I said that I supposed the men he referred to were the same as his fifteen armed horsemen.

Blandison laughed, and replied that, although he liked those loyal lads and admired their high spirits, he would not think of laying any such responsibility upon them. The men he had in mind, he said, were for the most part members of that great band of smugglers, "free-traders," "owlers," or "gentlemen of the sea," who made their livelihood in defiance of the laws laid down by merchants for the protection of merchandise. One and all, they were adventurers, chance-takers, lovers of danger, and Jacobites. For obvious reasons they kept in close touch with France. During the Forty-five they had given much help; but now they were many times as strong, they were organized, and knew what they had to do. In conjunction with the London mob they could and would do all that was necessary.

"The range of your social acquaintance," said I, "is amazing; but I fail to see how the mob of London could help in restoring the Stuarts."

"Naturally you would not see that, for, as I pointed out on Sunday, you do not know London. Though native there, and for most of your life a resident, you have closed your eyes to most of it, stopped your ears, held your nose. That may have been wise, but it has left you ignorant of the cesspools into which men broken by the wars, rotted by the peace, uprooted by the enclosure acts, or else merely poisoned by gin, drain down and fester and spawn. You do not know, and will scarcely believe me when I tell you, that there are districts of London even smaller than this small estate of yours in which ten thousand people are herded together. You have scarcely heard of the hell's kitchens and rats' cradles of St. Giles where crime is a profession and vice the only pastime. You could not even name the kinds of villainy that flourish there among pimps, fences, nickers, scourers, duffers, cut-throats for hire, and leaders of the dodge. Yet those are the people who make up what Justice Fielding called the Fourth Estate. Against them, on the side of the law, there is only the contemptible handful of Bow Street Runners, whose speed is not in pursuit. —Do you begin to see how the London mob might help?"

"But, to turn London over to the criminal classes—"

"How much worse would that make it than it is now? Do you not see that those classes are merely the reflection, in a puddle of filth, of the corruption about and above them? —But there is no intention that the mob shall be for a moment master. It will be used for what it can do, and then—away with it, forever."

"And used how?"

"To throw the city into confusion, so that no warning or message or help can be sent through the streets. Meanwhile a band of chosen men will capture the Tower and others will take the Palace of St. James and the two Houses. The Usurper and his family will be by that time in our hands, strongly guarded and ready for shipment to Hanover."

"So this is what you mean by 'glory'! It is to this riot of crime and horror of anarchy that you extend me an invitation!"

"Hear me out. What I want is order in England, and crime in high places and low overthrown. In this blow the mob will be used to destroy, among other evils, itself. And how? By destroying, first, that power of the money-changers out of which come poverty, vice, and crime as inescapably as a man is dogged by his shadow."

"But the mob is a wild beast, and if once let loose—"

"It has always been the excuse of the sluggard to say: 'There is a lion in the streets. I will not go forth.'"

I told him that these were wild and whirling words, that he talked like a man in a dream; but, as though to prove it, he paid no heed. "We are not now to consider," said he, "whether this blow shall be struck. The preparations are made, and the hour is set. You might as well try to check or deflect a thunderbolt. Our question is whether you can be counted upon, when once the necessary violence is over, to help in the restoration of that political and social order, that 'safety' if you prefer, which is at least as dear to you as to me."

I gasped. "Do you mean that is all—"

"That is all I now ask of you, or have at any time really hoped for."

You can perhaps understand, William, how startling, in its context, that sudden moderation must have been. It was, so to say, explosively quiet. Imagine one who has been nerving himself to refuse a highwayman's demand for his money, his watch, his clothes, and then hears himself politely invited, instead, to discuss a temporary loan over a bottle of wine! —Oh, sir, the effect of that sort of thing upon one's moral fibre is, I assure you, extremely relaxing.

Blandison may have been aware of this, as he was of most things. At least he had given me ample time in which to picture myself on a tall prance-aboutable horse, entangling my legs in a sword, knocking people's brains out with a pistol-butt, and finally cutting the throat of the poor old King, before he explained that all such details would be attended to by subordinate persons, and that my dignified function would be, simply, to look and sound pleased with the results. —Or no, perhaps there was a little more than that involved. I would be asked to see certain persons and to write a number of letters, mostly to leading Whigs, advocating the acceptance of a *fait accompli* which, by judicious management, might be turned to our political advantage. In short, as Mr. Chute said later on, I was being asked to serve as a "trimmer," much as the Marquis of Halifax did in the time of the Revolution. This is a role, in no way disgraceful, for which I may have some talent; and if I were not at least slightly inclined thereto perhaps I should not now be writing in quite this way to a Tory.

Of course I objected that this proposal was based upon a grossly exaggerated notion of my political standing and powers of persuasion. "No one," I remember saying, "pays the least attention to my opinions, so that more and more I give up the trouble of having any." But he seemed to think he knew more about that than I did, and went on to say various pleasant things about me and mine, which were greatly at odds with the harsh remarks recorded above. He told me, besides, that he did not require an immediate answer; and to me that meant that I should have time to consult Mr. Chute.

I leaned far back in the shell and breathed as though for the first time that morning. In Kitty's garden two butterflies, Whig and Tory no doubt, still clung to their respective roses red and white—hung motionless there with gorgeous fans outspread, being too exhausted now by political debate, or else too drunk, to fly away. My private skylark, invisibly high overhead and unmistakably intoxicated, was singing mostly for the angels yet so that a note or two now and then could be underheard by sinful man. From down-river at Twickenham Landing I heard the light-toned bell of the barge that comes up every Tuesday from Richmond, dragged by a ponderous horse. It is part of our weekly routine at Strawberry Hill to watch that barge crawl by; and now merely to know that it was near at hand, punctual as the sun at high noon, gave me somehow an assurance that the dreadful things Blandison was threatening would never happen. For further evidence of the same sort there was the gilded weathercock, still unsmitten, standing proudly and all ablaze on his pinnacle, incandescent with noon-shine.

Blandison had the look of a man who, having done his moral duty for the day, felt free at last to sink back to the level of ordinary men and women. I recall that he made a casual inquiry about the barge-bell and looked somewhat surprised at my answer, but with that exception he sat for some minutes silent. So did I. —And of course you see what that meant. When two people sit side by side for two minutes in an unconstrained and unresentful silence they are travelling fast and far on the road to friendship.

*   *   *

Into this quiet there suddenly broke a swift thudding of hooves, and half a dozen horsemen dashed through the Madlands gateway and plunged down the road toward the river. Blandison sprang to his feet and strode after them, walking diagonally across the lawn at such speed that I could scarcely keep up. "Some slight interruption has occurred, Mr. Walpole," said he, "but pray don't let it alarm you. My companions will soon have everything set to rights and the guilty persons punished."

I was not, in fact, excessively alarmed when, reaching the bank and looking downstream perhaps fifty yards, I saw who the "guilty persons" were. First came the huge old dapple-gray horse, splashing through the shallows and planting his shaggy hooves in the deeper places with sagacious deliberation. Half asleep on his broad back sat a red-haired boy of eight or nine summers. Next came the towrope, slack and dripping, and then the round bows of the barge, painted red to resemble a ripe apple. The deck was cluttered with country produce, including a sow and her nine farrow. A sail, feebly flapping in an occasional zephyr, gave enough help to what tide we have in Twickenham Reach so that the horse, like the boy, was obviously in the enjoyment of a sinecure. But this general effect of ease, somnolence, and *dolce far niente* came to a climax in the "Capting," as he calls himself, who was lounging aft with his left hand—the only one he has—on the tiller. Anyone with the least discernment would have seen at a glance that he was not the man to cause an interruption by any overt act; but then a second look might suggest that neither would he placidly endure being interrupted by others. He looked emphatically the quite indispensable kind of Englishman who knows his place, and in every sense means to keep it.

I wish you knew the Capting, William, for few men of his like are to be encountered, I think, in ecclesiastical circles. His language differs radically from that employed in the oratory of the pulpit, and about his dress you may judge for yourself. He had on that day, as always, a stocking-cap of faded blue against which his face, bronzed by the river-dazzle and vinously ensanguined, shone like the Archangel Michael's in a painted window. This cap he wears in memory of his wife whose stocking it was long ago when she still wore such things, and I judge that he is as inseparable from it, even at night, as Master Jenkins from his water-dog wig. The rest of his garments were, are, and always will be, strangely miscellaneous and nondescript —strangely, that is, to those unaware that he collects his wardrobe piece by piece, here a waistcoat and there a shoe, as he floats along. So, at least, Kitty avers after many confidential talks with the Capting while his horse and grandson were munching the sugar she has taken down to them for bait. She also reports that the "scholard's gownd" in which we see him wrapped on chilly days was taken from what was left of an Oxford student who had "went and drownded hisself only for the love o' wimming, seemingly."

But I fear that, the more I tell you about the Capting, the less you will think him worthy of mention in a dignified history concerned with high matters of state. What has happened, perhaps you are asking, to

that sensitive regard for social gradations in which I am commonly
not remiss? Well, sir, absurd as it sounds, I must ask you to blame
Father Thames, that great leveller inveterately determined to make
the high places low and quite unconcerned whether it be a "scholard"
or a bumpkin that he is drowning, the King's barge or the Capting's
that he bears up. Recall, if you please, that the river and I have been
neighbours through most of my life—at Eton and Windsor and
Downing Street, in Arlington Street, and now at Strawberry Hill.
When I look out of the windows even in the House of Commons, there
he is, though cluttered and sullied by trade, still majestic, mysterious,
familiar, and strange. What wonder, then, that the sight, sound, or
smell of him, the thought of his vast age and perduring youth, his hues
ever changing and his everlasting flow, should bemuse my wits and
confuse my firmest opinions? Be warned of this weakness, and make
whatever allowances, corrections, and deletions may be required; for
just here the river takes command of the story and sweeps it along
not my way but its own.

First of all, probably, you will wish to delete the Capting, and therefore I shall no longer strive his merits to disclose. The tale of how he
lost his right arm, though worth half a dozen sheets of foolscap if
only he were a gentleman, need not detain us here. Neither shall the
"Battle of the Barge," as we now call it, in which he was the conquer-
ing hero. Rather a pity it is, though, that a mere social prejudice of
yours should deprive Posterity of that short, sharp encounter: first,
the smooth-sliding bow-gurgling approach of the vessel with a snowy
convoy of swans about her and a little old straw-bonneted woman
perched high and sole among her tea-things on the cabin roof and the
old horse edging gradually in toward Walpole Landing expectant of
sugar and the red-haired boy looking vainly for Kitty Clive and the
long slack *drip-drop-drip* of the towrope past us and then past the
group of Blandison's derring-doers gathered near by on their stamping horses except for Sir Edward on foot, alert and brow-knitted and
stern; then, second, the brief parley, abrupt, peremptory, stentorian,
wherein the Capting, having been told to go back where he came from,
not only refused so to do but, in regrettably disrespectful language,
recommended to Sir Edward a different and more distant destination;
and last, as if an angel had dropped from out the clouds to turn and
wind a fiery Pegasus and bewitch the world with noble horsemanship,

how Sir Edward vaulted to the saddle and led a splattering swan-scattering charge at the barge and came within inches of glory, when, instantly following some wind-swift sweep of the Capting's left arm long accustomed to do the work of two, he was ignominiously taken in the pit of the stomach, doubled up, all but unhorsed, by a violently hurled, unerringly aimed, mangel-wurzel.

"Low," you say, and I forehear you, and cannot wholly disagree. In fact a clear majority of the ever-quarrelsome House of Commons in Horace Walpole casts the same vote, and, two weeks ago, would have insisted upon having all mention of that vulgarly cacophonous vegetable expurgated from the record. Yet now I bring in the above minority report, even wishing that it were ampler so that you also might enjoy the momentary look of discomfiture on Blandison's face, the dejection of the mounted gentlemen, the agitation of the old lady at the moment of onset, the slightly stressed nonchalance of the Capting as he returned to the tiller, the lustre of the water-drops each enclosing a noonday sun on the wings of the swans again statelily sailing, how the river smoothed itself out and the last bubble burst and then there was only the laughter, clear silvery peal upon peal, of— where had she come from?—Kitty Clive.

She waved a hand to the Capting, called out "Bon voyage!" to his passenger, and then turned all her guns of sarcasm upon Blandison in a raking fire. So, said she, he had at last found something for his brave men to do. How fortunate that the Capting's cat had not been on deck, or the sow running free, else his losses would have been more severe. The next time Sir Edward rode forth, hadn't he better put on one of the iron suits Horry had upstairs, or at least an old-fashioned stomacher such as she could easily provide from the wardrobe at Drury Lane? Oh, she made me ache for him, especially when she pointed out that in two days and nights the fame of this exploit would reach both ends of the Thames. Soon all England would know that some astonishing person at Twickenham, apparently a guest of Horace Walpole, was pretending that he owned the river Thames. Just how that report would advance his plans or conduce to our safety she could not guess.

Six or eight of the horsemen, meanwhile, had been riding slowly along the bank, keeping abreast of the barge. They were by this time perhaps two hundred feet from us, moving in single file in and out of the tremulous willow-shade. It was evident that they had not abandoned their purpose, and were now seeking a place from which to sally forth and stop the horse or cut the towrope.

Kitty saw and understood this, no doubt, but said nothing of it as we three walked along the path the horsemen had taken. She was listening to Blandison's acknowledgment that a serious blunder had been made, and to his opinion that it could be amended now only by holding the captain, the boy, and the passenger captive for the rest of the week. I heard her breath drawn sharply in between her teeth when he said this, but for the moment could not guess how she would take it. All I felt sure of was that she would tolerate no such insolence.

"Why, Parson," I heard her saying after a second or two in which she must have considered and rejected several other possible replies, "I think that would be perfectly delightful! We could keep them in my summerhouse, horse and all—in irons, of course, and properly gagged so that they couldn't talk with the servants. Such an arrangement would be pleasant for me especially, because, as you know, all four of them are old friends of mine. I could drop in and talk *to* if not *with* them for hours every day. You might even allow me to take them something to eat occasionally—under suitable supervision."

Blandison's voice did not show how he was taking this ridicule when he replied: "As I understand it, madam, your summerhouse is preempted for quite different uses, at least in the mornings. —Is there no other place where they might be kept?"

"Not at Strawberry Hill, and Madlands is already crowded to bursting with highwaymen. No; it really must be the summerhouse. Dear old Mrs. Thistlethwaite will love it. She'll die happy."

"Die, madam?"

"Oh, certainly. She's almost ninety-five, you know, and a thing like this can't fail to carry her off. —But, no matter; it will be one last adventure, as good as a play, and for many years her only diversion has been this sixpenny voyage from Twickenham to Hampton and back with the Capting."

I glanced at Blandison's face. It had a look of bewilderment, quickly followed by one suggesting a not unpleasant kind of pain. Then, suddenly letting go of Kitty's arm, he began to laugh. Something inside the man was breaking up and dissolving like the ice of the river in springtime. We had never liked him so much before.

What he was laughing at is for you to find out, in terms of what you know about the man and the whole situation. While you are about it you will please also imagine how he called off his horsemen and we three returned to my landing and sat down there under the willows and laid our heads together. Ten feet away the little waves were whispering "Hush!" among the reeds. We said much the same thing to one another, and wished that we might to the Capting.

Blandison introduced his highwaymen as they came up. They bore good names, old names, but were themselves surprisingly young. Their manners were deferential toward Blandison and easy toward Kitty and me. In their language I heard none of those oddities which Louis had collected the night before from his roommate, but some traces of what may some day be called the Oxford dialect. Indeed I thought that they must have come not from London's haunts of vice and crime but from those colleges up the river in which the lost cause of Jacobitism still flourishes like a weed that can do without soil, rain, or light. There were the ingredients of a gentleman in each one. As they gathered about us with their horses stamping and blowing they showed a true courtesy in their assumption that Kitty and I were on their side, almost of their number. —Yes, and here's an odd thing: both of us felt flattered.

Of Blandison's astonishing notion that he could stop the flow of traffic on the Thames without bringing the whole country down upon us I need say no more than that it was another example of the ignorance we found again and again amid the wealth of his information. The Battle of the Barge and Kitty's ridicule had taught him better. Our problem now was to prevent the story of that battle from spreading, and also to make sure that no such thing could happen again. This would involve overtaking the Capting and the use of methods much gentler than those the highwaymen had employed. It would also require a change of orders to the men who had been stationed by Sir Edward Livermore upstream and down. The first task was assigned to Kitty, and Blandison undertook the greater part of the second.

Our conspirings were brief, and the mounted gentlemen dashed away on their several errands. Kitty Clive then started up-river in my little skiff, rowed by Louis and munitioned with sugar for the horse and the boy, tobacco for the Capting, and tea for the little old lady. Then there was Mrs. Margaret to be told that she need not prepare tea or dinner; there was Mr. Chute and his tyrannical toe to be persuaded; there was George Selwyn to be got out of bed "in the small minutes of the day" and teaed (how do you spell it?) heard, answered, and bundled into the chariot. My cousin firmly refused to leave the house "with all these ruffians about," and we had to leave him. Then, to cap all, Blandison insisted that he must walk, and I with him. Well, no; he did say that I might ride Sir Edward Livermore's charger and then he, Blandison, would go on his black stallion; but I replied that if I was to meet my death before we got home—and already I felt decidedly "fey"—I meant to do it on my own feet.

" 'Fey'?" said he, his eyes lighting up. "I learned that word in the Highlands ten years ago, and have scarcely heard it since." —As though that had anything to do with my vexation, my all-but prostration, after being hectored all morning, witnessing a battle, hugger-muggering with king-changers, getting George up and down and out, all the while treading the very brink of "glory"! And now, instead of the tea I had earned and a moment or two for collecting my wits, I "must" set forth on a long swift walk with the man who had brought these tribulations upon me!

Blandison ignored my ill humour as we strode along, at twice my normal speed, on the road to Hampton Court. The word "fey" had roused in his mind a swarm of memories, all concerned with places the very names of which were, like John Chester's "Gungywamp," an incantation. Take, for example, Loch-na-Nuagh, Eriskay, Uist, Benbecula, Uskavagh, Kossinich, Raasay, and Jubhard! Something like that must have been the way the Weird Sisters sounded in *Macbeth,* and Shakespeare was only translating. I supposed at the time that Blandison was making them up, like Dean Swift in *Gulliver's Travels,* but since then I have glanced through Martin's book about the Hebrides, and find them all there.

He did not reel these names off for the mere sound of them, as most clergymen do the litany, but filled them, as it were, with weather, faces, talk, adventure. Boats went and came through the mist from Rum to Eigg and to Canna from Muck. Fires were lighted in Cluny's Cage where the treasure-chest was, and in the haunted cave of Glen-moriston. It was astonishing how these recollections rushed forth at the beck of a single word. Everywhere woven in with them was a girl, a young woman, perhaps a lady, whose name he did not mention. She it was who first used the word "fey" in his hearing, and explained that it applies to one who foresees his own approaching death, with the place and manner thereof. So the bagpiper McRimmon had done, said she, when he led the march against the Castle of Moy and declared before setting out that the rest would return but the McRimmon would never. And there was this odd fact in addition, that the men marching behind the McRimmon saw him shrink from six feet to one and then to an inch until the blast of the blacksmith's musket from the top of the rocky pass blew him out altogether as one does a guttering candle.

"Hold!" I cried at this point—or, more probably, panted, for I too was guttering and there close at hand was Teddington Tavern. "I must have tea!"

"Tea!"

Into that syllable Blandison packed more amazement, disgust, and reprobation than I had thought any word could hold, and his stern glance showed how ignorant I was of the beverages proper to heroes. He led me firmly by the arm past the tavern and down to the weir, meanwhile narrating how an unnamed young man and woman once walked I forget how many Scotch miles across the moors on a wind-swept day and broke their fast at evening on a cow's head they found in a cave, eked out by a loaf made of oatmeal, brook-water, and the brains of the cow.

The story, though interesting enough, did nothing to allay my own pangs—nearly as strange to me as those of the gout then were—of hunger. Since dinner-time of the night before I had consumed one cup of tea and a thin slice of bread—nothing else. It was now well into the afternoon of a day spent out of doors in strong and constant excitement.

At the weir, and again at Hampton Wick half a mile farther up-stream, Blandison stopped to speak with rough-looking men who seemed to be on watch there, under his command. Then we turned away from the river and into Bushey Park, where certainly I should find nothing to eat unless the King invited us to tea with him at the Palace. On several accounts that seemed unlikely, and therefore I resigned myself to starvation before we should reach Molesey Bridge. That, to be sure, is not much over two miles as the crow flies from Strawberry Hill; but by the way we were taking it would be more like five. Ordinarily I do about that much walking in a week. Blandison was allowing me an hour.

You have seen how boldly this man could come to the point when that suited his purpose; but when it did not he often showed a remark-able fluency in talking about matters remote from his real thought.

An example had been given us in Sunday night's game of whisk, and now, as we approached Hampton Court Palace, even my breathless exhaustion did not prevent me from observing another. His eyes, I could see, were taking sharp notice of roads, paths, ponds, elevations, and distances, as though he might be drawing a map of the region in his mind. Meanwhile he told me how four young cavaliers, imprisoned on the rock-fortress called the Bass, a barren island in the Firth of Forth, had risen suddenly against their guards and captured the rock for King James. They had kept the Stuart colors flying for three years, he said, while the rest of the country grovelled under the heel of Dutch William ; and I too began to look at Bushey Park somewhat as he was doing and saw how readily an army might hide in those thousand acres and then go marching straight down the avenue that leads from Teddington to the Palace, and how they were joined by men who had escaped from William's massacre at Glencoe—men whose chieftain had been slain in his bed by the Southrons after they had lodged with him two weeks and had torn his Lady's rings with their teeth from her fingers—and two of William's ships of sixty guns bombarded the Bass and ran for safety, their rigging smashed and their sails in rags, as Blandison and I emerged from a clump of shrubbery within fifty feet of Hampton Court Maze and saw at its centre, where the two low trees and the benches are, the fat, red face of an elderly man, motionless, stuck there like a daub of crimson meant to illumine an otherwise dull painting of landscape, surmounted by an ill-combed old-fashioned wig.

*   *   *

You have seen the Maze, William. In fact I remember the day when you stood precisely where that old man was standing, and in much the same perplexity. Therefore I need not describe the faded beeches, the red-brick pile of the Palace, the sombre hue of the yews in the hedge, black married to green, with a few golden leaves caught among them. As for the man, let me correct what I said above, that we saw his face. The hedge forming the Maze is exactly five feet high, so that only his eyes, brow, and wig—some three inches in all, were visible to us. He made me think of the bagpiper McRimmon toward the end of his dwindling. But that was disrespectful of me. Had I been a Tory I should have remembered that he was at any rate "every inch a king."

And yet if you had been there you would certainly have felt, as we did, that even His Majesty's resplendent brow was but dim in comparison with the Gentleman of the King's Body Guard of the Yeomen of the Guard—that full title is none too long for the seven feet and upward of his red, white, purple, blue, black, and gold plume, cap, ruff, tunic, cross-belt, breeches, stockings, and rosetted shoes—standing gorgeous, gilt-sworded, steel-halberded, at the entrance to the labyrinth. There indeed was a sight, as some old poet says, to make the rash gazer wipe his eye. He made me feel, as we approached, that I should like to find a convenient wormhole to squirm away into. But Blandison, having just brought his story of the Bass Rock to an end, paused at three paces from this magnificent creature, slightly bowed, and said, making the words ring: "Pray congratulate the Elector of Hanover upon his having found so good a hiding-place. Tell him that he will need it soon."

Had it not been for his huge flaring ruff, heavily starched, the guardsman's mouth would have dropped open. Wooden before, he was now astonied. There was no speculation in those eyes which he did glare withal. We watched him struggle for utterance, but no words came. At length Blandison told him that he might have a chance to reply later in the week, and we moved on.

The King must have heard every word. Furthermore, he had English and wit enough to understand something of what was meant. That being so, there was the question how he would take it, what his women would advise when he told them, and what the Yeoman of the Guard would do. Although the King and I were not officially acquainted, for never once in the twenty-eight years of his reign had I kissed his hand, he might well think that he knew something about me. Bold in action, quick in wrath, a stickler for punctilio, proud as only a little man can be of his soldierly exploits at Oudenarde and Dettingen, he could not be expected to take such an insult with patience.

All this and more I said to Blandison, vigorously. But he and I had exchanged moods since the morning. It was I, for a change, who did the berating and he who refused to be serious about anything. In my opinion I spoke rather well, and I enjoyed the turning of the tables. To be sure I was a mere wraith of myself, breathless, parched, starved, and had far less time for breaking him down than he had taken with me.

And so we came at last, I limping and Blandison bounding, to the new wooden bridge that Sir James Clarke, lord of the manor, built across the Thames two years ago between Molesey and Hampton. A commodious row-barge was awaiting us there, with Kitty and Mr. Chute and George Selwyn already at ease on its cabin-roof. Half pushed from below and half pulled from above, and the rest of me carried by a stout bargeman, I was soon up there also, and seated, panting. A few minutes later the members of the Club of Jenkins' Ear walked across the bridge and joined us. Just as Henry the Eighth's huge astronomical clock boomed two from Hampton Court the rope was cast off, the four bargemen or smugglers or highwaymen dipped oars, and we were off downstream.

*   *   *

Now at this point I should put in a sigh, if only I knew how to spell one—a sigh not of sorrow nor yet of patient endurance but the kind that a hero heaves when, after long pursuit of glory on an empty stomach, he reaches his goal, his guerdon, and finds it to be not a vain empty thing, as moralists assert, but a pin—that is, a caskin, a keglet, a baby barrel—containing about five gallons of Abingdon ale. At any rate, that is what I found when at last I opened my eyes. It was waiting for me there, already broached and dripping great brown beads from the spigot into a pewter mug. I say "waiting for me" because no one had yet had any of it, and Blandison—clearly our host and the master of ceremonies from this moment onward—announced that it was mine to handsel. The only stipulation he made was that I should give myself a few more minutes to cool off and then take, at first, only a few sips at a time. This initial moderation, he said, could be atoned for later on, and it would make all the difference between sudden death and a rapid improvement both in my state of mind and in my bodily health.

He seemed to realize, and did not exaggerate, my ignorance of ale. To be sure, I had always kept a beer cellar for my servants. From boyhood, also, I had been aware that ale was my father's favourite drink, and that too of the many fox-hunting cronies who used to gather about him at Houghton for their Gargantuan feasts. Indeed, it may have been the recollections of those revels that had so long kept me away from ale, even at the distance of iced water. But now at last I was to learn that true temperance lies in the exact mean between water and gin—namely, in the ale that is brewed in the ancient town of Abingdon on Thames according to a monastic formula handed down from father to son—that is, I mean from uncle to nephew!—through at least a thousand years. And if, in the first rapture of this discovery, I carried moderation perhaps a few quarts too far, that was because the ale had to serve as both food and drink.

It did; and before I saw the bottom of that quart mug I began to feel, unmistakably, those ameliorations which Blandison had prophesied. The problems of the morning, though I did not put the answers into clear words, were solved without effort. The vexation I had felt against Blandison gave way insensibly, swiftly, to the recognition that I had in him a companion of inestimable charm, wit, and kindness.

You are not to suppose that I drank the whole pinful myself. Kitty Clive took a little for companionship, but made a face. Selwyn, Byron, Morris, and Adair took a quart each, without faces. John Chester found it necessary to consume several quarts before he could make quite sure that the ale of Abingdon is the equal of that brewed in Connecticut. After his first quart Jeremy Tinker delighted us all by beginning to chirp like a robin in March when the frost thaws out of his throat. Blandison, during the first half-mile, was talking with the oarsmen. Mr. Chute, as usual, enjoyed his drink by proxy. We were all amused to see that he had brought his pencils and note-paper with him. For my part, I was glad, for it seemed probable that some things said and done on this voyage might escape me.

* * *

"Well, sir," said Kitty when Blandison had returned to us and was drawing himself a mug of ale, "I have done what you asked of me. Neither the Capting nor his boy nor his passenger nor his horse will breathe a word about that disgraceful attack. It appears, however, that no sooner do we get you out of one scrape than you drag us all into another. I now understand from Horry that you have grossly insulted the King of England and let him know that you mean to run him out of the country."

"The King of England, madam? Surely, there must be some mistake. —Or can you mean that half-human peacock I spoke to for a moment at the entrance to the Maze? —Why, this is dreadful! I took him for a Yeoman of the Guard."

"You know perfectly well what I mean, and it *is* dreadful. It's a violation of hospitality and a breaking of promise."

"Oh, Mrs. Clive!" and "Oh, Kitty!" exclaimed two voices so nearly in unison that you could scarcely have known and it does not matter which one of us said which. The suggestion that Blandison had been inconsiderate toward his friends was to me, by this time, simply shocking.

But Kitty continued. "First," said she, "you ask us to help save your precious head, and we consent—at a cost of thirty thousand pounds. Then the next thing we know you are putting in jeopardy all the heads at Strawberry Hill."

"What's that? Thirty thousand pounds!" John Chester exclaimed, leaning eagerly forward. "D'ye mean jest for one scalp? Where—Who—"

"Now, Kitty," I cut in, hastening to bury that topic, "you make too much of it. There's no danger. The guardsman never saw me before, and the King is half blind. Besides, he prob'ly doesn't know me by sight."

"Nonsense! There can't be two men in England that look like you. Yes, and from now on the whole Court will know you've been hobnobbing with the—"

Once again she was on the point of divulging to the club members her conviction about Blandison, and this time it was George that saved her. "From now on, Horry," he said, "you will be the most no-Tory-ous person in England. The whole company of the King's Body Guard will be waiting for us at the gate when we get home. I believe they already have Margaret and Louis in irons."

"They could keep them," said Blandison, with a gay smile at Kitty, "in Mrs. Clive's summerhouse."

"Of course they may prefer to take us on the river," Kitty said, glancing backward and round about.

"Only one thing is certain," George mused. "The carpenters are starting to build an extra-large scaffold on Tower Hill."

I was sorry that most of this had to be lost upon the members of the club. Byron and Adair would understand some of it; but the seagoing farmer from Connecticut was obviously bewildered, and Jeremy Tinker's sad little face was a study. To neither of these honest fellows, I suppose, had it ever occurred that the King of England might contribute somewhat to the merriment of his subjects. They were, in other

words, complete Tories, not as the result of thinking but the lack of it.
—Is there any other kind?

I, on the other hand, was thinking profoundly, and whether it was
inspired by the ale or was one of those serendipities—a word I may
explain to you at some less exciting moment—for which I have a
natural talent, there came to me all at once what I regarded as a brilliant idea. "Hush, now," said I in peremptory tones, "and let us hear
no more of this matter. I shall simply ask General Conway to call
upon the Captain of the King's Body Guard of the Yeomen of the
Guard and assure him that it was not me."

Mr. Chute's notes assert that this remark was greeted by an explo-
sion of laughter, but I recall nothing of that. What I do remember is
the look on Kitty's face, ranging through all the degrees of incredulity,
shock, and alarm.

Clearly the ale, or else the serendipping, would have to do better at
once. "Well then," said I, "we can have my cousin tell the King that
if he will consent to forget the whole affair, never mentioning it to
any one, then I'll do the same."

George called this a "handsome offer," but Blandison feared the
"little red-faced man" would be too stupid to accept it. Kitty agreed.
Twenty-seven years of being treated as King of England, she said,
had reduced the little man's intelligence, not remarkably high to begin
with, to a point well below the human level. This, she felt, was not a
thing to laugh at, but to be sorry for. It would happen, under the
circumstances, to any one, however brilliant he might be.

"Just think of it, Parson Blandison," she exclaimed. "Try to put
yourself in— Well, no; but try to imagine twenty-seven years of royal
humdrum and jog-trot, with every one bowing to you, lying to you,
pulling you this way and that, telling you what to say and then saying
it for you, and meanwhile never going anywhere without an armed
guard, never having a friend you can trust! —It's a dull life, sir, and
makes dull people."

Blandison agreed. Almost serious for a moment, he said that only
an ignorant fool would wish to be a king on his own account, but that
there were a few men left in the world to whom kingship was an
obligation.

But I had caught Kitty's drift, and wanted to help. "You haven't
heard the worst of it," said I. "D'you know, Blandison, they only let
the old gen'leman out for an airing once a day, and then he has to go

like a dog on a leash. I mean, there's always this guardsman along to see that he doesn't get lost or torn to bits by the London mob. It's pitiful, Blandison! —And so what does he do in his half-hour of half-liberty? Why, he always makes straight for the Maze, and then for its centre where we saw him today. Years ago he learned how to get that far; but he has never been able to find his way out again. The guardsman has to go after him when his time is up. —Don't you think that's pitiful, Blandison?"

"Another mug of ale," said he, handing me my third, "will help you bear the thought of it. —As for me, I pity the Yeoman of the Guard even more."

"And so," said George, sighing, "do I. They work that poor fellow to the bone. It's hard enough just to remember how to get into and out of the Maze; but after that, as soon as he can change his clothes, he becomes a Yeoman Bed-Hanger and must oversee the preparation of the royal couch according to a formula laid down by King Canute. Then, to be sure, he has a little time for recreation with the chamber-maids; but at two in the morning, when His Majesty has finished counting the pennies his courtiers have let him win that day at loo, this same miserable slave, in a third uniform, turns into a Yeoman Bed-Goer."

"What a long speech, George!" said Kitty. "But there's a sinecure that was made for you."

"Sinecure? Nonsense. He has to light the King to his chamber with a candle and see that he is disrobed according to another formula worked out by Edward the Confessor. Everything is done by rules, I tell you, and they can't be changed even by act of Parliament. Then he locks the bank, puts the key under the royal pillow, pulls the bed-curtains, and, just before blowing out the light, pokes under the bed to see whether the Young Pretender is hiding there. —No, no; he has to work. I shall not apply."

"Wal!" exclaimed John Chester as George sank back, exhausted, "I'll be . . . But don't he say the King's prayers for 'm?"

"Years ago," Kitty replied, "the King learned a prayer by heart. He says: 'God save the King.'"

"And that prayer he owes, oddly enough," said Mr. Chute, "to Charles Edward Stuart. The words were taken from a song—I don't know who wrote it—that grew popular in London just at the time when the Young Pretender came storming down to Derby."

But Blandison, to whom these remarks on the inevitable stupefaction of monarchs were of course directed, was not paying close attention. Having borrowed a pencil and paper from Mr. Chute, he sat down a little apart from us and began taking notes of his own. They had no bearing, apparently, upon our talk. From time to time he glanced out over the King's Home Park, six hundred acres in extent, or back at the Palace, which even at our distance loomed enormous. Kitty asked me in a whisper whether he was drawing a map, but I thought that would not explain his faint smile, his wandering gaze, or the way he now and then ran his fingers through his hair. I said that he must be writing a poem.

Seeing that our trouble-maker was innocently occupied for the moment, the rest of us also quieted down. Neither on the stream behind us nor along the banks was there any sign of pursuit. We had the regular beat of the oars to lull us and the continuing susurration of little waves. Every naiad of the river, every hamadryad half hidden among the leaning willows, held a finger to her lips as we floated by. And then, too, Abingdon ale is not a loquacious drink. At most it induces an inward soliloquy which, though profoundly philosophic, lies either below or above the level of words. It makes a man wise without the effort of thinking, and leads him to conclusions for which he scorns to give any reasons whatever. Reasons bubble up from the wines of France, along with theories, debates, babblings, and other such foreign nonsense. Meanwhile we English drink more and more ale, say nothing, and rule the world.

How strange that I had taken so many years to learn what my father's example might have taught me! Stranger still that the lesson should come from one strongly bent on destroying my father's work! And you will not fail to admire the simplicity of his method: first to browbeat, then to starve and exhaust me, then to endanger, and finally, with only a tacit "Drink or die!" to set me down beside that ale-pin and its five gallons of silent meditation.

I should like to feel that I meditated to some purpose, for hitherto my friends have seemed to disregard my philosophic profundity. They have called me "arch," "sprightly," and "voluble," none of which adjectives has quite the right ring. But now that I know about ale I hope to be praised for the deep things I might say if only I would.

Ordinarily, as I think you will agree, I am an observant person, eager to hear and see and report whatever is going on. That is the favourable way of putting it; but in a Tory caricature I might be shown as a quidnunc, mostly eyes and ears on a long thin stalk, forever bustling up to my friends at the club or on paper with "Here's another thing!" But a different mood possessed me during that voyage and the strange evening that followed. Though not wholly oblivious of external objects and events, I attended mostly to the persuasive, comfortable voice of Abingdon ale. Wonderful things it said—or so they seemed at the time. Of that you shall be the judge; but pray remember that any effort to put such matters into words is like showing a handful of pebbles and shells gathered two weeks since on the strand. They may look rather dull, perhaps hardly worth keeping, with the sea's moist breath and the roar of the breakers no longer about them.

*   *   *

We were rounding now that bold bend of the river where, after the many gropings and tergiversations of its upper course, it turns with definite purpose and makes as straight as Ham Common will let it run for Strawberry Hill. The most delicious landscape in England, perhaps in the world, was slowly opening and unfolding before us, gliding evenly past us on either side, and dimming away astern. The sun, now at our backs and halfway down the western sky, cast a mellow splendour upon every object near and far. Much the same serene and golden light that had glorified my library for a moment on Sunday afternoon was now irradiating the sky, the earth, and the water. It slumbered on the wooded heights of Richmond four miles away, gilded the smooth-nibbled lawns that sloped to the banks, and found out here and there a blunt old church tower, a bronzed oak standing majestically single, or the long liquid furrow cut by the barge's prow. Though the afternoon was not yet old, there came an almost overpowering sense that this beauty, having reached its fragile perfection, had before it now nothing but death. Nay, it was visibly dying from moment to moment as we floated on through the numberless, nameless colours that lay on the stream. It was a fading glory that we saw about us. All the air was laden with farewell.

And yet October, that afternoon, quite won my heart away from the season of syringas and nightingales. I saw how much kinder, wiser, and, so to say, more human, its beauty is—how much more it

says to the heart because it too has felt the touch of time and heard
its final summons. I realized that my devotion to high-bosomed June
and the flaunting pride of midsummer had been inconsistent with my
preference—well known to all who know me—of old women to young.
For that preference there are a dozen good reasons, any one of which
would justify those lines whose author you probably recall but I
forget:

> No spring nor summer beauty hath such grace
> As I have seen in one autumnal face.

The point is that if we're to love old women or old months at all
there's no time to be lost. Have I told you about my friend and neighbour Lady Suffolk—older than God and just as wise and almost as
deaf? Probably not, and at present I won't, except to say that my
affection for her is the stronger because I always feel when we meet
that we may never meet again. Well, and just as I treasure up each
thing she tells me about the court of the first King George—she was
once his favourite mistress and lives here in a house he gave her—so
that day on the Thames I strove against all the downy-winged legions
of sleep to catch and hold every line, hue, and motion. —Isn't that the
right way of looking, as though you would never have another chance?
Because, in fact, you never will.

*　　*　　*

Does this make any sense to you, William, or do you suspect that
I am losing what wits I have had? My own opinion on such a matter
has no value, but perhaps you can judge from the following list of
things I saw that day, saw clearly, and still vividly recall: a flock of
sheep on the riverward slope of a hill near Kingston, each one of them
clad by the western sun in a fleece of gold; a sudden jostle and scurry
of water-hens near the bank, starting a tiny tempest there and setting
the waves all asparkle; an old cart-horse, tired, alone, clumping down
to drink at Hampton Wick, nosing the water, and sending out toward
the barge a series of expanding half-circles; four swallows perched
on a reed, bending it down, until along came a fifth and the reed went
under; heavy moss on the piles at Teddington Lock, intensely green,
bearded, dripping; a swan, pale ivory set on blue as in a cameo, glid-

ing leisurely toward us with a motion soft as the oncome of sleep; and then, I've forgotten where, a shimmer of late sunbeams cast up from the waves against the wall of a whitewashed cottage.

Or again, there was Blandison's poem entitled "The Toying-Place." Put to the test, I could now reword the matter of it perfectly, even though I heard it but once and the author, after reciting it—standing there uncommonly handsome, methought, with the paper in one hand and the mug of ale brilliantly sun-smitten in the other—tore the manuscript into shreds and tossed them overboard. Whole couplets come back to me, and especially that one where the King, having patiently heard his Queen's objections to the Walmoden, replies,

> With all the majesty of five-feet-three,
> "I know you must love her, for she loves me!"

But no more of that, William! If any one is to laugh at the House of Hanover—and that is of course inevitable—I prefer to do it myself. You must be content with my assurance that Blandison's verses, composed and published and suppressed in ten minutes, were a masterpiece of mockery which would have brought your every drop of Tory blood to the boiling-point. What is left of it must by this time be rocking on the Bay of Biscay.

"What's a 'toying-place'?" John Chester wanted to know, and he looked completely unenlightened by the reply, helped out by a Hampton-Courtward wave of the mug: "It's a pasture, overlooked by the palace windows, especially designated and set aside for the amorous dalliance of Hanoverian monarchs."

"What d'ye mean, 'overlooked'?"

"The overlooking," said George, "is done not by the windows but by the Queen."

"An' then, that 'ar 'am'rous dalliance.' What's that?"

"Never mind," from Kitty.

"Ah. I thought so." And John Chester gazed back with quickened interest at the royal residence. "Wal," said he at length, summing up his reflections, "fine place fer it."

All of those memories are superficial, and I am well aware that a good mind, like Mr. Chute's, does not stop at surfaces. I have set them down only to prove that the Horace Walpole you know was there that day, undisguised by the ale, still eagerly snapping up unconsidered trifles, incorrigibly this-and-thatish, and quick as a kingfisher skimming the froth of the river.

*   *   *

And yet Abingdon ale enabled me to sit still for a while on that Tuesday afternoon and listen to a vaguely comforting voice that seemed to come from inside me. It must have been really the voice of Blandison, for he, after reciting his poem, had taken a chair at my side and had gone on talking—not contentiously now, or brilliantly, but in a drowsy tone and a lulling rhythm scarcely distinguishable from the beat of the oars and the whisper of waves. His actual words are irrecoverable, but here's a hint, no more, of the effect they had upon me at the time: "There is nought to regret or forget or lose but all to choose and use as your own while you float and drift and the colours shift and the river draws you the way he knows by rote as he goes with a song and every several note that flows each into the next bears the burden along in the never-hastening drift and float to some deep close where all song sleeps in the safe low place whither now you are drifting with oars uplifted and have no steersman but only the river is drawing you down and down and whether you hasten or linger the thread of the river will surely sing you and bring you securely forever and lay you in that dim willowy island and tavern of twilight and long narrow shadowy room of dark rafters."

That murmur came to me on the verge of sleep, and from there the voice led back through the winding valley of time and showed me scene after vivid scene of the river's history. It gave me to see the rafting upstream of the huge monoliths now clustered at Stonehenge; Julius Caesar rushing at the British pikes with his short sword drawn; Queen Boadicea drinking poison amid the heaps of her slaughtered bowmen; King John signing Magna Carta at Runnymede Ait, and the great Cardinal building the first palace at Hampton Court.

Cardinal Wolsey's red hat—undoubtedly the very one I now have in my collection—vouched for the truth of this entire vision, much as the leathery feelth of Jenkins' Ear in my pocket validates all I am telling you in this letter. The Cardinal himself I did not see face to face; but oh, the monks, William!—hundreds of them, thousands, Benedictines for the most part and mainly engaged in the consumption of ale and eels. This went on in my vision for the eight hundred years and more during which the Thames was a monastic river, as much a tributary of the Tiber as it is in our day of the Elbe; but then there came a man with the wildly heretical notion that England herself should have the use of her central stream. —I'm not sure what your feeling may be toward the King who dissolved the monasteries, but if you had seen him that day come sweeping up the river in his royal barge, his forty oarsmen keeping time to the music of shawms and sackbuts, you would have recognized the advisability of agreeing at once with whatever opinions he might hold on matters temporal, spiritual, or even marital. Tall and broad-shouldered he was, fork-bearded, high-coloured, standing at the prow with his feet wide apart and his thumbs in his belt, garbed all in green for the hunt and making, ah, such a contrast with the tame German kinglet I had seen that day lost in the Maze! The cold blue gleam of his eye as his barge foamed past made me feel for the moment almost a Tory.

*   *   *

Mr. Chute, of course, should have been busier than ever while I was plunged in these deep meditations, but he declares that Blandison's remarks about the history of the Thames were so inaccurate, conjectural, or purely imaginative as to be unworthy of record. He has recorded several paragraphs of what Blandison said on the way down-river about the voyage of the *Centurion*, beginning where she lost sight of the *Wager* off Cape Horn. On several accounts you might expect me to quote this passage in full; but I shall not do so for reasons that will soon appear. A main one is that the story is not well told. Its eloquence rings hollow.

Far more interesting than Blandison's narrative were the interruptions of it by Master Chester. Why was it, he wished to know, that the Parson said not a word about the scurvy and its killing a dozen men a day while the storm was at its height? Why did he make no mention of the time when Commodore Anson ordered all the able-bodied men into the foreshrouds to serve there as a human sail? Again he asked how Blandison had managed to forget the sailor who had been blown off the yard into the sea. Chester himself had tried for years to forget him, but never would. Even now in his dreams the picture often came back, he said, of how they all stood there at the after-rail watching the lost man for minute after minute—for hours, it seemed—while farther and dimmer away in the flying spume he kept unbelievably afloat, still breasted the rolling crests, perhaps still hoped that help might come, until at last it was not his strength or courage that failed but the eyesight of those who stood and prayed and cursed and wept and could do nothing to save him.

I judge that John Chester's wrath at these omissions was not due to mere disagreement with Blandison's narrative method. It went deeper, to the level of moral indignation—that level, I mean, to which we English, and evidently the people of Connecticut also, try to reduce all differences of opinion. Of course he had never heard of the "epic style" or the "grand manner," but with equal certainty he detested its bland ignoring of all sharp-angled fact.

I find a passage where Blandison, no matter in what connection, quotes that empty balderdash with which Samuel Johnson opens his "Vanity of Human Wishes":

> Let observation with extensive view
> Survey mankind, from China to Peru.

Now you may be sure that the lines are rolled forth in Blandison's golden voice with a magnificence that would deceive nine cultivated persons out of ten into the belief that they must mean something. But the Connecticut farmer is not satisfied.

"Whoa, thar!" he calls out, raising a hand. "I don't git that. Put them words into English, Parson, an' let's see what they come to."

The notes give Blandison credit for a brief pause, after which he offers this really honest paraphrase: "Let observation with extensive observation observe the human race extensively."

Then Chester sums up: "Ah! I thought so! Them words don't mean a damn thing. They're jest wind on the stummick."

Here at Strawberry Hill we are now agreed that Blandison had no part in the *Centurion*'s voyage, and that everything he told us about it on that Tuesday was drawn from the well known account—I know you have read it, as I have also—written or compiled by one Richard Walter and published some years ago in London. Mr. Chute was the first to discover this interesting fact. His record of Blandison's narrative ends, after four or five paragraphs, with these words of his own: "For the rest, see Walter."

Thus far, I say, we agree; but there has been much debate about the bearing of this matter upon the question of Blandison's veracity. On the one hand he seems never to have said in so many wards, even when describing the landscape of Juan Fernandez to me on Sunday, that he had taken the voyage. We cannot, therefore, charge him with explicit prevarication; but my cousin sternly insists that the man certainly meant to deceive us. The honest thing, he says, would have been for him to admit that his narrative was based upon a book he had recently read, eked out by his own imagination. Yes, and he goes farther than that—much farther. Having convinced himself that Blandison was "lying" about the voyage, he infers that he lied at least by implication and innuendo about everything. "Remember," says he, "how the fellow never told us right out that he was Charles Edward Stuart, and yet again and again . . . Well, doesn't that prove that he wasn't?"

There's something about that argument, though I am not the man to say precisely what, which I fear would not stand logical examination. For my part, I rest upon Mr. Chute's recollection that Blandison seemed "not a whit put out" by Chester's attacks, but rather, if anything, invited and deliberately incited them. Apparently he was not much concerned to convince us that he had sailed with Anson, but because of his agreement with me he really did want to have the major naval exploit in the War of Jenkins' Ear well told. At the same time he must have realized that Master Chester's talents lay not so much in continuous story-telling as in wrathful interruption and objurgation. At any rate, the bland superficiality of his own tale, whenever he had a chance to go on with it, gave ample opportunity for the other's outbursts.

Any one of these, as they stand in the notes before me, would make a lively letter by itself alone. Mr. Chute had now begun to "get the hang," as they say in Connecticut, of Connecticutensian English, and even in his diluted rendering it has a pungency, a force, and a strange new sort of humour, which I wish we might import from our American colonies. And then too, apart from the man's racy speech, there are the remarkable and at times all but incredible things he asserted and related, piling wonder upon wonder until his listeners could only surmise that the age of myth-making had come again. Take, for example, his account of the never-ending war on Robinson Crusoe's island between the goats introduced by the Portuguese and the dogs brought in by the Spaniards to kill the goats so that English bucca-

neers would be unable to replenish their supply of meat after rounding
Cape Horn. You, as a true-born Englishman, will be glad to know that
the dogs have been unable to exterminate the goats, so that our noble
countrymen are still able to renew their strength on Juan Fernandez
and sally forth from there to the slaughter of Spaniards and Portuguese alike. Your national pride would be flattered, too, by the tale of
how fifty-eight Englishmen took the treasure-town of Paita—somewhere on the coast of Peru, I think—merely by shouting. Your heart
would be moved by the story of how the flagship was driven from her
anchorage somewhere in the Pacific with only a dozen men aboard,
all of them invalids, and how the rest of the ship's company stood and
watched her disappear beyond the horizon, bidding adieu for ever as
they thought to their country, their friends, and all their domestic
endearments.

But haven't I crowded enough different kinds of things into the
three hours, more or less, since I climbed to the cabin-roof of the barge
and drank that first mug of Abingdon ale? If I should now start in
on the stories John Chester told us you would soon feel as unable as
I was at the time to distinguish between our ten-mile voyage down the
Thames and Commodore Anson's circumnavigation of the globe. One
of us has to keep his head during the rest of this chapter, and that
one must be you. Therefore let it suffice that shortly after sunset on
Tuesday October the fifteenth, seventeen hundred and fifty-five, His
Majesty's Ship *Centurion* dropped anchor in the port of Canton and
Blandison's barge at the same moment nosed quietly alongside the
small wooden jetty, tottering, mouldering, smothered in moss, of
Twickenham Ait.

*   *   *

This ait, this alluvial isle, river-born and for hundreds of centuries
fed on the fat of the river, lies less than a mile downstream from
Strawberry Hill. Considering how few feet it rises above high-water
mark and how the roots of its lush vegetation must drink directly
from the river itself, one may call it both solid and liquid at once.
Long and narrow like a great ship moored in the midst of the current,
it often lures me into the notion that it is beginning to move, setting
forth on some unimaginable journey. Often too in the dark of the
moon I have heard, or thought that I heard, wild voices calling from
there in no known tongue, have caught glimpses of lights that seemed

to move in solemn procession. Thus little by little there has grown in my mind a vague guess, half a wish, that Twickenham Ait, so grossly substantial, may yet be a place bewitched, enchanted, perhaps the last refuge in England of those sinister quercine gods anciently adored by the Druids in rites of human blood.

Observe that I call this "a vague guess," and admit that it is "half a wish"—a wish born no doubt of the need we all feel, in an age that grows tamer year by year, for strangeness and danger and distance. And yet you well know how inadequately superstitious I am, and how hard it is for me to maintain belief in things that simply are not so. This weakness, indeed, you have often bemoaned in our discussions of political and religious questions; and therefore you will understand the reason why, until that evening, I had never set foot upon Twickenham Ait. I had feared that my dream of the place would be shattered by the fact, as a bubble instantly bursts upon contact with a solid object.

But now, as we moved along the dim path from the jetty, my friends going ahead and I supported on either side by stout bargemen, I was rewarded in full for this long protection of my own ignorance. Twickenham Ait, seen thus for the first time in the last light of day, had the air upon it, or had at any rate the effect upon me, of immemorial magic. Instead of preserving a dream I found myself walking into one. We had not gone fifty feet among the shadows before I knew that there, within a mile of my home, was all the distance and strangeness I craved. Darkness exhaled as it were from the sod, and silence dripped from the boughs. The ancient pollarded willows, I thought, were holding their breath until we passed. I was dimly aware of presences that had no form, no voice. I felt that we were watched, overheard, and were intruding upon a solemnity beyond our conception. The voices of my friends seemed almost a sacrilege. Kitty's laughter, for once, sounded shallow and thin.

Give me credit, then, William, for a minute or two of religious awe, even though the deities concerned are supposed to have been ousted from England long since by bell, book, and candle. But then the path brought us out from among those brooding trees, and we saw before us not another Stonehenge, as you may be expecting, not a group of priests clad in mistletoe with their sacrificial knives ready drawn, not a band of satyrs dancing about a wineskin, but the most opposite thing to all these that you can imagine—a tavern.

Any house of public entertainment in a place apparently so world-forgotten and given back to the elder gods would have been surprising enough; but to me as an amateur of all things old this particular house would have been astonishing if my faculty of wonder had not been by that time somewhat dulled. You and I, in our antiquarian ramblings, have visited many a Norman castle in which the effect of antiquity is obtruded, even paraded, by shattered windows, broken towers, and cobwebbed halls; but now I would have you imagine a structure, by no means a ruin, which has been in continuous occupation for a time much longer than those baronial halls have been standing. See it as a thing worth attention not on account of any bygone pomp but because it has been used and worn and rubbed smooth by hundreds, thousands of our countrymen dead and gone—yes, and also because in the come-and-go of numberless seasons it has grown to be as much a work of nature as of human art.

I recall the tavern of Twickenham Ait as a long, low structure, hooded with mouldering thatch. Some parts of it were of stone, I think, and others half timbered. Whether there was also some wattle-and-daub in the oldest portions, I did not make sure, on account of the ivy that mantled and swathed it from ground to gable. Such a luxuriant upthrust and cascading of ivy I have never seen—for methinks it is by nature a pagan plant—upon any church-tower or abbey wall. Its verdure was somehow exultant, as though it confidently expected to see all mankind to bed. Faintly lustrous in the early star-shine, it seemed to transform the tavern into a dark green rock, and one fancied that when the fabric of human hands should crumble wholly away the ivy would flourish there alone for ages with no change of shape.

Yet the rock, if it was one, was hollow, and inside it there was a fire. Through the low latticed windows as we came out of the woods we saw a dance of huge shadows and red leaping light on the walls within. There poured into the dusk a confusion of shouts and laughter, raucous bursts of song, a stamping of feet and banging of tables. A woman screamed. The squeal of a violin vainly strove to cut through and ride down the clamour. There was an effect of sadness, even despair, in that uproar, as always there is for me in the sound of revelry heard from a distance. Also there was no slight hint of evil.

Kitty glanced for a moment at Blandison as though asking for assurance. I saw him reply with a slight smile and a nod of the head.

We moved on slowly, stumbling, hesitant. The door of the tavern was open, and filling the doorway, tar-black against the glow of the room behind, the huge square-shouldered figure of a man stood straddle-legged, burly, masterful, with his thumbs hooked into his belt.

But now you must expect no more descriptions, introductions, reflections, or explanations of how this and that came to happen. Instead, you must simply learn what you can as you go along, and when you come to something that you don't understand you may safely conclude that neither did I. The fact is that long before that evening was over I gave up trying to understand anything, and contented myself—as you should also—with believing everything. Here is your chance, indeed, to practise what you have so often urged upon me: first of all one must have faith, and belief will follow.

When we got inside the door and began to peer about in the long, low, narrow room—at the huge fire of logs, the layered smoke, the strange heavy high-backed chairs, and the faces of our fellow guests now all at once silent and wondering—the thing that caught and held my attention was the smell of the place. I cannot help you to imagine that smell, compounded as it was of numberless scents and stenches among which only the odour of sanctity seemed to be lacking; and in any case all the others were submerged by one mysterious ingredient. Even about that one I can tell you nothing to the purpose except that its effect was to bring my hunger all at once to the pitch of starvation. —For surely you have not forgotten the hunger that had been growing in me all the afternoon in spite of my efforts to drown it in ale. Now it changed to famine, and I was ready to eat any item in the larder of Wager Island, whether it were raw cormorant garnished with tobacco, roast dog, rotting seal-meat, boiled shoes, or even—if there was any nourishment in them—the sins of Jacob Grindling.

Our host—his name was Hal Pudsey, by the way, and he wore a forked beard, turning white—seemed to understand my condition at once, and what to do about it. Apparently he understood everything: our names and connections one with another, where we had come from, how we had come, and perhaps—though that was more than I knew—even why. Moreover, he had made his preparations, so that within five minutes after crossing his threshold I was seated at a long table in front of the blazing hearth and earnestly engaged upon a dish the name and nature of which I had not paused to inquire. There had been no time for such idle curiosity, or for the delicate discriminations I sometimes try to make when my housekeeper gives me a choice. Hal Pudsey, I think, had not suggested that there was anything but that one dish to be had, and I saw that every one else at the table—excepting Mr. Chute, of course, who probably had a leaf or two of lettuce—was eating the same thing with evident relish.

At first I took it for a pie, because of the crust; then I realized that it was also a soup. This soup contained onions beyond a doubt, and there was also a strong suspicion of garlic. As for the tertium quid, the main substance of the whole concoction, I was wholly at a loss whether to call it fish, flesh, or fowl, and could only make sure that it was savoury, gustful, lickerish, toothsome, delicious—in short, good to eat.

"What is this, Kitty?" I asked, reaching for my tankard of ale.

"Never mind," said she between mouthfuls.

"Never mind!"

It was the same thing she had said that day to John Chester, and I could not honestly reply: "Ah! I thought so!"—I was not accustomed to such answers from Kitty. It discouraged whatever other attempts at conversation I might have made.

But no one could have conversed during that dinner. I am told that more than thirty persons, most of them facing the fire, were seated at the long table made of loose boards laid on trestles. Our own company, counting the bargemen who had brought us down-river, made thirteen of these; and then there were several of Blandison's horsemen, not including the disabled Sir Edward. The rest were a rough-looking, bedraggled lot, evidently habitués of the place, whom I can only call river-people. They, and especially the women among them, were making most of the noise. The effect of our entrance had soon worn off, and now to the babel of many voices trying to outshout one another there was added the clatter of knives and spoons—we had no forks, by the way—and the rattle of dishes mostly of wood, the banging of tankards, slamming of doors, stamping in and out of servants, and a fierce altercation of wild animals, possibly cats and dogs, over something to eat they had found under the table. —Well, no; it was not a time or a place for the refinements of social discourse. At home, supposing that it could have arisen there, I should not have endured such a din for a moment, but now it was none of my affair. I was learning to take things as they came, and the rapid improvement of my inward condition was rendering me more and more indulgent toward the outer world.

The virtues of tolerance and serenity were well exemplified by our host, who was sitting at the other end of the table with Blandison on his right. Apparently unaware of the uproar, the heat, and the smoke that could not escape through the wide-open door and windows, he was paying exclusive attention to the creature comforts before him. Everything indicated that Hal Pudsey was a good trencherman; and his table manners were correspondingly atrocious. Even I could see that his use of the spoon was decidedly slapdash; and the results of this precipitation were clearly visible, Kitty tells me, on the bosom of his Tudor doublet.

Those last two words will surprise you; but the fact is that our host was dressed that evening in the most extravagant fashion of the court of Henry the Eighth. It was as though he had sent his tailor to study the portraits at Windsor Castle. The sleeves of his scarlet jerkin were so hugely puffed and bombasted that, when standing, he looked as wide as he was long. Even at table he kept on his head a flat velvet cap adorned with a feather and a buckle of massive silver. Now this sartorial antiquarianism was astonishing enough in itself, but of course it looked all the stranger in combination with the habits of a glutton and a sloven. One could only wonder in gazing at the spectacle—or, rather, I wonder now—whether the splendour of those old days may itself have been somewhat squalid.

Sitting there thus gorgeously apparelled and with the full light of the fire beating upon his placid, broad, slightly bloated face, Hal Pudsey was not a sight that even I could ignore. Every time I looked up from my trencher or drank from my tankard, there he was, drawing and filling the eye—filling the whole room, I might say, with argent, sable, and gules. You suspect, perhaps, that he may have been the creature of a disordered fancy; but even in my most sceptical mood I cannot disbelieve in three hundred pounds of illusion. There is also the fact that my friends saw him as clearly as I did. They too had the feeling that they had seen him before, that he was in fact almost as familiar as he was strange. And if all this does not silence your doubts, O man of little faith, I can think of nothing for it but—despite my promise—a description.

Hal Pudsey's head and face, even when seen above the great

shoulders of his doublet, looked large, but his mouth and eyes were small. His complexion seemed to me unwholesomely gray. One guessed that he had once been decidedly handsome, active, and strong, for even now, at seventy and upwards, he was by no means feeble or bad-looking. His square powerful hands were well kept. On the right thumb he wore a large ring—I think a signet. Coarse he certainly was, and yet somehow he escaped vulgarity. No doubt the beard helped a good deal; but there was also the man's calm self-possession, and the feeling that whatever hopes and fears he might once have known had now lost all hold upon him. —Oh, yes, let me add that within his reach as he sat at table there hung from a beam in the ceiling a large bronze bell, green with age, which had once belonged, he told me later on, to Abingdon Abbey. It was with a stroke of a wooden mallet upon this bell that he brought the dinner to an end, summoning the servants to clear the table and put aside the boards and trestles.

These details remain with me now not because I was at the time at all sharply observant of such things but only as the image of the setting sun lingers on in the eyes for some moments after one has looked away. For consider the vicissitudes through which I had that day been dragged willy-nilly by Jenkins' Ear, and the effect the sum of them could not fail to have upon a constitution which, though robust enough for ordinary purposes, yet differs from that of a cart-horse. The strain of the morning, the Battle of the Barge, the five miles on foot, the taunting of the King, the long day in the open air, the ale I had drunk on the river, the voice and the visions and the haunted forest, those astonishing garments, and then more ale and still more, a heavy dinner of I knew not what, the heat, the crowd, the smoke, the stench, the din—all these had reduced or raised me to a harmony of body and mind and spirit hard to define or even to name. I should not call it torpor because it was so pleasant. "Exhaustion" is not the word, for I did not feel even weary. Do you suggest "intoxication"? Nonsense, sir! I am the son of the man who could drink all the Tories in Parliament under the table—that is, except Bolingbroke—and then six hours later stand up in the House and beat Bolingbroke himself in debate. No, there really must be something in heritage after all, for I find that I carry my ale rather well. But if there's no single word, I can at least say that I had a beatific sense of security and well-being. I laid aside and forgot all the anxieties, dreads, doubts, regrets, and forebodings that torment my daily life, fully confident that my friends and Blandison, assisted at need by this potent and deeply experienced host of ours, would let me come to no harm.

Do you see what I mean? For an hour or two I gave myself up, rested back and down, let the world run itself as best it knew how. Nothing disturbed or surprised me. The noises of the room came to me as though from farther and farther off. The habiliments of the river-people looked less and less outlandish. The seamed and battered or swollen faces that looked in from time to time at the open windows and then were lost in the dark, the tall slouch-hatted man with the knife and pistol who leaned against the door-jamb in close whispered talk with Pudsey and Blandison, the maudlin prostitute more coarsely beringed and beraddled than Lady Madlands herself—yes, and even that tremulous ancient clothed in slime and with weeds in his beard who came staggering in to dump a basketful of loathsomely writhing creatures into a barrel by the door—I saw them as though I saw them not, or at any rate with no horror, no shrinking or reprobation, perhaps somewhat as they are seen by Whosoever had made them what they were and let them be.

* * *

"I hope, Mr. Walpole, that you enjoyed your eel pie."

It was Hal Pudsey. He had drawn a chair close beside me in front of the fire, and now, while I was collecting my wits, he told a servant to bring us two tankards of ale and began filling his pipe.

Eel pie! What I chiefly wanted my wits for was to let him know how utterly, all my life, I had loathed the look, the name, the mere thought, of eels—and that as for eating them . . . But then, as I gradually came to myself, of course I saw what his question implied. I *had* eaten them, in considerable quantity, and moreover had found them exceedingly good. That realization was dreadful to me, but I felt that it would be absurd for a man who must be by this time in no small part composed of eels to declare that he hated the creatures. What I did say, evading the question, was that I had eaten at least four helpings, and possibly five.

My host expressed his gratification. He had long felt, he said, that if only I would give his pies a chance . . . But for some reason . . . Well, at any rate and at last, here I was, and he was delighted to make my acquaintance.

Of course in a way he knew a good deal about me already, after all the years I had lived at Strawberry Hill. People would talk; and whatever they said on the river, upstream or down, was sure to be heard before long at Twickenham Ait. Take only the Capting now, going up and down twice a week and always stopping in for a mug whichever way he was heading. Well, that single one-armed man with an over-aged horse and an under-aged boy to help him, could gather and report more solid information than all the six newspapers in London.

Oh, yes, indeed! What with the Capting and the gentlemen of the road and the gentlemen of the sea, not to mention what the servants brought in and the talk of the village and that of gentlefolk crossing on the ferry, many things about the Honourable Horace Walpole had come to Hal Pudsey's ears, by no means all of which he had believed. No, indeed; not by any means all. Now take what some people said about—ah—well, about my relations with Mrs. Clive, for instance. Some people—he could mention names, but that was never good for the trade—would say anything, but he, Hal Pudsey, knew better, partly because of the Capting but then too, now that he'd had a look at me, because he had eyes in his head. After all, Hal Pudsey hadn't kept a tavern on Twickenham Ait for sixty years—and a tavern, by the way, with a convenient toying-room upstairs—without learning to tell at a glance whether So-and-so was the kind that had relations or, contrariwise, the other kind.

Hal Pudsey, who had seen all kinds, was convinced that each of us should live and let live and attend to his own affairs. To be sure, a little neighbourly gossip over a mug now and then was a harmless and pleasant thing, but when it came to dowager-talk and sitting in judgment and trying to make bad blood, he drew the line. Now take all the jeers and the fleers about the house I was building up there on the hill, which was a thing quite different from having relations because it was done in public and so every one thought he and she had a right to speak his mind. Well, to be sure, he himself had never seen my house close to, let alone inside it, and it might really be as odd a place as people said, but Lord love you, wasn't an Englishman's house his castle, and if he tried to make it look even more like a ruined castle than a house fit to live in had I ever heard of any law on the books that could stop him?

No, and neither had he; and if Parliament should enact and try to enforce such a law then he, Hal Pudsey, would wish to be the first

Englishman to break it because if such a thing once got well started there was no place for it to end short of the horrors of the bad old Puritan time when Parliament even tried to tell people how they must and must not dress. Of course he had inherited his house as it stood from a long line of Pudseys reaching back to ages before the Romans came, and he wouldn't like to make any changes, but when it came to the clothes he wore—

At this point I roused myself to inquire whether his way of dressing, for which I expressed a strong admiration, was not almost as much an inheritance as the house he lived in.

"Ah," said he, speaking in a deeper tone and in far more cultivated accents than he had been using as a tavern-keeper, "so you also see that, Mr. Walpole!"

"But how," I asked, "could any one help seeing it?"

"Many do. Almost every one does, in fact, somehow 'help it.' The public, sir, is now so deboshed by seeing on the throne of England nothing but oafish German squires that a man who looks like a king for the best of reasons, and dresses accordingly, is to them a monster."

He had moved a little away, and had laid down his pipe and tankard. I thought he squared his shoulders slightly, and his thumbs strayed toward his belt.

"Your first name," I said, "is Hal."

"That is so. I am the sixth Pudsey of that Christian name born in this house since the night, well over two hundred years ago, when King Hal was stopped here by a storm on his way from Westminster to Hampton Court. The Tudor strain, as you see, is a strong one. It keeps coming back, in son after son of this house—though never before, perhaps . . ."

He paused there; but his thumbs had now found his belt and I saw what certainly looked to me—though of course you must still allow for many things—like the original of Holbein's portrait of Henry the Eighth.

He held that royal pose only for a second or two and then, with a shrug and a smile suggesting a sort of contempt for such boyishness, slipped back into the tavern-keeper. Two more tankards of ale were brought us as he drew his chair back to my side and set his long-stemmed pipe once more alight. Blandison also was smoking, I saw, as he sat with some twenty others at the far end of the room. All those

twenty, with my friends among them, had apparently forgotten Hal
Pudsey and me. Their gaze was upon John Chester, who I judged had
by this time run away with Blandison's story and was really "taking
them there." Even the river-people were quiet, were fascinated, it
seemed, as they listened to this strange, wonderfully vivid New England English. The eyes of the bargemen shone. The highwaymen from
Oxford were more deeply absorbed in the tale of the *Centurion* than
any of them had ever been, I warrant, in the talk of the learnedest
tutor. Now and then a sentence or two of Chester's story reached me,
and I was tempted to join the group about him. That, however, would
have cost some effort, and, besides being perfectly comfortable by the
fire, I wanted to know more about my present companion. I saw that
Mr. Chute's pencil was racing. Kitty Clive turned halfway round,
smiled, and waved a hand. There was no beckoning in her gesture.

Hal Pudsey was saying that certain tavern-keepers he knew of
tried to profit by the legends, true or false, that Queen Elizabeth had
slept for a night or two in their houses. Well, but what if she did?
Nothing ever came of it, and there was nothing to show for it after
she was gone—except, of course, the bankruptcy of that particular
house, because Queen Elizabeth never paid her score. On the other
hand, when her father stayed overnight with almost any one you
might expect something to happen, and, nine months later, something
to show.

I replied, politely, that it showed even two hundred years later, but
then went on to suggest—still politely, I hope—that his evident pride
in the bar sinister was somewhat unusual.

His answer would have delighted you, William, if only for its erudition. Good heralds, he quietly informed me, did not say "bar" but
"bend sinister," or else "bastard bar" or "baston." Thus your pupil
was corrected by an innkeeper, and John Guillim's *Display of Her-
aldrie* proves him right. I fear, however, that you would be less
pleased with his remarks upon bastardy in general—and in his opinion
it is general indeed. He asserted that if the truth were known, and
also told, by the College of Heralds there would not be one coat-of-
arms in the kingdom without its bastard bar. And then another thing
he said, even more disconcerting to one's family pride and notions of
social rank: that if you could trace through twenty generations all the
blood that has poured into any one family-stream, say that of the Wal-

poles or the Pudseys, you would certainly come to the conclusion that every one now alive in England—not counting, of course, such recent comers as John Chester—is related to every one else.

But now once more about that bastard bar on the Pudsey escutcheon. My host's feeling was that the family, already in King Hal's time an exceedingly old one and somewhat "run-out," had profited by this engrafting with a wild young stock like the Tudors, recently imported from Wales. He thought that almost any kind of bastard was good for a family now and then, but that one sired by Henry the Eighth—for weren't his people themselves mostly illegitimate to begin with?—was likely to be more than commonly rejuvenating.

But this was not the only benefaction to the Pudsey family for which my host felt grateful to his royal ancestor. Another one was that he had brought about the Reformation in England, and consequently the dissolution of the monasteries, thereby checking the rapid depletion of the eels in the Thames upon which the Pudseys had always mainly depended for their sustenance. You may not be aware of the connection, William, and I think historians seldom mention eels among the causes of our break with Rome, but Hal solemnly assured me that if the monks had been allowed to live beside the Thames in such vast numbers for another hundred years there would not now be a single elver between Thames Head and the Nore. He did not assert, but perhaps expected me to infer, that King Hal had ousted the Church of Rome at the special request of the family.

As my host was by no means an unintelligent man, I suspect that there was a good deal of humourous exaggeration in his talk, perhaps not wholly unlike that which Master Chester was at the same time displaying in his tale of the *Centurion*'s voyage. And yet Hal Pudsey was really, without knowing it, an extreme instance of what foreigners mean when they speak of our English "insularity." The fact that his island is scarcely greater in area than my own estatelet on Strawberry Hill, instead of diminishing, hugely enhances this effect. Not merely his diet, his habits, his knowledge and ignorance, but even his moral and philosophic opinions—for he is not devoid of such—are founded upon Twickenham Ait. Montesquieu could scarcely have found in all the world a clearer example of his notion that men's thoughts are governed not by reason or common sense but by the place where they happen to live.

Hal Pudsey has lived on the islet all his eighty-four years—that, at any rate, is the age he claimed for himself—and his people have been there apparently since just after Noah's flood. Nothing, I judge, has happened to them in that time except for the one brief invasion of the Tudors already mentioned. No danger has ever threatened them, and one does not see how anything short of another universal deluge could do them the least harm. Absolute monarchs of their tiny realm, ringed about by the ancient willow-copse, set apart from the stain of the world by the river's everlasting lustration and yet not so far away but that they could know long before the king on his throne whatever wickedness was toward—ah, surely I need not even try to say how soothing the mere thought of their security was to a mind outworn by its own endless to-and-fro! There was a strong inducement to sleep in merely imagining those numberless Pudseys spawned in the mud of the isle since time began, each of them eating his quantum of eel and drinking his portion of ale and sinking back again to enrich that same mud so that others might do the same. The slow, soft, indolent voice beside me droned on and on like the voice of the river itself, floating down and down like a barge on the river laden with poppy and lotus and mandragora and all the drowsy syrups of the world, speaking of eels and the mystery of whence they come and whither they go and by what manner and means past any man's finding out they reproduce themselves, praising the wonderful goodness of Abingdon ale, asserting that the best firewood in the world was that which the Thames brought down and lodged on Twickenham Ait as a pure largess, revealing the ancestral secret that in making eel-pie one must boil the eels until they lie still and then use plenty of garlic, inveighing against the folly of worldly ambition and especially of wishing to be king, declaring that back in 1688 when the Stuarts ran away or again in 1715 after the death of Queen Anne it would have been easy for an unmistakable Tudor to seize the throne, averring that such action would have been absurd in one already seized of a moated realm completely equipped with everything they had at Hampton Court except a maze to get lost in, ridiculing the folly of the Boy in his supposition that he could prevent people like the Capting from their lawful and immemorial use of the Thames, conjecturing nevertheless that the Boy would probably succeed in his ridiculous purpose if only he could avoid making any more such blunders between now and Saturday, confiding that the word had been passed on to him from One Who Ought to Know that he, Hal Pudsey, would do well to bake at least

a bargeload of eel-pies against Saturday because most of London—or
at any rate the hungrier part of it—would be coming up-river on that
day to eat them, confessing that if there was one thing about the river
which he did not like it was floods, reminding me of the deluge of four
months ago in which it had seemed that all the refuse of London was
floating upstream, prognosticating that a not wholly dissimilar inun-
dation might now be imminent, hinting that if I had any goldfish in
my Chinese ponds which I should dislike to have eaten up by eels then
I had better dip them out before Saturday, which would be the
eighteenth of October otherwise known as St. Luke's Day on which
strange things such as Horn Fair were known to happen and by the
pricking of his thumbs . . .

*   *   *

"Is Mr. Walpole asleep?"

"I've been talking to him steadily for at least an hour, and he has
not once opened his eyes or his mouth. Besides that, he has drunk, to
my knowledge, three quarts of ale."

"Mr. Walpole has probably inherited, though seldom used, a remarkable capacity for that beverage. His grandfather, a Norfolk
squire, used to say: 'Come, Robert, you shall drink twice to my once.
I cannot permit a son of mine, in his sober senses, to be a witness of
his father's intoxication.' —Your talk, however, has no doubt been
sufficiently soporific, and he has had a hard day. Let's move our chairs
a little aside, and speak softly."

I went on not opening my mouth or my eyes, having been completely
convinced by this time that a wise man does nothing but sit and wait,
confident that every thing he needs will come to him. It was the easiest
eavesdropping I had ever done. Voices were now coming to me from
both sides, and were making that same odd effect of simultaneity in
things far asunder which I had observed more than once before that
day. With my left ear I heard for the most part tones of reprobation,
an old man's counsel of caution, warnings that Blandison would certainly fail unless he gave more heed to the customs of the river, repeated and emphatic assertions that failure would be after all the best
thing for him—all this intermixed with talk about smugglers, the
Upright Man, St. Giles', scholars on horseback, Horn Fair, and
preparations for Saturday.

John Chester, meanwhile, was pouring into my other ear the capture by Commodore Anson of the Spanish treasure-ship *Cabadonga*, in June, 1743, somewhere in the rolling waste of the Oriental Ocean. He sat farther off than Pudsey and Blandison, but his voice was proportionately louder. An audience of river-people listened eagerly to every word, no doubt misunderstanding at least one out of three and yet gathering the general sense. Remarkable linguists those Thames folk are, scarcely inferior to the Swiss in their working knowledge of many languages and dialects.

Now what ought I to do at this point, with Mr. Chute's paraphrase before me of Chester's vivid tale and twenty pages behind me—that is, on the floor—of steadily down-flowing drowse and dream? Chester's story fairly bristles with actuality, like those tiny vignettes I gave you awhile back of scenes snapped up on the river. It takes you—if I may again borrow Byron's phrase—there. And that's precisely the trouble, for in going halfway round the world to view the sea-battle you must temporarily leave and forget Horace Walpole sitting almost asleep less than one mile from home. He is not, I admit, an exhilarating sight, nor has his conversation its customary sparkle; yet the fact remains that this Tuesday is his day as Monday was Byron's. Its last moments must not be snatched from him.

Perhaps you think I might splice the story that Chester told into my own, somewhat as I combined Blandison's tale of Bass Rock with our approach to the Maze. Well, I'm glad to have that passage admired, even belatedly, but carrying on two widely disparate narratives at the same time takes more energy than I can summon at the end of a hard-writing day. Therefore I accept Kitty Clive's suggestion—she has just been in here and pondered the problem—that I do the *Cabadonga* capture in Blandison's effortless way of telling things and yet telling them not.

John Chester saw the battle from end to end, looking down upon it from his favourite perch on the *Centurion*'s foretop beside his friend Prince Uncas. Those two youngsters caught the first sight of the Spaniard's uppermost sails as they came swaying up at dawn on the last reach of the voyage to Manila from the mines of Mexico. They yelled down to the watch on deck. For the twentieth time they made ready their muskets. They watched the *Cabadonga* wallowing on through the drizzle after the foe was sighted, and then, beyond all expectation or reason or hope, making ready for battle. She fired a warning gun, set her spritsail yard fore-and-aft for convenience in boarding, and began to toss cattle and chests and lumber into the sea. The confusion and hurry on her deck made Chester think of an anthill suddenly torn open.

The Spaniard had thirty-six portholes for great guns, besides twenty-eight swivels on the gunwale. Anson had sixty guns but, after the ravages of scurvy, not enough men to work them. Yet all below there on Anson's deck was quiet now, with every man in his place. Two men stood by each gun instead of the needful eight or ten, each ready to do the work of four or five shipmates whom the sharks had long since eaten. Remembering that they were Englishmen, they were not in the least dismayed by their diminished numbers but astonished, rather, that these mere Spaniards should dare to face them.

A squall of wind and rain hid the *Cabadonga* for some minutes, and when she emerged the Royal Standard of Spain was straining at the topgallant masthead—a purple flag with a shield of gold in the midst, surmounted by a golden crown. Up then at once went our colours and broad pennant, and Anson fired with his bow-chasers and overtook her and gained the weather-gauge and lay within pistol-shot on her leeward bow and began to rake her deck. The great guns began to speak their grave authoritative language, the Spaniards firing in broadsides widely spaced while we answered with one gun at a time and thus kept them from their known tactic of falling flat on the deck whenever they expected a concerted fire. Chester saw Bill Cheney leading a party of a dozen men from gun to gun—running out the piece, taking careful aim, and touching it off. The two men remaining at the gun just fired then immediately began to sponge and reload.

Bill Cheney took careful aim, I ought to say, because the *Cabadonga* was a treasure-ship, and he had no wish to sink her. Captain Byron was delighted to learn that he used in his gunnery the same precise knowledge of where and how hard to hit which he had shown at Portsmouth in swinging his "twig" against skulls.

Chester said that his friend Uncas gave a special kind of yell whenever he "picked off" a Spaniard with his musket from the foretop; and I judge that this noise, of which we were favoured with a startling imitation, must have contributed not a little to the defeat of the foe. It is also to be remembered that these two young men came from a country where powder and lead are scarce, so that if you miss your shot at a wild turkey's eye you are likely to go supperless to bed. At any rate, the yells came in quick succession, and Uncas gave three of them when he felled the Spanish Captain. Shortly thereafter all the ants that were not lying about on the *Cabadonga*'s deck in attitudes of complete nonchalance began scattering down their runways—all of them, that is, except the one engaged in striking the Spanish standard, and his life was spared by the marksmen from Connecticut only at the special request of the Commodore. Even so, sixty-seven of the enemy already lay dead, and on the supposition that John Chester and Prince Uncas accounted for most of them that would provide a sufficient number of yells. Two Englishmen had also lost their lives, not because of enemy action but through the accidental dropping by a cabin-boy of an armful of cartridges.

And then came the booty—two hundred and twenty-seven bags of silver and gold, besides one hundred and ninety-two chests of the same. According to George Selwyn the whole treasure amounted to a million and a half of dollars. Precisely what a dollar is worth in real money, I have long meant to inquire; but when I do so it will not be of George Selwyn.

However, it happened oddly enough that he was the only member of our group at the tavern who could describe as an eyewitness the final disposition of the Spanish treasure. As Surveyor of the Melting of the Mint he had been officially requested to be present on a certain day in April, 1744—I think well after the hour of noon. Probably no such indignity had ever been put upon him in all his years as a sinecurist; but he went, and was rewarded by a spectacle not of course to be compared with the execution of the Scotch Lords but still memorable enough to draw from him a vivid description of the thirty-two treasure wagons, crammed with gold and silver, rumbling up from Portsmouth under armed guard, jolting through the city with thousands at gaze, jingling along Cheapside and up Tower Hill and along Tower Wharf and through Middle Gate and over the moat and into the dismal fortress which you tell me was not built by Julius Caesar.

Let us say, then, that when the last treasure-wagon had been unloaded and the final bar of gold stored away behind lock and bolt and bar and several armed Yeomen of the Guard, Jenkins' Ear had been paid for in full. Half the treasure went to the King, and Anson's share made him wealthy for life; yet even the one hundred and thirty-nine officers and men that survived out of the almost two thousand that had sailed from England four years before got something. I have a print by William Hogarth showing one of the *Centurion*'s men on the top of a coach with a bagful of Spanish gold beside him.

* * *

This is a somewhat cavalier way of handling almost the only event in the War of Jenkins' Ear which an Englishman can remember with patriotic pride. Nowhere in this narrative, however, am I at all concerned to make that war seem anything but what it was: contemptible in motive, disgraceful in conduct, and futile in outcome. Besides that, I want you to remember that the *Centurion*'s circumnavigation of the globe seemed to me a trifling matter as I sat there by the tavern fire half dreaming and half awake. For I too had made my voyage that day into far-off seas and countries. Like Byron I had come to a strange island, had eaten sin, and had won through at the end to a peace of body and mind more precious by far than thirty-two wagonloads of gold and silver.

WEDNESDAY

"Louis," said I, as soon as I had opened my eyes and closed them again because they could not bear the light, "go and take that huge black hand off the balustrade."

"A hand, sir!" he gasped, and between lowered lids I saw his look of alarm—not on his own account but for me.

"A severed hand, yes—or a gauntlet of iron, and gigantic."

"Are you ill, Mr. Walpole? Does your head ache? Have you a fever?"

"Never mind. Go at once, please, and quickly, before the balustrade breaks down."

He obeyed, but was gone much longer than the errand seemed to warrant. I had several minutes in which to realize that my head did ache atrociously, and also that Louis must think me insane. Just as I began to reflect upon the unwisdom of revealing one's dreams to servants the young man returned, with a large steaming bowl not of tea but of something quite different, with a really delicious odour.

Here, I saw, was a chance to evade the question about what, if anything, he had found on the staircase. "What is this, Louis?" said I.

He smiled indulgently and said: "It's a wholesome and comforting drink, your Honour, by the name of 'flannel' which Mr. Selwyn has taught me to prepare for him when he is in your present situation."

I looked at him closely, letting him stand there with the hot bowl in his hands. " 'Situation,' you say. What can you possibly mean?"

"Perhaps you would prefer me to say 'in your condition,' sir."

"Certainly not! The next step would be to call it a 'state.' "

"Oh, no, sir! Last night, to be sure, when Richard Beston and I lifted you out of the barge and carried you up here and put you to bed with straws in your hair . . . But this morning, I am happy to see that it is, at most, a 'condition'—one, sir, which will yield surprisingly soon to flannel."

221

He held the bowl toward me, almost under my nose, with an ingratiating, even a "coaxing" smile of which I did not at the moment realize the magnanimity. Its odour improved upon closer acquaintance, and I really longed for it, felt that it was indeed just what I needed; but such was the violent throbbing in my head and the feeling in my eyes that they were being bored out with hot irons, I must first be sullen and contumacious.

"It's too hot," said I, not looking at it or lifting a hand. "Where's my tea?"

"Mrs. Margaret will send up your tea by a servant in due course. The flannel should be taken first."

Well, I took it, sipped it, liked it, drank it all down, and wished there were more. Louis said, however, that one bowlful would be just enough, and confided that the ingredients were gin and beer seasoned with nutmeg, ginseng, sugar, and brought to the boiling point. I believe he said something, too, about "a hair of the dog that bit me," but that, of course, was based upon a wholly erroneous notion.

I told Louis how much I disliked the tendency of some people to explain all the ills that flesh is heir to merely in terms of what that same flesh has eaten and drunk. This, I said, was a degrading materialism which I was sorry to see in him. He ought to consider, I said, that his master had many anxieties, many toils of the mind and spirit, quite sufficient to bring on headaches, bad dreams, and— But I decided not to mention straws in my hair.

Louis was not paying close attention. As my headache gradually yielded to the flannel and then was dispersed by tea, he let me know that I was not the only one who had suffered mental and spiritual anguish on the previous night and day. Mrs. Clive, after they two had talked with the Capting, had sent him back on foot to look for me. The rest of his day and most of the night he had spent in a more and more frantic search, rewarded only by a rumour that some one had caught a glimpse of me hobbling past Teddington Inn some yards behind a tall, powerful stranger dressed in black.

What was he to think, and what was he not to fear? By midnight he had nearly given up hope. "It was terrible, sir!" he summed up. "I thought of everything that might have happened."

"Except," said I, "that I might be at Twickenham Ait."

"But how could I think that, your Honour? I was not aware that Eel-Pie House is a place in which gentlemen would care to be seen, to say nothing of a clergyman. Besides, we all know your aversion to eels and to ale, the only two things to be had there."

"Eel-Pie House," I mused. "So that's what it's called."

Louis' hands went up, and his eyes also. "Do you mean to say, sir, that you didn't know even that much? Haven't you heard that it's a haunt of smugglers, a thieves' kitchen, a resort of watermen and fishers for eels, not to mention the business of the toying-room?"

Of all that, I told him, I had been quite ignorant. I also said that I was sorry for the anxieties I had innocently caused him, and that I thought we had both better try to forget all about these matters and mention them no more to any one. "Especially," said I, "let us say nothing about that—ah—"

"You refer to the strange object that was not on the balustrade?"

"Precisely."

"Very good, sir. But I make bold to mention three things which should not be forgotten. The first one I have mentioned before: Parson Blandison is not to be trusted. The second is that you never can tell what may happen when I am not there. The third, that Twickenham Ait is a good place to stay away from."

"Yes," said I, making ready to rise, "and the fourth is that when I don't stay away from there the thing for me to drink first of all the next morning is flannel."

*   *   *

But enough of that. It's an odd thing, William, that here I've been writing to you for day after day, thinking about you all the time, seeing you there by your library window reading these pages, and yet have been able to edge in scarcely a word such as one friend says to another. That's not my way, you know; nor is it a good one. Moreover, you must have felt that few of these pages are written in what I may call my style, which is really no style at all but only the easiest way of chatting across the miles and the years. And so you are somewhat perplexed, though I hope not offended. "What sort of letter is this?" you grumble. "The one good thing about a letter from Horace Walpole is that he gives you himself, but here . . . Has the castle of Strawberry Hill been stormed, overrun, and sacked? Has my friend been thrust from the throne of his mind by half a dozen pretenders at once?"

Not for a moment have I forgotten that this is a letter, addressed to the one reader of whom I am assured. Clearly, steadily, as I sit here writing by my library window, I see you reading by yours, some fifty miles north-northwest. Except when you lift or lay down a page, you sit there motionless in your elbow chair whilst the wintry sunshaft travels from west to east across the room. So still and absorbed you are that one might almost take you for a picture—by Rembrandt, probably—of a man reading. You have on that rusty old snuff-stained gown which your housekeeper has so many times tried to destroy and you have as often retrieved from the dustbin. But these are trifling matters, and I do not expect my friends to dress as though for an appearance at court before reading a letter from me. It is the face that counts in a portrait; and your face it is that I watch, study, and strive to interpret.

Are you surprised at this? Considering how many other people I have to watch, do you doubt that I can also pay strict attention to you? But, sir, I have already claimed, and you know that I possess, the power of inhabiting several minds at once. This is so strong in me as to raise the question whether I have any mind of my own. If I have, it is the mind of a man incorrigibly social, with no talent for thinking, talking, or writing to himself. The lack of a listener leaves me dumb. I cannot drive the quill without help. It must also be pulled—just now, by you.

And how pulled? Why, of course, by my intuition of how you will take this scene and that, how such and such an event will move you to wrath, pity, or admiration. I leave out much that would certainly go in if I were writing, say, to Horace Mann, and so could count upon his intimate knowledge of European politics. Blandison's purposes, perhaps even his character and identity, would be less mysterious to him than they are, and may remain, to you. On the other hand, I pause in this letter upon many a scene that would have little meaning to our Ambassador in Florence. He would regard sin-eating, for example, as only a savage superstition. Well, perhaps it is; and yet I think you will never again administer the central sacrament of your faith without some recollection of that wild scene on the coast of Patagonia.

Do you object that remarks of this sort are clearly not drawn by but aimed at you? I am not sure of that. What does iron do to lightning? In any case they show again the steady trend of my thought toward Bletchley Parsonage. They confirm my assertion that you are doing no small part of this work.

You do it, William, by providing me with a reader upon whom nothing that I can say or suggest will be lost—nay, one who is all the time far on before me, expecting and demanding more than I can perform, building up the hints I give into larger, loftier castles of the mind than I have imagined. You do it by supplying my deficiencies, by succeeding where I fail, by making connections and drawing deductions undiscerned by me. You know so thoroughly well how ungifted, untrained I am in extended narration, how inept in portrayal of character and even of how people look. You know my inability to sustain a mood for two minutes together, and that the course of my thought— to call it that—is as erratic as the flight of the flittermouse. And so —even as I often do in the House of Commons while listening to some stammering speech which has almost atoned by its earnestness for a woeful lack of skill—you say to yourself: "This fellow means well, but he needs my help."

Thanks, then, once for all! And may it be your reward that you will create a better story than I am telling. May this hope come true, that when you lay down the last page you will have a deeper understanding than any one else of these recent events at Strawberry Hill. May that week survive in your mind like a picture, a song, a poem, a cathedral, or any other work of man's art wherein the order that underlies and overarches life's apparent disarray is partly disclosed.

But just now, William, you are pulling perhaps a little too hard at the quill. The fact that Horace Walpole is addressing a clergyman does not warrant him in trying to preach. What I mainly want to say is that, like John Chester and his Indian friend, we two and we alone are embarked on this voyage. You stand watch in the daytime, and I in the night; I struggle from wave to wave whilst you look out over the sea; but we are bound together by a mutual trust. I suppose there can scarcely be a closer companionship than this of ours, withdrawn as we are from all other concerns and wholly enclosed, absorbed, in our single dream.

Ah, yes; I can see that you too are possessed by these voices, spellbound by this vision. Your face is that of a man entranced, ensorcelled. The shouts of the village boys on Bletchley Green come to you from amid the crash of Pacific breakers. When you glance out of window to rest your eyes it is not the ivied wall of your little stone church that you see but the agonized *Wager* struggling with storm on the other side of the world. The clock on your bookshelf strikes unheeded.

Your tea is brought in and grows cold whilst you sit, plunged in thought, on the desolate summit of Mount Misery shaped like a skull.

To a stupid reader I should need to explain many things which you understand at once—as, for example, that the narratives of Byron, Blandison, and their companions are all subordinate to the really momentous contest going on here at Strawberry Hill. Just there, in the defence of our castle against a marauder, I should have to tell him, lies the heart of this story. You see that without being told; and also you will discern that the narratives of the Jenkins' Ear Club, though subordinate, are by no means mere entertainments like those of the Arabian Nights, but play each one its part in the central struggle. By this time I think you may even begin to realize that my story as a whole, which at first you thought would fall apart, deals in fact with a single action occurring in one place in a brief and continuous time. You are watching time past flow into the present. You are discovering strands of influence that connect persons and events apparently wide asunder. Now and then you catch a glimpse of that meaning in life which, according to Captain Byron, we must either find or go mad. —Such it is to be a good reader, provided, of course, that one has something in hand fit to read.

How comfortable it is, like your old gown and slippers, not to be writing a book and yet to write! What a luxury to indulge oneself in all the real delights of authorship without assuming any of its responsibilities! Book-writing suggests Grub Street, long words and short commons, stupidity on stilts, and vulgar devices for drawing attention. Success at it brings the suspicion that one has made money by hard work, and failure marks one down as a fool. No; a man of breeding will always hold ink at arm's length, never letting it get into his veins. To bathe in it, to drink of it, to become a corpulent, slightly animated inkpot like Sam Johnson—faugh! Give me, rather, a steady diet of stinking seal-meat! And what shall be said of Samuel Richardson's way of manufacturing letters as merchandise and selling them over the counter? Why, of course, that it amounts to sheer prostitution of the most delicate, dewy, and virginal art, the shyest and yet most confiding, that men have ever devised.

When a gentleman writes at all let it be to his friends; and yet even then, the quill can make but a ghostly squeak compared with the living voice. I keep that in mind, and accordingly postpone many a question. I say to myself that there will come a winter's night, at your fireside or mine, when you will turn and ask: "Now, about that Parson Blandison—who was he, do you think, and what?" Well, sir, that will be a night on which we shall go late to bed. Also I look forward to some green and gold afternoon of next May when we two shall be walking down the shallow valley of the Ouzel from your door to Fenny Stratford—having been invited, probably, to drink tea with the Curate there, or perhaps even with Dr. Browne Willis, that highly estimable rich man and scholar. By that time our left legs will be in good walking order again, and we shall be taking steps to see that the gout will never return.

A breeze from the southwest will be ruffling the reedy stream and turning gray as hoarfrost the leaves of those ancient willows. In the cottage gardens we pass, in the sloping meadows, and standing thick and tall on the Ouzel's banks, there must bloom all the flowers that Ophelia so daintily drowned among. Let us also have a blackbird in full song, a nightingale or so, and, if it can be arranged, a kingfisher fleeting along the "glassy, cool, translucent wave" like a tiny rainbow that has suddenly sprouted wings. See what can be done to have the bells of St. Michael's ringing as we approach, for there's nothing like a peal of bells to make a man rejoice that he is English. Well, and then, as we walk through that picture and hear the heart of our country still beating unconquered and unafraid, perhaps I shall say: "This, William, is what we tried to defend during that week of last October."
—Or, again, I may not. Is it friendship to explain what one's friend knows already?

Let me mention one thing, however, which you might not draw from my written record. I mean the fact that, during all this contest in which both sides perfectly understood that vast issues were involved, we kept our tempers and acted like ladies and gentlemen.
—Ah, mind you, we struck shrewd blows and told home truths as we saw them; yet there were few angry words spoken, and seldom did any voice grow shrill. To ask whether we avoided what, in other circumstances, might be called "cheating" would be to inquire too curiously. You must remember the great issues involved, and the sort of man we had to deal with.

Was it cheating for Mr. Chute and me to repair once more on Wednesday morning to Kitty's summerhouse? We had a right to that seclusion; and if Kitty and Blandison chose once more to sit in the shell outside the half-open window we could no more forbid them than we could help overhearing. What we heard, I set down from Mr. Chute's record:

BLANDISON: It's a comedy we're acting here, don't you think, Mrs. Clive?

CLIVE: H'm. Perhaps. We shall see. I have heard Horry say that all the world is a comedy to those who think, but tragic to those who feel.

BLANDISON (audibly astonished): Mr. Walpole said that? Well, but that is good. Remarkably good. Why, Dean Swift, Pope, Voltaire even, would have been proud of such a *mot*.

CLIVE: Yes, no doubt; but Horry, you see, wasn't trying to be clever. He meant what he said, and so doesn't deserve any credit.

BLANDISON: He meant it? You mean, seriously? But in that case—

CLIVE: Oh, how should I know what Horry meant? Just now I can only feel the bitter truth of his words—to me.

BLANDISON: Ahem! Ah . . . Madam, shall we walk?

Would it be superfluous to remind you, William, that Kitty knew that Blandison knew that every word they spoke under the window was overheard? Perhaps it was only to tease us that she accepted the invitation. At any rate, she rose, and they two walked about the garden. Thenceforward we heard only snatches of their talk. Here is one snatch:

CLIVE: Well, sir, the fact is that although you have been living here for two days and three nights, and in that time have not been noticeably silent, there are now five theories held about you by the people of Strawberry Hill, no two of which resemble each other.

BLANDISON (laughing): But *you* know who I am, don't you, Mrs. Clive?

CLIVE: Oh, naturally! Not for a moment have I been in any doubt. It's only that the others won't believe me.

BLANDISON: Too bad! Too bad! —They must be stubborn indeed to stand out against . . .

And here is another snatch, spoken after an interval of several minutes during which Kitty must have been told that a change of monarchs would be to her professional advantage:

BLANDISON: Yes, indeed. It was the Stuarts who first brought women on the public stage.

CLIVE: Ah, but they sometimes took off again those women who had won the royal approval.

BLANDISON: True. There was Nell Gwyn, for example. She left the stage when she was twenty to become the King's mistress, and never regretted the promotion.

CLIVE: No, I'm sure. We all remember King Charles' dying words: "Let not poor Nelly starve!" But I have none of her qualifications for that exalted office. I was not born and reared in a London rat's cradle; my mother was not a drunkard; I am able to sign my name; and, worst of all, I am somewhat past the age of twenty.

BLANDISON: All such defects will be ignored, dear Madam, by any Stuart who once hears you talk. —But now, to be serious for a moment, may we count you on our side?

CLIVE: This whole temptation, or whatever you may call it, reminds me of how George Handel once tried to induce a famous soprano to sing a part which she thought unsuited to her voice in his *Messiah*. He promised wonderful things—even to marry her—but she wouldn't believe him. Then he argued and stormed and threatened, in vain. Finally he thrust her out of a window and held her there, dangling, far above the street, meanwhile shouting down: "Now, vill you mine music singen? Vill you, I say! —De vort ist 'ja,' oder ich let you to drop!"

BLANDISON (laughing): And did she?

CLIVE: Did she what? Drop?

BLANDISON: No. Sing it?

CLIVE: Oh, I forget. Perhaps I never heard.

BLANDISON: But it's awkward to leave her dangling there. —What would you have done?

CLIVE: I've often wondered. On the one hand there would have been my strong dislike of being coerced, even by a great musician.

BLANDISON: And yet he had offered her an important part in a really magnificent work.

CLIVE: True. But so brutally!

BLANDISON: I don't hold with those German methods—for of course Handel is a German, and a docile servant of the Hanoverian usurper. Now I, as a Jacobite gentleman, believe that there are better ways of persuading a lady.

CLIVE: I agree.

BLANDISON: But again I say, what would you have done?

CLIVE: The right answer to such a brute would have been: "Very well, let me drop, for I will not sing." But about those better ways that you mention I would say: "Please let them continue."

BLANDISON: You can give me, then, some hope?

CLIVE: This much: there are few things that a lady enjoys more than the gradual process, managed by a gentleman, of being persuaded.

*   *   *

More than once in these pages I have referred with little respect to the tribe of writers whom we are learning to call "novelists"—a new-fangled name for creatures equally upstart. Now let me admit that I am finding it hard to maintain contempt for a craft whose secrets I so much need to know. How do these fellows manage—if indeed they do—to suggest the continuing activities of all their people at times when the story must fasten upon only a few? Supposing, now, that the summerhouse scene from which we have just reluctantly turned away had been presented not by a mere gossip-monger, an eaves-dropper, but by a man who really knows how to write. What then? Why, then you would have in mind at this moment not only what Blandison said and Kitty Clive answered but some notion of what George Selwyn was doing meanwhile—that is, sleeping—and Henry Conway also, and my man Louis, and the Club members down at the tavern, even Blandison's highwaymen.

Yes, emphatically; if I were a good story-teller you would know by this time whether those highwaymen are to have a part in the tale that will justify their keep or are merely to stand about looking more or less ornamental and dangerous. Also you would have heard a remark or two from Jeremy Tinker and James Adair, if only to prove that they are not deaf-mutes. For another thing, you would have been told just how it was arranged, to the general satisfaction, that Lady Mad-lands should do her sneering and her Lord his slumbering in their own castle rather than mine. A much longer list of my shortcomings might easily be made, but I fear its effect would be an overwhelming sense of the number of things you must try to ignore, or pardon, or do for yourself.

Yet take the problem of time as an example of my perplexities. Here's the week at Strawberry Hill, from Sunday morning to Saturday's sunset. Ought that interval to be filled like a trunk into which one's valet has thrown everything in sight and then sat on the lid, or only with those articles that may be of use on the journey?

Strike out the vulgar metaphor if you wish, but see what I mean. The question faces me now: Shall I move steadily on at the even pace of time from the summerhouse scene through the dinner hour and so to our gathering in the library at two o'clock? Much might be said for, and by, that method. It would enable me to relate, for instance, how Jeremy Tinker fell into the goldfish pool, was heroically dragged therefrom by Richard Beston, and emerged from the house ten minutes later in a suit of aldermanic broadcloth, many sizes too large for him, which Beston had almost certainly acquired at the pistol's point on some lonely highway. Quite as good in its different way was Blandison's confidential whisper to me that George Selwyn had called me a "mummy," and then his surprise at finding that I like that nickname. At dinner, moreover, we heard from Louis the explanation of those nocturnal explosions which had mystified us ever since Blandison's arrival. It appeared that the highwaymen encamped among us had so terrified one of our Twickenham dowagers that she had ordered her servants to fire muskets out of the upper windows of her house at regular intervals during the night. We made Blandison promise that either he or Sir Edward Livermore would wait upon this lady at once with assurances of her personal safety.

Clearly, any one of these stories would suffice for the main substance of an ordinary letter by Horace Walpole. You can imagine how that carver of cherry-stones would work up the anecdote about Jeremy. He sees the bleared eyes of that embattled dowager suddenly brighten, and thirty years fall from her, at the vision of a handsome highwayman in her drawing-room, sipping tea. But, sir—and here you are to imagine a sigh—after a lifetime of trifling and ladytalk, Horace Walpole has been suddenly called upon to produce nothing less than a prose-epic. Of his utter inadequacy for such a task he is keenly aware. Hence these cries for help, these agonies of the metatarsophalangeal joint, and dreams of gigantic armour. But grandeur, always his abhorrence, is thrust willy-nilly upon him. The Lilliputian is cast ashore on Brobdingnag. Farewell, then, oh, farewell, the steaming cup and what-are-trumps! Farewell to malice and to masquerade, to have-you-heard and so-they-say and who's-with-child-by-whom! Horatio's occupation's gone!

In other words, I find that I must leave out a good many delectable matters and get back to the history of Jenkins' Ear.

*   *   *

"I'm a sailor," says Isaac Morris, standing straight and tall behind the Speaker's Chair as though at the wheel of a ship. The steady peer of his dark eyes through the window and far beyond says the same thing over again, and so do the large bronzed hands, one of them lividly scarred, that grip the back of the chair. And yet it is not that he needs support. He stands there perfectly self-possessed, neither humble nor proud, basing his claim to attention upon what he is, knows, and can do. There's no nonsense about him, and not much whimsy, but the occasional twitch of his thin-lipped mouth gives promise of humour. His shoulders are broad, square, high, and his arms remarkably long. His beard, like someone's in Chaucer, is "yshave as nigh as ever he can," so that the bronze of his cheeks is mingled with blue. One lock of his black hair, drawn together behind in a cue, is pure white. In the lobe of each ear he wears a droplet of gold about the size of a pea.

"I'm a sailor," he says. "That's all I be, or have been, or look to become. Behind me there ain't no mouldered house like Newstead Abbey, no palaces and towers like Parson Blandison's in God knows where, nor yet an old fame and long havage and learning got in a school. Those be good things, and they make good men; but all I am come out o' the sea, as likewise some day it will be going back there, I hope, on the wash of a green wave over the bow."

Feel the slow roll and sway of those words, William. Hear how they abound in the "colloquial barbarisms, licentious idioms, and irregular combinations" of which Samuel Johnson has laboured, I hope in vain, to purge our language. In speech of this sort there is no pretence, and therefore nothing vulgar. It is a language not learned but earned, full of weather, loaded with things seen, heard, smelt, touched, tasted, and done.

"Down to the tavern last night," Morris goes on, "I had me a tell with Cap'n Byron. I told him how I felt about standing this trick at the helm. 'These good people up to the house,' says I, 'they don't know fo'c'sle talk, and more by token they do use a mort o' words I never yet laid a tongue to.'

" 'Talk your own language,' said Cap'n Byron. 'It's sound English, and they'll soon larn it.'

" 'Well then, so much for words; but look you,' I said, 'how this tale has come all atangle. Take one thing: here you get these people worked up about Wager Island and then go away and leave untold a good half, or the worst half, of what happened there.' 'Oh, that's all right,' you say, free and easy. ' 'Tis true that Chepe murdered Cozens on the island along with a few little things like that; but I have to get on with my seal-meat, and so let Isaac Morris tell 'em.' Likewise later on you end your story whilst swimming somewheres on the coast of Chile, like as if you'd gone the whole v'yage just for a bath. But won't folks wonder if you wasn't drownded out there, so's 'twould only be the spectrum o' the Honourable John Byron talkin' here at Strawberry Hill?'

"He laughed. 'Oh, well,' he said, 'I had to stop somewhere, and if I'd gone on—'

" 'Yes,' I said, 'and if you'd gone on you'd 'a' had to sound cheerful and prosperous-like, the which would 'a' guv you a pain. And so it's left for Isaac Morris to tell 'em how you lived on the fat o' the land out there in Santiago and got adopted and wined and dined and dressed like a prince and dandled by the Gov'nor and all the girls wanted to marry you.'

" 'I didn't s'pose you knew about that, Isaac,' he said. 'O' course you exaggerate, but . . . Where'd you hear it?'

" 'No matter where,' I said. 'Point is, I have to tell it. Likewise Mr. Selwyn has gone and guv these folk to think Jenkins' Ear must 'a' dried up and blowed away 'bout the time that 'ar Spanish gold was dumped into the Tower. But not by a jugful it didn't. It went on a-workin' for months and years of wanderin', drowndin', starvation, disease, sudden death, and lyin' in prisons until you wished you was dead. I have to tell that, too; not to mention how everything come out at the last.'

" 'H'm,' he said, 'That's so. You must tell the end of the story and most of the middle and no small part of what happened fust. This really is a tangle.'

"The Cap'n called for more ale and smoked and thought a spell,

and then he said: 'Isaac,' he said, 'here's what I'd do. I'd begin at
the end,' he said, 'and read the record o' the Court Martial you showed
me last night. That way you can get it all in from start to finish, using
the very words that every one spoke. Of course if you want to add
something now and then as it comes along—say about how you got
those earrings—why, that will be your privilege.'

" 'God's truth,' I said. 'A man that wears earrings at Strawberry
Hill, he really did ought to explain 'em. O' course,' I said, 'there's
things like Injun buckskins that ain't been explained, but we mustn't
be unpatient.'

"Anyhow, that's what I'll do. I'll begin by readin' a thing called
'The Deposition of Isaac Morris, Midshipman.' It was made three
days before the Court Martial held on the flagship of Admiral
Steward, then lyin' at Portsmouth Harbour, on the eighth day of
June, 1746. That was nine years and four months ago, with a few
days left over, and I'm glad I don't have to try and remember just
what the Judge Advocate said to me and what I said back. As for
makin' things up like some people not a thousand mile off at this
moment, or else rememberin' what other people wrote in a book, I
can't do that at all.

"I disremember the name o' the Judge, but he was a mite of a man
with little pale eyes and a sharp nose, and choke-full o' fidgets, like a
white mouse. Yes, a white mouse he was on high heels and wearin' a
hugeous wig to make him look taller, with some ten or a dozen long
white hairs by way of a beard—the which hairs wasn't enough to
hide that he had no chin. He come in with a strut and a puff and a
glare into the dark, damp cabin where I was kept and waved me out
o' the only chair and told the man with him to sit on the edge o' the
bunk. Long, lank, and yellow this other man was, but with big laughin'
eyes. Daniel Dickens of Portsmouth he was by name, a wig-maker by
trade, and a master shorthand writer like Mr. Chute.

"Dickens lighted the candle that stood in the sconce and then took
out a sheaf o' paper and five or six sharp pencils. The Judge was
moppin' his brow with a linen hankcher and starin' hard at me. I
folded my arms, leaned me against the bulkhead, and stared back
at 'im.

" 'Take this down, Dickens,' the Judge said, like a white mouse
growlin'. 'Take it all down, and don't you dare change a word.'

" 'Very good, your Honour; I have it: Take this down Dickens. Take it all down and don't you dare change a word.'

" 'No, no! Use your common sense! That's no part of the deposition. Cross it out.'

" 'Very good, your Honour. I have it all down, and I've crossed it out.' "

JUDGE ADVOCATE (to Deponent) : You seem amused, sir. What are you smiling at?

DEPONENT: Nothing. —Or almost nothing.

J.A.: Well, you'd better not. You'll soon see that this is no smiling matter. —Your name, I'm told, is Isaac Morris.

DPT.: So I also have been told.

J.A.: Well, don't you know?

DPT.: Not to be sure. I have only hearsay.

J.A.: Well, I'll be— That is, bless my soul! Never heard o' such a thing! —But perhaps you know whether you are a member of the crew of His Majesty's Ship *Wager,* wrecked off the coast of South America on May the—ah, yes, the fourteenth, 1741?

DPT.: I sailed on that ship on her last voyage.

J.A.: Don't beat about the bush. How old are you?

DPT.: About twenty-five.

J.A.: Don't say 'about.' Answer exactly.

DPT.: I don't know exactly.

J.A.: Surprising. Improbable. Where were you born?

DPT.: In Topsham, Devon.

J.A.: Now there's the kind of answer I like What was your father's position in life?

DPT.: I don't know.

J.A.: Well, then, your mother's?

DPT.: I don't know.

J.A.: Don't try to hide anything from me. We'll get it out of you.

DPT.: You'll never get out what isn't there. I have nothing to hide.

J.A.: Then why don't you tell me about your parents?

DPT.: I never knew them, nor anything about them. I was born a bastard and brought up a foundling.

J.A.: What's that? A bastard! —Take that down, Dickens. Don't change it. —And do you freely admit you're a bastard?

DPT.: I say so.

J. A.: Bless my soul! —And brought up a foundling, eh? Where?

DPT.: Wynnard's Hospital, Exeter.

J.A.: Well then, no wonder you're on the way to— How many other crimes have you been charged with?

DPT.: I have never been charged with a crime. Not even now. I'm being held here on no charge whatever. That's against the law. You know it.

J.A.: Ah. Ahem. We'll see about that in good time, my man.

DPT.: I hope you will, and soon.

J.A.: Insolence, you'll find, will do you no good. Now tell me how long, all told, you have spent in jail. —And remember, we have the records. There's no use lying.

DPT.: If you have the records, why ask me?

J.A.: Answer the question.

DPT.: About three years.

J.A.: Aha! But you said just now you had never been charged with a crime. For what, then, were you imprisoned?

DPT.: For being an Englishman.

J.A.: I will not be fobbed off with nonsense. —Dickens, put it down that the deponent tries to evade my questions. —Now, sir, I give you one more chance. State precisely in what jails or prisons or other places of detention you have been—ah—incarcerated, and also the reasons therefor.

DPT.: You have no right to ask that question, but I am willing to answer it. First, I was held prisoner for eight months by the horse-eating Indians of Patagonia, in their village called Chief Town. That was for me a "place of detention," but I was treated there with far more humanity than is shown in England to known foundlings and bastards.

J.A.: Humph! Is that so! Why did they hold you prisoner?

DPT.: They wanted to adopt me.

J.A.: A strange taste! Well?

DPT.: Next, for two years and over, I was imprisoned on the Spanish ship *Asia,* because my country was at war with Spain. Also, and for the same reason, I have spent four months in a dungeon, living on bread and water, at the Spanish port of Corunna which we call The Groyne. —And now, as you see, I find myself detained on a ship of that Royal Navy which I have served since I was a boy. The reason for this detention, I have not been told.

J.A.: Yes, yes. Just so. —Dickens, you may as well cross out those last few questions and answers. Just say that deponent has been a prisoner of war. —You have been in His Majesty's Navy for how many years?

DPT.: Fifteen.

J.A.: In what rank did you enter it?

DPT.: As a cabin boy under Captain Dandy Kidd.

J.A.: Indeed! A good man, that. Had he lived, he would have gone far. He was a close friend, I believe, of Admiral Anson.

DPT.: Yes. And my friend, too.

J.A.: Come, come! I happen to know that Captain Kidd was a gentleman. As such, he would not be likely to choose his friends from among cabin boys, to say nothing of bastards and foundlings.

DPT.: Sir, we are in this room alone, and you might be seriously injured before the guard could come to your assistance. —Don't suggest again that I am lying.

J.A.: Ah. . . . Mutiny! —Dickens, call the guard! Tell him— But, no. No! Come back here. Sit down. We can't let this get all over the ship. Cross it out. Especially those times I said— You know. Oh, God bless my soul. Where were we?

DICKENS: Deponent was saying, your Honour, that the late Dandy Kidd was a friend of his, and you were saying that he was a bastard.

J.A.: No! No! I said the deponent was a bastard!

DICKENS: But you told me to cross that out.

J.A.: Look here, Dickens, I don't like the tone you're taking. Now you throw all the notes you've taken thus far on the floor, and start again. What I said was that Captain Dandy Kidd was a good friend to have. —Is that in?

DICKENS: Yes, your Honour.

J.A.: Good. Let's see, now. Oh, yes. Deponent will please state whether he had, or has, any other—ah—friends in His Majesty's Navy?

DPT.: Many.

J.A.: He will kindly mention their names.

DPT.: First of all, there was John Bulkeley, the Gunner of His Majesty's Ship *Wager,* and the best friend I have ever had. He may be dead. I don't know. Next came Henry Cozens, Midshipman, killed on Wager Island by Captain David Chepe. Next there was the Honourable John Byron, also a Midshipman. I am not sure that he is still alive. Then, too, there was, and still is, George Anson, once my Commodore and now—as I've heard—one of the Board of Admiralty.

J.A.: Good God! Admiral Anson! Do you say he was your friend?

DPT.: If you doubt it, ask him.

J.A.: Well, of course I don't doubt your word; but for a great man like that to make friends with a common seaman— Most unusual.

DPT.: He was once a common seaman himself. Besides that, I was a Midshipman when he knew me.

J.A.: A Midshipman!

DPT.: Commodore Anson gave me a berth at the request of Captain Dandy Kidd.

J.A.: Oh, great God Almighty! A Midshipman! —But, my dear Mr. Morris, why didn't you say so?

DPT.: I wasn't asked.

J.A.: True. True. *Mea culpa.* —Dickens, tell the guard to bring us in another chair. Have him bring in two chairs, so that you can have one. Yes, yes. Now we know where we are.

* * *

"I don't quite understand," Mr. Chute spoke up at this point, "about the document you have in hand there. It's your deposition, I know, made just before the Court Martial, and you say it was taken in short-hand by one Daniel Dickens of Portsmouth. Later on, I suppose, it was written out in longhand, perhaps by him, so that you and others could read it."

"That is so, Mr. Chute. Me and a few others paid Dickens to make us copies, the which we reckoned would turn out useful in our business. They have."

"But the passages which the Judge Advocate directed Dickens to strike out are still there, apparently."

"Dickens left 'em in this copy o' mine, but took 'em out o' the copy he showed the Court."

"I see. and did he also change your own language a bit here and there—not the meaning, of course, but the words?"

"Ees, fay. He didn't ought to, but I s'pose he reckoned it a kindness to make me talk so cruel bookish. Times here I can't hardly spell out what I must 'a' meant."

"Thank you, Lieutenant Morris. That makes everything clear. Please continue."

"Well, Dickens, he was out o' the cabin and back so's to hear me say 'No, thank you' to the Judge's snuffbox. He moved like a gull on the wing, that man. In less 'n half o' no time there was they two chairs and Dickens and me down on 'em and him once again writin' down, like this:

J.A.: Good for you, Mr. Morris. Never begin the habit, and you'll never have to try and leave off. It's bad for the health and ruins a man's lace. —But don't put that in, Dickens, Certainly not.

DPT.: I should like to know on what charge I am being held.

J.A.: Oh, let's not call it a "charge," Mr. Morris. Rather say that your services are desired as a witness of the wreck. The Court Martial to be held in the great cabin on Tuesday next, beginning at nine, will try to determine the cause, no more, of that event. A trial may follow when the facts of the case are found; yet as a Midshipman and a friend of Admiral Anson . . . You see what I mean.

DPT.: I'm asking why I was taken off the *Carlotta Snow,* which brought me from Portugal, and put into this hole below water-line with a guard at the door.

J.A.: I had nothing to do with that, but I suggest that the officers who —ah—detained you were unaware of your—ah—rank.

DPT.: It would have been enough if they had recognized me as an Englishman reaching home after six years of serving the King. As for the wreck, I should gladly have come many miles, on foot, to tell what I know about that.

J.A.: Are you willing to tell it now?

DPT.: Certainly. Here it is. The *Wager* stood a good chance of being wrecked from the start because she was badly fitted and found, overloaded and undermanned, and was sent off too late in the year. All that, of course, was the fault of the Admiralty. And yet—

J.A.: Now, Mr. Morris, let me advise you as a friend not to say that.

DPT.: I do say it. And yet she might still have lived if her Captain had been an able, sober, and honest man. In my belief, he was not.

J.A.: But, sir, you strike right and left. Every word makes an enemy. To say nothing of the Naval Commissioners, who will read this report and who control your whole future, there is Captain Chepe. Don't you know that his single word will carry more weight than all that can be alleged against him by all his officers and men?

DPT.: Well?

J.A.: But suppose he brings against you the charge of mutiny? Can you deny that the words you have just spoken have a mutinous sound?—There's still time to have them expunged from the record.

DPT.: I heard you tell the secretary to take down every word, and not to change one of them.

J.A.: Oh, yes, but between friends—

DPT.: Later on, I think, you will ask me to swear that I have told the truth, the whole truth, and nothing but the truth. Is that so?

J.A.: But the law can't force a man to incriminate himself.

DPT.: If telling the truth as I see it is a crime, then I am guilty—and ready for the consequences. Have you any other questions?

J.A.: A few. But let me urge you to keep it in mind, while answering them, that mutiny is a serious matter. The penalty, you know, is death.

DPT.: Your next question is?

J.A.: Ah—yes, the next question is—ah . . . Were you a witness of the events, all or any of them, leading up to the death of Henry Cozens, Midshipman?

DPT.: I did not see the shooting of Cozens, but less than five minutes after it I was at his side. From then until his death, fourteen days later, I was with him as much as possible, and saw how he was treated.

J.A.: How was that?

DPT.: With barbarous cruelty and neglect.

J.A.: On the part of whom?

DPT.: David Chepe, formerly Captain of the *Wager,* the man who shot him.

J.A.: Do you assert that Captain Chepe shot Mr. Cozens?

DPT.: I do. Chepe himself, I think, has never denied it.

J.A.: Are you acquainted with any—ah—extenuating circumstances?

DPT.: Henry Cozens had been drunk for days, on liquor provided, in my belief, with Chepe's knowledge and in the hope that he would make trouble. He did. He quarrelled with the Purser and then with Chepe, accusing them both of piratical intentions. It was the Purser who first shot at Cozens, meanwhile calling out the word "Mutiny!" The Purser's aim was spoiled by the Cooper's jogging his elbow. Chepe then ran out of his tent close by, clapped a cocked pistol to

Cozens' face, and shot him through the cheek without asking a question.

J.A.: Perhaps to prevent a riot.

DPT.: If you like. One can always say that. On the other hand, Cozens at the time was unarmed, and there were only two or three other men within hearing. Riots do not start in that way. Neither are they quelled by leaving men to die by inches, lying on the ground uncared for, in the rain. Cozens might have lived if Chepe had allowed us to move him to shelter, or had not forbidden the Surgeon to take the pistol-ball from his jaw.

J.A.: Do you see that you are charging your former Captain with something like murder?

DPT.: With murder, yes. I think he had arranged with the Purser to shout that word and then to fire at Cozens.

J.A.: This is terrible. I fear that some one must hang for this—probably not the Captain. —Can you suggest any motive?

DPT.: A day or two before the shooting one of our seamen overheard an angry talk between Cozens and Chepe in which the name of Captain George Shelvocke was mentioned several times. The Midshipman must have charged the Captain with the purpose of turning pirate, as Shelvocke did after the wreck of his ship.

J.A.: Ah! No wonder Captain Chepe shot him. He couldn't have that sort of thing.

DPT.: As you say. And all the less if it happened to be true.

J.A.: Now really, Mr. Morris, you can't mean to bring that worst charge of all, far worse than murder, against Captain Chepe.

DPT.: Not now. I don't know, and you would not tell me if I should ask, what other members of the *Wager*'s company will be present at the Court Martial. If there's no one who can do it better than I, then I shall try to prove that Chepe meant to turn pirate.

J.A.: In that case, you will certainly be hanged.

DPT.: So I have been told by several persons since I reached home. The thought is not new to me. During all the years of my struggle to get back home I have known that a rope might be the reward.

J.A.: Then you must have felt guilty.

DPT.: Of what?

J.A.: Well, of—ah— How should I know? Say of harbouring evil thoughts against your Captain.

Dpt.: Have you any further questions?

J.A.: Oh, bless my soul! Let's be friendly, Mr. Morris. Surely we can work this thing out if only you won't be so—ah—I think I will say so—hard.

Dpt.: I shall answer your questions.

J.A.: Is it true that a ship's gun was fired at Captain Chepe by members of the *Wager*'s company?

Dpt.: A quarterdeck gun, a four-pounder, was fired twice by Boatswain King and eight or ten others who had remained on the wreck after the rest of us had gone ashore. They had spent the night looting the ship's stores, and all of them were drunk. The balls passed just over the Indian hut in which Chepe and his friends were sheltering from the rain.

J.A.: Did they mean to kill the Captain?

Dpt.: I was not one of them, and cannot say.

J.A.: Please state your opinion.

Dpt.: They had for some time been signalling for a boat to take them off the wreck, but because of the violent storm none had been sent out. Perhaps they only wanted to attract attention, or to show that they could command it.

J.A.: But shooting at the Captain! Surely, that was mutinous.

Dpt.: It is not for me to decide.

J.A.: Is it true that Captain Chepe was taken prisoner by his men and held for some time in captivity?

Dpt.: After the death of Cozens, who had been greatly beloved, there was hot indignation against Chepe among the ship's people. They did not, however, arrest him. That was done by Captain Pemberton of the Marines, who charged the man with murder and meant to take him to England for trial. Except for a certain amount of reviling by Boatswain King, Chepe was well treated during his imprisonment.

J.A.: Did Captain Pemberton bring him to England?

Dpt.: No. Chepe was left on the island at his own request.

J.A.: That is not the way men imprisoned on the charge of murder are usually treated. Is it not a fact that he was deserted by the larger number of his men, and left to die on the island?

Dpt.: It is not. The fact is that he could have been taken off only by force. He wanted to remain and, as I have said, turn pirate.

J.A.: Captain Pemberton of the Marines presumably had the force. Why did he not use it?

DPT.: He was persuaded by Gunner Bulkeley not to do so. The Gunner pointed out that if Chepe went with us he would divide the men in the *Speedwell* into warring factions—as he had often tried to do on shore. We could not take that risk, on a long voyage in a crowded boat.

J.A.: The Captain had, then, a certain following?

DPT.: Yes: of some twenty men, ten of whom had previously plotted to kill him, for which they were driven out of camp by Gunner Bulkeley. For various reasons, those twenty agreed with Chepe's plan to go up the west coast of South America, cut out a Spanish vessel, and go on the account.

J.A.: You do not think, then, that his real purpose was to join the Commodore, say at Juan Fernandez?

DPT.: No. He refused to make for that island, but was always talking about a rendezvous at Del Socorro. For reasons that still seem to me good, I never believed him.

J.A.: Please state those reasons.

DPT.: First, he lost the Commodore's light, I believe by deliberate intention. Second, after losing it, he failed to fire signal-guns according to orders and general custom. Third, he lay to for four nights running when he should have been trying to overtake the Commodore. In all this he followed closely the example set by George Shelvocke, when he turned away in the night from Commodore Clipperton. Fourth, Chepe let his ship drive on the rocks many leagues south of Del Socorro. That was not accident, for he had been earnestly warned more than once that we were nearing the coast. Fifth, he lingered on the island for five months to my knowledge—and I know not how much longer after I was gone—without lifting his hand to hasten the departure, thereby giving the Commodore ample time to abandon hope of the *Wager*'s survival and to proceed without her. Sixth, Chepe never consulted with his officers, never took them into his confidence, never accepted their advice, and never until too late told them the sailing orders given him at St. Julian's by Commodore Anson. He would seldom come on deck to see conditions for himself, and neither would he believe the reports of his officers. Lastly, I knew the man. He was incapable either of command or of obedience. He was violent and weak at the same time. He thought only of David Chepe, instead of his men, his ship, and his country.

*　　*　　*

Mr. Chute had long since laid down his pencil, realizing that if Morris could read these words so could I. At this point he interrupted again. "Lieutenant Morris," said he, "that last answer of yours would do credit to a barrister at law. How much of it did you actually say?"

The twitch of Morris's mouth was engaging. "All of it and more thereto," he replied; "but what I said in good sound Devon this linkister o' mine, this Daniel Dickens, he must needs put into law talk. He meant clever by me, o' course, but some things he changed a bit, and other some he left out."

"Can you give us an example of things omitted?"

"Back there a few leaves where I was telling how the Boatswain shot a ball over Chepe's hut I recolleck sayin' that even when sober the man didn't have brains enough to load down a flea. Then too I said that in times o' trouble Chepe always showed the mud he was made of. 'Tis heavenly truth I spoke there, and it did ought to be wrote down. It ain't."

"Perhaps," George Selwyn suggested, "your friend Dickens thought if he took out a few insults there might be a chance of saving your neck from the rope."

"I be a thought put about to answer that, Mr. Selwyn. Insults I had not spoke, but only what I was to swear to. I ban't one to blacken any man's name out o' wrath, let alone for pleasure. Slander and scornin' with sneers I lack the craft of, along with all other drawin'-room havance. —About Chepe I told what I'd paid dear to larn. If I died for it, well then, I died; but not as a liar."

"There's no use, Lieutenant Morris," said Kitty then. "Every one knows our George has a wonderful wit, but there's a hole in his head where you think the kind of things you have just been saying. —Besides, he's jealous. 'Showed the mud he was made of' is something he wishes he'd thought up himself."

"Many thanks, dear Kitty," George murmured with one eye open, and sighing. "Now do go on, Lieutenant Morris. I hope we come to the executions before long."

"Well now, when it comes to the rope and all that, Mr. Selwyn, you may be in for a dish-down. Same time, there's other kinds o' dyin', mayhap less public but just as unpleasant to do. Most o' them kinds we tried, an' they made God's plenty o' corpses."

"That's good! Bring 'em on."

* * *

J.A.: Perhaps we have heard enough, with something to spare, about Captain Chepe. Now there's the voyage of the *Speedwell*. The Admiralty wants to learn everything possible about her remarkable voyage.

DPT.: Because of its bearing upon the wreck of the *Wager*?

J.A.: No; but for the help it may give in future navigation of those strange waters. What can you tell us about the vessel itself?

DPT.: The *Speedwell* had been the *Wager*'s longboat. She was carvel-built, single-masted, thirty-four foot long, and of a flimsy construction.

J.A.: Would she have been useful, say, in a piratical expedition?

DPT.: No. A single shot below the water-line, where the planks were less than an inch thick, would have sunk her. Yet she was by far the largest vessel we had left. Most of the men who left the island would have to go in her.

J.A.: I see. Interesting. Did Captain Chepe agree?

DPT.: At times; but then he would change his mind and refuse to let us have her. Again and again it was pointed out that since she was of no value for his purposes she ought to be used for the preservation of life.

J.A.: Yes, but let's not get back to the Captain. Once more, about the *Speedwell*?

DPT.: When some eighty of us agreed to go for the Brazils we saw that the longboat must be made to hold more men. The Carpenter cut her in two, increased her length by eleven feet, and gave her another mast so that she was rigged like a schooner. He decked her over from stem to stern, laying the deck on the thwarts. This left a four-inch gunwale all round the deck, but took five inches or more from the head-room below. The hatchway, amidships, four foot square, was the only opening in the deck.

J.A.: What did Captain Chepe think of these changes?

Dpt.: I go back to the Captain at your request. He was a prisoner during most of the time these changes were going on, and so could not stop them, but at least three attempts were made to kill the Carpenter while he was at the work. As he was the only man among us with any skill in the use of shipbuilding tools, his death would have left the rest of us with the choice between going with Chepe and starving to death on the island.

J.A.: But the Carpenter, I judge, survived, and was not discouraged.

Dpt.: Only once did we see him even disturbed. That was when he found that the *Wager*'s anchor-stock—a sound piece of English oak which he had been saving for a breast-hook—had been split up and used as firewood by one of Chepe's followers. Then, for a few days, he was out of his mind; yet he had the work done within four months after the wreck. That, we all thought, was a wonder, considering that he had worked alone, mostly with the materials that had washed ashore, while standing outdoors in the dead of winter.

J.A.: Yes. And how large was she when finished?

Dpt.: Forty-five foot long, ten foot eight inches in beam, and much less than half that in depth from deck to keelson. She was ugly and crank and weak, and her waist was too thin for her length.

J.A.: You said that some eighty men planned to leave the Captain. Surely, that number could not be crowded into the craft you describe.

Dpt.: We started out not with the *Speedwell* alone but also with the barge and cutter. They carried twenty-two men. The barge soon turned back, however, and the cutter was lost when we were three weeks out. Then eleven men, preferring almost certain death on the land to the crowding and stench in the *Speedwell*'s hold, were set ashore at their own request. This left about sixty aboard by the time we found and entered the Straits of Magellan.

J.A.: Sixty men, you say. But even then—

Dpt.: For one thing, death was steadily reducing the number. For another, Gunner Bulkeley arranged, and for a time enforced, a system of four watches which left not more than forty-five men below at one time.

J.A.: But I fail to see how even forty-five men could be packed into a hold the same number of feet in length.

Dpt.: When below, the men lay by twos and threes on either side of the keelson, which was necessarily covered from end to end with half-barrels, casks, and kegs. Forty could be stowed when we put two men on either side of the keelson, foot to head, though none of them would be able to lie at full length. With three on either side we could get in sixty; but then the third men outward from the center, lying well up the slope of the bilge and tightly wedged under the thwarts, were often stifled or else crushed to death.

J.A.: Bless my soul! Why did they not sit?

DPT.: They tried to, but soon grew too weak. After months of exposure and destitution on the island, these men were still starving. Also, they were now suffering the agonies of cramp, caused in part by their inability to move and in part by the fact that their clothing, for three months at least, was never once dry. Add the dark and the din, the foul air, the torment of vermin, and, worst of all, the stench, and you begin to get some notion of what a few of them— I have never learned how many—survived.

J.A.: But foul air, stench, on the open sea?

DPT.: The *Speedwell* had been decked to make her watertight. Of course she was not, but in times of rain and rough water, when the hatch was drawn down, little fresh air got into the hold.

J.A.: And therefore the Gunner arranged that each man should spend six hours out of twenty-four on deck?

DPT.: Yes; and so that the people might move about and get over the cramp. In theory it was a good plan. It included a frequent shifting of the men below, so that those in the next watch would be nearest the hatchway. The plan soon failed, however, because too many, while on deck, fell over the four-inch gunwale into the sea. Also there came a time when the men below could not, or would not, make this shift—some of them being dead, others dying, and still others too weak or indifferent to move.

J.A.: You don't mean that dead men were allowed to lie among the living!

DPT.: It was only when we went ashore that they could be removed. At one stretch of fourteen days and nights we did not once sight land.

J.A.: God bless my soul! —And you, Mr. Morris, lived through all that!

DPT.: For three months I sat, leaned, or lay on the Carpenter's tool-chest in the hatchway, so that whatever fresh air came into the hold reached me first of all. Gunner Bulkeley had assigned to me the duty of guarding that chest. It contained all our tools, all the weapons belonging to the men, and a small black book out of which the Gunner and Carpenter read their prayers. I sat there heavily armed. Captain Pemberton of the Marines, also armed, was close beside me. He kept order among his men, who lay aft of the hatchway. Lieutenant Beans had charge of the seamen. He too sat near the chest, and was armed, but he failed to control his people.

J.A.: How was that? Did they start a mutiny?

DPT.: Mutiny? Huddled there in the dark, starved, thirsty, unarmed, unable to stand or sit, even to crawl? Really, sir, you seem not to picture the situation. No; but while they had the strength they fought one another with bare hands, so that more than one of the corpses we dragged out and buried from time to time bore marks of murder. After that they reviled their officers, especially the Gunner. Day and night they lay there and shouted and screamed and murmured and whispered against him. Even if he wanted to, and of that I am not sure, Lieutenant Beans could not silence them. Cursing the Gunner was the chief occupation and last earthly joy of many a dying man.

J.A.: Aha! The Court will wish to hear about that. Get it down, Dickens, that the Gunner was hated even by those he had led astray. —For there has been a rumour, let me tell you, Mr. Morris, that this Gunner Bulkeley began and led the mutiny on the Wager. Perhaps that is why the men disliked him, when they saw what their revolt against Captain Chepe had led to.

DPT.: As I have said, there was no mutiny on the Wager; and that was largely because the Gunner was there to prevent it. On the *Speedwell* he was hated—certainly not by all, but by many—for several reasons. One was that he had stood out against those who wanted to kill Chepe, and another that he rationed our food and drink in the hope of saving our lives. Moreover, he seemed to keep his normal health and strength whilst others were dying, and this led to the suspicion that he was filching more than his share of the stores. No one, it was thought, could maintain the cheerfulness that Gunner Bulkeley always showed, when he came below deck, on the pitiful ration of brandy he allowed to others. Some held, however, that brandy alone could not maintain such joy, and that he was in fact exulting in the sight of their present misery and at the prospect of seeing them hanged if he ever got them home.

J.A.: What was your own opinion, Mr. Morris?

DPT.: I doled out the rations, and I know that the Gunner had never a drop or a crumb more than fell to his share. If more had been offered—on the ground that he was doing more hard work than all the rest of us together—he would have refused it with anger, and would have taken the rationing away from me.

J.A.: Indeed. You surprise me.

DPT.: Also I know that John Bulkeley was not always so cheerful as he tried to appear while talking to the men. In fact, he was often sad.

J.A.: An uneasy conscience, perhaps?

DPT.: He would have said so, yes; but he would not have meant what you do. He blamed himself for many a thing which he could not possibly have helped.

J.A.: Such as?

DPT.: For one thing, the death of Henry Cozens.

J.A.: Ah! Indeed! But you have deponed that Cozens was shot by the Captain. How is this, Mr. Morris? —Dickens, get this down exactly.

DPT.: John Bulkeley, like most sailors, was a childless man. He had loved Henry Cozens—who, indeed, was beloved by all that knew him—somewhat as a fond father loves his son. He had known the lad's weakness for drink, and had certainly done what he could to protect him against temptation. When Cozens was dead, however, he could not rid his mind and heart of the feeling that he might and should have done, somehow, more. He felt that, at the least, he should have detected in time the devilish plot of those who had plied Cozens with drink in the expectation that he would make trouble. And then too, in addition to his sense of failure, there was the agony of his struggle against the hatred he felt toward those who had laid the plot.

J.A.: You mean, I suppose, that he hated the Captain.

DPT.: And I also mean that he triumphed over that hatred—God knows how. He came to feel sorry for David Chepe.

J.A.: Well, Mr. Morris, of course I don't doubt your word, but this is hard to believe, even to understand. —What else was the man sad about?

DPT.: That Midshipman Byron had stayed on the island with Chepe instead of sailing with us. He puzzled about this for months, and made many conjectures. Once, while talking with me in a low tone, late at night, sitting there on the chest, he suggested that Byron also might have felt guilty of Cozens' death, and might have punished himself by staying with the men who, he believed, wanted to kill him also. Another guess of his was that Byron had wished to protect the *Speedwell* people against the charge of mutiny which he knew that Chepe would certainly bring if he ever got home to England.

J.A.: A highly improbable guess, I should say. How could he hope to "protect" them—supposing for the moment that he should wish to— by staying behind when they went away?

Dpt.: That would show, for one thing, that he had taken no part in their alleged "mutiny," and also it would enable him to watch David Chepe until he got home.

J.A.: And then, again, why should a gentleman like the Honourable John Byron put his own life in danger to save the lives of common sailors?

Dpt.: The Gunner felt that objection, and yet there had been certain things in the Honourable John Byron's conduct toward his shipmates that could be urged on the other side. He had been kind to them all, and friendly, refusing to take any advantage on account of his rank. Among his closest friends had been a certain John Duck, a negro; but closest of all, with the possible exception of Cozens, had been the Gunner.

J.A.: Humph! Odd! —But now you say that the Gunner blamed himself for everything that went wrong. What were some of those things?

Dpt.: A great many things can go wrong on a voyage of thousands of miles through uncharted seas in a craft like the *Speedwell*. Whatever misfortune happened to us—for example, our blind fumbling about for a month off the Straits of Magellan—he laid to some fault of his own. On the other hand, he never took credit for anything that went right. Thus, after his skill and vigilance had saved us a dozen times from disaster, his only remark was that any one who had seen these providential deliverances and still doubted the existence of a Supreme Being, thereby lost all title to God's love and mercy.

J.A.: Was he pious? Was he enthusiastic?

Dpt.: At any rate, he was deeply religious. Not content with holding "prayer-meetings" on the deck, where he and the Carpenter and Cooper and Master's Mate gathered at every interval of calm weather, he never let slip a chance to talk about what he called "salvation" and "the tender mercies of God" whenever he came below.

J.A.: Those are topics, it seems to me, highly unsuitable for the time and place.

DPT.: So they seemed to Boatswain King and a number of others. It angered them to be told that their miseries of the flesh were meant to prepare their souls for eternal bliss. And the happy smile with which these things were said was misunderstood. Many felt that the Gunner was exulting at their pains and woes. "Souls," he would say to those starving men lying unseen in the darkness to left and right—"Souls, what a blessed privilege is ours to be thus set apart from worldly temptation, and not to be cloyed by riches, dignities, or honours of any sort."

J.A.: Most extraordinary language for a mere gunner—or, indeed, for any man in the circumstances! Where can he possibly have picked it up?

DPT.: Some of it, I think, from a little black book called *The Christian Pattern*. It was kept under lock and key in the Carpenter's chest, along with our tools and weapons. Gunner Bulkeley, although he had it by heart, often took it on deck with him in fine weather, at the same time carrying a leather bottle of ink and a quill. He told me once that the book had been given him by the Reverend John Wesley, and that it was the most precious thing he had in the world.

J.A.: Did you say John Wesley, that ignorant heretic, that wild enthusiast, that rabble-rouser? Why, sir, this Bulkeley must be a Methodist!

DPT.: He never said so; but shortly before the *Wager* sailed he had heard this Wesley preach and had been, as he put it, "converted" by that one sermon.

J.A.: "Converted," eh? That proves it. He belongs to a riotous sect of Papists and Jacobites who want to give England back to the Pope. That little black book—its real name, by the way, is *The Imitation of Christ*—is Popish, Mr. Morris, distinctly Popish. Of course I've not read it, but so I am told.

DPT.: I doubt whether John Bulkeley knew that, and also whether he would care.

J.A.: We'll show him cause for caring. —Dickens, don't fail to set down that Gunner John Bulkeley is a Methodist. The Court will see that a man who has already joined a mutiny against the Church of England is just the man to start one against his captain.

DPT.: May I ask whether John Bulkeley is alive, and in England?

J.A.: You may ask it, Mr. Morris, certainly—and the question will be answered in due time.

DPT.: I answer your questions at once.

J.A.: True; and in the way of friendship I should gladly reciprocate. I am bound, however, by my duty, as you are by yours. —What more can you tell me about this Methodistical trouble-maker?

DPT.: Gunner Bulkeley, sir, was my friend. If alive, he still is my friend. Your further questions will no doubt be answered in due time, by him.

J.A.: Oh, Mr. Morris, really now—

*　　*　　*

Kitty's laughter broke in here. "Oh," she cried, "this is as good as a play—and I mean a good play. Can't you see the little judge fidgeting in his chair, pulling two or three precious hairs out of his beard and then offering Midshipman Morris his snuffbox again?'

"Yes, ma'am," John Chester put in. "An' Midshipman Morris not only but likewise the friend of Admiral Anson, the which was even more to the p'int. —Good for you, Leftenant Morris! Y' oughter come over an' live 'longside o' me on the Connecticut Thames. That's how we talk up to our jedges."

"Or, you might come out among the Choctaws," Adair suggested.

"A good notion," said my cousin Conway, in a tone perhaps too dogmatic. "I don't know much about the Choctaws; but in civilized countries mutiny is considered a serious matter, and officers of the law are treated with respect."

Kitty glanced at me, and I saw—rather than heard—that she was sighing. If she were not almost as fond of my cousin as I am . . . But I wander.

Master Morris told us a number of things about John Bulkeley which he had withheld from the Judge. Putting his account together with Byron's, we began to feel that we knew this Bulkeley rather well. We could see him sitting there beside Morris, with the sunlight falling through the hatch upon his grizzled head and his thick, gray, constantly moving eyebrows, a man half starved, worn by toil and anxiety, and yet for some reason happy, gay even, and all the time smiling as he talked with the "souls."

In the natural course of things Lieutenant Beans would have commanded the *Speedwell*, and he did in fact claim the title of Captain. Beyond that, however, he was content to lie quiet in the hold and live like a bear in winter on his accumulation of fat, leaving most of the decisions and all the work to Gunner Bulkeley, Carpenter Cummins, Cooper Young, and John Jones the Master's Mate.

The men just named were on deck, by two and two, four hours at a time, one at the tiller and one handling the sails—no one else, I judge, making any attempt to leave the hold whilst the vessel was on the open sea. This activity, and the realization that everything depended upon them, kept them well and cheerful on a three months' voyage of three thousand miles during which about half of their shipmates died, some by starvation, some of stifling, and others in mere despair. The real command went to the Gunner, not because he wanted it or had any official claim but on account of what he essentially was. Mr. Chute questioned Morris rather closely on this point, and seemed much interested in the result. I think he saw in it another instance of the general problem of leadership with which, during the week, we were often concerned.

Knowing your feelings, William, about John Wesley's rag-tag-and-bobtail—and, for that matter, fully sharing your contempt mixed with fear of the endless riot he has stirred up amongst us—I am sorry to report that all four of the men who sailed, steered, and governed the *Speedwell* were Methodists. The seeds of this pernicious heresy had been brought aboard the *Wager* by John Bulkeley, in whose mind they had been sowed by Wesley himself in a sermon delivered in an open field near Bristol before several thousand miners and collier seamen. Blessed or cursed with a tenacious memory, he had retained the larger part of Wesley's remarks *verbatim,* along with the words of a hymn and fragments of an extemporaneous prayer. This prayer he would use as a charm in such miscellaneous exigencies as thunder and lightning, high winds, scurvy, threats of insurrection, and the results of excessive indulgence in strong drink. By dint of hearing it a hundred times repeated, Lieutenant Morris had the prayer by heart, and it ran thus : "O God most mighty, O Lord most holy, most merciful Father, thou most worthy Judge Eternal, suffer us not to depart from Thee at our last moment for any pains of death."

You see that, like all other such abracadabra, the words are nearly
devoid of meaning. No doubt that was the main cause of their compelling effect upon the ignorant, fear-ridden men huddled there in the
dark. They took it for a magic formula which could bind and loose
the powers of evil like the Lord's prayer recited backwards—a belief
natural enough after they had seen the Gunner bring them through the
Straits of Magellan with no map, no landmarks he had ever seen,
nothing that they knew of to depend upon other than that one prayer.
Therefore even the obstreperous Boatswain was cowed into silence
whenever, in the midst of some outcry of his for more brandy, the
Gunner intoned "O God most mighty, O Lord most holy," and so on
to "pains of death."

There's an interesting comparison to be made between Bulkeley's
prayer going up from the eastern coast of South America and the sin-
eating carried on by Chepe's company at about the same time and a
few meridians farther west. That lies in your territory, William, and
I leave it to your reflections. You will not forget that the prayer was
offered by rank heretics, while the sin-eating was done by a group of
churchmen so thoroughly orthodox that, according to Byron, they
never once mentioned the name of God except "in vain." And there
was this further difference: the prayer seems to have worked, literally,
"like a charm."

Bulkeley felt that the hymn he had heard at the Methodist meeting
would also have been highly effective if only he had been able to recall
the tune. Unfortunately, like most Englishmen, he had no ear. His
attempts to fit the words to the only tune he knew, "The Coasts of
High Barbary," were unsuccessful. The words of the hymn, as Morris
recalled them, were as follows:

> Jesus, Lover of my soul,
>   Let me to Thy bosom fly
> While the nearer waters roll,
>   While the tempest still is high;
> Hide me, O my Saviour, hide,
>   Till the storm of life be past;
> Safe into the haven guide;
>   Oh, receive my soul at last.

For preaching of the rough-and-tumble Methodist sort, however,
the Gunner had a natural gift. As you too are a preacher, you may
wish to see a sample of the man's abilities in this kind. Listen, then, to

Bulkeley as remembered by Morris, translated out of Devonian into English by Chute, reported by Walpole, and—who knows?—perhaps to be echoed by the Reverend William Cole in his next Sunday's sermon to the squire and villagers of Bletchley.

"Souls," the Gunner would say, coming down through the hatch and seating himself bolt upright, with folded arms, on the tool-chest, "good morning, souls!"

"You go to hell, Gunner," a voice would shout back from the darkness of the bow. " 'Tain't a good mornin', an' ye know it damn well, y' old liar!"

" 'Tis foul weather on deck, that's true, Boatswain; but not in the soul. The wind's coming stiff from sou'-sou'east, with rain in flaws and the sea rising; but the winds and the waves obey His will. Every wave goes over the deck, but He remembereth his own."

"Like hell it do! Half of every wave comes down in here. We want brandy!"

"The dirl o' the waves on the side makes it hard to hear you, Boatswain."

"Yah, ye're deafer 'n a nadder when we claim our God-guv rights: but iffen some poor damn fool was to whisper as he wants to give his soul to Jesus, ye'd hear him in a hurricane."

"That's true, I hope; and so would that soul's Maker. But let us not bicker now, Boatswain. Those of us that's left, let us think how we're bound together in brotherly love. 'Tis dark in here, and wet, and we're famished all of us alike and together, and whereso we may be on the welter o' waves there's only One knows or cares. Aye, we're lost to this world, souls, and our next landfall may be heaven. Then let us go singing, I say, and come into port with a cheer."

"We'll sing him enough bawdy songs—eh, lads?—iffen only he'll broach the brandy. And we knows the chunes to 'em, like he don't for his Methody hymn."

"Souls, He hath said in His Word that whom He most loveth He chasteneth most. Think, then, how He must love us. He hath humbled the pride of our strength and dilvered the lust o' the flesh and set us a far ways off from the world and its wickedness. —All this is for our salvation, iffen we will but ask and have."

"I'll trade any man my chance o' salvation," the Boatswain yells, "for only one nip o' brandy."

"By what devilish wiles are they caught and entrapped whose feet take hold upon hell? If it be by wealth and the goods of this world, then surely are we the poorest of God's children. If by longing for power or fame on men's lips, then we are the humblest, the least, and by men the most forgotten. If by lust o' the groin and the gut, there too we are little tempted. If by comfort and ease that lull the soul into sleep everlasting, we are saved from that danger also. Thus God hath so wrought that for us there is nothing but holiness left."

"You lie, Gunner. There's brandy, and we want it now."

"Do you shut your foul mouth now, Boatswain, or we'll shut it for you," another voice yells in the darkness. "We've seen you crazed with drink afore, and by God we won't have it here."

(I should have explained, William, that two political parties had formed in the hold of the *Speedwell*. The Conservatives, led by the Gunner, were for rationing the stores of food and drink. Their opponents, among whom the Boatswain was the most vociferous, argued that since they must all soon die the sensible thing would be to die happily in one magnificent final bouse. You will recognize the profundity of the question involved, and how it underlies most of the questions that have agitated political assemblies since the sons of Noah combined against their bibulous parent. More than once it was put to the vote on the *Speedwell*, and disaster was averted only by last-minute discoveries that Boatswain King was speaking for men who had died, but whose bodies had not been removed, since the previous count was taken. —Thus it is that under conditions apparently most adverse we English reproduce those methods of government, even including the system of rotten boroughs, upon which our liberties securely rest.)

"Let us lovingly bear," the Gunner continued, "with our dear brother the Boatswain—that frantic, foolish, loud-mouthed, and jug-bitten man. Pay no mind to his dark and damnable oaths. Think not that 'tis he who so jangleth against God's love, but the devil within him. Let us make it a means of grace and a help to salvation that he spews forth night and day the language of hell."

"Don't ye bear that Methody blather, messmates! Ram his little black book down his throat!"

"To you, Brother King, I have a few words to say; and whilst I speak them may the spirit o' brotherly love keep me from anger. That body o' yours, made of mire to last but a little while, is miserable here in the dark and the damp, we all know. It is foul, tormented by lice, racked by pangs of cramp and hunger, and agonized day and night by its longing to get at the brandy there in the keg wedged into the fore-peak just beyond your head. In calm weather you hear the brandy washing from side to side of the keg, and then your body's longing rages within you like a wild beast caught in a cage. You have worn your nails away and filled your finger-ends with splinters, trying to claw through the wood.

"These things I do not say in triumph, but rather in pity for one who, thinking that his body is all he has, yet finds that body brought so low. I say them in wonder that any man should so gnar and grutch as you do at a day-lived pain of the flesh whilst he boldly faces, and hourly draws nearer, the flames of hell.

"Far worse than the longing for drink is the poison of envy and hatred and fear within you. Here in the *Speedwell* as on the *Wager* and during our stay on the island, you strive to spread this poison of yours amongst other men. You say that we who keep watch on deck are taking more than our share of the stores. We all know that to be false. You say that we live at ease on deck whilst you are here packed three deep, each breathing the breath of all. Boatswain King, you may come on deck whenever you like, and for the first time in many months do your share of the work. You will find that the man at the tiller must sit on the deck and brace himself with his toes curled over the gunwale whilst every wave we ship rushes round him and often over his head. You will learn that the *Speedwell* is not a good sea-boat. You will learn what it means to grope one's way along a strange coast with no chart, no compass, and, as now for ten days, without even a land-fall or so much as a glimpse of the sun at noon.

"Bear these things in mind, Boatswain King, when next you are tempted to envy, or to spread falsehood against those who are striving to save your body and soul. Or remember the shipmates we've lost on this voyage, who had less time than you, though also less reason, to repent of their sins. There was George Bateman, sixteen years old, who starved before we came to the Straits. Three days later we buried the small bones, like a bird's, of Tom Caple, aged twelve. Next there died Thomas Thorpe, Thomas Woodhead, and Peter Delroy, all on one day and all good men. Then came the turn of Mr. Harvey, of whom it may at least be said that he was probably the first Purser in his Majesty's service that ever perished of hunger. —Twenty-one men and boys we've lost since we left the island, but you, John King, are still with us to curse your friends and blaspheme your God. This is a mystery which we shall not understand until Judgment Day; but one who values his bodily life as you do yours should at least be grateful.

"But now there's enough o' dying, and 'tis o' the soul that lives for ever that we did ought to be thinking. Why for have we been saved from the snatch o' the sea, from scurvy, from ravin of beasts and the clutch of treacherous men? What for are we still let to live through the flat o' the wind and the claws o' the rocks and the thundering crash o' the billows? Who showed us those herbs of singular virtue that cured our sick? Who kept us alive on a desolate rock? Who wafted us out o' great storms into harbours unknown, unhoped for? My brothers, 'tis scant credible when ye come to count the mercies to us unworthy of Him who hath His way in the whirlwind and worketh His wonders upon the deep. All this He hath done not to save our bodies, which may yet in His good time be lost in the sea or broken upon the gallows. He has done it for the love of our souls.

"Shipmates, you all know me for an ignorant, sinful man, unworthy to lay a hand to the Gospel tiller. Should any here fail of salvation—aye, even the Boatswain—'twill be, I know, by my fault. Could I speak to you now as John Wesley spoke that day, my words would be as a fire and a hammer, and your hearts as white iron on the anvil. 'Twas raining that day, and two thousand stood in the rain to hear him. Some had gone—and I, God forgive me, among them—to throw dirt and stones at the preacher; but not a hand was raised. No one spoke, no one moved for an hour whilst we stood and listened, and the mercy of God came down in that drench of rain and washed our sins away. And then came the hymn with the tune I shall always strive to recall. But no—'tis gone. Even my Bible is gone. On the day of the wreck it was taken from the gun-room—I know who did it—and destroyed."

"Ye're a liar," shouts the Boatswain. "I never did!"

"But one good book I saved. It was in my pocket. Nay, it was even then written clear in my mind and heart where thieves break not through and steal. Souls, I give you these words from *The Christian Pattern,* and do you take them—"

"Choke him!" the Boatswain cries. "Don't let him say 'em! That little black book is witchcraft hot from hell!—Oh, God, iffen I could get at him—"

"You have heard the Devil, souls. Now hear the voice of the Prince of Peace, even of Him who said to the waves of Galilee: 'Peace, be still.' This is what it says to us: 'Holy men have served our Lord in hunger and thirst, in cold and nakedness, in wakings and fastings, in persecutions and many reproofs. Yes, many and grievous have been the tribulations of those who have hated their bodily lives that they might save their souls unto life everlasting. They gave up all manner of riches and honours and earthly power, and cared for no thing of this fleeting world. Scarce they took what was barely needful, and were sorry to serve the body in its necessities. God's poor they were in outward things, but inwardly rich in grace and in ghostly comfort.' "

*   *   *

By this time, William, you will heartily agree with the Boatswain's suggestion that Gunner Bulkeley ought to be choked. On the *Speedwell* there were practical difficulties, but we can do it here.

And yet, after a talk on this topic with Mr. Chute, I begin to fear that no disdain of ours will finally silence such voices. Our scorn does not reach these people. Perhaps they do not even know that we are, quite pointedly, not listening. Whilst you and I are sunk in our dream of the Gothic ages, they go on changing the England that now is into that which is to be.

But changing it how, by what means? Of course not in the direction of the "holy poverty" so fulsomely praised in the Gunner's little black book. That, to be sure, is an idea "distinctly papistic," although my own observations at the Vatican suggest that the Bishops of Rome have usually been content to leave it in the realm of pure idea. No; but in this Methodism there is a notion even more corrosive, subversive, poisonous to the England we know and love. I mean the notion that in every human being—prince or beggar, sot or saint—there exists what these enthusiasts vaguely call a soul, and that in the estimation of God every soul is as precious as any other. Well, sir, to a man of your perspicacity I need not point out how tempting such a theory is to those who certainly have nothing but a soul, if indeed they have that, to base their pride upon. You see at once to what levelling, what high-flown insolence—in a word, what "democracy"—it must lead.

Do you say that there is nothing new in this doctrine, and that it is visibly present in original Christianity itself? True enough; but hitherto all sensible Christians have seen that such pretensions to equality must be postponed to a "better world." You will correct me if I am wrong, but I seem to remember a petition in our prayer-book that the Lord may make us content with that station in life to which He hath called us. That is good English common sense—which consists, of course, in a mingling of ideal theory with the knowledge of what will really work. But this John Wesley is an impatient man, and he is making multitudes impatient. His theory is well enough; but the trouble is that he wants to do something about it, here and now.

He is already doing much. It is astonishing how far, and into what unpredictable corners, this enthusiasm has already spread. You have just seen it at work in the hold of the *Speedwell*, and I suppose that in such a place, among such people, anything might happen. But, sir, I could if I would name you three ladies of really exalted rank who show marked Methodistic leanings—even to the entertainment of cross-eyed George Whitefield at their dinner-tables. In short, there's no telling to what this will lead. I live in dread lest even my Louis— that model and masterpiece of social decorum—may some day inform me that he is prayerfully concerned for the welfare of my immortal soul.

You think these fears absurd, but let me tell you that during tea-time on that same Wednesday afternoon I found I had under my roof two defenders, and one of them a devoted follower, of John Wesley. This second person was Jeremy Tinker, who had known Wesley for upwards of twenty years—had, in fact, crossed the ocean with him, and had been in some sort his protégé in the Colony of Georgia. Jeremy's praise of the man, from whom he had apparently received much help both material and spiritual, was easily explained, but Blandison's—yes, I have written and you have read the name correctly—was indeed surprising.

You would have thought that these two, in speaking of Wesley, had two different men in mind. In Jeremy's eyes, as he spoke of his friend, there was much the same look of adoration—entirely misdirected, of course—which I see in those of my little Ponto when he comes to my chair and looks up at his master. Blandison, of course, has none of that feeling. For John Wesley's doctrines, whatever they may be, he probably has as little respect and sympathy as you or I; but about the man himself he had a number of shockingly favourable things to say. You will not believe any more than I do that Wesley is a scholar, a gentleman, a wit, a person of polished manners, but if you had been here your main question would have been why Blandison should assert such things. Recalling the common belief, I asked whether he was not praising a fellow-conspirator against the Royal House. This, he assured me, was not so. "Oh, no!" said he. "We Jacobites would gladly claim the Reverend John Wesley, but the fact is too notorious, and is indeed the main blot upon an otherwise almost blameless character, that he is obsequiously and disgustingly loyal to the German usurper."

And so, what was I to think—at least, until I had a chance to get Mr. Chute's opinion? When I did so I found that Blandison's admiration of Wesley was chiefly due to the man's mastery of assemblies, or rather of mobs—to his power of facing a crowd of men eager to kill him and sending them away with tears in their eyes.

Well, there you are. Who would have thought of that except Mr. Chute? For my part, I had not previously realized that the power of handling a mob is in any way admirable. Now I saw that it takes qualities of courage, self-command, and quickness of wit which are certainly not in me. And also I saw that Blandison and John Wesley do indeed overlap, in that both are chance-takers, lovers of danger, each willing to stand for one against thousands, and face them down.

Mr. Chute went further. Using the voyage of the *Speedwell* as a text, he made what sounded almost like an apology for Methodism. "Let's think a moment longer," he said, "about the situation of those men crowded there, and some of them crushed, in that dark stifling hold. I know it's not pleasant, but try for a moment to imagine the din of the waves along the vessel's sides, and the tumult within of voices quarrelling, groaning, screaming. Think how it would feel to be pent in the dark for week after week, unable to move, scarcely able to breathe, eating rather less than you are eaten, and all the while knowing that the lamed, leaking, sea-worn vessel may at any moment go down. If it doesn't, if by some miraculous series of divine interventions you do get home alive, then you have the prospect of being hanged.

"Come now, Horatio," said he, "you who so much enjoy imagining the Middle Ages, think your way into the *Speedwell* for a moment, and whilst doing so remember that this isn't a dream of the past but a fact of our day. I mean not only that countrymen of ours did really live through this horror less than fifteen years ago, but that multitudes of other English people are living now in much the same miserable way. And the worst thing about this must be the feeling that you are lost and forgotten on a desolate sea, that no one knows or cares in the least about your woe. That is horrible indeed. Many men, many women, have sung and rejoiced in the midst of the flames because they felt that their torment was known somewhere, that it would count, that it had a meaning. But to feel that it means nothing whatever . . . Well, you remember Byron's outcry: 'That way, madness lies!'

"But then, let us say, there comes into that foul den of torture a man—call him Bulkeley or Wesley or Christ—who does know and care about your suffering because he shares it. He comes with a smile, not a sneer. He smiles because he is happy, on your account as much as his own. He is happy because he believes there's a meaning in this misery—a meaning so deep, high, and everlasting that no bodily anguish can matter in comparison at all. He believes that the main thing about a human being is not this handful of dust but the soul that lives for ever, and that each soul has an infinite worth. Now let us assume, if you like, that he's wrong in so believing. For my part, I hope he's right; but what I know is that such a conviction will be extremely contagious in places like the hold of the *Speedwell*. There are many such places. One of them is that part of London which, as Blandison has correctly said, you know nothing about. I myself know shamefully little. I suppose, however, that human nature is quite as prevalent there as in Mayfair or at Strawberry Hill. If so, then there must be people there too who long to know they're beloved, even if only by God.

"John Wesley knows more, I suppose, about those people in St. Giles's than any other living man. He knows their like in a thousand cities, towns, villages, hamlets, and thorps from end to end of England and across. He knows them not as a mass but as individual men and women and children, each one with a soul and each soul with a past and present of which, in many instances, he can give an exact account. His friends say that he has vast erudition, but certainly he is learnedest of all in the great book of souls. Wherever he goes—and he goes everywhere—he says, like John Bulkeley, 'Good morning, souls. The weather is extremely bad, and we are starving, lost, and rejected of men. Praise the Lord!' "

And so, back to the *Speedwell*.

But no; on second thought I've decided to put down another remark of my wise old friend which I left out above in consideration of your

feelings. You're not so sensitive as that amounts to. He said that
Methodism could not have happened if only the clergymen of England, each inside his own parish, had been minding their proper business. He said "Don't blame Wesley for Methodism. He probably
dislikes the necessity of it as much as we do. I don't suppose he enjoys
preaching in the open fields, or being reviled and hauled before jus-
tices of the peace, or riding fifty miles every day and sleeping in a
different bed every night of the year. No; it's only that he sees a certain necessary task being neglected by several thousand persons who
are paid to do it, and so he says: 'Here am I, Lord. Send me.' Then
he mounts his spavined old nag and rides off though the rain, armed
with a hymnal written mostly by his brother Charles, to do battle in
the everlasting war against Satan's Kingdom. —Well, I mean to say,
Horry, that if it's chivalry you're looking for then you and William
Cole don't have to go back to the Crusaders."

Of course I might have mentioned Don Quixote, even Hudibras,
but I didn't. As usual on such occasions, I was crushed. Thus the
answer is left to you.

Keep this in mind, though, if you do attempt a reply: John Chute
of the Vyne is a Methodist in no sense or degree. The worst that can
be said of him is that, like Shakespeare's Malvolio, "sometimes he is
a kind of puritan."

*   *   *

But now, we really must return to Lieutenant Morris—or rather,
try to overtake him. It's amazing how far the man has got with
his adventures while I—pulled back, of course, by you—have been
maundering here about Methodism and other such quite unjenkins-
earesque tediosities.

Behold Morris now, after three months and two days on the Carpenter's chest, reclining at ease on the eastern coast of South America,
breathing fresh air, drinking fresh water, and with "any God's quantity" of good fresh seal-meat waiting about on the beach, asking only
to be knocked over, sliced, and cooked. He has seven men with him,
to wit: Guy Broadwater, Samuel Cooper, Benjamin Small, John
Andrews, John Allen, Joseph Clinch, and John Duck, a negro. He has
also five candles, five gun-flints, a hatful of powder, seventeen musket-
balls, four muskets, one hatchet, and a scuttled puncheon.

This is affluence, one sees; and still more important is what he has

not: bad smells, noise, corpses, vermin, Methodism, and Boatswain
King.

With regard to the vermin, there appears to be a method of macera-
tion between two stones which—which I need not detail because it
can be of no practical use to you. And then there's the question how
Morris and his men happen to be there in Freshwater Bay near Cape
St. Anthony, Latitude 37.25 South, Longitude 55.25 West, and some
three hundred miles southeast of Buenos Ayres. But really, sir, must
I know everything—and not only know but tell it? Why can't you
suppose, for example, that they went ashore to fill water-kegs and,
while they were thus engaged, a storm came up which blew the *Speedwell* out to sea and then, by breaking her rudder-head, prevented her
return? Well, sir, in that supposition you would be right in every
detail. Why not continue, then, to use your excellent imagination in
matters of this nugatory sort, and so save time for both of us?

I should have told you that I have drawn up a brief list—I say a
brief one—of matters on no account to be mentioned, or at any rate
fully discussed, in this letter. This news may rejoice you, but only
until you learn that there stands at the very top of my *index expurga-
torius* the word "armadillos." I now regret this, feeling sure that you
have never so much as heard the name of the luscious small creatures
that scramble and sprawl and slumber in the South American landscape awaiting the advent of castaway sailors—preferably English.
Your ignorance is the more a pity because the armadillo serves equally
well for a meal or a sermon, whichever may be one's more immediate
need. Thus a clergyman at a loss for a topic would find in her—she is
exclusively female, by the way, so as to be more tender and toothsome—a complete demonstration of Divine Providence. How else,
except for the mercy of God and for the behoof of starving Englishmen, are we to explain the thick horny shell she comes in, thus providing the dish as well as the meat, ready for baking? According to
Lieutenant Morris, this shell guards her back and comes down on both
sides of her, meeting under her belly but yet leaving suitable aper-
tures for four legs—a convenient arrangement, considering that she
is, after all, a quadruped. The shell guards her, I say, from the attacks
of tigers, Indians, and other such vermin, until the English arrive.
Her head is smallish, nosed like a hedgehog, and carried on the end of
a pretty long neck which she thrusts out before her body when she
walks. This, to be sure, is a way of using the neck observable in other

animals, but a peculiarity of the armadillo—that is, if we forget about turtles—is her clever device of drawing both neck and head back under her shell upon the approach of any danger.

Here, obviously, is a hint for another sermon—not so much about armadillos, though suggested by them, as about people. You might say that there are three kinds of people: first, those with no necks and consequently no heads, like Madlands; second, the Blandison sort that thrust forth the neck and keep it so thrust; and, third, armadillo people, like me.

You may think I'm boasting, but I admit that the armadillo reminds me a good deal of Horace Walpole. Her shell is jointed in the middle of the back, says Morris, so that she can turn the fore part of her body whithersoever she pleases, but I judge that the hinder part has not this autonomy; it merely follows, or goes along. This is true of me also. Furthermore, when the armadillo is frightened, and that is most of the time, either she digs an extremely swift hole in the ground and climbs into it or else, even more in haste, she curls herself up into a rapid ball and, however you may pelt her with stones or kick her about, she will not move herself in the least but only lie stock-still, and pretend she's dead.

As for diet, a few green leaves and a tongueful of ants content her, and the result of this is that her disposition, like mine, is a model of mansuetude. It follows also that her flesh eats exceeding well—tasting, I'm told, somewhere between turtle-soup and sucking-pig, roasted.

It is a curious thing—don't you think so, William?—that we should spend so much of our lives wondering how we look and sound to other people, perhaps even smell and feel, but never give a thought to the question how, suitably cooked and garnished, we might taste. Never, I say. This more obvious and elementary kind of good taste is with us not even an object of aspiration. Can you tell me whether the nobler minds in cannibal countries are in this regard somewhat more altruistic?

So much, then, as a brief indication of what you lose by my leaving armadillos out. Lieutenant Morris and his seven companions did not do that. For a month they lay about the beach and stuffed themselves with armadillos baked, roasted, and boiled, until they too acquired a natural instinct for curling up in the sunshine and lying stock-still. Realizing, however, that winter was coming on, they at last made an effort to walk the three hundred miles to Buenos Ayres. They failed, possibly because they were too fat, and were back again in five days. Then they built themselves a rude hut under the seaward-facing cliff and waited three months. Toward the end of May they tried again, and failed, to make that journey on foot. More and more, as the mild winter passed, they felt that they might never get away from that desolate place. They began, therefore, to make themselves as comfortable as possible by capturing a number of wild hogs and dogs for breeding purposes. These creatures soon grew so tame that they followed the eight men whenever they went out hunting, and lodged in the hut with them at night.

But presumably, William, you remember the shifts and devices, the industry, the dull patience, whereby Robinson Crusoe kept alive in circumstances not greatly different from these. To me, at least, they make a tedious tale which I shall not attempt to emulate. What does it matter, at least to the story of Jenkins' Ear, that part of the cliff crumbled down upon the hut, that the men were once terrified by what Morris called "a great tiger" but terrified the beast even more, or that they shot what he called "a lion," cooked his heart and ribs, and found them "very indifferent eating"?

More to the purpose is an incident that occurred toward the end of the winter. Morris had been out all day hunting limpets with three of his companions, the four others remaining at the hut. As they were returning through the dusk and got within a stone's cast of the hut, Morris saw that the dogs were "very busy" about something that lay on the ground, and were "wagging their tails in a fondling manner." At the time he paid little attention to this, but went on to the hut. He found that it had been plundered. The muskets and powder and ball, the hatchet, the knives, even the one or two cooking utensils, had disappeared. The four men who had been left in the hut were gone, the fire was out, and the handmade stools were smashed.

This was disaster. It had come without the least warning. These men had survived tigers, lions, falling cliffs, and a number of other such trifling dangers since coming on shore, but until this moment they had felt safe from man's deadliest enemy—man. I suppose that Morris's consternation as he stood there in the door of the hut must have been somewhat like that felt by Crusoe when he saw a human footprint in the sand.

He rushed out to call his three companions who had been with him on the day's hunting. They were now standing at a little distance, apparently trying to drive the dogs away. Morris ran to them and found there the body of Guy Broadwater with his throat cut, and that of Ben Small, stabbed through the breast. The dogs had been at these bodies. Of Joseph Clinch and John Allen, who had also spent the day at the hut, there was no sign.

You picture them, don't you, William?—those four men there on the sands with night striding toward them across the Atlantic, all in tatters, shaggy-bearded, gray-faced, hollow-eyed, each looking blank interrogation and wild dismay at the others but at first saying not a word. They are struck dumb by this blow, benumbed by the horror. Now and then one of them tries to kick the dogs away from the two corpses, but the beasts have turned wild again at the smell of gore, and keep coming back. They dart in with sharp eager yelps. Do you hear them? The boar is drawn down by the odour of blood. The sow comes waddling, with her farrow. A grave must be dug, and dug deep, at once, and with bare hands alone, for every tool has been taken.

We stand there and watch, you and I, while the bodies are hastily huddled away with no ceremony, no prayer nor word, and only the beasts for mourners. Then we go back to the hut with the four men and the beasts and stare into that darker hole in the darkness. It has been home, and is now a ruin. It has held all that these men have owned, and the difference between little and nothing is—infinite. And then, too, if we are to put ourselves really in their place, we must flood our minds with the questions "Who has done this thing?" and "Where are they now?" and "What will they do next?" There's the mystery about John Allen and Joseph Clinch, whose bodies have not been found. Are they dead or alive? and, if alive, where? It is full night now, with no stars. The night is cold, and the fire is out, with no flint or steel or living coal to light another. —Oh, let's get away from this dreadful place, from the smell of the blood and the loudening cry of the breakers!

*   *   *

My hope is that you will come upon that passage when you are sitting close by your prospering fire, with 'Busy' in your lap, and one of the blue and white teacups I sent you from Paris in hand. My own situation is as comfortable as the gout allows, although Ponto is not in my lap—is never, in fact, allowed there, and perhaps does not even aspire to such eminence. I have just had tea. Anne Boleyn's little clock is at this moment striking five. Louis has briskened the fire, has picked up from the floor and arranged a few score of these sheets—unable, poor fellow, to read more than a word here and there with my stern gaze upon him—has solicitously inquired about my metatarso-phalangeal joint, and then, reluctantly, after snuffing the candles, has left the room with the tea-things.

And so, as Lord Hamlet says, to thinking—or, if you prefer, imagining. Is there a difference? and, if so, precisely what? The common belief that imagination is a wild, uncontrollable, all but savage faculty of the mind which civilized man should ignore, or something like a flawed mirror distorting each thing it reflects—what are we to say of that?

John Locke, now, in his *Essay Concerning Human Understanding* . . . But why be pedantic and old-fashioned? Horace Walpole says, in his latest and longest letter to William Cole, that imagination, rightly so called, is the highest, deepest, and altogether noblest kind of thinking. Other kinds are mainly concerned with facts and their consequences, but this with the truth. Other kinds set two facts side by side and coolly observe their differences. This kind brings the same two really together, and, before you can look twice, by the blessing of God they've produced a child! Most thinking looketh upon the outward parts, but imagination upon the heart. It pierces to the quick, the core. It lifts almost any gray cooling ember from the fireside of life—like John Chester, say, when lighting his pipe—and blows or sucks it back again to glow as a crimson gleed. If Kitty Clive were here now, looking over my shoulder, she'd say: "Why not say it right out, Horry, and call it a kind of love?" —She went to London this morning on some dreary Drury Lane business, but she'll be back for dinner.

A notion occurs to me at this moment which I may as well set down at once. Two hundred years from now—and you are to make sure, remember, that it can't happen earlier—some misguided person or persons may think of turning the present epistle into a book! I don't say this is likely, but I hope you won't think it impossible. In all modesty let me confide to you that I do not expect my name to die quite out of human memory in that space of time. The thousands of letters I shall leave behind me will not, I think, be wholly ignored. Most of them, taken singly, will be trifles of course; but in their sum they will contain a mass of gossip, scandal, anecdotes, and characterizations which no historian will ever dare to neglect.

And how will the world know about these letters? Sir, if Alexander Pope could cheat a publisher into printing his correspondence while he was still alive, how much more readily will Posterity be persuaded to preserve that of Horace Walpole! —And then, just when they think they have every scrap of me safely housed between covers, to come down on them with this epistle, characteristic in most respects but dealing for once with a vast subject of utmost significance, and all of it quite unknown! —Do you see it?

Well then, there will arise the question what to call that bantling of ours, orphaned well over a century before its birth. Others will decide, but a suggestion to be so wedged into our text that it cannot be ignored will not be unwelcome. First let me say that I hope they won't call it 'A Week at Strawberry Hill'! My ghost would walk and its gorge would rise—if ghosts have gorges—should the not impossible popularity of the book bring in the profane vulgar to trample my terraces, frighten my duo-centenarian goldfish, scratch their names on my painted glass, and whisper with sniggers in corners: "Now which room was it, exactly, where . . ." —Oh, no, William; not that! I've had enough of that, as you will learn in due time, to last me for one eternity.

Something tells me that your vote would go for the title "Jenkins' Ear," and I do not deny that the suggestion has merits. The sound of those words, once heard, is ugly enough, Apollo knows, to stick in the ear for ever, and if you add an *s* to the possessive case you can make it also a jaw-breaker. This title, moreover, is nasty, brutish, and short, as Thomas Hobbes truly says the language of most men is wont to be. It names an object of antiquarian interest such as one amateur of the past might well snatch out of time's enormous grab-bag and hold up and describe and evaluate, as I am doing here somewhat elaborately, to another. And then, finally, it is an honest title. With that omnific, ubiquitous Ear the book will really be concerned as a whole and in every part—aye, even to that scene on Cape St. Anthony to which, let us hope, we may soon return.

And yet, if I could have my way . . . I wonder if you recall what Kitty Clive said back there on Monday when Blandison asked what she hoped to teach him. "Oh," said she, drawling the words ever so little, seeming to fumble her way through them as if not quite sure— though she was to a nicety—just where she was coming out: "Oh, something—about—love."

That's what this book will be, and there's the title I would choose.

But I can see that you don't like it. "Love," you are saying, "is an ambiguous word. It lies either below the dignity, or else above the personal knowledge of Horace Walpole. —In short, then, No, as Lord Madlands emphatically says, No!"

Very well; do you decide the title, and I'll write the book. But I cannot possibly write it without the sympathetic imagination which enables me in some degree to enter and share other lives. If Kitty wants to call that sort of thing by that dubious name, we can't stop her.

*   *   *

Under the circumstances, what could Morris and his three companions do except try for a third time to cover on foot the three hundred miles between Freshwater Bay and Buenos Ayres? They were barefooted now, their clothes had rotted away, they had no weapon or tool, not even a knife, and no means of making fire. Their dogs and swine, useless for food because they could not be cooked or butchered, went with them. On the way up the coast they found a dead whale, many cockles, and the stranded wreck of a man-of-war, apparently Spanish. By great effort they got as far as the Cape of the River Plate, less than a hundred miles from their destination, but there encountered a multitude of creeks and muddy swamps which in their enfeebled condition they were quite unable to struggle through. For two days they lingered there, tormented by flies and mosquitoes, striving to find a way up-river, often sinking shoulder-deep in the bogs. At length, nearly starved and exhausted, they turned back for the third time to Freshwater Bay.

Three northward attempts on the eastern coast as on the west, and then on both sides of the continent a despairing return to the first point of departure with the expectation of dying there; the wild ceremony of sin-eating on the one side and the ravin of beasts on the other; a dwindling on each side of the number of men involved until there are left only four—these parallels, William, have not been devised by me to make a symmetrical pattern. Account for them as you may, they are in the story as it was told. More important than those I have mentioned, though less apparent, is the fact that on the Pacific and Atlantic coasts alike these countrymen of ours were tormented by every woe, one would say, that fiends could devise or human flesh endure. If you will but think back to the start of the *Wager*'s voyage and list their miseries one by one, realizing how unlikely either of us would be to survive the least of them, you will comprehend why it was that neither Chepe's company at Wager Island nor that of Isaac Morris at Freshwater Bay had any strong desire or expectation, following their last return, that they might live.

And yet living, one knows, is a habit that needs no support of reason. Morris, Andrews, Cooper, and Duck took up the task with little zest, but perhaps with a sense of obligation. They rebuilt their ruined hut, made themselves new shoes and a rude sort of cape and breeches of seal-skin, and listlessly tried in sundry ways to render their physical condition less miserable. Having no arms to defend themselves against wild beasts, they never ventured far abroad. For a month or more they lived chiefly upon their dogs and swine, killed by stones and eaten raw. About a quarter of a mile from the hut they found a dead horse of which, by way of change, they took now and then a morsel.

The story grows dull at this point, I know; but so was the living— that is, the waiting for death. One must consider that these men had been together now for a long time, so that their stock of stories, ideas, opinions, and witticisms had been exhausted. Neither was there any prospect of an early replenishment. Of society—after the dogs and the swine were gone—they had none. No cards had they, no theatres or masked balls or little dinner parties, no books or newspapers or letters coming in and going out, no servants, no gossip, no gout, no . . . Forgive me for labouring the obvious. I'm only trying to realize their situation, to imagine it, to put myself there. And I find that I can't. For a moment I think I've grasped it, and then in a twinkling it slips like a ghost away.

To be sure there are always—or so the poets tell us—the consola- tions of nature. This hut of theirs stood close up against a forty-foot cliff of gravel and clay, to get what shelter was possible from the incessant wind. The prospect was toward the sea, on which there appeared for month after month not one sail. Do you suggest that there must have been a solemn grandeur in the music of the breakers, and a beauty in the many-hued crumbling of the foam? I reply with the query whether these undeniable splendours are not more readily discerned and enjoyed when one has a hope of seeing and hearing, some day, something else. And then if they climbed the cliff and walked abroad over the land, what was there to see? An almost perfectly level and featureless plain, covered with tall grass in summer and thistles that grew beyond the height of a man. Underfoot were sand, gravel, and rounded pebbles, so that there was no need of the many shells that snapped and cracked to make a man feel that he had, after all, been drowned long since and was walking now on the limitless floor of the sea. The sky was a vast blue bowl inverted, as empty of cloud for day after day as the land below was of trees.

For month after month in winter and summer, no change, no life, save of tall grass blown by the wind; but then of a sudden they would hear from many miles off a gathering thunder of hooves, a frenzy of screaming, and wild horses by tens of thousands, sometimes with black cattle among them, would sweep across the plain with streamers of fire leaping behind. No life, and then life in unimaginable profusion, with death following after—yes, that was the notion we got from Morris of those South American plains—the Pampas, I think he called them. 'Twas a new word to me, either Indian or Spanish. The horses had been introduced by the Spaniards, he said, long ago. He thought they were of the Barbary breed. —Think of it: a few beasts born in Northern Africa are taken across the sea, and perhaps two, male and female, escape from their masters, say a hundred years ago, and now their progeny run wild by the million in that new land! —Scarcely less a wonder, Morris said, were the multitudes of birds that flew north and south in the spring and autumn migrations, often so darkening the sky all day that one doubted whether the sun had risen. He had not supposed there were, or had been since the creation, such numberless myriads of birds.

These last few pages are clearly an exception to my general rule that what I should find tedious to read I refuse to write. Frankly, I am bored, perhaps quite as much as you are, by all this futile tramping up and down the eastern coast of Patagonia, and not the less because we have already seen much the same kind of thing on the western coast. I agree with you that if we are to have any more consumption of decayed animals, whether roasted or raw, whether horses, seals, whales, or even armadillos, I shall either fall asleep or burst into tears. And yet there's the problem, how to give the effect of monotony without being monotonous, and how to bring home to ourselves the amazing endurance of these men without enduring some slight tedium on our own account.

That's a question, you say, for writers of fiction, perhaps of history, but I suggest that it bears quite as much upon letter-writing, even conversation. 'Tis a law of the mind that a single incident, person, or object—and the more singular it is the better—has more meaning and interest than a thousand. Think, for example, of those numberless horses, those inconceivable multitudes of birds. At best they are an idea in the mind, not an image. But now were I able to make you see just one great rosy flamingo or a single wild horse on the dead run with fire behind him, why, then, I think, you would be in no danger of dozing.

One morning, while out on the hunt, having ventured much farther from the hut than usual, the four castaways found in that treeless land the dry fallen trunk of a large tree. Well instructed as they had been by Gunner Bulkeley, they saw at once that it must have been placed there—had been especially transported perhaps from the far-away Andes—by Divine Providence, and this undoubtedly with the intention that they should make a boat of it, fit the boat with sails of sealskin, and then, lying at their ease and regaling themselves on the way upon the flesh of armadillo, let the south wind waft them up the coast and into the River Plate, and so to Buenos Ayres.

To all four this seemed an excellent plan, and they would have set to work upon it at once had it not been for a few difficulties of execution which Divine Providence had apparently not considered. One was that the trunk, weighing several tons, lay several miles from the coast. Then there was the fact that they had no fire to hollow the trunk in the Indian way. Neither had they an axe, a hatchet, a knife, or any flake of metal to serve for gouging, cutting, splintering even.

You see the situation, and it may be that the more you think about it the more you will wonder why these interpositions of Infinite Power should be so incomplete, suggesting less the spirit of love than they do the punishment visited by a jealous pagan deity upon Tantalus the Titan. These four men, however, were neither philosophers nor clergymen. Therefore they set their wits awork, and at last John Duck, the negro, had an inspiration. He reminded his companions that some eleven months before, at the farther end of their first attempt at Buenos Ayres, he had thrown away his musket—a miserable weapon in any case and weighing some twenty pounds. But circumstances alter cases, and now the musket that had not been worth the trouble of bringing back was thought well worth the effort of walking sixty miles and more north to get. —You will be glad to hear that on the way homeward they found several ostrich eggs in the sand. This must have been providentially arranged, for Morris earnestly insisted that during their previous residence of over a year on that coast they had not seen a single ostrich!

I don't know whether you have ever made a hatchet out of a musket-barrel with only a stone for hammer and a rough rock for your anvil. If not, let me tell you that, first, you beat half the length of the barrel perfectly flat and smooth. This will take you about a year, counting in the time spent in recovering from aches and bruises. Next, you whet an edge on this flattened half, using the rock as a whetstone. The other half will serve as a handle, and then you will be prepared to spend the rest of your life in trying to change a log into something resembling a boat.

Our four English sailors with nothing else to do—no sermons to write, no ruined abbeys to visit, no interminable letters to read—made better time on their hatchet than could be expected of a gouty clergyman. They worked at it, I judge, with a sort of concentrated fury from every dawn to dark, no doubt feeling that each blow brought them nearer the white cliffs of Dover. Indeed there are few scenes in the annals of Jenkins' Ear that come so clearly before me now as the picture in the mind of these four naked men standing close together there by the anvil-rock, their shaggy hair falling in elflocks over their faces but not hiding the fierce intensity of their gaze at that scrap of iron more precious to them than gold. —And not the intensity alone, but the patience of it, William! They walk sixty miles north and sixty miles back in order to beat and grind and whet and hone in order to chop and split and gouge in order to sail and paddle away in the clumsiest imaginable craft in order to give themselves up to their Spanish foes in order to rot in prison for months or years in order to be sent home when peace is signed in order not to miss their excellent chance of being hanged.

But that, after all, is only my comment, my thought and feeling. I must try to stand out of the way and let the facts speak. There's that smashed finger of Cooper's, for instance, and the splitting of the blade along the edge so that for a time the men thought all their labour lost. I want you to see the dull gleam of the pounded iron, the glitter of stone dust on the anvil, the dark gouts of red on the trampled sand, but most of all those faces, those eyes. Do you hear the clamour of the gulls overhead? Do you catch that nameless odour given forth—I know not by what, but I have smelt it and smell it now—when two stones are strongly clashed together? Do your arm and shoulder ache with the shock of that pounding, I say, and does the sweat stand out on your brow?

I may be going too far, but surely I have made clear what I mean by the transmuting power of the sharply particular instance, by the unique, unpredictable, irregular, chance-born event. Surely you can see that this incident is more revealing than a hundred pages of abstract and generalized statement. Well then, if that is true, what sense can be made of Samuel Johnson's pontifications concerning what he calls "the grandeur of generality"? —But posterity will not remember Samuel Johnson, and so let us take an example from a poem of our own time which will never be forgotten. One line of it, "the short and simple annals of the poor," will serve our turn, and you will please compare those words with the picture of four men furiously at work turning a rusty musket-barrel into a hatchet.

These men are "poor" enough for the purpose, God knows, and here is one representative scene from their "annals." Now observe that so long as you stand off at a gentlemanly distance you can keep your description of the scene admirably simple and short. You do so quite easily—nay, 'tis easier than not—by the mere preservation of your ignorance. But, sir, beware of drawing closer! At every step of approach some gaud or trapping of "grandeur" will fall from you, some human sympathy will take its place, until by the time you catch sight of Cooper's smashed finger and see the stain on the blade —it is not "blue blood," of course, only red—you may feel that the annals of these four men are by no means simple and cannot be briefly told.

But whither away, Horace Walpole, and what is happening here? How comes it that an innocent question about how to write a story leads you on to these gross indiscretions? Nay, at every turn of this tale, meseems, your thought goes shirking off and down into some democratico-methodistical enthusiasm, some new treachery to your breeding and birth and class. Draw your self, if you have one, together! Drag the Walpole antelope home and tether him there, if need be with a ring in his nose! What is Cooper's smashed finger to you? In a word, what would Louis say!

* * *

It is written that the ways of Divine Providence are inscrutable and past finding out. Don't ask me, therefore, why it happened that after the log had been miraculously provided, and also the ostrich eggs and the musket barrel and the smashed finger—in fact, just when the hatchet was finished and ready for use—the whole heavenly plan was changed and the hatchet was never used at all.

(I'm not quite sure of that, William; but it sounds well. It rounds out the period. There's a possibility that Cooper used it for cutting off his finger. Who knows? Who will care, two hundred years hence? Certainly it was not used for making a boat.)

How this happened, I know. I continue to translate Morris's Devonian, which at this point grew even wilder. Cooper, Andrews, and Duck left him alone at the hut one day while they went down to Long Point after limpets. As dusk came on he was sitting there by himself—fireless now, dogless, hogless, perhaps even hopeless—when he heard the soft thudding of hooves on the sandy beach outside. But horses, here by the sea? Wild horses, perhaps? If so, Heaven-sent as another means of reaching Buenos Ayres! You see him dart to the doorway and peer into the half-light. Yes, a dozen horses dark against the foam and all of them screaming it seems to him as they come rushing headlong straight for the hut. Not until they are almost upon him does he see that each horse has a rider crouching so close to the animal's back that beast and man look one. Each trails a long, slender lance, pointed at him. The screams have come from the men, not the horses, and they are meant not to express but to induce the emotion of terror. They succeed in that intention.

But this quill is not for such tasks, and there's no need to elaborate an event which filled less than a minute. Enough that Morris, bewildered and helpless, was surrounded by a band of huge, copper-coloured, vile-smelling fellows who stared down at him unpleasantly from the backs of tall half-wild horses. Their looks suggested nothing more agreeable than instant decapitation, dismemberment, and boiling in a pot. It was, I judge, an awkward moment.

From the hugest of his captors, a magnificent giant later on to be known as Orellana, Morris caught an intelligible word or two from which he guessed that he was being taken for a Spaniard; and by great good fortune he had enough Spanish not only to dispel that vile suspicion but to make it clear that his country was presently at war with Spain. Then at once there went up a jovial shout of "Amigo! Amigo!" and with roars of laughter and much vigorous back-thumping he was hoisted to the crupper of Orellana's horse.

That was the first time in his life, Morris said, that he had ever bestridden the noblest of beasts; and the strangeness of his position was not lessened for him by either the sight or the smell of his horse-mate's majestic back. One can see that, after a long period of humdrum, shocking things were happening to Midshipman Morris in too swift a succession; but it seems that this smell was at first the most nerve-shattering experience of them all. He was soon revived, however, by the arrival of Andrews, Cooper, and Duck, all mounted like him and looking as cheerful as could be expected of English sailors on horseback with their arms tightly clasped about naked Patagonians. They too had evidently made their explanations and had been promptly accepted, horsed, and run off with, as "amigos."

John Duck sang out as he came jolting up: "Don't be afraid, Isaac. It's all right. We're all here." —So, indeed, they were, and so, apparently it was. The Patagonians, at any rate, were delighted, as though by some excellent jest. Their swart wild faces shone with glee, and they laughed like children at play. This happiness, moreover, seemed to be unconnected with cannibalistic expectations, for instead of rubbing their own bellies they thumped their new-found amigos on the back as though to congratulate them and to express their joy in a mutual good fortune.

Now I need not remind you, William, that every good Englishman grows cautious in proportion to the boisterosity of his welcome, wishing of course to satisfy himself about the social status of his welcomers before he lets himself go. But this takes time, often many years, and the four examples of English reserve sitting there on horseback were not given minutes for making up their minds. Besides, it was not a question of letting themselves go; they were taken. All at once Orellana gave a great yell, whereupon he and his men coalesced once more with their steeds—changed back, if you like, into centaurs —and then, clapping heels as it were to their own sides, scrambled up the cliff, reached the plain above, and darted away southwestward, jolting the poor sailors, as Morris said, "woundily." He himself felt on that wild ride that he must be coming in two. He forgot about the smell of Orellana and clung to him closer than does the proverbial but probably non-existent brother. He told us, in fact, that he never recovered that smell in anything like its pristine vigor, perhaps because he acquired it—and you will soon learn how—himself.

Night fell, and the Southern Cross shone bright, whilst the little band of centaurs, stormy-maned, thunder-footed, rushed like a terrene tempest across the plain with yells and gay calls and laughter and noises meant for song. Not in haste but in pure joy of speed they raced and ran through the dark, going smoothly and evenly now as birds on the wing and ever more swiftly it seemed as they caught a glimpse from far on of a glowing and growing wonder of wind-blown flame, aye, of fire, the beautiful stranger dropped down from the sun to help men fight the cold and the dark and the dread. And Morris forgot his fear and pain at the sight from afar of that glory of flame once known, long lost, and now strangely found. Ah, it bloomed as they rode, as they rushed, like a great crimson flower in the dark, with petals up-reaching, flaring, and all round it the beautiful moving bodies of men black in shadow and red in the glow and huge and naked and wild with hair hanging shagged and shining eyes and mouths that laughed and sang in the midst of a circle of horses, hundreds of horses unbroken but hobbled and tethered and struggling, screaming, afroth with the wine of their freedom still working, and hating man's will and the change coming on them from horses to centaurs as in through the struggle of wild Pampas horses they rushed and they rode to the edge of the fire and . . .

*　　*　　*

Just there, William, having got well started into that sentence and while my quill was careering across the page like an unbitted and unshod steed, I caught a glimpse through the corner of my eye of a vague shape moving, of a gray and vapourish figure half hidden in the shrubbery near my window, making gestures of aesthetic anguish. Ponto began to growl. The short hairs at the back of my neck stood on end. Shivers ran down my back. My hands shook. My quill fell to the floor. Quite forgetting the gout, I rose and stood by the window, trembling.

All these, you will understand, were the signs not of fear but of wrath, for this thing had happened before. Again and again during my residence here, when my quill had broken free and was going at its own gait in prose or verse, there had occurred the same insolent trespass by a hunched four-foot wisp that had once been a human wasp. Thirteen years in the grave had not convinced him that his reign was over.

For ten seconds perhaps I stood there and watched him twisting, writhing, grimacing in the dusk, striving to convey in sign-language his contempt of my headlong sentence—his scorn which would once have gone into a couplet sharp as a dagger and with poison on the point. Then of a sudden I bethought me that two could play at this game of literary criticism by dumb-show, and also that in his own expressions of opinion he had never felt restricted by the canons of good taste, politeness, or even decency. Therefore, slowly, deliberately, gazing steadily at him the while, I raised my right thumb to my nose and, while holding it there, gently agitated the four fingers in the manner which you may recall from the years we spent together at Eton. Never, of course, did you and I employ that gesture; but we observed it with interest as used by the sons of butchers and other such vulgar persons. I think we called it "cocking a snook."

This gesture appears to be of great antiquity, and universally intelligible, even in the spirit world. At any rate it was immediately understood by the ghost of Alexander Pope. With a look of incredulous horror which I cannot describe, the spectre faded, vanished, and took itself off.

"Excellent, sir!" you say. "Alexander Pope is put in his place. Yet I observe that your style is still prancing about on a tall wild horse; and how you are to climb down again . . ."

William, you see the difficulty at once. Kitty Clive has just stepped in for tea, and I've read her that passage about the ride. "Cross it out!" she suggested at first. When I wouldn't, and wanted to know how I should go on from there, she said: "Well, now, a bad writer of plays, when he gets into trouble— Do you know what he does?"

"No. Tell him, Kitty."

"He seats his people at dinner; and then the audience—if it's an English audience—forgets how bad the lines are because it's so much more interested in what those people are having to eat."

Very well; that's what I do—or rather, it's what the Patagonians did when, by jocular poking of ribs and congratulatory thumps they found that their guests were emaciated to a pitiful degree. Orellana shouted orders; three Indians slipped away from the shine and into the dark struggle of horses, with knives agleam in their hands; others threw on the blaze huge armfuls of dry thistles so that the flames shot high in a torn flapping cone and the stars went pale. The Englishmen, blue with cold, their jaws chattering, drew close to the fire with tremulous hands outstretched and saw as they stood there a wonder, an awe, an astonished conjecture leap up in the glittering eyes of their hosts whose bare bodies, much farther off, were shining, streaming with sweat. "What can they be thinking, planning, these shaghaired, white-toothed, probably man-eating giants?" And then, on the other side: "Whence come these pallid starvelings, so avid of fire? Must they not be wandering gods of the sun, or priests of that holy flame? —Let us feed them and treat them well."

The scream of a horse in death-agony shrills in from the dark, and then, minutes later, four collops of flesh are handed to the sailors. They stare at them, horrified, and hunger changes to nausea; for though they have learned to eat seal, horse, whale, and armadillo in various stages of decay, the mere thought of consuming flesh still aquiver with life is strange to them, and repugnant. Their quick-witted hosts are soon brought to realize, if not to understand, this prejudice, and, whilst the horse-meat is roasting, they are regaled on whortleberry wine in huge goblets of horsehide. This is a wine which I am unable to compare with the products of Oporto, Xeres, Bordeaux, or Madeira; but according to Lieutenant Morris its effect is to induce a rapidly mounting confidence in one's companions and more cheerful views of one's situation in general.

Better, perhaps, even than Kitty Clive's suggestion for an author in difficulties is the expedient of getting one's people comfortably drunk, and then to bed. This, in fact, can be safely left to the imagination of one's reader, even though his personal habits—like yours, William, since your undergraduate days—are by no means riotously convivial. You can see, hear, and smell for yourself how that evening under the stars went on, with first the goblets of horsehide going round, then the roast horse going round, then again the goblets going round and round, then the dancers and the singers and the drums-of-horsehide-beaters white and red and arm-in-arm going round, then the fire itself going round, until at last every barrier and distinction of race, colour, creed, smell, and language, even that possibly oldest and deepest discrimination between men of the land and those who go down to the sea in ships, was lost out of mind as a trifling matter compared with the wonder of fire and the glory of wine and the boon of comradeship.

All that, I say, you can see for yourself. I add only one detail which had lingered in Morris' otherwise somewhat confused recollections of that evening. He told us how, when the fire was dying, Orellana picked up little John Duck, now soundly asleep, carried him to a tent of horsehide, laid him gently down on a horsehide mattress, and drew over him a blanket of horsehide. Then he himself lay down at the door of the tent and immediately fell asleep. All the other Indians, some thirty in number, slept by the smouldering fire, surrounded by horses. So did Morris, Andrews, and Cooper.

* * *

Here, then, was an intervention of Providence, a turn of Fortune's wheel, or, if you prefer, a twitch of Jenkins' Ear, as sudden and startling as any to be found in this veracious chronicle. Not even the Honourable John Byron's prosperity in Santiago, if he had been inclined to describe it, could have provided a sharper contrast with miseries undergone before. Between the dusk of one day and the dawn of the next, these four men passed from despair to delight, from solitude to multitude, from starvation to repletion, and from nakedness to the prospect, at least, of horsehide breeches!

I would have you pause upon this felicity of theirs, and perpend, and learn from it—what? Why, to be sure, that I, having given you some notion of the woes lived through by Morris and his companions all the way from Portsmouth harbour to their arrival at the camp on the Pampas, now find myself balked, stammering, embarrassed by the fact that they are, at last, happy.

"Oh well," you say, "they'll soon get over it, and then the tale can go on again."

True. And, seeing that you know so much about these matters, I shall let you imagine that sunny interval between the cloud that had passed and the cloud coming on. A few hints from Morris' narrative will meet all your needs—especially if you keep in mind as a background such things as the hatchet-making, the hold of the *Speedwell,* Wager Island, the wreck, the storm, the scurvy, Boatswain King, Captain Chepe, and Midshipman Campbell.

Orellana's band of horse-eating Indians wandered westward across the vast South American plain for some six months, traversing in that time a distance of a thousand miles and gathering up as they went not only a number of other such bands but fifteen hundred wild horses. Time, to them, was a matter not of clocks but of suns, moons, and seasons. Their work was also a dangerous and a thrilling sport, with much contest and rivalry in it of man with man and of each band with all the others. It required expert horsemanship and a skill in throwing the plaited horsehide lash at which Morris and his companions never ceased to marvel. Morris said that this lash—in Spanish, lasso—is of two kinds, and is used in two different ways. The first is about two inches broad and fifty feet long, with a running noose at one end, which is whirled by the horseman as he rides at top speed after his quarry and then thrown over the head of the beast and drawn tight. The other kind is a narrow strap of horsehide, eight feet in length, to either end of which is fastened a ball of stone or iron. One of these balls is whirled round the head of the hunter until he arrives within the right distance, and then is thrown in such a way as to entangle the legs of his game.

Our four sailors now had God's plenty of fresh air, space, horse-meat, and wine of whortleberry, so that they rapidly regained their weight and strength. John Duck, indeed, grew positively obese by constant overeating and underwork. What saved him from gout is a mystery, for the Indians set so high a value upon him—apparently because of his black skin and his habit of sitting even closer to the fire than his white companions—that he was never called upon, or allowed, to exert himself in any way. As for the other three, all of them quite useless, of course, in the capture and taming of horses, they seem to have done as they pleased—now and then skinning a horse or bringing water or gathering thistles for the evening fire.

More valuable than these contributions, however, was the amuse-ment they gave to their hosts in falling off horses and trying to throw the lasso and the bolas. Thus they kept the whole band for months in laughter. Without intending it, they served in the dual role of demi-gods and clowns—or as messiahs, one might say, sent expressly to save mankind from boredom. Accordingly—although this showed a total ignorance on the Patagonians' part of how to treat messiahs—they were well cared for, treasured, perhaps even beloved.

Our countrymen did not at once understand this. There was the initial difficulty which every true Englishman experiences in realizing that, to foreigners, he may look slightly ridiculous. Then, too, it may be that their former miseries had blunted their sense of humour. Finally, we may ask how well they had been prepared in the England of our time for the really complicated situation they were in.

We English feel that the clown, like the poet, is born, not made. He owes his success, we believe, not to anything like art but to his misfortune. We misinterpret the earnest, absorbed expression of countenance with which all the best clowning is done and assume that the clown is stupid. Now the Patagonians also went wrong, but more intelligently. Witnessing the agonized efforts of our countrymen to hurl the lash and to stay on the backs of wild horses, they were unable to conceive that grown men could do those things so badly, or could so ludicrously fail to do them at all, unless for purposes of entertainment. They were accordingly entertained, and all the more as the efforts of Morris and Cooper and Andrews grew more grimly determined. With every fall from a horse, every snarl in a lash or blow on the head from a bolas, they gave themselves up to a purer joy of laughter and a more affectionate pride in their Englishmen.

As I have said, all this was at first perplexing to the newcomers. Failing to recognize that they had already been granted exalted rank as clowns, they must needs puzzle their heads about their social station and ask themselves whether, besides being captives, they were regarded as slaves, guests, friends, or potential members of the tribe. Still another and less pleasant possibility was suggested by the pampering of John Duck—a thing not easily comprehensible except on the supposition that the Indians meant to eat him, and then, at convenient intervals, the rest of them.

John Duck seems not to have troubled his head with this conjecture; but it disturbed the white men, who in other regards felt increasing contentment with their situation. One must consider that until the day of their capture they had heard scarcely anything about the Patagonians except the Spanish report, put about with commercial motives, that all of them were giants and that their food was man. Most of our countrymen believe this today, I suppose, and regard the alleged cannibalism as another dietetic oddity of foreigners on a level with the French liking for snails. In the minds of Morris, Andrews, and Cooper there was a more personal and immediate concern. Not content with mere rumour, they wished to know.

It was at least partly with this question in mind that Morris did all he could to win the friendship of Orellana—that rather magnificent barbarian, somewhere in the neighbourhood of seven feet tall, whom he already liked and admired. To this end he made all possible speed in improving his command of the mingled Spanish, English, Patagonian, and sign-language in which he and the chieftain conversed. One evening, as they two were reclining together beside the fire, he put the question directly—no doubt because his vocabulary did not allow of circumlocution—whether he and his companions were destined for the knife and the pot. The Indian, when at last he understood, was hugely amused. He rose to his feet and with both arms made a wide sweeping gesture toward the ten or twelve hundred horses standing hobbled and tethered all about the camp. "Ah, no! No, amigo!" he shouted. "Habemos muchos caballos!"

You observe, William, the courteous implication that so long as the horsemeat held out it would be absurd for the band to fall back upon so inferior an article of diet as the flesh of Englishmen. One does not see how that information could have been conveyed with greater delicacy of feeling.

Another reason why the Englishmen were not eaten was that the Indians needed them as gambling stakes. John Duck, to be sure, was never wagered, for it seems to have been agreed from the start that he was royal property; but the other three often changed hands several times in a single night's play at dice. Morris told us that he was wagered at one time, successfully, against a pair of spurs, and at another was lost to an Indian who had bet a handful of ostrich feathers. On that same evening, however, another Indian bet a brass pan against him, and won.

This must have been bewildering, perhaps even a little humiliating, yet such exchanges made no appreciable difference in the situation of the three sailors. However their nominal masters might change from game to game, they remained the property, guests, friends, or partners of the whole band.

These barbarians gambled with utmost eagerness, but rather for the excitement than with any thought of personal gain. Indeed it would seem that their notions of property are extremely vague and undeveloped, so that whatever belongs to one member of the tribe belongs in some sense to all. Thus a man may wager and lose at dice everything he has in the world—that is to say, his saddle and stirrups, his lasso, bolas, knife, breeches, and lance. Now in our best London clubs, of course, a gamester in this situation promptly blows out his brains; but not so on the Pampas. There it is perfectly evident that each member of the tribe must be suitably equipped, not only on his account but for the common good. Accordingly, the ruined man of the night before rides forth in the morning with breeches, lance, knife, bolas, lasso, stirrups, and saddle, fully prepared once more for the duties of life and another ruinous game at dice.

You will recall my mention of a smell that Morris encountered, or was attacked by, on the evening when he and his fellows were run away with from their hut on the coast. It was the smell, you remember, of Orellana; yet Morris soon found that it was not peculiar to the leader, but, like all things else, was equally shared by all members of the band. Later on, he was to discover that it was the tribal, the Patagonian, smell, so distinctive and idiosyncratic that a herd of wild horses feeding at night on the Pampas and suddenly catching that taint from ten miles upwind would at once turn tail and rush through the dark in frantic stampede. Always, therefore, they had to approach a herd from down the wind; and the skill required in horse-hunting was thereby much increased.

That much Morris told us about the potency and effect of this smell, and you will admit that the suggestion is vivid; but when he tried to suggest how the smell actually smelt he failed entirely, not through his own fault but through that of the English language. For indeed it is surprising, when one considers our wealth in eye-words and words of the ear—nay, even of touch—how meagre, weak, and unprofitable is the vocabulary of the nose. How to explain this linguistic discrimination against an organ so prominent, so useful, and, in health, so inoffensive, I do not know. If only we could enlist the assistance of your Busy and my Ponto, with what wonderful new-found words of the nose, unknown to Samuel Johnson, we might enrich and refine our native speech! As matters now stand, however, Lieutenant Morris had to content himself, in describing the Patagonian smell, with the inadequate adjective "terrible."

This was to express his own feeling at the time of the first assault. During his wild ride with Orellana, as I have said, he thought of other things, and he found also on his first evening by the campfire that the smell grew less obnoxious at each circulation of the horsehide goblet. When he awoke at dawn of the following day, however, amid some thirty recumbent Patagonians, there it was again—overpowering, frightful, intolerable. He might have tried to run away if he had not been so fascinated by the conduct of the Indians as they awoke and caught their first conscious breaths of the morning air. Each of them first rubbed his eyes, then sniffed suspiciously, then suddenly sat up with mingled astonishment and disgust, gazed about for a distracted moment or two, fixed his eyes upon the Englishmen—not counting John Duck—and then held his nose, meanwhile making derisive nasal noises.

I judge that nothing more completely unintelligible had happened to Morris, Andrews, and Cooper in all their travels; and a swift analysis of the reasons for their bewilderment shows that the sum of them was indeed overwhelming. In the first place they were of course aware, like all true Englishmen, that foreigners don't bathe. They knew also, or believed, that among foreigners in general the Indians of America are the unbathingest. Moveover, of this conviction they had at the moment what seemed irrefutable olfactory proof. You see, then, how shocking it was that the most odoriferous of Indians should be holding their noses, actually, at Englishmen—and at Englishmen, too, whose only diversion for months had been a daily plunge into the surf!

But let us not brood overlong upon this absurdity. Orellana himself at last awoke, sniffed, sat up, and looked about him, aghast. At once he saw, or smelled, what was wrong. Moreover, he did not, like his followers, content himself with mere diagnosis or criticism. Accustomed as he was to prompt and responsible decisions, he issued orders which, in little more time than it takes to say it, resulted in the smearing of Morris, Andrews, and Cooper from head to toe with an oleaginous substance which, they later learned, was a rancid grease composed largely of horse-fat. —As for John Duck, he seems to have smelt well enough already.

This was the only occasion, I think, on which the Patagonians used any violence upon their captives. In itself and also in its immediate effects, it was an unpleasant experience, but, as that first day in the camp wore by, the Englishmen were delighted to find that the insects from which they had so longed suffered disliked the smell at least as much as they did. They felt cooler than formerly, in the heat of the sun, and when night came their coating of grease kept them warm. More and more, as time passed, they took comfort in having a smell which, however unpleasant, was the same as that of the men about them. Little by little, then, they forgot it—or, when it came to mind, remembered only its advantages. Scarcely more than a week had passed before the smell of the tribe had come to seem a decidedly good smell to them—a smell, indeed, orthodox, established, necessary, the absence of which amounted to an indecent exposure of the person.

But just at this point I see that I have written down "Indians" on my brief list of omitenda. Besides, you will remember that I mean to give only a few hints for your own imaginative picture of that long wandering across the plains. Let me hasten on, then, to the end of it, and to the arrival, just before winter set in, of those hundreds of men and their thousands of horses at Chief Town, Patagonia's capital city and royal seat.

You will paint that arrival as you see fit, but let me suggest that virility and splendour are called for, and some hint at the brave wild things we have left behind on the road to civilization. Try to render the mysterious immensities of level and empurpled distance out of which Orellana and his band are now riding homeward, westward, and a little upward, bringing in their numberless harvest of horses and their three English sailors and their inestimable John Duck. The sun, as they ride, drops behind the crests of the Cordillera de los Andes—what a magnificently mountainous name for mountains! —and among all the pigments of the imagination you will find no crimson too sanguinely encrimsoned for representing the long jagged line of light far up that quivers and throbs for a moment upon that lofty crepuscular snow. And then it is gone, and at once a thousand-mile shadow leaps from the crests to the eastern sea. At a gulp it swallows the Pampas down, its colours and forms and motions, yet leaves aloft and afloat for a while the gold of the cloud of dust moving steadily westward above the dull hoof-thunder. But behold, and see as they saw it, another sun born in the shadow far on there, far up, where in Chief Town the bruit of their coming has now been heard, that cloud of gold has been seen, and their King has kindled a dry-thistle fire. It sears a great ragged welcoming hole in the dark, that fire, as they ride and laugh and shout and sing towards their women and home after six months away and numberless wandering miles. You must somehow contrive to paint their voices, that joy of return out of man-time, good as it is, back into the time of women and warmth and home. Paint also their jubilant speed, the thrust of their spurs, the flog of their quirts, and the plunging shoulders of foam-spotted horses. But see now, again, how far on, far up, the great fire gives birth to a score of torches that wave for a moment, then mount, and come streaming down. Can you show that meeting, that trample of horses, those thousands of eyeballs agleam? Go on, then, to the arrival, the great fire, the women and children, the shouting of old names, the holding aloft of new babies, the circle of horsehide huts, and the gracious greeting of the King.

The King of Patagonia—I'm sorry that I cannot give you his name, armorial bearings, or even the name of his dynasty—was apparently almost as much pleased by the four sailors Orellana had brought him as by the muchos caballos. He received them almost at once in the royal hut, enthroned on a pile of horsehides and holding a long-stemmed pipe in lieu of a sceptre. On the one side of him lay a javelin, on the other a bow and arrows, and about his middle he wore as a robe of state a loose mantle of red cotton cloth. His crown was of ostrich feathers some three feet long; and, as these surmounted a figure gigantic to begin with, the total effect must have been truly regal.

And yet he was affable too, and hospitably inclined—having already learned from Orellana that the three palefaces were not, after all, Spaniards, but belonged to a country at war with Spain. When these three assured him, in reply to a question, that they were all "great men" in their country, his affability increased. The spot of white in Morris' black hair convinced him, as it had Orellana, that Morris was the greatest of the three—although, to be sure, it did not lift him to a rank approaching that of John Duck, so wonderfully black all over. His Majesty contemplated John Duck's colour with a sort of rapture. At the close of the audience he gave orders that a horse should be roasted at once for the three white men and that the negro should have a whole roasted horse to himself. Also he assigned to each of the white men a Spanish wife, chosen from a number of captives he had recently taken in a raid upon a Spanish settlement. To little John Duck, however, he gave an Indian wife about twice his tallth—and there's another indispensable word unknown to Johnson. The King, said Morris, could not bear the thought of a man with such a beautiful colour "bangling away his time on a white woman." (To "bangle," learned sir, is Devonian, or perhaps Druidic, for *to waste*. My Louis asked Morris particularly about it, and has since informed me.)

*   *   *

And so there you are, in spite of your gout, striding about in seven-league boots a good five thousand miles from home. In terms of strangeness—in difference, that is, from Bletchley Parsonage and Strawberry Hill—you have gone even farther. You rub your eyes, you pinch your better leg, you ask how ever you got there, and also how you will ever get back again.

But why come back at all? Lemuel Gulliver, as I recall it, was extremely reluctant in returning to this human world after his three years among the Houyhnhnms, those noble horses. Now the Patagonians have, to be sure, a few human traits still clinging to them; and yet they eat horse, they smell of horse, they laugh like horses, they cloth themselves, sleep upon, and build their houses of horse. In short, they are doing their best. You are profoundly interested in chivalry, and these men are admirable cavaliers. Already they have reached the stage of the centaur, half man and half horse, and beyond that they are unmistakably aspiring to complete Houyhnhnimity.

What? You won't? You want to return? —Ah, well, your friends would have missed you, and you would have missed the ruined abbeys, the cross-legged alabaster knights in old churches, and the letters awaiting transcription.

There arises the question, then, about your route of return, and for that you may safely trust to Jenkins' Ear. For the Ear, remember, has thus far led you all the way from the Painted Room in Fleet Street to the horsehide palace in Chief Town, and it remembers every turn we have taken in those many labyrinthine ways. My fingers, moreover, are firmly closed at this moment upon that Ear as it lies, all passion spent, in my pocket. I may tell you that my father's son has little mercy upon the auricular organ that caused my father's fall. My left hand is a very Torquemada in exacting confession—if need be, by torture. With pinches and wrenches and wringings it keeps on asking "What hast thou done?" whilst the right hand sets down the answers. —Ah, yes; we shall get home.

To be hopelessly, helplessly lost, sunk in darkness, distance, and oblivion like those men in the *Speedwell*—surely that is the ultimate horror. It goes beyond even the nightmare of Dante, whose damned souls know at least that they are in hell. But there's a lostness of another kind—temporary, local, delightful. How luxurious, almost, it is to wander away into that long dismal turmoil of the ages when Christians smote Paynims and Popes smote the Emperor and thou-

sands of heretics were burned or thumbscrewed back into the Faith—
to fumble and grope for a while in that midnight of time, I say, and
then to ring for tea!

You see the analogy, and I think it may suggest a reason why
people read novels, romances, even long dry-as-dust letters like this
one with nothing to recommend them except their strict fidelity to the
facts. What the good reader wants, I take it, is to be lost—not irre-
trievably. He delights in a safened danger, in a wilderness reaching
never too far from the lights of home. He likes to ride wild bare-
backed horses at furious speed through the night without laying down
his tobacco-pipe or lifting his bandaged foot from the buffet-stool.

*   *   *

For a time, then, at Chief Town, the Ear loosed its hold upon Isaac
Morris and his companions. It had drawn them there, and would in
due season draw three of the four men away again; but in the meanwhile they were left to their own devices. I am telling the story of
Jenkins' Ear, always refusing to be drawn aside into any extraneous
matters. Therefore you will not learn from me how the white sailors
learned to ride and to throw the lash and to hunt the fleet-footed
ostrich, how they raided Spanish haciendas and rode for their lives
before Pampas fires and helped to bring in magnificent harvests of
horses, and how finally, and to him best of all, Morris became the
trusted companion and closest friend of Orellana. He did not himself
dwell upon these matters, but only sketched them, and then looked
about the room to see whether that was enough.

Kitty wanted to hear something about Mrs. Morris—how she
looked, dressed, talked, and the like. It was clear to any one closely
watching that this was the one topic Morris had hoped to avoid; and
yet, after a momentary pause, he did his best with it. I also do my best,
as a bachelor, in the following paraphrase.

Mrs. Morris, it appears, was about seventeen, but definitely nubile.
She was somewhat languorous and slow-footed, except when dancing
before the fire at night with the castanets clip-clapping in her hands
and the drums of horsehide thudding and a hundred male voices shouting the time. Many Spanish songs she had by heart, and could sing to
a tiny guitar slung from her middle, swaying a little as she sang in

tones softly hoarse that drew a man's blood as the full moon pulls the
tide. Her black hair fell to her knees like night coming down, and her
eyes were pools of midnight. She seemed to be Night's daughter. Her
body, under the dusk of her hair, was not so pale as an English
woman's nor yet so bronzed as an Indian's, but like old elephant-tusk
or as though she had never eaten anything but olives. For the rest, she
was "a woman tall and well turned," Morris told us—by which he
probably meant that she was small in the right places and elsewhere
sufficiently large. In short, he gave us the impression that she was
exceedingly good and easy to behold in her simple garment of horse-
fat. As for talking, she did little of that, nor was there need of her
doing much. In character, he said, choosing a word usually applied to
the weather, she was "sultry."

Kitty thought this account had covered—or should we say uncovered?—the main points; and so we did not learn how, except for
the horse-fat, Mrs. Morris dressed, or what her Christian name was,
or whether, as Kitty would say, she was "really a good girl." You in
your turn, reverend sir, will have to do the best you can with the hints
provided. To my fancy this long-ago, far-away lady is somewhat dim,
but I surmise that in Morris' recollection she was still vividly dark,
languorous, unencumbered by raiment, and seventeen. I judge that he
actually loved this woman, and that through all the years it has been
his dearest hope to return some day to Chief Town, not only to be
with her but to see for the first time his child and hers. The earrings
he wore had been her gift. His simple statement that he had been
unable to give her anything whatever was, I thought, one of the most
touching things in his story.

*   *   *

The Ear had not forgotten Morris far away there on the eastern
slopes of the Andes, riding wild horses, chasing the ostrich, watching
Mrs. Morris dance in the firelight, gorging himself on roast horse, and
often, it may be, somewhat overtaken in the dark blue wine of whortle-
berries. It irked the Ear, we may well suppose, to see a bastard, one
brought up in a poorhouse, thus bangling away his time. For it is, I
need scarcely tell you, a moral Ear, an Ear puritanical, middle-class,
and therefore strongly inclined to ethical unrest at the sight of a poor

man enjoying himself. Besides, it may have felt a suspicion that Mrs. Morris had not come by that title through regular proclamation of the banns and blessing of Holy Church.

Moreover, I fear it cannot be urged on Morris' behalf that idleness was forced upon him. Why, for example, could he not have bestirred himself in the collection of that medicinal bark of the cinchona tree, so abundant in the Andean uplands? Was it not his moral duty as an Englishman to convert the Patagonians from their wild-horse-hunting and whortleberry-drunken ways into—well, let us not say "slavery," because that is what the Spaniards do, but profitably industrious habits? You know how dear this bark now is, and how hard to get in the unadulterate state. The demand is enormous, the market insatiable.

Why, sir, one's fancy kindles at the thought of the man's opportunities. He might so easily have cornered cinchona, as John Law tried to make the Mississippi flow into his pocket, after which there would have been trade-routes to establish across the South American continent—his friendship with Orellana being put to some practical use at this point—and then warehouses to build in Buenos Ayres, ships for ocean transport, wholesale houses in London, Antwerp, and Boston, a dozen quack doctors to proclaim for suitable fees that cinchona bark is more sovereignly panacean than Dr. James' powders or Bishop Berkeley's tar-water even, so that by little and little the smell of horse-fat would give way to the odour of millions and King George would dub him Knight of Quinine and on his alabaster tomb in Westminster Abbey men would carve once more, as in the time of William the Conqueror, the title which had been rendered illustrious: "Isaac Morris, Bastard."

But see, now, instead of that splendour, a vivid example of "bangling" and what it leads to. Isaac Morris came out of the Land of Cinchona as poor as he went in—except, of course, for two earrings, worth less than a guinea, given him by a woman of dubious virtue.

*　　*　　*

To a man of your coat, William, it should be a joy to observe the vigour of the Ear's action when its moral indignation had been thus aroused.

There came a time when the three white sailors were riding with Orellana on the horse-harvest many hundreds of miles to the eastward of Chief Town. John Duck was not with them because the King refused to risk so precious a man on horseback. Of the ten or twelve Indians in the band I caught the names of only four, and I set them down here because they are all that is now left in the world of that company. One was called "Ostrich Legs," another "Brains in His Belly," the third "Afraid of a Snake," and the last one "Very Big Fellow." Boyish names they are, like the cognomens we used to invent for one another at Eton, suggesting a rough but not unaffectionate comradeship in danger, work, sport, drink, and laughter. Since childhood, almost, these ten or twelve fellows had been riding with Orellana. They were the same men who had captured the sailors. —Oh, yes; I ought to say that Orellana's own name was probably not baptismal. To my ear, at least, it has not the right Patagonian ring, and I adopt from Blandison, who knows everything, the suggestion that it was given to or taken by him in memory of a certain Francisco de Orellana who, well over three hundred years ago, sought for El Dorado in the South American jungles and named the Amazon. Mr. James Adair told us that American Indians would naturally use the name of such a man, even though an enemy, in the sense of "War Chief."

I judge that Midshipman Morris was happy in this companionship, and looked back from it with no regret upon such civilized and Christian associations as those of the Exeter poorhouse and the hold of the *Speedwell*. In the exchange of "Midshipman" for "White Spot" he felt no degradation. He may even have been a little proud of winning admission to the band by learning to throw the lash and, though brought up a sailor, to ride wild horses. —Well, of course it is true that men have done less than that for membership in White's, the House of Commons, the English Clergy, and other such honorificabilitudinities; yet no one is better aware than you and I that earning a thing by hard work takes away all merit in its possession. Neither do we forget that pride is a deadly sin, and one to which foundlings and bastards are by no means entitled. Jenkins' Ear, equally sound on that point, saw to it that Morris' pride, happiness, or whatever, was soon punished by a fall.

As they approached Buenos Ayres on that long eastward ride, Orellana and his followers seem to have thought less and less about wild horses and more about Spanish women. We bachelors may surmise that their motive was religious—a wish to convert a few feminine souls, preferably young ones and well housed in the flesh, to the true faith of sun-worship. If so, their missionary efforts were easily successful. Going from farm to farm—"haciendas," I think Morris called them—they soon collected a sufficient number of novices who seemed not unwilling, after a few simple instructions, to assume the horse-fat. Thus provided, the Indians were about to turn back toward Chief Town when, in the middle of the night, they and their women and horses were suddenly overpowered and captured by a detachment of Spanish soldiers.

Morris said nothing about his own anguish in passing from the freedom of the Pampas to solitary confinement. His compassion was for his Patagonian friends, who never had known imprisonment of any sort or bowed to the will of any man. He was kept in chains for some months in Buenos Ayres and then was transferred, along with Andrews, Cooper, and sixteen other English prisoners to the Spanish man-of-war *Asia*.

This vessel had been Admiral Don Joseph Pizarro's flagship in the squadron sent out years before to intercept Anson. She was, in fact, the only survivor of that ill-fated squadron, not one member of which had rounded the Horn. Now, all but falling apart, she was riding at Monte Video, a hundred miles or so down-river, trying to make up a crew for the homeward voyage.

But a crew, Morris said, does not "come running" to a waterlogged, rat-riddled ship with a record of nought but disaster. Admiral Pizarro, besides, was known to be not a sailor at all but a soldier whose notions of seamanship scarcely went beyond frequent use of the lash and of a noosed rope slung from a yardarm. Spanish sailors feared him, Portuguese despised him, and as for the Indians of the region—none of whom, to be sure, had any knowledge of the sea—they hated his very name because it reminded them of the bloody-minded brute who, two centuries earlier, had drowned old Peru in blood.

You would think that this hatred could not last so long among a barbarous people; but Morris assured us that he had often heard Orellana execrate Pizarro, the so-called Conquistador, as though he were a living man, and that he had been present at many conferences in the horsehide palace which were solely concerned with plans for capturing Don Joseph Pizarro—completely identified by the Indians with Francisco of that surname—and putting him to as many different kinds of death as could be brought to bear upon one man.

We asked Morris why it was that with nineteen captive Englishmen aboard, nearly all of them sailors, Pizarro should have looked any further for a crew. The answer, delivered with sundry quick twitches of the mouth, was that the Admiral, having had experience with Englishmen, probably felt it would be too dangerous to set nineteen of them free, though unarmed, amongst hardly more than a hundred Spanish soldiers. For those soldiers, the remnants of the force with which he had sailed years before from home, were all that he now had to depend upon, the other four hundred men aboard having been "pressed" by methods like those John Byron had witnessed at Portsmouth.

Morris and his two comrades in misery were confined on the orlop deck of the *Asia*. The darkness, the damp, and the stench reminded him of the *Speedwell*'s hold. The insects were much the same as those he had formerly known, and rats took the place of the Boatswain. But other and more recent memories must often have come to the three as they lay there, in chains—recollections of the horse-hunt and Chief Town and great fires of thistles, of Mrs. Morris, Mrs. Andrews, Mrs. Cooper. And then there would be the thought of John Duck far away to westward, busily propagating Indians of his own admirable hue and also the gospel according to the Wesley brothers as delivered by them to John Bulkeley. Even more frequently, we may be sure, they thought of Orellana and his band, naming those friends over, man by man—yes, and getting in the name of "Sings in the Dark" which returns to me at this moment. A good name it is, and one they had good cause to remember.

To Morris, Andrews, and Cooper the thought that their Patagonian friends might still be languishing in some Spanish prison became so intolerable that they agreed not to mention it. They chose to assume, rather, that all the eleven had somehow broken free and were now once more scouring the plains. That is, they gave up Orellana and his companions as for ever lost out of their own lives, and it seemed to them a poor exchange when they discovered that Alexander Campbell, once Midshipman on the *Wager*, was aboard.

Campbell was so overjoyed at finding his three old shipmates living now in misery as prisoners of war that he gladly gave them an account of the adventures which had brought about his own prosperity: how he had quarrelled with David Chepe and left him, had turned Catholic so as to gain the confidence of the Admiral, had crossed the continent from Santiago to Buenos Ayres with Pizarro, and was now going home with him in expectation of securing a commission in the Spanish Navy. He spoke bitterly of Chepe, and said that he was a dying man who would never reach England. Of Byron he would say nothing whatever except that he was still alive.

The reason for this silence was made clear in several long conversations, held mostly at midnight, between Morris and a Spanish carpenter's mate whom he called Pablo—a somewhat elderly man who had spent most of his active life on the western coast of South America and was well acquainted in Santiago. It appeared that the Honourable John Byron had prospered mightily there. Almost from his first appearance, a mere skeleton clad in sealskins, he had lived with a certain Dr. Gedd, a Scottish physician, who had treated the young man as he would have a son. Pablo believed, in fact, that the childless old doctor would long since have adopted Byron if the Governor of Chile had not been equally desirous of doing the same thing. This Governor, or President—I think we did not hear his name— wined and dined the Honourable John at the official mansion, introducing him there to the best society of the province. He took him along on many a "progress"—if that word is sufficiently dignified for the travels of a Spanish potentate on mule-back—up and down the coast. In every possible way he showed the people of Santiago that Byron's broken Spanish was the language he most delighted to hear.

Pablo had left the city before this amicable contest was decided; but of one thing he felt sure: these two old gentlemen would never let Byron get away; or, if he did somehow manage to slip from between their four outstretched hands, then the señoritas of the region would hold him fast. Half a dozen flattering proposals of marriage, Pablo asserted, had been made—always through Dr. Gedd—to this penniless foreigner of whose origins nothing was known except that he had come almost like a corpse washed in by the sea.

How much of this Morris was "laying on" in a friendly attempt to embarrass Byron, we could not tell; but certainly it had that effect. Byron twisted and writhed, grew red in the face, thrust his hands through his hair and then made hearts with them, cried out "Ha, hum!" once or twice, and finally: "Get on with your story, Isaac! It's past six o'clock." In short, his confusion was so engaging to watch that we easily believed all we were told about his popularity in Santiago.

All of us believed it, that is, except my cousin. To him it seemed an odd thing for a Spanish city to be so hospitable towards an Englishman whilst England and Spain were at war, and especially to an Englishman who had crossed the sea with a definitely hostile intent. Whatever he may have felt as a man, General Conway as a soldier did not like to think that the animosities proper to the serious conduct of warfare, perhaps even to its very survival, could be thus ignored and forgotten.

Lieutenant Morris, it appeared, had particularly asked his friend Pablo about this matter, and had received a reply so significant that I fear I shall be tempted to lay it some day, with suitable precautions, before the House of Commons. Pablo declared that the people of Chile did not feel toward England in the traditional way of the Mother Country. If anything, it was Spain that they hated; or rather, the bigotry, greed, and oppression of French Bourbon rule in Madrid. In his opinion that rule could not last much longer, and would certainly not survive a vigorous blow. If only Commodore Anson—whose humane treatment of his prisoners had aroused universal admiration in the Pacific Colonies—had been able to put ashore a few hundred able-bodied and well armed men, he might easily have taken that whole western coast and then, little by little, South America.

Here was independent testimony from a man born and reared in Chile, and from one with no motive for juggling the facts. He was not trying to show that a far-away King had let slip an opportunity in every sense golden but only to explain why the people of Santiago had received John Byron hospitably. They had treated him well, Pablo meant to say, not solely on account of what he was but because, though coming from a strange land far to the eastward, he was neither a Spaniard nor a Frenchman.

Think of it, William! Mexico and California would soon have fallen to us, and then we should have had only France to deal with in order to make ourselves the masters of the Western Hemisphere all the way from Tierra del Fuego to the North Pole.

Oh, sir, here was "bangling" on a really grand scale. Now you begin to get some conception of the workings of Jenkins' Ear. While the "Patriots" plotted and the *Craftsman* sneered and Anson's squadron lingered for long precious months in Portsmouth harbour, taking on now a few knotty masts and then rotten cordage and at last a consignment or two of jailbirds and dotards and yokels who had never pulled a trigger—while England, I say, was mainly occupied in shouting "Down with Old Bob!" there was slowly passing away our chance of a dominion more vast than Alexander the Great ever dreamed of.

But enough and to spare of a speech I might make in the House if I would, but probably never shall. A far more persuasive orator than I am is Clio, Muse of History. Let her speak for me, and let Posterity decide as between my father and those who dragged him from power.

There's the question, of course, what we English would have done with a vast empire if Gunner Bulkeley's Divine Providence had entrusted one to our care. The bad fist we've made in our American Colonies is suggestive, and there's also an adage that he who would rule others should first learn to rule himself. Imagine Horace Walpole, for example, helping to enact laws for the Western Hemisphere when it is obvious that Strawberry Hill is too much for him, and that even this letter is constantly getting out of hand.

*   *   *

Pablo, one midnight, stealing into the filthy den where our three sailors lay, brought exciting news. The *Asia*, he said, would sail on the morrow, the Admiral having at last scrambled together a sufficient crew by impressing eleven Indians recently captured on the Pampas. He had seen these Indians brought aboard that evening, all of them fettered, and held together by a heavy chain fastened to their iron collars. Though powerful men, one of them almost a giant, they were pitifully gaunt, Pablo said, and hollow-eyed. He felt sorry for them, not only on account of their present misery but because he knew Pizarro's plan to make them help work the ship and, after reaching Spain, to sell them for galley-slaves. Pizarro, in fact, had set this plan in motion at once by ordering that each man should be given thirty strokes with the cat and that salt should then be rubbed into the wounds.

There followed a long talk, at the end of which Pablo agreed to see the Indians before dawn, to let them know that they had friends on board, and to smuggle into their hands a dozen Dutch knives and as many long strips of horsehide.

On the next night Pablo appeared again. He reported that Orellana and company, having steadfastly refused to obey any orders, had been flogged several times during the day, so that now the mere sight of their backs turned a decent man sick. They laughed, he said, and jested with one another, whilst the thongs swished and thudded and the blood ran. The Spanish soldiers, convinced that this laughter was in ridicule of them, were infuriated by it, and took turns at the whips. Also the Indians, as they stood there with their arms outstretched and bound to the masts or the gratings, had now taken to singing, in uproarious and hilarious concert, a strange wild song. The words of that song, wherever the tune may have come from, seemed to be English. There was one word in it, or at least a name, which Pablo had heard before. He thought that even Admiral Pizarro, who was always present to watch the flogging, must recognize it too. It was the name of Jesus.

Before the carpenter's mate left the English sailors on that second night he agreed to begin at once the by no means safe or simple task of providing the Indians with at least twenty-two small cannon-balls, each weighing three or four pounds. For this service and all the other help he was giving, Morris offered him the only thing of value that he possessed—his earrings. Pablo would not take them. Spanish though he was, at least in ancestry, the man had been revolted by the cruelties he had witnessed. Though a Spaniard in blood he was also a child of that western world in which freedom and independence—I think we English had better make up our minds to this, William, and act accordingly—are not, as with us, a luxury allowed only to the few, but the indefeasible right of all men. Lieutenant Morris, of course, did not say this. As an English bastard and foundling he would scarcely have thought it. I mention it as a possible explanation of Pablo's strange conduct in putting his own life at hazard for a set of mere heathens, dark-coloured people, soulless and already damned.

The *Asia* was now well out at sea, so that the Admiral was at liberty to create in her that close imitation of hell which, Morris said, is often produced on shipboard by commanders at once bloody-minded and completely free to do as they please. Byron cut in at this point to remark that he understood it to be just the other way about, and that hell takes lessons from the captains. However that may be, it seems certain that Don Joseph Pizarro had a model in mind when, on the second day out from Monte Video, he abandoned the crude cat-of-nine-tails and turned to more ingenious methods of inducing these horsemen to do the work of sailors. And whither would a faithful Christian most naturally look, in such a situation, for hints and suggestions? To that vast body of precedent and tradition, of course, which had been accumulating for five hundred years in the Holy Office, otherwise known as the Inquisition.

No doubt there was something incongruous, and perhaps you will think even sacrilegious, in Pizarro's use of devices originally meant for the saving of souls as though they had no higher purpose than to make a stubborn Indian climb a mast. The incongruity, to say nothing of sacrilege, is not of my making. For that you must blame Pizarro, Orellana, or Jenkins' Ear. —Yes, by all means, blame that irreverent Ear, and the cynical joy it has always taken in pulling old sanctities inside-out. As for me, I only report, as a faithful translator of Isaac Morris, that Pizarro did try upon these eleven Patagonians certain of the most refined subtleties of torture that Christians have yet invented for the spiritual salvation of their fellow men.

I have to report also that these methods of persuasion, sanctified by so many ages of Christian use and wont, failed. Explain it how you may, Orellana and his companions were unimpressed by them. They looked on at their own physical torment, the details of which I forbear to mention, as mere spectators, mildly amused. For the most part they smiled indulgently, as though wishing not to discourage the well meant efforts of boys; but then, of a sudden, perhaps because one of them had mentioned some ludicrous happening of long ago on the Pampas, they would forget their pain in hilarious laughter, or else, remembering the campfire at Chief Town and the horsehide goblets of whortleberry wine, would chant in chorus that hymn by Charles Wesley set to music by John Duck—every word of it mispronounced, not a word of it understood, but echoing from end to end with the name of Jesus.

Thus the second day at sea and the third, wore by, and in all that time no Indian had climbed a mast, pulled a rope, or lifted so much as a marlinspike. The Admiral's authority had been flouted—or, as he probably felt, even derided. He could not allow this to continue. At sunset of the third day he ordered that every man aboard, including the prisoners, should be on deck two hours later, there and then to hear his last words to the Patagonians and to witness a scene no one present would ever forget.

When Morris was led up from his prison, so weakened by long starvation and inactivity that he could scarcely bear the weight of his shackles, his first thought was that the *Asia* must be on fire. A river of red light was flowing down the companionway; and on every rung

of the ladder he climbed lay the colour of blood. Yet he heard no
shouting or screams, no tumult, in the vessel. The ship was unusually
quiet, he thought, and there was even an effect of religious ceremonial
as he and Cooper and Andrews were ushered to the quarterdeck and
there placed, among the other English prisoners, so that they might
have unobstructed view of whatever was about to happen in the waist,
a little below them and some thirty feet off.

A great fire—apparently of driftwood to judge from the blue and
green hues of the flame—was burning there in what seemed to be a
blacksmith's forge on wheels. The smith was working at the bellows.
All round the fire, but held away from it by ropes, stood fifty or more
wild cattle, momentarily terrified into silence. They filled the waist of
the ship, except for the gangways reaching on either side from the
quarterdeck to the forecastle. The gangways were crowded with men.
So was the forecastle at the other end of the ship. On the quarterdeck,
besides the prisoners, were gathered the officers, all excpt Admiral
Don Joseph Pizarro. In all, some five hundred men stood there waiting, silently intent and expectant in the red leaping light. Their faces
were red, their hands and their garments, as though soaked in blood.
So far as Morris could see, they were all unarmed, even the soldiers.
He guessed—as it turned out, rightly—that Pizarro, wishing to take
no chances that his spectacle might be cut short by violence, had
gathered in every weapon to be found on the ship.

Pizarro, in fact, had apparently thought of everything, and everything was done with that decorum, decency, and order which had
marked his namesake's preparations for the slaughter of the Peruvian
Inca and his followers. To be sure, the elder Pizarro had slain his
tens of thousands *ad gloriam Dei,* and this burnt offering on the *Asia*
would be, in comparison, a rather pitiful affair; but no doubt the
Admiral was familiar with the story of the widow's mite, and was
doing what he could with what he had.

But besides the piety of Pizarro's arrangements for the burning of
idolaters—the fact that they had refused to obey his orders, and that
he had a problem of discipline to solve must have dropped by this time
out of mind—there is also to be considered the sheer art of them, the
thoughtful calculation of effect.

Here in England we are mere barbarians in such matters. In spite
of all that George Selwyn has told me about the great processions by
which our condemned criminals are brought to Tyburn tree, the

wagons they ride in, the "last dying words" in printed form hawked about in the crowd before the execution, the high prices paid for balconies and rooms that command a good view, I still feel that our main concern in these affairs is, simply, to kill people and get them out of the way. When a bull or a bear is killed for sport we let the dogs do it, and when we kill dogs in large numbers it is done with clubs and at night so that one sees only the results as one rides the next morning through the streets. Burning people for theological reasons has been more and more neglected amongst us in proportion as the power of the clergy has declined. Of course I know that the fire is still prescribed by law, on the ground that it is "more decent" than hanging, for women found guilty of certain offences, but the last execution of that sort I know of occurred over forty years ago, and in Scotland. Furthermore, there was no dignity about even that event. The culprit—a witch, by the way—was first "worried at the stake" and then burnt.

"Worried"! —Now if that meant no more, as the ignorant might suppose, than that she suffered some anxiety as she stood there bound, watching her executioners pile the fagots head-high all about her, then one might feel that the decencies of the occasion had been preserved. But, sir, it really means that they first set dogs upon her, and, to my taste at any rate, that takes away all the charm. I hope we English didn't do that when we burned Joan of Arc.

The Spanish people, on the other hand, have a long, rich tradition to guide them in such matters. When they kill a bull they do it, I hear, in an elaborate dangerous sort of dance, in which every step and stroke is prescribed by rules as strict as those set down by the late Alexander Pope for the composition of poetry. Bull-killing with them is an art in which the performers are held at the pitch of perfection by the hisses or plaudits of critical thousands. Similarly, when they burn a heretic, a witch, or even a Patagonian, the thing is done as though the eyes of all bygone burners of human flesh were upon them. It is not the mere suffering and death of the victim that they mainly consider, for that could be managed with a club or Hamlet's "bare bodkin," but the dignity, the ceremonial pomp, the spectacle, of his— what shall I say?—his departure.

Obviously, these are my reflections. Isaac Morris had other matters to think about as he stood there in the silent crowd, waiting. He waited for what seemed to him a long time. Admiral Don Joseph Pizarro was

giving his commanded audience ample leisure for appreciating the
excellence of his arrangements: the great fire, the beasts, the silence,
and that blood-red light striking up the mainmast and far out over the
sea. Even the Patagonians, when they did appear, seemed at last to be
doing his will, to be collaborating with him in his effort to produce the
utmost dramatic effect.

They came marching from their prison in the head of the ship, along
the starboard gangway, each of them with a soldier on either side,
Orellana in the lead and Very Big Fellow at the end of the line. They
were nude except for their loin-clothes. Their feet were free of irons,
but manacles still enclosed their wrists. They came along the gangway
with strong, confident strides, their arms folded, their heads held high,
and looking eagerly, cheerfully about them. Man after man as they
came—Orellana first and then all the others—caught Morris' eye for
a moment and then looked away. They turned in toward the fire and
descended from the gangway to the deck on which stood the forge.
The smith threw more driftwood on the flames and turned again to his
bellows. In half a minute the eleven Indians and the twenty-two
soldiers were standing in a circle about the fire, surrounded by the
closely packed herd of cattle. Orellana stood facing the quarterdeck. His head was battered and bloody. His body was discoloured by
many bruises. He was smiling to himself as he gazed into the flames,
no doubt thinking of campfires far away, and on the instant when he
saw that smile and interpreted its meaning Morris heard himself
shouting, in Patagonian: "Don't be afraid, brothers! We are all here!"
One of his two guards smote him hard on the mouth.

Morris admitted to us that it had been a foolish, almost a meaningless, thing for him to say. After all, it was little more than a quotation
of John Duck's cheering reassurance at the time when the four sailors
were captured by Orellana's band. And besides, what could the three
Englishmen now do, fettered and guarded as they were, for their
friends?

Orellana did not reply, or even glance up at Morris.

Now the Admiral came out the door of the great cabin, dressed in
the full regalia of a Spanish General, and slowly made his way among
the officers and the shackled Englishmen toward the break of the
quarterdeck. Even in the ruddy light of the fire his face looked pale.
His large black eyes were flashing. His mustachios, also black, and
pendulously long, had been newly waxed at the ends. It was clear that

his wrath, though controlled, was now of that most terrible kind known as "righteous," and that he felt the responsibilities upon him of an extremely dignified occasion.

All the ship was perfectly still, Morris said, while for several seconds Pizarro stood there at the rail gazing sternly down at the Patagonians. No man spoke or moved. From the sea there came no murmur. The herd of beasts was still. Only from the blood-red sails did there come the faintest sigh. It must have been a moment of beauty made perfect, one of those tiny eternities that come and go within five ticks of the clock.

But Brains in His Belly, insensitive to such refinements, must needs shatter that perfection with a jolthead jest. This campfire, said he in Patagonian, speaking so clearly that Morris in the quiet heard every word, was good enough to look at but was getting uncomfortably warm. He wished that John Duck were there to enjoy it—that Beloved Black One who had always been able to stand so wonderfully close to the fire.

It is not for us, William, to sit in judgment upon Patagonian humour; and with regard to this sample I suggest that we make haste to laugh lest we begin to weep. The main point is that it proved entirely successful with the other Indians, and, soon, with Brains in His Belly himself. Picture, then, eleven huge, nude Patagonians all bloodied and battered from head to heel now wholly abandoned to the pure joy of laughter, while twenty-two Spanish soldiers stare at them sternly, quite unamused, and Pizarro, the frustrated artist who has striven so hard to create there a piece of perfection, glares at them, helpless, from over the rail.

Pizarro could only suppose that they were laughing at him, though the fact was that their ridicule was levelled at a personage even more august; namely, Death. The Admiral's voice trembled with rage as he leaned far forward and gave the Indians what he called their "last chance." Either they would set to work at once in cleaning the cattle-pens, he shouted, or else they would burn.

Orellana raised his right hand high in a noble gesture which was immediately seconded by his companions. He began to speak in Patagonian, using not a word of Spanish and yet looking steadily all the while at Pizarro. "White Spot," he called in a great voice, "we had thought to have you with us by many more campfires, but this is the last. Be strong, be free, be happy, and do not feel sorry for us."

There he paused, and ten voices said, "Do not feel sorry for us."

"Beloved brother," Orellana went on, "you must find your way back some day to Chief Town. Tell the King we have gone to catch many wild horses, many beautiful women, and that every time we sit by a campfire we shall drink one goblet to him. Tell our sons that we died like men. Tell our women not to mourn overlong. Tell the Beloved Black One that we sang his song about Jesus as long as we could, and it made us feel happy and strong."

"Happy and strong!" the chorus repeated.

"We thank you, brother, for sending us the tool that has freed our hands. We thank you for many good stories, and for being our friend."

"Our friend," said the other voices.

"We are not afraid because we are all together. We are going away together now, but before we go we shall have one last good time. You stay here and remember us, White Spot. —Farewell!"

"Farewell!"

Then the eleven hands fell, and Pizarro screamed from the rail: "Soldiers! Your duty!"

The arrogant confidence was gone from his voice now he saw that the hands of these huge dark men were free, that the manacles in which he had thought their wrists tightly locked had somehow been opened and had become deadly weapons. The heavy handcuffs swinging on the ends of their two-foot chains were, indeed, not unlike bolas, and at least equally good for the crushing of skulls.

But these words are too slow, as the dutiful soldiers were also. The Admiral's shriek was yet ringing along the deck when a single warwhoop overtook, overpowered it, and each Indian instantly reaching out on either side caught his two Spanish guards by the necks and crashed their skulls together with such concerted precision that the whole performance, swift to behold and delicate to hear, suggested the carefully simultaneous cracking of twenty-two eggshells. For that you may count three seconds, and then perhaps thrice as many for the subsequent tumbling, tossing, cramming, and stuffing of twenty-two dead Spaniards into the flames—all done in time to the music composed by John Duck for the words by Charles Wesley:

> "Jesus, Lover of my soul,
> Let me to Thy bosom fly."

Thus the soldiers are cast for a role quite different from the one Pizarro has planned. Their simple duty now is to put out the fire, or at least to darken the ship, and they do it merely by lying all huddled together there in the forge, somewhat uneasy at first but gradually quieting down. The colour of blood drains off the sea, drops down from the sails, dies out of the crowding hundreds of faces, and gives way to night, deep night, in which the few widely scattered and dim ship's lanterns serve only to show how dark the night is. Take your stand where you may on the *Asia* now—up the shrouds, on the forecastle, along the gangways, or at the rail of the quarterdeck beside Pizarro—there is little that you can see unless yours powers of vision, like a Patagonian's, can almost instantly change from the eagle's to those of a hunting owl.

Listen, then; for wherever you may be on that terror-struck ship, or within earshot of her, leagues off in the dark, there is much to be heard, guessed at, imagined. Hear the dreadful rumble and roar of the beasts maddened now by the stench of burning flesh, dashing their horns against the stanchions, thrusting against the barriers, shaking the deck in a frenzy of thwarted stampede. That sombre reverberant bellow is the ground-bass, the *basso ostinato*, of the music. Just above it, less continuous, more scattered, coming first from the gangways and then rapidly spreading out toward the quarterdeck and the forecastle, you hear the shouts, yells, screams, and agonized cries of men. By these sounds alone you know that Death is ransacking the darkness, striking suddenly here, there, wherever he will—at the hatchways, along the rails, among the maddened cattle, but oftenest on the quarterdeck where, one minute ago, Pizarro and his richly uniformed officers stood awaiting a spectacle of gorgeous cruelty. Now the plans have all been changed. Now, instead of the odour of frying horse-fat there spreads from the forge another smell—call it essence of Spaniard. Now the air is loaded with thunder of blow upon blow at the great-cabin door of Spanish oak triple-planked, spiked with iron. Who is in there behind lock, bolt, and bar, wildly firing a pistol through the broken window? Someone hammers and thuds at the door with a snatched-up spar for a battering-ram and sings as he beats and beats again a terrible heart-stopping song:

> "Whilst the nearer waters roll,
> Whilst the tempest still is high."

The words, though barbarously ill pronounced, come clearly enough through the bellow of beasts and the screams of stricken men. They pervade the ship, so exultantly shouted they are by eleven masterful voices, some near at hand and others far off in the dark, but keeping the time and the tune as though the musicians were side by side.

The music is holding the band together, as often before it has done in headlong races across the plains and at night by the thistle-fire. It tells each man where each of the others at every moment is playing, and that Ostrich Legs, Very Big Fellow, Sings in the Dark, Brains in His Belly, Afraid of a Snake, Orellana himself, are still feeling strong, still happy. No one need feel sorry for them, the song says; they are having a great good time. It binds them and guides them and leads them as though in an intricate swift-footed dance of death, with clash of chains and thump of handcuffs against skulls to mark the beat.

Isaac Morris, standing in his chains at the rail of the quarterdeck, seeing little or nothing of how the fight goes but listening, guessing, interpreting, has to clamp his jaws tight to keep from adding his voice to the triumphant chorus. He has heard that song, or the words of it, put to pious uses on the *Speedwell*; he has known it to serve the needs of many a jocund, bacchanalian, and erotic occasion; he knows how much it helps in driving wild horses and hunting the ostrich; but never has he dreamed that it would be most efficacious of all as a battle-cry inciting to slaughter. That, no doubt, is because he has some conception of what the words mean and even of where they came from; but the Patagonians, ignorant of all that, and far more moved by the tune than by the words—wasn't that what Gunner Bulkeley had foreseen?—are singing the hymn with a ferocity calculated to turn a man's blood to ice. Orellana, not twenty feet from Morris and dimly visible to him as he lunges with his spar at the door, is shouting with the voice of a giant trained in the horse-hunt:

> "Hide me, O my Saviour, hide,
> Till the storm of life is past!"

There's no telling how much time has passed, whether two hours or two minutes, since Pizarro's well laid plan gave way to Orellana's, and the wild broke in on the tame. To Morris the time seems long because of the change it has brought. The ship grows darker still as the last tongues of flame in the forge die down. Except for that dreadful war-chant, it is growing quieter now that the screams give way to groans. Morris surmises that all the Spanish soldiers, about a hundred in number, are either dead or dying, and that the Indians do not mean to slay the many unarmed Portuguese aboard, or, for that matter, the other English prisoners. The English, Portuguese, and Indians are there against their will, and hate the Spanish with one accord. Quite easily, therefore, any determined and intelligent man free of chains—Alexander Campbell, perhaps—might draw these polyglot hundreds together and, after silencing Pizarro, command the ship. Ah, yes, what a chance of striking a blow for freedom and England! Where is that Campbell? This is the moment for him, if alive, to blot out all recollection of his former cowardice and treachery.

Command of the ship means nothing to Orellana. Since the slaughter began, and before it, his one thought has been to come face to face with Pizarro, and then to do whatever the moment may inspire. Three or four of his companions, having completed their duties elsewhere, offer their help at the spar with which he is still striving to beat down the ironbound door. He shakes his head and they stand aside, starting in on perhaps the fiftieth repetition of "Jesus, Lover of My Soul." Orellana is not singing now. He is saving his breath. He needs it. The topmast is twenty feet long. It weighs a hundred pounds. He goes back to the rail for his run, and stands there for a moment, poised. A pistol-shot sounds from the cabin window. He waits a moment longer. "Your white weapons bite like a wasp, O White Spot," he shouts, and rushes again at the door.

The blow breaks the upper hinge, crashes through the third plank, and leaves the door crazily sagging. From inside comes a dull rumble as of wooden wheels bearing a heavy weight. A lantern is lighted in there, and a gleam through the window catches the war-chief crouched by the rail for his last run—naked, glistening, his hair tossed wild, his eyes on fire, and with a long narrow ribbon of blood striping down from his chest across the dark skin. He is laughing now as he stands for half a second with the ram laid level between his two hands. Another pistol is fired, this time from the splintered gap in the door—and misses. Some word that he shouts to his companions, whether because it is so ludicrous or on account of their pride in him, almost silences their song; but then they recover themselves and go on to the end of the stanza:

> "Safe into the haven guide!
> Oh, receive my soul at last!"

For a long time, now, it had been dark in the library, Louis and I having forgotten to feed the fire and light the candles. All of us, I think, had nearly forgotten Morris, as beyond a doubt he had lost all thought of himself. We could not see his face; but apparently, as he sat there, perfectly still, he was staring at the night that pressed close to the window. He had dwindled, sunk, you might say, to a voice, to a low, tired voice, speaking without emphasis, with no least concern for rhetorical effect, in the idiom of his childhood. I cannot imitate either the strangeness or the simplicity of his language, and of course Mr. Chute could take no record. Whatever artifice may be discernible in my account must be charged, therefore, against me. It is due to my effort to render what Morris gave us to see of his vision. As for him, I am not sure that he cared at all whether he was "taking us there." He was there himself, first in a darkness, then amazed by a blinding flash, and after that lost in another darkness deeper than any he had thought could come down on this side of the grave.

* * *

The hymn having ended, and before the singers could begin again, Orellana made his final rush at the tottering door. The speed of his run and the weight of the spar wrenched it loose from the lower hinge and drove it inward, downward with a shattering crash, to the cabin's deck. Lantern light poured out through the gap it left. It shone, inside, upon a scene of consternation. Through the opening, Morris saw half a dozen uniformed officers cowering back toward the farther wall. Alexander Campbell, a sword in his hand, was with them. Pizarro lay flat on the floor behind a quarterdeck gun aimed at the doorway.

Who could name in an hour, or exhaust in a lifetime of meditation, all the thoughts that flooded the mind and heart of Isaac Morris during the second in which he moved a little to one side to avoid the shot that he knew was coming? It was the kind of second in which a man grows suddenly old—that is, if he sees, as Morris clearly saw, all the issues that hung upon it. For there on the hither side of the fallen door stood the best friend he had in the world, stood now in his moment of triumph, eager, crouched, ready to spring, with empty hands outspread, his dark body turned to ebony against the glow. Orellana's face was invisible, but Morris could imagine the fierce exaltation with which he confronted at last the man whose very name he had hated since childhood. But oh, dear God, let him spring at once, for the iron object on wheels behind which Pizarro is apparently trying to hide is not, after all, a meaningless lump of metal. It throws a double-headed three-pound shot which at a distance of three paces . . . And Morris cried out to his friend as he saw Pizarro's right hand, with his pistol in it, reaching up toward the vent of the gun. A single spark from the pistol's flint falling into the gun's powder-pan . . . He cried out; but his warning was lost in a deafening roar, and Orellana threw both his hands high, falling backward.

For a moment, then, time seemed to stand still. The cabin lanterns had been blown out by the concussion, so that the quarterdeck was again dark. The ship was strangely quiet. Orellana, dimly visible from where Morris stood, was lying perfectly still. Then a man not in uniform, a man with a sword, ran out of the cabin and began stabbing the prostrate body.

The ten members of Orellana's band were all gathered by this time on the quarterdeck. They had been stunned, no doubt, momentarily, by the death of their leader, but now either Brains in His Belly or Very Big Fellow leapt at Campbell, lifted him high, and dashed him back into the cabin. Pizarro and his officers began to fire at the Indians from the window and the doorway. Ostrich Legs was wounded, then Sings in the Dark, and two or three others. They paid little attention, apparently, to these wasp-stings. The song about Jesus began again—sung not ferociously now but proudly, with a kind of solemn joy, while the ten men stood in a ring about their leader and the lead pelted in upon them. When the last line was ended they took up the body and walked with it to the quarter rail. All ten of them stepped over the rail, still holding the body, and leapt with it into the sea. They were more than a hundred miles from land, and not one of them, Morris knew, could swim.

*　　*　　*

For a while we sat there silent. It was not that we expected Morris to go on again, or wished him to, but that any word we might say would now be a word too much.

The clock struck seven, and George Selwyn did not remind us that it was time to dress for dinner. Still no one spoke, or moved—excepting, that is, my little dog, who came to my chair to suggest that the room was strangely dark and was growing cold. I knew that already.

At last we overheard one faint, brief sentence from a man who, thus far in the week, had scarcely opened his mouth. Strangely eloquent, I thought it, and the best possible comment upon Morris's story: "Yes," sighed Jeremy Tinker, "that's the way it is!"

* * *

No one dressed for dinner that Wednesday evening because the members of the Club, at my earnest invitation, stayed with us. We did not even sit at the table, but moved freely about while we ate in my new Refectory—a really beautiful room just below the Library, as I may have told you, wherein a subdued magnificence is happily married to comfort.

Something had made me wish that this occasion should be as bright, warm, and friendly as I could possibly make it. The fire, *à la* Twickenham Ait, was built of Thames driftwood well seasoned, of which I have a good supply. It flourished and crackled and leapt up the flue in eager emulation of a sixty-foot flame of thistles. On the dinner-table and round about there was scattered a galaxy, a fallen skyful, of tall wax candles; and every mirror in the room, every lozenged window-pane, wineglass, knife, spoon, but Kitty Clive's eyes most of all, shone back like tiny constellations. Neither was there any perceptible dearth of Madeira, port, Bordeaux, brown sherry, and other such bottled cheer and wit that we English bring in from foreign lands. Louis produced from the servants' cellar enough ale for half a dozen John Chesters. As for me, I sipped ice water, and poured some of it into Kitty's claret to demonstrate the moderation of us both.

If anything was lacking to make the evening go as merrily as wedding bells are said to, it was music; and even that was added about ten o'clock when the members of the Club—not counting Blandison, of course—stood up by the fire and rendered, with some approximation to harmonic laws, first "Ye Gentlemen of England" and then "The Coasts of High Barbary," the tune of which, you recall, Gunner Bulkeley had tried to employ for "Jesus, Lover of My Soul." The second song had to be repeated because Kitty and I so much enjoyed seeing Jeremy Tinker vigorously stamp out the time as he sang. Then he alone rendered "My Boy Willie" in a high, thin voice like a bird's, and was just starting in on "Jesus, Lover of My Soul" to Charles

Wesley's tune, which he said he knew perfectly well, when George Selwyn had the presence of mind to hand him another glass of Madeira.

And yet this same George Selwyn endangered the success of the evening—or so I feared at the time—by pointing out that now we had heard two stories which, although interesting enough so far as they went, had been brought to no satisfactory conclusion.

By this time we were all sitting together by the fire, some of us eating apples and John Chester filling his pipe.

"You mean," Kitty said, "to an execution."

"Well, things did seem to be heading that way, but then they broke off."

George's gaze, first at Byron and then at Morris, suggested both critical disapprobation and personal grievance; but neither of the two made any reply.

There was a pause while we watched Master Chester lay a live coal on the tobacco in his pipe. "Why, hell," that worthy remarked, "Jim Adair, hyar (puff), knows all they is to know 'bout the end o' them (puff) stories. He said so last night, down to Pudsey's (puff). Let him tell it."

Byron and Morris looked surprised at this. Indeed, I suppose we all did, for no one in the group seemed less likely to know anything about the sea than this denizen of the American forest. Yet Adair did not deny that he had this information. He sat silent, gazing into the fire, as though waiting for permission from the two persons most concerned.

"Please do," said Kitty. And then the sailors—perhaps a little reluctantly—nodded their consent.

Adair began with the courteous remark that we must not expect him to end these stories nearly so well as his two friends had begun them. He had, to be sure, some knowledge about the final outcome of the *Wager*'s disaster, but we had recently seen how unconvincing mere information must always be in comparison with the record of actual experience.

All this being understood and allowed for, he would try to think his way back, through nine years and more, to the month of June, 1746. At that time he was lodging at the Blue Posts on Portsmouth Hard, the tavern in which, six years earlier, the Honourable John Byron and his friend Augustus Keppel had meant to sleep, but, instead . . .

However, he had not chosen the Blue Posts on account of those illustrious associations but because it was a convenient place in which to
await the sailing of the merchantman that was to take him back to
America. The time spent there had not been wasted, because he was
able to spend several evenings with his English factor, Daniel Dickens
by name—a peruke-maker who eked out the slender earnings of his
trade by preparing legal documents for the officers of his Majesty's
Navy and keeping accounts for certain American importers of English goods. This versatile Dickens was at the time extremely busy
preparing papers for a Court Martial soon to be held in one of the
great ships in Portsmouth Harbour, and could meet Adair only in the
evenings. Not only was he occupied in the preparations, but he was so
excited by them that on the evening before the session of the Court he
could scarcely bring his mind to bear upon the current prices of
trucking-cloth, vermilion, and peltries.

Dickens, in fact, was indignant and wrathful at the prospect of a
gross injustice about to be done to innocent men. Naturally inclined to
a fervent expression of his own feelings, he spoke his mind freely in
condemnation of a certain Captain Chepe and in praise of one John
Bulkeley, a Gunner, and a Midshipman by the name of Isaac Morris.
Dickens had by this time written out the depositions of all three, and
knew that the Captain was blaming the wreck of his ship upon these
two men and a few others who had managed to get back alive from
Patagonia. More than that, he was charging them with mutiny, for
which the punishment was death. Dickens quoted Chepe word for
word: "I have nothing to say for nor against these villains until the
day of trial; but then it will not be in my power to be off from hanging
them."

That sentence, Adair said, had been lodged in his memory not by its
oddity of expression alone. There was also the tone of bluster in it,
the vindictiveness, the hint that the speaker was still Captain and so
had the power of life and death—or, rather, that after a long debate
within him between Mercy and Justice the decision that these men
must die had already been reached irrevocably, so that the Court Martial had nothing to do but ratify his judgment and ask him to perform
the hangings with his own hands.

All this, said Adair, would have made little impression upon him if
he had spent his previous years in a country much inclined to let the
rope take the place of thinking, one in which the least step out of line

by a poor man was a step toward the gallows, and where public executions had become a spectacle, a diversion, a jest. We must allow for
the fact that in Northern Ireland, in Scotland, but most of all in the
American forest, he had learned to think of human beings not as
always too many but as too few. Yes, and he asserted that all a man's
thinking, his conduct, even the way he fights in a battle and either
aims his musket or only pulls the trigger with his eyes shut, depends
in some degree upon the average population per square mile to which
that man is accustomed.

There's a notion, quite new to me, which one might expect to find,
but does not, in Montesquieu, Voltaire, or David Hume, but scarcely
in a man dressed like a Chickasaw chief. Adair brought it in, however,
only to explain why he had been shocked by what Dickens told him.
He said that his informant's powers of mimicry and description
brought Chepe, Morris, Bulkeley, Cummins, and also the little mouse-
whiskered Judge Advocate who had questioned them, all but bodily
into the room. It was absurd, he thought, for a man to waste his life
recording the words of other men when he had in him such words of
his own as this Daniel Dickens.

At any rate, before that evening was over and the last glass of
rum-punch drained, Adair himself was indignant, excited. Most of
that night he sat alone in the tavern parlor, reading the book Dickens
had left him—*A Voyage to the South Seas,* by John Bulkeley and
John Cummins, published in London some two years before.

Ill written as it was in some respects, but manifestly honest,
minutely exact, and pervaded by patience, fairness, and Christian
charity, this book brought Adair's interest in the men of the *Wager* to
a still higher pitch. The result was that by ten o'clock of the next
morning he had gained admittance as a secretary to assist Dickens in
recording the trial in the great cabin of Admiral Steward's flagship,
and was gazing hard at Morris, Bulkeley, Cummins, and also a shattered hulk of a man with a red bulbous nose who, as Dickens told
him, was Boatswain King. These, along with perhaps half a dozen
others whose names he could not recall, were the men who, according
to the universal opinion of Portsmouth and perhaps their own as well,
were about to be hanged. If they did think so, that was the one respect
in which their former Captain, now sitting next to the Judge of the
Court at the table, wholly agreed with them.

David Chepe himself, eaten out by poison and strong drink and fever, already looked much like a corpse. His little ferret eyes suggested to Adair that for years he must have lived mostly on hatred—waiting for this day.

In the chair of the Judge or head of the Court sat George Anson, now a Rear-Admiral of the White. He had come down from London for this occasion because of his former acquaintance with several of the persons concerned and also his wish to learn all he could about the loss of the *Wager*. He conducted the trial, Adair thought, with no remarkable intelligence but certainly with patience. This was shown especially toward Boatswain King, who, convinced that he was in any case about to die, meant to improve his last hours by making himself obnoxious to every one. Anson, however, seemed to feel that the sole, or at any rate the chief, business of the Court was not to hang people, but rather to get at the truth. To the evident disappointment of David Chepe, he postponed the charge of mutiny until he had in the record abundant testimony that the *Wager*—badly built and fitted, overloaded, undermanned, and crowded with invalids incapable of any service—should never have been sent on the voyage. Turning then to the question of the wreck, he found that Chepe had grossly neglected his duty in not keeping the deck night and day during the storm, in bringing Midshipman Campbell into his cabin and using him as a spy and a trouble-maker among the crew, in failing to investigate the complaints brought to him by Gunner Bulkeley, in ordering the Gunner to distribute pistols among the officers instead—if the thing had to be done at all—of doing it himself, in allowing the aged Sailing-Master to take command of the watch after the old man told him he could not see to keep the ship in position, and still worse, in failing to fire signal guns when the *Centurion*'s lights were lost. Was Captain Chepe unaware of that universal custom of ships sailing in a squadron? Had he forgotten the strict orders given by the Commodore to the Captains at St. Julian's? Why, after losing the *Centurion*, had he seen fit to lie to, four nights running, when he knew that the other vessels must all be before the wind, making straight for the first rendezvous? Was it possible that he was trying to get free of the Commodore? That suspicion was not quieted, certainly, by his conduct in running his ship on the rocks of a lee shore after repeated warnings from the Gunner. One could scarcely say that it was silenced by his shooting the one person who was known to have charged him with deliberate desertion of the squadron and intent to turn pirate like Shelvocke.

The killing of Cozens, Anson said, was not a matter for the present Court to pass judgment upon, but the charge of mutiny, desertion, and breach of duty in his Majesty's ships at sea did lie within its jurisdiction. He was in doubt whether to consider first the charges brought by Captain Chepe against certain members of the *Wager*'s company or to take up at once, while the evidence was still fresh in mind, the derelictions of that same officer. He declared a brief intermission so that he might get the advice of the Judge Advocate.

*   *   *

It was now late in the afternoon. Many officers and Marine guards, as well as the prisoners and judges, were crowded into that cabin which had been built for the comfort of the Admiral and his few guests. The room was close and hot. Boatswain King, having shouted himself hoarse, looked exhausted. John Bulkeley was sitting bolt upright with his arms folded, quietly talking with Carpenter Cummins. Chepe's face, which had looked in the morning like a sheet of soiled foolscap, was flushed. Every few seconds, his head jerked suddenly sidewise and backward. His eyes were bloodshot. His long dirty fingers clawed at the table-top. Several times he half rose from his chair and then sat down again.

When Anson returned to his chair he asked Daniel Dickens, Clerk of the Court, to read Chepe's deposition, in substance an accusation of mutiny against all the men who had left Wager Island in the *Speedwell*. Then came the deposition of Isaac Morris, of which I have given you some notion. Bulkeley and Cummins, in their statement, said that they had nothing to add to what they had already written and published in a book called *A Voyage to the South Seas*. Upon that record they rested their whole case.

The Admiral had read the book, and so had Captain Piercy Brett, formerly his Lieutenant on the *Centurion* and now sitting with him as a member of the Court. (This is the man, William, who drew the illustrations for Richard Walter's book, and who later had a chance, but lost it, of capturing the Young Pretender in the Channel.) To both of them it seemed a perfectly honest document, with nothing in the least "mutinous" about it. Indeed, said they, the two writers had shown a respect for their Captain, a patience with him, and a wish to give him the benefit of every doubt which, under the circumstances, were really remarkable. They felt, too, that a record of this kind, carefully and regularly kept from day to day while the events were fresh in mind, was far more dependable than any man's recollections could be after the lapse of six years. If Captain Chepe had kept a similar diary, presenting the facts in the case as he had seen them, this would be the time for him to lay it before the Court.

Captain Chepe, now on his feet and speaking with the condign indignation of a man who abhors a lie, replied that of course he had no such thing. During the storm off Cape Horn and those terrible months on the island, his mind had been occupied by matters far more serious than diary-keeping. He ignored Boatswain King's shouted accusation that he had been mainly concerned with keeping all the brandy to himself, and went on to say that it would have been impossible for him or any other man to write a journal on the island because there was no ink, no quill, and not a scrap of paper left on the *Wager* after the wreck. " 'Cause why?" the irrepressible Boatswain broke in again. "On account o' yer orderin' me, just arter we struck, to take an' tear up an' toss over the rail all the paper I could find, the which I went an' done faithful; an' then ye tried to drownd me or mebbe die o' thirst so's dead men couldn't tell no tales; but anyhow that's where all the paper went by Chepe's orders, the which ain't mutiny but good Admiralty law an' I knows me rights even if I do swing for it."

Pray excuse me, William, for allowing such vulgarity to intrude upon these decorous pages. And yet certainly it has as much right here as in a court of law. Anson seems to have known, or cared, simply nothing for legal procedure. Apparently it was his notion of a Court Martial that every one should be allowed to talk at once, on any subject, as wildly as he pleased, and that from the resulting chaos the judges should then—by instinct, I suppose—extract or deduce some rough approximation to justice.

Anson probably had in mind for a model the no-methods used by some uplandish Justice of the Peace in his native Shugborough. Well, what of it? Four-fifths of our English law has for centuries been administered in this blundering, muddle-headed way, often by men who had never opened a law-book, or who would in any case have been unable to read such a thing; yet here by the Grace of God, or perhaps of the Goddess Fortuna, we still are with our throats uncut. Besides, it is to be remembered that this Anson, now First Lord of the Admiralty and a peer of the realm, began life—unless I have been misinformed—as a sailor before the mast. Now, naturally, I deplore and resent all such intrusion of men who merely "earn" advancement upon the ranks of those to the manner born, yet I can see how the general principle that persons in authority are always right and their subordinates should not be allowed even to speak may have been modified in Anson's mind by memories of his own years in the forecastle.

At any rate, there was the question before the Court, and every one discussing it at once, whether the Bulkeley and Cummins journal was admissible as evidence. Chepe hotly and roundly declared that the Boatswain was a liar, that no order to destroy the papers on the *Wager* had ever been given him, and that it was the storm, and the wash of breakers over the ship as she lay stranded, which had carried off all the written records, including the logbook.

At this point Samuel Cooper, one of the two men who had come from Patagonia with Morris, stoutly demurred. No storm and no breakers could ever have torn paper into small square bits such as he and others had found in great numbers, washed up among the rocks of the island. Carpenter Cummins added that neither could wind or water have taken a bundle of written paper out of his sea-chest while leaving all the rest of the contents undisturbed.

Thus with charge and countercharge and abusive epithets the hearing in the great cabin moved farther and farther away from the question and, correspondingly, more and more resembled a debate in the House of Commons at midnight when the Tory members are being unusually obnoxious and pig-headed.

At length, taking advantage of a momentary lull, Anson said that he now agreed with Captain Chepe that all, or nearly all, the written paper on the wreck, and perhaps the blank paper as well, had been destroyed by some one, or under the orders of some person, who did not wish the record of the *Wager*'s voyage to survive. Mr. Dickens would kindly make a memorandum of this matter for the use of whatever Court might in future be interested in the motives and methods of that person, at present unnamed. Just now he, the Judge of this Court, was mainly concerned with the question Captain Chepe had raised: whether the published Journal which bore the names of John Bulkeley and John Cummins could have been written by them at the time of the events it described. If not—if, for example, it should turn out that this journal had been composed by some professional voyage-writer in Grub Street—then there would be strong suspicion that they two had tried by means of this book to conceal some serious guilt of their own.

"The guilt of mutiny, yes!" said Chepe in a shrill harsh voice which reminded Adair of the shriek of a hawk. He slapped the table with his spread hand as he spoke, and his head twitched backward as though jerked by a wire.

"For the moment, Captain," said Anson, "the Judge of this Court has the floor. Let me say that I foresaw while reading this published journal that the question now before us would arise. Therefore three days ago—and I now wish it had been earlier—I wrote to the only man I know to be alive in England who might help us to a decision. My letter was sent by special messenger, who was to ride post night and day and to bring back to this session the man to whom the letter was addressed. —Mr. Dickens will please go to the stern gallery and see whether there is a boat holding a gentleman in captain's uniform approaching us from the Hard."

Imagine for yourself, William, what must have been the guesses and conjectures, the few hopes and the many fears, of the men whose lives depended upon the identity of this "gentleman." Does it not look as though Jenkins' Ear had determined to protract their apprehensions to the last possible moment? They were able to think of only four "gentlemen" who might now be alive and at home, entitled to a captain's uniform, and aware of what had gone on six years before on a certain bleak rock in the sea. There was Captain Pemberton of the Marines, who had returned to England with John Bulkeley. There was Lieutenant Hamilton, also of the Marines, who might by this time be a captain. Again, it was not impossible that Midshipman Alexander Campbell had turned his coat once more and secured a captain's rank in return for a promise to support his old commander at the trial. For certainly it must be to the interest of the Admiralty and Navy discipline that Captain Chepe should be proven right, and all the ignorant seamen wrong. Think of the confusion that would follow if this Court were forced to decide that a captain must not run his ship upon the rocks or shoot his midshipmen!

Finally, it would not do to ignore the one chance in a hundred that the Honourable John Byron had survived, had perhaps come all the way home with Chepe, and in the intervening years had won a command. He would still be rather young for such authority, of course; but then his friend the Honourable Augustus Keppel was still younger, and had been appointed a commander at nineteen. Yes, it might be Byron or Campbell that the Admiral had sent for; but more probably it was Hamilton. For the present life-and-death purpose it made little difference which one it was, because all three of these men—even Byron, mysteriously, heartbreakingly—had sided with Chepe back there and remained with him. Oh, then, that it might be Captain Pemberton, if indeed it was any one, who was coming!

Pemberton knew nothing of the journal, of course; but at least he was an honest man, and one whose testimony would be heard because he was not among the accused or in any way subject to this Court. Had he not arrested and confined David Chepe back there on a charge of murder, intending to bring him home for trial? It had taken days of argument to dissuade him from that purpose, and now he might be expected to confront Chepe's charge of mutiny with the vigorous wrath it deserved.

But probably he would not come. The long day was waning now, the sun hung low over the Solent, and Dickens came back to report that he had seen only one small wherry coming out from the Hard, with one man in it—coatless, hatless, wigless, and rowing like a Thames waterman for a wager.

Anson seemed to sigh. Again he regretted that a great press of business at the Navy Office had belated his letter, and also that he was obliged to be back in London early on the following day. In a tone of manifest anxiety, almost of pleading, he asked Bulkeley and Cummins whether they could think of any way of proving that their journal had been composed, at least in large part, during the period it was meant to record.

John Bulkeley, up to this time, had spoken only in reply to direct questions, and then briefly. Adair told us that, to judge from the man's face and attitude, he might have been less involved, less concerned, than any other person in the room. Now he rose and took from his pocket a small black book. "Yes, Admiral," said he, speaking quietly, slowly, "there comes a notion of a way. This little book"—he held it up, open, so that every one could see how the pages were filled at the top and bottom and margins and even between the lines with minute hand-written characters—"has helped to save my soul, and mayhap a few others. Why then may it not also help to save my bodily life and the lives of my friends, the which is an easier thing to do and far less important? Here in this book are two things as different as noonday from darkness. First, in print, there are the words that God spoke to holy men long ago. Second, there are the words of a sinful man, John Bulkeley by name, written in with a gull's quill wherever the words of God left the smallest room. 'Twas a bold thing, and mayhap wrong, for me to use a holy book so, but I had to think not for myself alone. That night on the wreck, when I saw that my journal and the Carpenter's were gone, along of the ship's log and all the blank paper, I had to think what this meant and would come to if so be in later days there was naught but the spoken word of simple men against the word of a Captain. John Cummins and I took thought of this together, and we agreed that our best hope would be in words written down at the time, and mayhap all the better hope if written, seeing that the Lord had left us no other place, in a holy book. 'For see,' said John Cummins to me as we stood there in the cockpit with one tallow-dip to light us and knee-deep in water and holding with both hands to a stanchion against the shock of the broadside billow, 'not the wickedest man in the world could set down aught but God's truth in a book like this *Christian Pattern*. Every word that we say here will be sworn to as though on your Bible, the which is gone.' —Is that right, Carpenter? Is that what you said?"

"I said that, Gunner; and now I say it again. A lie wrote down in that book would damn a man's soul for ever."

"Ah, true! But we told no lies neither then nor now. That same night of Thursday, May the fourteenth, 1741, we made our first jotting here on the flyleaf with what little ink I had left. The struck ship was fetching great jerks and leaps in a tumbling sea whilst I wrote, and the Carpenter held the candle and the ink-bottle. At the best o' times John Bulkeley is but a poor clerk, and 'tis no wonder that the handwriting is crazed a bit by the steep tilt of the cockpit floor and the suck of water at my ankles. Yet I did write these dozen lines until we were attacked by the Boatswain's drunken gang, who forced us to stand upon our defence, and then was our candle douted and the last o' my ink spilled down the page. —Admiral Anson, you can see from where you sit the great blot it made."

Chepe cried out that Bulkeley was now caught in an unmistakable lie, for if all his ink was gone how could he have written the rest of the book full of words on the island and during the *Speedwell*'s voyage? For his part he was now confident that the Gunner had first secured the book when he got back to England, and had then written in these notes to support the lies he had published.

In reply to a question from the Admiral, Bulkeley said that the published journal was based in every particular upon these rough notes, and that he would be glad to have the court compare the two versions and make sure that this was so. Then, with reference to Chepe's accusations, he declared that all the notes in his little black book were written, as the colour would show, in what he called "cuttlefish ink" or "sepia," which every good sailor knew how to prepare for writing purposes. He was walking as he spoke toward the end of the table, and, having reached it, suddenly thrust the book under Boatswain King's nose. The Boatswain shrank back with his open hands outspread, almost upsetting his chair and yelling: "Take it away! Take it away! It's witchcraft!"

Bulkeley closed the book, smiling, handed it to the Admiral, and then said in a pleasant voice: "It seems that the Boatswain has seen this book before. That could not have been in England, for until today he and I have not met since he tried to have it taken from me by force in Rio de Janeiro."

It developed, however, that Boatswain King had never seen Bulkeley writing in the book, and, excepting the Carpenter, neither had any other man who had been in the *Speedwell*. Isaac Morris testified, indeed, that the book had been kept during that voyage in the chest under the hatchway on which he had sat, and that in fair weather the Gunner or the Carpenter would often take it on deck together with the gull's quill and the leather bottle of cuttlefish ink; but he had not seen them writing in it or even known for certain that it contained handwriting—although every man in the vessel suspected Bulkeley was writing prayers in it.

The Admiral asked whether, before the *Speedwell*'s sailing, the Gunner had told any man on the island about the use to which he was putting his little black book. Yes, said Bulkeley, he had told one man—or rather, at the time he had been hardly more than a boy. Toward that person he had felt as he supposed a father might toward a son, and had trusted him completely. Therefore with no hesitation he not only had told him about the journal but had shown it to him, explained its purpose, and asked for his help in making it as full and accurate as possible. Adair recalled that Bulkeley had said this with less than his accustomed cheerfulness, and that his tone had been really sad when, at the Admiral's request, he gave the name of this one-time friend: the Honourable John Byron, Midshipman.

"Dickens," said Anson, interrupting another outbreak from Chepe, "please go to the entry-port and see if any one has come."

As the secretary left the cabin, Chepe went on to remark that the Gunner's claim to have been at any time or degree on friendly terms with Midshipman Byron was of a piece with all his other falsehoods. The proof of that, said he, had been given when Byron let the *Speedwell* sail away without him and had stayed with his Captain as a close and faithful friend through many tribulations. He was giving instances and examples of this fidelity when Dickens returned to the cabin, ushering in a tall, lean young man without a coat or hat, his hair blown awry, breathing hard, who, in spite of his smile, looked on the verge of exhaustion.

There was a moment, William, which, if this were a work of imagination, I should dearly like to describe. Anson's relief at this last-minute appearance of a gentlemanly captain, the mingling of joy with hesitation in Bulkeley's face, the blank dismay in the face of David Chepe, the astonishment striking the Boatswain dumb, and then the warm gaze of Byron upon only one man in the room, Byron's crooked smile, his handclasp, his embrace, all showing more clearly at last than a thousand words that the years and the meridians had wrought no change in his affection for one who had been to him more than a father—I say that here was one of those richly compacted moments upon which the mind loves to dwell, which it longs to illuminine and perpetuate. Thinking of it, I begin to discern why it is that some men write fiction and others paint pictures. They too must feel, some of them more intensely than I do, an awed, half-religious sense of this and that moment's uniqueness, significance, inexhaustibility—in a word, its beauty, brushed by an angel's wing.

Oh, sir, the time may come, and you may be surprised, shocked even; but in this letter I am still a slave of the facts. I cannot pause upon Byron's entrance because Adair did not. He hastened on through the questions put by the Admiral: Had Byron ever seen this little book, and if so when and where? Had he ever read any of the handwriting in it? Could he swear that it was done by the Gunner? Did he know for what purpose it was intended? And did the first page or two of this writing tell the truth about the loss of the vessel, to the best of his knowledge and belief? The answers, all of them supporting the Gunner's previous testimony, led on to the crucial question: Why, then, had Byron remained with Chepe on the island, letting Gunner Bulkeley sail away with the sad conviction that he had been deserted by his closest friend?

Byron replied that he had actually started with Bulkeley on the first fifty miles or so of the *Speedwell*'s voyage, but had then been sent back with certain others in the barge to secure some necessary canvas. Upon their arrival at Wager Island the oars and sail of the barge had been seized by Chepe and Campbell, so that Byron could have returned to the *Speedwell* only on foot, alone, and with the strong likelihood of dying on the way. Besides that, he now saw that Chepe, with the barge in his possession, stood some chance of eventual return to England. That would mean a charge of mutiny, with Midshipman Campbell to support it, against all the men in the *Speedwell*. In such an event, Byron saw, the only chance of saving those men from the rope would be that some one of equal rank with Campbell, and untainted by the charge itself, should be present at the Court Martial to confront Chepe's allegations with the truth. Therefore he had clung for months and years to a man he despised, doing him menial service, enduring his brutal abuse, carrying his bloated body through the swamps of the Chilean coast, tending his fever at Chiloe and in Santiago, returning with him to England in a Spanish vessel and then, because Chepe could not endure the journey from Plymouth to London, riding on through the southern shires alone and at top speed through the turnpikes because he had no money to pay the tolls. At once he had told the Navy Office of Chepe's return and made arrangements for his support, saying also that he himself would be at Newstead Abbey, ready for immediate response to any summons. That summons had come less than twenty-four hours ago, since when he had ridden one hundred and eighty miles on five different horses and had rowed two miles against the wind in a boat. He was happy to have arrived in time and now, after such toils and pains and lapse of years, to declare that among all the men he had ever known there was not one more completely honest, faithful, patient, kind, and no one less capable of mutinous conduct even against a bad captain, than his friend John Bulkeley.

Even now, William, I find myself racing through these remarks as Byron did through the turnpikes because I have so vivid a recollection of how he suffered in hearing them repeated by Adair. We now saw the real, or at any rate the deepest, reason for his refusal to conclude his own story. That would have involved a public confession that he had done something noble.

Moreover, for once in the world, nobility had all the reward it had sought or dreamed of. Byron held the great cabin breathlessly silent for three or four minutes, not more, and when he had finished—this was quite the most irregular and reprehensible thing in the whole proceeding—there was a moment of applause when every one joined in except the Boatswain and Captain Chepe. The Admiral then thanked Captain Byron for his attendance, glanced at his watch, and told the Marines to clear the room.

Adair thought that the Court did not take more than five minutes in reaching its decision. He heard that decision read after his return to the great cabin, and that evening got an exact copy of it from Dickens. He assured us—and I am so particular on this point because I find the thing as hard to believe as you do—that these were its exact words: "We do honourably acquit Captain David Chepe, together with all his officers and men, from the loss of His Majesty's Ship the *Wager,* excepting Lieutenant Robert Beans, who has disobeyed his captain's orders by not setting the main-sail and letting go the Anchor, as ordered; however, in regard to his hardships and misfortunes, do also acquit him with a reprimand from the Court."

Ah, sir, did ever mountain so labour to bring forth a more ridiculous mouse? To be sure, Chepe was given quite definitely to understand that this verdict did not by any means exonerate him of the charge of murder; but then neither did it even allude to his allegations of mutiny. Oh, from any one's point of view, what a lamentable conclusion was here, and how stupid beyond belief was this foisting of all the blame upon Robert Beans for his failure to execute an order which, Captain Byron himself has told me, only a madman would ever have given and the result of which would have been to tear out the mast. But then of course there had to be some one found at fault after all this pother, and I suppose the Court chose Beans on account of his disgusting name, or else because he was fat, or more likely still, because he had always tried to agree with every one.

Your sympathies, I am sure, will be with George Selwyn, after all his sanguine hopes deprived of an execution. And yet if you could have heard how David Chepe was led out of the cabin by a guard, all but frothing at the mouth because he knew that he would never see John Bulkeley dangling at the end of a rope, and knowing also that he himself might soon be standing trial for murder, perhaps you would not feel unduly sorry for George.

THURSDAY

During the last ten minutes, William, I've been glancing back through some of these pages, reading aloud here and there, testing sentences as one does coins to hear whether they "ring true." My rueful answer is: Now and then, but not often. The effect of living talk, which is all I ever aspire to in writing, is too seldom caught. —Or rather, though there is talk here, methinks I catch too much the tone of Horace Walpole—frivolent, flippous, overanxious to please, to shine, at least to glitter, and always playing merry hob with the English language as though it were still a growing thing and our own.

Horace Walpole we have, like the poor, always with us; but here I have wanted to send on those other voices, utterly different from mine, and the language they used which I should never have thought of. Why, sir, 'tis but a few days ago that in this very room, now silent except for the brush of my quill, we heard the stormful impetuosity of Byron, Chester's acrid vernacular, the sound *sermo pedestris* of James Adair, Jeremy Tinker's plaintive chirp, and the magniloquent harmonies that Blandison often made as though by all instruments playing at once. Where are they now, those sighs, those sudden glories of laughter? What has muted and hurried them all away into what deep oubliette, or drawn them back to the earth's dark roots and made them one with the throb of Sappho's lyre?

Take the story Morris told, where I fall farthest short of my purpose. To be sure, it is mostly translation; and yet I did expect it to sound more like Morris than Pope—ye gods of Olympus!—does like Homer. Is there something in the air of this region that dwarfs all grandeur to the Twickenham scale, as the Chinese grow a centenarian pine-tree in a pot?

But gloomy thoughts of this kind are what come of looking back, which is a thing as bad for my literary health as it was for Lot's wife or the husband of Eurydice. Indeed, I suspect that both of those myths were made to show what happens when a writer reads over what he has done, falls out of conceit with himself, begins to revise, and thus loses the very life he is trying to save.

As for that prevalence of my own voice, it simply cannot be helped. Who, in fact, does conceal his proper tones and idiom beneath those of another? Suppose you bring me an old manuscript of a play you have just discovered in some mouldy archive—a play about Wat Tyler, say, with no author's name and nothing to show when, where, or why it was written. Well, you read me five lines in which Wat himself is supposed to be speaking, and at the first line I prick up my ears, at the second thrills race up and down my back, at the end of the third I am certain, during the fourth I am speechless, but then I gather strength to shout "Shakespeare!" and not all the pundits of Oxford and Cambridge could rid me of that conviction.

Ah, well; the less a writer thinks about how writing should be done the less badly he will do it. Three rules should suffice him: (1) Ride the horse of the moment always on the dead run. (2) Change horses at every stage. (3) Never look back. —Oh, yes; I keep another one in mind, lest these three should grow tyrannical. It reads: never have any rules, unless to break them.

*   *   *

All that, you say, is obviously true with regard to your friend's way of spoiling paper, but when it comes to his way of life he's a man of utmost regularity. Every one of his days at Strawberry Hill he begins with a chat in his bedroom with his man Louis; and then the scene moves to Mrs. Clive's summerhouse, where two people eavesdrop two others and take notes on their conversations. You recognize that this is an admirable routine which you would never tire of reading about, and yet you fear that no man, even a bachelor, can maintain it for ever. There will come a time when blind chance steps in, or fate, or Jenkins' Ear, or the divinity that roughhews our ends smooth-shape them how we will, and thrusts him back upon life's mere welter and disarray.

So it happened on that Thursday morning. I awoke without Louis' help or knowledge, and not in bed but out beside the staircase in my nightgown. My first thought or feeling was one of profound relief at the discovery that there was not, after all, a gigantic leg and foot, encased in armour, monstrously incumbent there on the topmost balustrade, by its sheer brutal ponderosity slowly cracking, crushing my delicate slender-limbed antelopes.

Soon, of course, I was asking myself why, in that place or in any, I had expected to find such a horror, and then I knew that once more I had been dreaming that old, old dream, the torment of my boyhood which had grown if anything more terrible with the years. Now at last it had lured me even to sleep-walking, and the end might not be yet. There came a vague sense of shame, and I turned and stole back to my chamber on tiptoe, carefully avoiding the floor-board that creaks, lest Louis—for it must have been almost on the stroke of nine—should hear me and draw his conclusions.

He was capable of that, I knew. There was no chance of his having forgotten that, only the morning before, I had sent him to look for a severed hand in a great iron gauntlet. Now, should he find that I had gone on a similar quest myself, barefooted, in complete dishabille, how could he not fear for my reason as I had feared for his when I heard him muttering thieves' Latin?

But these apprehensions, though timely, were misdirected. When I pushed open the chamber door Louis was standing at the window and peering out toward the river through my perspective glass. Even his back, though he stood perfectly still, looked agitated, and some low exclamation drew me to his side. Down there at my landing two hundred feet off, a dozen horsemen—Blandison's apparently, most of them dismounted, some with swords drawn and others with pistols—were violently repelling the attempt of a bargeful of people to come ashore, were bundling them back, men and women alike, into the barge and pushing the vessel off with shouts from both parties that came up the hill as a confused hubbub while the bargemen struck with their oars at whatever head or hand came within reach and a woman screamed. Louis handed me the glass. The people were gaily dressed, as though for an occasion "to be enjoyed *al fresco*." At first I did not recognize any of them; but there was one man, on the roof of the cabin, looking down upon the tumult, laughing, who . . . Ah, no! No! —But then he lifted his right hand high in an unforgettable gesture of farewell which I had seen him make a score of times on the stage, and it was David Garrick!

I too made a gesture, equally theatrical—that of smiting the brow. I groaned. I staggered to the bed, lay down, and allowed Louis to draw

the covers over me. "Oh, Louis," said I, "this was to have been the
day!"

He knew well enough what I meant, but at first his only reply was
to bring me a cup of tea. When I had got it down, by a process which
I think Lieutenant Morris would have called "slorping," he poured
me another and then said, firmly, but with a cheerful countenance:
"If I may presume to emend your tenses, sir, this *is to be* the day."

"Nonsense," said I. "The thing is done. We can't change it. He's
gone. He'll spread the story everywhere. He'll get his friend Sam
Johnson to write a burlesque about me, and play it at Drury Lane.
Oh . . ."

Louis let me run on in this wild way as we let women weep, partly
because we can't stop them. He poured me a third cupful—a thing
I seldom take but always hold in reserve for emergencies—while I
was unnecessarily reminding him of the really delightful party to
which Garrick had invited me two months before, with the Duke of
Grafton there, Lord and Lady Rochford, Lady Holderness, the Spanish Minister, two Regents, and the wife of the Secretary of State.
That had been at his villakin up the Thames, and he had there and
then accepted my invitation to take breakfast with me the first time
he went down-river in his barge. This was the day we had agreed
upon, and here was my return of his hospitality! What would Mrs.
Clive say when she heard about this?—for all at once I recalled her
engagement to go into town with Garrick and his bargeful this day
for certain rehearsals.

Louis calmly replied, in the first place, that

> Presence of mind and courage in distress
> Is more than armies to procure success,

and, in the second, that when we heard what Mrs. Clive had to say we
should know what we had to do.

"That's true," said I. "Get her here immediately, and all the gentlemen—even Mr. Selwyn, and certainly Parson Blandison. Tell them
to come in their nightgowns if they have to, but to come at once, to the
Library."

*   *   *

Kitty was there first—not in her nightgown but in tears. She
already knew all that I did, having witnessed the whole dreadful affair

from her own windows, and something besides. She had recognized Mrs. Susanna Cibber, one of her "dearest friends" and deadliest foes, on the barge. Perhaps you don't know, William, why that should be important, but then you must be the only literate person in England who is unaware of the fierce contest between these two women for the leading part of Polly in *The Beggar's Opera*. Kitty made that part and, upon the whole, has held it for at least twenty years, but often it has been a matter between these two almost of tooth and nail; and now to see this hated friend provided gratis with a story so completely apt for the destruction of a feminine reputation . . . !

"Well, Horry," said she, between a laugh and a wail, "if you decide to spend the rest of your life with Mr. Horace Mann in Florence, please remember that I'm going along! What's the sense in being called a bad woman if you don't get any enjoyment out of it?"

Mr. Chute had to be told what had happened, and, when he was so, began hobbling up and down the room—his gout was bad that day—and thinking. George Selwyn, for a wonder, came in next, rubbing his eyes, yawning, treating the whole affair lightly with pishes and pshaws. My cousin, taking it seriously enough, averred that a little more of this sort of insolence and we should have the dragoons down upon us. He reaffirmed that the only thing to do was to "call this fellow out." It was just then that Blandison came in—looking, I thought, rather pleased with himself, and bidding us all a cheerful good morning.

I am not going to tell you what Kitty told him. It was severe, it was harsh, it was unjust, and as nearly unkind as one friend can be to another. For a moment or two one almost thought she meant it, and Blandison's smile slowly faded into a look of honest perplexity. What had he and his gentlemen done, he asked to know, to warrant such vexation? Had they made another mistake like the one about the Capting's barge? It had been agreed after that event that the ordinary and legitimate traffic of the river should not be interfered with, but surely it had also been understood that no one was to come ashore at Strawberry Hill. Indeed from the very start we had known—had we not?—that during this delightful week simply nothing and no one would be allowed to disturb us. Well, then?

"No," Kitty shot back, "if there's any disturbing to be done you want to do it all; and I will say that you seem to need no assistance. Now that you've insulted the King you go on to make Horry look ridiculous and make trouble between me and David Garrick and give all the help you can to the woman who would like to tear me apart."

"But take me with you, madam. I really . . . Did I hear you say David Garrick?"

And then it came out—a thing I should not expect you to believe if this were a work of fiction—that Blandison had not recognized the foremost actor of our age. Perhaps he had been too preoccupied or excited; but that would not be like him, and I incline to think that he had never laid eyes upon Garrick before, either in London or in Paris. How that might bear upon our whole question about who he was and where brought up, we had no time to consider.

Twenty minutes or thereabout had now passed since the repulse of the barge, and all that while Garrick had been going steadily downstream with the current, rowed by four powerful oarsmen. He had got by Twickenham Ait, no doubt, and would now be approaching Richmond Hill while we stood here bewildered, at cross purposes, with no plan. —What then? Were we helpless? Could we do nothing? What did Mr. Chute think?

He asked us how long Garrick would probably take, at the rate he was going, to get from Richmond Hill to his landing place in London, wherever that might be, and then from there to Drury Lane Theatre. Blandison thought it might take him about two hours and a half, and also said, in reply to another question, that his man Richard Beston could ride from Strawberry Hill to Drury Lane in, at most, one hour and a half. "Then," said Mr. Chute, "we have an hour in which to write a letter of apology, expressing our sincere regret for what has happened and assuring him that no discourtesy was intended."

George Selwyn, now at half-past nine more nearly awake than we usually see him at noon, said that of course our regret was sincere enough, but that mere sincerity, whatever that word might mean, would not serve the turn. All the rest of the letter must be pure fabrication, concealing not only the fact that we had quite forgotten the engagement but also the nature of Blandison's so-called "gentlemen" and their nefarious purposes. Mainly, though, we had to prevent Susanna Cibber from spreading slander about Kitty Clive—a thing which could not possibly be done by telling the truth but only by means of what were sometimes called lies. Therefore he suggested that Mr. Chute and Henry Conway, disqualified as they were by an incorrigible veracity, should have no part in composing this letter. We must put our trust in Kitty because to the natural gifts of deception she had as a woman were added the talents and experience of a great actress. Besides, to what lengths and ingenuities of prevarication would a woman not go in defending her "honesty"? Let it be Kitty's letter, then, in the main; but Blandison might perhaps contribute a few falsehoods. I of course would write the thing out, and he would do the criticism.

We had to laugh at hearing George Selwyn, the habitual drawler, thus teaching the doubtful battle where to rage and rattling out his plan of campaign as fast as his tongue could trip. Briskly then, almost gaily, and with no little of the satisfaction that always comes of wholehearted fellowship, we set to work. For me certainly, and I think also for Kitty and George, there was a kind of happiness in feeling that Blandison, who had brought all this trouble and danger upon us, was now our comrade. We were a quartette, you might say, vaguely similar to the one that sang to us the night before in front of the fire. Kitty carried the air, Blandison harmonized, George added various grunts and growls, and I stamped out the time like Jeremy Tinker.

But away with these whimsies, for there was serious work on hand. In less, far less, than an hour—I'm a dab at swift writing—Richard Beston pouched our missive, swung into the saddle, rowelled his steed, plunged away and was gone into Twickenham, over Pope's grotto, past the isle of eel-pies and on into Isleworth and filthy Brentford and pellmell through Turnham Green with no stop at the Pack Horse but on into Chiswick, Hammersmith, Fulham, Chelsea, until he should snuff his familiar St. Giles and make ready to fling himself upon the swarming labyrinth of London. —I had never before imagined what a comfort it might be, occasionally, to have a private highwayman living in one's own house and ready to speed off at a moment's notice on any errand.

I picture the dispatch of our letter before telling you what was in it because of my doubt whether its contents, had you seen them, would have had your full approval. However, here is what it said, in substance, over my signature: that I was shocked, grieved, overwhelmed with regret and embarrassment, by the all but unbelievable event which had robbed me of the pleasure of Mr. Garrick's distinguished company, so eagerly awaited for so long, at Strawberry Hill; that, although I must assume the blame for what had happened, I had really known nothing of the affair until it was nearly over; that the persons immediately concerned in the repulse of his barge were as innocent of any intentional discourtesy toward him as he himself was of the many murders of old Polonius which he had enacted in the part of Hamlet; that these persons were here rehearsing their lines for a new comedy, perhaps to be called *Something About Love,* which I hoped to lay before him in the not distant future—a comedy designed to take, in the second half of our century, somewhat the same place that *The Beggar's Opera* had filled in the first except that it would be far more genteel, enormously more lucrative, and would have in it not two or three but fifteen highwaymen and highwomen, all mounted, and each of them provided with a solo to be sung on horseback, besides various choruses for mixed voices not omitting the equine; that the aforesaid persons had in a few days grown so enamoured of the parts assigned them that they occasionally lost all sense of the distinction between the play and real life; that their regrettable treatment of Mr. Garrick's barge had been an instance of this excess of histrionic enthusiasm which, they hoped, Mr. Garrick would comprehend and, if possible, pardon; that Mrs. Catherine Clive must beg to be excused from rehearsals at Drury Lane until the following Monday for imperative reasons involving her personal safety; that the leading feminine role in the comedy *Something About Love* had been from the start designed, at Mrs. Clive's earnest request, to suit the charming voice, the beautiful face and figure, the affectionate and charitable character, of her beloved colleague Mrs. Susanna Cibber; and finally, because I had recently heard the remark commended, that life is a comedy to those who think, but a tragedy to those who feel.

*   *   *

We went down into the Prior's Garden and sat on the bench there, or walked up and down, or pretended to be interested in the flowers. Nothing much was said for some time. We were ill at ease, and each of us had in mind so to speak a moving picture in which a river-voyage and a horseback journey converged upon Drury Lane Theatre. Would Beston get there first? He certainly would if "the Roscius of the Age" should stop in at a tavern, a chocolate house, or one of his clubs; and that would be the natural thing for a man to do who was both empty of breakfast and bursting with such a story. —But then if Garrick began to talk before he even read our letter . . .

"That letter," my cousin broke out at last, savagely beheading an aged rose with a swish of his cane, "would not deceive a stupid child."

"It was addressed," Blandison quietly replied, "to an intelligent man, and was not meant to deceive anyone."

"Humph! What then?" growled the General.

"Why to amuse, and so to placate him; to let him see that we are in a slight difficulty here, not at present explainable, and must therefore request his indulgence."

"Humph! Indulgence!" And several more senile roses bled to appease my cousin's wordless wrath. Some such expression as "forsooth" or "quotha" would have been helpful to him, but as neither was in his vocabulary he had to let his cane speak for him.

"Tell him, Kitty," said I, for I cannot bear to see Henry Conway unhappy.

"Oh, what's the use? I'd rather ask him what he would have said, or done. Yes, General; do for pity's sake leave those poor flowers alone and produce, for once, an idea!"

"You know perfectly well, Kitty Clive, that I'd never have got into this—what does John Chester say?—this mess. Right at the start I said the only thing to do was—"

"Never mind. I asked for an idea, not a prejudice."

Swish!

"Now, children," I pleaded. "This is no time for hard feelings. —Henry, kiss Kitty."

"Humph!" But he obeyed, and she looked round at the rest of us, and perhaps a little especially at Blandison, to see whether that was going to be all.

"In my opinion, General," said Mr. Chute, ignoring this byplay, "the letter to Mr. Garrick meets the many and complex demands of the situation as well as could be expected of a document composed under great emotional strain in half an hour."

"Humph!" said my cousin, less indignantly than before but still showing that he was not persuaded.

"Very well, then. I put it to you that, being unable to tell either a lie or the truth, we could only resort to that sheer and obvious nonsense for which our friend and host has so remarkable a talent, natural and acquired."

At this point my three collaborators bowed to me, and I replied with a chuckle and smile combined which may as well be called a smuckle.

Mr. Chute resumed in his most chuticial manner. "Consider, now," said he, gazing earnestly at my cousin and counting off his points on the fingers of his left hand with the index finger of his right, "the probable effects of this letter upon the brilliant mind of David Garrick, highly trained in the comprehension and interpretation of all literary effects. At first he may surmise that our friend is somewhat light-headed; and if he does think that it may not be for the first time. The rumour of it, at least, will have reached him before. But, sir, when he comes to that passage about the fifteen highwaymen, fifteen high-women, and thirty horses, the suspicion of mere frivolity will not suffice. He will then be confronted with this dilemma: either the Honourable Horace Walpole, M.P., has gone stark mad or else David Garrick—if I may borrow a vivid expression from Master Chester—is having his leg pulled. Now, sir, he will undoubtedly conclude that the second of these alternatives is the safer one for him to adopt."

My cousin, seeing that some response was expected, remarked "Ha!"

"In other words, it will be apparent to him that if any stories are to transpire with regard to this morning's strange incident at Straw-berry Hill, he will be unable to invent any explanation more extravagant than those likely to emanate from the place itself. Now, will you consider, for example, that shrewd thrust in which we express not only regret but astonishment that Mr. Garrick should have mistaken a piece of mere acting for the thing itself—should have been deceived by theatrical pretence to such a degree that he actually rowed away. How could we have foreseen, we said, that our amateur efforts had brought us to a pitch of histrionic proficiency that would delude the greatest actor and stage-manager on earth? —I'm sure you follow this, and see its cogency. Our strategy has been like that of a general who discourages attack by making a show of force somewhat greater than he can, in fact, command."

"Ahem!" said my cousin, still reserving judgment.

"And therefore Mr. Garrick will say nothing about the matter. As for Mrs. Cibber, although she may have felt a short-lived elation this morning when she thought of spreading the scandal that Mr. Horace Walpole now keeps an armed guard to conceal his amours, she will not fail to detect the tone of raillery in that fulsome language about her

voice, her face and figure, her charity. The scars of old battles will
admonish her that not so would Mrs. Clive speak if she were in the
least uncertain of triumph in any new conflict that might now arise.
Therefore she too will, I think, say nothing."

My cousin was mopping his brow with a "bird's-eye wipe," although
the day was not oppressively warm. "I see what you mean," said he.

Of course he didn't, dear fellow, at all; yet Mr. Chute's analysis of
the situation was not wholly in vain. Kitty Clive was considerably
cheered by it. The laughter came back into her voice, and again we saw
the dauntless gay look in her eyes as of two stars dancing. "Why, at
this very moment," said she, "dear Susanna is probably singing that
old duet of ours, and applying it all to herself."

"Sing it, Kitty," said George.

And she stood up and bowed and did:

> "I'm bubbled, I'm bubbled!
> Oh, how I am troubled!
> I'm bubbled, bamboozled, and bit!
> My mind is bemuddled, my feelings befuddled,
> I fear I shall fall in a fit,
> Oh, oh,
> I fear I shall fall in a fit!"

*   *   *

But you would not be interested, William, because neither am I,
in what we talked about, thought, imagined, and feared, in those three
hours of waiting. Blandison left us for a time, perhaps to draw up
with Sir Edward a new set of rules for traffic on the Thames. George
went to sleep on the bench. Mr. Chute delivered an Addisonian essay
by word of mouth on "Sincerity"—a word which he declared to be
one of the most difficult in the language. I observed that the windows
of the servants' quarters stood wide open, and inferred that the established custom of eavesdropping at Strawberry Hill was not being
allowed to lapse. Our minds were filled with questions. Had Beston
delivered our letter? Was he bringing back a reply? That picture of
the converging river and road was changed to one of a half-asleep
horseman loitering back through St. Giles and Chelsea and Fulham,
forgetting his errand, perhaps losing his letter, and pausing at every
tavern to drink. Would he never come? For a man who had spent

the best years of his life in killing time, I did it badly. Time was killing me—not neatly, at a single stroke, as George likes to see such things done, but with patient persistence. The Twickenham clock struck eleven, and then, several years later, twelve. Well on into eternity we heard a swift pounding of hooves in the road just over the garden wall and saw Richard Beston dismounting stiff-legged at the gate from a horse that looked ready to drop. He stumbled toward us holding out a letter addressed to me, and I took it and tore it open with a jerk and read, aloud:

> Drury Lane Theatre
> Thursday noon, Oct. 16, 1755

To the Honourable Horace Walpole, Esq.,

Sir: Nothing cd more effectively assuage the disappointment of my hopes for a bkfst at Strawberry Hill than the letter now before me. I have long wisht to have in my cabinet of curiosa, small but select, a specimen of that epistolary art for wh you are justly famous, & now to have acq'd this highly characteristic example at the cost of only one bkfst makes me a proud & happy man indeed.

Equally, perhaps, has it overjoyed those members of my company who were with me this morn in the barge, & most of all Mrs. Susanna Cibber. She bids me extend her best wishes for the "personal safety" of her beloved coleeg Mrs. Clive & applauds that lady's discretion in avoiding the snares that London sets for young & beautiful women. "What a virtue must that be," she cries, "wh requires a guard of 12 armd men, to say nothing of the Hon Horace Walpole's solicitous supervision!" She thanks Mrs. Clive for so generously granting her the feminine lead in *Something About Love,* but pts out that no actress in the world cd compete for attention with the mere spectacle of Mrs. Clive on horseback. This alone, in her opinion, wd, as the saying is, "bring down the house."

Your messenger—did I not see him this morning in your troupe at Strawberry Hill?—stamps in jack-boots up & down the room with his hat pulled low, answering no questions in no intelligible tongue. What an actor, dear sir, you have there! What miserable pretenders in comparison are all the Macheaths, Jemmy Twitchers, Crookfingered Jacks, & Nimming Neds I have been able to train in the last twenty years for *The Beggar's Opera!*

I must now waste the afternoon instructing a group of mere professionals how to read their lines in an inferior play by one William Shakespeare. Heaven speed the day when *Something About Love* will be brot to my door post haste by this same mounted messenger armed with pistols. Meanwhile I remain, sir, your most humble & most obedt servant

DAVID GARRICK

* * *

What a comfort it was to be back in the Library at two o'clock with the Club members present, the fire in flourish, the Connecticut tobacco-pipe aglow, and Ponto courteously greeting us one by one! Oh, now, we said to ourselves, or at least I did, for a session thoroughly anti-climactic, tame, dull, and with no more barges!

Blandison, in the Speaker's Chair, seemed to realize this wish and need. For once, he prosed. He began by saying that in our conversations thus far we had made fewer references to Jenkins' Ear than might have been expected in a company of friends who owed their association to that organ alone. Had we lost faith in the Ear, or did we now take its pervasive influence for granted? To be sure, our thoughts had been somewhat distracted by incidents—that delightful evening at Twickenham Ait, for example—with which it might seem at first glance that the Ear had nothing to do. But were we sure of that? For his part he firmly believed that the left-hand auricular organ of Master Jenkins—or was it the right-hand one?—had been working for now almost exactly sixteen years to make Mr. Horace Walpole acquainted at last with the eels of Twickenham Reach and the virtues of Abingdon ale. But "working," he felt, was a word grossly inadequate. The mathematics of Newton could not compute, nor could the imagination of Shakespeare conceive, the all but infinite series of arrangements which had finally produced a letter, written less than three hours ago, by Mr. David Garrick in London.

"D'ye aim to say suthin' afore long, Parson, or (puff) can I go to sleep like I allus do back home in church?"

Slowly drawled, in a flat, low tone, without the least suggestion of a smile, these words had the effect of instantaneous deflation. "You are entirely right, Master Chester," said Blandison when our laughter had subsided, "and my professional habit of turning everything into a sermon simply must be overcome. Let us go back, then, to the facts of history and recall a few of the numberless events brought to pass by the Ear shortly after it was shown to a committee of the House of Commons. The war with Spain, the fall of Sir Robert Walpole, the voyage of Anson, the wreck of the *Wager* and its consequences, we have already in mind. Yet these things were but the first rudimental fumblings of the seed, now well planted in time, and germinating there, splitting in two, beginning to send down thin white rootlets and to reach with its feeble infantine branches upward. Have patience with it now, for the Ear itself is patient. It does not hasten, but neither does it rest. Like those of the mystical Yggdrasil, its roots are groping toward the realms of death and fate and the gods of darkness. Daily, too, and hourly, its branches strengthen as though they foreknew that soon they must bear the weight of many dangling men."

"I never did hear tell o' no sech a thing," remarked John Chester. "I don't (puff) believe it."

"Before the *Centurion* had reached Cape Horn another series of events had begun, stemming directly from the Ear, in a contemptible principality, befogged and dismally overhung by clouds of tobacco-smoke, called Prussia. Few Europeans at that time had heard its ugly name, and little more was known to any one than that it was peopled by thick-witted semi-barbarians whose main passion in life was to find and enthrone and slavishly obey some complete barbarian in whom stupidity had been brought to its unadulterate essence. All their aspirations in this regard had recently been fulfilled by a certain Frederick William; but now his son, Frederick the Second, was beginning to show that if anything can be more dangerous than stupidity on the throne then it is a low, selfish, and brutal cunning. The wickedness of this second Frederick might have waited long for its chance to spring had it not been for Jenkins' Ear, but now he saw his opportunity in England's preoccupation with Spain and her serious losses under Vernon at Cartagena. With no declaration of war, breaking many promises and pledges and treaties, flouting every principle of chivalric combat worked out in a thousand years, he suddenly invaded the realm of the young Archduchess of Austria, daughter of the late Emperor Charles the Sixth."

"Bless God we don't have all them emp'rors and suchlike back home," said John Chester, rising to knock the ashes out of his pipe. "Jest hearin' the names of 'em makes my head swim."

"Among the innumerable contrivances of Jenkins' Ear I suppose that none will have a more degrading effect upon times to come than that attack. Then indeed the world bade farewell, like Othello, to the 'pride, pomp, and circumstance of glorious war that makes ambition virtue.' For Frederick struck like the blackguard he is at whatever was left in his time of knightly honour. He turned the art of manly conflict into a dull mechanical business of killing people and riding over their dead bodies to what he called victory. He won the base kind of victory which lies open to any man who is willing to use base means. And those filthy means, we know, have made him today the most powerful man in Europe, so that to his natural barbarism there is now added the vulgarity of overwhelming success. This would be no great matter if Prussia alone were involved; but in fact every other nation that maintains its freedom must adopt his methods, and worse, and still worse, until—"

"One moment, if you please," said Mr. Chute. "I agree with what you are saying about King Frederick of Prussia, whom some people are already beginning to call 'Frederick the Great.' What puzzles me, for the moment, is that you trace his iniquities back to that same Ear of Master Jenkins which, on an earlier occasion, you seemed to regard as a boon to England if not to mankind."

"Ah, sir," Blandison replied, smiling, "your alertness in discerning an inconsistency is matched only by your courtesy in pointing it out. I suggest, however, that the inconsistency may be in the Ear itself, or rather that it provides the opportunity both for good and for ill, according to the nature of those who come under its influence. Captain Chepe of the *Wager* was ruined by it, but Gunner Bulkeley at the same time rose to a simple nobility which he might not otherwise have attained. I myself exulted, as I have told you, in the first effect of the Ear; but that does not bind me to approve all, or nearly all, of what it has since done and will do."

"Thank you, sir; I am answered," said Mr. Chute. "Please continue."

"When Frederick of Prussia struck without warning at Maria Theresa that great and beautiful woman was twenty-three years old. Her father had been only two months in the grave, her treasury was exhausted, her ministers were old and irresolute, her army was widely scattered, and she herself was with child. At her age, moreover, it was natural that she should place some trust in the solemn pledges

made to her father by ten or a dozen nations, including Prussia, that
they would support her in her just claim to the Hapsburg realm. We
may be sure that Frederick pondered all of these things like a chess-
player planning a checkmate before, in the Christmas season, when
such treachery would be least of all expected, he suddenly marched
into Austrian Silesia with thirty thousand men. The Queen could
muster at that time only three thousand soldiers. By the end of
January, Frederick had brought almost the entire province under his
control. He then wrote to a member of the Queen's court: 'My heart
has no share in the mischief my hand is doing.'

"If this is not enough to show what kind of man Frederick was and
is, consider his conduct in his first real battle. In April, 1741, the
Prussians, favoured by flurries of snow, stole upon a much smaller
body of Austrians near the Silesian village of Mollwitz. Frederick
had not only the advantage of surprise and of numbers but his infantry, trained to a machinelike speed in loading, could fire five shots to
the enemy's two. His cavalry, however, was routed by a furious Austrian charge, all his baggage was captured, and he himself rode off
the field at top speed with a group of his officers. Ten miles of headlong retreat brought him to the village of Oppeln where a handful of
Austrian hussars sallied out against him and his party. 'Farewell,
gentlemen,' said he to his companions, 'I am better mounted than you
are,' and again he rode away in the general direction of Prussia. It
was many miles farther on, and late in the day, that he heard a
mounted messenger shouting behind him: 'Sire! Sire! Come back.
We have won the battle!' "

*   *   *

Over against that picture of a thoroughly new-fangled knight riding away from a battle which, meanwhile, his own foot-soldiers are
winning for him, Blandison set another picture, old-fashioned even to
the Gothic degree. It showed, in the royal castle of Hungary, three
hundred feet above the Danube, a vast medieval hall of cut and carven
stone, full of shadows on high among the ancient rafters but lighted
along the walls by flambeaux. Gathered there in the ruddy flicker was
the whole nobility of the kingdom, silent, waiting for the purple curtains to open on the musicians' gallery overhead. They waited long,
hearing the faint hiss of the sap in the torches, each man hearing the

breath of the man standing close beside him, before, and behind. Their Queen had summoned them to assemble in Diet on this night of September the eleventh, 1741, and they would wait for her until dawn, if need were, without a word or a sigh of impatience.

At last the curtains were drawn aside and the Queen, whom they proudly called their King, stood before them and somewhat above, looking majestically down. Her dress was simple and black, in mourning for her father. She wore the eight-hundred-year-old crown of St. Stephen with the bent cross atop—that strangest crown in Europe, in part the gift of a Pope and the rest of it a token sent by a Sultan in acknowledgment of some act of clemency in the time of the Crusades. In her right hand she bore the jewelled scimitar of state.

After the roar of welcome and acclaim by which she was greeted in a thousand voices, another silence grew and deepened. She was striving to speak, and could not. At length the First Lady of the Bedchamber stepped between the curtains and put in her arms her month-old son, and she held him up before the assembly and the tears streamed down her face and she began to speak, using the Latin tongue which is still the language of state in that country, saying that now she had been betrayed by all who had sworn to defend her except this one most dearly beloved land in whose faithful love and proven valour she now put her entire trust. She spoke briefly, simply, mingling the monarch with the woman, and when she had spoken a thousand sabres flashed in the torchlight and the great hall rang with *Moriamur pro Rege nostro Maria Theresia.*

Thus I try, and fail, to reproduce the grandeur of Blandison's language in describing that scene, Mr. Chute's notes on the passage having been lost, mislaid, or, it may be, purloined by Louis, who is studying shorthand and Latin at the same time. My version, however, is not so bad but that you can discern the speaker's purpose: to draw a sharp and painful contrast between the kind of monarch who appeals to the chivalric tradition and the sort that asks no better support than the ability of his soldiers to fire their muskets at great speed.

Blandison reminded us that England's sympathies at this time had been with the beleaguered Queen, and that Sir Robert Walpole had done all he could to break the confederacy against her. He had even sent the English Ambassador, Lord Hyndford, to suggest that Frederick be a little magnanimous toward a young and inexperienced woman. "Don't talk to me of magnanimity," Frederick replied. "A

Prince must consult his own interests. I am not averse to peace, but in return for it I mean to have four Duchies."

Thus the King of Prussia. His cousin, the Elector of Hanover, sometimes styled King George the Second, was able to control his sympathies for the Queen by much the same dutiful consideration of what he owed to himself as a Prince. Her case was hard, to be sure, and he could almost have wept the German tears that come so easily to think of all the wolves in Europe rushing upon that tender and helpless woman; yet he must not forget that Hanover, his one ewe-lamb, lay exposed on the one side to France, largest wolf of them all, and on the other to Prussia, the hungriest.

"And now at last the Ear," said Blandison, "no longer content with keeping Master Jenkins in drink and arranging for the consumption of Jacob Grindling's sins, did really begin to vaunt and to flaunt itself. Almost one might have said that it aspired to the throne of old Chaos, or to some dark constellation of midnight whence it could rain everlasting confusion upon mankind."

"Ho, hum!"—from John Chester. "Sounds like it mought mean suthin', but 'tain't Connecticut talk."

Louis threw him a look of mingled fury and disgust. Why ask for meaning, it seemed to say, when one is given such magnificence? Blandison's sheer eloquence had drawn our fervent young verbolator for the moment to his side.

"Other wars had no doubt been confused and confusing," Blandison went smoothly on; "but for blind turmoil and fracas and pellmell of forces hurled one upon another they knew not why, and of voices crying 'Lo here!' and 'Lo there!' in the dark, history has no parallel that I know of to what we now call the War of the Austrian Succession. Certainly not one in a thousand of the men who died in that struggle had any clear idea of its causes and purpose; and even now, looking back upon it, perhaps the most sensible thing we can say— and many have said things far more foolish—is that these multitudes suffered and died on four continents and two oceans because, ten years before, a Spanish sea-captain had cut or torn off the ear of an English shipmaster.

"For the mind has the same need of reasons that the eye has of light. The thought of blind chance is intolerable, and equally abhorrent is the thought that such things are visited upon us by a divine power. What, then, is left? We accept the theory of Jenkins' Ear as those starving men on the coast of Patagonia did their rotting seal meat. On account of that Ear, we say, English and Dutch Protestants began killing the Lutherans of Prussia in order to preserve the Catholic realm of Maria Theresa, while the Catholics of France and Spain slaughtered those of Austria in the hope of tearing that realm apart. Yes, the Ear divided the nations into hostile camps: on the one side England, Austria, Russia, Hungary, Holland, Saxony, Hanover, and Milan; on the other Spain, France, Prussia, Sweden, Bavaria, Sardinia, Scotland, and the Kingdom of Naples."

"But don't ye go an' leave out New London agin Louisburg," said John Chester.

"Oh, I didn't know. Was that a part of the War?"

"Eeah. We took her."

All of us laughed at this succinct account of a military campaign. Blandison praised it as "brief, clear, and sufficient." It reminded him, he said, that he had been talking too long, and he would now resign the chair to our friend from the American forest.

This sounded courteous, but three or four of us knew that just here was the place for my cousin's stories about the battles of Dettingen and Fontenoy. Kitty had promised him that he should tell those stories, and Blandison knew that we expected to hear them—not so much on our own account as to give the General a speaking part in our "comedy."

You know how I love to have Henry shine, and thus far in the week he had not quite done so. The fact is that in everyday social encounter he is seldom at his best, Nature having designed him not for a carpet-knight but as a hero of romance. And even in battle, though brave as a lion, he is dogged by misfortune and, as it were, a forgetfulness of the part he was created to fill. Thus on the field of Lauffeld, in '47, just as he was beginning to carve a glorious name upon the bodies of the foe, he was suddenly dragged off his horse by some low rapscallion, thrown down, trampled upon, and while one French hussar held him by the hair another was about to stab him when up rushed an English sergeant with a common soldier and killed the second hussar but was instantly killed himself, leaving the soldier to fend off a dozen more Frenchmen so that Henry Conway could escape, as he did, but could not find his horse and was captured and disarmed by a mere corporal and led away to prison.

There's an instance, clearly, of what Blandison means by risk,

danger, loss, and ruin perhaps; but, beyond a doubt, the tragic grandeur surrounding those of whom the world is not worthy. For you
must understand that Henry Conway would have had no trouble in
beating all the hussars, rapscallions, and corporals in the French
Empire, were it not that heroes can have no dealings with any such
canaille. His whole trouble was that he could not find another knight
worthy of his steel. —Such is the predicament of the true hero in
our time.

Need I add that men of this stamp are apt to be most dearly beloved? They arouse no envy, but rather a strangely mingled sense of
admiring compassion. We love them not for their wisdom and wit,
which are wont to be deeply hidden away, nor yet for their deeds, their
power, their fame, or any advantage that may accrue to ourselves, but
solely for what they are. —Why, yes; there it is, and of course I'm
only playing variations on the piercingly beautiful passage where
Montaigne tries to tell us why he loved Etienne de La Boétie: "If any
man should importune me to give a reason, I find it could no otherwise
be expressed than by making answer, 'Because it was he, because it
was I.'"

All of which, you complain, is nothing to the point, and keeps Adair
and Blandison awkwardly marking time between two chairs until I
am through with my digression. Very well, I agree, and I care not,
and furthermore if I hear any more complaints of this sort I shall
straightway digress into an essay in praise of digressions with Montaigne's example before me. Besides, any place in a letter is a good
enough place for me to bring in Henry Conway, especially when other
people are trying to leave him out.

*   *   *

James Adair is now sitting in the Speaker's Chair with the light of
the triple-arched window beating full upon him. The azure, vert, and
gules of the upper panes change his pearly doeskin jacket into a
Jacob's coat of many colours. There is a splotch of red on his folded
hands. He sits quite motionless and speaks in a clear low voice with a
hint of music in it as of wild water far off.

"We have all liked," he begins, "the way Byron and Morris and
Chester have told us who and what they are, where they come from
and why, and then have gone on to relate what they themselves have

seen and heard, thought and done. I shall try to follow their good example.

"I was born forty-five years ago in the northeast corner of Ireland, but of Scottish parentage. As you see, I am what is called a 'black Scot'; and for that I give the perhaps fanciful reason that there is some thousand-year-old strain in me of wild Pictish blood. The fact that we know little about the Picts, except that they were wild and lived a long time since, has left all the more room for imagination. The thought of them has shaped my life and coloured my thoughts with the glamour of the past. Even as a boy I felt more at home on the desolate summits of Slemish and Slieveanorra than in the town of Carrickfergus where I lived. During my student years in Scotland I spent my holidays by choice in the Highlands and Hebrides, lodging with the natives in smoky huts of stone and adding a little Gaelic to the Latin, Greek, and Hebrew I was learning from books. When I went back to the Highlands nine years ago, and again last month, it was a pleasure to find that I could still make a shrewd guess at what was said to me, though my answers might show now and then a tincture of Chickasaw or Catawban.

"Have I suggested why, when the time came for choosing an occupation, I decided to become an Indian trader in America? That would provide wilderness enough, but you may ask why a lover of the past should emigrate to what is called the New World. In my conviction America is as old as Europe, the main difference between the two in this regard being only that the antiquities of the western hemisphere are as yet undiscovered. Something of this I knew as a young man. Also I had been caught by the notion, from which I have never since escaped, that the natives of America are children of the Ten Lost Tribes of Israel. Thus antiquity and the wilderness came together, and at the age of twenty-five I went to America as agent for a family of Scottish merchants by the name of MacGillivray."

Mr. Chute had to be told how to spell that barely credible name, and then we learned something about the extremely old family or clan which, in spite of such an encumbrance, has done decidedly well for itself in the West Indian trade. Some members of it, I judge, still make a bare livelihood by running off with the property of Lowlanders and Southrons, but most of them in recent years have engaged in that more modern form of brigandage known as "trade." They send out hatchets, knives, tiny mirrors, spangles, vermilion, and the like, and receive mostly peltries in return. The profits, according to Adair, are considerable. When George Selwyn asked him whether he would go so far as to call them "handsome," he did not demur.

"My first voyage across the Atlantic," Adair went on, "comprised most of the miseries suffered by the men of the *Wager* and the *Speedwell*. We had little scurvy, and I do not recall that we ate any sins; but the good ship *Simmonds* was tossed and beaten and blown off her course by a continuous succession of tempests, finally rising to a hurricane, from the time she left Gravesend until, three months later, we landed in Georgia. Captain Byron has given us an enthralling account of the storms off Cape Horn that finally destroyed the *Wager*, but I can tell him that for weeks at a time we should have welcomed almost any rock in the sea that was large enough to be wrecked and to starve upon. Lieutenant Morris has made much of that one man on the *Speedwell* who had once heard John Wesley preach and had learned the words but not the tune of a Methodist hymn. Let me tell him that we had on board John Wesley himself, preaching several times a day, and also his brother Charles who had written those words and composed that tune."

"Dreadful!" George groaned, with his eyes shut.

"The Wesley brothers began their day at five in the morning"—here George groaned again—"and from then until midnight they were preaching, praying, exhorting, expounding, composing and singing more hymns, but mainly saving souls. In between souls John Wesley taught Greek to one of his converts so that he could read the New Testament in the original, and taught himself German so that he could preach to a group of Moravians we had on board. Meanwhile he was much exercised about the sad spiritual state of our Portuguese Jews. I suppose he might have addressed them in Hebrew, but instead he learned enough Spanish to change a few of them—or so he intimated to me—into good Methodists. I then pointed out that there were also a few Highlanders amongst us, in all likelihood little better than Papists; but just as he was starting in on Gaelic under my tuition we sighted land."

George opened his eyes and gazed at Adair with horror. "Good God!" he gasped. "This fellow must have been far worse than scurvy! Why couldn't you have had the foresight to toss him overboard?"

"Oh, no! No!"

"Why not, Jeremy? It would have saved no end of trouble."

But Jeremy Tinker, having inadvertently launched himself upon his maiden speech, would not turn back. "Why," he exclaimed, red in the face and his voice quavering, "the Reverent John Wesley 'e's prob'ly next to the best man alive! Didn't 'e get Gen'ral Oglethorpe to pay my debts—twenty-seven shillin's sixpence three farthin's—an' take me 'long with 'im to Georgia? Can't I see 'im this minute steppin' down through the puddles from the colleges to Hoxford Castle where they keeps the debtors, an' me in the cage where they let us stand an' beg from passers-by, an' 'im stoppin' to look an' 'Good mornin' to you, my friend,' says 'e with the right 'and o' fellowship reached in through the bars, an' from then to this hour I've loved the Reverent John Wesley the way iffen one or tother must go overboard may the blessed Lord let it be me!"

"Oh," said George, visibly embarrassed, and then "Ah," and finally: "Very well, then, let him remain—but with the distinct stipulation that there's to be no more of this getting up at five in the morning."

"But, Jeremy Tinker," said Kitty, with her warmest smile, "you haven't said anything before about being a—a Methody."

"No, ma'am, 'cause o' not bein' worthy. I do try in my weak way, but all them bad 'abits I larned in my tinkerin' days an' likewise when livin' with the Romanies, they keep comin' back, ma'am. Now an' then I touch a glass, or smoke a pipe, or mebbe even turn a card, the which I well know to be sinful—not for others but for me. Fack is, I ain't saved, Mrs. Clive, even thof the Reverent John Wesley do 'ave promisin' 'opes for my soul."

"Jeremy Tinker and I," said Adair, firmly, "have been close friends ever since that voyage of twenty years ago, and if there's any question about his soul, either here or at the Last Judgment, I hope to testify in its favour, emphatically."

"Oh, James, now, you know—"

"Yes, I do; and so let's get on toward the American forest and Jenkins' Ear. To that end I hasten through our first few months in Georgia. Jeremy's efforts to turn himself into a farmer were not highly successful, partly because the trustees of the Colony, back here at home, insisted that only those things should be grown there—wine grapes, for example, and hemp, mulberry trees, and medical plants— for which England was dependent upon foreign countries. He did succeed in falling in love, but that is for him to tell later on if he wishes.

"My business at the time was to learn Indian languages, and at first

I made slower progress than Jeremy's mulberry trees. There were no dictionaries, of course, no grammars, no books of any kind to help me. Besides that, I made the mistake of beginning with the Catawban, merely because I found near Savannah an Indian of that tribe who knew a little English. There was no one to tell me that the Catawbas, few in number even then, were rapidly dying out on account of the extreme ferocity and boldness of their warriors. No one knew that their language, somewhat like that of the Five Nations far away to the north, was unrelated to anything spoken by the southern tribes with whom I expected to trade. And yet the time I spent upon Catawban, far more difficult for me to learn than Hebrew had been, to say nothing of Greek, was not wholly lost. It was something, in later years, to be the only trader in the forest who knew that dying speech, and it has meant much more to be a friend of the famous Catawban warrior whose name means, in English, New River. —Mr. George Selwyn may be familiar with that name."

George had never heard of such a person, and did not even seem to want to.

"Ah, well," said Adair, smiling, "it is no matter. I'm not sure that New River has heard of Mr. Selwyn. He will be interested, though, I think, when I get back to his country and tell him about his landlord."

"What's this?" Kitty cried. "You don't mean that our George owns land over there! —George, why haven't you told us?"

George's grunt was no answer, but finally we got it from Adair, whose business it is to know such things, that "Mr. Selwyn inherited from his father, four years ago, some two hundred thousand acres of land which are described in the grant as 'lying in the extreme parts of North Carolina, near the mountains and the Catawba Indians.' "

"Two hundred thousand acres!" exclaimed the farmer from Connecticut in a tone of all but religious awe. "Why, hell, that's more 'n we got in the hull o' New London. And then, too, I hear tell they got gold down thar in North Car'liny."

"Yes, indeed," said Adair. "The sights of my Deckard rifle are made of Carolina gold—probably from Mr. Selwyn's estate."

George's eyes were by this time open, and I knew as well as if I had been sitting inside his brain that he was thinking about White's Coffee House and a wonderful hand at loo and a wager upon that hand which would make him famous for ever. He might lose his gold-mine, of course; but George, as I trust you understand, is a hero in Blandison's strict and exacting sense: one who lives for "risk, danger, loss, and ruin perhaps, but, at any rate, glory."

His eyes stayed open while the trader described the superb collection of scalps, twelve of them taken in a single exploit, to be seen in New River's cabin. We were being rather minutely informed about the mounting and decoration of these trophies when Blandison asked for the story of that one exploit. But Adair would not tell that tale, on the ground that it had no connection with Jenkins' Ear. The best thing for the Parson to do, he said, would be to call in at New River's cabin whenever he might be passing by. There he would find the whole thing told in pictures on the stem of the hero's tobacco-pipe. Also he would be able to examine the scalps themselves—an exceptionally valuable set because they were all Senecan in origin and the Senecas, besides the fact that they usually put up a fierce resistance to scalp collectors, were rarely encountered on Mr. Selwyn's property.

Adair also refused John Chester's request that he "put a price on this heer set." The scalp-market, he said, was extremely variable, and had not as yet been developed to anything like the extent of the market in peltries. The money-value of scalps fluctuated with time and place, peace and war, race and nationality, and even with the individuals from whom they were taken. Since the opening of the War of Jenkins' Ear there had been some effort to standardize the price, the English settlers and traders occasionally offering one pound sterling for a well authenticated French scalp in good condition, and the French perhaps half as much for an English. But little had been accomplished in this way because the Indians could not be brought to see that a severed scalp had any value except to the man who had taken it. To him, indeed, a really distinguished scalp at his belt or dangling from his pipe-stem was the equivalent of a title of nobility; but all the more on that account he was likely to be disgusted with the white man's tendency to regard such trophies as articles of commerce. Yes, disgust, he thought, was precisely what his friend New River would feel if any one should offer him, say, a thousand pounds for his round dozen of Senecan scalps.

*   *   *

Adair spent some time with the Catawba Indians on George Selwyn's estate and then a longer period with the Cherokees, farther south. He told us that, unlike most English traders, he lived actually with the people of the forest, adopting their diet and dress, taking part as far as they allowed in their dances, festivals, religious rites, even their wars. My impression is that he married an Indian woman, but even Kitty learned nothing about Mrs. Adair.

Thus, little by little, this man born in Ireland and highly educated in a Scottish university came to think and feel somewhat in the manner of his barbarous companions. He found much in them to condemn, deplore, or pity; yet as the years went by he was more and more inclined to take their side against the white settlers who were ousting them from their hunting-grounds, putting under the plough their cornfields once worked with a clam-shell hoe, and sowing strange notions and diseases among them. Had it not been for his occasional returns to this country, his visits to Savannah and Charlestown, and the correspondence he kept up with various European scholars, he might well have sunk into barbarism himself. Many instances of that, he said, are known; and he told us about a woman of English ancestry who, after living for years as a captive in a northern tribe, pled pitifully not to be returned to her people.

Meanwhile Adair extended his trading operations, acquired the pack-trains and mule-drivers needed for transporting his wares back and forth across the mountains, and increased his acquaintance with Indian languages, politics, and diplomacy. Another occupation was the gathering of evidence that the American Indians are descendants of the "Chosen People." The best proof of that, I should say, is the principle stated in Holy Writ that "whom the Lord loveth he chasteneth"; but Adair found much besides. He is in fact writing a book in which all his proofs, as he puts it, will be "irresistibly adduced," and writing it under conditions almost as difficult as those that confronted Bulkeley and Cummins in their literary efforts on the *Speedwell*. His study is a trading-post beside the Yazoo River into which any member of the Chickasaw tribe is free to enter at any moment without knocking. That may not sound serious unless you know that to the American Indians all black marks made on paper by white men are extremely "bad medicine"—an opinion for which the written treaties we have made with them, and then consistently broken, may lend some support. The very devil, they say, is in these lying black marks, even when made by a friend, and the only way they know of driving him out is to burn him.

Think of that, William! My Louis—and perhaps your Andrew as well—may steam open a letter now and then, or temporarily purloin a page or two for purposes of self-improvement, but he would no more lay a manuscript of mine on the fire than he would his right hand. As for the gout, it is a sedentary if not a sedative disease, admirably conducive to the writing and reading of long letters. But most of Adair's writing has to be done after midnight, and he must hide his manuscripts in hollow trees if he can find any, or under rocks—but there are no rocks where he lives—and in caves. There are no caves.

*   *   *

More to the present purpose is the mounting anxiety felt by Adair in those early years with regard to the huge shaggy continent about him. For some obscure reason, even though he had personally witnessed our misgovernment of Ireland and Scotland, he strongly felt that England should control North America. That, of course, is what all true-born Englishmen feel; but we differ from Adair in having a blind confidence that a just and beneficent God will not allow the New World to fall into the hands of inferior nations. He was not so sure of that. The more he went about among the tribes, learned the lie of the land, and talked with other traders, the more possible, even likely, it seemed to him that England might be crowded out. And this anxiety was not solely due to the firm grip of France upon everything to the north of the Great Lakes and the strength of Spain in the south and west. Neither did he have it primarily in mind that our colonies on the Atlantic coast are weak, poor, divided, dissimilar, and almost as ignorant as we are here at home of the vast territories at their backs. No; Adair's main notion about America came to be, and still is, that whoever controls the Mississippi River will eventually, and soon, be master of the country as a whole. Our coastal colonies, he asserted, could not possibly hold out for any length of time if either France or Spain, but particularly France, should once dominate that river and the valley it drains. He took no credit to himself for a notion which he described as obvious, elementary, and written clear on the map itself for any one to read. He did wonder, though, that this notion had apparently never occurred—and my observations in Parliament support him here—to persons in England who could do something about it. But France, said he, has for more than a hundred years understood the importance of the Mississippi, and has acted—slowly, to be sure, and feebly—in accord with her understanding.

My cousin interrupted at this point, perhaps a little brusquely, to say that he did not at all agree with the speaker. "His Majesty's Government," said he, "is well aware of what both France and Spain are doing on the Mississippi, and is not in the least concerned. When the time comes we shall simply sail up that river and blow them out of there."

Until that moment Adair had made, I think, not one gesture, and had, in fact, scarcely moved. Now he raised his right hand for a moment so as to cover the lower part of his face. Possibly he was smiling, but his eyes were serious as he inquired how familiar his Majesty's Government might be with the navigation of the river. My cousin said the Navy would know all about that. If not, then the Army could march up both banks of the stream and oust those foreigners. He did not anticipate much trouble in crossing any of the tributaries Adair mentioned—Mr. Chute got down only the names of the O'Hara and the Misery—or that there would be much difficulty in the four-hundred-mile march from the Gulf to the river's source.

Adair's hand dropped to his lap. He was not smiling. His eyes grew even more serious as he gazed for several seconds at Henry. Then he said: "You will be happy to know, General, that when, two weeks ago, I waited upon the Duke of Cumberland—now mainly in charge of our military affairs—he expressed an opinion almost identical with yours. He too thinks that the Mississippi is about four hundred miles long, instead of four thousand as an Indian friend of mine once told me."

"Naturally," my cousin replied. "The Duke—say what you like about him on other accounts—is a good soldier. It's his duty to know about such things. He doesn't depend upon wild men for his information."

"Obviously not; nor for his military tactics, which I believe he takes from his cousin Frederick of Prussia. —By the way, did the Duke lay the plans for General James Braddock's recent march through the wilderness toward, but I think not quite to, Fort Duquesne?"

Unlike his cousin Horace Walpole, my cousin Henry Conway is not a man of many words. He now contented himself with only one: "Probably."

"Ah. And it need scarcely be said that in the laying and execution of those highly civilized plans the opinions of 'wild men'—that is, of

George Croghan and George Washington, for example, who know that wilderness at first hand—were not considered. They would not have advised General Braddock to drag a battery of cannon through swamps and thickets for a hundred miles or more. George Washington, I believe, advised him not to do so, but General Braddock had his orders from the Duke of Cumberland. In consequence, General Braddock is now dead. So are most of his officers, and more of his men than one likes to think of. His cannon are stuck in the swamp, and Fort Duquesne remains in the hands of the French."

My cousin is really at his best when he uses no words at all. That is what he did at this point, and the rest of us likewise. For several seconds he and Adair sat gazing at each other, making no attempt at a compromise between the latest methods of slaughter and those still effectively practised in the American forest.

It seemed to me as the silence lengthened that here was a moment for what military people call a "diversion." Therefore, with a smile at each of the gazers and a side-glance at Blandison, I remarked that General Braddock had died, at any rate, like a hero of whom the world was not worthy. Finding that no one smiled, I went on to say that in any case suicide ran in Braddock's family, his sister having hanged herself after losing all her money at cards. But no; my cousin's gaze was hardening into a glare, and the Indian trader was clearly indisposed to reduce the length of the Mississippi by a single mile. What then? How then? Well then, I told them the only amusing story I know about this James Braddock, who was after all an extremely dull dog: how he went back for the hundredth time to the lady who was just then keeping him—God knows why, and I know her name, but never mind—with a demand for money, and, when she told him he had already taken her last shilling, snatched her purse, found two guineas, pocketed them, threw the purse in her face, and so flung out of the house with, just before the door slammed, "What! Did you think you could *cheat* me?"

It fell flat. The only effect was to transfer my cousin's glare to me. Perhaps every one was thinking *De mortuis nil nisi bonum;* but then too, of course, the prosperity of a jest depends as much upon the time and place as upon its intrinsic absurdity. —This is a thing I know and yet know not, Fate having ordained that I shall be absurd everywhere and always.

* * *

The awkward interval was ended when Adair moved on into a eulogy of the founder of Georgia, in his opinion one of the noblest figures of our time, General James Edward Oglethorpe. He had not gone far, however, before Jeremy Tinker, having now found his tongue, shrilled out:

"But, James, why not call 'im by the right name? 'E's James Edward Stuart, an' by rights King of England. I've told you a thousand times."

"Yes, Jeremy," was the gentle reply, "but, you see, I thought these good people might not understand. They might think he was only another Pretender. You wouldn't like that, and neither would our friend. He never told us, you know, about his being the true King."

"But 'e didn't 'ave to. Any man could tell jest by lookin' at 'im as 'e must be Majesty 'Eaven-sent. Same time, we did oughter call 'im proper, an' not in vain."

"Hey!" John Chester burst out, his eyes prodding at us one by one. "What's a-goin' on hyar? I don't git this."

Kitty Clive, after some lightning-swift survey of all that was involved, shook her head at Chester, effectively. Adair, who had given us our cue, sat silent. My cousin was obviously perplexed, and so was Morris—but not Byron. There were a dozen things I wanted to say, especially to Blandison, and he looked like a man well stored with answers; yet neither of us spoke. George Selwyn suppressed no one will ever know what devastating pungencies, gazing steadfastly the while at the Walpole arms in the ceiling.

To you, William, the whole delicately complex situation will be instantly clear, as I suppose you have read the once-famous and still notorious Shaftoe Narrative about the "Warming-Pan Prince." Call it a Whig fabrication if you like, but it served the turn in its time as Jenkins' Ear was to do later on. Our question is, however, whether Posterity will know that old story alleging an interchange, in 1688, of Stuart and Oglethorpe infants. How can we make it clear to readers of two centuries hence—that is, without seeming to inform them— that even in our day many simple-minded people think the Old Pretender, and of course his son as well, is really an Oglethorpe, and that the Oglethorpes in turn are of the true Stuart line? —None of this, to be sure, properly applies to the founder of Georgia, for he must have been born some years after 1688; but you know to what lengths we are often led by the wish to believe.

Don't you think some credit is due to a group of Whigs for their refusal to break the heart of a congenital Tory by exploding an old Whig hoax? Jeremy Tinker, we knew, had never had much in life, and now there were left him only a few shreds of illusion. Therefore we sat there in concerted silence, biting back and swallowing down any number of things we wanted to say, rather than weaken his faith that he had seen, known, loved, and served the Lord's Anointed. Sir, if there be sins of omission, why may there not be virtues and holinesses also—yes, and triumphs?

One thing, Adair said, that might raise a doubt whether this man was in fact the true King of England was that he looked and acted so kingly. With a really magnificent appearance, tall, shapely, at once gracious and grand, mingling the manners of a gentleman with the directness of a soldier, he had the kindness that goes with strength. And yet, like the rest of us, he had his social preferences; namely, for the weak and poor, the outcast, the persecuted. To the friendless, he was a friend. To any man in prison for debt, he seemed to think himself a debtor. He would own not one acre of land in Georgia, we were told, and hired the house he lived in at Savannah—a house twenty-four feet long by sixteen in width, made of rough boards, unpainted.

What there is so remarkably royal about that, I do not understand; but a story Adair told us about Oglethorpe's youth was more to the point. He was dining one day in Flanders with a company of gentlemen upon whom a certain Prince of Württemberg had managed to foist his presence. This Prince, with the delicate sense of humour for which the Germans are famous, took up a glass of wine and, with a flick of the finger, splattered a few drops in Oglethorpe's face. What was the young man to do? Should he challenge the boor, the answer would be that Princes of the Blood do not fight their social inferiors. On the other hand he could not avoid the imputation of cowardice if he let the thing pass. His decision was instantly right. Leaning forward a little and looking the other in the eye with a pleasant smile, "My Prince," said he, "that's an excellent jest, but in England we do it differently and, I think, better." With that he flung a whole glass of wine in the Prince's face, and every one at the table except the Prince himself broke out laughing.

Adair lingered fondly upon the early years of the Georgia plantation, as though there had been something idyllic, even Edenic, about them. To be sure, there was the curse of toil, and the Wesley brothers would see that there was plenty of talk, at least, about sin. I judge,

however, that the sinfulness did not get much beyond talk, opportunities for the practice of it being so restricted. Whether on that
account or because of some obscure woman-trouble—from which
Eden itself, you recall, was not immune—the Methodist leaders finally
left the place. Jeremy Tinker seems to have fallen in love as soon as
John Wesley was out of sight. At any rate he had his own small farm
and worked it as well as you could expect a man half a gypsy and half
a tinker to do. For the first time in his life he had a house of his own,
many friends, some creature comforts, and a sense of safety. That was
much more than he had ever expected. His cup ran over, though not
with rum because there was no such thing to be had in Georgia; his
head was anointed with oil, or at any rate might be as soon as the olives
came into bearing; and he may even have entertained "promisin' 'opes"
of dwelling in the house of the Lord for ever.

Just how long the felicity of Adam lasted is a thing which you
clergymen doubtless know. I do not. I have a notion, though, that
every time a man says "for ever" he is overheard by something that
has other plans. During those few happy years in the Georgian Paradise, Jeremy Tinker was unaware that a bibulous shipmaster called
Robert Jenkins was keeping himself in drink by exhibiting in the
taverns of far-away London a loathsome shred of gristle.

                    *   *   *

The news that England and Spain were at war came belatedly to
James Adair, then living among the Cherokees in the Great Smoky
Mountains. It came by special messenger from Oglethorpe, several
hundred miles away, and with it an earnest plea for help against the
Spaniards of Florida, who were making ready to attack the Georgian
seaboard. In particular Oglethorpe asked for a contingent of Creek
warriors to offset the Seminoles with whom the Spaniards of Fort
Augustine were in alliance.

Adair was not yet well acquainted among the western tribes; but
one of the MacGillivrays who had close trading relations with the
Creeks finally secured audience for him in the "old beloved town" of
the Creek nation called Coosa. This was a privilege seldom accorded
to white men, and it would not have been granted if the younger
Creeks had not just then been nearly desperate for something, almost
anything, to go to war about. For the war season was close at hand, the

quivers were full, and the scalping-knives whetted. The braves had been suitably barbered and painted and otherwise bedizened for slaughter passive or active. All that was lacking was a *casus belli* which the peace-party, the White-sticks so called, deemed sufficient.

Creek politics are not hard to understand if one keeps in mind the situation here in England when a raucous group of Young Whigs and the whole baying pack of the Tories were assailing my father's policy of peace. On the one hand there is always the party of older, wiser, and better established men who already have enough scalps in their possession to assure them of political power and social respect for the rest of their lives. Almost invariably their vote is for peace, if only because they know that every fresh scalp brought in by a younger man reduces in some degree their own preeminence. For scalps newly taken they feel an abhorrence not wholly unlike that of an English gentleman for "new money." Their notion seems to be, indeed, that scalp-taking is a brutal business which ought from henceforth to be prohibited, and that every one should be contented with the trophies he has already acquired.

Now this attitude, enlightened as it seems to us, is deeply resented by those who have comparatively few scalps, or, in cases of extreme destitution, none. Asserting that the motives of the peace-keepers are wholly selfish, they do not scruple to revile them in public speech, Adair told us, with a ferocity that goes beyond even William Pitt in his fire-eatingest days. Not content with invective, they beat war-drums all night round the fire in the great square of Coosa, keeping every one else awake. They plaster themselves with vermilion, brandish tomahawks and knives in public, dance dreadful dances, gnaw their own flesh, and try to paint everything red. Also they hold long councils wherein they magnify into an intolerable insult whatever discourtesy, real or imagined, has ever been shown by any one toward any Creek.

These malcontents, these Red-sticks, had arranged for the appearance of James Adair at Coosa. They may not have had great hopes of him, but everything and every one else had failed. I doubt whether Adair himself was overjoyed at the opportunity, for he, you remember, was a White-stick—partly, perhaps, for humanitarian reasons but also because scalp-taking tended to distract the Indians from their proper business of collecting peltries. However, I suppose he thought mainly about his friends in Georgia and resolved to do his best.

Behold him standing now just before the council-cabin on the western side of the great square at Coosa. The cabin is open toward the square, and inside it some thirty old men recline on benches or beds of strewn cane. They look drowsy, and most of them are fat. You can judge from their faces that they are men of many scalps, men satiated with glory, to whom risk and danger, loss and ruin perhaps, have come to seem rather boyish and barbarous. Chief among them, because he has more scalps than any one else, is the Miko or King of the nation. He is clad in white doeskin and holds a long white staff. Pictures of men and animals, all painted in white, adorn the inner walls. White eagle-tails and the snowy plumage of the trumpeter-swan depend from the rafters and eaves. Round and round every pillar and beam coil white carven snakes, the Miko's emblem. Thus the colour of peace is everywhere blazoned, flourished, flaunted, as though in a storm of snow.

Bathed in blood on the north side of the square is the Red-stick cabin, filled with fierce young men, lean, wide awake. Other cabins there are for boys and for men extremely aged; but these do not count. The square, except for the place occupied by the central fire, is crowded with women, children, and black slaves. Most of them are gaily dressed, for this is their festival of the young corn. Only yesterday they finished burning the last bones of the old year—it included all their used clothing, their furniture, their utensils, even the embers on their hearths—and brought up a new year out of the river. Now they are standing quiet, expecting a speech from the white stranger to correspond with the nobility of his bearing and the splendour of his attire.

You see all that, I say, and hear the rush of the Coosa River a hundred feet below, with the harsh roar now and then of an alligator basking down there on the bank. You wonder about the long shining strips that hang from Adair's left arm, and I have to tell you that they are belts, six feet long, of wampumpeague—tiny shells, black and white, threaded closely together, often used as money—which he has brought as gifts for the Miko. —I say "gifts" to be polite, but if you as a Tory wish to think of the twelve thousand pounds that were paid as a bribe to reduce my father's majority in the House of Commons, that is your privilege.

And now he is beginning to speak, in Choctaw, addressing the Miko directly but in a voice that can be heard in every corner of the square.

He speaks slowly at first, with utmost dignity, and about matters as remote as possible from his real theme, praising the grandeur of Coosa, the wisdom of her Miko, the fame of her warriors, the wonderful beauty of her maidens. Then he pauses, advances, lays a black belt at the Miko's feet, and returns to his former place.

"Ugh!" says the Miko in courteous acknowledgment, and slightly bows.

Adair devotes his next section to the praise of peace, and of all the great, good, and wise men such as the Miko himself who have done their best to preserve it. This goes on for some time, and then another belt is laid down and acknowledged.

But really, William, all I need tell you is that Adair has brought with him seven belts; a man of your experience in the pulpit can make up the rest of the speech for himself. Thirdly and fourthly might be given to the well known virtues of the English people and the corresponding iniquities of the Spanish. Fifthly should contain a panegyric of Master Robert Jenkins. In sixthly, reaching your climax and using appropriate gestures, you should describe the atrocious attack upon Master Jenkins and the reaving of his precious irreplaceable ear. Seventhly and finally, you extend to the peace-loving Creeks a cordial invitation from the Great White Father across the sea that they join with him in visiting condign punishment upon these Spaniards. The best way to do that, you suggest, is to send off at once a large band of Creek braves to attack and destroy the Seminole tribe which has wickedly allied itself with the Spaniards in Florida. Only thus, you conclude, in tones that tremble with the sincerity of your emotion, can the pure white dove of peace, now so grievously affrighted, be lured back to her favourite perch and induced to resume her accustomed coo on the ridgepole of the council-cabin of Coosa. —With that you lay down at the Miko's feet your last long glittering belt of wampumpeague and await the applause.

"Ugh!" says the Miko. And all the other scalp-satiated White-sticks reclining beside and behind him on their couches of cane appear to be of the same thoughtfully considered opinion. They do not, to be sure, go so far as to say so, even by means of that most readily uttered of all monosyllables. No indeed; for there is a rule, an unwritten law, the like of which is certainly operant in our own mercantile class, that the more scalps a man has the more he keeps his mouth shut and brings his features under that stern control most perfectly exemplified by a corpse. Nevertheless, a unanimous silence can be as expressive as a vociferation.

On the other hand, the Red-sticks one and all have been completely convinced by your logic, and brought to a frenzy of wrath by the fervour of your sincerity. They are for rushing forth at once with wild yells after that brutal Spaniard—or, if they fail to find him, any other man of the same nation, any Seminole, any one with a scalp. But the Red-sticks are not in command of the situation. Their attempt to start a war-dance round the central fire is firmly quashed. Their yells gradually subside into growls and then to sullen mutterings. At length the Miko, as calm as he is white, slowly rises from his couch and begins to speak.

His remarks are courteous, dignified, highly metaphorical, and extended. Beneath the polite phraseology Adair catches here and there a hint of irony. The old man hopes that his friend the Irish trader will express to Master Jenkins the deep sympathy felt by the Creek nation upon hearing about the loss of his valuable ear. He feels confident that Master Jenkins will bear this loss like a man, not forgetting that there are a number of Englishmen in the American colonies who have lost both of their ears, and some even their noses, through no fault of the Spaniards. He reminds the Irish trader that among the Indians an ear is often removed more or less in jest, particularly when a number of young braves are happily overcome in the joys of firewater. He points out that the tearing and biting off of ears is a recognized practice in the manly sport of ball-play, and is taken by the losers not as a thing calling for sanguinary reprisals but in the gamesome spirit in which it is meant. He suggests, therefore, that Master Jenkins, at the time of his loss, may possibly have been drunk or else engaged in some rough kind of game. In any case, the information should be conveyed to the Great White Father that the warriors of the Creek nation, perhaps because of their natural stupidity, are unable to comprehend why they should go out and kill Seminoles merely because a man born in Ireland has made an extremely eloquent speech of seven belts about a Spaniard's attack upon an Englishman's ear.

When the Miko sat down, all the people in the square—the old men in their cabin, the boys in theirs, even the Red-sticks—were quiet. The crowd began to disperse. Adair heard the rustle of the evening breeze among the boughs of the forest crowding close up against the cabins.

An alligator's roar from some pool far down the stream sounded to him like gigantic laughter.

* * *

I realize, William, that a man in your situation estimates letters mainly by their length, but I fear that my gout would not last me—it weakens apace, by the way, and at the present rate of writing will soon be gone—if I should relate every phase of Adair's one-man war against Spain and then France with the particularity which I have lavished upon that scene at Coosa. Besides, it's not only you that I have to think of, but my country. Parliament meets in a few days, and every sane man's vote will be needed if we are to hold the Tories within any reasonable bounds.

Yet the problem how and where to save time is not simple. As I read through the notes on Adair's narrative I am once more impressed—"oppressed" might be a better word—by the extreme intricacy of what he tried to tell us. This effect is not due to any fault of his but, partly, to my own ignorance of the places and persons concerned. The name of Oglethorpe I have known, of course, all my life, and indeed the General himself is almost my neighbour in London; but such cognomens as Oconostata, Willenawah, Outacite, and Attakullakulla are less familiar, and I am not much helped by the information that they mean, respectively, Great Warrior, Big Eagle, Man Killer, and Little Carpenter. I have a vague notion where Savannah is, and Charlestown; but the only map of North America I have here does not show the town of Coosa or even the Yazoo River where Adair now lives. All I feel sure about concerning those places is that they must be hundreds of miles from anywhere else, and that in travelling those miles you go not in a chariot or coach along a post-road but on foot, following a "trail" about twelve inches wide and often as many deep. This trail abhors a straight line. It brings you, at every few feet, either to a swamp or else to an old hurricane tree which you have to climb under or over or along. There are no inns or taverns beside it. At twilight, if you happen not to be pursued, you build a tiny fire by the trail and roast the squirrel you have shot for supper—there are no armadillos in North America—and then fall asleep listening to the cry of the panther and feeling thankful that it is not a scalp-yell. If you are pursued no directions of mine can help you because you won't find it out until too late.

Do you begin to see why it is difficult to simplify and shorten Adair's story? The scene of it is the vast American forest, composed of trees which the tallest elm in England could scarcely come to the knees of, and standing so thick that a squirrel might go from the Atlantic coast to the Mississippi without touching the ground. One does not really see the forest because there are so many trees; and just so in Adair's narrative, the outlines are blurred by sheer multiplicity. Every Indian settlement he mentions seems to have its separate language, religion, customs, and tribal antipathies. The alliances and diplomatic interrelationships of these settlements are intricate beyond anything we know in Europe, and they are still further complicated by a system of clans or "totems" of which I can make no sense whatever.

All things considered, then, I feel justified in driving a straight road, so to speak, across this wilderness of a story—a road which will certainly leave out a good many interesting things on either side but will at any rate be fit for the travel of a gouty clergyman and a hastening quill.

*   *   *

In a more and more anxious effort to assist the endangered people of Georgia, Adair appealed for help to the various tribes, but found that most of them, if they were to do anything in the "white man's war," preferred to fight on the side of the Spaniards. At last, however, he found a small group of Cherokees who lived so well hidden away in the Great Smoky Mountains that they had never been maltreated by the English traders and apparently did not even know their reputation. By good fortune, also, these people had long cherished a grudge against the Seminoles of Florida. After due debate, therefore, and acceptance of wampumpeague, dancing of war-dances, beating of war-drums, fasting and purification of the warriors, some thirty of them started off in a considerable frenzy of blood-thirst to avenge Jenkins' Ear upon the bodies of their Indian foes. Adair felt at the time that he ought to go with them; but instead—being anxious, I suppose, about Jeremy Tinker—he went directly to Georgia.

Arriving there in June, 1743, he found Oglethorpe well fortified and entrenched on a small coastal island called St. Simon's, I don't know why. Not far off on the mainland and at the mouth of the Altamaha lay the military settlement called Frederica, I fear I do know why and don't like it any better on that account. Carolina,

Georgia, Frederica—what will Posterity think of us for plastering such names upon the pristine wilderness? Why not call the whole country Hanover and be done with it? And think of the names we might have had if we had only listened to the Indians! Do you listen for a moment to "Altamaha" and see whether you don't begin to hear the murmur of numberless little waves. After that you can try "Susquehanna," and "Monongahela," two of the most delightful clusters of melodious vocables that I have ever heard.

Oglethorpe had with him some eight hundred men, three-fourths of whom belonged to a regiment recently raised and trained here at home. Most of the others were Scottish Highlanders from a settlement down the coast called Darien, each of them a good example of the tough northern breed that somehow convenes, like wasps at the smell of sugar, whenever a fight is toward. There was also a sprinkling of "rangers" dressed in green—an exceptionally ferocious lot of men who differed from the Scots in that they could not wait for a fight but went after it. Many of them had come from the debtors prisons of England, so that they feared nothing earthly or hellish. Among them, said Adair, the leading spirit was Jeremy Tinker.

"Now, James!"

"Now, Jeremy, you've done nothing but find fault with the way I'm telling this story. If I hear another interruption from you I shall set you down here in the Speaker's Chair and let you tell—"

"Oh, no!"

"—how you got an Indian arrow through your hand while leading those men in green against the Seminoles, how you climbed the mast of Oglethorpe's schooner to get above the battle-smoke at Cumberland Sound and directed the fire of the English guns, and then about the Battle of Bloody Marsh—"

"I say no, James. I won't—"

"—how you led those thirty rangers in green and all the wild McNabs round to the rear of the Spanish column and waited in ambush and shot them down and chopped them up so that not one in three ever saw Fort St. Augustine again. And don't you say 'won't' to me."

The threat was affectionately spoken, but it succeeded. Rather than take the chair Jeremy would do almost anything, even hear himself praised. Adair went on to show that the man England had cast aside as mere human debris because he owed some one a few shillings had been transformed by his years in Georgia—that is, by associating with others in a common enterprise, and by finding himself liked, respected, even needed. Jeremy had fought bravely in defence of a country he loved and in the service of a man he adored.

Just here, if I had the time for it, belongs the really astonishing story of how Oglethorpe with his eight hundred men and a schooner and two sloops fought off five thousand Spaniards in some fifty vessels of various sizes and sent them back to Florida far less arrogant than they had come. And yet it's not wholly a matter of time. That story does not lie on the straight road I am building.

This is rather a pity, for I judge that few events in the War of Jenkins' Ear were more creditable to England—in the degree that she can claim as hers a handful of Highlanders and jailbirds whom she had been glad to get rid of—than the defence of Georgia. Had it failed, the two Carolinas and Virginia might well have fallen to Spain. After hearing Adair's story of the Battle of Bloody Marsh Mr. Chute declared that it should be called the Thermopylae of America. —And why, then, have we heard nearly nothing about the affair on our side of the water? I will answer that if you will explain why we know and care scarcely more about the Rebellion of Forty-five, which came almost to our doors. Is it because we are such a courageous people that no danger moves us, or because we are too dull to bring home to ourselves anything that does not pinch our proper bellies and purses?

Life was not dull for Adair as he scrambled through thickets and swamps and crammed powder and shot into three-pounders, helping Jeremy Tinker defeat this new Spanish Armada. The White-stick seems to have taken on, for the nonce, a tinge of red. Yet these people that he and Jeremy were killing, he told Oglethorpe, were after all only Spaniards. What if the French should come in now, beginning the last phase of their long struggle for the continent, throwing the weight of the western tribes against Georgia? That would mean fighting on two fronts, with hundreds of miles between them. He felt that he should be in the Great Smoky Mountains, using what influence he had there to hold the Cherokees neutral if not to win their help.

With Oglethorpe's approval he leaves the seaboard settlements and is at once engulfed by the ancient, mysterious, whispering forest. All society, civilization, the total history of mankind, drops away, and he becomes one man, alone. Try to imagine it, William, for this is a sort of experience that you and I know simply nothing about. English versifiers have indited a good many foolish odes to Solitude in the last fifty years—didn't Pope compose something of the sort as a boy? —but this is the thing itself. You will not forget that the man stepping westward at fifty miles a day is a scholar, well stored with Latin, Greek, Hebrew, French, Spanish, Gaelic, and a startling theory about the Ten Lost Tribes of Israel. His life depends, however—and who shall say how many other lives as well?—upon what he has acquired of the different but really extensive erudition of wild men.

More and more as he goes on, and especially at night by his little fire, he thinks about the war-party of Cherokees that set off some weeks ago against the Seminoles. Where are they now, those virtuous young men who so minutely observed every rule of preparation for combat: beating the war-drum, dancing the war-dance, tearing old scalps with their teeth, drenching themselves with the black drink, fasting for three days and nights, and sitting down only when the sun did? He imagines them glimmering along the war-path, never snapping a twig or dislodging a pebble, making no more sound than the fall of a withered leaf. At nightfall each one takes his only meal of the day, a handful of parched corn doled out to him by a special officer whose duty it is to see that the warriors do not overeat. Then he drinks from the brook and sleeps for a few hours with his back against a tree. There is something definitely ascetic, all but saintly, in the devotion of these men to the task of slaughter. Like the holy hermits of the Gothic Ages, or Elijah alone in the mountains, they feel that by starving their bodies they bring down strength from on high.

We had an interesting discussion of that likeness between the saint and the warrior which unfortunately does not lie on our road. I can only tell you that Blandison, in the course of it, pointed out how the knights of the Gothic Ages—Sir Galahad, for example—often combined the two characters, and how they too fasted and kept vigil before going into battle. Adair said that Indian warriors are always remarkably lean. He expected his friends in the forest to be amused almost to the point of unmanly laughter when he told them that the present Captain General of England's army—the Duke of Cumberland, of course—is one of the most corpulent men in the kingdom.

And now let me give you in Adair's own words his mental picture of the battle which might already have taken place down there on the Cape of Florida. "As they approach the Seminole hunting-grounds," says he, "the Cherokees redouble their caution, dispersing to the farthest distances from which they can hear one another's signals. When they must pass a broad grassy plain they proceed in three rows, each man lifting his feet high so as not to beat down the herbage and each row making only one man's track. The scouts on ahead have thrown over their backs the skins of buffaloes and bears, perhaps have fastened to their hands and feet the paws and hooves of those animals, and so for miles together they go on all fours, winding here and there as the beasts do.

"Thus in every possible manner they seek to take their enemy by surprise; but, if at last they are discovered before they can charge, then from both sides there go up boastings of all the barbarities committed by either party upon the other in years gone by. Meanwhile the Cherokees are stripping themselves for battle. If they have the time they renew the paint on their faces and breasts, for an Indian brave longs above all to be gorgeous in death. Each has taken cover behind a tree or in a cavity of the ground. In imitation of the Hebrew trumpets, the leaders on both sides blow their whistles of willow, and the war-cry, the scalp-yell resounds. Ten thousand wild-fowl are instantly on the wing. A herd of deer rushes by. Chewed bullets are flying, bowstrings twanging, and arrows singing their death-song. A red-handled tomahawk twirls end over end through the air. The blade sinks deep into a shaven skull. A Seminole leaps from behind a tree with his scalping-knife drawn, but before he can reach the stricken man he himself is transfixed by an arrow."

Have you doffed your clerical robes, William, and adorned yourself with pitch and vermilion? Are you somewhat more aware for the moment of your scalp than of your great toe? There are swamps all about you, I believe, and in the swamps are many alligators, so that every Seminole you bring down must be scalped at once or there will be nothing to show for your pains. Also I understand that these alligators are no less fond of white men than of red, and have no prejudice against clergymen.

*   *   *

Thus hoped, or rather dreamed, Adair on his way to the Cherokee village from whence his band of warriors had set forth. If the attack on the Seminoles had prospered, then others might follow, and perhaps the Creeks and Choctaws might be persuaded to share in the harvest of scalps. Upon reaching the village, however, he was greeted with nothing but evil looks. He learned that the war-party had never reached within striking distance of the Seminoles. While passing through one of the English colonies they had been attacked without provocation, some twenty of them had been butchered, and their scalps had been taken. Blood now cried for blood. Either Adair must see to it that twenty fresh scalps were quickly forthcoming, to be delivered to the injured families, or else the young Cherokee Red-sticks would proceed to collect far more than that number of trophies from the English colonists.

Here was a problem for Oglethorpe; but Adair found upon returning to Savannah that the General had sailed for England, taking Jeremy Tinker with him, to gather recruits against the expected French invasion. He sought help in several places, and finally struck a bargain with Governor James Glen of South Carolina whereby that dignitary was to request the proper authorities in London to ship him a kegful of scalps taken from persons recently hanged at Tyburn. In return for this favour Adair agreed to remain for some time in Charlestown and give Governor Glen the full benefit of his experience in trading with the Indians.

I shall not go into all the charges made by Adair against this Royal Governor, a chubby little man much given to rubbing his smooth white hands together and discussing the vast profits to be made in the exchange of glass beads for peltries. In their sum these charges amounted to the accusation that Glen was far less interested in serving his country than in lining his own pockets. At any rate, he seems to have been a sufficiently coarse and hardened character, well fitted for success in mercantile transactions. When Adair found out that he had paid the current prices for enemy scalps to the settlers who had murdered and mutilated the Cherokee warriors, Governor Glen's only comment was that he had been liberally remunerated out of the Royal Treasury and had, in fact, made a neat profit in that piece of business. Months later, when it became clear that the Cherokee Red-sticks would soon begin their own scalp-collecting, the Governor admitted that the kegful of Tyburn scalps he had sent for would probably never arrive. "I wrote for them," said he, "to Daniel Dickens of Portsmouth. You know the man. He has a sharp eye for his own interests. A wigmaker can always use hair."

A few days after this, Adair happened to see several large parcels of peltries delivered at the Governor's mansion at a time when his host was detained in council. He was somewhat surprised at this, not having heard that Glen was employing any traders for himself. He admired the pelts, and turned one of them over to see what trader's mark it bore. What he saw, burned into the soft leather, was the mark of the fleur-de-lys and the name of a French trader who operated, he knew, in the region of New Orleans, chiefly with the great western tribe of Choctaws. The meaning of this was unmistakable. The Royal Governor of the British Colony of South Carolina was being paid by French traders for such services as turning the Cherokees against the English and also, it might be, for holding an English trader in semi-captivity. —On that same day, although the winter was well advanced, Adair walked out of Charlestown on the way to Western Waters.

This, I judge, is the boldest and most dangerous journey that Adair has ever made. The distance he had to go was well over a thousand miles, most of it on trails he had never travelled before. The weather, he told us, was worse than Scotland's, so that he had rain all the way except when it was snowing. This made less difference because he was most of the time either swimming or wading. A main difficulty was in keeping his powder dry, and another in finding anything to eat. For the first hundred miles he was pursued by two Cherokees sent after him—or so he believed—by Governor Glen, and toward the end of his journey a party of hostile Choctaws tried to turn him back. In short, it was a thoroughly delightful excursion, of which he seems to have enjoyed every minute—especially that one in which, standing beside some nameless western stream, he drank two swallows of rum out of his leathern bottle to the health of his Choctaw pursuers on the farther bank, and then, after thumbing his nose at them, plunged into the thicket. The gesture of "cocking the snook" seems to be understood even by savages, for the yells of the outraged Choctaws were terrific.

On this journey, run, swim, wade, flight, or whatever it should be called, Adair had to go directly through the country of the Cherokees, who by this time had lost any fondness for him they may once have felt. Yet it was among these people, so grievously wronged by Daniel Dickens' retention of that kegful of Tyburn scalps, that he was accorded the only welcome he found on his long way. In the cabin of the Cherokee warrior and sage called Attakullakulla, or the Little Carpenter, he sat by a fire, ate bear-meat, drank ginseng tea, and slept for one night in a bed. Also he had much interesting discourse with this famous old man who could not only talk English but read it, and had spent some months in England long ago and even dined with the King. Attakullakulla brought forth for his guest's inspection a bundle of letters from Governor Glen which he called "an heap of black broad papers which ought to be burned in last year's fire." Opening the first, he observed that it contained a small bit of truth, probably due to the Governor's being perplexed with a press of business when he wrote it, "but count," said he, handing over another, "the lying black marks of this one!" Adair read them all, and found unquestionable evidence that Governor Glen had long been doing his best to drive the Cherokees away from the English and into the arms of the French. He was clearly the sort of Englishman who could not love his native land so well if he did not love money more. Attakullakulla's contempt for such treachery was equalled only by his pride at the thought that this "little white liar" had tried so hard to deceive him.

A day's journey farther on, but still in the hunting-grounds of the Cherokees, Adair reached the cabin of another friend, a German by the name of Christian Priber, with whom he had a different kind of talk. This man was thought by the English to be working in the French interest, and the French in turn were convinced that he was in the pay of England; but in fact he had the almost incredible notion that both England and France were intruders who should be driven out of a country belonging to the Indians alone. Both parties had tried several times to arrest him; but such was the man's popularity among the Cherokees that they might as well have attempted, Adair said, "to capture the Pope in the Vatican." What Priber wanted was to draw the tribes together in a Kingdom of Paradise in which there would be no wars, no private property, no trade, no firewater, no slaves. Strangest of all, he had made it clear that he would not be king of that Paradise, whose builder and maker would be God. —You will not be surprised to learn, William, that some years after Adair's visit this wild enthusiast was taken prisoner by English traders—he was visiting in the Creek country at the time—and safely lodged in prison at Frederica. He died there, I believe, and his poisonous manuscripts— among them a dictionary of the Cherokee language—were burned.

Now there is an example of how difficult it is to draw what I have called a "straight road" through this story, avoiding everything in which you might take an interest. From now on I must do better. I leave it to your imagination how James Adair, having reached the country known as Western Waters, established a trading-post.

there among the fierce Chickasaws of the upper Yazoo, married the daughter of a chieftain, and began to wage war against France by means of his English trade-goods and such Indian allies as he could gather; how he drew the northern half of the Choctaw nation over to England's side and then struck at the French dominion of the lower Mississippi with a flotilla of fifty canoes of birch-bark light as an eggshell propelled by paddles made from oaks struck by lightning for reasons I cannot pause to tell you; how his Indians burned at daybreak a French trader's town within sight of New Orleans and his friend Chief Red Shoes, sixty years old, saw a trader escaping from the town on a good horse and started after him on foot and ran the horse to death in twenty hours and brought back the trader's scalp. While you are about it you may as well throw in an attempted assassination of Adair by two French ruffians which was foiled by the skill of his Chickasaw wife in wielding an axe. By doing these things for yourself you will enable me to finish this tale before Louis comes in with the candles.

*   *   *

The name of Robert Dinwiddie, Lieutenant-Governor of Virginia, must have been familiar to you for some time, at any rate if you have been as deeply interested as I have for the last year or more in the situation of our American colonies. He seems to be about the only man we have over there who realizes that the French mean to drive us off the continent if they can, and for a long time he has been trying to get the other colonies to cooperate with Virginia in defence of the western frontier. I believe he has had most success with Governor Shirley of Massachusetts, and decidedly least with Governor Glen of South Carolina. Here at home it has long been known that Glen and Dinwiddie were constantly at odds, but until I heard Adair's story I had never guessed the reasons. I should now say that Dinwiddie despises Glen as an honest man does a liar and a thief, and that Glen hates Dinwiddie out of fear. That would be natural enough, considering that Dinwiddie won his spurs by exposing the corruption in the West Indian Customs Service. From such a man the rather crude dishonesty of the Governor of South Carolina could not long lie hidden.

Pray excuse these remarks somewhat in the manner of a Member of Parliament. Their purpose is to explain how it happened that Adair, last April, made the journey from Western Waters to Virginia, and there busied himself under the direction of the Lieutenant-Governor in preparation for the approaching campaign of General Braddock. Dinwiddie had invited him to come because he was familiar with wilderness fighting, and because it was thought that he could gather Indian recruits, but perhaps mainly on account of his former association with Governor Glen.

General Edward Braddock arrived at Hampton Roads, in Virginia, toward the end of last February. Perhaps you are unaware that he crossed the ocean in Anson's old *Centurion* under command of that same Augustus Keppel whom you have already had a glimpse of in his boyhood. There were at least two other ships under Keppel's command, and in them were two regiments of the line recently quartered in Ireland. My cousin Conway was well acquainted with the officers of those regiments, the Forty-fourth and the Forty-eighth, and all of them, he told us with some emphasis, were excellent soldiers. Adair replied that even if he had ever felt any doubt of that, he would not at present express it, seeing that most of those officers were now dead. By the same standards Edward Braddock, he said, had also been an excellent soldier, at least in the expert opinion of the Duke of Cumberland. He had for years enjoyed close association with the corpulent Duke, and had shaped his own notions of soldiership upon that hero's conduct at Dettingen, Fontenoy, Culloden, and the butcheries in the Highlands. The insolence of Braddock's manners, Adair said, and his stubborn refusal even to hear the advice of people who disagreed with him, bore the marks of a German origin.

At this point there was an exchange of disagreements between my cousin and Adair into which I simply will not be deflected. It lies off the line of the story, and Henry Conway, as usual, did not shine. Neither will I pause, as Adair did, to illustrate Braddock's cold contempt for everything American: the colonial legislatures and governors, the provincial troops and their commanders, the weather of the country and the wines and the women, but, most of all, the hopelessly ignorant notions they had over there about how to fight a campaign.

This attitude was a little hard to maintain when Braddock's Quartermaster General, Sir John St. Clair, disgracefully failed in his task of providing stores and transportation for the army, and had to be saved from disaster by a certain Benjamin Franklin of Philadelphia with whose proverbs, vulgar but frequently apposite, my Louis is strangely familiar. Braddock got round that by asserting that Franklin was the only man of sense in America—in which case it would be interesting to know what Franklin thought of Braddock.

There was also a Colonel Washington, not much over twenty years of age, in whose favour the General made another exception. This youth, of whom I have spoken or written in the past with less than due respect, resigned from the military service of Virginia last year upon learning that colonial officers of all ranks would thenceforth be juniors to officers of even the lowest ranks who bore the King's commission. Braddock did a sensible thing when he invited the young Virginian to serve on his staff with the rank of Colonel. Had he also paid serious attention to what Washington told him about wilderness warfare . . . But Jenkins' Ear had other plans.

James Adair, meanwhile, was encountering many difficulties in his effort to bring in the Cherokees. The slaughter of the war-party he had recruited among them some time before was by no means forgotten. There were many indications, hard to prove and yet unmistakable, that Governor Glen had used the intervening time to drive the Cherokee nation still farther toward alliance with the French. It could not be proved against him, though Adair had no doubt of it, that he brought about the brutal massacre of a group of warriors who were actually on their way to join Braddock's march.

Of that march itself, and of the inevitable disaster at its farther end, what can I tell you that you do not already know? The news of it reached England only two months since, and is still painfully remembered by every thoughtful British subject. Yet James Adair told us a number of significant things—he went the whole way with Braddock and saw something of the battle itself—which I, at least, had not previously heard. My impression had been, for example, that there were many Indians on our side, but Adair affirmed that Governor Glen's machinations had left us with no more than fifty, most of whom soon ran away. Never had I heard—yet it is unquestionably so—that Braddock plunged into that primeval wilderness of swamp and forest encumbered with all the howitzers, twelve-pounders, coehorns, horses, and artillery-wagons that might reasonably have been taken by a general making ready for engagement on an open plain. His conviction was, one sees, that the military methods of Frederick the Great were applicable under all circumstances. He stopped to bridge every brook and to lift every rock out of the road his pioneers were making half a mile ahead of him. What wonder that he moved forward less than three miles a day and took a month in going the hundred miles or so from the Potomac to the Monongahela? I suppose it might be said his men were beaten before they got there.

That reminds me of a thing which probably no one but Adair would ever have mentioned, or perhaps even thought of. He said that Braddock's army—not the Provincials so much as the two regiments brought across the sea—were daunted, even terrified, by the mere silence of the forest about them, by the enormous height of the trees, and the unbroken day-long shadow through which they moved. He saw them startle at the waving of a frond of fern in no breath of air; and at night they huddled together at the cry of a panther or even the song of a bird which he called the Whip-Poor-Will. And it was not only that these sounds and sights were strange to them. They had a conviction, increasing from day to day, that they were intruding upon the domain of some nameless Power which resented and might not long endure their presence. I knew, or thought I did, what he meant; for something of the sort I myself felt long ago, when Thomas Gray and I were travelling through the high Alps. I think Byron also knew, and had a vision, while Adair was speaking, of Mount Misery on Wager Island.

Yet, however the men might feel, they were held under strict control. General Braddock relaxed not one point of military discipline. In the fierce heats of the Virginian June and July he required his soldiers to wear their heavy woollen coats tightly buttoned about them as though they were on parade. He took them across the Monongahela to martial music, and brought them up toward Fort Du Quesne with all the pomp and pride he could muster. "No doubt," said Adair, "they made a deep impression upon the Ojibways and Ottawas and Hurons and Delawares who were watching them on either side."

Adair made us see that crossing of the river, six hundred feet wide but shallow, with glitter on the musket-barrels and splashing of horses and scarlet of King's coats vivid in the sunlight of early afternoon. We saw the lurch of the white-topped wagons, and how the horses strained to drag the twelve-pounders up the farther bank. Then on and up they go in something like battle order, for the fort is close at hand, with the guides and engineers and light horsemen leading the way. The road is still only twelve feet wide, a mere tunnel through the leaves, so that the ravines on either side of it are unseen, unsuspected. The horses are stumbling over stones, and the men cursing at

the heat and flies, when suddenly one of the engineers catches sight of
a group of Indians just ahead and a Frenchman, evidently their
leader, waving his hat as a signal. He is wearing a fringed hunting-
shirt and has a silver gorget at his breast. He looks to be a young man.
But now, in response to his signal, there comes from each side of the
road a burst of musket-fire. Three engineers are down, and a horse
breaks away at a run. The fire is answered by the light horsemen, and
the young man in the hunting-shirt falls dead. At once his place is
taken by another Frenchman, and the fire from both sides increases.
No enemy is visible through the leaves on either side, but the grenadiers return the fire at random, falling back meanwhile upon the main
body. Savage yells and screams are heard above the musket-fire. The
grenadiers are huddling in a compact mass. General Braddock is beating the Provincials with the flat of his sword when they try to find
shelter behind trees. Five horses are shot under him, and he is riding
a sixth when he is struck in the breast by a bullet. Washington rides
up and down unhurt, although two horses are killed under him. The
grenadiers are firing into the air. Half the twelve hundred men who
waded the river ten minutes ago are now dead. Of the officers hardly
one in four is alive. Still the lead sleets in from both sides, and every
bush, every tree, seems on fire; but no foe is seen. All at once the
horror passes beyond what men can endure. Panic fear springs upon
them and drives them headlong away through the thickets and down
to the river and across it. Their dead and their wounded, their coehorns and howitzers and tall mitred hats and burnished Tower muskets
are all that remain in the tunnel of leaves.

*   *   *

Louis has not yet come in, and I am writing by the fag-end of God's
candle with straining eyes and a weary hand. No doubt the scrawl I
am making will indicate that much. People say that my hand-writing
would be legible enough if only I would leave a little more space
between words. I try to, but it shrinks from year to year. When I'm
seventy my letters will make no sense at all; but of course they never
have made much, and perhaps the gradual disappearance of meaning
will not be discerned.

There's enough twilight left in which to bring Adair's story to a
close. Shortly after the rout of Braddock had confirmed his worst

fears he took ship at Savannah, bringing Jeremy Tinker with him, and came home. He did this partly in the hope of suggesting a few adjustments of German military tactics to the conditions of wilderness fighting, but his recent audience with the Duke of Cumberland has convinced him that France will soon drive us out of America. Before that happens, however, there is strong likelihood—if he follows the directions and presents the letters I have given him—that South Carolina will have a new Governor.

Adair and I had a long talk on that Thursday evening, toward the end of which Jeremy Tinker joined us. In two minutes' time I made and Jeremy accepted the proposal that he should stay on here at Strawberry Hill and make himself useful in any ways his varied talents might suggest. You will soon learn with what vigour and promptitude he went to work. After the lapse of two weeks and a little more this arrangement seems to be highly satisfactory to us all— perhaps especially to Ponto.

But now it is almost dark, and I can write no longer. What in the world has become of that Louis?

FRIDAY

On Friday it rained, with a vigour and persistence evidently meant to atone for five days of uninterrupted sunshine. The windows streamed; every gutter gushed; pools formed on the terrace, married, and begot and gave birth to small Mississippis; my Chinese ponds overflowed, and my favourite goldfish—Confucius, no less— was washed down into the Thames and is now either changing into an eel or else is on the way back to the Celestial Kingdom.

We spent most of the morning in the blue breakfast room, idly watching the downpour. There was nothing else to do. Even our eavesdropping, Blandison pointed out, was being done for us. The pun was not much, but it showed what progress had been made toward a mutual confidence and understanding. Looking back over our days together, we felt, or I did, that they must have been as many months. Looking forward . . . But we tried not to do that, for tomorrow would be our last day.

As you probably realize, the question about Blandison's identity had by this time faded almost out of mind. And the reason was that in some sense we had found the answer: he was himself, our friend, and one of us. No doubt we felt this with different degrees of warmth and certainty, Kitty most of all and my cousin least; yet it was our consensus. Moreover, I am glad to be sure that Blandison not only knew this but was happy in the knowledge. There had not been much in his life, I think, of the kind of companionship we gave him in the little time we had. That he wanted it, needed it, and valued it at something like its inestimable worth, there can be no doubt; but, for whatever reason, it had not come his way.

We talked at random, with friendly silences between one topic and another. What was that thing, Blandison wanted to know, that Kitty was sewing. With a gasp at such ignorance she told him that she was knitting, and that the "thing" was one of a pair of bed-stockings meant for a friend of hers who suffered with cold feet at night. Then we rambled on about Jeremy Tinker and how glad we were that he was going to stay with us, Kitty suggesting that the destroyer of the Georgian Spanish Armada might help to defend me from my head-gardener, who is a Scotchman. We discussed the prospective reunion of the Morris family, and were confident that Master Chester would grow rich on his traffic in the Patagonian bark that is good for gout. George came in about then and remarked that cinchona bark is no doubt extremely profitable but you have to work for it, whereas gold-mines . . . He yawned.

At length Blandison, turning to me, asked how I was progressing with my Memoir, and whether I thought I should have enough material. I stared, having temporarily forgotten the vague plan which had brought the whole week upon us, but then: "The Memoir, I mean," said he, "of the War of Jenkins' Ear."

I sighed at the mere thought of such toil, and Kitty let her knitting fall to her lap. She sat gazing out at the rain, her hands hanging slack from the arms of her chair, and the rest of us gazed at her. What she wore that morning I forget, except that it was blue, hoopless, un-furbeloved, and perfect for playing the part of Kitty Clive, her best role.

"Oh, no!" said she, looking round at us and surprising in five pairs of eyes the affectionate pride she knew was there. "What does Horry know or care about wars? Besides, his Memoirs are dreadfully dull. They simply won't let themselves be read. Reason is, in hist'ry you have to stick to the subject and keep yourself out, which of course he can't. —Well then, if there must be a Memoir, let General Conway do it."

This was a sound suggestion, and I said so. People aren't aware of it, but my cousin writes well—for a soldier. He once wrote a poem, not nearly so bad as you might expect. —At the time, to be sure, he was in love.

"But this week," Kitty went on, "has been more interesting than a thousand wars. I mean it's been more human, deep, kind, with more laughing in it, not to mention a few tears. If it's risk and danger you want, loss and ruin perhaps, and certainly something about love, why, then . . ."

She left the sentence hanging. It was one of those incompletions that say more than a rounded paragraph.

"Only think how it was last Sunday," said she, holding her palms upward for a moment and looking from face to face. "That afternoon one of us was using all his astonishing boldness and wit to storm this castle so as to use it for purposes we could only guess. Meanwhile the rest of us were saying: 'Well, we can't keep him out. This may cost us our heads, but we must risk them.' —That was five days ago. gentlemen, and now here we sit."

"With our heads still on," George added. "Of course, though, the week isn't yet over."

"No; and we're glad there's more to come. Parson Blandison tells a story this afternoon—tells it much better, we hope, than he did that one about the *Centurion*—and then for tomorrow he has, no doubt, some interesting plan. Still, even these five days—wouldn't it be selfish of us to keep them all to ourselves? Only think of nobody else ever hearing about them, so that when we are gone they might as well never have happened! —Oh, that would be wicked!"

I don't understand how that woman manages to express so many of my thoughts and feelings half a second before I can find the words for them.

"But, Kitty," Mr. Chute objected, "you forget that we mustn't tell any one. We can't."

"Why not? What prevents our writing it in a letter to somebody we can trust and asking him—for of course it couldn't be her—to see that it's kept secret somehow, and sent on for say two hundred years? Horry's a dab at letters. He'd have Mr. Chute's notes to help him, and Louis, and all of us that can stay on for a few days. Parliament doesn't meet for three weeks, and that's all the time he'll need. In a letter, you see, he won't have to do any thinking, but can just be miscellaneous and incompetent and natural. He can even bring himself into it all the way through, and that will make it one of the most delightful letters in the world."

"At any rate," said I, beginning to like the idea but not wanting to say so, "it would have to be one of the longest."

"No, no; it mustn't be long, but a number of short ones strung together. You can write it for those wonderful unborn people you prefer so much to us. That's what you always do, anyway. You address your letters to Horace Mann, George Montagu, Richard Bentley, and so on, but of course they know what you mean."

It's a delicate matter, William, to object and hesitate just long enough when a flattering proposal is made which you mean to accept. Not to do it at all is a breach of etiquette, but when overdone there is the danger that people will lose interest, or even take you seriously. However, I let Mr. Chute persuade me when he pointed out that, in addition to his notes, I could use Richard Walter's *Voyage of the Centurion,* already in the house, and could send for the printed *Journal* of Bulkeley and Cummins, perhaps even for the book by Midshipman Alexander Campbell. —He evidently had in mind something much more scholarly than the letter you now have in hand. In any case, I have found that Campbell's narrative was suppressed, probably by the Admiralty Office, soon after its publication, and that the Bulkeley and Cummins is out of print. Richard Walter's account I have scarcely opened since I sat down to write.

Thus we came to the question about the immediate recipient of our letter, the man we could trust in the present and for the future. We agreed that he must be a man of sterling character, great erudition, discriminating taste, vivid imagination, and endowed with the power of recognizing a literary masterpiece when he sees one even though it be written by a contemporary and—this is harder still—a close friend. We were seeking, in short, a man who could read, and I pointed out that no one can really do that unless he has at least tried to write. Now writers, I said, though they can read, seldom do so—and I gave the whole baker's dozen of reasons.

The field of choice was narrowing. Some one mentioned Thomas Gray, and much was said in his favour. You are well aware how I have always admired Gray, praised him, quoted him, helped to publish him, but—well, I finally objected that he would spend far more than the allotted two centuries in correcting my quotations and emending my grammar. I also felt that if I was to have only one reader in my time then it ought to be a man for whom my letter might do some kind of good, if not by way of instruction then at least in that of distraction.

Thus the problem was reduced, as Mr. Chute would say, to its simplest elements: what sterling, learned, and so forth friend of mine, not distracted already, most needed to be so? Just then, as I asked that question, I felt a sudden fiery stab of pain in my great toe—a pain the like of which I had not supposed could exist—and upon that inspiration I all but shouted: "The Reverend William Cole!"

Anything I might say about the rest of that session would be anti-climactic. Imagine for yourself how I was congratulated upon the felicity—or, as I should prefer to say, the serendipity—of my choice.

*   *   *

We hear the hard pelting of raindrops against the panes as we wait in the Library now for Blandison to begin. I doubt whether he, at the window, can see twenty feet through the downpour. The members of the Club have come in a covered vehicle, but have been considerably dampened in their short run from the gate. Now they sit close to the fire, steaming. John Chester is tending the fire in place of Louis, on the ground that he knows more about such things than any one "not brung up in Connecticut." Then too, he points out, this will set Louis free to fetch from the beer-cellar that pin of Abingdon ale which he understands the Capting delivered today at my landing. "Tote it right in hyar," says he, "iffen 'tain't too heavy for you an' Dick Beston. Iffen 'tis, I'll do it myself. Then the Parson can tell a tale bad as he done at Hal Pudsey's, but the arternoon won't be wasted."

Louis' eyebrows are all but lost in his hair as his gaze shifts, astonished, from Chester to me. Thus faced with the dilemma, which of these two young men is to be affronted, I look at Kitty. She says quietly, firmly:

"Ask Mrs. Margaret to mull us a large pitcher of ale. Bring it in piping-hot. Then no one will catch cold while we listen, without saying a word, to Parson Blandison's wonderful story."

"The story begins," says the voice at the window, "in the late afternoon of July the twenty-second, ten years and three months ago. There is fog and mist on the sea, slowly changing to rain, as the little *Du Tellier* comes groping up through the Outer Hebrides with no chart, no pilot, and not one man aboard who has ever made this voyage. Now and then, in brief gleams of sunlight, the young man at the bow catches a glimpse of many scattered isles, and of dark rocks empurpled with heather-bloom and golden with lady's bedstraw. There is no sign of human habitation, nothing to show that these islands exist outside his own dream. Then the fog and the mist and the rain return, and the brig fumbles on like a ghost that is strange to the ways of death."

Blandison is talking as though to himself. He seems not to know, or at least to care, that the members of the Club have their backs toward him. His voice is low, yet every word comes clearly to our ears above the sound of the raindrops.

"The young man," he says, "is wearing the garb of a Church of England clergyman. His seven companions address him as 'Douglas.' They are mostly old men, and all are Jacobite exiles embittered by many years of poverty-stricken life in foreign lands. They have no faith in one another, and little hope that 'the Reverend Douglas,' not yet twenty-five, can bring them back their own. Youth, to them, is a thing forgotten. After thirty years of hoping they have come to prefer despair. If asked why they have joined this hare-brained expedition they might reply that even despair may be disappointed. During the seventeen days and nights since the *Du Tellier* set sail from France they have watched the young man with suspicion, expecting him to break out in some boyish audacity that will bring them all to ruin."

Now John Chester has turned halfway round and is facing toward Blandison. "But look hyar," says he, "iffen that's the Young Pretender ye're talkin' 'bout, why don't ye tell how his big ship *Elizabeth*, full o' muskets an' cannon an' powder, was stopped by the *Lion*, Cap'n Piercy Brett, late Leftenant o' the *Centurion*, an' them two fought a draw an' turned back an' left the lad to go on without no guns nor powder nor money nor food nor men nor—"

Chester's breath gives out there, or else he realizes that he is making no progress. After a brief interval Blandison continues: "We are obliged to Master Chester for reminding us of the naval aspect of this expedition. Surely, though, the present company has heard enough for one week about ships and seafaring. The young man there at the prow, the Prince, the Chevalier, sometimes called the Young Pretender, is not unduly concerned with such details. From the start he has understood that success or failure will depend not upon the weapons or other supplies he may bring from Europe but solely upon the loyal help of his subjects in his kingdom. Above all he longs to set foot for the first time in his life upon British soil and to meet his unknown friends and companions.

"Toward sunset the fog lifts for a moment, and he sees on ahead, half a mile away, a pile of gray rocks with a silvery strand below them and a blood-coloured ledge reaching into the breakers. Soon the longboat is launched, and the waves bear it in toward the desolate strand. His first step into his kingdom is upon that stain as of blood that will never wear out.

"He is not expected. There is no one to welcome him. Before nightfall, however, he and the seven old men are sitting on the floor of a hut roofed with thatch, beside a fire of peat built in the centre of the only room. The smoke is supposed to escape through a hole in the roof. There is not a grain of meal or an inch of bread in the hut. An hour goes by, and their host comes in with a mess of flounders. He lays the fish on the bare embers. He is a short, hairy, muscular man, like a bear, this Angus Macdonald. His bright eyes look merrily out from between the hedge of his brows and the forest of his beard. He is wearing only a tattered kilt, which may once have shown the colours of his tartan. Even in this rocky place his feet are unshod, for where there is no grass there can be no cattle—and, without cattle, no leather, no shoes.

"The Prince, accustomed all his life to the open air, is nearly blinded and choked by the smoke and the fumes of the roasting flounders. Again and again he is obliged to run out at the door for a breath of air and to wipe his streaming eyes. 'What ails that fellow,' Angus asks the Duke of Atholl, 'that he will neither sit quiet within nor stop outside the hut?'

"The flounders at last are sufficiently blackened and burnt, and the hungry men fall to eating with their fingers. While they pick the bones the night comes down and the rain patters more loudly on the thatch overhead. It streams down the rough walls of stone and gathers in pools on the earthen floor. Soon the Prince is putting his old tutor, Sir Thomas Sheridan, to bed. He himself lies down on a heap of straw near the open door, but all night is unable to sleep.

"He has come thus far from the land of his birth toward the place where he should have been born. All his life he has been in some sense on the way. Since early boyhood he has been laying vague plans for this adventure, hardening his muscles, training himself to endure long marches in hard weather with little sleep and food, gaining skill as a horseman and swordsman and marksman, studying old battles, talking with old soldiers, and seeing a little of actual war. Much of this has been merely boyish, but the sense of obligation has played its part. Deep affection for his mother, and the wish that she might wear a crown like her ancestors, one of whom saved Europe from the Turk—

that, no doubt, was the beginning. Always, too, there had been the example of his patient, laborious father—a man not gifted in action but faithful to the limit of his powers in what was to him a holy task.

"Yes, that belief in a divine ordination—so the young man says to himself as he rises and lays another lump of peat on the smoulder—must never be lost out of mind in the days and weeks ahead. Though he cannot fully believe it himself, he must act in the faith of his father, of his grandfather, and of all the Stuarts before them, that kings are named and supported by Him who said, 'Let there be light!' He must act as though in obedience to an almighty bidding which easily overpowers, as dawn the darkness, every notion or whim or selfish contrivance of fallible men.

"How has it come about, he wonders, listening to the beat of the rain and the sea's hoarse calling, that the faith which has always been so clear to his father's mind is now dim in his own? Perhaps it is that the father has been reared in the doctrines of one church only, but the son in those of two. Yet their love of England has drawn and held them together. He recalls how the man and the boy, long ago, drew a rude map of England, not copied from books but out of their heads, setting down all the English names they could think of in the places they thought they should be. He remembers how they questioned the English visitors at the Muti Palace in Rome—a steady stream of Jacobites, with a few supercilious yet inquisitive Whigs—about this and that aspect of life in the home country. Correspondence had also helped, and the services of a few expert though ill-paid spies. By such means they had gathered a considerable knowledge of England, much of it inaccurate but all of it warmed by love.

"Of Scotland the young man knows far less. Even the language of these islands and of the wild hills to eastward is stranger to him than Greek. It is a fearful impediment that he will be unable to speak to his own people, when he first meets them, in words they can understand. Besides that, he will come among them as a stranger, penniless, friendless, unarmed, unsupported, with little but a dream to offer. Every cautious man he knows, even his father at first, has pointed out the perils that will confront him. They have been right, those timid old men, in terms of what they understand. Lying there on his bundle of straw while the window changes from black to gray the young man admits that his chance of success is as one in a thousand. But that one chance—what is it? His heart fills with joy as he reaffirms the faith he lives by. He believes that loyalty is still a living and potent thing, and that the spirit of glory has not died out of the world.

"He leaps to his feet and rouses his companions. He has come thus far. He is on the way."

*　　*　　*

Here there was a pause. Blandison stepped to a table and stood there sipping a glass of wine. Louis came in with two large pitchers of mulled ale. The members of the Club moved their chairs so as to face the speaker. We were all feeling that this tale promised to be better than the one we had heard at Twickenham Ait. That picture of the exiled father and son bending over their homemade map had been effective. There was also the novelty of seeing these things, however Blandison had learned them, as though with the eyes of Charles Edward himself. Though we all knew a little about the main events of the Forty-five, none of us had ever quite realized that the Young Pretender had been, in the good sense, so really young as the story was making him out. —On the other hand, I wished that Blandison would talk to us rather than to himself. I felt, too, that ten minutes or so of the historical present would be, for a while, enough.

"Sky and sea were swept on that first morning," he resumed, "by a great wind bounding out of the west. The cliffs of Borra loomed clear to the southward. On the north we had Boisdale, South Uist, Benbecula. Eastward we looked to Skye and Eigg and Rum, each a jewel set in azure. The air was filled with the wings and cries of numberless waterfowl. It was a day that brought far places near and made the impossible seem easy of achievement. When an old man urged the Prince to go back home he was given at once the right answer: 'But, sir, I have *come* home!'

"That was true, but his welcome was not heartening. Old chieftains of the western clans came to stare at him on the deck of the *Du Tellier* when she reached the mainland. They did not know him for the Prince because he was still wearing his clerical garb, but they met his promise of Charles Edward's coming with questions about the arms he would bring, the money, and the soldiers from France. When he answered that the Prince would come alone with no arms or money, they turned aside and muttered among themselves behind their plaids. Bishop Hugh, the Vicar Apostolic of the Highlands, declared that without help from France there could be no chance of success, and the young man replied that the Prince would refuse to lead French troops, even if he had them, in an invasion of his own country. The Jacobites of Edinburgh sent a messenger to urge the Prince not to land, and telling how the leader of Clan MacLean had already been arrested. News came that the Lairds of Sleat and Dunvegan now refused to keep their pledged word and would give no help. There was even a rumour that one of these two powerful men was already in correspondence with the Hanoverian Government.

"Here the Prince stood, then, at last, in the very centre and home of whatever enthusiastic Jacobitism there might be left in the realm, and this was his reception. The prospect was dark indeed. Any man who had based his expectations upon the gathering of a mighty host would certainly have despaired. But Charles Edward was not that sort of man. He had been taught in childhood, and still believed, that the spirit—even in things of this world, and in battle—is mightier than the flesh. What he was hoping for, as he stood there on the crowded deck in conversation with the leaders of Moidart and Lorne and Skye, was not at all a great army of soldiers well equipped and thoroughly trained which might meet and defeat by German methods the German host that would be sent against him. He was looking for half a dozen men, perhaps two or three, in whom the spirit of loyalty was still alive. He thought they would be young men, not chieftains, not powerful or wealthy or famous, and that he would know them by some gleam in their eyes, some note of exultation in their voices, possibly by some hint that they recognized him.

"In this he was not disappointed. First there was young Ranald Macdonald, who had just brought the news that Sleat and Macleod would not come in. The lad's angry tone as he spoke of their treachery made the Prince cry out, 'But *you*, surely, are with me, if they are not,' and back came the answer, 'I am, Sire, though not another man in the Highlands should draw his sword!' This meant that Clan Ranald as a whole would join, and soon it brought in Young Lochiel, the noblest and most beloved spirit in Scotland. Thousands would follow wherever he led. And then came a third, yellow-haired, yellow-bearded, gigantic and magnificent in the red-and-black tartan of the MacGillivray clan. 'My name,' said he, 'is Alasdair, and I am with you to the end.'

Blandison paused again for a glass of wine. "I knew that man," said James Adair, "and he was indeed magnificent. He stood six feet and eight inches tall, and his long yellow hair was like a banner in the wind. Nearly all the other members of his family were merchants, both at home and in America, but Alasdair, their chieftain, held to the old ways. He died at—"

"That is so," said Blandison, "but he lived, while he lived, like a man. When the Prince went ashore at Borradale, sending the *Du Tellier* back to France so that no one could mistake his determination to stay, it was Alasdair who carried him in through the breakers.

"For several days and nights they waited there by the sea, a slowly increasing band of companions held each to each by a common hope and danger. It took some time for the news that the Prince had come to spread out and over those many islands, up through the lochs and glens, and into the small rocky fields and the castles and shielings and bothies where the men who could help him dwelt. When they heard the news these men would not loiter, but there would be much for the chieftains, at least, to arrange, considering that this might well be their final departure. For one thing, what should be done about the approaching harvest? Could the women and children and tottering old men bring it home to barn without help? If not, then whatever fighting men should return would be the only survivors. Yet little by little the rumour of Ranald's words was bruited abroad. It came to be known beside mountain tarns and on crags where the eagle nested that Prince Charlie had come home to his people and Gentle Lochiel was with him and Great Alasdair was his closest friend. Then one by one —sometimes alone but oftener with a troop of elflocked caterans straggling behind, the chieftains came down to the tent on the beach and put their hard brown hands between the hands of the Prince in that ancient and beautiful act of fealty which has nothing subservient about it but only the mutual recognition of mutual duty and need. There came Keppoch with the warm, brown loyal eyes, and Glencoe tall and dark and lean. Stuart of Appin came and did homage not to his Prince alone but to a superior in his own clan. Kinlochmoidart came in, the elder brother of young Ranald, and wise Glenaladale, wild Scothouse, and dreamy Morar.

"These were poor men one and all, with little to offer their Prince except their lives. They came in footsore and weary from the steep rocky paths and the moors and the glens. They had slept on the way in their plaids, with the rain beating down upon them. Some of them must have been hungry all their lives, so thankful were they for a few bannocks of graddan-meal and a cup of whiskey. Some came from half-ruined castles jutting gaunt from the crags or dark by the ocean's edge, and others from bothies of stone and sod half hidden under the ground. Their country itself was a castle broken and rifled by strangers. Whatever national pride they had left must look far back for its source. In the dull and timid sense of goodness they were not good men—that is to say, docile, meekly industrious, vulgarly sub-servient to wealth and power. Enough that they were true men, with a spark of ancient loyalty glowing in them which could yet be fanned into flame. They had kept the sense of glory, and so could follow a banished Prince—a poor man with little but a dream to offer—in support of a cause which they believed to be lost and hopeless.

"This was the old way. Thus it had always been. The message was carried from glen to glen, from isle to isle, and then the claymore was buckled on, the sporran was filled with what provision might be found, brief farewells to wives and children were said, and up from the loch and down from the crag and over the heath they strode by tens and dozens and scores, the men who had never been humbled or hired or bought. They strode to the beat of the wild old songs handed down from the days of Wallace and Bruce and Douglas the scourge of the Border. Their women, looking after them from the doorways, saw their round wooden targets banging against their backs, saw their blue woollen bonnets pulled slantwise over the black or red or yellow hair, caught the gleam of a clumsy Lochaber axe or of a scythe-blade bound with rawhide to a wooden shaft, until at last there was nothing left to be seen and only the dying skirl of the pipes to be heard. Then the women turned and closed their doors and began to pray and to wait."

*   *   *

No one interrupted Blandison after he got well into his story, and I hesitate to break in even now upon the words he spoke as they lie before me in Mr. Chute's manuscript. I shall leave out many details of the long march from Borradale to Edinburgh and of the gradual process whereby a crowd of men accustomed to fighting one another was shaped into a band of companions. I cannot stop to tell you of the friendship that more and more firmly bound Alasdair and Lochiel and the Prince together, or bring the individual chieftains and caterans and gillies before you as we were made to see and hear them. I am reduced to the mere assertion that Blandison somehow took us inside these men, so that for the first time we understood the motives of the Rebellion.

For us of Strawberry Hill, clearly remembering how we had felt when the Highland forces grew and struck and rushed toward London, all this was a strange experience. It was startling, I mean, to learn that "the Boy" and his followers had been, after all, so human.

Let me give you one more scene, and positively the last one in this letter, of a fire by night. Those dreadful men who are on the way to capture London and overthrow a dynasty have just killed a half-starved cow somewhere in the wilderness, and a dozen ragged gillies are now gathered about a pile of burning peat with collops of beef spitted on the points of their dirks. You see the red light striking up over gnarled hands and gaunt bearded faces. It glitters on the steel pistol-butts in a chieftain's belt, on the yellow cairngorm in the brooch that fastens a plaid, on the iron or brazen bosses set in the wooden shields. Off to one side, in the shadows, you catch the glimmer of many faces, intent, absorbed, with shining eyes. The men are listening to a bard who is chanting in Gaelic one of the ballads of Ossian— a poet unknown to me but, according to Blandison, the Homer of the North.

One month from the day of his arrival in the Hebrides the Prince raised his standard—a white unicorn on blue, with a crescent moon and four white roses—in a valley called Glenfinnan, not far from the sea. There he read a proclamation from his father, whom Blandison called King James, giving him power to act as Regent and calling upon all loyal subjects of the British Crown to assist him in every possible way. By that time the Prince had with him an army—badly armed and provisioned, to be sure, and devoid of anything like military discipline—of about a thousand men. General Sir John Cope, with fifteen hundred men well armed and trained, was then setting forth to prevent his approach to Edinburgh. On the day his standard was raised the Prince learned that the Ministers of King George had offered thirty thousand pounds for his head. He immediately offered precisely one-thousandth of that amount for the head of the Elector of Hanover.

You remember that General Cope's small army was reduced by desertions as he marched northward while that of the Prince was rapidly growing from day to day. Cope, also, was outmanoeuvred, and was finally obliged to take ship at Aberdeen and return to the neighbourhood of the city by sea. Charles Edward, moving swiftly across the land, reached it before him.

On the seventeenth of September, less than two months after his landing, the Prince, in the early dawn, sent Lochiel with a party of his Camerons to the Netherbow Gate, which lies farthest from the Castle. They had no means of forcing an entrance, but the gates were suddenly opened from within to allow the passage of a deputation from the magistrates to the Prince. The Highlanders rushed in with Lochiel at their head, shouting their battle-cries, but they found no one to fight. As the wakening city became conscious of the blue bonnets and bright tartans in the wynds and streets, window after window was thrown up in the tall houses, face after face peered forth, and shouts of welcome were heard. Soon the citizens were bringing provisions to their unexpected guests. One of them, out for his morning's walk, found a Highlander sitting on a gun. "Do you belong to yesterday's guard?" he inquired. "Oh, no, she be relieved," was the reply.

"Thus easily, and without striking a blow," said Blandison, "the Prince came home to his house. A place had been made ready for him in the hearts of his people. On every hand he heard them shouting their welcome to 'Bonnie Prince Charlie.' The Cameron pipers blew 'The White Cockade' and marched through the Canongate with Macleods and Macgregors behind them and Stuarts of Appin and Grants of Glenmoriston and Macdonalds of Clanranald, Glengarry, Keppoch, and Glencoe. They moved into Parliament Close as though they owned that place, and stood in a great circle about the Market Cross to hear the Declaration of King James while the townsfolk peered over their shoulders. Seldom had so many clans stood together, and never had the citizens beheld such a congregated might of men half wild yet controlled by a single purpose. For once they caught a glimpse of glory, tattered and begrimed though it was, as they stared at those tanned lean faces, the long beards and hair hanging in elflocks, the bruised and scratched bare knees, and the weapons of times gone by.

"They stared, but did not understand. The beautiful woman on a white horse, tossing white cockades among the crowd with one hand while she held a bared sword in the other, was to them a meaningless spectacle. And yet, if they had but known it, there was the last chance that Scotland would have of saving herself from foreign domination and degradation. The Prince was partly to blame that the chance was not taken, for he made no address to the people. It was a grievous error of an inexperienced youth.

"The moment passed, and Charles Edward rode through the city toward Holyrood Palace with the multitude shouting acclaim. On his right rode the Duke of Perth, and on his left Lord Elcho, whom he did not trust. His own horse, recently taken from a Hanoverian officer, was a great black stallion. He had long since doffed his clerical garb and was now wearing a tartan coat, velvet breeches, a blue bonnet with a cockade of white satin, and the Star of St. Andrew. Just as he caught sight of Holyrood, the home of his ancestors, news was brought him that General John Cope, with three thousand men, was on the way from the coast to meet him in battle. His heart gave a leap of joy."

*   *   *

"And then," said my cousin to me in a low voice, "came Preston-pans." I nodded, well remembering the fright that event gave London ten years ago, and the quandary of a certain young Whig placeman with my name about how, if we had a few more such battles, he might earn a living. A good many details of that strange fight I still had in mind; but they had never seemed to me consistent with one another, or quite comprehensible. My hope was that Blandison would now make them so, as he had thus far done the earlier events of the Rebellion. To be sure, he was looking at everything, and trying to make us do so, through the eyes of one man, the Young Pretender; but in that simplification there were definite advantages. Its results were startlingly different from those of the miscellaneous rumour and gossip and political falsehood we had thus far heard. Allowing as we easily could for his prejudice, we were now for the first time seeing the Forty-five, and living through it, as an intelligible series of events. Our knowledge of how it finally turned out did not in the least detract from our interest in why it had done so.

Blandison had been walking up and down the room, with swifter and longer strides than one usually takes in libraries. Now he came to a stand again by the window and gazed out into the storm, which was by this time subsiding. His voice, when he spoke, had once more the tone of soliloquy.

"All that afternoon and through most of the night," said he, "the court of the Palace was thronged with people eager to catch sight of the Prince, to hear a word from him, but not, apparently, to give him any help. Ladies and gentlemen came in coaches and sedan chairs to wish him success—most of them hoping that this would place them on the winning side, whichever it might be. He received them courteously; but two months of association with men had made him impatient of triflers. His thoughts were upon the battle which must come soon, but which he was determined should not be fought within the city walls. Between two conversations about European styles in hairdressing he sent out directions that the Highlanders should make ready to march at dawn, and also for the assembly of medicines, surgeons, and wagons for the care of the wounded in both armies.

"Three days later, at sunset, the two armies came face to face on a moor above the fishing village of Prestonpans. Looking down the gentle slope toward the sea, Charles Edward saw that Cope had chosen ground well suited to the evolutions of regular, well trained forces. And a force of that kind, Cope had. His army, though scarcely larger than the Prince's own, was composed of cavalry, infantry, and artillery in the right proportions, each in its proper place and each supporting the others. The red and white of the foot soldiers made a brilliant show down there. So did the helmets and sabres of the dragoons on their handsome horses, and the polished brass barrels of the field guns.

"The Prince's heart was heavy as he turned away, though not for himself and his fortunes but for the lives in his keeping. By what right could he ask these friends of his—men with whom he had laughed and raced and wrestled and gone wet and hungry for week after week in the mountains—to stand up now in the blast of grapeshot, to wait for the trampling hooves and the flash of sabres and the thrust of the bayonet? He knew they were willing to die for him, but how could he let them?

"They were cooking their evening meal when he returned and moved from fire to fire. They called out to him in Gaelic, and broke into merry laughter at his attempts to reply in kind. What were those six long tubes of brass that the Southrons had over there, they wanted to know, and why had they fastened long knives on the ends of their muskets? They had been much amused by the gaudy dress of the footsoldiers. How were they going to kill those men, they inquired, without injuring their uniforms? In the eyes of them all there was a strange wild look of joy.

"At length he found the four friends—Alasdair, Lochiel, Young Ranald, and Gillies Macbean—upon whom he now chiefly depended for counsel. They assured him that his fears were groundless, and hoped that he was not growing cautious in his old age like Lord George Murray, who knew nothing of war except how to retreat. In any case, said they, it would not now be in the power of any man to prevent the Highland charge. The clans would somehow come at the foe, if they had to wade the marsh up to their eyes. In spite of Cope's sabres and horses and cannon they would reach him and beat him and put him to rout—not because their Prince had asked them to but for sheer delight in battle and as a matter of immemorial habit. Gillies Macbean asked what purpose the Lord could have had in creating Southrons if not for Highlanders to fight on every possible occasion?

"Somewhat encouraged by this manly talk and banter, the Prince lay down at midnight on a heap of damp pease-straw. In three hours he was awakened to hear the news that a path had been found through the marsh, and an hour later still the men were moving slowly, silently, in single file, toward the enemy's lines. Somewhat before dawn they were standing ready for battle in the stubble of a newly harvested field. The Macdonalds, as the most powerful of the clans, had been given their traditional place of honour on the right wing. The Camerons formed the left. A heavy mist hid the two armies from each other, but the voices of Cope's officers showed that they had not been taken by surprise.

"Standing then before his three thousand, and hoping that Cope's army also might hear him, the Prince drew his sword in the half-light and shouted: 'Gentlemen, I have thrown away the scabbard. With God's help and yours I shall set you free from the foreign usurper and make you once more a proud and a happy people. You will win this battle because you will be fighting for your true King and Prince against the hirelings of a hireling. Many of them are here against their will, and many more for pay. Some of them are my subjects and your fellow-countrymen. Spare as many of them as you can, and bring them in as captives so that they may join our ranks. —And now, may the Lord of hosts uphold the right!'

"A light breeze of the dawn was swiftly dispersing the mist as he spoke, and the two armies were revealed to each other. They were some four hundred paces apart. On the Hanoverian side no orders were called. The redcoats did not move. The dragoons were holding their excited horses in check. Not a hand was lifted by the men at the field-guns. For several seconds it lasted—that astonishing, almost shocking inaction. One could only surmise that the Prince's few words had convinced all the men over there that they were on the wrong side. But no; there was also the possibility that the long wooden wall of bossed shields now rushing at them had frozen them fast in terror. For the Highlanders had waited for no command. The mere sight of the foe had roused them to sudden fury. At once when the mist blew away they had started forward at a swift walk that soon quickened to a trot, with a mutter of Gaelic to one another as they went which did not at first drown the rustle and crunch of stubble beneath their bare feet but gradually grew and grew as the trot increased to a run until the battle-cries of the clans rang out on all sides of the Prince while he ran and heard Alasdair at his right hand shout 'Dunmaglas! Dunmaglas!' and then the Macdonalds yell 'Creagan an Fhithich.' From the Camerons, now well in front of the line slicing sidelong for the guns, came a blood-chilling scream which in English meant 'Sons of the hounds, come here and eat flesh!'

"Still Cope and his many stood dazed before the onset, not lifting a hand or pulling a trigger or loosing a rein. Dreadful seconds went by with the steadily growing patter and pound and beat of six thousand feet coming at them behind a wall of iron-studded targets and flash of claymores and Lochaber axes and incomprehensible cries until they could only think of the numberless lies they had heard from Whigs of far-away England that these shaggy men of the bosk and the dune and the dell ate human flesh only and ate it raw and still reeking of life on the points of their dirks. For the worst they had heard of the men of the north since the woaded Picts first raided the Saxons was now confirmed by this brash breaking of all the rules of civilized war which required that they should stand off at a respectful distance to be shot at with field-guns and muskets until on one side or the other there should be no one left to shoot. Worse still, these men were fighting not by the book of instructions, not under orders, not like machines invented by Frederick of Prussia and approved by his Hanoverian cousin, but as though they had some cause to serve or some person whom they loved and wished to help.

"For perhaps a minute after the Highland charge began the field-guns remained silent, but then an officer ran forward and touched off several of them in the faces of the clansmen. James Mor of the Macgregors fell with five slugs in his body but immediately raised himself on his hands and cried: 'My lads, I'm not dead yet, and by God I shall see if any man does not do his duty.' The Highland line paused for a moment in its rush and then poured on and round and over the guns like a wave of the sea.

"A company of Cope's dragoons was ordered forward, and the Camerons let off a popping fire at them from their old fowling-pieces and blunderbusses. The horsemen did not even discharge their pistols but turned about and rode down the artillery guard and so thundered pellmell to the rear. Gardiner's dragoons were brought from the other flank, but they too had long since learned the art of retreating and soon followed the other horsemen. Colonel Gardiner himself tried to make a stand with a few foot-soldiers but was cut down by a Highland scythe.

"Though both ends of Cope's line were now unprotected, the clansmen made no attempt to turn his flank. In the midst of the battle they paused, pulled off their bonnets, and made a short prayer. Then they cast aside their firearms, drew claymores and dirks, and rushed at the infantry. The Hanoverian line wavered, and broke, and ran.

"What we call the Battle of Prestonpans was in fact a rout. It lasted five minutes, and at the end of that time five hundred of Cope's well equipped and disciplined soldiers, many of whom were veterans of Dettingen and Fontenoy, lay dead on the field. One thousand of them had been taken prisoners, and nine-tenths of these were wounded. The rest escaped only because the Prince had no cavalry. To General Cope remained the honour of reaching Berwick-upon-Tweed well ahead of his best mounted dragoons and there announcing one of the most shameful defeats that English arms have ever suffered."

*   *   *

To that word "shameful" my cousin took such vigorous exception that Blandison finally withdrew it, admitting that in forty years of Hanoverian rule its meaning had changed almost out of recognition. Henry was not satisfied with this apology, and was about to say so when I interposed with the remark that General Cope, at any rate, had not been in the least ashamed. On the contrary, he had wagered ten thousand guineas that the first man sent in his place against the Highlanders would be as thoroughly beaten as he had been. "After

Butcher Hawley was routed at Falkirk," said I, "Cope collected his guineas and regained his honour at once."

Even my cousin could smile at that; and all of us were amused by Blandison's account of the booty collected by the Highlanders and their speculations about various articles they saw for the first time. There was a group of them that wanted to haul home a couple of field-guns, one of which they called "the mother of muskets," perhaps with the hope that nature would take her course and those two would multiply and replenish the earth. A cateran from the northernmost wilds fell in love with a small yellow object which he found on the body of an officer he had just slain with an axe. Quite unacquainted with mechanism of any kind, he was much impressed by its arms that moved in a circle and its low steady voice like the sound of an insect boring into wood. Even more wonderful was the faint song it sang, like a far-off bird, when its arms came over two of the markings. At first he showed it to no one, feeling perhaps that here was a personal friend with a voice for him alone. Next morning, however, he found that this friend had fallen asleep and that no pleading or shaking or shouting would wake him. At last he cursed it, and squeezed it so hard in his fist that the little knob at the side broke off. Thus it died, and he turned it over to Young Lochiel.

The Prince spent most of the day on the battlefield, arranging for burial of the dead and care of the wounded on both sides. Upon his return to Edinburgh he forbade any celebration of the victory, declaring that he himself took no delight in the slaughter of his own subjects. —And this, said Blandison, was a difficulty which Charles Edward encountered at every stage of the Rebellion. His Hanoverian enemies could and did regard him, quite simply and frankly, as a foe to be destroyed, along with all his adherents, by any means fair or foul. He on the other hand, besides the weakness felt by any gentleman in contest with oafs, felt always a strong reluctance to strike as hard as he was able at those whom he wished to make his friends.

There was also in the Prince, Blandison told us, that defect of intelligent minds—for a serious defect it is, said he, when aggressive action is called for—which obliges one to see every situation as it looks to one's opponents. This weakened him in his debates with Lord George Murray, a cold and cautious man twice his age whose knowledge of tactics gave him great influence in the councils of war. The impulse of the Prince after Prestonpans was to rush at once upon

London, taking full advantage of his victory and of the fact that King George and the Duke of Cumberland were in Europe with most of their armed forces. He urged speed, boldness, and that fierce dependence upon a headlong plunge into the thick of difficulty which the clans had shown in the battle. Keep these men on the charge, said he, and they will batter the gates of Hell to flinders; but if you bring them to a stand they will drink themselves stupid and forget their errand and only remember their women far back in the bothies and how the little fields of oats are growing more golden every day for the slash of the sickle.

But then "Ah, yes," Lord George would say, looking sidewise from under his graying eyebrows, "all that, your Highness, is most eloquently said as a young and inexperienced man—I speak with all due respect—would say it. On the other hand, if we may now return to common sense, I would respectfully point out . . ."

In short, the Prince and his Highlanders waited there in Edinburgh for a month or more after Prestonpans while King George and his bellicose Billy came back to these threatened dominions and General Wade marched northward and the clansmen drank themselves happier every night.

After lingering for five precious weeks in Edinburgh, to no advantage except that his army grew to five thousand men, the Prince set forth on the road to Carlisle. He went on foot with his mountaineers, leaving his horse to Lord Elcho, "a gentleman of fashion," and his private carriage to an old Laird who should have stayed at home in bed. Every morning he was the first man astir, and made sure that the army was on the march before the break of dawn. Alasdair and Gillies Macbean walked beside him until they reached the Border, which I think at that point is either the river Esk or else the Liddel. Then they shook his hand and said that if ever he should care to return to his own people they would gladly give their lives in his support, but that they would not lift a finger to make him King of England.

He went on from there, somewhat sadly, and took Carlisle without a blow. A Lancashire squire, John Daniel, brought him some forty recruits. Young Dickson, one of the soldiers captured at Prestonpans, and later converted, rode ahead into Manchester and there, with the help of a drum and a blunderbuss and a girl companion, gathered a regiment of three hundred men before the Prince arrived. At the river Mersey, near Stockport, he found waiting for him an aged

woman who said that she as a child, eighty-five years ago, had witnessed the return of the second Charles. She was a Mrs. Skyring, and
the Prince knew her name because during all the Stuart exile she had
sent half her income every year to the Stuart court in Rome. Now
she had sold her jewels, and here was a little money to help the man
who would some day be Charles the Third on his way to the throne.
The Prince kissed her cheek, and she said: " 'Lord, now lettest thou
thy servant depart in peace.' "

Well, William, my political convictions remain as firm as ever, yet
I am sometimes a little envious of the monopoly you Tories hold upon
such scenes as that.

*　　*　　*

"And now," said Blandison, "you will picture the young man sitting
at an upper window in the town of Derby, well over halfway down
from the Scottish Border to London. He is wearing the Royal Stuart
tartan and the badge of the oak and thistle. His face is older by years
than that of the dreamy youth who waded ashore on the blood-
coloured ledge of Eriskay less than five months ago. It is the face of
one in whom the dreams of youth are beginning to encounter the facts
of experience.

"There is a group of Highlanders standing in line before a cutler's
shop just across the narrow lane, waiting to have their weapons—
claymores and dirks, scythe-blades and axes—sharpened. They are
merry down there in the sunshine, telling the townsfolk and one another what short work they will soon be making of London Tower.
For the Tower, they point out in their Gaelic, will not run away like
Cope's soldiers, nor will Lord George Murray be able to dodge it
as he has the armies of General Wade and the Duke of Cumberland.

"From the room behind the young man comes the tired voice of
Lord George Murray: 'The clansmen have done all that could be expected of them, and more. They are now worn out and homesick. They
are beginning to desert. If ever we should reach London there would
be none of them left. Besides, we have Wade's army at our rear, and
the Duke's veterans on our flank. We must hasten back at once, lest
they cut off our retreat.'

" 'Homesick'? They do not look it, those laughing men down there
at the shop-door. They are not talking of home but of London and
how they will soon be battering at the gates of its fortress. After

travelling a thousand miles on foot they are by no means so 'worn out' as these eight or ten chieftains at the table who have ridden most of the way. They are weary, to be sure, but not of battles. If they are sick, it is of Murray's senile caution. If they are deserting—and this is doubtful—it is because their longing to seek out the foe and rush headlong upon him has been baffled at every turn by a man to whom war is like a game of chess.

"Oh, that Tullibardine were here to answer Lord George, his younger brother!—to say to his face what he for months has been telling the Prince, that these retreats and evasions and procrastinations are parts of a deliberate effort to betray the Cause. Lord George, the Prince now knows, had been in close consultation with General Cope less than a month before Prestonpans, and that battle had been a Jacobite victory not because but in spite of him. He had learned there, if he had not known before, that the clansmen could not be cowed by superior numbers and equipment, so that the only way of serving his Hanoverian masters would be by delays, by retreats, by letting hunger and weariness and jealousy do their work. He it was that had insisted upon that costly lingering in Edinburgh. On the way southward it had been he that thwarted the Prince's strong wish to fight Cumberland and Wade. Now that he had passed them by, this same man was urging that their position in the rear necessitated immediate retreat.

" 'But "retreat," ' the Prince exclaims, stepping from the window to the table, 'is a word you have learned from some book of tactics, Lord George, and not from the clansmen or from me. Why in God's name should you talk of retreat when we have no enemy before us and behind us nothing but success? From the start it has been clear that our hope lies only in steady onrushing attack. You know this, and therefore the question cannot be avoided whether it is retreat that you really want or our defeat.'

"But Lord George is more than twice the Prince's age, and so are most of the other chieftains at the table. Each of them, and Lord George also, is the unlimited ruler of his clan. Any one of them can march away at will with all his men, and no power on earth can stop him. The Prince is dependent upon these chieftains. He cannot issue orders.

"Young Lochiel says nothing, but the Prince knows that even he has always been hesitant about this expedition into England. So were

Gillies Macbean and Alasdair, he remembers, far back there at the Border. Or rather, they did not hesitate; they simply and firmly refused to share in this adventure because its success could mean to Scotland only the loss of one whom Scotland was learning to love. He feels now that those two friends were at least halfway right, and that only his will and sense of duty have driven him thus far southward through towns and cities and shires where the people gape at him as they would at a raree show. With a sort of longing he thinks back to the dearth-stricken country two hundred miles north."

"In that case," said Mr. Chute, laying down his pencil, "how comes it that this same man, the still so-called Young Pretender, is now again attempting—let us say by your help—to gain the throne of England for himself or his father? You see what I mean: ten years ago he was somewhat in doubt whether he wanted that throne, but now . . . In short, one can scarcely avoid the question whether the man knows his own mind."

"Mr. Chute, in those ten years a country and a man have grown, the one of them worse and the other wiser. It is not, I assure you, that the Prince has any more wish for the throne on his own account than he had then, but that England needs him more, and ought to know that she does. For ten years longer she has had the spectacle of Hanoverian stupidity and brutality before her. Have you enjoyed it, sir? Have you admired it? Do you feel that a member of England's Royal Family who tries to bring it to an end is acting wickedly, selfishly? Suppose that his loathing for what England now is has been overcome by his love of what she has been and might again be. Is there anything blameworthy in that?"

I looked from one face to the other, and back again. Neither man was angry. Both were trying, I thought, to understand and to be understood. There was respect on both sides, and personal liking. The whole thing, lasting several seconds, was fascinating to watch. At length Mr. Chute took up his pencil and said, with a faint smile:

"Please continue."

*   *   *

Would you agree with me, William, that altogether the strangest thing about the Rebellion of Forty-five was the Prince's retreat—that's not quite the right word, but 'twill serve—from Derby? Again and again in these ten years I've asked myself, and sometimes other people, why it was that he turned away, after making all that effort, just when success was at last within sight, almost in his grasp. With Wade behind him and Cumberland far off to one side, nothing stood between him and London except that ridiculous camp of apprentices at Finchley, improvised at the last moment, of which Hogarth has given us a well known print. His toils and perils were over, and ahead lay only the goal. —Why, then, did he not march on?

The simplest explanation is that the Tories of northern England did not flock to his standard in any such numbers as he had expected; but to that I think we should reply that he never had thought in terms of numbers or mere military power. Add the fact that just before reaching Derby he had received, in the "Manchester Regiment," a considerable addition to his forces. This explanation, therefore, does not really explain. It is by far too simple. At least a dozen other things must be kept in mind, among which I should lay some emphasis upon the fact that the Highlanders, though not "homesick," were at any rate much farther from home than any of them had ever been before. Their fighting, for ages, had been a matter of sudden short forays, never of long campaigns. To be sure, they would follow their chieftains anywhere and for any length of time; but at Derby the chieftains themselves began to realize, if they had not before, that there was little for them to gain in the substitution of the House of Stuart for that of Hanover. One cannot doubt that they really loved the Prince; but that very affection soon led them to ask, "Why give him up to the English?"

Thus I might go on to a tedious length, not forgetting to say that between the rash Prince and the calculating Lord George Murray there was a chasm in which the whole enterprise could scarcely fail to be engulfed. At the end of a dozen reasons, however, I should still have to say that the about-face at Derby is to me a mysterious thing. I think it was that even to Blandison, who knew so amazingly much —or thought he did—about Charles Edward. At any rate what he told us was only what we know: after that session in the upper room at Derby the return to Scotland began.

You have not forgotten, I suppose, what this meant to England. The apprentices at Finchley Common, when they heard of it, returned thankfully to their shops. The banks ceased to pay in red-hot sixpences. The Prime Minister came out of the locked room in which he had been trying to compose a letter of enthusiastic welcome to the

House of Stuart. The royal yacht which had been lying for days at Parliament Stairs, ready at a moment's notice to set sail for Hanover, was sent back to wherever she came from. The bonus of six pounds per man which the Government had offered for enlistments in the army was withdrawn. George the Second—who, to be sure, had never been much disturbed—returned to the Maze or the Toying Place, and Horace Walpole gave up all thoughts of earning his livelihood.

These are a few of the numberless consequences of that decision which we do not, and never shall, understand. Let me name one more: on the way back to Scotland the Prince rode a horse among the chieftains, having as little as possible to do with the men on foot. Instead of being the first man abroad in the morning he was now the last. He spoke little, seldom smiled, never laughed.

Scouts and skirmishers of Cumberland's pursuing army were now occasionally encountered. Green-uniformed fellows they were, and under the immediate command of General Oglethorpe, who had recruited them for service in Georgia. The Prince, when he saw them, began to hope that he could force a battle upon Murray during the retreat, especially if he himself was not present. With this in mind, he remained in bed even later in the mornings, and insisted that all the cannon and ammunition taken on the advance should be carried back into Scotland. Murray could not well object to this, for he had often praised the superior power of artillery as compared with foot soldiers. True, he had no gunners worthy of the name, and the powder would soon be too damp for use; yet the guns were dragged along through river and marsh, and every Highlander was paid sixpence for carrying cannon balls up Shap Fells.

The ignorant peasantry, having heard a rumour that the northern men had been defeated, now began to show their fangs. Beacon-fires flickered from the hills at night. Fear and hatred ran ahead of the host. A sleeping boy, the youngest of the Manchester recruits, had his throat cut as he lay exhausted by the side of the road. When the probable murderers were discovered in a hut close by, their clothes covered with blood, the Prince would not let them be hanged because he had no certain evidence of their guilt. He also pardoned a man called Weir who had been captured while trying to escape with much valuable information to the Hanoverians. "This man," said the Prince, "has merely obeyed the orders, however vile, of his masters. I shall defend his life, if necessary, with my own."

Oglethorpe's green-clad men pressed closer and closer. In many a village the Highland rear guard marched out to the music of church bells ringing to welcome their pursuers. On the eighteenth of December, at Clifton Moor, General Murray was forced either to fight or be taken. He sent a message to the Prince, two miles ahead, asking for reinforcements and orders. The Prince sent back a thousand men and orders to retreat. Therefore General Murray let loose a sudden charge of Highlanders out of the hedges at cock-shut time which sent Oglethorpe reeling backward and kept Cumberland at a respectful distance until the Border was crossed.

It was a gallant picture that Blandison brought before us of the fording of the river Esk: a hundred men abreast, their clothes held high, wading the water that reached to their waists, holding hands for support against the current, with another hundred stepping behind them, and then a third, until all were over and dancing to dry themselves while the pipers blew a reel. They were hungry still, to be sure; but that they had always been. The main thing was that they had invaded a foreign land, had beaten every foe they met, and now were bringing their Prince back home. At every step from now on they would touch the soil of Scotland. Once more the men of the Highlands were happy and, given half a chance, invincible.

"Clouds cover the peaks," says Blandison. "Fog drifts down the glens like ravelled tatters of white cloth. Rain, sleet, and snow are slashing at them, freezing on their faces, wetting their powder, blotting out the landmarks, glazing the upland paths. The men laugh and sing in high glee as the weather worsens. The sting and scream of the north wind is what they have missed on the fat level lands below. And all the gayer they are when they learn that the Hanoverian army is lumbering after them back at the Border and searching about the feet of the mountains, wheezing and snuffling like an old blind hound. It is led by General Hawley, a man who strives to outdo even the monstrous Duke of Cumberland in brutality. Already he has built a score of gibbets in the streets of Edinburgh for the hanging of Jacobite prisoners not yet taken. He has brought a dozen hangmen with him.

"On the afternoon of January 17, 1746, the villagers of Falkirk, halfway between Edinburgh and Stirling, saw General Hawley's army of ten thousand men climbing a hill close at hand, first the cavalry and then the infantry ascending, line after line, until they disappeared in a dark cloud that covered the top. A storm from the opposite side of the hill was evidently driving in their faces as they climbed. Then suddenly the murk was illumined by red flame, and there followed a long roll of musketry. Two or three minutes went by as the villagers stared upward, and then the cavalry began spilling out of the cloud and rushing back down the hill with the infantry after them, throwing away their muskets as they ran and tumbling and cursing and yelling for quarter. Last of all in this pageant was the downsweep of Highlanders, like a cascade, which drove the Southrons through the village and far out on the road to Edinburgh with claymores, dirks, axes, and hurled stones. When Hawley got back into Edinburgh that night he ordered that thirty-one of his dragoons should be hanged on his new-made gibbets, and thirty-two of his foot-soldiers shot for cowardice. He was not satisfied with having left seven hundred of his men lying dead on the field, besides the thousand more that were wounded or captured."

* * *

Perhaps it has not occurred to you, William, that the document you have in hand is, among several other things, the history of a war. If not, then one reason is that I have shown somewhat the same skill in avoiding battles which Blandison found fault with—or was it the Prince?—in Lord George Murray. Think of how I skirted the edges of the *Centurion's* fight with the Spanish galleon and had John Chester narrate the whole siege of Louisburg in three words.

One battle in this war, however, will submit to no such offhand treatment, and the only escape I can find for myself is to present it in Blandison's own language.

"After Falkirk," says he, "it was the strong wish of the Prince and of every stout-hearted, keen-minded man he had with him to pursue General Hawley into Edinburgh and break his shaken force once for all and take and hold that city. By this time, however, the spirit of defeat and retreat had won such a dominion over the older chieftains, and especially in the mind of Lord George Murray, that it could not be dislodged by victory itself. Within two weeks after the Battle of Falkirk the Jacobite army, now ten thousand strong, was streaming northward toward Inverness as though in a frenzy of flight, leaving wagons and cannon scattered along the way. At every mile, it seemed, the weather grew worse. Icicles hung from the men's hair and beards. Sleet and snow drove so fiercely against them that they could scarce see their own hands and feet. And hunger, even worse than the storm and the bitter chill, made strong men weak and turned young men old.

"This hunger was different from that which most of them had known all their lives. It was more like famine. Under the best of conditions it is no easy thing to feed ten thousand men on the march; but these conditions were the worst. This march, as the Prince had foretold, was directly away from any source of supplies, through a desolate country fast-bound in ice and snow. The commissariat of the little army, such as it once had been, had now broken down. The ration of oatmeal—and that was all they had—was reduced from day to day until it came to less than a handful. —See then those men of the mountains, their legs blue with cold, wading in muddy inlets of the coast in search of shellfish that may have been overlooked by the fisherfolk. When one has been found and brought ashore, how the thin hands tremble that hold it! How feebly the dull blade fumbles for the crack! How slowly the blood comes oozing from the flesh when the knife slips from its mark! Yet he carefully sucks the blood from his hand, missing no drop, and then, laying the clam on a rock, shatters the shell with a stone. He licks at the mass of shards and pulp with a bloody tongue, and rests, and gathers strength, and crawls again toward the sea.

"It was with that hunger, tampering with the wills of men and dragging them back to less than the strength of children, that the final battle began. Meanwhile the Duke of Cumberland was moving up the coast from Edinburgh with the ponderous tread of a thousand elephants. He had with him a host of professionals, Hessians mostly, who had been hired by the French, then captured by Austria, and finally bought with English money to keep the Elector of Hanover upon the throne of England. Those men were well fed. A small squadron of English warships, amply stocked with English roast beef and pudding and beer, sailed up the coast at the leisurely pace of the Duke's line of march, steadily maintaining the patriotism of his German heroes at the highest pitch of ferocity. To any faithful Hanoverian it would have been a delight to look from the starving Jacobite there on the rock to those floating Whig kitchens two miles out at sea, and therefrom to deduce a perfect confidence that his comfort, his liberties, and his sinecures would be preserved. There was, moreover, a frank, blunt brutality in the Duke's manner of trampling and burning and crashing his way from town to town which quite fulfilled certain notions of what a prince and a soldier should be. He had no nonsense about him, made no pretence that a man is better than a beast; and this left him free to show that one man, at any rate, was considerably worse."

"I don't like this!" my cousin broke in, angrily. "I think some respect is due to a prince and a soldier who—"

"You are entirely right, General Conway, and no true Englishman can 'like' it. The more highly one thinks of royalty and of the soldier's calling, the more one must abhor a man who degrades them both.

"To the Jacobites, now at Inverness, there came news on the fifteenth of April that the Duke had reached Nairn, ten or twelve miles away, and was advancing to meet them. One biscuit, made of the mill's last sweepings, was immediately given to each man and officer for his day's ration, and the army drew up on the moor called Culloden, close at hand, expecting battle. This level and open field was ill suited to Highland tactics; but in no other place could Inverness be defended.

"The army waited there for some hours, most of the men lying down in sheer exhaustion, until the intelligence arrived that the Duke was giving a feast at Nairn that night in celebration of his birthday. At once the Prince felt a longing to attend this feast, though uninvited, and—so as to make it a really memorable occasion—to appear there with all his men at about midnight, when the Hanoverian brandy was in swift circulation. There was no demur to this plan, even from Lord George Murray, and at eight o'clock that evening the expedition set forth.

"In all those thousands there was scarcely a man who, in the time of his strength, would have been unable to make the distance from Culloden to Nairn in two hours, but now midnight came, and two o'clock, and Nairn was still ahead. Lord George Murray was in the van. The Prince was moving up and down the line, lifting exhausted men to their feet, wakening sleepers, doing all he could to hasten the march. At a little after two the Duke of Perth came galloping back from the front line to report that Lord George Murray had ordered a return to Culloden.

" 'But what does this mean?' cried the Prince. 'By what right does he issue orders without consulting me?'

" 'As to his right, Sire, of course he has none; but he declares that it would be impossible to reach Nairn before dawn.'

" 'Let us fight at dawn, then, and at Nairn! Pray tell Lord George to march on!'

" 'I fear it is too late for that, Sire. The front line has been on the retreat for nearly an hour, by a shorter path back to Culloden.'

"The Prince reached Culloden at six in the morning to find that Murray and his clansmen were already there. They had gone to the far side of the long narrow strip of moorland that stretches between the Firth of Moray and a stone wall bordering the local road. Many of them were asleep on the boggy ground, half hidden among the heather. Other men came straggling back by twos and threes, too exhausted to seek or even to ask for food. The Cromartys and Mackenzies and Macphersons, with half of the Frasers, were absent through no fault of their own. The Prince had with him some five thousand men, none of whom on that sixteenth of April were fit for battle. He knew that his enemy, ten miles away, had nine thousand, well fed and well rested, and also was greatly superior in cavalry and guns. The one thought in which he could take the least comfort was that the Duke, after his birthday feast, would scarcely attack on this dreary morning with a chill wind off the sea. At nine o'clock, shortly after the Prince had sunk to the ground for a little rest, a messenger rode up through the field of sleeping men and told him that the redcoats were close at hand.

"He leapt to his feet, shouting the names of the chieftains. Pipes sounded, drums rattled, orders were called, here and there the clansmen sat up and rubbed their eyes and staggered to their feet. While yet half asleep they began forming in line of battle, clan by clan, in the same order they had followed on the futile night march to Nairn. This meant that the Macdonalds, who had marched last, were now on the left and the men of Atholl under Lord George Murray held the right. But since the time of the Bruce all Scotland had known that the place of honour at the right of the front line belonged to the Macdonalds. They could not but resent being thus displaced, and the thing was all the more an insult because Lord George had usurped their traditional position for himself and the Murrays of Atholl—the one clan that had shown an inclination to desert. It must have been with this in mind that Lord George had hastened back from Nairn; and perhaps he had been planning it even when he started out at the head of the marching column. In no way could he have done more to ensure defeat in the coming battle.

"Lochgarry, Scothouse, and Keppoch rode up to the Prince and demanded that he use his influence with Lord George to get the Macdonalds returned to their rightful place. The Prince replied, looking closely in the faces of the three chieftains, that if they recalled the retreats from Derby and Falkirk they must understand that his influence with Lord George, or, for that matter, with them, was extremely slight. He told them that he regretted and indeed resented the change in the line, but that it had at any rate one advantage: Lord George would not be able to retreat in the midst of the battle with the eyes of the army upon him.

"But now there was no time left for such considerations, for Cumberland's fifes and drums could be heard in the distance, the sound of them borne on a northeast wind with a black cloud behind it and bringing mist and rain. The Union flag came in view, far and dim at the end of the moor, and slowly behind and about it there grew an army of redcoats moving almost at the pace of a dead-march in two long lines of foot-soldiers—fifteen regiments in all—with strong cavalry on the two flanks. They were coming forward with the precision of clockwork, timing their march to the slow advance of the field-guns moving two-by-two in the gaps between the regiments. Scarcely human they looked in the distance, but more like wooden soldiers gaudily painted. The northern men gazing at them through the mist were amazed that so many could move as one. For minute after minute they stood and watched that strangely retarded charge. In the pauses of the drums and fifes there came the rumble of gun-carriages and the steady dull thud of many thousands of feet. Then a horror, not of fear but of foreboding, spread through the ranks of the starved and exhausted men, not a few of whom had the gift or curse of second-sight. Perhaps it was not their own deaths alone that they vaguely foresaw, but the irresistible crushing of that wild liberty which was all they had left. They saw, it may be, and shuddered at the sight, that men can be broken and melted and welded into a dreadful machine for the destruction of men—a machine that moves on many legs, strikes with many hands, and kills with no purpose.

"The Prince, from his place in the middle of the second line, saw the clansmen begin to waver as though they felt that this was not their battle. But it was, he knew, and he sprang to the saddle and called for pipe music and rode along the front of the army facing the men, naming clans that had fought under Wallace and the Bruce, shouting to his friends such as Alasdair and Gillies Macbean who stood among the Macphersons until the skirl of the pipes and the war-cries drowned his voice. Hundreds of blue bonnets were flung in the air and a shout went up like a chant of 'Charlie! Charlie!' From the Southron line far behind came cheer after cheer. A song broke forth from the little regiment of Stuarts of Appin:

> " 'The salt sea we'll harry
> And bring to our Charlie
> The cream from the bothie
> And curd from the pan!'

"I saw him there," said my cousin, while Blandison paused to drink a glass of sherry. "His mount was a gray gelding, and he had on a tartan coat and a vest of buff. His knees were bare. He carried no weapon that I could see. A brigade-major who was marching beside me said: 'How a man could fight for a leader like that!' His name was James Wolfe, and he was eighteen years old. He began the cheering, and the rest of us joined in—not for the Young Pretender but because we knew that many men over there were going to die."

"And those men knew that too," said Blandison, setting down his glass. "The Prince saw that they knew it when he drew rein before the middle of the front line and looked from face to face. There was no fear in those faces, but neither was there any hope. Many had lost their wooden shields and crude weapons in the night-march. Many stood bare to the waist in the rain now changing to sleet and snow. Their bare feet and legs were blue with cold. Scarcely any of them had eaten a meal for two days and nights. It was a wonder that they could so much as stand; yet they did stand firm now that they saw their Prince before them. Two or three score, awakened by the skirl of the pipes, were getting up here and there from the heather and finding their places. It was a sight to break the heart."

"Sir," my cousin broke in again, "I saw them myself, and a more tatterdemalion, bedraggled, and disreputable crew has never pretended to be an army. They were thieves, drunkards, barbarians, some people said even cannibals, and rebels against their King. Why, sir, I heard their yells, and they could not even speak English."

"The sound of the pipes died away," Blandison continued, "when the Prince raised his hand and spoke, using what Gaelic he knew: 'Highlanders, you have come home. This is your land—the best land in the world to live in and die for. Behind you, and guarded by you, are the little rocky fields you have tilled and sown, the women and children you have loved, and all the years that have made Scotland's glory. Before you is an army of men better trained than you are, better clothed and fed and weaponed, and twice your number. They are strangers here. They come to ravish and burn and slay. Most of them have been hired in a foreign land to maintain a foreigner on the throne of England. They will be fighting for hire. Let us fight for home, for love, for glory, and may God save the right!'

"There was no cheering but a low hum of voices as he returned to his place on a low knoll just behind the small battalion of the Earl of Kilmarnock. From there he could see that the redcoats were now much nearer, but still beyond reach of a Highland charge. The field-guns on either side began their parley."

"We scarcely knew on our side," said my cousin, "that the barbarians had any field-guns. We could not hear them, and I think they hurt no one."

Blandison ignored the interruption. "The Battle of Culloden Moor," said he, "was less a military engagement than a slaughter. For more than an hour the Duke stood off beyond musket-range and pounded and tore the Jacobite lines with round-shot and grapeshot to which his opponent could make no effective answer. The Highland cavalry found cover in a shallow valley close at hand, but the men on foot had no recourse except to throw themselves flat on the ground. Few of them did that. Most of them stood and faced the storm of lead as they did the sleet from the sky. Standing still for an hour under heavy fire is an ordeal which few bodies of disciplined troops have ever endured. The clansmen were not disciplined, and their accustomed way of fighting allowed for not a moment of inaction."

"Why, then," asked my cousin, "were they required to stand? We have always wondered."

"At first to give time for Colonel Roy Stuart to cut round the enemy's flank and attack him in the rear. When it became known that he had failed in this, the distance between the armies was still greater than the men, in their condition, could run at top speed.

Neither could they retreat, for that would bring them to Inverness, which they felt obliged to defend. They could only hope that the enemy himself would charge, and he did not."

"And yet we were all the while advancing," my cousin said, "so that finally we came within musket-range."

"True; and before that time the Prince had made three attempts to get the clansmen in motion. The Macdonalds on the left, still incensed at the affront put upon them by Lord George Murray, did not move in response to the Prince's request that they lead the charge. Two messengers sent with the same request to Lord George himself either did not reach him or else were disregarded.

"Thus the dreadful minutes went by, and the Prince had to stand and see his men falling about him, had to hear their screams and see their bones protruding from the torn flesh. Many of them he had long called by their Christian names: Raonull and Fearchar and Ringean and Eachunn. They had called him Tearlach. For months he had marched among them, and told his tale by their campfires. He knew that they were poor and ignorant men, but also he knew that they had loved him, as he loved them. They were tattered and bedraggled, but they were not vulgar. They were gentlemen one and all, and knew a true Prince when they saw one.

"If it is a dreadful ordeal for men to stand still under fire for an hour, not once lifting a weapon, what shall be said of one who not only does that but feels his responsibility meanwhile for the deaths of many friends? The Prince had his equal share of danger. At the very start of the cannonade the head of his groom, standing six feet from him, was shot away. But bodily danger was as nothing compared with the struggle between his impulse to lead the charge himself and the realization that his death would ruin all. For minute after minute the strife within him went on between ought and ought not while the field-guns thundered and bodies were broken in two until, looking straight forward above the men of Kilmarnock, he saw the blown yellow mane of great Alasdair where he stood in the centre of the front line amid a cluster of clans that had always been too brave to be large. Alasdair was looking back at him as though pleading for orders. On the instant it came to the Prince that what he could not do for himself this good friend would delight to do, and he made with his right arm and hand a strong forward gesture which could not be misunderstood.

" 'Dunmaglass! Dunmaglass!' rang out then above all the noises of
battle, and Alasdair MacGillivray was charging from the Jacobite
centre toward Cumberland's left with Gillies Macbean behind him
and then Mackintoshes, Macleans, Camerons, Stuarts of Appin,
Frasers, Gordons, Farquharsons, and Chisholms. Far over at the left
the three clans of Macdonalds under Keppoch, Scothouse, and Glengarry, were moving uneasily about, still sullen but unwilling to endure
the disgrace of inaction. For long they had been torn by cannon-fire
in their flank as well as in front, and now a body of dragoons stood
ready to rush upon them as soon as they charged. Such a challenge
they could not ignore. Suddenly, angrily, a man leapt forward—yes, it
was Keppoch himself, and Scothouse followed a moment later. Their
clansmen followed grimly, reluctantly.

"Alasdair and Gillies Macbean, sweeping Lord George and his
Atholl men along with them in their rush, were fighting now at the
hot mouths of the guns, were beating the gunners back from their
pieces, were past the cannon and breaking through the supporting
regiments and thrusting against the levelled bayonets of the second
line. They were throwing stones and clods of peat in a fierce effort to
break down that hedge of steel when Wolfe's regiment wheeled and
took them in their flank, but Gillies Macbean killed fourteen men in
the breach of the stone wall. Wolfe kept firing, and Gillies leapt upon
the bayonets and pulled down half a dozen by the weight of his body,
and the regiment was firing into the flank. Alasdair went double and
then rose to his full height and hurled first his claymore and then his
target full in their faces as he went down, and the cavalry swept in
through the broken wall, and Lord George was under the hooves of
the horses.

"On the other side of the field the Macdonalds were facing the
muskets and guns of the Southron right and centre. The wind was
blowing a tempest now, and the snow flew level; but when for a
moment they could see they found that a regiment and a troop of
cavalry had come round upon their flank. They staggered into the
crossfire, came to a halt, began to lie down. Already Scothouse was
dead, and his people were drifting away; but Keppoch gave a great
shout and burst from the crowd of his men and ran straight forward
with his round wooden shield on his left arm and his claymore aimed
like a lance at Cumberland's line. He was hit, and fell; rose again
and walked forward, but was hit a second time and fell to his knees

and crawled slowly on into the shower of grapeshot with his claymore clenched in his teeth.

"When at length the Prince could look about him he saw that he was standing alone on the storm-swept field amid many low mounds of white, some of them still stirring a little. He felt lost, bewildered, forsaken. A great longing came upon him to be with Alasdair and to go where Keppoch had gone. He turned his horse, drew his sword, and plunged through the blinding snow toward the sound of Cumberland's guns."

*   *   *

There, William, was the end of Blandison's story. No entreaty or interrogation could induce him to add one word. He left us to suppose, if we wished, that Charles Edward had found the death he went seeking there in the storm—in which case there would be the further question: Who was the man now making another attempt at the throne? Yes, and who, for that matter, would be the hero of that romance or legend or myth about the Prince's wanderings through Scotland, after Culloden, as a hunted man?

Speaking of myth recalls a strange tale drawn forth by Adair from Jeremy Tinker, who we found had been present with a number of Oglethorpe's recruits at the Battle of Culloden Moor. In substance it was that he and a score of other soldiers had seen, shortly after the guns fell silent, a white figure on a great white horse riding up and down beside the broken wall where most of the Highland men had been slain. They could not see the figure clearly through the pelting storm, nor had they any wish to go closer; but the ghost came upon and cornered one soldier prowling for booty in a pile of dead men and asked whether he had seen there the body of a giant with long yellow hair. The soldier gasped out that such a man had been found, still alive, in the midst of a circle of dead redcoats, and that he had been dragged, along with some forty other wounded prisoners, to a barn close at hand which was then set on fire. The ghost made no reply, but hung its head and rode slowly off through the storm.

Blandison listened to that story with no change of countenance. He was now sitting in the Speaker's Chair, watching through the window the hurry of clouds before the west wind. He looked as it were withdrawn, or perhaps a little sad—although it may have been only that his effort to recall and relate those ten thousand details of

FRIDAY   415

the Prince's adventure, however he may have learned them, had, for the moment, tired him. One could not make sure from his face that he heard Jeremy's halting recital of the atrocities committed after the battle by Cumberland's orders: how bands of redcoats went about the field stripping the dead, stabbing the wounded, cracking the skulls of prisoners with musket-butts. These little matters had never been mentioned by my cousin Conway in his frequent references to Culloden. I glanced at his face while Jeremy was talking and then looked quickly away.

James Adair took up the tale where Jeremy's quavering and reluctant voice left off. I have already told you that he was on this side the ocean in the spring of 1746. It chanced that in April, two months before the court martial at Portsmouth, he was visiting in Scotland among his friends, employers, partners, or whatever they are, of the MacGillivray clan. He went with them to Culloden a few days after the battle and found the charred bones of their chieftain, Alasdair, in the barn. Several hundred unburied bodies were still on the field, most of them with smashed skulls. These they gathered and put under ground in a place they called "The Well of the Dead." Then for a few days they followed the trail of Cumberland's army—a thing not difficult for a man of Adair's experience to do because it was well marked by mutilated corpses, smoking ruins, men and women crippled for life by torture and flogging, and little groups of starving children looking for parents they never would find. The Germans, we know, are a wonderfully thorough people, and I think we shall do well at this point, William, to keep it in mind that Cumberland's army, in no small part composed of Germans, was led by a German. Perhaps that explains the odd fact that the Duke burned to the ground not a few sacred buildings of the Established English Church and, in a final paroxysm of thoroughness, forced a perfectly orthodox English clergyman to clean a stable!

You, no doubt, will remember that event longest, but I think I shall keep in mind a picture Adair painted for us of a stretch of tidewater beach guarded by redcoats, and on the sands a ploughman driving a clumsy wooden plough through and through the shellfish beds which are the main source of food in that desolate region. A single ox, hardly more than a skeleton, drags the plough. A soldier walks behind the ploughman, prodding him from time to time with a bayonet. The villagers, mostly women and children because their men are either dead or in hiding, look on. —I am glad to have my cousin's word for it that these people are barbarians, and starvation of course will be no new thing to them. In any case they must be taught a lesson, these terribly dangerous women and children, which they will not soon forget.

The Duke was actuated, no doubt, by the loftiest of patriotic and filial motives, and it seemed to him after three months of butchery that he had only begun his task. "All the good we have done," he wrote from Scotland to the Prime Minister, "is but a little blood-letting, which has only weakened the madness but not at all cured it. I tremble with fear that this vile spot may still be the ruin of this island, and of our family."

And yet, as we know, the Duke's thorough methods did not achieve a thorough success. Although he burned and raped and flogged and slaughtered his way through the Highlands with complete fidelity to the House of Hanover, yet the man he was looking for, the quarry of this whole hunt, somehow eluded his search.

And is not that a mysterious thing when you look at it squarely? The huntsmen were ten thousand in number; they had and they used every means of intimidating the natives that imagination could suggest or heart desire; they continually held forth their huge bribe of thirty thousand pounds to a people who had always been bitterly poor—and yet they failed! For five months—at least according to the legend of which I have heard a brief incident here and there—the Prince lived on in Scotland, constantly associating with men and women who knew that by a word, a look, a gesture, they could lift themselves from poverty to riches, yet not one of them even tried to betray him. On the contrary, scores and hundreds of them endangered their lives in protecting him.

This is, I say, one of the strangest things that history records. In trying to account for it I have thought of two possible explanations. The first is that Charles Edward died at Culloden, as Blandison gave us to understand that he wished to do, so that the legend of his later wanderings is concerned with his "ghost," or, more sensibly speaking, is one of those popular superstitions of the Highlands about which, I am told, the mad poet William Collins has written an unpublished poem. If that theory will not serve—I myself am not strongly inclined to it—then our only alternative is to remember once more that the Highlanders are mere barbarians and therefore do not compre-

hend the value of money. When my father said that "every man has
his price" he was thinking, of course, only about civilized people as
he had known them in England.

*   *   *

Tea helped to alleviate the slight leucocholy—Thomas Gray's
learned word, not mine—induced by the stories of Blandison and
Adair. So did the mulled ale, the Madeira, the fire on the hearth, and
the vivid sunshine striking almost level across the tree-tops outside.
Yet I should not call that last tea-time of the week a merry occasion.
Kitty Clive, for once in her life, looked positively sad. Blandison had
apparently talked himself out for the day. My cousin seemed almost
as thoughtful as Mr. Chute. Byron and Morris and Chester stood at
the far end of the room discussing how to wear a ship under bare
poles. I played with Ponto, trying to make up for several days of
comparative neglect. Adair, standing near me, was urging Jeremy
Tinker to tell us something about his recent stay in Georgia.

Jeremy would not do so, at least in the way of a solo performance.
By dint of many questions, however, and as many tremulous, hesitant
answers, we learned all we cared to know about the series of events
that had saddened his life. He had returned to England with Oglethorpe to help in recruiting men for the protection and development
of Georgia; but no sooner had a few hundred such men been gathered
than they were commandeered by the Duke of Cumberland for his
campaign against the Prince. Their hearts were not in that campaign,
and they fought so feebly at the Battle of Clifton Moor that Oglethorpe had to face a court martial. This meant that he never returned
to Georgia. Some years ago he gave Jeremy Tinker enough money to
defray expenses of a voyage to the colony, asking him to make a full
report upon all that he saw there. Jeremy found that a place originally
designed for poor men was now largely in the possession of rich
planters. Negro slavery, prohibited in the original laws of the colony,
had been widely introduced with the explicit approval of the English
evangelist George Whitefield. The work of the Wesley brothers,
whom Jeremy had adored almost as much as he did Oglethorpe, had
been undone and forgotten. Men who had been saved from the debtors
prisons of England were now sending fellow Christians to jail for
debt. The woman whom Jeremy had hoped to marry was dead. The

poor people who had been his friends had left the tidewater region for the western wilderness. He sought a few of them out, and found them so miserable that he gave away, little by little, all the money he had left. Adair found him living, far up in the mountains, with a Scotch-Irishman by the euphonious name of Jake McNab and helped him to return to England, where he made his peace with Oglethorpe, and so was free to come to Strawberry Hill, to stay on here, and to provide the subject-matter of what I trust is the least enlivening paragraph in this epistle. —Let me add that since the Friday of which I speak a considerable sum of money has been collected here from a large number of contributors. As Jenkins' Ear was the cause of their involuntary contributions, it seems appropriate that Jeremy, one of the Ear's most pathetic victims, should be the beneficiary. I have already invested the sum in such a way as to ensure that his financial tribulations, at any rate, are over.

John Chester was surprisingly helpful in drawing Jeremy's story into the direction which we of Strawberry Castle wanted the talk to follow. With some heat of indignation he asserted that millions of men had been hurt by the War of Jenkins' Ear much as Jeremy Tinker had been, and that for his part he had never been able to see how that war had brought any good to any one. Connecticut had got out of it mainly headstones of young men who had gone to help Admiral Vernon in the West Indies and had never come back. New England had taken Louisburg away from the French and then had seen it given back to them in the treaty of October 18, 1748, nine years to the day after the declaration of war.

"Yes," said I, "and seven years ago tomorrow."

Chester asked whether any one knew how much the war had cost Old England in money, and I was able to answer at once that the bill had come to sixty-four million pounds.

"And what did she get for that?" he went on. "Did Spain stop searchin' our ships at sea?"

"She did not. She is searching them still."

"Did Spain pay her debt to England?"

"Not one pound of it."

"Did France straighten out the boundary of Canada?"

"Since signing the treaty she has never once mentioned the matter."

"Did that treaty bring real peace?"

"A new war with France is now beginning."

"Did Cumberland put down the Young Pretender so as he will never try again?"

"Of that there is still some hope; but we are not yet sure."

"Ah. An' so it turns out Old Bob was right arter all, and the folks that made such a noise about Jenkins' Ear was wrong. Back in Connecticut we liked Old Bob. We can stand most any kind o' king over thar on account he's so fur off an' kings don't count much anyhow; but iffen they's much more nonsense like this about the Ear, why, then Connecticut—do you mark my words!—will have to make what they call other arrangements."

You may recall our hope of Sunday afternoon that the stories told by the yet unknown members of the Club might help to dissuade Blandison from whatever it was that he meant to do. Now, five days later, it did seem that the Goddess Fortuna had been on our side, and that if Blandison had a heart, as Kitty had declared, it must have been touched by the narratives of Byron, Morris, Adair, Jeremy Tinker, perhaps most of all by his own. A little more evidence of what the Rebellion had cost in human suffering might turn him away from his present purpose.

With this in mind I described the trial of the Scotch Lords Kilmarnock and Balmerino, certainly the most dramatic and melancholy scene I have ever witnessed. George Selwyn went on from there with the execution of those same rebels on Tower Hill, telling the story with his accustomed gusto and in minute detail. You may doubt whether such an occasion can be presented so as to make an effect of grandeur, even nobility, but that is because you have never heard George in his best form on a topic worthy of his talent. He is in fact so wonderful at such things that although I was in town on the day of those executions, about the middle of August, 1746, I was more than content that he should do the eyewitnessing for me—he had hired for two guineas a place at the window of the next house to the scaffold —and then report. My friends at White's laughed at me for this, but who would not rather read Dante's account of hell than go to all the trouble of a personal observation?

That story, then, was profoundly affecting, and to Blandison all the more so perhaps because Balmerino and Kilmarnock had been closely associated with Charles Edward. George threw in for good measure a description of the hangings on Kennington Common where a number of rebels died, you recall, in one day. It seemed to me that in this

scene his brushwork was a trifle heavy and his colouring a thought
too high; but of course I know that taste differs widely in such matters. He began by reminding Blandison of a certain Colonel Townley
of Manchester who had joined the Prince, bringing many others with
him, shortly before the retreat began at Derby. Blandison said that he
knew the man well. "In that case," George went on, "you will be interested to know that after Townley had been hanging for six minutes
he was cut down, and then, because he had life still in him, the hangman gave him several blows on the breast with a club. As this did not
have the desired effect, the executioner cut Townley's throat, ripped
him open, took out his bowels and heart, and threw them into the fire.
Last of all he slashed the four quarters and stuffed them into the
coffin. As for the head, you can see it impaled on a spike above Temple
Bar when next you visit the Rose. Of course it doesn't amount to
much nowadays, having been there for nine years and more; but I
understand that we shall soon have another rebellion, and then we
can get some fresh heads."

When George strikes at all, you see, he strikes hard. Now it was my
turn—for we had thought out the order of our several parts—to do
the same thing. Frankly, I did not want to. I would have given a
good deal not to have been there at all. For this was to be no mere
attempt to beat down another man's opinions. It meant hurting him
in his memories, invading his dreams, taking from him some part of
what was left of his youth. Yet I rose, walked across to a bookcase,
and took from it an object wrapped in paper. "Blandison," said I,
going over to his chair, "that name of Townley reminds me of the
silver plate in which, last Tuesday, you showed such a keen interest.
Louis has since found it, and here it is. Pray keep it as your own if
you like."

The eyes that looked up into mine for half a second were those of
a man deeply troubled. "Thank you, Mr. Walpole," said he, and rose
and went to the window, stripping off the paper. For minute after
minute he stood there in the fading afterglow, gazing at the plate,
turning it slowly round and round in his hands. His face gave little
sign of what he was thinking and feeling, but three or four of us
could make a close guess. Somehow, somewhere, he had been misinformed about this rose of silver, so that for years he had been
thinking of it as a token of Jacobite loyalty on the part of men still
alive. Now, at the centre of the rose, he saw the engraved words:

"Martyred for King and Country, 1746," and on the petals he was reading the names of thirty-five men, with that of Townley among them, who had been hanged on Kennington Common.

We sat and watched him in a long silence broken only by the somewhat monotonous comment of Anne Boleyn's clock, which has been saying the same thing for two hundred years without ever being quite understood. At length he laid the plate down on a little table and turned and gazed out of the window. Perhaps half a minute more went by before Mr. Chute, in a clear, quiet voice, summed up our experience of the afternoon. "For the first time, now," he said, "each of us can see the Rebellion of Forty-five in its full gallantry, glory, and sadness. How strange that a thing so beautiful should have happened in our time! How glad we should be that its beauty was untainted by success! For now the story of the Young Chevalier, the last of the world's true knights, is a story the world will never forget. No one, surely, will mar its perfection by making another such attempt."

Blandison's face was pale, and his eyes looked unusually large when he turned toward us. For a moment he seemed about to answer Mr. Chute, but then he said: "Mrs. Clive, I think the terrace must by this time be dry enough for walking. —Shall we go and see?"

*   *   *

Many hours later, at three or four o'clock of Saturday morning, I tapped softly at the door of Mr. Chute's room. "Come in, Horace," was the immediate answer.

He was sitting up in bed as I entered and took the low chair at his right. Near the bed on the left-hand side a candle was burning, as it does every night and all night long like a tiny light-house. It threw most of his face in shadow, but outlined sharply the high-arched bridge of his nose and the broad sweep of his brow. I remember wondering whether it was the shadows or perhaps some exceptional spell of pain that made him look so worn. But one does not put such questions to Mr. Chute. You might live with us for a month and never hear the word "gout."

He had been reading, I saw, and the index finger of his left hand still kept his place in the *Encheiridion* of Epictetus, one of his favorite books. He knows it almost by heart, of course in the original Greek, so that perusal of it by candle-light is no great strain on his eyes. For the most part he merely catches a phrase or two and then lays down the book to proceed with a long meditation.

This room of his always makes me think of a tent used by a soldier on a campaign, so small it is and so bare of decoration. Yet there are a few engravings on the wall, one of them showing the Ponte Vecchio in Florence where he and I have spent many a happy hour. For some reason he has painted nearly everything red and black—just the colors, you remember, that are favored by the young scalp-hunters of the Creek Nation. The bed is low, narrow, and hard. There are two chairs, a writing-desk, and a shelf holding some twenty books. —I've never thought of it before, but that's the number possessed, or aspired to, by Chaucer's Clerk, and he too liked to have his books bound in black or red.

This visit of mine was not so unseasonable as you may think, for Mr. Chute seldom falls asleep before dawn. Only then, having fought his battle, does he reach for the little black box of opium that lies beside the candle. Think of it, William! Although your gout is by no means so bad as his, and I believe you never take opium, you must know what heroism is implied in that abstention. You can imagine how often he yearns for the gray light at the window which tells him that he may put off his armour. Also you understand why he is glad of almost any interruption, at any hour, of his dialogue with pain. In these matters I am still an ignoramus, but he has assured me that I shall learn.

There was something that would have made a brave man smile and Kitty Clive cry in the way he reached out his hand to me after I had told him about the torment of my last few hours. I felt that he was welcoming me into some broad and ancient brotherhood whereof all I needed to know was that it must be noble because he was in it. "Yes," he said, gently, "that's the gout, Horace. That's the way it first comes —like Lucifer, with fire from heaven. Some would say from hell, but I think not."

I heard no tone of pity in his voice while he told me what I had to expect. This attack, he thought, would not last long, and indeed I might hope to write it away in my letter to the Reverend William Cole. So far he was right, and no doubt he foretold the remoter future with equal accuracy when he said that the disease would return at shorter and shorter intervals, each time with a pang more fierce and a more diabolic knowledge of how to shake and shatter my manhood.

"In that effort it will certainly fail," said he. "You have on your side that precious faculty of laughter which I have so often envied, and now you will learn to laugh not only at pain but at yourself for having it. Then too, there's your power of throwing yourself into other lives. While writing to Cole, for instance, you won't be thinking about your gout but his; and he in turn will forget his misery while sharing that of Byron, Morris, and Tinker. Yes, and Blandison's even. How sad he looked last night when he came in from his walk with Kitty! And she too, you remember, could scarcely bid us good night, her voice was so choked with tears. —In things of that kind you will more and more lose the thought of your pain, or at any rate will recognize it as your share of the human lot. Thus you will never sink into self-pity, that most contemptible weakness, and when your suffering is keenest you will remember that out of the same root which gives us our word "agony" the Greeks made a word meaning a wrestler, an athlete, a champion."

That is not *verbatim,* but it shows the general drift of his thought. In a way, of course, he was sorry that his friend should be doomed to suffer somewhat as he had long done, yet I caught now and then a tone almost of congratulation in his voice, as though he felt that suffering was a new thing to me, and what I needed. He knew better than that, as you do also, and in a word or two I reminded him of that incurable ache at the heart which began when you and I were boys at Eton and remains with me still, night and day.

"You mean," said he, "the foul Tory lie that you were not your father's son."

I did mean that, and went on to say that anyone who had borne since childhood the knowledge that his mother's honour had been thus aspersed, and yet could do nothing to refute the scandal, could not even mention its existence, was a man not unacquainted with pain.

Mr. Chute's answer was given in an untranslateable glance, a warm slow smile, and a momentary pressure of his hand upon mine. A good deal of our communication is of that wordless kind. In the fifteen years of our friendship we have gone beyond words.

William, you once saw my mother, in our house at Chelsea. You must remember how lovely she was, how merry and kind and true.

Think, then, what it must have been all these years, and even more after her death . . .

Never before have I alluded in writing to that dreadful experience. Mr. Chute is the only one with whom I have ever discussed it. That you know it, and Gray and West and George Selwyn, of course I have always been aware. As for Posterity—well, perhaps the present hint may induce a few people of two centuries hence to think better of Horace Walpole than they would otherwise have done.

Before long I was telling about my armour dreams—the two that you have already heard about and another, much more terrifying, that came on Thursday night. In that last one a tremendous helmet with black plumes was crushing the roof just over my head. I woke to find myself at the open window, looking up and trying to call for help.

Dreams of that sort—that is, of ponderous objects crushing things feeble and flimsy—are recurrent with me, as Mr. Chute knew. More than once we have agreed that they are somehow related to my feeling of inadequacy to the name I bear, and possibly also to the contrast between the gigantic palace my father built at Houghton and this card-castle of mine. The special form they took on this occasion was probably due, he thought, to the frequent mention of armour during the week—"a week," he added, "in which the past has made a determined effort to invade the present."

"That reminds me," I replied, rising from the chair, "of the dream I had tonight. Just before coming in here I found myself standing again at my open window, this time gazing down at a beautiful white creature with a long horn of ivory tapering up from its brow. I saw it dimly, for there was no moon, yet with no uncertainty about what it was. For a minute or more it stood there, perhaps a hundred feet off among the trees. It was looking toward me, with its head held high. I have never seen a thing more majestic. At last it turned and went slowly away toward the river. —I woke up with a sense of overwhelming loss and impoverishment. The world seemed to me a poorer place."

Again Mr. Chute took my hand. "That dream, if it was one," said he, "needs no interpretation. I might have had it myself. —And now, Horry, here is something that will help you to sleep. Good night, and God bless you!"

SATURDAY

With the help of Mr. Chute's opium and certain vigorous instructions given by him to Louis, I slept right through the next morning. Ah, sir, what a blessed oblivion! For six hours my bosom's lord sat lightly on his throne, and if I had any dreams they were such as presage some joyful news at hand.

I awoke to hear the Twickenham clock striking twelve, to see the curtains of my bed sliding back, and to behold at the bedside a pallid and tremulous Louis holding toward me a cup of tea partly spilled and positively chattering in the saucer. To and fro across the little room behind him strode Richard Beston in top-boots, his hat pulled low, his breath coming in audible gasps, his hands restlessly clutching and letting go their respective pistol-butts, the very picture of anxiety, dismay, and all the other emotions to which gentlemen of the road are supposed to be immune.

"Drink this," said Louis, spilling a few more drops down the side of the cup as he shoved it—I regret the vulgar word, but it was that kind of action—toward me.

I stared at him.

"Drink it!"

The tone was brusque, harsh, peremptory, without the least echo of those amicabilities which on every earlier day of our acquaintance had cheered my first waking moments. However, I took the tea, sipped it, found it cold, and said so.

"Get it down!" growled Richard Beston, looking pistol-shots at me from under the hatbrim.

I did so. When it was down, "You tell him," said Louis.

"I'll see 'm damned fust. He's your marster, not mine."

"Ah, but your marster did it, not mine."

"I dunno 'bout that, an' no more do you; but I'll lay you a bull to a fadge as 'twere that damned blowen wi' the ogles what snagged 'im!"

"Are you losing your mind? Do you mean to suggest that Mrs. Clive captured your queer Tom Pat and hopped the twig with him against his will? Nonsense! You talk like Tom o' Bedlam!"

"Arrr!"

"See here," said I firmly, lifting myself in bed so as to look more formidable. "What do you two mean by bringing your miserable quarrels into my bedchamber? If you have anything to tell me, do it now—and then leave."

"Your Honour," Louis replied, looking rather firm on his own account, "though not wishing to appear unrespective, my conscience is clear. If any one is to confess the terrible thing which Parson Blandison has committed it will not be me—that is to say, in other words, I."

Well, at any rate, Richard Beston finally confessed that his master had "cut his stick, along o' that 'ar rum blowen wi' the ogles." Freely translated by Louis, this appeared to mean that neither Blandison nor Kitty Clive was anywhere to be found—not in her house or mine, not in the summerhouse or in the Gothic sarcophagus, not at Madlands or Twickenham Ait or Pope's grotto or the beer cellar or under any bed, to say nothing of what I always say nothing of when writing to a clergyman. My little boat was tied up at my little landing, so that they could not have escaped in that. They were not in either of the goldfish pools. The Capting had been interviewed at Twickenham and had seen "neither hide nor hair of 'em, but wished 'em j'y." Furthermore, he had cheerfully agreed to "shut his bone-shop" about the matter while at the same time keeping his peepers open. Similar asseverations and promises had been made by Hal Pudsey, by the landlord of the King's Head, and by the various dowagers of the neighbourhood to whom Louis had addressed discreet inquiries. Beston had drawn the cover—if that is the right hunting term—of Bushey Park, and had drawn a blank. They were not in the King's Maze; nor had the Yeoman of the Guard who had such good reason to remember Blandison set eyes upon him that morning. In short, these two devoted young men had travelled many miles on foot and horseback during the last three hours, had asked hundreds of questions—all of them, Louis assured me, extremely "discreet"—and had learned simply nothing. From the start they had felt that I ought to be told, but both of them stood in awe of Mr. Chute. He had fallen asleep shortly after issuing his directions about my slumber, and they had not dared to wake him.

So there was enough news for one day, and you see that my sleep had been dreamless because one never does dream of such things until after they happen. But the disappearance of Kitty and Blandison was not all, nor was it in Beston's opinion by any means the worst. All the horsemen were equally gone, with their horses, and no one at Madlands knew why or whither. Sir Edward himself had sufficiently recovered from his honourable wound to "tip a mizzle" on horseback. All that was left of the band of highwaymen, in fact, was Blandison's great black stallion, which had been found quietly munching oats in the Madlands stable and making no disclosures. The Madlands coach and four had disappeared.

And then Beston came to what he considered the really serious phase of the situation, for which he had been gradually preparing me all along. This was, as I soon discovered with Louis' knowledge of thieves' Latin to help me, that "they" were coming, had probably started already, and would soon be upon us. With Blandison gone and the Upright Man far away, there would be no one to hold "them" in check, so that what "they" would do to the treasure of Strawberry Hill and Madlands House and Hampton Palace and the poor old King put an intolerable strain upon Richard Beston's imagination and vocabulary.

With his own safety, I judge, the highwayman was not primarily concerned, but he did hate to see pearls cast before swine. Like all true conservatives, he wanted wealth to remain in a few pockets—until he got round to collecting it himself.

Ever since an unpleasant event of some years ago in Hyde Park I have hoped that I might live to see a highwayman in real perturbation of mind. Now that I had the spectacle before me, however, I found my enjoyment much diminished by my own apprehensions. For "they," I suppose, is the most terrifying word in the language. All my life I have lived in dread of what "they" might vote, think, feel, say, whisper, suspect, or laugh at; and now "they" were on the way, mewards, in overwhelming numbers, out of control. To my question about who "they" were, Beston waved his arms, and began a long list, of which Slamming Ned, Three-Finger, and Harry the Skiv are all I can remember. Louis stopped him, and told me, as if I should

have known, that "they" were all of St. Giles' from Saffron Hill to
Seven Dials, and from Bloomsbury to the River. "They" were the
nickers and running rumblers and cock-a-brasses and blue-pigeon-
flyers and foot-scamps and sharps and flash boys of London. "They"
were what some people called the Mob, although that term was really
applicable only when "they" went mobbing. Ordinarily, Beston said,
he was not afraid of them—as indeed why should he be, considering
that he was to the manner born? —but when "they" turned out for
Horn Fair without their Upright Man, and came up-river instead of
going down, why, then . . . Oh, Mr. Walpole!

Thus there was depth beyond depth to the horror which Beston en-
visaged, presaged, and shadowed vaguely forth to Louis and me. I
say "vaguely" because words failed him, and likewise gestures, grimaces, blank stares, and attitudes of dismay. For not yet had he fully
disclosed the perilous stuff wherewith his heart was burdened. At
first he could not, then would not; but finally he must, and it came
out that he was now the only conspirator left on the scene of action
who knew the Plan, had the means in hand of its execution, and
could either set it awork or else let the preparations of many months
and minds for ever fail. With him alone it now rested, or so he believed, whether a certain elderly personage should have a few more
chances to find his way out of Hampton Court Maze or, on the other
hand, there would be left of that personage at nightfall only a few
disjecta membra regi: here a tooth, there a limb, and yonder perhaps
a wig even more than formerly awry. Oh, dreadful dilemma! Oh,
fearful decision! —How would you, William, decide?

And yet I would not have you spend all your sympathy on Beston.
Think also of me, lying there with the mounting realization upon me
that if the highwayman should be unable at last to make up his mind
then the final vote would have to be cast by Horace Walpole, to break
a tie. Yes, it might not be enough for Jenkins' Ear that my heart
should be broken. Greatness of some sort might still be thrust upon me,
either as the champion of the House of Hanover or as a regicide. The
latter alternative, now that Blandison was gone, would put me squarely
in the seat of Oliver Cromwell. People would soon forget the supposed
iniquities of my father while they prepared to suffer under the tyranny
of his son.

Pray try to imagine the effect upon a mind just aroused from sleep
of those vast dim words: "they," the Plan, the Upright Man, and

Horn Fair. None of them conveyed a clear image or idea, and yet in each one there was somehow—I mean at the time, in the circumstances—an overtone of mystery, danger, and threat. Taken together they induced almost that sense of awed foreboding by which I had been overwhelmed in my dream of the Plumed Helmet. There was the feeling, too, that in some manner they portended a continuation of that dream. I seemed to hear a monotonous voice talking, murmuring, whispering beside a campfire in the dim-piled crespuscular Great Smoky Mountains of sleep and telling me about the wild saturnalia called Horn Fair and a flood of the Thames in which the water came not so much down the stream as up with the filth and debris of London afloat on its sullied current and how "they" themselves were coming on Saturday from London to eat huge quantities of eels and raw goldfish and I on my hill and he on his Ait would do well to make ready because "they" would come with a Plan if not with an Upright Man as both the gentlemen of the sea and those of the midnight roads had warned him.

And this was Saturday, October the eighteenth, our last day. This was St. Luke's Day, when the witches' cauldron of London boils suddenly over and stenches confined to one place through most of the year spread contagion far and wide. This was the day when the beast in man is let loose to roam and prowl and yelp and do its beastly will. In other years they had gone downstream to Cuckold's Point and Ratcliffe and Charleton, but now "they" were on the way to Strawberry Hill with masks on their faces and horns on their heads and the demon of riot within them. Sixteen years ago the Fair had been postponed for a day so that the mob might stand outside the Houses of Parliament and shout "Down with Old Bob!" and "We want War!" —Had Blandison helped to arrange that postponement? Was he working now to destroy the son as he had the father, and with the same foul weapon?

I did not, of course, believe any such thing. All I am attempting is to indicate, swiftly, the mob of thoughts that rushed through me pellmell with hideous cries and gestures in those first moments of apprehension. A man is not wholly responsible for the thoughts that enter his mind by this and that postern. His duty is done when he takes by the collar those that he thinks unworthy and incontinently throws them out again.

"Louis," said I, "you and Richard Beston have been more zealous

in this matter, and far more anxious, than the situation demands. I
do not blame you for that, but I ask you to make no further search
or inquiries, to say nothing about this matter to any one, and to quiet
the talk of the other servants. You have my word for it that Mrs. Clive
and Parson Blandison have gone on an errand meant for our common
good, and that they will be back in due season. Beyond that statement
I do not care to go just now; but you will soon see that I am right."

William, you would have been surprised at the confidence of my
tone and bearing. The two young men were visibly impressed, relieved, and subdued.

"Louis," I went on, "please ask the gentlemen to meet me in the
breakfast room at half past twelve. Ask Mrs. Margaret to serve
breakfast there at that time. Tell the shepherd boy to drive the cow
and the sheep up the road and to pasture them well away from the
river. Then step over and tell Mrs. Clive's housekeeper that I hope
she will find it convenient for me to call upon her at one o'clock.
Finally, you will dip all the goldfish out of the ponds and bring them
into the house, keeping them well away from the cat. Ponto, of
course, I shall want to have with me at breakfast. —For the present,
that is all."

You will think from these many words—reduce them if you can,
William, for I have not the time—that our conference must have
lasted an hour. In fact Louis and Beston were with me about ten
minutes; and in less than that I was dressed and downstairs and Mrs.
Margaret, just returned from Kitty's house, handed me a letter. I
pulled it open and read:

Dear Horry Time presses & will Ownly saye am doeing What one
poor Woman can forr her Countrie till Deth doe us Part yrs in gt Hast
Cath Clive. P.S. tho This be Madness yet theres Method int

"Method"? Oh, yes indeed, supposing that mystification had been
her purpose, and to leave me wandering in the wilderness of conjecture. If we were not now in the millrace of this chronicle, helplessly
hurried along toward its final plunge, I could enumerate nine different
ways in which those words, ostensibly so incondite, might be taken.
One of those ways was comfortable enough, but I could think only of
that intolerable worst. Picture me standing there in the lower hall and

peering at the sheet in the dim if not religious light of the Gothic lanthorne, straining my eyes and spraining my imagination to find or fancy some period, comma, or dash after the word "Countrie" that would make all the difference. But, to be honest with myself, there was none. Thus was I punished in full for all my punctuational errors of commission and omission.

And yet was this an inadvertent error of Kitty's, due to "gt Hast" or to that strong dislike of writing which, as she so often had said, put her all of a twitter at the mere sight of a quill? I tried to think so, but could not. No mere pen-fright and no pressure of time had brought in that phrase from the marriage service and then left it so tormentingly ambiguous. This was the sort of thing that old Horace had meant by *ars celare artem*. This was method concealing itself, not completely.

But why, you ask, should so good a friend leave me thus bewildered? Why write at all, if only to heap fear upon fear? Sir, you may well ask that question, and I may well decline to answer it. The explanation would take us deep into that interminable Book of Woman whereof you, as a bachelor, know barely the title and which I, as a betweenity, have read only halfway through. Be content, then, with the hint that in becoming my friend Cath Clive had by no means ceased to be a woman—or, in so far as it is different, an actress.

*   *   *

Our breakfast was not a merry affair. My friends were stunned by the news which they had heard already from Louis. They made as little sense as I did out of Kitty's letter. Mr. Chute at first said nothing, and when I reported Richard Beston's prognostications his silence deepened. In other words, he was thinking; and at such times the rest of us do not interrupt. From George Selwyn there came not one quip, crank, or wanton wile. He did not even yawn. The only memorable remark was made by my cousin when he said that this was what came of not calling the fellow out, or of letting him in to begin with.

The day into which, after breakfast, we wandered listlessly forth was worthy of a better mood than we brought to greet it. Yesterday's rain had revived every hue, for indeed it is one of the salient charms of October as an aging beauty that her colours do not wash off.

There were half a dozen new roses in Kitty's garden, each supplied with its amorous butterfly; her pigeons glistened high and white in the blue; the blackbird sang and the skylark towered and the dew-drunken cricket scraped at his tiny fiddle as only creatures could that had not yet heard the news. The day brimmed over with beauty as though to make us feel all the more how empty it was of Kitty Clive. Take one more thing, a trifle and yet strangely touching: on the table by the window in the summerhouse we found her blue knitted scarf with Congreve's *Way of the World* lying open beside it.

Ah, so she had been there that morning while we were asleep. Louis had not told me whether she had sung her "Come hither," but Blandison had probably found her there. He had learned the way, and could now come without calling.

We heard the Twickenham clock strike one. Recalling my engagement with Kitty's housekeeper, I excused myself and left the summerhouse. Walking swiftly round the corner, I had just come to the oaken shell by the window when there reached my ears a faint far-away rumour, a delicate medley of many sounds at first so thin and ethereal, so sifted by distance, that they might have been only a rustling of leaves in a gust of the west wind or a sudden burst of the skylark's ecstasy on the topmost round of his ladder. The blackbird stopped his song to listen, and I my walking. Ponto ceased to snuff here and there for Kitty and looked up at me with that expression of lifted ears and bared upper teeth and head cocked left-sidewise which, being translated into human, means more clearly than you and I can say it, "Aha !" And, of course, he was exactly right. I postponed the housekeeper, sat down in the shell, and agreed with him—if not heartily, at any rate completely—that "they" were coming.

You may say, perhaps, that he smelt them, but I doubt it. The slight breeze we had was from the west, and I judged by the sound that "they" could not be closer than Richmond Bend, or, at most, straightening out into Twickenham Reach. No, it was pure deduction on Ponto's part, and unless you begin with a due respect for his intellectual powers you will quite fail to comprehend what I have to tell you about his conduct during the rest of this day.

Ponto and I sat there for perhaps a minute, wishing to make sure before we said anything that those distant sounds were really coming up-river. But they were so, beyond a doubt. The rumour, as I have called it, gradually increased into a confusion of noises in which I could distinguish shouts and yells intermixed with the tones of musical instruments, shrill of whistles, blare of horns, clatter of rattles, beat of drums. Clearly this was no mere revelry on Twickenham Ait, nor could all the people of the villages round about have raised a clamour which, without being noisy, gave such an effect of vociferous multitudes. This was London's hoarse, voluminous roar invading the peace of the upper Thames.

Ponto growled, deep in his throat. I rose, turned to the window, and spoke to my friends. They too had been listening. They came out of the house. We walked to my terrace and looked down-river. Something was moving there, or rather a thousand things like one. Just on the hither side of Richmond Hill, perhaps two miles away, the stream was so choked with craft that it looked as though a man might walk from bank to bank without wetting his feet. It was hard to see how so many barges and wherries and skiffs could move at all against the current, tightly wedged together as they appeared from our distance to be. Yet move they somehow did, though slowly. Perhaps two hundred feet in advance of them, and steadily maintaining that interval, there came on a long line of glistening white.

Mrs. Margaret arrived on the terrace, smiling with pleasure at the interruption of her daily routine. Louis came, several shades paler, several years older, than I had ever seen him before. One week of Jenkins' Ear, I saw, and of sleepless nights and fierce concentration upon thieves' Latin, had broken his youth; and I feared that if the Plan should go through he would be positively senile by nightfall. I sent him back after my perspective-glass. He ran.

Then Richard Beston came, saw, and trembled: "*Oh,* sir!" gasped he, standing close at my side as though for protection, and then again, "Oh, *sir!*" The momentary deviation into English was highly effective.

But what could ail the fellow, professionally bold yet now the image of fright? Perhaps the Plan was far more terrible than he had given me to suppose—for, after all, it was he, not I, that knew that Plan, and Horn Fair and St. Giles' and the Upright Man and "them." Very well, then, said I to myself, let Beston do the being afraid, and do you, Horace Walpole, occupy yourself with other matters. "Go and get your master's stallion out of the Madlands stable," said I to Beston, "and bring him across the road. On your way, tell the Madlands people to lock and bolt their doors. —Don't frighten them, though. Merely say that most of the crowd will go on to Hampton

Court and kill the King. Tell them that all of us here at Strawberry
Hill are to be hanged and quartered, but that good Jacobites will
not be molested."

Beston seemed pleased at having something else to do than shake in
his boots. He was just turning away when my cousin touched him on
the arm and quietly said: "You won't need those pistols. Kindly leave
them with me."

"But . . ." replied the Gentleman of the Road, probably intending
to retort that surrendering property to other persons was not in his
way of business. A brief glance into the General's steel-blue eyes,
steady as the Pole Star, convinced him, however, that the present
occasion was exceptional. He handed over his implements of slaughter
and drooped away with his hat off, mopping his brow, for the time
being little better than a law-abiding citizen. I doubted whether John
Wesley himself had ever converted a sinner with more dispatch.

But this was an interlude, and meanwhile the noise from down-
river had been steadily increasing. We began to hear a rumble of
wheels along the road just over my wall—a sound to which in the
last four or five days we had grown unaccustomed. A dozen, a score
of vehicles flashed by the open gate with whip-snapping, curses,
laughter, tooting of horns, and yells. Down in Twickenham the chime-
bells were ringing, and not, I assure you, with that learned observance
of the campanological rules which you and I so delight in, but wildly,
drunkenly, as though a pack of fiends had got hold of the ropes. The
Spirit of Misrule was rushing upon us. The Accursed Cauldron of
London—to scatter my Capital Letters abroad in the manner of Cath
Clive—was boiling over. In short, They were invading Us.

One of the vehicles mentioned above as flashing by the open gate
did not do so. It stopped there, and six persons—I think that is the
exact term Louis would have employed—descended. Two of these
were unmistakably, even conspicuously, female. The others were pretending to be so at least to the extent of hoop-skirts and a liberal use
of padding. All of them wore masks, had horns on their heads, and
were slightly intoxicated. The contents of the large hamper they had
brought with them suggested that the word "slightly" would not long
apply.

They lugged the hamper in through the gateway, set it down on a
flower bed, and then stood looking about them like people who have
reached, as the learned say, their *terminus ad quem*. It was evident

that they had been at some trouble to get here, and did not think the effort wasted. Because of their masks we had not their facial expressions to guide us; but their squeals and guffaws and pointings-out of this and that clearly showed that Strawberry Hill and its residents fulfilled their expectations.

Ponto preceded us, barking furiously, as we walked across the lawn. "Throw them out!" growled my cousin to me. "Just show them your pistols, Henry," said George. "Please do not," I replied. "They are our guests, and we must be polite." Mr. Chute squeezed my arm when he heard me say that. Not often is he so demonstrative.

We bowed as we approached, and I introduced my friends. No introductions were offered by the other party, but the true females tittered and a pseudo-one remarked, briefly, "Horns!" Then there was laughter, prolonged and uproarious, while we of Strawberry Hill stood there looking awkward, mystified, red-faced perhaps. I simply did not know, and none of us did—not even Mr. Chute—the correct and expected reply to "Horns!" This ignorance put us at a disadvantage. It made me feel, even though I stood on what I had been accustomed to regard as my own property, like a soldier who has not heard, or has forgotten, the password.

Every reader of Shakespeare knows that "Horns!" had once an insulting sense, universally understood, in which it applied to a wronged husband, or, to be plain with you, a cuckold. Now one sees, of course, how ludicrous it is, and how conducive to social merriment, for a man to be deceived by his wife; but surely that is one disgrace to which we bachelors are not liable. Moreover I believe that in this sense the word is obsolescent in England, possibly because the condition to which it refers has become so common. Therefore the mystery remains, what it was that these persons were laughing at. I have only one suggestion to make, and it is based upon the fact that all six of them were wearing horns while we four—a smaller number, you observe, a minority—were not thus provided. That may not seem important, but do you wait until the six cornutes become six hundred, six thousand, six and so forth, and then go among them with your brows absurdly, not to say obscenely, unadhorned! Sir, you will find yourself a laughing-stock, an object of contempt—in short, an outsider.

To that hint I suppose you will object, in your captious way, that on this occasion there were no thousands, or even hundreds, of horned persons present, but only six; yet those six laughed. True; but I reply with crushing cogency that in these matters physical presence is not required. 'Tis enough for a shallow laugher to feel sure that he is on the laughing side, and these six were positively arrogant in that confidence. They knew that hundreds, thousands, and so forth, were coming by road and by river to back them up, to amplify their laughter into a cachinnation, and to send the cry of "Horns! Horns!" reverberating from bank to bank of the terrified Thames from Hampton Court to Richmond Hill. They laughed as harbingers, as forerunners, as samples of what we had to expect. They laughed in unison, as I suppose the beasts must do if they laugh at all.

And we four friends standing there bare-browed, nonplussed— what had we on our side wherewith to confront this insolence? Not unanimity, I assure you, for, apart from the indignation which all of us felt, you would scarce find a quartet of friends in the world less like each to each than we were. Each of us, consequently, had to fight and lose his own battle, unaided. Like that already famous flower of Thomas Gray's, my extreme politeness of welcome wasted its fragrance upon a desert air. General Conway looked like massed artillery, which he was not permitted to fire. George Selwyn aimed with his eyes shut some satirical remark which might have done damage if only it had been heard. Mr. Chute always needs time, and there was none. That left only Ponto to speak and act for us, but a Ponto enraged, rampant, latrant, reboant, horrisonous, and indeed, considering that he is hardly two feet long even if you count his tail, making a good deal of noise. The six called him sundry names, none of them really applicable. At last a pseudo-female tried to kick him, and that was too much. I scooped him up and indignantly, with no bow or word of excuse, bore him away. Both of us were trembling in every fibre. Our three friends came after us. So did Louis, with the perspective-glass. So did the triumphant cry of "Horns! Horns!" Our retreat was orderly but inglorious.

During this encounter I had been too much occupied to observe that some sixty more persons, masked and horned, had come in at the gate or leapt over the wall or else wandered across from Kitty's garden. Half a dozen vehicles had come to a stand in the road and were discharging their semihuman contents. As many riders, horned and masked, sat their horses just outside the wall and looked over at us and laughed and shouted "Horns!"

You will please understand, and so save me the nauseating repetition, that this cry continued during most of the afternoon. We heard it chanted in chorus and screamed and bellowed. When there came a lull at Strawberry Hill we heard it from Madlands, from Bushey Park, from the river, or from Ham Common on the Surrey side, always followed by a harsh shallow laughter with no merriment in it but only a shrill derision.

Was it not King Solomon who said the laughter of a fool is like the crackling of dry thorns under a pot? I wish I could write like that royal author, for then I might give you some notion of how it sounds when fools get together by thousands and laugh. I had known before that laughter can be sad, but this had the tone of despair. Intermixed with the iteration of one stupid syllable, it suggested insanity and gave me a new understanding of the term "horn-mad."

To the true spirit of carnival, even when it approaches the frantic and bacchanalian degree, I am by no means averse. In fact I have never felt happier or more at home than during that pre-Lenten season in Florence long ago when for many days and nights I was seldom out of a domino except when I was in bed. That was in the brief springtime of my life, to be sure, which happily coincided with springtime in Italy; yet even now that I begin to hobble toward forty a masked ball is to me a king-delight. There is something so frank and brave about wearing only one mask for a whole evening instead of the dozen or twenty that I should otherwise don and doff in that time. And then all those other people, about whom one has the darkest suspicions that they must be So-and-so, pretending that they are monks and nuns and clergymen of the Established Church! Yet we English are too prone to leave off our manners when we put on disguises. In our masquerade we tend to show what we should do and say in real life if we dared. The present occasion will show what I mean.

I suppose you know that the carnival and masquerade called Horn Fair is one of those quaint old customs which, in their sum, compose our notion of Merry England. It is thought to commemorate King John's munificent gift of a tract of land, tax-free, to a certain miller whose wife he had seduced. This tract lies a few miles down-river from London, not far from the Isle of Dogs, and until recent times it was marked by the antlers of a stag affixed to a pole, which pole in turn was stuck into the mud at what we still know as Cuckold's Point.

There for ages on every St. Luke's Day the denizens of London's garrets, cellars, slums, and stews have gathered to celebrate the generosity of the monarch and the complaisance of the husband. They go equipped with horns either artificial or natural, the latter kind being secured from the butchers of Smithfield. Also they carry various instruments for making a hideous din, and here the cow's horn and its various imitations in metal comes again into play. Most of the men are dressed as women, and the women as prostitutes. Of late years the Fair has been more and more attended by ladies and gentlemen—as mere spectators of course, always masked. It is even said that the Royal Family has lent its countenance, suitably disguised, to this festival of royal foundation. The fashion of masking has recently spread to the lower classes, and they express their preferences in bestiality with a remarkable profusion of pasteboard snouts, jowls, tusks, and muzzles wherein it would appear that their favourite beast is the hog. For diversion they have, first, a mumming or crude stage-play which includes a king and a miller and their respective wives. This is said to be extremely amusing for those who are amused by that sort of thing. Then follows a sermon in Charleton church, of which I suppose the same remark may be made. Next they have a meal *al fresco* and get thoroughly drunk and shout "Horns!" and laugh and beat one another over the head and tear off whatever clothes the prostitutes have on and laugh again and see to it that the quaint old customs of cuckoldry and kindred amusements shall not lapse through mere desuetude—elegant language that, William!—and then by river and by land straggle back from St. Luke's Day to St. Giles' in London—some of those old saints would scarce recognize themselves in their modern patronymics—and reluctantly put away their horns, their masks, and the satisfaction of looking, sounding, and acting like what they really are.

Most of this erudition I have from Mr. Chute, who has spent much time since that memorable Saturday in reading and thinking about Horn Fair. He holds, by the way, that the attribution to King John is highly dubious, and opines that what we have here is a debased version of the ancient Bacchanalia, ineffectively prohibited by the Roman Senate some two centuries before the Christian era. In support of this view he points out that the Bacchanalia were at first for women alone, and that when men finally were admitted they had to wear feminine garments. The god Bacchus himself did this when he

attended, and he also wore a single horn on his brow. All the partici-
pants were masked, and Mr. Chute is writing to Thomas Gray to ask
whether they wore horns. That they drank a good deal in honour of
their patron deity may be assumed, and so may their arrangements
for the perpetuation of the species. The Roman Senate was not opposed to any of these practices, but it tried to put a stop to the
Bacchanalia on the ground that they were being used as a blind for
political conspiracies and attempts at revolution.

I am sorry, William, to unload all this learning upon you at a time
when our story is so exciting, but I have to get rid of it somehow. At
least it illustrates Mr. Chute's habit, in his antiquarian capacity, of
taking everything farther and farther back. He seems to think that
nothing ever began, or—what is even worse—will ever end.

*   *   *

Looking down-river from the terrace through the perspective-glass,
I saw that Richard Beston's "Oh, sir!" had been accurate enough.
More vessels of more different sorts than I had thought the Thames
could float were making deliberate way up from Twickenham Landing. Like the Spanish Armada, they were coming in the shape of a
crescent moon with the convex side upstream. A few had stopped at
the village itself, and more at the Ait; but hundreds moved steadily
on as though borne by a slow tidal wave. On before them rode a huge
flotilla of white swans—not hastening but certainly not lingering, and
less as though they were driven than with the effect of a proud avoid-
ance, by cleanly creatures, of sordid communications. All the swans
between London Stairs and Twickenham Ait must have been there.
They were a noble company, and on that very account they were
having as little as possible to do with Horn Fair.

The vessels came on in good order, held in firm control by a huge
man standing at the prow of a barge that kept slightly ahead, like a
flagship. Whenever an impatient wherry or skiff broke ranks and
moved a yard or two forward of the van, this admiral or commodore
sent it instantly back to its place, perhaps with some shouted order
which I could not hear but also with an imperious sweep of the arm
and a peremptory finger.

I rested the glass on Louis' shoulder and gazed at the commodore.
He was indeed a large man and burly, but not so tall as I had thought.

The impression of great height was given in part by the lift of the stem but still more by the straight, yard-long, and moon-white horn that sprang from his brow. Not only did that horn add a cubit to his apparent stature but somehow it invested him with an air of dignity. It seemed a natural and inevitable thing that the herd of bicorned creatures pressing about him on either hand and crowding behind like cattle at the pasture-bars should obey without question a horn so proudly single.

The upper half of his face was hidden by a visor of black cloth. He was dressed in plain brown, not quite like a gentleman nor yet in the manner of one whom Louis would be likely to call a "person." His wig, I think, was of the species known as "scratch," and his stockings were black. These details, however, were of no moment compared with the bearing of the man, his self-confidence and poise. I was just thinking that he had in him something decidedly like human grandeur when, of a sudden, I saw him violently convulsed and shaken by some agony that contorted his mouth and twisted his hands and fingers, his entire frame, as I have seen a stately tree all at once sway and writhe in a blast of wind. It was a painful thing to watch. I was glad to have my attention drawn away by a lady who rose at that moment from a thwart among the oarsmen and stood beside him, smiling up, with her hand on his arm. She too was wearing a visor, but I think there is no mask in the world that could prevent me from recognizing Kitty Clive. Neither could I doubt for a moment that the handsome man in black who rose and stood at the commodore's left hand was Parson Blandison.

*　　*　　*

I once heard a great painter declare that nothing was more important in his art than knowing what to leave out. A good picture, said he, is what remains when everything in the world that is not indispensable to it has been excluded. That remark applies equally well, of course, to the art of writing; and it must have been apparent throughout this chronicle how steadily I have held it in mind. Now, however, in my record of those catastrophic last hours of the week, I must select and reject even more stringently than hitherto. For example, I shall not report what I said to Kitty Clive and she to me when I helped her off the barge. The curt colloquy between Blandison and his host I pass over without a word. I set down with no comment the fact that Kitty, taking the unicorned admiral of the fleet by the hand, led him up to me and introduced the Upright Man to the Honourable Horatio Walpole, after which there was a formal exchange of bows but nothing spoken. For your information merely, and as though I were writing only a memoir, I tell you that Blandison dragged forth from the barge and up-ended and presented to me an unmistakable person by the name of Master Robert Jenkins—a youth, said he, by no means unknown either to fortune or to fame who had graciously come along with his bottle, his water-dog wig, and his celebrated Ear to impersonate himself in the final act of our comedy.

These, sir, are exclusions so drastic and expensive that you can only wonder by what wealth of other resources they can possibly be justified. It is as though you should find me throwing out of my collections the tobacco-pipe of Tromp, the hat of Cardinal Wolsey, the clock of Anne Boleyn, and the original manuscript of Gray's ode "On a Favourite Cat Drowned in a Tub of Gold Fishes," to make room for—what? Well, sir, in those improbable circumstances I think I should ask you to wait and see.

Meanwhile I ought to confess that not all of my exclusions are deliberate. Many things happened that afternoon of which—thank Heaven!—I knew nothing, and others made no impression. My faculty of shock, fright, and horror had been blunted, all but worn out. For instance, I felt no astonishment at the sudden emergence from myth into actuality of Master Jenkins. It was only that I looked and there he was, precisely as he had been portrayed, and I was not even surprised. Just as in a bad dream we take the worst possible happenings for granted, so by that time did I. Nay, I was ready for the impossible. Suppose Kitty had whispered in my ear that the Upright Man was really, in private life, a certain Grub Street dictionary-maker whose name has already sullied these pages a sufficient number of times. Do you think that would have disturbed me? Not at all! I should have replied: "Well, my dear, he's our guest. We must be polite. Please ask Mrs. Margaret to brew him a gallon of tea."

That, of course, is a wild supposition, chosen because of its wildness. For one thing, Kitty would never have told me even if it had been true. And yet, amid all those horns and masks and female disguisements, who could say of a certainty who was not there? For my part I felt perfectly sure of only one absentee: the King. According to the Plan as I vaguely understood it, he would have to wait in the

Hampton Court Maze, as patiently as he could, to be killed. His journeys and junketings were over. Distracted as I was by my own cares, I felt almost sentimental about his Majesty standing there imprisoned by a five-foot hedge, hearing the distant cry of "Horns! Horns!" and perhaps remembering that this was the Day of St. Luke, possibly wishing that he too might sink for a time into the anonymity of a horned head-dress and hoop-skirts and a visor, now and then fidgeting a little, calling out more and more plaintively and then with mounting wrath for the Gentleman of the King's Body Guard of the Yeomen of the Guard. But no answer would come, and no guidance, to the little man from Hanover who had always been so adept in getting himself into difficulties and so doltish when it came to getting out again. There would be no Sir Robert Walpole to help him out now. The splendidly polychromatic functionary who knew the way out of the Maze had by this time been disposed of by Blandison's highwaymen. To that end it was, no doubt, that the still disempistolled Beston had been sent off posthaste with a message as soon as Blandison stepped off the barge. —Or, again, the message might have been addressed to the King himself. Perhaps he had been told that he would have one hour, say, in which to solve the secret of the labyrinth which had baffled him for all these years, and then to set off for Hanover in the royal barge, never to return. Should he take more than an hour, then there were the two trees at the center of the Maze, both of them small but sufficient for the purpose.

You will not blame me so much for these violent imaginings, William, if you put yourself in my place. Pray sit with me there for five minutes on the bench beneath the willows while I catch my breath, slow down the frantic speed of my heart, and try to comprehend a little of what is going on. Listen, now, to that hideous uproar, incessant and increasing, in the place where I for so many years have been wont to hear only bird-song, rustle of leaves, and the comfortable chuckling of ripples. The crowd, already hundreds strong in a place made only for dozens, is growing from minute to minute. Horned people are streaming through the gateway, swarming over the wall, wading in from their boats to the bank, lurching down across the terrace from Kitty's summerhouse, coming indeed from every direction except, possibly, the vertical. Through the embrasures of the garden-wall I see only a jostling of horns. The Twickenham Road is so thronged with coaches, chariots, curricles, and horned bipeds, some of them astride of quadrupeds, that forward motion is clogged. Over in Madlands every visible open space is clotted with human beasts, making short work no doubt of the pagodas and baby-houses and noseless classical deities. All the swans have now disappeared up-river, but the fleet is still pressing on toward Teddington, Kingston, Hampton, and the Maze where the King stands waiting. For Strawberry Hill is by no means the sole object of this invasion. Indeed, one can scarcely say that it has any object or goal. The fleet moves with the blind impartiality of a flood, and the crowd with no more conscious purpose than one of those vast straggling herds of bison on the plains of North America that James Adair told us about. Blandison alone, working with a few men he can trust, has decided the destination and the deed.

You recall that Richard Beston trembled when he spoke his eloquent "Oh, sir!" That was because he knew, or thought he did, what was about to happen. But fear of the known is one thing and that of the unknown quite another, for which we need a different name. I would call it terror, and to suggest what the word means to me I remind you of Milton's "two-handed engine at the door" that "stands ready to smite once, and smite no more." No one can make sure why that vague image is two-handed—a not infrequent phenomenon among those that have hands at all, but engines are seldom so equipped—or precisely how and when and whom it is to smite. Such questions are left to the reader's imagination, as the Plan has been left to mine.

I have an imagination, and during the present week it has been vigorously exercised, but nothing in those visions of Tuesday night on Twickenham Ait, or in my dreams of armour and the vanishing unicorn, has prepared me for the actualities of Horn Fair. This is by far more fantastic, mysterious, and terrible than they were. In a sense, it verifies them. It is the incredible fact of which they were the dim adumbrations. Why, yes, even Louis, that hardened sceptic, must now see that my "condition" on Tuesday midnight was due not to Abingdon ale but to my prophetic soul.

"And yet, surely," you say in your cool manner, "things aren't yet so dreadful as to call for quotations from Milton." You turn halfway round on the bench and report that not much harm has yet been done: a few flowerbeds trampled, certain young North American pine trees knocked over, a battlement or two on the wall perforated by walking-sticks to make sure that they are made of plaster, and the like. You think that the lawn is likely to suffer most because it has not had time to dry off since yesterday's heavy rain, but that probably the total expense of repair will not be more than Blandison can win from Lord Madlands in a single rubber at whisk. No one has entered the house, or is likely to do so while General Conway stands at the door with Beston's pistols conspicuously displayed. Moreover, the members of the Club have now arrived and have stationed themselves at the windows to see that no painted glass is pilfered. Jeremy Tinker, armed with a garden-rake and assisted by Ponto, is talking back to the roughest members of the crowd in a language they understand. Young Louis, pallid with wrath, is shouting at them in the same argot. Parson Blandison and Kitty Clive are chatting like old friends with the Upright Man at the entrance to the Prior's Garden. They are merry together, you tell me. Nearly every remark of the huge man with the single horn makes Kitty Clive shake all over. Now Parson Blandison is thumping her on the back. Now the three of them go into the garden to have their talk out in seclusion.

Thanks, William. It is most comforting to have you take these things so calmly. I too prefer the cheerful view for as long as it can possibly be maintained. But let me draw your attention to the two maskers now approaching our bench. They represent King John and his wife Isabella, stock characters in the Horn Fair mumming. A second glance shows you that they are mummers extraordinary. Their costumes suggest no little knowledge of how kings and queens bedizened themselves six hundred years ago. Instead of horns they are wearing royal crowns—of gilt and paste, to be sure, and yet so cleverly made that in the light, say, of the Drury Lane candelabra they would look convincing enough. But now take a third look, and in the degree that you have been a frequenter of the London stage in the last fifteen years you become aware that you have seen these crowns, these costumes, these very same mummers, often and often before. You know who they are, and that they know me, and unless you have forgotten what happened here on Thursday noon you begin to realize that bland optimism is not always a sufficient philosophy.

"Why, here is a man without any horns!" the queen exclaims as they come to a stand before us—ignoring you, naturally, because you are here only in imagination.

"Hush, my dear," says the king. "He can't help it. He's unmarried."

"Oh, to be sure—now that I look more closely. —But why isn't he wearing a mask?"

"Look still more closely and you'll find that he's wearing several—indeed, many."

"Ah! They must have grown into his face. But then, too, he's in male costume. That's against the rules."

"For men, yes."

"You mean—"

"Certainly not!"

"Well, then you must mean that this is Mr. Horace Walpole. He's an exception to all rules, male and female."

"Nonsense! You know perfectly well that Mr. Walpole always vanishes when people come to see him at Strawberry Hill."

"But why?"

"Be innocent of that knowledge, dearest chuck. Let the fact suffice you that the more visitors he has the less visible he becomes; and today he has ten thousand. —No, no! This fellow is a pretender. He's only acting the part of Mr. Walpole—badly."

"Now, your Majesty, why can't you ever say a kind word about other people's acting? —I think this fellow, as you call him, is pretending decidedly well."

"What? Merely sitting there and looking embarrassed, saying not a word? Why, the true Horace Walpole would have done all the talking, for fear we might mention that little affair of Thursday noon. By this time he would have told us the whole plot of his new play, *Something About Love*. Also he would have introduced his cast of highwaymen, highwomen, and I forget how many horses."

"H'm," says the queen, swiftly surveying the crowd at our backs. "Highwomen, indeed! If I know anything about *low* women . . . But, your Majesty, I see that you are right, as always. The true Mr. Walpole certainly would not let Mrs. Clive out of his sight for a moment with all these Londoners about. Besides, this fellow is blushing, and Mr. Horace Walpole never does that. —Shall we leave him?"

"That would be kindest, yes."

*

And now, William, being thus encouraged and refreshed, let us stroll about the grounds together and mingle with these our fellow-citizens who, in despair of our ever visiting them, have so generously come to us. You will not be endangering your clerical reputation, and I, even if I am recognized, have no dignity left to lose. Let us go as antiquarians, if you like, and with the expectation of learning something about the great city down the river which is not to be found in Stow's *Survey of London,* even though one should look for it in the Reverend John Strype's recent and enlarged edition.

Stow, writing in the time of Elizabeth, seems never to have realized that London is several cities in one, and that each has its separate interests and language. You and I have learned that much in the few minutes we have sat here. Already we have heard the quite distinct accents of the court, the club, the drawing-room, the market-place, the rookeries, and the stews. "Why, neighbour"—do you recall that flat shallow voice from Cheapside?—"this Mr. Walpole is a warm man! He sits very pretty indeed! This proputty, now—what 'd you say it might bring?" And then from St. Giles': "Ha! Better 'n a rum squeeze at the spell! We'll frisk the ken for fams and gobsticks." A moment later: "No, sir, Thomas Gray is a dull fellow. He has, to be sure, a sort of strutting dignity, but it comes of walking on stilts made by other men." Thus the talk goes on and on until we realize that London is a modern Tower of Babel, and recall why that tower fell. For the language oftenest heard here is that ruffian argot or thieves' Latin of St. Giles' which I first became sharply aware of only five days ago. Louis and I then regarded it as a mere curiosity, and laughable. It seemed to us a foreign tongue, as far away as the Chinese. I know better, now that I hear it spoken at Strawberry Hill. There is menace in it, and a portent of things to come.

The people in this crowd, you see, are at play, and therefore off guard. They are revealing their true nature all the more freely and fully because of their disguises. Keep that in mind as you look and listen and wonder. Keep it in mind that people are to be known not so much by their work as by their amusements, and that the present activities of this multitude are thought to be amusing.

I have already named a few of them. Not for a moment has there been a lull in the cry of "Horns! Horns!" or in the empty laughter or the jangling of the Twickenham bells. Now, as we edge and dodge from the bench toward the terrace a score of metallic horns are thrust in our faces and blown with a deafening blare—whereat, of course, and especially because I cannot conceal my dislike of such conduct, there is much raucous glee. Two things, you observe from behind your robe of invisibility, are hugely comic to our compatriots: making a din over nothing and causing discomfort or pain to their fellow-creatures. I find that the first of these was mentioned in Elizabeth's time by a German traveller called Hentzner. "The English," said he, "are vastly fond of great noises that fill the ear such as firing of cannon, blowing of horns, beating of drums, and the ringing of bells; so that it is common for a number of them that have a glass in their heads to get up in some belfry and ring the chimes for hours together, for the sake of the exercise." Think of a German saying that about us—and getting it right, except that of course we do it not for exercise but out of sheer insolence!—George Selwyn tells me that these drunken ringers are sometimes caught round the neck by a noose in the bell-rope and thus jerked away into eternal silence; but he adds, unnecessarily, that this happens not often enough.

With regard to the delight we take in causing and witnessing pain there's no need of quoting old authors, and I prefer not to mention my good friend George at all. Perhaps the treatment of me by the impersonators of King John and Queen Isabella will suffice for an example. If not, I reluctantly draw your attention to the fact that over there in the angle of the garden wall a cock has been tied by one leg to a stake and that a dozen men—all of them horned, masked, and attired as women—are throwing cudgels at him. The first prize will go to the thrower who strikes off the bird's head; but already a lesser award has been won by a cast that broke both legs. You must have heard the shout of glee that went up when that happened. The cock's legs have been hastily splinted now, and he stands there awaiting the next throw. The hurled stick crushes his breastbone, but they lift him from the bloodied grass, prop him, thrust a nail down his throat so that his head is still held high, for after all they have brought only six cocks with them, and not one must be wasted; and again he stands there waiting, motionless but not yet dead, burning his image into my memory like a brand that will not wear out before my latest breath.

Now a shapeless man-mountain of fat lumbers up to the line and stands there a moment, thirty feet from the cock, with his oaken club drawn back for the throw. The grotesque hoop-skirt he has on, and the wadded bodice, do not so much disguise as reveal him. The swinish snout he wears as a mask is but a slight exaggeration of the actual face it covers. For I know that ponderous paunch, that bull-neck and sagging jowl. I could pick the man out of a million. He was here in my house not four months ago, making my towers tremble. This is the Duke of Cumberland, the hero of Culloden and scourge of the Highlands, sometimes called Billy the Butcher. This is the man who will rule England—barring a return of the Stuarts—if the old George dies before the young George comes of age. Ah, how heroic and royal he looks now, each one of his three hundred pounds compact of martial valour, as he fiercely looks his foe in the eye and aims and—

But that's enough, William! Don't look at him any longer! See Blandison over there, standing a little apart from the cock-killers and gazing not at the tortured bird but at them, at Billy the Butcher. How pale he is! and his eyes, how wide and all ablaze! See him start forward and take two long strides toward the Butcher and then suddenly stop as the stick is thrown and the cock's head snaps off and there goes up a shout of acclaim. For this is interesting, William, exceedingly. Don't miss an instant of it, or the slightest change of expression in Blandison's face. He looks older, and for the first time weary, if that is the word, or perhaps overwhelmed with disgust or a kind of shame. Look closely, I say, and try to make sure what that new expression means.

Ah well, he is walking away now, slowly. In the long week of our acquaintance I have not before seen his head so bowed. His characteristic gesture has been a gay tossing back of the head, somewhat reckless in effect and utterly self-confident. Not once hitherto have I caught in his face or manner any hint of a change of mind. Yesterday afternoon he did look thoughtful, even pensive, while George described those executions and little Jeremy stammered out the tale of his broken life. Then, too, there was his silence while he gazed at the silver plate and gave it back to me as though he wanted never to see it again. He was then like a man counting the cost of a thing which he still considers worth its price, but now—Well, what do you think?

You think I am making too much of this. New thoughts never come all at once, you say, ignoring the clear instance of Newton and the apple. No thoughts of any kind, you continue, are likely to be suggested by a group of ruffians throwing sticks at a barnyard fowl. You remind me that Blandison is keenly interested in cockfighting as a spectacle, as an ancient game lasting on into the modern world, and as an opportunity for laying wagers. This boyish enthusiasm, you say, led him down there to the angle of the wall, but when he found something quite different going on he turned away, disappointed. That is all we are sure of, and you think we had better stop there.

William, I don't agree with you. If we stop with the things we are sure about we shall never understand anything. I suggest that Blandison's fondness for cockfighting is somehow connected with the high value he sets upon courage in confronting great odds. The courage of the fighting cock is to him a symbol of what he means by "glory." It reminds him of the virtue, as he calls it, which makes some men greet danger like a friend. Suppose I am right, and then imagine the effect upon him of seeing not the battle of feathered knights he expected but a poor bird tied by the leg, unable to defend itself in any way, slowly and brutally done to death by a gang of oafs for their sport. If you think he could stop with the mere spectacle, pitiful though it was, of that bird's agony—could fail, I mean, to recognize in it something vividly symbolic of the obliteration in our time of all splendour and glory—then a good many of these pages have been written in vain.

*   *   *

So much, then, for one of our sports and pastimes. If you like the sample I can also show you a whistling-match, a smock-race, a dancing dog, a learned pig, a posture master, a balance mistress, a running at the quintal, a grinning through the horse-collar, and a tossing of quoits on my terrace where the sward has for years been rolled and mowed and weeded with affectionate care, one might almost say, for each several blade of grass. —Don't get the notion, though, that the terrace alone is suffering. Under these thousands of stamping heels my whole lawn, and the meadow below it, is becoming first a quagmire and then a dark green soup. A good deal, in fact, of what was yesterday Strawberry Hill is now smeared on the garments and hands and faces of my guests.

As an antiquarian you will see that most of these diversions come down to us from the time, whenever that was, of Merry Old England. Older still, and even merrier, is the sport of butting at other butters with one's horns to the accompaniment of sundry grunts, bleats, snorts, bellowings, and similar appropriate noises. There is another amusement, still more antique, which I cannot exhibit because, so far as I am aware, it is being pretermitted or at least postponed today at

Strawberry Hill. Mr. Chute's presence may exert a chilling influence, or those two pistols in my cousin's hands—and, by the way, if I have said above that Milton's image of a "two-handed engine at the door" is in the least vague, then I take it back. Some dissuasion there may be also in the very spirit of this place, dedicated to a celibacy not devoid of feminine companionship and to a monasticism held a little short of extreme rigour. At any rate, the auspices are not propitious, and if you insist upon that sort of thing you must go over to Madlands, where, as a horror-stricken Louis has reported, "the adulteration is extremely ubiquitous."

Though shocked at this, I am not surprised. What can you expect with all those marble gods and goddesses scattered about in the wilderness? If they expected anything else, Lord and Lady Madlands must have forgotten their Greek mythology.

And now that you understand the situation more clearly you begin to wonder not at my excitement but at what, in the circumstances, may be more properly called my calm. I thank you, and I explain that the secret lies in letting others do my agitation for me. This method is closely similar to the one I have used nearly all my life in the various offices—sometimes vulgarly called "places" or "sinecures" —which I hold under the Whig government. It involves no more than the hiring of some practical person to do all the necessary work for one-half, or thereabouts, of the stipend. Thus he is employed, the work is far better done than I should do it, I am left at leisure, and all but the Tories are pleased.

Most of my deputies have served me well, but only, as the Italians say, *con industria*. Today, as you can see for yourself, Louis and Jeremy and Ponto are worrying *con amore*. They put their hearts into it, as though they were quite as much concerned as I am. And indeed they are more so. To Louis, that stickler for decorum and minute observer of social rank, this taking-over of a gentleman's estate by the rabble of London is no mere intrusion but something more like the end of the world. I begin to fear for his reason. On the one hand he wants to hear every word uttered by the Upright Man, but then also he must needs rush continually about in the crowd telling every one in every one's own language that he has no right here and must leave at once. Thus he contributes his full share to the hilarity of the occasion.

Jeremy Tinker has now been in my employ for somewhat less than

two days, much of which he has spent in listening to stories, and yet
he has acquired a sense of proprietorship in these buildings and acres
with which my own feeble grip upon property of any sort cannot compete. I shall never outgrow the feeling that I am merely a visitor at
Strawberry Hill—endured by the goldfish because I feed them, toler-
ated by the blackbird because I admire him, ignored by the butterflies
as cousins are wont to ignore each other. But Jeremy has already
taken root. Every blow of a quoit slicing into the greensward is to him
as though it fell on his own flesh.

And Ponto? There is probably not one of us, even my cousin, for
whom this experience has meant a more violent assault upon every
sense of decency. Take the matter of horns. He's accustomed to them
on four legs; but now to find them on two, and indeed to be able to
find scarcely any two-legged creature that is not thus transmogrified,
is a shock. Take skirts also, and petticoats. Since puppyhood he has
known about them, allowed for them, harboured no prejudice against
them, but always on the supposition that they would be at least evenly
balanced by breeches, smallclothes, or whatever euphemism he uses.
Well, he has been back here several times to make sure that I am
still wearing breeches, but the paucity or obsolescence of them elsewhere is causing him extreme disquietude. Then there are the Twickenham chimes gone mad, the cries, the drunkenness, and chiefly the
smells. Yes, it must be the stenches, mainly, that drive him frantic.
Think of a dog tenderly reared in the odour of lilacs, roses, and river-
water—of a dog accustomed to having the air of the breakfast or
dining room incensed after every meal—now confronted with all the
fetors of St. Giles'! What wonder that he rushes wildly about, growl-
ing at Jenkins, snapping at the Upright Man, barking furiously at
every one?

You see, then, that what would otherwise have been my anxieties
and perturbations are being quite competently attended to, and you
understand what enables me to look down with so philosophic an
eye upon this lower region of turmoil. —Or, rather, what you really
understand is that a man all aquiver with apprehensions is doing his
best to maintain an attitude of Stoic unconcern. For serenity, poise,
composure, is what the times to come will expect of us, and we must
try not to disappoint them. Think also of times gone by, of Marcus
Aurelius with the barbarians everywhere rushing in upon his realm,
undismayed, preserving at the heart of the storm one region of calm.

Though utterly unlike that great emperor, I may still act like a gentleman. Philosophic calm is beyond my powers, but at least there is always frivolity.

We have with us today a perfect example of that serenity, smugness, insolence, or whatever its true name may be, which comes of being uninvolved. I mean the Upright Man. —This name, by the way, is perhaps derived from the first paragraph of the Book of Job, where we read: "That man was perfect and upright, and one that feared God and eschewed evil." If so, then we also have an example of how injurious perfection is to a man's character, and still worse for his manners. Mr. Chute, indeed, has shown me a passage in an old book called *The Fraternity of Vagabonds,* 1561, where we are told that "an Upright Man is one that goeth with the truncheon of a staff, which they call a Filchman, and is of so much authority that, when meeting with any of his profession, he may call them to account and demand a share or snap unto himself of all that they have gained by their trade in one month." Now I do not understand how any man, however perfect, can at the same time eschew evil and also be the leader of a gang of thieves; but it is certain that the one-horned person standing by the gateway with an admiring throng about him—do you see Kitty Clive there beside him, smiling up, and also the reverent Louis?—does carry a Filchman, and his remarks are rolled forth with an authority that cows every other noise and seems to say: "When I ope my lips let no dog bark."

Perhaps we can edge a little closer, so as to overhear without being seen. For my part, I don't want to recognize the fellow's presence, but then on the other hand any friend of Kitty's . . . Yes; we can stand here just outside the gateway, hidden by the wall. —Please be careful, though, not to trample that white rose. By nightfall it may be the only rose I have left. —Now if only Ponto wouldn't bark quite so furiously we should be able to hear well enough.

People are asking him questions, as though he were an oracle. His replies are made without a moment's hesitation, as though by a mind already made up about everything. "No, sir," says he, "Fielding was a blockhead. He was a barren rascal. He had no invention, sir. Any page reads like any other page."

A surprisingly sound opinion, William! He must be quoting some man of sense. And now, apparently, some one has asked whether the author of *Tom Jones* had not great knowledge of life, for the reply thunders back: "Aye, sir; and so has a breeder of cattle great knowledge of life—of the same sort."

H'm! Well, really! Aren't you glad we came? —But now listen again, for "No, sir!" he shouts. "If England were honestly polled, the present King would be sent back home tonight, and all his adherents hanged tomorrow."

I had never thought to hear such a remark, however true it may be, at Strawberry Hill.

Now some one, of course with malicious intent, must have asked whether he thinks my recent letter to David Garrick an admirable production. "Aye, sir," says he with a laugh, "for it is no easy matter to write a thousand words without once deviating into the truth. That letter, sir, is a masterpiece perfectly consistent with Strawberry Hill. Nothing in it is in fact what it pretends to be."

Surely we have heard enough, William. —But hark! He goes on: "I have had the honour of informing Mrs. Susannah Cibber that, whatever she may allege about Mr. Walpole, the least hint of slander against Mrs. Clive is a thing I shall not patiently endure. For to her I owe more than I can ever repay. She has made me laugh when I was saddest."

Ah. Sweet and sour, you see; but fundamentally right. —I do wish that Ponto weren't quite so vociferous, for now all we hear is something to the effect that folly, like murder, will out, and that, of all the forms it can take, the architectural is the least injurious. Evidently he is talking about my house, for we catch these words: "As a building meant for human habitation the structure does indeed leave everything to be desired; but considered as a baby's bauble, sir, it is very well. Scarcely anywhere else will you find a thing so monstrous on so small a scale, at once so trifling and so pretentious. Strawberry Hill, sir, has this not inconsiderable merit: it enlarges one's notion of what is credible."

* * *

It was probably Blandison's idea, though the Upright Man proclaimed it, that the Masque of King John and the Miller's Wife should be performed in front of Kitty's summerhouse. This is the best place we have for the purpose because the wide sweep of lawn reaching down to the river provides room for a multitude of spectators. We shall need all the room there is, for more herds of horned creatures are thronging in every minute and from every direction to view the mumming. Mr. Chute, looking back and downward over the crowd, says to me in an undertone that the scene reminds him of the cattle-market in Smithfield, partly because of the numberless clashing horns and the bellow but also for the reason that Wat Tyler's Rebellion and the plot to kill the King came in that place to its head. I also glance back, and my heart misses a beat. Here at last I am really seeing the London mob, or at any rate the materials of which a mob might easily be made by almost any incendiary word. Yes, indeed; if there be any man here who has a dreadful Plan to execute and who knows the right word and how to speak it, how gladly will these creatures, half bestial already, sink back into beasts complete and rush forth in stampede to do his bidding!

Meanwhile we are doing our best not to vex them in any way, and not to let them think us inhospitable. Here on what we call Kitty's grounds, as on my own, there are a number of young trees for them to break down, and several flower-beds to be trampled. In the small rose-garden which has figured more than once in this chronicle the last blossoms of the year are already trodden into the soil, no doubt with a faithful-unto-death butterfly or two among them. The cricket's violin is broken; the afternoon is bereaved of a blackbird; Kitty's pigeons have flown away, and if any skylark is singing above us I cannot imagine why or to whom.

And yet it is a comfort to be with my friends once more, even though I cannot keep it out of my mind that this is the last time I shall see Blandison, Byron, Morris, Adair, and Chester. We are standing in the front line of the crowd, some twenty feet from the oaken shell and the painted-glass windows. Louis and General Conway have remained at my house to protect it from burglars, but George Selwyn is here, and Mr. Chute. Ponto is in my arms, quivering. Jeremy Tinker is vainly striving to keep people off the flower-beds. Kitty stands at my side, and Blandison just beyond her. They two are chattering about their excursion to London after the Upright Man. It appears that they found him at his house in Gough Square off Fleet Street, not yet out of bed. He complained that Mrs. Clive, as an actress, should keep him up late at night and then rouse him at dawn or thereabouts to ask for his help in a political plot. You may not see the point of that witticism, William, but Kitty and Blandison are laughing as though it had one. I deduce also that they stopped at

Twickenham Ait on their way to or from London and tried to get
Hal Pudsey to join them. He refused, on the ground that people might
take him for another Pretender and try to make him move into
Hampton Court Palace. He said no Pudseys ever leave their Ait;
and Kitty now sees his point, asserting that we should be grateful to
that bulky man for not coming. They laugh at that also, and indeed it
is surprising how merry they are today. Would you say that they look
a little excited? I myself can't make sure. Blandison's face may be
slightly paler than usual, but it tells me nothing about his mood or
purpose.

But why, you ask, should I be in doubt on that score? He has told
me in clear terms what he intends to do, even suggesting the means
and the method. Since then there has been no retraction, and if he
has given any hint of a change of mind it is only in failing to ask for
my final decision. But that, surely, is a slight and even negligible
matter. We have had no chance for talk since yesterday evening; and,
besides, he may well feel that the show of force he is making now is
his strongest possible argument, calculated to overpower my last
hesitations. For here are the means in sufficient quantity, whatever
may be said of the kind. He holds in his hands at this moment, I have
not the least doubt, this weapon. Why then should I doubt that he will
use it?

Well, sir, I think I have not said that I do so. How can it be
doubted? The evidence is overwhelming. Consider the long preparations he must have made, reaching back to the Jacobite Court in Rome
and including collusion with France, perhaps also with Spain and
Sweden. Imagine the provision of funds, the bribing of this rabble-
leader and that, secret conferences with smugglers and highwaymen
and killers for hire, the gathering and training of the band of horsemen under Sir Edward Livermore, to say nothing of what has been
done or attempted during this week at Strawberry Hill. There, at the
least, is a year's hard work. Does any man in his senses put himself
to such toil, come so close to a long-sought goal, and then, for some
scruple of conscience or weakness of will that shows itself in no
other way, turn aside?

Let us hear no more, then, of doubts. In Blandison's face there is
not the least sign of uncertainty or wavering. Now more than ever
in my knowledge of him he has that air of splendid audacity which I
have striven in vain to describe. In his eyes, his face, his whole bear-

ing, you see that here is a man who plays for the highest stakes in contempt of prudence. He lays great demands upon life, and will not be refused.

Thus I try to entertain you while the mummers are busy in the summerhouse at their disguisings. But they have kept us waiting a bit too long. The crowd is growing restless. The foul and blasphemous shouts, yells, and caterwaulings increase behind us and coalesce into a hoarse concerted roar as it were of one beast unimaginably huge, savage. Ponto's trembling is instantly stilled. He lies limp in my arms, barely breathing, but the short hairs at the back of his neck and along his spine stand on end. For ten seconds, perhaps, the roar grows and grows; but then Sir Edward Livermore rides out at a footpace from behind the summerhouse and brings his mount to a stand not far from us, facing the crowd. He says nothing, makes no gesture, no motion, but only sits there calmly looking out and down. It is enough. One man on horseback is enough to quiet that brutal roar. But there are more horsemen—many more than I had supposed Sir Edward had under his command. They come riding out slowly, one by one, and take their stations here and there on the edges of the throng. They surround it, daunt it, make it ready to be delivered to a single purpose and will. They are imposing a plan upon chaos, stamping the shape of a mind upon the mindless. How deliberately they move, and with what perfect confidence that nothing can thwart them!

Even Richard Beston, as he comes on foot round the corner of the summerhouse, is deliberate. All his perturbation is gone, now that Blandison has returned. He carries a wicker cage holding three slate-blue pigeons. A faint hum and stir of curiosity runs through the crowd. Only those in front can see what is going on, but all the rest want to know. Even you and I would like to know what it means. Beston sets the cage down by the oaken shell and goes back where he came from, taking plenty of time. You observe as he walks away that he has somehow reacquired two pistols since we last saw him. The brim of his hat is once more pulled down so low that he seems to have no brow whatever—and indeed even when uncovered his forehead is not extensive. In a moment he returns, leading Blandison's black stallion by the bridle. The horse dwarfs the man to insignificance, and when the two of them come to a stand beside Sir Edward Livermore's steed you can scarcely see Beston at all.

And now at last the four mummers appear at the door. They are greeted by a shout like that one in Milton which tore Hell's concave and, beyond, frighted the realms of Chaos and old Night. Ponto once more nearly dies, and only some assurance that I am not quite ready to do so revives him. Meanwhile King John and his Queen Isabella are taking their places on the level ground halfway between us and the summerhouse. They are not more than ten feet from us as they go through the first motions, for the most part amatory in significance, of their pantomime. Then the other two figures advance from the doorway and I hear John Chester remark: "Thet 'ar fat one is him that knocked the head offen the rooster."

Yes, William, if my translation is correct, then so is my friend from Connecticut. The part of the Miller is being taken today by the Duke of . . . But no; it sounds more respectful to say that it is taken by Billy the Butcher, a nickname which Posterity may not understand. Don't tell them who is meant, or how well the name fits him. Why he, the most infamous rake in England, should play the part of the complaisant husband I do not know, unless it be on the ground that all things are reversed on St. Luke's Day; but the cause of the delay is now clear enough. It would naturally take some time to divest him of the hoop-skirt he wore at the cockshy and make him presentable as the Knight of the Golden Horns. —As for the adulterous Wife of the Miller, it matters not who she is. Probably she was brought along as one who could do the part without further training.

I ought also to say—and a skilful narrator would have worked it in some time ago—that the Upright Man is standing somewhat behind and to the right of the actors. There's no telling what he thinks he is there for. He can scarcely be a prompter because the play we are about to witness is in dumb show. If it is his duty to keep the rabble in order, then why did he not quell that roar of five minutes ago? I doubt, in fact, whether he has any real authority, power, or function. His presence here is more probably due to a habit of making himself conspicuous and obnoxious on every occasion.

No, I really don't like the man. Of course I never thought I should, but now that I've met him . . . Oh, but I forget! You don't know who he is, and I have no intention of telling you. After all, I've confessed to enough things in these pages without admitting to Posterity that this man, with a name of which the future may not be wholly ignorant, once spent an afternoon at my country house and made such and such impertinent remarks about it. Therefore, as King John said to Queen Isabella, "be innocent of that knowledge."

*   *   *

I linger out these preliminaries because I am reluctant to plunge into the final scene, startling and for ever memorable though it was, of our week together. Finalities of any kind, and even such mere phrases as "for the last time," always touch me to the quick. Every farewell is to me like a little death. Let this suffice as a hint of the mood in which I stood there with Morris, Adair, Chester, and Byron. Our time together had been brief, but none of it had been wasted. How much they had shown me which without their help I should never have known! How many doors of the heart and mind they had opened which I had not even guessed were there! Now they would soon be gone, those doors would close, my memories of the week would fade, and I should sink back into what I had been.

As I approach the end of my narrative, that strangely commingled feeling of thankfulness and sorrow grows stronger. For three weeks I have held these men steadily before the eyes of the mind, seeing and hearing and understanding them really better, I think, than when they were with us in the flesh. But I can hold them no longer. They are really going now, each one setting forth again into the mystery out of which he came. Tomorrow I myself must return to other scenes and companions.

*   *   *

The story of King John and the Miller's Wife need not detain us. Wholly concerned as it was with the so-called humours of adultery, it could not fail to be at once dull, in spite of all that two good actors could do to save it, and also hugely entertaining to the spectators. From their guffaws and other noises of amusement you might have inferred that marital infidelity was quite a new notion to them, instead of the staple of their daily gossip. I tried not to hear those noises, or even to look at the dumb-show. Kitty's face was better worth watching as she in turn watched her chief rival without the least envy, for once, of the part that rival was playing. And Blandison's face! He gazed steadily all the while at Billy the Butcher, the cuckolded husband of the play. I saw his contempt slowly deepen into loathing.

Thus the flat, stupid bawdry dragged on for minute after minute. I sustained myself as well as I could by reflecting that the annals of cuckoldom are of necessity short and simple. Before long, I was thinking, we must come to the sermon, quite as traditional a part of Horn Fair as the play. As a usual thing my appetite for sermons is not keen, but I longed for this one because, though I had not heard who was to preach it, I felt sure that it would be a change. It might even be decent, cleanly, and those are qualities for which I have a fairly consistent predilection.

The change, though not the decency, came sooner than I had expected, and with shocking force. All at once I heard the player queen speaking, as of course she had no right to do in a pantomime. That was shocking enough, but what she said, in a loud, clear, carrying voice, was far more so. I shall not set down her actual words, partly because she has since apologized. You should know, however, that her remark, gratuitously foisted upon the dumb-show at just the point where she thought it would do most harm, was in substance an insulting allusion to Kitty Clive and to me and the possible uses of the summerhouse. The innuendo was instantly understood by a few persons at least in the crowd and a titter began here and there. With astonishing speed it grew into laughter, rose to a yell, hoarsened into a roar, and I saw in a swift glance over my shoulder and down the slope that the entire multitude below us was stirring, surging, beginning to move as a vast dark wave with cries thrown up like spray of violence and disaster. The herd was swiftly changing into a mob. It was coming up the hill. What it meant to do, it would find out by the time it reached us.

But this was not all I saw. Before the player queen's words were out of her mouth the Upright Man was rushing at the four actors with a shout and his staff upraised. He snatched off Queen Isabella's crown, dashed it to the ground, drove her and her companions into the crowd, and then started back on the run toward the oaken shell. But Blandison was there before him. Already he had made some sign to Sir Edward which had the effect of holding not only him but all the other horsemen immobile. Chester and Morris, meanwhile, at his request, had brought the shell forward some ten feet from the summerhouse windows. All this had taken far less time than I do in the telling. He was now standing in the shell with his right hand held high. The rest of us—twelve in all counting Ponto, for my cousin and Louis had just arrived—stood near him to right and left. The Upright Man, after a moment's hesitation and some blinking of his nearsighted eyes, came to my side. "Mr. Walpole, I—I assure you, sir," he stammered out. Then Blandison began to speak.

There are some voices that almost make one believe in the legend of Orpheus, how by his singing alone he moved rocks and trees and made wild beasts follow him at heel. I have heard one or two such voices in the House of Commons; and another I heard that day.

Seeing that Blandison's face was white with wrath, I expected him to begin with a shout of denunciation. On the contrary, his first words were spoken softly, gently, though with such distinctness that we could all but feel and see them spreading effortlessly out and out to the verges of the crowd like ripples in a pool of quiet water. The roar died down, and the crowd stood still. They all wanted to hear every tone of that golden voice; and, if they were to hear, then every one must be silent even to breathlessness. They were so, and the voice went on to remind them, courteously, that they were the guests of Mr. Horace Walpole, son of the great Sir Robert of that illustrious name. To the father, it said, every Englishman owed the boon of twenty years of peace during which England had grown powerful and wealthy. To the son every man and woman here present owed at least that consideration which all decent people show to their hosts. The land on which they stood, it said, was the private property of Mr. Walpole, and private property in land was one thing which English people still knew how to respect. Some damage had been done here, not intentionally but because certain persons had not been taught to behave themselves. In order to defray the expense of repairs the armed horsemen would see to it that no one should leave by road or by water without making some contribution, great or small. The largest sum ought to come from the largest man in the crowd, not only because he had done the most damage but for the reason, also, that he was the wealthiest. Who that man was, every one must know, for he had just been enacting the part of the cuckold.

There was good-natured laughter at this, and some one called out: "Make Billy pay pound for pound, and it'll cover all the charges!"

Seeing that he now had the crowd with him, Blandison changed his tone. "There are some injuries," said he, speaking more loudly and with an unmistakable ring of anger in his voice, "that are committed in sheer ignorance and stupidity. But others are done with calculating malice. The first kind may sometimes be atoned for in money; for the second, nothing but public confession of guilt will suffice."

He paused there, and for several seconds stood silent, looking here and there in the front ranks of the throng as though for a particular individual. When at length he had found her he went on, without once shifting his gaze. "I have lived for one week at Strawberry Hill," he said, "as a guest of Mr. Walpole. I came here a stranger, at my own invitation, but from the start and increasingly I have been treated as a friend. And that has been due to no merit of mine but to the fact that this place is a shrine of friendship, than which there is nothing nobler in the world. It would be a poor return for such kindness if I should let Strawberry Hill be sullied by deliberate slander."

I too had found her now in the crowd. She was not meeting his eyes. Her pallor showed through the grease-paint.

"Of Mr. Walpole," Blandison continued, "it is enough to say that he is an honourable gentleman. To some of you, at least, that will mean that there is a certain kind of misconduct to which he could not possibly stoop. Mrs. Catherine Clive is an honourable gentlewoman. These two are, and have long been, close friends. Their friendship does honour to them both. It honours humanity also by giving clear evidence that the beastly conduct represented in the dumb-show of this afternoon is not the only possible relationship between men and women."

So this was the Horn Fair sermon I had been waiting for, and really it was not in the least dull. When Blandison paused again and lifted his gaze and looked about the crowd no individual in all that multitude looked for a moment aside. One could not have imagined, beforehand, that so many thousands could be so silent.

"It is known to some of you," the preacher resumed, "that I have had something to do with this holding of Horn Fair up-river instead of down. To that degree I am responsible for the gross insult here offered to our hosts. I have no intention of bearing that responsibility for one minute longer. Therefore I request Mrs. Susannah Cibber to step forward and stand in my place and admit, in as clear and loud a voice as she used a few minutes ago, that she has been guilty of insolent slander of two honourable people, both of whom she will name. She will tell you the truth : that she really knows nothing against those people, that she regrets and retracts what she has said, and that she will not say that sort of thing again, so help her God."

Mrs. Cibber, for once in her theatrical career, seemed not to hear her cue, or perhaps it was that she suffered a sudden attack of stage-fright. There was a considerable interval, during which I thought I heard a note or two of the skylark's rapture. At length, however, the poor woman was escorted to the shell by Sir Edward Livermore, and from there she did say, though in tones far less resonant than she had used before, approximately what Blandison had dictated. I helped her down from the shell when she had finished, and shook hands with her. So did Kitty. Then Blandison led her back to David Garrick.

While he was returning I heard a sudden commotion just behind us and looked round to see Jeremy Tinker and Master Jenkins scuffling on the ground just below the windows where the oaken shell ordinarily stands. Jeremy was seated astride of the famous mariner's stomach and, with both hands gripped round the hero's throat, was methodically beating his head against the side of the wicker cage containing the three pigeons. Jenkins was beginning to whimper. His legs lashed furiously in the air. A sailor's clasp-knife, open, lay on the grass a few inches from his right hand.

I judge that Ponto took in this situation, and understood it, at least as quickly as I did. Besides that, it had already been agreed between him and Jeremy Tinker that they too should work together as much as Ponto's responsibility for me would allow. At any rate, he leapt from my arms with a sharp, eager yelp and in two or three bounds reached the scene of the fray. When there, seeing that Jeremy was at least holding his own, he did not hesitate for an instant about what he should do. A slower-witted dog, or one less thoroughly instructed in recent history, might have attacked the stockings of Jenkins, in which case the world might never have known the aston- ishing fact which I, with his help, am about to reveal. Being who he was, however, Ponto approached the opposite extremity of the pros- trate man, ripped off his water-dog wig with one swift twitch, and ran away with it round the corner of the house. —I may as well add in this place that the wig has not yet been found.

"Why, Jeremy!" I exclaimed, on the spot now, and employing the tone of moral reprobation which with me, and perhaps a few others, is meant to conceal a secret delight.

"Well, sir, 'e war a-scratchin' a pitcher of 'is dod-blasted ear on the painted winder, an' it come over me all of a suddent all the 'arm an' 'urt that ear 'as done an'—"

It was a pity that the longest sentence Jeremy Tinker has ever ventured upon should be interrupted. I suppose he was going to say that under these provocations he temporarily forgot being a Methody and that vengeance is mine saith the Lord; but at that moment up strode Blandison with no time to spare if he was to keep control of the crowd and took one startled look at Jenkins now struggling to sit up and rubbing his shaven pate so that I looked again and discovered with astonishment his complete normality, symmetry, conformity to the human pattern, or, not to hold you overlong in suspense, that he was as two-eared a man as one would find in a proverbial month of Sundays.

Ah, how I envy that presence of mind which instantly brings to bear upon the moment every pertinent thing one knows! Ponto had shown it, and so had Blandison, but I suppose that Jeremy and I might have stared at the dewigged Jenkins for half a minute without realizing what was so villainously wrong—or, if you prefer, so intolerably right—about him. Two-earedness was for us so much the accustomed and expected thing that we were blind to the wild anomaly, the iniquity, the horror of it in this particular instance. No man in the world, we should have known, had less right than Master Jenkins to the possession of two ears—at any rate, *in situ*. He owed his whole fame, now world-wide, to the supposition that he had but one, and both Jeremy and I had spent the past week in exploring, with others, the consequences of that supposition.

Yes, those consequences! The fall of my father's ministry, the ruin of the peace he had built, the rise of the brutal Frederick and his lock-stepping Prussians, the dismemberment of Austria, the embroilment of Europe, the rape of the Highlands, the invasion by rich men of the poor man's refuge in Georgia, the numberless broken lives, the toils and privations and meaningless deaths of innocent men by the thousand—all reaching back to a calculated fraud, a stupid lie told over and over and persisted in for year after year. This came to me item by item, and I felt in my veins a mounting wrath which helped me to understand how mobs are formed and murder is done. Jeremy Tinker must have been before me in this, for I saw his hands reach again for Jenkins' throat. I knew what he longed to do, and doubted whether any command or entreaty of mine could prevent him.

But Blandison pulled him off. He jerked Jenkins to his feet, stripped the coat from his back and threw it over his shaven head—meanwhile reaching for half a second, I thought, into one of the pockets. Then he said to Beston and Louis, who had just come up: "Take this man into the summerhouse and keep him there with the door and windows closed. The crowd must not see him." All this was done as it were at once, and then there was a moment in which Blandison stood gazing at some small object in his half-open hand which I could not see. His smile was to me indecipherable, and so were the words he murmured: "The beginning, and the end."

*   *   *

What that smile meant, and the words as well, grows clearer to me as Blandison takes command again of the crowd. His mood has changed, his tone, his whole bearing and manner. If in his earlier remarks there was any effort to flatter and cajole this rabble there is no such thing discernible now. He is a man through with trifling who has important engagements elsewhere. His words are gathering speed and force. They are falling like the blows of a boxer who, though roused to wrath, yet remembers all his skill.

Something there is to begin with about the glory of England when she was glorious—in the time of Cressy and Agincourt, in the persons of Edward the Black Prince and Henry the Fifth, in the archers and pikemen who followed their lead. Montrose, Dundee, Prince Rupert, and Sir John Byron of the Civil Wars are brought before us in swift characterization. Then, against that background, we are given a picture that sears the brain of a huge mass of blubber aiming a cudgel at the head of a cock tied by the leg to a stake. With the death of that cock, says Blandison in a voice that must have been clearly heard across the river, there was snuffed out the last spark of true courage to be found in all this crowd. "Need I tell you," he goes on, "who killed him? Your affectionate name for him is 'Billy the Butcher,' but he is also known as the Hero of Culloden because on that field he shot down from a safe distance a number of starving Highlanders whom he outnumbered two to one. From there he marched bravely through Scotland, burning houses and barns, starving children, flogging women, hanging old men, putting boys to the sword, leaving everywhere a trail of desolation and of blood. For the most part this thoroughly German hero commanded German mercenaries because the people of England were too fat, too sluggish and stupid, to fight either for or against the Stuarts. The English people did not complain when this professional killer was made Captain General of England's military forces; and should he ever become King of England they would accept even that indignity with a yawn."

Billy the Butcher's huge round face is as red as the sinking sun. He is standing not twenty feet from the speaker, whose eyes are fixed upon him. Princes of the Blood are not accustomed to such attacks. Never before has he been so berated. The recollection of his last visit to Strawberry Hill makes this one all the more a shock. And yet what can he do except stand there silently, as a mummer should, taking what comes? The guards and the horsemen, for once, are not on his side. Neither will the crowd be if this tirade continues a few seconds longer. The reputation for bravery he has won by ordering his gunners to shoot down other men is now of no avail. This is the man who strove with his captains for day after day to make them give four hundred lashes to a soldier-boy whom two hundred had all but killed. He loves blood like the leech he so closely resembles, but now he must be content with what he has—and most of it is going to his head. This is the man who brought the beautiful Savoyard Girl—do you remember Hogarth's portrait of her?—from London to Windsor by coach, offered her a hundred pounds for one night, and then, when refused, let her walk back on foot. Even brutality, however, seems not to apply on the present occasion. Captain General Nolkejumskoi, hero of Culloden, simply does not know what to do. He can only grow redder and redder, and even of that he is already approaching the limit. —All at once I see Midshipman Campbell in the cockpit of the *Wager* with his head banging back to the count of "twenty-three, twenty-four" against the bulkhead, and then comes Kitty's cry: "I'm sorry for him!"

"Some of you suspect," Blandison is saying, "that Horn Fair has been brought up-river to assist in capturing a certain Hanoverian squire and in bringing back England's legitimate monarch. You hope that is true, not for reasons of loyalty but because you delight in turmoil. Others have heard that a French fleet is making ready at Dunkirk for an invasion of England. You hope it will come, because an invasion would bring bloodshed on a grander scale by far than a cockshy or even the execution of the Scotch Lords. Throughout the afternoon—in the pauses of jangled chime-bells and torture of cocks and shouting of "Horns!"—you have been regaled by rumours of an impending attack on London Tower, of a conspiracy among the smugglers and water-men to block the Thames until a Stuart is crowned, of help coming at need from Sweden and Spain and the mountains of Wales and the Scottish Highlands. All this has been as good to you as strong drink. Like a quart of gin it gives you a temporary illusion of value and meaning in lives otherwise empty.

"There is, however, the question, how much of this talk a sensible man can believe. Does one gather the strength of a unicorn to crush a fly? In order to change the occupant of the English throne, what need of bringing the force of confederate nations against a people that does not know the difference between a true king and a blundering foreign yokel? A Jacobite rebellion against the House of Hanover might begin in this place at this moment and be completed before yonder sun, now less than half an hour above the horizon, goes down. It could be done without the least help from you, and against your will if you had one. Not a man in this half-human crowd would dare to raise his hand or his voice against it. —If I am wrong, let that man speak now."

The only voice we hear for three or four seconds is that of the blackbird chanting his vespers from the summerhouse ridgepole. So quiet are those ten thousand—I accept King John's estimate of the number—that the bird probably thinks he is alone. At any rate, there seems to be no connection between his song and what is going on.

"No doubt you have heard," the sermon continues, "that Prince Charles Edward Stuart is now in England. It is even said, for I myself have heard it today, that he is here at the Fair, mingling with the people he was born to rule. If that be so, then his heart is broken and the dream of his life is ended. For I know this man. Not to say it boastfully, I know him well, and I can tell you that the love of England has been his master passion. Though born in exile—and yet in part for that very reason—he has always dreamed of this country as his motherland, homeland, holy land, which it would be his dearest joy, as also his duty, to serve. Hitherto he has been obliged to learn

of her largely through books and the talk of travellers and what his
tutors could tell him. With her past, her times of glory, he is well
acquainted; but such knowledge has not prepared him for what she
now is.

"Think, then, if you can, with what loathing such a man must have
witnessed your bestial conduct in this place during this afternoon. As
a Stuart, he cannot be a Puritan. To the spirit of revelry and carnival
he is by no means averse. Old customs—ancient, indeed, handed on
through the ages from history's dawn—are what he would expect
at Horn Fair, and delight to see. But stupidity, cruelty, the ways of
the wallowing hog, and, worst of all, your horrible mirthless laughter,
he has not been prepared for. Are these the people, he cannot but ask,
whose King I have longed to be, whose love I have hoped to win?
Is this herd of swine and cattle the means I have planned to use for a
noble purpose? —I will not! I can not! It is too filthy a tool!

"But then comes the thought that he can do this thing alone. Two
miles away the Elector of Hanover, that red-faced little man, stands
waiting at the centre of Hampton Court Maze. Nothing could be
easier than to ride there, strip off his every mark of usurped authority,
substitute the far more suitable horns and snout, and then turn him
loose among you as one of the least distinguished members of this
multitude. He might fume and fret for a while, and absurdly call
himself king of the country, but the only evidence that he had ever
been known as George the Second would be his inability to pronounce
the simplest English sentence. You would laugh at him, as you do
now, but I think you would soon learn to like him as one of your own
kind, and he in turn would feel at home with you. —Ah, yes: it would
be a pity to separate you from the man you call your king. You and
he deserve each other."

If silence gives consent, then these thousands are admitting the
truth of every word. There is not a murmur from them as Blandison
pauses for several seconds and looks about him. When he speaks
again it is in the voice of a man announcing a firm decision.

"Thus the Prince," says he, "clearly sees, if he is here, that the
crown is within easy reach of his hand. He will not stretch out his
hand to take it. Of his reasons it is enough to say that he now beholds
the people whom as King of England he would have to rule.

"For the rest, I can assure you that Prince Charles Edward will
soon leave England, and that no further attempt to restore the House

of Stuart will ever be made. You will hear many false tales about this man in the future as you have in the past, for the House of Hanover and its salaried liars will go on striving to make it appear that the legitimate heir to the throne is even more dull and corrupt than the German usurper. In the Prince's youth you were told by these same liars that he was a weakling, a cripple, an imbecile. From now on you may confidently expect to hear that he is a drunkard, that he wastes his little substance upon loose women, that he has lost whatever mind he may once have had, and that he is dying of a broken heart. All this will please you, no doubt, and certainly it will be well paid for out of your pockets. Furthermore, the House of Stuart may even assist these hired liars by providing the Prince with a double of whom the worst that can be said will be true. Why not? Why disappoint those who prefer to believe that the unicorn is really a rhinoceros? Why disturb the slumber of those who will have nothing left but the comfort of a sluggish and stupefying life? It will be better for them never to know that somewhere in the world, in at least one heart and mind, the passion for glory which England once had and has now utterly lost is still living on. The true Prince will remain a free man, going his own way, choosing his companions, keeping his self-respect, saving himself from the contamination of power and vulgar success. —Thus endeth the second lesson."

Blandison glanced for a moment at the Upright Man and then at Sir Edward Livermore, both of whom nodded as though in assent. Then, with an imperious and sweeping gesture of his right hand . . .

*　　　*　　　*

Just as I was writing those last words, William, I was interrupted by one of my favourite Twickenham dowagers who wanted my advice about the indigestion of her lap-dog. She stayed for more than an hour because the malady had a number of complications to be considered one by one. When she finally left it was obvious to Louis, and he made it fairly clear to me that I should not be able to finish this letter at Strawberry Hill as I had hoped. "Parliament convenes to-morrow," he reminded me in that much more autocratic tone of voice than he used to have which he may have acquired from the Upright Man along with a considerable addition to his vocabulary, "and therefore we must depart without further procrastination." Well, to be sure, there was no need of any such haste because, as I could have told him, the House of Commons regularly fritters away several days before it gets down to business in perambulating back and forth after the Black Rod, electing a Speaker, finding out whether his Majesty is graciously pleased to approve the said Speaker, swearing sundry oaths prescribed by law, and then meeting with the Lords in joint-session to hear the reasons why his Majesty has been graciously pleased to call them together.

At any rate, here we are now in the House of Lords, and are supposed to be listening to the King's Speech delivered in the King's own English. Would you like to hear some of it? I give you a sentence which I have just noted down, letter for letter: "I hope by bidisters vill be able to dot sped de whole rest of de sessiod upod dese sobjicks."

Even you, William, as a Hanoverian Tory, will observe certain peculiarities in the royal pronunciation. We have long understood, of course, that the English *th* is not to be expected of our German-born sovereigns, but this conversion of *m* into *b* and of *n* into *d* is due, I believe, not to his Majesty's place of birth but to the fact that he stood hatless in the Hampton Court Maze for several hours on St. Luke's Day and was dewed upon, so that he caught a severe cold in the head. That much I learn from a dowager who knows a Lady who is the wife of a Lord who was present at Hampton Court at the time; but no reason is suggested in this account why his Majesty should thus imperil the Realm by the exposure of his royal person to the rigour of the twilight dews. One can only surmise that he was engaged in the contemplation of the beauties of nature, or perhaps in composing the speech through which my colleagues of both Houses are now peacefully or stertorously slumbering and I am writing to you on my knee.

This House of Lords, let me tell you, is by no means conducive to literary effort. Dark and damp at the best of times, it is today overcrowded, and a chill gray fog is seeping in from the river through every crevice and cranny. The King's crimson face—it ought really to be done in gules for a painted-glass window—is barely visible to me, and the great silver unicorn in the royal coat of arms above his head has disappeared altogether.

In these untoward circumstances I do not at once recapture the mood that held me during the three weeks at Strawberry Hill in which I wrote, often at white heat, the earlier pages of this letter. Several days and dinners and games at loo have intervened since the last of that writing, and with each of them there has been some loss of outline and hue in the vision that once stood so clear. I am slipping back, as I feared, into what I have been. I begin to wonder that this and that event or person or scene should ever have moved me so deeply. Therefore I make haste, at the first opportunity, to set down what I still remember.

Louis came up with me to my house in Arlington Street, and we had a pleasant talk on the way about the friends who had left us for ever. He suggested that one or more of them might still be found at the Rose Tavern in Fleet Street; but I did not encourage that notion after I discovered that his ulterior purpose was to call—with me, of course —upon the Upright Man in Gough Square. I wanted, besides, to keep undisturbed my mental picture of Chester and Morris sailing off together for the plains of Patagonia, of James Adair far out on the trail through the Great Smoky Mountains, and of Byron either reclining under the vast oaks of Newstead or setting forth again toward Wager Island. I felt, and do still, an indescribable charm in those images faintly lustrous and slowly fading, each of them ennobled by distance. For a long time to come, I think, they will bring into my trivial nights and days some hint of life's possible grandeur. On many a midnight tormented by gout they may lead me as gently as opium into the castle of sleep.

There is, to be sure, that Painted Room at the Rose which you and I, as antiquarians, must some day examine. We shall go there, of course, not to verify Mr. Chute's opinion of the picture but to trace with our own eyes the series of degradations it represents from the conversion of St. Paul to the fraud of Robert Jenkins. A strange and saddening compendium of our English centuries, that painting must be; but let us postpone our visit until we are sure that Jenkins has gone to his everlasting reward.

You remember Blandison's order that Jenkins should be confined in the summerhouse under guard of Louis and Beston, but you do not know what happened during that by far too brief incarceration. Louis says that Richard Beston, with pistols, stood outside the closed door, and that he himself, also armed, went inside with "the old sot." For a time he seems to have stared, perhaps severely, at Jenkins' disgraceful two-earedness; but then, thinking of my collection, he demanded that the third ear, the famous one, should be turned over to him. Jenkins firmly refused, even at the pistol's point, so that there is no saying what it might have come to if Jeremy Tinker had not just then torn open the little back window and started to climb in. Concerning Jeremy's motive the expression of his face left no doubt. It was not a desiccated ear that he was after but that throat, that windpipe, upon which his thumbs yearned to complete their operation. Jeremy's Methodism was at low ebb, and the hero who had turned back the Spanish Armada in Georgia was emergent. Jenkins saw this, and quailed. "Don't let him come in!" he screamed. "He'll kill me!"

"Well then," said Louis, meanwhile giving Jeremy a few temporizing knocks on the head with the pistol-butt, "if I keep him out you will hand me that ear at once."

I leave to your imagination, William, the question in Jenkins' mind whether 'twere better to die slowly for lack of rum—for without the ear that would be his dismal prospect—or to die on the spot, of thumbs. The struggle in his mind, however, did not last long. He fumbled in his coat pocket, and his face went pale. He fumbled again, and went white. He pulled the pocket inside out, and it was empty. So were all his other pockets, unless you wish to count a tobacco-pipe with a two-inch stem, a twist of sailor's tobacco, and three farthings. But Louis was inexorable and thorough. Not until Master Jenkins stood before him in nothing but tears would he admit that the third ear was gone, was lost, and had probably been nipped in the crowd that day by a nimmer.

Louis had wanted that ear, he has since assured me, not for himself but for me; and now, finding that the tangible object had escaped him, his next thought was to gather information about it which might be useful in my memoir. "Where did you get that object?" he demanded as Jenkins pulled on his breeches. The familiar question brought forth at first the familiar reply, but Louis cut it short. "I want the truth," said he, "or else I go out at the door and Jeremy comes in at the window."

There is something about the Swiss people, due perhaps to the high, cold, pitiless light in which they mostly live, which cannot but seem to us English a little harsh and abrupt. Their notion is that things are either true or false, and they want to know which; but we feel that they ought to be both at the same time. When Louis spoke of the truth he meant, of course, the facts. And Jenkins, at last, understood him.

"I—I cut it," he stammered, "offen a Spaniard."

"Was he alive?"

"Naw. A dead un."

*   *   *

And now I shall write at top speed, relating only what I must. The King's Speech cannot last much longer, and I can take no pleasure in what is left to tell.

The strong broad sweep of Blandison's right arm meant both rejection and dismissal. It brushed those thousands away like so many gnats. I recall a shouted sentence or two from the Upright Man and some activity of the horsemen, but the multitude knew already that Horn Fair was over, that night would soon be upon them, and that something else for which they had no name had come to an end. There was no more laughter now, no blare of tin trumpets, not one cry of "Horns!" At last they understood that they did not belong there, and they went away by road and by river like a scurry of withered leaves with the west wind behind them. Had you looked out from the summerhouse windows at sunset you would have seen not one intruder left but only a loathsome litter and debris of trampled food, smashed horns and snouts of pasteboard, and numberless broken bottles. Eight men and one woman were standing by the shell, gazing at Blandison.

He had taken three bits of paper from his pocket and was writing or drawing on them with a pencil, swiftly. In half a minute he handed these slips to me and I saw that on each of them he had sketched a unicorn's horn, broken in the middle. There were no written words, nor did there need to be. My friends, looking over my shoulder, understood what was meant as well as I did. They said as little as I did—and that was nothing—when I handed the papers back. For one of them at least, as for me, our victory had already turned to dust and ashes.

Now Richard Beston lifted the fluttering pigeons out of the cage and held them while his master wrapped the strange symbolic message about the leg of each, covered it with oiled cloth, and bound it with cord. When all three were ready for flight Blandison took them in both hands and tossed them upward. They rose in wide circles and emerged into sunshine and straightened out on their several ways, one flying

southward, one east, and one to the north. The thing was more beautiful than I can say, and sadder.

We stood and watched—all except Kitty, whose eyes were flooded
with tears—while those arrowy messengers dwindled and dimmed
and evening washed round them. When the last one disappeared I
was suddenly overwhelmed with the full realization that what might
have been could now never be. We had saved England, yes; but from
what, and for what? The thought lay heavy upon me of my responsibility, small or great, for the passing of England's glory. That weight
is not yet quite gone. "I vant for by bidisters to dese dings," the King
is saying at this moment, "deir ferry special achtung—dot iss, atten-
tiod—to giff."

Louis came back from my house with a tobacco-pipe for John
Chester, a knife for Adair, a watch for Morris, a perspective-glass
for Captain Byron, and for Blandison a beautiful small copy, bound
in green leather, of the Odes of Horace. Kitty also had gifts—knitted
things made by her own hands—for them all, and a looking-glass set
in ivory for Mrs. Morris. After that there was not much left to say.
We went down to the landing together, and the members of the Club
got into the boat that had been sent for them from Twickenham Ait.
Master Jenkins was thrust in with them at the last moment, and a pin
of Abingdon ale. When they caught sight of the pin they gathered
round it and sang us a Rose Tavern song about Jenkins' Ear to the
tune of "The Barley Mow." Then they pushed off. Jeremy Tinker's
face was a study as he watched the departure of his friends, the ale,
and the windpipe all at once. Dusk was falling now, and by the time
they reached the main current their features were only a memory.
Yet we saw four hands go up out there in the gloom and clearly
heard their cry: "God save the King!" James Adair's coat of moony
doeskin and the bare pate of Master Jenkins were the last of them.

Again there was not much left to say—or, in other words, there
was everything—as we walked with Blandison up the slope to the
gate. Beston was leading his master's black stallion. Our farewells
were spoken on the way. In bidding me goodbye Blandison put his
arms about me in the formal European manner and kissed me on the
cheek. I had not been thus saluted, I think, since I left Florence, and
the slight embarrassment of it caused me to ignore whatever else he
did, say in the region of my right-hand coat-pocket, at the same time.
Just at the gate he dropped to one knee before Kitty Clive and kissed

her hand. Even in the twilight I could see her go suddenly pale. "Sire!" she cried in surprise and mild reproof; and then again, more softly, "Sire!"

For as long as the beat of a kingfisher's wing it lingered, that moment too lovely to live or to die. Then he was on his feet again, smiling, tossing back his head, looking swiftly, intently, from face to face. "I thank you, my friends," he said, and bowed with such a gracious dignity of the old times that one could not but imagine a cavalier's hat swept downward and a white plume brushing the grass. A moment later he was in the saddle. After a brief thunder of plunging hooves the twilight took him, and then the silence.

*   *   *

We stood there at the gate for some time, while the stars came out and a maidenly moon, like the one on Blandison's silver ring, slowly brightened above the hills of Surrey. The day's last lark was returning to earth, stair by stair, from his final glimpse of the sun. A white rose, untrampled because it grew just outside the gate, was gathering into itself all the light there was left in the world. It seemed to glow with a cool inward fire, which might well outlast the night.

My cousin broke the silence with "Well, Kitty was right about everything, and we have won."

It stood there for a moment to be considered—that statement so clear, simple, and downright. There came a sigh of the evening breeze from the willows. We heard the nibbling of my few sheep, now at home again, in the meadow. Among the reeds of the river-bank the water was whispering "Hush" and "Hush."

Then came the answer, in a tired, low voice: "I am still right, and we have lost—everything."

The air was growing chill. Louis brought Kitty's shawl from the house, and I laid it over her shoulders. I put my hands in my coat-pockets.

"Humph!" said my cousin.

There was something in my pocket that did not belong there. It was flat, smooth, leathery, and loathsome to the touch. I pulled it out, held it close to my eyes, and peered at it with disgust.

"Now, children," said I, "don't quarrel. You are both right. We have lost a king and won an Ear."